# THE
## *Council*
### SERIES

**VOLUME TWO**
# KRIS BUTLER

The Council Series
Volume Two
**Kris Butler**

First Edition: June 2022
Copyright © Kris Butler 2021

Proofreading: © 2022 Owlsome Author Services
Cover Design:© 2022 Incognito Scribe Productions
Formatting: © 2022 Incognito Scribe Productions

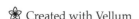 Created with Vellum

Tara,

much love from your

BCSH family

Kris Butler

# THE
*Council*
S E R I E S

# KRIS BUTLER

# contents

## fractured futures

## bosh bells & epic fails

# box set bonus

# foreword

This book has sexual scenes meant for adults. It is a reverse harem romance that has MM. The steamy scenes are steamy. If that's not your thing, then this book is not for you and that's okay. That is the great thing about books, there are many different kinds and we can all find ones we love.

This book uses the F-word a lot, so if you don't like foul language, then this book might not be your cup of tea.

It has been mentioned that this book may make you laugh out loud at times, so be careful when reading while drinking or eating or it may cause spewing accidents. This also goes for the hotness... grab your partner or some batteries. It's gonna get hot up in here.

This book highlights mental health in a positive light and the characters have positive coping skills that they will use from counseling. While they may be helpful, this is not a self-help book and if you feel you need help please reach out to someone you trust, or you can find some help here at https://www.samhsa.gov .

Triggers might include sexual abuse, human trafficking, drug abuse, and kidnapping. This book does dwell more into this.

If you don't like this book because of those reasons, don't say you haven't been warned. But I hope you love it because this series is very special to me.

*To having the future you've always wanted, and believing you deserve it.*

**Dum Spiro, Spero**
*"While I breathe, I hope."*

# fractured futures

Book Three

# Fractured

## FUTURES

# KRIS BUTLER

# blurb

*"It was time to take a stand and show the Council we weren't going away. They could try, but they had already taken too many people in pursuit of their own agenda, fracturing futures as they went. It was time the Council felt some of that pain."*

The Council had gone too far. All the secrets revealed had left us shattered and as we picked up the pieces of our damaged dreams, we hoped we would make it out alive to live the futures we all had planned. We would need to work together if we had any chance of stopping them, but it was obvious now that we were in way over our heads.

Could we trust the Agency? Could we trust each other? Would it be enough?

Join Sawyer and the guys as they fight for justice for them all against the Council. This is a contemporary reverse harem sports romance intended for 18+. This, why choose romance, may have some themes that are triggering to readers. Please read the foreword for more details. This is book 3 in the series and books 1 and 2 must be read first. This will end on a HEA.

# prologue

. . .

ONE WEEK EARLIER

## elias

BLINKING, I rubbed my eyes as the overhead speaker announced our landing. I'd gotten on the first flight out of Salt Lake City Friday night, and twelve hours later, I landed in London, England. Due to the time zone differences, it was already Saturday evening. A whole day had been lost between traveling and jumping multiple time zones. The lack of sleep felt worth it, the sacrifice a wage I'd willingly pay. This meeting was vital to surviving the Council and important I made it in person.

If I could secure this ally, I would be one step ahead of my father, and more importantly, the Council. It would effectively ensure my *chosen* family was safe. Sawyer and the guys

5

wouldn't understand my reasoning for leaving, but I knew this had to be done alone. I hated leaving in the middle of the night, but hopefully, they'd forgive me in time. The risk was preferable to them being dead.

Making my way through Heathrow, a sense of nostalgia wafted through me. The simple act of returning to the UK was a balm to my tortured soul. I'd forgotten how much I loved it here. London had been my home for fifteen years, and before the guys and Sawyer, it'd been the only place I'd fit in.

Stepping out of the airport, the London air welcomed me. The balmy, warm air wrapped around me in a familiar hug. With only my satchel, I headed for the taxi I'd reserved. I hadn't known how busy it would be on a Saturday evening, and waiting around wasn't something I could afford. Time was of the essence.

The black cabs idling at the curb were a welcome sight as they came into view. Luck was on my side when I spotted the number the car app had given me straightaway. I let myself take a moment of pleasure at being reunited with the things I loved about the UK—elegance, manners, and, most importantly, tea. At last, I was in a country which appreciated a good cup of tea. Bloody Americans and their microwaving. Smiling at the memory of Mateo asking how to make tea warmed something in me. Those were the kind of moments I found myself fighting for.

Reminiscing on my love of this city, the first time I arrived here bubbled up to the surface. It'd been scary stepping off that plane that first day since I hadn't been born in the United

Kingdom. But then I spent fifteen years of my life here, influencing my likes and dislikes, and well, my standards. Opening the taxi door, I slid in and nodded at the driver.

"Where to, mate?"

"Princes Gate, Knightsbridge."

Settling back, I reviewed the points I wanted to address with my benefactor. I wasn't positive how convincing I'd need to be, but I hoped he'd rally to our cause. It was the only way I could put any other steps into motion, and it started with exiting the Fitzroy family.

The cabbie pulled up to the elegant building, and for a moment, I soaked in the beautifully crafted architecture. London had something other cities lacked regarding history and aristocracy. A doorman opened the taxi as I paid the fare, making sure to leave a generous tip.

"Thanks, mate."

Taking in the street, confidence mingled with hope as I took a step toward my future. I was ready to take on the world for my family if I had to. For once, I had something bigger than myself to fight for.

"Good evening, sir. How can we help you today?" the concierge asked when I stepped into the foyer of the building.

"I'm here to see Mr. Hawthorne."

"Of course. I'll inform Mr. Hawthorne of your arrival. Is he expecting you?"

"No, but tell him it's Elias."

"Very well, sir. May I offer you any refreshments while you wait?"

"That would be lovely, thank you."

The woman smiled, walking over to a bar area. It didn't surprise me he had one in the waiting room. The fact Mr. Hawthorne even had a waiting area made me laugh. He was one man living in a ten thousand square foot monstrosity. However, despite his wealth and grandiose life, Mr. Hawthorne wasn't pretentious, well, no more than any other Londoner.

The concierge brought over a tumbler of amber liquid, placing it on the small table. Relaxing back, I sipped what I assumed was expensive whiskey as I waited. I wouldn't put it past him to make me sweat a bit for showing up here unannounced. When the concierge motioned for me to follow, I downed the last bit of the liquor, the burn coating my throat as I did.

She stepped into the lift, pulling out a unique key for the top floor before hitting the button. The ride up was quiet; there wasn't even any elevator music. I guess if you had a private lift, you could take the awful Muzak part out. The ding resounded, my heart beating in rhythm with the sound as it announced our arrival. The doors slid open, an ominous feeling emerged as she gestured for me to exit.

"Have a good evening, sir," the concierge spoke before the doors closed on her, descending back to the ground floor.

Turning around, I observed the grand foyer with the large centerpiece of fresh flowers and the sparkling chandelier that hung over it. The dark marble floors shone brightly as I made my way across them, looking for my host as I walked further into the dwelling.

"Mr. Hawthorne?"

"Elias."

My name sounded out behind me, surprising me. Spinning, I came face to face with my mentor, my confidant, and my secret benefactor. A wide smile spread over my face as I gave the man a warm hug.

"What brings you here, old friend?" he asked kindly.

"Old? I believe you own that title."

"Come, let's talk in the study. I'll have some food prepared. I bet you're dying for a cup of tea."

"Ah, tea. It's glorious being back in a country that understands it properly," I laughed.

"Very true. I missed it as well during my stay at TAS. Tell me, what's new on campus? Any new things in town?"

Settling down, I updated my old friend on the changes around the school since his last visit to Utah. Food and beverages arrived, and we dug in as we chatted. I found myself famished and devoured everything. Once we'd filled ourselves with tea, I laid out my reason for visiting, addressing all the points I'd practiced. When I finished, Mr. Hawthorne assessed me for a few minutes before he spoke. Dread filled my stomach the entire time I waited.

"Whatever you need, I will help with, Elias. The Council won't be allowed to hurt any more people," he attested with an intense ferocity I hadn't heard from him. "Mark my words."

Relief filled me for the first time in weeks at his proclamation. *We could do this.* My plan would succeed, and I could show Sawyer the man I wanted to be.

Before I slept, I wrote a letter putting my first step into

play. When morning came, I found myself sad to leave so soon despite my urgent need to begin the fight. Perhaps returning to London would be a trip I could make with Sawyer and the guys.

Popping into my favorite shop, I bought tea and treats I couldn't get in America. On my way out, I spotted a post box and slipped in the letter I'd written last night, hope blooming in my chest.

Heading back to Heathrow, I thought about all the pieces that had started to move into place, and a giddy excitement filled me. As I settled in for another long flight, a sense of accomplishment for achieving what I'd set out to do spread through me. In addition, this time, the time zone math would work to my advantage. When I landed in Connecticut Monday morning, I'd be one step closer to Sawyer, one step closer to the family I've always wanted, and one step closer to dismantling the Council for good.

The game was afoot, and I was about to 'smother mate' the king. They would never see me coming.

# one

. . .

## rhett

"MOM, BE HONEST WITH ME," I pleaded, my brow furrowed, and stare intense. Crossing my arms, I stared down at my mother before asking, "Did you know?"

Rhonda Taylor looked at me, resignation on her face, telling me everything I needed to know, but hadn't wanted to accept. My heart raced as I paced back and forth in the kitchen with what this meant. She'd snuck out with Rowan the other night before I could question her more and had conveniently been busy all day Friday. It was now Saturday, the day of the expo, and I needed answers. I couldn't sleep with the uncertainty of not knowing any longer.

"Mom!"

"Calm your tits, Rhett. Geez, you're worse than your sister with the hysterics," she exhaled, her body sinking at the question. Swallowing, she peered at me from the kitchen island where she was sitting. "No, honey. I didn't know about the Council. Your father, well, his family didn't tolerate him too much. If they are the same Rothchilds, which based on that Agent guy, they are, then it's doubtful Ryan was much involved with anything on this level," she finally shared.

My shoulders sagged at the news. I didn't know what I'd wanted as an answer because despite finding out my father's side of the family was part of the Council, it didn't look like mine was directly involved. I should've felt relieved, but I didn't. My father was a whole bag of mixed emotions on his own. I hadn't seen him in three years, and even then, it was only for a brief moment when I'd stopped by the house and found him snooping, looking for something. He left when I challenged him, but not before hitting me up for money. Whether for drugs or gambling, Ryan Rothchild was not a good man and more trouble than he was worth.

The day he left this family was the first time he did something right, even if I hadn't seen it that way at the time.

"I remember her, you know," I whispered, my eyes cast down on the countertop, scared to admit this truth.

"Oh honey, I always wondered if you did." She reached out, grabbing my hand, "You were so young at the time that part of me hoped you hadn't. I'm sorry I never asked. It was just as hard for me."

Squeezing her hand, I looked up into the eyes of my mother. I hated that I'd once seen her as weak for staying with him, I understood now. I saw the strength she had to try to hold it all together, to give us a family unit. When I was four or maybe five, we'd visited Grandmother Rothchild. Rowan hadn't been born yet, so it was just the three of us.

Granny Rothy, as she'd told me to call her that summer, was the type of grandmother all kids dreamed about. She was kind and giving, smelled of cookies, and listened to what I had to say as a precocious child. Granny Rothy always carried candy in her pocket for me and would tell me amazing stories. She'd thought I hung the moon, and I felt the same about her. That summer was the first time I lost someone.

Granny Rothy lived in a massive house on the coast of California, the beach only a few steps away. She was technically my great-grandmother, my father's grandmother. Even at my young age, I picked up on her disdain for my dad. I was just starting to figure out that he wasn't the father I thought he was. He would often miss my baseball practices and smelled of the sour juice he drank when he did show up. Ryan couldn't keep a job and did nothing to help around the house, and I saw the stress my mother was under trying to keep it all together.

That summer, I got to live a dream childhood every little boy should get to experience. I was surrounded by a granny that loved me, endless fun, and every type of toy under the sun. We went on adventures to the zoo; I learned to swim and ride a bike. Granny and I were the best of friends, and I was sad when I thought of leaving her. The last weekend of the summer, my parents came to stay before they took me back home. We'd planned a beach picnic, but Granny hadn't felt well, so she'd stayed behind.

While we were out on the beach, I'd dug up a shell I wanted to show her. My father had returned to the house earlier, so I figured it was okay to as well. Creeping into the back patio door, I heard shouting coming from Granny's no-no room, the one place I wasn't allowed to enter—the office.

"I heard them fighting, Mom. I'd run back to the house to show Granny my shell, and that's when I heard the shouting. I don't remember what was said, just that Granny sounded sad and scared," I recalled, the same fear gripping my chest. "I crept along to the hallway and hid in the corner where I could see into the room. She was sitting at her desk, and dad was ranting about something, pacing the office, he-he-he," I paused, the emotion thick. I had to clear my throat before I could try again. "He slammed his fists down on the desk, leaning over it to get in her face, threatening her. The sound and movement made me gasp, and she heard me. She looked right at me, Mom."

Once I'd permitted myself to remember, the memory flooded me, overwhelming my senses. I'd hidden it away for so long, that now it felt so vivid, like I was that small boy hiding in the corner again. My mother had tears in her eyes as she listened to me retell the story. Both of her hands grasped mine, trying to offer me support.

"Her eyes were so sad. I saw a tear fall, and I wanted to go in there and tell Dad to stop making her cry. But she was braver than me. She stood up, told Dad he was acting like a child and wouldn't be getting what he wanted because she'd made sure," I rambled. "That's the only thing I remember because, at that point, she came over and shut the door. Before she closed it, she looked right at me and mouthed, 'I love you, moon. Run!' When it latched, I heard Dad scream profanities, and then there was a thump. I didn't want to get in trouble or disappoint her, so I took off running and ran—"

"To the beach. I remember… I always wondered where you'd gone because you seemed so scared that you were shaking when you returned, but you refused to talk about it."

Nodding, I held my mom's gaze, this shared secret finally being spoken out loud. I might not have connected the dots then, but as we stared at one another, it was clear what we both presumed. Ryan Rothchild had killed his grandmother that day, my Granny Rothy. He was more dangerous than I'd ever imagined.

"I'm so sorry you had to see that and keep it to yourself, Rhett. I'm so sorry," my mom cried. Moving around the island, I wrapped her in a hug, and we held one another, comforting each other the best we could for a woman who hadn't deserved to die.

"Oh my God, that reminds me. A letter came for you a few days after her funeral, but it said not to be opened until you were older. I'd put it into the safe and forgotten about it until now. Let me get it. I think it was from Granny."

Mom ran to the back office and was back in minutes holding out a slightly aged envelope to me. The front was addressed to My Moon, Rhett Turner Rothchild. My father's mother had been the Rothchild, and her maiden name, making my father's surname Turner when she had married. It was probably another reason the family hadn't respected him. He wasn't a true descendent carrying on the lineage but had wanted his due anyway.

My hands shook slightly as I peeled back the seal, the crackling sound from the aged glue sounding around the kitchen. Enclosed was a letter addressed to me, dated a week before her death. She'd foreseen a need for this; that thought alone made me sad and scared for what awaited me on this particular branch of the family tree.

*To my moon,*

*I hope you don't read this letter for many years, or that its contents don't come true for a long time. But I fear this is one time my family name cannot help me. You have been staying with me this summer, moon, and it has been the best summer of my life, getting to create stories with you, exploring new things, and basking in the love you have for the world. I hope you never lose it and I'm around to see it. You have a sensitive soul and I can tell you will be a true romantic at heart. Even at five, you love to watch the classics with me. I love watching you during them, your look of awe and study as you try to remember every detail.*

*There are things about our lineage that I'm not proud of. The biggest ones are the things my son, Ronald, has gotten the family involved in. Before him, our name and family have been on the right side of history, using our money and status to make things better. If you study our family history someday, you will see all the things we have been part of, and I hope it makes you proud.*

*I fear that you won't get to see those things, though, because, by the time you are old enough to understand them, our family will be polluted with the poison my son is infecting into it. Your father, unfortunately, has become part of that poison. He is involved in dangerous things, and I pray that my plan works for you and your mother. She is kind and deserves better than my grandson, and I hope I can help with that.*

*Your father is demanding to see the will and what assets he will be gaining upon my death. I believe my son has put him up to it for a favor. I've kept it under lock and key and hired an outside lawyer to handle everything, so neither my son nor your father can tamper with it.*

*I hope I get many more summers with you, moon. This has been the best one of my life. You're the son I wished mine had been. You're kind and sweet, and always watching out for the little animals and kids on the beach. Rhett, my moon, you're a natural protector. You're creative and talented, and I hope you do something with that. The stories we made together were brilliant, and if they are the last things I remember, I will die having the time of my life.*

*You are strong and intelligent, and I see so much for your future. Don't limit yourself, and while I hope I'm around to meet the person you fall in love with, whether boy or girl because I believe love is love, I know you will worship the ground they walk on. Just make sure they do the same for you too, moon. Don't settle. They need to be amazing to capture you, my moon.*

*I've set up a fund for you to use for school or whatever you desire. I know even at five, you won't be irresponsible. If you want to travel for a year, you can. If you want to go to school in Europe, you can. If you want to start your own company, you can.*

Nothing but your own imagination will limit you. Dream big, my moon, and you will go far.

I've also made you the trustee of my estate, meaning this house, the possessions within, and the cars will all be yours someday. It will be taken care of by a trust until you turn twenty-five. I want you to have time to enjoy your life and for there to be enough time that my wretched son forgets and moves on. I don't want to make him your enemy; that is not my wish at all.

The last thing I've changed is that I'm hoping to help your mother get out of her situation. I know she will never accept anything from me, but I've given her the name and number of a trusted friend. If she is to ever reach out to them, they will see that she is granted a quick divorce, protection and will be given money to start whatever she needs to. It's my way of showing her she can do this if she wants it.

Despite Ryan and my Ronnie turning out to be nothing but trouble for the family, you have been the best gift I could've asked for. I love you for spending your summer with an old woman and making her feel young again.

I hope it doesn't come to this moon, but there might come a time when you might be called on. I've tried hard to disconnect any association from me and you; all the documents will be routed through a shell company, but I don't doubt that Ronnie has his ways of finding information when he wants it. So, if my fight bleeds onto you, I pray you are more successful than I have been.

Enclosed is a key to a safe deposit box I've had set up at your local bank. Inside will be key codes, passwords, and contacts of all the information I've collected over the years on a group called the Council.

*My son is part of this group, and it's not a good one. The whispers I hear give me nightmares, and I hate to think what it will be like in the years to come as their corruption expands more and more.*

*I pray that you can be separate and live your life, but if you cannot do that, hopefully, this will help point you in the right direction. Be careful, moon. Never forget my love.*

*To the moon and back, little one.*

*Granny Rothy*


"Holy shit."

Mom and I both looked up at the same time, our faces ashen. Several emotions filtered across my face. She'd known and had tried to stop it, and not only that, but she'd left me information that could help.

"Mom, do you know what this means?"

"She was the one who gave us the money for this place…" she trailed off, deep in her own memory. Granny Rothy had given us freedom from the grave and hadn't even known about Rowan yet. If I did anything with my life, I hoped it was enough to honor her.

Kissing my mom on the cheek while she was lost in her own memories, I gathered up the pages and rushed out the door. This was huge, and I wanted to see what was in the box. I had a few hours before the expo, and maybe I could find something that might be useful.

Rage filled me as I pulled out of the driveway and headed to the bank. Reaching for my phone to call the guys, I realized my pocket was empty, and I remembered I'd placed it on the kitchen counter earlier. Shit. I would need to run back and get it.

Later though.

Now, it was time to go behind enemy lines and gather intel.

It was time to take a stand and show the Council we weren't going away. They could try, but they'd already taken too many people in pursuit of their own agenda, fracturing futures as they went.

It was time the Council felt some of that pain.

# two

. . .

## soren

LISTENING TO RHETT'S VOICEMAIL, I had a sick feeling in my gut.

*"Soren, there's been a change of plans. I can't go into it right now, but I'm not going to be able to scope out the students with you. I'll catch up with you after."*

We weren't supposed to deviate from the plan. Bad things always happened when you did! I'd read enough books to know that. No one ever took people who read seriously enough, in my opinion. I knew things they'd never imagined.

Everyone else was already in position, so there wasn't anyone I could reach. Ty was meeting with his dad, Rey and Sawyer were skating, Ollie was with his uncle in the box seats, and Mateo was watching surveillance with some of Agent Bossypants' team back at HQ. After his showdown with Sawyer, we'd started an ever-changing nickname game for Agent B to see who was the cleverest.

Rhett and I were to infiltrate the student section and chat with them to gather any information we could while they didn't think anyone was listening. It was easy and safe, but now that he was changing the plan and not telling me why, it could only mean bad news.

This was uncharacteristic for Rhett, so I had to assume it was something significant, or he wouldn't be doing this. I didn't like it, though. Nope—not one bit. This wasn't the plan, and now I was reeling with what to do. Sighing, I started toward the arena when my name was called by a voice I'd hoped never to hear again.

"Soren, baby, it's Mom," cooed the addict parading as my mother. Hanging my head, I sighed and turned.

Pamela Stryker looked awful. Her hair was greasy, unkempt, and stringy, it even appeared to be three different colors. Her body was frail, and she'd lost a lot of weight to an unhealthy level. Her clothes were provocative despite the cold weather, and I'd garner she was prostituting herself in that outfit. Her fishnets had a tear up one leg, her shoes looked beyond scuffed and perhaps even the wrong size. Her shirt was low cut, sleeveless, and showing off the numerous track marks up her arm. *Fucking hell*—this spelled disaster. Bad things came in threes, so what was next?

"Pamela," I sighed, not moving any closer to her. She'd lost the title of mother years ago. She didn't seem bothered by the use of her name, probably more concerned with getting whatever she needed from me.

"Hey baby, come and give your momma a hug."

She stumbled toward me, arms outstretched as if she expected me to want to hug her. I stepped back out of her reach before she could touch me. Pamela was further gone than I'd ever seen her. Quite frankly, I didn't know why I continued to hold out any hope she'd magically transform into a decent mother. She hadn't been interested in being one my whole life, the only appeal I had for her was what she could gain from me. Pamela was a user, plain and simple, and it didn't matter if it was drugs or people.

"Cut the crap and drop the act, Pamela. What do you want?" I asked, my voice full of exasperation. I was already tired of this game.

"I need your help, baby. These guys are, they're serious, and I'm in a bit of trouble," she started, just like she always did. It was always someone else who was the problem. "You just have to give them the girl, that's it. Then I'm free. We can be free, baby. Don't you want that?"

She had the audacity to smile at me with hope in her eyes. Her words shocked me long enough that she'd managed to walk forward and grasp my hands, pleading with me. *Pamela Stryker was fucking insane.* The sheer audacity of her thinking I'd ever give Sawyer up just to protect her. Maddening—not happening, Mother dearest.

I shouldn't have laughed, but it bubbled up out of me before I could control it. Her returning slap, though weak, still caught me off guard.

Stepping back, I looked at the woman who'd birthed me and wondered how I'd gotten so lucky to avoid that future.

Whoever my father was, he must have strong genes because I was nothing like *her.*

"Let's get something clear, *Mom,*" I sneered, over this tirade. "I will never, in a million years, pick you over anyone in that house—my real family. Actually, go ahead and add the entire fucking planet because there's no way in Hell I would ever choose you." Breathing rapidly, I stared down at the woman who'd hurt me in so many ways. "You're officially absolved of any 'motherly' duties you feel because, let's face it, you're shit at it. Begone, woman. If I never see you again, it would be too soon."

I was seething; rage and hatred dripped from my every word. My body was taut with anger and tension as I stood over her, and glared down at the sniveling skeleton parading as Pamela Stryker. She started to open her mouth, with what I was sure to be a horrible insult, when someone who I did consider a mother, intervened.

"Soren, is that you, dear? Everything okay?"

Rhonda Taylor walked up, placing her hand on my bicep, sending her calming waves through me, instantly relaxing my body. Her words held more kindness and love than Pamela had ever managed. Keeping my gaze locked on Pamela, I knew I'd crack if I looked at Momma Taylor right then.

"Just saying *goodbye.*"

Looking at my mother for the last time, I turned and walked away with Rhonda following me. When I got inside the hockey rink, I took a turn down a hallway until I found an empty office and walked in. Rhonda followed me inside, as I expected she would.

Staring straight at the wall, I took deep inhales, trying to hold it in. Her soft touch on my back broke the dam, and the sobs were coming before I could stop them.

Rhonda turned me and wrapped her arms around me as I broke down in her embrace. She cooed reassurances to me, but all I could hear was my utter heartbreak as it poured out of me.

I cried for the little boy who'd only wanted his mom to be happy, to be proud of him.

I cried for the teenager who lost his innocence way too soon in a despicable way.

I cried for the man who would never share a mother/son dance at his wedding.

Lastly, I cried for the mother I'd never had.

When all the tears had fallen, I pulled back, and Momma Taylor's hands bracketed my cheeks as she stared at me.

"I'm taking that woman," she swallowed, gathering her own emotions, "she was your mother?"

I nodded; words didn't need to be said.

"While we don't get to pick the family we're born into. I've always believed we do have a choice on who we consider *family*. I didn't get it at first, you know; the relationship you all have with Sawyer," she soothed, wiping my tears. "I always knew you boys had a unique bond, and I felt lucky to be a surrogate mother to you all." She smiled, proving she was more *mothering* than Pamela ever had been.

"This week, learning all the things we did and seeing you all interact the way you do, *I got it.*" Her hands rubbed soft circles into my cheeks, wiping away tears when they fell. "Sor, honey, you guys have made the best family unit. All of your jagged edges fit one another, and together, you're whole. I saw it in the room that day, and I couldn't be prouder of you all." She smiled warmly now, wiping the tears left on my cheeks.

"That being said," she hedged, making me hold my breath as I waited. "I would be honored to be your mother-in-law. Is that how it would work? You'll be brother husbands or something?" she teased, causing me to chortle through my tears.

"I would be honored to have you as my mom, too."

Now, she had tears in her eyes, and we held one another. A few minutes later, we pulled back, both drying our eyes. It might seem like I lost my biological mother today, but in reality, I'd lost her years ago. The greater picture was what I'd gained, and *that* would be what I focused on.

I had a mother, two sisters, and a brother now, along with my best friends. I knew others would be included as time went by, and that thought made me hopeful. I gained a real family, and that outweighed any biological connection to me. I could live with that.

After our cry fest, Rhonda looked puzzled and asked me where Rhett was. She'd been part of the planning meeting and knew everyone's roles. Relaying the voicemail he left, I felt it was stupid to keep secrets at this point. She had a look of concern on her face, making me even more worried.

"Is everything okay?"

"I don't know. We discovered some interesting information about Rhett's father, and he had left in a hurry. He went somewhere, and when he returned to the house, his face was ashen, a look of fear on it. He grabbed his phone and walked out, not saying a word. I don't know what he discovered, but I don't think it's good."

Dread filled me, and I prayed it was nothing, but Rhett was always steady. That was something I could count on and trust in, and this wasn't the norm. If Rhett was scared, what was going on that we didn't know about? I squeezed her hand tight as we parted and hoped she wasn't right. I wasn't sure how many more surprises we could take.

Rhonda went to sit with Charlie, and I headed to the student section. I grabbed some popcorn and a drink, wanting to have some props to help me blend since I was alone now. Plus, popcorn was just awesome.

A few students greeted me as I found a seat, most not even paying attention. Maybe it was better to be alone, since Rhett's big ass wasn't as inconspicuous. The program started a few minutes later, the mother confrontation almost making me miss the beginning. As the skaters began, most of the students quieted. As the different performers came on, it was interesting to hear what they thought of their peers. It made me even more grateful for the family we had. I'd forgotten how petty people were.

*"Her outfit looks like Godzilla made it."*

*"I heard she slept with the whole hockey team, and they're now calling her breadbasket because any shot makes it in."*

*"Johnny told me that Austin has a micropenis. Do you think that's true?"*

*"Who do you think is the hottest instructor? I miss the hot tutor."*

*"Do you think she was sleeping with the director? Or do you think what Phil said was true?"*

Finally, something useful, I kept trying to pick out the voices it belonged to, but they would get covered at times by others.

*"I heard she had photos of them doing things, and Phil found them and blackmailed her."*

*"No way!"*

*"Yeah, also, that Phil was jealous, but not of Jill, but the Director because they were secret lovers!"*

*"Shut-up! You're bad, Misty."*

*"Oh look, that slut Sawyer is up next. I hope she falls. I heard what she did to Adelaide, stealing her boyfriend and everything. Skank."*

Anger filled me at whoever said that, and I knew it had to be Bitchelaide's doing. When I heard Mateo call her that, I'd felt it suited her. We'd all adopted the nickname, and it reminded me how glad I was she wasn't hanging around the house anymore. There had been numerous times I found her trying to sneak into our rooms or leave her underwear for us —fucking gross.

The announcer came on, and I focused on the ice to the two loves of my life. I couldn't wait to see them skate together. From the moment they stepped out, it was obvious they were special. Everyone quieted down and concentrated on them. Their music suited them, "Imperfect" by Shadows of Mayhem. It was a band Rey and I'd found last year, and the song had hits of fast and soft moments.

As they moved and glided over the ice, I found myself jealous of it. It was almost as if they were making love to it as they skated, and if anyone was going to be the third piece of that awesome sandwich, it would be me. It was odd being envious of frozen water, but the way they floated over it was like a lovers' caress. I was transfixed as I watched Sawyer and Henry skate, creating a beautiful love story—theirs. It was the most beautiful routine I'd ever witnessed. It had their heart written throughout it all, making it more than just a dance of seamless moves. *It was them.*

The crowd agreed by erupting into applause as they finished, lost in their world and each other. I had to focus to not sport a boner right then surrounded by students, but seeing the two people I loved, doing what they loved together, was breathtaking. It gave me all the feels. My skin agreed as it broke out in goosebumps.

Gathering my trash, I made my way out of the stands so I could go and congratulate them both with a kiss. The naughty things we could do began to fill my mind. Dumping my stuff in a trash can, I picked up my pace toward the locker rooms. Halfway there, my phone vibrated in my pocket. Thinking it was them, I pulled it out with a grin on my face, already formulating a naughty text I could send in return.

Except the message wasn't from them.

**Unknown:** Hello little Soren, have you missed me?
You should've listened to your mommy and done the

exchange. Now, this has to get messy. Just remember you had a choice, and you chose wrong.

**Unknown:** *pic attached*

**Unknown:** I'll be in touch.

The pic showed Finley and Rowan unconscious, their hands bound and a gag in each of their mouths. They looked to be in a trunk. Bitterness filled my throat, and I barely made it to the trash can before I was expelling all the popcorn I just ate. Wiping my mouth with the back of my hand, I shakily texted Rhett.

**ME:** They're gone. Finley and Rowan. They've been taken.

I didn't think about anything else as I took off running, needing to find Rey and Sawyer. They would know what to do. They would—

An arm came out from a dark corner and pulled me back. I thrashed wildly against the person holding me as I tried to break free.

"Soren, calm down. It's me," breathed Agent Backstabber.

"Let me go," I fumed. "I need to find Rey and Sawyer."

"You can't. If you do, they won't go to the Alumni dinner, and our plan will be ruined."

Tired of this fucker underestimating us, I head-butted him, giving myself enough leverage to get out of his chokehold.

"No, I don't keep secrets. *Not from them.* You can't ask this of me. You can't. It's time you start remembering we work better together and trust them to make the right call with all of the information. It isn't your choice to make. It's theirs, and I'm not hiding this from them."

With that, I turned and stalked off, leaving him holding his nose and not even caring if it was bleeding. I didn't even care if he was some super-secret badass agent. This was my family, and we fought together. Try to hurt one of us, and you got all of us.

The captor had messed up. I knew who he was now. He'd shown his hand, and I was going to use that to my advantage. I'd been known as The Stryker for a reason, winning more medals than anyone my age. I didn't do that sitting on my ass, and yet, they continued to underestimate me. Soren Stryker meant business, and I never missed when I struck.

*Ten years ago, age 14*

*"Hey Stryker, you want to go to a party?"*

*"Really? That'd be so cool!"*

*"You just gotta steal some drugs from your mommy. That's if you're not too scared," teased one of the older kids.*

*I was the youngest on this trip at fourteen, and my mother had tagged along. She constantly embarrassed me around the others. She would hit on all the coaches and dads. I wished she'd stayed home so I wouldn't have to lie about who she was to me. But now, these kids were inviting me somewhere. I could steal whatever they wanted if it meant I got to hang out for once.*

*"I'm not scared. You're on. I'll be right back."*

"Better hurry. We leave in ten minutes, and we're not waiting."

Dashing to the room, I forgot one of my rules about listening for sounds before entering. I wasn't supposed to disturb mom's "business," as she called it either. The sounds of moans filled the tiny hotel room, and I could see movement from the bed. Covering the side of my eyes, I tried to block out the noise as I tiptoed to the dresser. I found several things lying about and grabbed something, not knowing what any of it was to begin with. I stayed away from this stuff after seeing how it made my mom act. I didn't want to be anything like her.

I made it back out the door and breathed a sigh of relief. She would be occupied for a while and wouldn't notice I was gone for at least a couple of hours, if she noticed at all. I had time to party with the big kids.

Feeling proud, I made my way back to the front of the hotel where I'd left them. When I arrived, there was a car zooming off just as I stepped outside, the windows down as they all laughed and pointed at me. Assholes.

I couldn't wait till I made real friends. Resigning myself to a night in, I grabbed the book out of my bookbag and found a seat in the lobby. I was almost at the last chapter when a dark shadow fell over me from behind, a hand covering my mouth, followed by a pinch in my neck.

When I woke a few hours later, it was strapped to a bed, naked, and a man was sitting next to me. He looked to be the same age as my mom but had a weird mustache and oily slicked-back hair. His eyes looked dead, and fear filled my body as he smiled at me.

*"Don't worry, little Soren, I'm going to take good care of you."*

*"Who are you?" I stuttered out in fear.*

*"Let's just say I'm a friend of a friend, and you can call me Morano. You and I will be the best of friends when we leave here. You'll get to live as long as you keep your mouth shut. Understand?"*

*I nodded, and tears started to fall. I didn't want this type of friend. I vowed to myself right then that I would become strong and brave. I would make my own family, and I would be my own hero. I never wanted to feel this way again.*

*I was Soren Stryker. I would decide how I lived, and it wasn't in fear.*

# three

. . .

*Two hours earlier*

## finley

"HEY, girl! Thanks so much for helping me. With everything going on, I didn't want to do this alone." I smiled, my hands fidgeting as I talked. "Plus, I know I'm already going to get yelled at by everyone as it is. I'd like to keep my beatings to a minimum because who has the time for that?" I joked.

I was nervous, and when I was nervous, weird jokes came out—at least I didn't have Sawyer's word vomit problem.

Charlie had regaled us with the story of the code orange origin and I'd laughed so hard the other night. It was classic Sawyer, and I loved how she spread her awkwardness wherever she went. I couldn't imagine her without it, actually.

"Yeah, sure! It's no problem, Fin." Rowan grinned. She

had such an ease about her. She was a good mixture of Rhett and Rhonda. "So, what are we up to? Classic home invasion? B & E? Falsifying some documents?" Rowan laughed, rubbing her hands together in intrigue.

When I didn't laugh back and only cringed, she dropped the playful act and looked at me seriously.

"I was only kidding, Fin. Sorry, I watch too many movies."

"Uh, about that." My cringe deepened as my face reddened. "So, I might not have been *100% honest* about my intentions." When she didn't say anything, I started to talk faster.

"You see, that girl that went missing, Jill? I think I found something, and I just need to step into an office and confirm it. Nothing major, just a *little B&E.* I just need you to be my lookout."

"Whoa, I... um. What do you mean by little?" Rowan asked, shifting her weight as she started to panic. Before I could assure her, she began her own version of a panic diatribe. "Ok, listen, I don't know if I'm really cut out for the spy lifestyle. I have a nervous bladder, and I'm not really supposed to be stressed, I uh—"

Rowan was melting down quickly, and I would lose my chance if I didn't act fast. Taking her arm, I dragged her to the spot I needed her. I'd been in the building for over thirty minutes before she'd arrived, mapping out the best lookout locations. Taking her by the shoulders, I squeezed reassuringly.

"You'll be fine. Just stand here and play on your phone. If

someone comes this way, send me a text. Simple. You won't be involved at all. Promise." I smiled encouragingly.

"Just send you a text," she repeated back slowly. Coming to a decision, she nodded her head. "Yeah, okay."

Rowan appeared a little dazed but pulled out her phone and held it as I suggested. It gave me confidence she wasn't going to run away, freaked out as soon as I went inside.

Slipping around the corner, I checked both directions to ensure no one was there before walking up to the door. I'd learned long ago that the key to pulling most things off was acting like you were meant to be there.

Taking out my kit, I inserted the lock pick tool and adjusted the pins as I listened for the clicks. It was a simple door lock, so I managed to unlock it in about thirty seconds. Not bad for being rusty. Folding my kit back up, I quietly slipped through the door, leaving it open a tiny crack so I could hear if anyone was coming.

Using my phone, I hit the flashlight button and surveyed the cramped space. For being the director, he wasn't very organized. Boxes of files littered the floors from wall to wall, making passage through difficult. If I hadn't used my flashlight, I would've face-planted two feet inside the door. That would've been embarrassing.

Finally, making it to the desk, I began to search through the items on top. Nothing stood out, but I wasn't banking on him leaving a "password here" Post-it. Flipping on the monitor, I got to work hooking up my encryption keycard to decipher his login. Thankfully, it found it quickly. The dumbass had an easy one—*skatinggold*. So original there, Director.

Scanning the files, I found the ones I needed and started to transfer them onto my thumb drive. I was about 80% done when Rowan squeezed in through the crack and latched it behind her. Her breathing was quick, and I couldn't make out her frantic whispers. Grabbing the drive when it pinged, I slipped it inside the secure spot in my bra.

Using my phone again to light the box labyrinth, I hurriedly made my way over to her. When I got there, she grabbed my phone in a panic, and it slipped from my fingers, crashing to the floor. Light scattered all around us like a disco ball.

"What are you doing? You're supposed to be standing guard," I angrily whispered.

Her hand came over my mouth as she placed her foot over the light of my phone, casting us into darkness. Seconds later, I heard what she'd apparently tried to whisper to me —voices.

*Voices were in the corridor.*

Shit.

They grew louder as they moved closer, and I could make out a man and a woman, but I wasn't able to hear their conversation from our position. Rowan had her back against the door, and I was pressed to her front, her hand still covering my mouth. We stood in an anxious quiet, waiting to see if we'd be discovered. Eventually, they walked past the door, apparently turning down another hallway as their foot-steps lessened. Rowan dropped her hand finally, her breath slowing as she exhaled in relief.

"Sorry, I panicked and forgot what I was supposed to do,

so I just ran in here." She cringed, her face making me chuckle. Which I instantly regretted when we heard more voices outside the door.

"Did you hear that?"

This time it was more distinguishable, making me realize it had to be closer. Double donkey balls, this was bad! Thinking on my feet, I retrieved my phone from under her shoe and shoved it down my pants to hide the light. Bracing her shoulders, I tried to send her confidence and strength.

"Trust me. Just follow my lead."

She nodded in response, but I could see the anxiety and fear written all over her face. I hated myself for putting her in that position. Rhett would never forgive me, and a small part of me agreed with him. Another one of my wacky brained schemes, getting us into trouble.

Hearing footsteps approaching, I reacted. Moving my hands from her shoulders to her face, I searched her eyes for a second before kissing her on the lips. Rowan was clearly shocked by the move but didn't push me away. We held our lips pressed together, eyes locked, waiting for the inevitable. When I felt the door pull open, I moved my body with the momentum so we would fall through the door.

Laughing as we fell, Rowan joined me, having caught on to my ploy. The man at the door stared down at us in shock as we laid at his feet in giggles, unsure what to do. Rolling off her, I acted clumsily as I stood.

"Oh my God, I'm so sorry, sir," I slurred, "The door was open, so we snuck away for a little private time, if you know what I mean." I winked at him, trying not to actually throw up on the despicable human.

Rowan stood as well, clutching my arm, giggling hysterically. I pulled her away, wanting to use the distraction and shock to our advantage before he realized we'd broken in.

As soon as we were around the corner, we both straightened and began to jog at a quick pace to put more distance between us. Once we were out of the admin building, I braced my hands on my knees, panting from the little exercise. Athletic, I was not. Rowan was doing the same, and I felt more guilt rise up when I thought about her illness and putting her in this situation. I really needed to ask for help sooner and not follow all my crazy schemes. I should've told Sawyer that day when she'd asked.

"I'm so sorry, Rowan. I really thought it would be empty and a quick in and out. Rhett's going to murder me," I grumbled.

"What are you talking about? That was flipping awesome! Oh my, I've never felt that alive before. It was great, and you thought so quickly on your feet. I was frozen, and then you're like, here do this, laugh, throw a wink. Oh my God, I'm in awe of you."

Looking at her oddly, I wasn't sure how to take her words of praise. I was used to being the screw-up, the reckless one who got into trouble. Hero worship was not my norm—far from it, in fact.

"Um, thanks? But let's not aspire to be me, and maybe don't tell your brother. He'd kill me and I would like to actually have sex with my boyfriend at some point."

This only caused her to laugh even more. The adrenaline and pure craziness of the situation had me joining her after a while. Her laugh was contagious, and it made me glad I'd asked her. After a few minutes, I tugged her arm to get moving toward the arena before someone noticed us missing.

I really should've seen this next part coming. Hindsight and all that though.

Turning the corner of the brick building, I was pulled back by force as a hand wrapped around my mouth and throat. I could see Rowan was also bound out of the corner of my eye, the fear evident on her face.

"Tsk, tsk, little hacker. Did you not take my gift as a warning? I'll make sure to be more precise this time then. It seems like you've been a bad little girl. Time to go see the boss. Oh, I can't wait to see what I get to do with *you*," breathed the disgusting voice into my ear.

He yanked me around where I couldn't see Rowan any longer, but I could hear her whimpers, and I hoped she was okay. Tears gathered at the corner of my eyes, and I was kicking myself for this whole stunt. I kept thinking I was a spy, that I could get away with shit. Instead, I made it worse and had to be saved over and over. I'd really fucked this up.

Fear filled my veins, paralyzing me, making me unable to use any of the self-defense moves I'd mastered years ago. Instead, a syringe filled with cold liquid was jabbed into my neck, and my awareness faded away. Shiticles. This wasn't going to end well for us, and unfortunately, I'd involved a kind and innocent person this time. Reckless-1, Fin-0.

# four

. . .

## sawyer

"THAT WAS INCREDIBLE!"

Henry picked me up and spun me around, making me laugh, throwing my head back. For this brief second, I could forget about the potential danger and enjoy the carefree moment we were having. I could pretend we were high school sweethearts, and headed for big things.

I could pretend, but it was only ever for a second. Reality was too real to pretend for too long.

Setting my feet on the ground, I hugged him tight. Our program had been flawless, and it filled me with the courage we needed to get through the rest of the night. I would be coming face to face with my biological father soon. Pretending I didn't know the despicable creature he was, would call on my best acting skills. Clapping from behind broke our celebratory reunion as partners.

"Well done, Mr. Reyes and Miss Sullivan. Well done, indeed."

The voice sent shivers down my spine every time I heard him speak now. I didn't trust him, and if I could prove he had something to do with Jill, I would gladly nail his balls to the wall. Stepping out of Henry's embrace, I turned to face the Director.

"Thank you, Director Donnelly. Excuse us."

I tried to walk past him, but he reached out and grabbed my arm instead. I sucked in a breath at his touch.

"I would let go of her if I were you," Henry said through his teeth, sending a very different kind of chill through me.

"Now, Mr. Reyes," Director Donnelly started, his stance taking on a different feel, "I don't think we need to resort to violence. I just wanted to make sure you both had accepted your invitation to the Alumni Dinner tonight. Several alumni are interested in meeting you both. It could be, let's say, *advantageous* for your careers."

When he finished, my arm was dropped, and he walked away. I swear I heard him whistling like some creepy villain from a cheesy horror movie. Rubbing the spot his fingers had gripped me, I tried to dispel the darkness his touch had left lingering on my skin. I could already see bruises forming in the shape of his fingers. Fuck, none of the guys were going to like that. Hell, I didn't like it.

Donald Donnelly would get his comeuppance one way or another, and I hoped I was the one to do it.

"Come on, let's go change and get this nightmare of a dinner over with," I grumbled.

Henry followed behind me, both of our moods soured by the filth parading around as our director. Stepping into the locker room, I walked over and sat on the bench, dropping my head down between my legs. Breathing deeply, I focused on what mattered—friends, family, and love. Thoughts of the last time Henry and I were in here sent flutters through me, and I used it to shake away the negative tendrils that had latched on to me.

"Smalls, we'll get to the bottom of this. *I promise.*"

Looking up, I found Henry leaning against the locker in front of me. His face was solemn, but I could see the truth shining in his eyes. Standing, I walked toward him, wrapping my arms around his waist as I rested my head against his chest. His steady heartbeat was a calming balm to mine.

Instantly, he wrapped his arms around me, engulfing me in his embrace. Henry made me feel safe, and I basked in that security, soaking in his faith. We stood this way for a few moments, his head on top of mine as we settled one another. The door banging open a few minutes later had us both jumping as we turned to see who was coming for us. Henry did one of those manly things where he expertly moved me behind him before I could even blink.

"Sor, what's going on?"

When he saw who it was, he relaxed, and I peeked around him. Soren stood panting as if he had run here, the look on his face causing me worry. Moving around Henry, I went toward Soren and wrapped my arms around him, giving him the peace I'd just gathered from Henry. He pulled me close, clinging to me as he tried to calm himself down.

A second later, I felt Henry wrap us both up in his arms, engulfing us. Wow, now this was nice. Before I started to get dirty thoughts, because, let's be honest, that position gave me all kinds of ideas; I withdrew enough to look at Soren. Pulling his head down, I kissed him gently and smoothed his hair off his face. I gazed into his eyes, offering reassurance for whatever plagued him.

"Hey, what is it Sor? Tell us."

"I... Fuck!"

Tears started to fall down his face, and he sank onto the bench next to him. Following him, I grasped his hands in mine, squeezing to let him know I was there.

"Sor, we can do this together. Just tell us, okay?"

He looked up, taking a deep breath, and delivered the message I hadn't expected.

"Fin and Rowan have been taken."

"What? I don't understand. Taken? Where? By whom?"

"I-I-I don't know everything that's going on, but Rhett didn't meet me, and then I ran into my mom," he rambled, a little hysteria in his voice. "She told me I needed to give you up, but I refused and told her to go to Hell. Then I ran into Rhonda, and she mentioned Rhett acting strange, but neither of us knew what for. So, we went our separate ways. I was sitting in the student section like we planned, and I was getting some info. Then you guys performed, and wow guys, that was incredible."

He took a moment to pause before the rest rushed out in

one stream of air. Once he had sucked in a new breath, he started again. Henry remained frozen against the lockers, his gaze intent on Soren.

"I was sitting there, amazed by your show. I started to make my way here, and I got a text. I thought it was you guys, but it wasn't. It was him." His body shivered in repulsion. "He gave himself away. Said I should've listened to my mom and then sent a picture of Fin and Rowan tied and gagged in the trunk of a car!" Soren exclaimed. Turning, he focused on me, pleading with me. "I started to run here, and Agent Dickhead grabbed me and told me not to tell you, that it would ruin the plan. But I didn't care; I took off after head-butting him because we don't keep secrets, we don't."

He was shaking, and the last part had been said in almost a breathless whisper. I was trying to put all the pieces together, but my brain had faltered on the Fin and Rowan news.

"What do you mean, they were gagged and tied?"

Soren looked up at Henry when he'd whispered his question. Soren's eyes were full of tears now, and I knew he wasn't making it up, not that he ever would. A small part of me was hoping, though, that maybe it was a joke.

*The fucking joke was me.*

My breathing came quickly as I thought about my best friend and boyfriends' sisters being taken.

"No, this isn't supposed to happen."

It was an odd thing to think, as if I got to choose what happened in the world. Shaking my head quickly, I tried to dispel it from my mind, to make it go away.

A loud boom broke me out of my panic, and I realized it was the door. It slammed against the wall again, making me jump. I wasn't sure there hadn't been damage this time based on the level of noise. My body tensed, not sure if someone was coming for us. Rhett stormed in, a pissed-off mountain of rage. If I didn't know how much this hurt him, I would've been scared, but I knew this was his biggest fear—not protecting the people he loved.

Without a thought, I got up off the bench and ran to him, hugging him tightly. I was getting in a lot of hugs today, their healing power incomparable to anything else. Rhett stood there breathing hard, body clenched, and for a second, I didn't think he was going to respond. Cooing noises came out of me as I rubbed his back, hoping to find his rage monster off switch.

Finally, he wrapped his arms around me and picked me up. I wrapped my legs around his waist and then remembered I still had my skates on, so I dropped them back down. He lifted me up more under my ass until I was eye-level with him. Placing my hands on his cheeks, I stared into his eyes.

"Hey there, Grump," I soothed away the wrinkle between his eyes, "they won't get away with this. We will find them. *I promise.*"

Rhett stared into my eyes, and I must've convinced him because he finally nodded, dropping his head to mine as his tears started to fall. Guess I'd found that off switch after all.

"I can't lose her."

"I know. I can't either. We'll find both of them. *Together.*"

He sat down with me in his lap a moment later, and I

turned and found Soren holding a shell-shocked Henry. He was just sitting there, staring blankly at the lockers in front of him. Locking away my own fear, I pulled out the strength I needed to get my friends back. I could freak out later, but now I needed to be strong for all of us. My crappy past had prepared me for this. I was used to it.

*I could do this. I could do this. I could do this.*

My mental chant filled me with the courage I needed, and I locked my fear and panic away until I had my sisters back with me. Climbing off Rhett's lap, I kneeled in front of Henry and grabbed his hands to get him to look at me.

"Henry, we're going to this dinner. We stick to the plan, and we get the answers we need. The Council isn't harming another person I care about." Power filled my voice and the confidence we could get through this.

"He knew."

"Who knew, Rey?" Soren asked, casting me a perplexed look.

"Henry, what are you saying?"

"My dad. When I was home before the semester started, I found something. It didn't make sense at the time. I thought something was going on, like maybe they were getting a divorce or something," Henry rambled. "They'd both been acting weird. But then Agent Blueballs revealed my dad was with the Agency, so I guess I just dismissed it. I didn't think it mattered anymore. But now, I think he knew...."

Ice filled my veins at what he was saying. His dad knew? Did that mean they weren't on the side of good? Could they have been responsible for my parents? How had we stayed under the radar for over ten years, though, and then R found us? But if that was the case, and the Agency said they weren't bad. *Who did we trust?*

"Does that mean your dad doesn't work for the Agency?" I whispered, fear evident.

"I think it means we can't trust *anyone*," breathed Soren, voicing the thoughts in my head.

"No, it just means you need to look at all the pieces together and quit only seeing half the board," a voice in the shadows proclaimed, stopping us all dead in our tracks.

"Who the hell is there?" Rhett shouted, his voice taking on that rumbly bear sound again.

Stepping out from another row of lockers, I think we were all momentarily shocked to find one of the Ashleys.

"Ash?" Soren asked, confusion on his face.

"Surprise!" She did a little jazz hand number. "I'm not the super bitch you thought I was." She smirked.

"No, just a bitch, apparently."

"Ah, that's the sweetest thing you've ever said to me, Sawyer. I do like you, you know." She sauntered over with all the confidence in the world. "I hope we can be friends after all this. If we don't all die, that is."

"Why didn't Agent Buttface out you then, when he outed everyone else?" questioned Soren. Yes, that! Thank you, Sor, for staying logical when all I could think about was wiping the smirk off her face.

"Let's just say," she paused, her grin widening, "it's above his pay grade. Some families within the Agency are cleaning house, so to speak. There's a secret order within the secret organization."

Raising my hand like the smartass I was, I waited for her to finish her monologue.

"Yes, Sawyer?" she sighed, her annoyance at me making me smile.

"First, why hang around Adelaide?" I ticked off on my finger. "Second, how much crazier can this get? Third, why should we believe you?" I finished holding up three fingers.

"Well first, *this* is my personality, and I was playing a part. Catch up!" She clapped her hands, rolling her eyes as she held up her own finger as she answered my questions. "Second, it's only crazy if you don't believe it. And third, because I know how to rescue your friends." She smirked again, one hand on her hip, the other waving three fingers at me. "But if you don't need help, by all means..." She started to stalk off in a classic bad guy way, giving me all the wrong kinds of feelings.

"Wait... ugh," I groaned, standing to stop Rhett from following after her. I placed my hand on his chest, telling him to wait. When he accepted, I faced her head-on. "We could use your help. What do you mean about pieces?"

She turned, a huge smile on her face, having no idea the threat I'd just saved her from. Though if she was Agency, she probably knew some secret kick move or something. Doubt clawed at my mind for a second, worried I'd signed on with the devil instead of the angel.

"Henry, your dad isn't the mole. That would be your *mother*."

She leaned back and inspected her nails, almost like we bored her. I wasn't sure I liked this version of Ashlee.

"What were they blackmailing her about?" I asked, but Henry answered instead.

"She was covering up a money trail or something. I couldn't make sense of it, just that it seemed odd and there were threats." He looked up finally, staring at Ashlee, addressing her. "Tell me everything."

"Yes, you're on the right track. The deposits you found were to an offshore account your mother set up years ago. She's been stealing money from the foundation she works for, but she hasn't always worked there."

"Raven Networks. She and my dad met there."

"Now you're getting the picture," Ashlee smiled.

"Care to share with the rest of the class? Our friends are missing. Let's get this whole 'secret spy bad guy' reveal moving along." I motioned with my hands before remembering to add the social niceties. "Please." I didn't like being left out on the outside of things and was starting to get a bit punchy again.

"Ugh, you're no fun, Sawyer." She pouted. I didn't think she knew how close she was to being pummeled. The thought of her knowing kung-fu was the only thing that stopped me.

"Sofia Garcia was a plant from the beginning. She was sent to Raven Networks to source out the Agency mole. She met David and fell in love with him. They married and had two kids. This part, you know, blah blah. The part you don't know is that she didn't discover David's identity, he told her.

He loved her enough to be honest with her; too bad she couldn't do the same. Sofia had a crisis of conscience and couldn't hand over her husband. So, she lied and pointed the finger at someone else. She almost got away with it too."

The pieces were starting to click, and I think I finally figured out what she was saying…

"But then my mom and dad disappeared from Latimer's organization. Sofia didn't just work for the Council. She worked for the Latimers too." Looking up, my brain was clicking faster than I could speak for once. "Sofia was placed at Draven's to find info on Victoria since she'd been sent to work for Latimer. When Victoria disappeared, Latimer blamed Draven. They must've known she lied at that point. How did she keep them off her trail for as long as she did?"

"Round of applause Saw. A+ for you, girl." She clapped again, and I wanted to wipe the grin off her face. "Yes, the Draven's knew when Victoria left, and I'd wager, they had their suspicions where she was. Latimer was furious and blamed them for insider conspiracy or some shit. Bad blood between those two." She cringed, enjoying telling the story. She started walking around like she was looking at stuff, but we were in the private staff locker room. There wasn't much here. When she'd left us in suspense long enough, she stopped and faced us all.

"It took the Council a few years to realize this. Props to Mama Reyes. Sofia was actually pretty good at lying to people. When Draven realized Sofia knew, they threatened her, and she renegotiated. Sofia either became a triple double-cross spy, or she committed to one of them. This part we don't know. But it seems in exchange to save David and her family, she turned on yours instead."

I looked at Henry and saw the pain reflected there at his mother's actions. I didn't hold it against him. I didn't even hold it against his mom to an extent. She made some bad choices, and my parents paid for that. It was hard to know the way out when you were surrounded by darkness. I understood that part of the equation and remembered her from when I was little, and how she made us cookies and bandaged our scrapes. I would forgive her someday, just not today.

"Rumor is that Nicholas Draven was the one who she was faithful to. She'd send him pictures of you, and it's said he looked forward to them, missing his daughter as he did. But, as secrets do, they never stay buried. Latimer eventually figured it out, and that's when Leon Rojas was sent, or 'R' as you knew him. Sofia was pressured to tell Leon where you were headed, or they'd kill David."

So, Sofia was the one to leak our escape. No wonder we didn't get far.

"The money is believed to have been her escape plan. She was stealing pennies off each donation, hardly noticeable at the time, but over the past fifteen years, that adds up to a lot. When word got out you were, in fact, still alive, they pressured her once again to get Henry on board."

"Why do they want Rey?" Rhett asked, vengeance in his voice. I was honestly surprised he'd been quiet this whole time and hadn't started Hulk smashing stuff. Ash wasn't one for quick monologues. She apparently saw the danger, though, and cut to the chase when he asked.

"They use skaters for various purposes. They probably wanted you to be a drug mule, basically taking things with you as you traveled the globe for events. Plot twist, you refused and then found Sariah, and well, all was lost. Their last threat hadn't been to spill to David or even kill him. Nope, they found a better option this time—sell her daughter to the highest bidder. Looks like they've finally had enough of Sofia and decided to collect. Abernathy himself sent his own man to do it."

By the end, we were all exhausted from the emotional upheaval and secrets she'd unloaded on us. I didn't get one thing though, why Abernathy? It seemed Soren had the same thought.

"Why Abernathy? You said it was a fight between Latimer and Draven."

"Ah yes, gold star for you too, cutie." She winked, Henry and I tensing at the action. "Relax, I'm not going to break up the throuple. I just recognize a good-looking guy when I see one."

"Get to the point, Ash. I'm running out of patience for you, and I get punchy when I do."

"I'd like to see you try, Saw. I think it'd be fun." She grinned, and I think she would actually enjoy it. Finally, she quit the games and answered, "Abernathy has been planning to overtake Hawthorne for years. He's trying to buy allies."

Fury built in me at her words. It always came back to Abernathy. His power and greed knew no bounds, and he wouldn't be satisfied until we all fractured into a million pieces to get what he wanted. We were nothing but collateral damage on his way to world domination. I was sick of it.

Mostly because I didn't understand why I was so special to them. I was just a girl... a girl who only brought devastation to the people around her. A girl destined forever to be alone, losing the ones she loved—a girl who knew what she had to do no matter what the cost.

# five

. . .

## rey

ASHLEE'S WORDS circulated in my head, and yet, all I could focus on was how my mom had a part in killing my best friend's parents. How she'd almost killed Sawyer, and was possibly responsible for Fin's kidnapping. There was nothing she could do to come back from this. There was no redemption for her—none.

Standing, I took in my family scattered around the room and focused on the now—Fin and Rowan.

"Are you here to help us?" I questioned Ashlee, trying to keep my voice steady, "Because while I appreciate the history lesson, we need to find the girls. *That's* what matters right now," I demanded, pointing my finger down at the ground to emphasize.

Rhett moved behind me, physically supporting me with

his posture. Ashlee swallowed, looking unnerved for the first time. I didn't blame her. His menacing stare, crossed arms, and massive frame would be enough to make anyone wet themselves; add in his intense eyebrows, and you'd spill all your secrets, which worked as she started talking, appearing flustered for once.

"I uh, yeah, I mean, that's why I'm here. *Duh*," she tried to redirect. "I wasn't just shoving your noses in it or anything, promise. I want to help. I *can help*."

Assessing her, I realized she seemed sincere for once, but it didn't matter. From this point forward, I only trusted people in our circle, and she hadn't earned that yet. So, I would listen to what she had to offer, but like Agent Buttface had learned, we decided together in the end.

"Fine. Meet us at the house in two hours. Sawyer and I have a dinner to attend. Soren, Rhett, you need to stick to the plan and meet back at the house when it's time. Contact Mateo and see if he can find anything while we're out. If I know my sister, she will have… Shit," I muttered, cutting myself off. Glancing at Smalls, it appeared to dawn on her at the same time.

"Fuck. I need a phone." She hung her head but stuck out her hand. Soren placed his phone in her hand, a confused look on his face.

She started dialing a number, and I wanted to tell her it was okay. Smalls had only known she had a brother for two weeks; it wasn't going to be natural to her yet to think of him in stressful situations.

"Hey, can you come to the staff locker room? It's important. Yeah… that's what I need to talk to you about. Okay, yeah. See you soon."

When she hung up, she handed the phone back to Soren and turned to Rhett. "What about your mom? Do we tell her now or wait until we know more?"

Rhett looked lost for a second as he decided before shaking his head no. He'd seemed to withdraw more into himself the longer this went on. I wrapped my arm around him in a one-armed hug, trying to give him some comfort. I was worried, but I didn't have that luxury. Finding the girls would only happen if we didn't screw up. Surprisingly, Rhett leaned into me and seemed to exhale some. He took care of us all so effortlessly, I didn't think he knew how to rely on others.

A knock on the door had Soren walking over to let Asa in. It wasn't locked, but I guess he was polite like that. He walked in, looking around curiously at all of us, picking up on the anxiety in the room.

"You said you knew where Fin was? She never met me before the show," he asked Sawyer, then seemed to remember her show, turning and hugging her. "Stellar performance, by the way." Sawyer clung to him, and I could tell she was trying to push her thoughts away, but every now and then, I could see her fear for Finley peek through.

"Hey, it's okay. What happened?" he soothed, rubbing his hand up and down her back. Asa looked up at me, and I guess my face wasn't hiding my fear enough either because he stilled, putting some pieces together.

"Where's Fin?" Asa's voice came out in a strained whisper, almost as if he was afraid to hear the answer.

"They were taken," Ashlee supplied nonchalantly. She'd leaned back against the lockers, casually inspecting her nails. Her delivery hadn't been soft or tactful, but it was to the point.

"What do you mean? Who? And why are you here?"

Sawyer finally pulled back from her twin to answer. "Fin and Rowan were taken. That's all we know right now," she explained, taking a breath. "We're going to get them back." Confidence and assuredness filled her statement, and it was hard not to believe her at that moment.

"What can I do?"

"Can you go and get Fin's computer and take it over to HQ? Mateo might be able to look at it to see what Finley's been digging into. I know she's been doing her own research, so we'll start there. Rhett and Soren will meet you there in an hour, and the rest of us after the dinner."

"You're still going to that dinner? How could you—"

"Because they're working very hard to keep us from learning something. We stick to our plan, and get our information. It's the only play we have at the moment. But don't ever think I'm not worried or fucking scared. Just don't."

Sawyer's voice was firm and had an edge to it. I could see the determination in her eyes as she stared at her brother, willing him to understand.

"You're right. I'm sorry. I'm just…"

"I know. But we can only do this if we all stay clear-headed and work together. No running off on your own." She pointedly looked at him. "We don't need to rescue more people, and the list is already too long at this point. So, let's all skip the great heroics and not go rogue. We'll find them together."

"*We'll find them together*," we all chorused.

"Well, this is touching and all, but I've got things to do, so… yeah. I'll see you at your house in a couple of hours. It's been real," Ashlee said, walking out of the room, swaying her hips as she did.

Shaking my head, I turned back to the group gathered. "Okay, I think that's the cue to get moving. Everyone knows the plan?" When no one disagreed, I continued, "Ollie and Ty are still doing their missions, so inform them when they get to the house. It's too risky to tell Ollie now, since he's in enemy territory. Any updates from either of them?"

Rhett and Soren shook their heads, both appearing lost in their own thoughts. I think we were all feeling the weight of the revelations in the past thirty minutes. Soren kissed Sawyer and me before heading to the door. He waited while Rhett hugged Sawyer, holding her for a long moment— almost like he needed to steal her strength. Eventually, he let go and kissed the top of her head before walking off. The guys headed out together, and I prayed we wouldn't be too late.

Twenty minutes later, Smalls and I were dressed and headed to the cafeteria for the Alumni Dinner. We were a little late due to our impromptu Operation ToePick meeting, but nothing could be done about it. Smalls and I were both quiet, unsure what we were about to walk into and who would be at this dinner. I was worried about how she'd respond if she came face to face with Latimer or Abernathy—especially Abernathy.

What would it be like to meet your biological father after learning he'd sold you?

I couldn't fathom it, but I also never thought my mother would sell out her best friends and their daughter. Parental crimes were becoming a bit of a bingo card. Cover a square if your mom wasn't your real mom. Cover a square if your dad worked for a secret Agency. Cover a square… it all seemed too out there to be real, and yet here we were. What was reality anymore? I was scared to find out what was next.

I opened the door and guided Smalls in. She was wearing a dress under her thick coat, and if this wasn't as serious as it was, I would've struggled to focus during this dinner. It was navy blue and had an open back to it. I didn't know anything else about dresses or fashion, but she looked stunning in it. Taking our coats, I hung them in the staff closet, making sure we didn't leave anything in our pockets. My paranoia was increasing, but at this stage, was it paranoia? No, I didn't think it was.

The first person we saw as we entered the private room was the Director. He'd always seemed slimy, but I couldn't ever pinpoint the reason. He grinned widely at our arrival, and I wanted to wrap Smalls up in my arms so he couldn't perv on her. She inched closer to me, and I momentarily felt a thrill run through me that she'd wanted the same thing.

"Miss Sullivan, Mr. Reyes. I was beginning to think you weren't coming. I'm so happy to have you join us." He was starting to come across as a cheesy televangelist. "Come, I have a table for you with some *special* alumni for you to meet."

Smalls and I walked solemnly over to the table, passing several others full of students and parents, a few calling out as we passed. We made it to the front of the room, and I instantly hated the position. We were practically trapped with no easy escape. I didn't like it.

Pulling out the chair for Smalls, I tried to comfort her as we took our seats. A couple of men and women were dispersed around the table. It didn't look like Abernathy was there, but I wasn't sure who the others were, and there were still some seats open.

"Ah, here are our special guests, our expo finale performers. Let me introduce you to some of our most *generous* alumni," Director Donnelly said. "Here we have the DuPont's, the Berkshire's, and Bellamy's. We're just waiting on—"

"Orson Abernathy."

It came from behind us, making Smalls and I tense. I felt her breathing start to increase, so I placed my hand on her leg, linking my hand with hers under the table. I began tracing my thumb in circles on her palm. By the time he walked around the table, his smarmy smile in place, her breathing had evened.

Kris Butler

"Ah yes, Orson Abernathy. Well, it looks like we're all here now, so I'll let them know. Excuse me," the Director clipped, walking off to do whatever he said.

I'd been focusing on the man who'd set this whole ball into motion. He was older than I'd expected after meeting Isla, but I guess she had only been eighteen, and he was in his mid-twenties when they married. Orson's hair was a chestnut brown with some silver streaks styled short to his head. It was the eyes that connected Asa and Sawyer to him.

The bright green was unique enough to stand out. He didn't even glance toward us; he merely looked bored at the fact he had to be at this table with everyone. It was curious that he was here. It didn't appear to be his type of thing based on what we knew. Abernathy sat next to Bellamy, and they greeted one another in a friendly manner, some interesting looks passing between them.

It was clear they considered themselves above everyone else and only chatted with one another. Next to Sawyer, a lady started to talk to her about the skating program, which then drew Orson's interest. He eyed her curiously, and I wondered how much he knew about her after he'd sold her off. Did he know Latimer had given her to a family? Did he know she escaped?

After a few seconds, he went back to his conversation, bored of his perusal of her. I continued to rub Small's hand, not letting up for anything. It was giving me comfort as well, grounding us together.

"My daughter skates in the same program, do you know her?" the woman next to Sawyer questioned.

Turning, I took in the lady. She appeared very unassuming. However, I watched as she tracked people, seemed to listen to the whole room, and was aware of her surroundings at all times. Her persona had to be an act, a ploy.

"Oh, I don't know. I'm still new to everything. What did you say your name was?" Sawyer asked politely.

"Berkshire. My daughter is *Ashlee* Berkshire."

I wasn't confident, but I felt like she emphasized Ashlee when she said it, clueing us into which Ashlee she referred to.

"Oh, yes, we teach one of the dance classes together. I don't see her much outside of the *locker room*."

Good girl, Smalls. Subtly dropping clues that we'd put together.

"Ah, that's lovely. Hopefully, she's been *helpful* as you've adjusted to campus."

"Oh, yes, absolutely. She's a real gem," Smalls said, sarcasm dripping from each word.

Surprisingly, Mrs. Berkshire laughed at her response, and I wondered if maybe the mom would be nicer than the daughter.

"Yes, you've definitely met her then if that's your response. She must like you if you've gotten her *real* personality," she whispered conspiratorially.

Food was brought out then, and we ate in relative silence as the alumni all tried to one-up one another with their achievements. It was quite dull, and I was beginning to feel restless. I needed to be actively doing something to find Fin. Peeking at my phone, I saw no new messages. Sending a text to Soren, I was hoping for an update.

**Me:** Anything?

**Sorbet:** Mateo is looking at the computer. Agent Bitch-slap stopped by before everyone else showed up. He's... well, let's just say I hope Sawyer throat punches him again. Rhett and I didn't find anything, but planted the bugs in the offices and common rooms. Those are running now. Ollie's was up for about 5 mins but then went offline. His phone is as well. Ty's worried.

**ME:** Shit.

**Sorbet:** Yeah. There's something else, but Rhett didn't want to say anything to Sawyer yet. But Elias was at the Arena, and he was with Adelaide.

**ME:** ...

**Sorbet:** Yeah, same. Ty's dad is here, though, and he's nicer than Agent Dickcheese. Charlie is up to speed too. They told Rhonda. She's a bit hysterical. Isla is sitting with her. Asa is... not good, man. How's the dinner?

**ME:** Boring. Ashlee's mom is here. So far, just the meal. I'm getting antsy.

**ME:** Orson is here too.

**Sorbet:** Fuck, how's our girl?

**ME:** She's staying strong. If we don't get asked soon about this tour, we will head back. I need to be doing something. I can't let...

**Sorbet:** We won't. I promise. I feel...

**ME:** Stop. This isn't your fault.

**Sorbet:** It feels like it, but thank you for saying that. I love you.

**ME:** I love you, Sor.

**ME:** I'm scared.

**Sorbet:** Me too. It's okay to be. But we will solve this together. We all will.

**ME**: I believe you.

**ME:** I'll keep you posted.

**Sorbet:** Okay, be safe, babe.

I pocketed my phone, and the movement caught Smalls' attention; she gave me a questioning look, but I shook my head. I didn't have anything useful to tell her. The news about Elias, I didn't even know where to start with that. It would need to be later and added to the ever-growing shit-to-do list.

It finally seemed like the dinner was about to be over when dessert was brought out. The Director had spent most of the meal schmoozing Abernathy. The interesting part was that he didn't seem to like Director Donnelly if Orson's expression was anything to go by. He seemed like he wanted this meal to be over just as much as we did.

The dessert was placed in front of me, and a note dropped into my lap simultaneously. By the time I realized it, the waiter was gone, and I had no clue who'd just given it to me. Discreetly, I opened it up under the table. It was just a bunch of numbers and a symbol. Even more confused, I put it in my pocket. Smalls looked at me again, and all I could do was shrug this time because I had no clue. It obviously was important, but who was it from?

Finally, the dishes were cleared away, and the Director got

up to give his kiss-ass speech to the alumni present and the families of the students. Director Donnelly was too much like a car salesman. Whatever he was selling, I wasn't buying.

"Now it's that time of the dinner where our next candidates for *clava oraculi* are revealed. If you were given a code anytime during the meal, then you've been selected by an alumnus. Welcome to the inner sanctum," he cheered, stretching his arms wide. Sawyer looked at me, a question on her face, and I nodded as Donnelly continued. "Thanks to all the parents and students for our wonderful expo today and for making the fall alumni dinner the most successful yet. We can't wait to see you all again in the spring! Have a great night."

With that, everyone started to gather their belongings as they prepared to leave. I turned to Sawyer, not sure exactly what it meant. Was it for both of us? Well, too bad. It was going to be. I squeezed her hand in reassurance as we waited for further instruction on what to do.

"Sawyer, have you had the *full* tour yet?" Mrs. Berkshire asked, a small smile on her face.

"No, Mrs. Berkshire. I don't believe I have."

"Well, let me show you. And please, call me Constance."

"Yes, let's go grab our coats."

"No need, dear. It starts in this building."

Smalls stood up, and I held onto her hand, glad they included us together. We supported one another as we followed our tablemates through some doors at the back. A few people from other tables seemed to follow us as well. We walked into a room and gathered with the others, all shuffling on our feet as we tried to figure out what was going on. I was surprised when it wasn't the Director who took over the meeting, but Constance herself.

"Welcome to the inner sanctum of the school and school board. You've been selected for *clava oraculi* because you possess something we admire and would like to welcome you into our ranks."

Constance touched a wall panel that disappeared into the wall, and a door with a key code appeared. I guess now the code made sense. I just wasn't sure what I was about to walk into. Smalls looked up at me, anxiety evident in her eyes as well. I pulled out my phone and used her body to cover me as I quickly sent off a text.

**ME:** We're headed in. 3492847

Then I dropped a location pin in case we lost connection, or worse, were taken. At least this way, they had somewhere to start. Fin had taught me a few things over the years, and I wasn't taking any chances. Let's hope this went as Agent Buttface predicted, or they might need to rescue more than two people tonight.

# six

. . .

"ANYTHING?" Asa asked for the third time in five minutes.

"Nope," I grumbled, the irritation evident in my voice, "and your hovering isn't helping me. I haven't done this in a few years, and it was just a hobby... so could you, I don't know, give me some space?"

"Sorry, I'm just..." He hung his head, the fear evident in his body.

"I get it. I do... I'm worried too, but I can't really help if you're making me more anxious."

"Right." He nodded, seeming to get it. "I'll go grab some drinks."

Asa walked off, and I felt for him. I didn't think I'd be as calm as he was; well, I guess he wasn't calm if he was bugging me, but he was controlling it better than I imagined I would. Typing in another sequence, I tried to unlock her secure folder. Finley had a stellar system, and I didn't think I was up to par; as much as I wanted to be the one who could do this, I wasn't so sure I could.

Soren walked over and took the chair next to me, and started flipping through a notebook, presumably looking for clues. The conference room was jam-packed with people, both friends and Agency. Hitting another error message, I decided to get some air. Soren watched me get up and nodded in solidarity.

Sometimes it felt like I was the useless one of the group, and then the moment I was given a mission in my wheelhouse, I couldn't even do it. My insecurities of not being good enough were being triggered under all this stress, and I didn't like it. I knew they didn't see me that way, so I needed to smack myself around a bit to remember it.

Rhett was pacing at the front of the room, making everyone avoid that section. Part of me felt I should say something, but I wasn't close to my siblings, and I had nothing reassuring to offer. Maybe after some air, a bit of inspiration would hit me. That could happen, right?

Despite the house being full of people, it felt *empty*. Half of the people who lived here were out doing something potentially dangerous, and I was here. No one had heard from Oliver yet, either. Ty was starting to show his nerves with both him and Sawyer gone. He tried to deny it, but I could see how tense he was in his body posture.

I'd finally convinced him to pack a bag and stay in Elias' or Ollie's room, so he didn't have to keep bed hopping or feel like he was missing something at the house. I think he was ultimately just glad to be asked, and I liked it had been me to realize that. I guess I did have my purposes.

Rhonda sat in the kitchen, staring blankly at the wall. She had a cup of something in her hand but didn't appear to be drinking it. Isla smiled softly at me as I walked past. She'd been trying to offer support to both Asa and Rhonda, but it was hard to know what to say to someone I imagined. Quickly, I grabbed a bottle of water and exited the kitchen, not sure what to do with all the suffocating emotions in the air.

Lucky was pawing at the door, and I realized we'd all forgotten about him. This was why we needed Elias and Sawyer. I hoped Elias would realize that soon. I missed him.

"Hey, Lucks, come on… I'll take you out."

He looked up at me, and I swear he smiled in relief. Opening the door, he scurried out and headed toward the grass. Yep, we'd neglected the poor dog. He was so quiet that sometimes I forgot about him. He typically stayed with Elias or Sawyer anyway, and now they were both out of the house, I guess he'd been lost in all the chaos.

Just as he finished, I noticed a figure heading up the drive-way. They were dressed in all black with a hoodie pulled over their head. Dread filled me, and I hurriedly jogged up the stairs. Lucky wasn't in any rush, though, and he continued to sniff around after he'd relieved himself.

"*Lucky*, come on. Let's go." Nothing. I motioned with my hands, trying to get his attention. I snapped, I clapped, but nothing still.

"Lucky," I sang, "time to go in." No response.

"Lucky!" I screamed in more of a panic this time as the figure grew closer—still, no acknowledgment from the dog. Scampering back down the stairs, I couldn't leave him to fend for himself. Quickly, I made it over to where he was sniffing and tried to pick him up, but he moved out of my grasp at the last second.

Now, he thought we were playing a game and continued to run away from me each time I'd get close to him as I tried to pick him up. I had to make a hilarious sight—ass up, arms out, chasing a white furball. The little shit was enjoying this, I bet. *This will be the last time I brought him out here, I huffed to myself.* I should just let him get killed by the creepy guy in the hoodie.

Diving for him, he moved again, and I bombed into the grass. Fucking great. Looking up, I could see the hooded guy standing on the edge of the pavement, watching me. His shoulders moved up and down, and I realized he was laughing at me. The creepy hoodie guy was laughing at me.

"Are you laughing at me?" *Why am I engaging with the psycho killer?*

"Sorry, dude. It's just so funny watching you chase that tiny thing."

His voice must've been some type of Pied Piper because Lucky trotted up to him and sat perfectly at his feet. The killer bent over and picked him up, Lucky licking his face in appreciation. *Oh, I see how it is, dog. Choose the crazy dude over me.*

Pushing off from the grass, I got to my feet, brushing off the blades and dirt, thankful there wasn't snow in this section. Turning in exasperation, I looked over the hooded figure. Maybe I could reason with him to give me the dog? Sawyer would never forgive me if anything happened to him.

"Could I have the dog back, please?"

"I don't think he wants to be with you, man."

Hanging my head, I was becoming frustrated. I couldn't do anything right today—not even take out the dog for a bathroom break. Why was Sawyer with me again?

"Well, if you're here to kill us all, you're going to have to go through me first. I know how this works, right... the virgin dies first? Or wait, was it last? You know what, it doesn't matter. You'll just have to kill me first, and I'm a screamer. So, I doubt you'll get far before a whole slew of people come out here."

I crossed my arms in determination and borrowed confidence and stared down the dog stealing killer. He barked out a laugh this time, throwing his head back and causing his hood to fall.

"You're funny, kid. Mateo, right?" he asked when he righted himself.

"*Kid*? How old do you think I am? I'm twenty-one, jackass."

"Sheesh. Sorry, it's just an expression. Look, I'm a friend of Finley's. We were supposed to meet up earlier, but she never showed. That's not like her, so I just wanted to make sure she was okay. Promise. I'm not here to kill you or steal your dog."

I scrutinized him, trying to see if he was lying. I wasn't an expert on the matter, but I felt like this would be something I could tell if he was. Feeling moderately relieved at his statement and accepting that Lucky appeared to approve, I relaxed.

"Fine," I grumbled, starting to get why Rhett liked it so much. It really conveyed a lot in a syllable. "Yes, I'm Mateo, though how did you know my name? Never mind." I waved my hands in front of me. Walking toward the front door, I gestured for him to follow. "I guess you should come in. There's been a bit of a *situation*."

My words had his jovial expression dropping and changing into a serious one.

"Tell me everything."

He took off toward me with Lucky, and for a minute, I thought maybe I'd misread the whole '*I'm not here to kill you*' thing, but when he bypassed me for the door, I jogged to catch up.

"Uh, do you have a name 'not going to kill me guy'?"

"It's kind of complicated, and I'd prefer to keep it to myself for the moment."

"Yeah, because that's not fishy or anything. Listen." I grabbed his arm, ready to defend my friends as I stepped in front of him, blocking the door. "There's a lot of shit going on. So, no. I'm not going to let some rando walk into our house like we don't have people after us. You either tell me who the hell you are, or you can't enter."

My eyes bored into his, my stare deadly as I held firm in my belief. These were people I would stand up for. And despite me looking like a geek, I was an athlete. I could probably take him on long enough to alert Rhett or someone.

He stared at me for a few minutes with a look of surprise. Well, get over it, *killer*. You'd just woken my dragon, and I was prepared to breathe fire. My menacing stare must've worked, because he relaxed his posture and conceded his position, stepping back.

"You're right. I'm sorry for not considering your feelings in all of this. I just... care about Finley, and I think I could help. I'm Cohen."

The name wasn't any I'd heard before on our watch list, but he could be giving me a fake one for all I knew.

"How do you know Fin?"

"We... sort of work together, okay. We have this shared history."

"Are you a hacker friend?" He looked momentarily stunned at my question before he responded.

"In a manner of speaking, yes. I promise I want nothing but good things for her."

"Okay, come on. You can help me with her computer. I can't crack her password," I admitted, turning to open the door. "You take one coding class, and everyone thinks you can hack," I mumbled under my breath.

I wasn't angry at them, but myself. I wanted to be better at this. Though, maybe this was how I could do it. This guy might be able to give us answers to what she was doing before she'd been taken.

"Just know there are a lot of people who are worried, so if you can help us, great."

Opening the door, I led him back through the house. Rhonda and Isla were still at the table, and Rhonda seemed to

77

have moved on to distractedly stirring her coffee now. I hoped Cohen was able to help as much as he believed he could. Soren looked up when I walked back into HQ, a confused look on his face at my shadow.

"Uh, I found this guy outside. He says he's a friend of Fin's, that he was supposed to meet her, but she didn't show, and that he could help us find her. So, I thought we could use his help," I rushed out.

Rhett turned at my response, studying Cohen. For being in a new place, Cohen took in the speculative glances from everyone and didn't even seem to bat an eyelash—better than I would've done. He almost seemed to enjoy it.

"If you can help, you can stay. If not, then leave," Rhett barked. Cohen nodded, appreciation in his eyes at Rhett's no-nonsense approach. Asa had perked up as well, having returned from his drink run.

"I'm Asa, Fin's boyfriend. Can you... can you really help?" his voice pleaded.

At the word boyfriend, Cohen tensed for a minute, and I realized he still had Lucky, who'd fallen asleep in his arms now. Walking over, I took the sleeping dog from him and placed him in the dog bed. Lucky gave a little huff at being moved but instantly curled up in his ball, snuggling down into the two shirts someone had placed in there—Sawyer and Elias'.

"Well, Asa, I'm Cohen. I didn't realize Fin had a *boyfriend*, but what a snack you are," he flirted, leaning against the table now that his arms were free.

Seriously, dude. This was so not the time. I rolled my eyes, but Asa didn't even seem to notice, so caught up in his distress.

"Cohen. Focus," I admonished.

"Sorry, he's hot." He shrugged, looking at me. My face must've said to cut the crap because he sobered and took a seat at the table. "Okay, give me the details."

"Fin was supposed to be at the rink, but never met up with Asa," I emphasized. "After the expo, Soren received a text stating that she and Rowan had been taken, and there was a picture of them bound and gagged in a trunk."

"Who's Rowan?"

"My sister," Rhett growled.

"Ah, okay. Pieces are clicking together. Here's what I know." He held out his hand to list things off. "One, Fin asked me last week to look into something for her. She was working on a case and needed help with one of the firewalls." Lifting a second finger, he continued. "Then yesterday, she contacted me again and said she needed a file on someone. Does Donald Donnelly sound familiar?"

"The Director…" Asa trailed off.

"Well, okay, I guess that makes sense," Cohen nodded to himself, lifting a third finger and continued as he spoke. "Fin was meeting up with a friend, I guess this, Rowan. They were going to retrieve some files from a computer. She'd erased them from a cellphone and cloud drive already but believed there were still some hard copies on a drive that suspiciously wasn't hooked up to the main network and instead was on a closed circuit with a crazy firewall." When he finished, Cohen had five fingers up and waved them before lowering his hand to the table.

"She was looking into the missing girl," Soren concluded.

"Maybe, it did involve a girl, I think." Cohen shrugged, unbothered. "Anyway, she was exchanging a drive I wanted for Donald's dossier. *Except* she didn't show, and so here I am."

"What was she giving you?" Rhett asked, suspicion laced in his voice.

"Oh well, nothing, just some files."

"Bullshit," I remarked, causing everyone to look at me. "I'll give it to you; you're good. You've told us about 80% of the truth. So, what's it going to be? Are you going to trust us and tell us the rest, or are we going to resort to what I promised outside?"

I crossed my arms, attempting to make myself appear menacing and as intimidating as I could, which probably was about as much as a poodle. However, he conceded again and placed his head on the table, softly banging it on the surface. After about a minute of this, he quietly stood up and shut the door.

Taking out a device, he started scanning the room. I guess it was one of those bug spyware things. When the room didn't beep with anything, he relaxed more. The only people in the room were Rhett, Soren, me, and Asa. I wasn't sure where Ty had gone, and the Agency tech person was no longer in the room either.

"I'm not trying to be an asshole. I care for Finley, and I want her back safe. Some things about me aren't going to make sense now, but I ask for the girls' sake that you trust me. Once we have them back, I promise to answer any questions you have. It's just that now is not the time, and I don't want to waste anymore. Deal?"

"You screw us over, and I'm punching your face. Do *you* understand?" Rhett grumbled, his voice representing a bear more than ever before.

"Understood. Now, the computer?"

I pointed to the one next to me, and he walked over and took the seat. The other guys went back to what they were doing before he came in and tried not to stare. I finally understood Asa's behavior earlier because all I wanted to do was watch Cohen.

"And I'm in… So nice of Fin to use my name as her password," he teased.

Asa rolled his eyes and chuckled, thankfully not buying into this guy's nonsense. I had to say, though, so far, he was holding up his end. We at least knew what she'd been up to, and now we were on her computer. It felt like a massive breach of privacy, but also, it was a life or death situation, so it felt justified.

"Looks like she was looking for pictures between Donald and a student named Jill. Ring any bells?" We all nodded, confirming what he'd told us earlier. "And it seems she stumbled upon something to do with Phil."

"Shit," mumbled Soren.

"Go on," I encouraged.

"Well, she was going to Donnelly's office to retrieve the files. Let me see if I can ping her location."

He typed away some more as we all watched him, not even pretending to do anything else now. Cohen was much better at this than me. I felt some pride that I'd been the one to find him, even if he'd technically found me.

"Okay, her phone shows her at the ice rink, and then it just goes offline after that…" he trailed off, confused.

"That's what Ollie's did. Do you think?" breathed Soren.

"Could be. It's just hard to know," I responded, the wheels in my head turning.

"So, what do we do now?" Asa asked.

"Well, I'm going to keep digging and see if I can find where the signal went."

"Wait," Soren interrupted, "Henry just texted me their location and a PIN. I'm not sure what it means, but I'm guessing it's the 'private tour,' and he's not sure if he'll have a phone connection."

"Give me!" Cohen exclaimed, reaching for the phone. He pulled out a cord from his pocket, connected the phone to the computer, and started typing code really fast.

"Yes! I got him. Well, at least those two, but maybe they'll connect to our other missing people. It looks like they're on that same closed network, but what the school didn't account for was his phone automatically connecting to it and giving me my in!" Cohen rambled almost incoherently, caught up in his nerd code speak. I saw why he and Fin were friends now. They both spoke fluent nerd.

"Through your phone, I can piggyback into the network. It should buy us some time, and it shouldn't trigger any interloper alarms."

"Dude, you're speaking Fin nerd speak," Soren interjected, confirming my own thoughts with a laugh. "Which makes me trust you marginally more, but no one else understands you. But it's not just Fin and Rowan. It's our girlfriend and my boyfriend too. Please, we can't lose anyone else."

"Okay."

"Okay?" Soren asked, confused he didn't argue.

"Okay. I get it. You don't know me, and it's an intense situation, but I am good at what I do, and I'm going to do whatever I can to bring all these people back. Which by the way, I think it's cool you're in a throuple. That's very progressive of you." Cohen smiled.

"It's actually… you know what, I don't even know the shape for seven, or is it six? Let's just go with poly. So much easier."

Cohen stopped what he was doing for a minute, and looked up at Soren, blinking. "So, you're all dating the same girl? Guy?" He asked, looking around the room.

"No, well, yes, but also no. We're all dating Sawyer. Well, me, Mateo, and Rhett are in this room, but Ollie, Ty, and Rey are as well, who are still out. I'm also dating Rey. Asa is Sawyer's brother, and he's, as you know, dating Fin."

"Well, it's like a regular *90210* up in here."

"Dude, how old are you? That show reference is so outdated." Soren chuckled.

"Um, I'm twenty-six, and I like the 90s. Does it matter?"

"I guess not. Any luck?"

Soren and Cohen continued to talk while Rhett and Asa just stared off into space, waiting for something solid. I watched Cohen work on the laptop, trying to make sure he wasn't doing anything he wasn't supposed to. Not that I had extensive knowledge, but it made me feel useful. There was that damn trigger again. I needed to make an appointment with my therapist to check in. It couldn't hurt at this point to talk to someone about all these changes in my life.

An hour later, all of us had given up small talk when Tyler came into the conference room. He looked at Cohen but didn't say anything as he sat next to me.

"Anything?" I questioned.

"No, I'm worried." He was biting his lip, his muscles bunched. I was about to offer him some comfort when we all jumped at a sound.

"Boom goes the dynamite!" exclaimed Cohen.

"What?" Rhett demanded. He'd been laid back, arms crossed, and jumped almost two feet in the air at the noise.

"I got something. I think I know where they are, or at least someone."

Relief flooded me at his words, and I hoped we wouldn't be too late.

# seven

. . .

## finley

AWARENESS STARTED to drift into my head as I began to come to. The cold floor was the first thing I registered, followed by the sound of something dripping. Blinking, my eyes began to adjust to the dimly lit space as I gathered my memories.

*The office... the files... kissing Rowan... being grabbed.*

Straining my neck, I tried to see if I could find Rowan. I didn't want to think about what it would mean if we were separated. Unable to see anything from my position, I attempted to roll onto my back. It took great effort, and I laid there panting for a few minutes before I could open my eyes again to look from my new perspective.

I was in a basement, or at least underground, based on the fact there were no windows and only cement walls surrounded me. An old spigot stuck out of the wall as it dripped slowly into a bucket, occasionally spilling over onto the floor, creating a small puddle. The room was small with nothing else in it outside that bucket, and I shuddered at what it implied.

A small noise to my left had me rolling more in the other direction to find Rowan. Relief washed through me when I saw her eyes open. She took a few minutes to gain her awareness, but when her eyes landed on me, I saw relief. *Rowan didn't hate me and was glad we were together.* Our arms were bound behind our backs and our legs together. It had made it difficult to move into this position, and I had no intention of moving anytime soon unless it was to leave.

A gag was in my mouth, but from my rolling, I'd managed to loosen it. Using my chin, I worked it loose some more until I could spit it out. The fabric had a weird taste, and I wanted some water as my throat ached from dehydration. Not enough yet to try drinking anything from *that* bucket—so gross. Licking my lips, I tried to gather enough saliva to ease the dryness.

"Rowan, are you okay?" The question finally croaked out after a few tries. Her nod was slow, but I could see the determination in her eyes to make it true.

"I'm so sorry. I never—" stopping myself, I couldn't head down that path of self-hatred right now. I didn't have time for self-loathing.

"Okay, I'm going to suggest something kind of awkward. Just… trust me, which I know is hard, but yeah…" *Shut up Finley, geez*, I internally berated myself.

Rocking forward, I moved until I was close enough to touch our bodies together. Rowan eyed me strangely, but didn't back away in fear. Gently, I started to pull her gag with my teeth. It was slow and awkward with me all up in her grill, but it was better than her not being able to talk. Plus, I felt the gags still had some drugs on them and no telling how long we'd stay awake with those in our mouths.

When I'd pulled it out a little, she started to work with me, moving her chin as I had. It probably took about thirty minutes as we painstakingly worked to pull and push the cloth. Eventually, I had it loose enough that I scooted back, and she was able to work the rest out herself.

Rowan went through the same routine I did of licking her lips and trying to gain moisture for her throat. I was never going to take brushing my teeth for granted after this, as I rolled my tongue over my fuzzy teeth. Man, that cloth had tasted disgusting.

When she finally had enough saliva to wet her mouth, Rowan stared at me. I expected to see hatred, but, surprisingly, all I found was admiration.

"Fin, don't you dare beat yourself up. You didn't orchestrate this so, just stop, okay? We're going to need your brains to get out of here in one piece. Thank you for removing that gag. I didn't know how much longer I was going to be able to stand it."

"It was the least I could do."

"Fin," she chastised my self-deprecating tone.

"I know, I know." I rolled my eyes, but we both ended up smiling. I reminded myself of the agreement I'd made to let things be, no sense in carrying around guilt at the moment, as it wouldn't be helpful.

"So, I think we're in a basement, and I don't think we went far. It doesn't feel like we were out for long, and while my body is sore, it's not sore-sore from having laid here for a day or anything, plus I don't have to pee yet," I stated matter-of-factly in a rush.

"Weird deductions, but they do make sense. That makes me feel better, too, knowing we could still be in town."

"Exactly. We just need to figure out who took us and where."

"Yeah, no problem." She chuckled.

"Well, obviously, it was the Council. That dude screamed *murder organization.*"

"Do you think they know what we did beforehand?" she asked, biting her lip.

"I don't know. Before he jabbed me, the guy said something…" I trailed off, searching my memory, trying to recall what he said to me right before I blacked out. *"Tsk, tsk, little hacker. Wasn't my gift a warning…"*

His gift, I mused. What could he mean by his gift? The memory of the photo of Sawyer flashing up on my screen came to mind. He was *the unknown number. Shit.* He must've planted something when we had the computer up. I thought I'd done a sweep, but apparently, this guy, or whoever they had that worked for them, wasn't the average hacker.

"I think it's the guy who sent us the pic of Sawyer and you know… telling us he was watching. It had to be him. He was telling me I'd been naughty, but really, that could have been about anything. So, let's hope they don't know. That might be the only thing that saves us."

"What was—"

Rowan's words were cut off before she could finish when we both heard the creak of a door somewhere. I hadn't been able to make out a door earlier, as it all blended in with the wall. Frantically, I nudged my gag back up into my mouth. When Rowan saw me doing it, she hurriedly did the same. We couldn't let them know we had them out. Closing my eyes, I prayed they didn't have surveillance in here, and they were just coming to check on us.

"Grab those two and take them to the showers. Time to get them ready for their debut. After all, they are special guests of Mr. Abernathy," a cold voice sneered, sending shivers through me.

Rough hands grabbed me, pulling me up, and I stumbled, trying to gain my balance, but the binds on my feet made it impossible, along with the drugs in my system. My captor didn't seem to care as he shoved me about, frustrated with my lack of coordination.

I heard Rowan cry out behind me, and I knew I'd never forgive myself for this. The name Abernathy began to sink in, and I realized it was Asa and Sawyer's father who'd kidnapped us. *Just fucking great.* I hoped I got to see him so I could deliver the same gift Sawyer had to Agent Buttcrack—a swift kick to the groin.

My abductor was dragging me by this point since my legs refused to work bound together. We came to an open room that vaguely smelled of chlorine and bleach. Well, that had to be a good sign it was at least clean. They tossed us down onto the ground and then turned to leave. I was getting tired of these bindings on our legs and arms. Straining my shoulder, I tried to move my hands some, but to no avail.

A few minutes later, two girls entered. They didn't look very old, and I had a sick feeling in my gut about what might be going on here. The pieces were starting to connect, and I wasn't a fan of it. They didn't say anything, keeping their eyes on the ground as they cut our feet free. Moving my legs, it felt nice to be able to stretch them at least. Water hitting me had me screeching in alarm since it was ice cold.

"What the hell!"

"Get under the water. It will be better if you just do as we say," one of the girls said in a monotone voice that was creeping me the hell out. *Okay, sure, Council puppet.*

Standing, I wobbled for a minute before stepping under the cold spray. My teeth started to chatter by the time I was thoroughly drenched head to toe with the frozen downpour.

I realized too late that the drive was still in my bra. Well, I assumed it was still in my bra, or I figured I'd be dead by one of the goons by now. One of the girls came over and cut the ties on my arms and then squirted some shampoo in one hand and soap in the other. They walked to the edge of the room, standing with their backs facing us. Well, it was nice to think we had privacy, but I didn't believe it for a second. There was no way guards or cameras weren't around.

Quickly, I rubbed the shampoo in my hair as I tried to hurry so I could get out from under the water. Rowan seemed to have the same idea, both of us leaving our clothes on for fear of being naked without anything, since we didn't see towels or clothes nearby. Hoping the shampoo was out, I quickly rinsed my body before jumping out from under the stream.

My fingers were frozen, my skin covered in goosebumps, and my lips undoubtedly had to be blue. It was almost hard to walk in the wet denim. I was so cold, and I realized the genius of their plan. They didn't have to keep us bound when we were frozen solid.

Shivering, Rowan and I walked toward the two girls. Upon closer inspection, they had to be teenagers. One barely sixteen, the other a little older perhaps, eighteen at the most. My heart broke a little for them being in this situation, and I hoped whenever we got out of here that they did too. No one deserved to be here.

"We're done," I shivered out, my teeth knocking together with such force I was worried I'd crack a molar.

They didn't turn around but just walked forward. Two guards stood on either side of the room we'd been in, and I knew my assessment had been correct. This place was heavily guarded. It was going to be difficult to escape on our own. I prayed that the team had figured out what had happened by this point. It was our only hope of surviving.

Entering another room, this one was drastically different from the past two. It had soft carpet, and we were dripping water all over. Expensive furnishings adorned the mauve room that resembled a bedroom. Dresses hung around the room on various clothing racks.

Taking in my surroundings, I hadn't noticed the girls

returning with a bundle for us. They gave one to me and Rowan, and I realized it was a fluffy robe. Not even caring at this point, I stripped out of the wet clothes as fast as humanly possible and snuggled into it.

It felt like heaven.

Rubbing my body, I tried to soak up some water, and I began to bounce on my toes a little to get circulation moving. Rowan was barely moving, and fear washed through me. Shit —her illness.

"Ro, are you okay? Stay with me. Focus on my voice."

Her eyes moved up to my face in slow motion. I walked over and helped her get her wet clothes off. She struggled to move her muscles and had a difficult time removing her clothes. Once I was able to get her shirt over her head, I wrapped the robe around her shoulders and belted it for her.

"Ro, I'm going to undo your pants, okay? Just hold onto my shoulders if you need help with balance."

She didn't answer, but I saw her eyes blink twice, so I took that to mean it was okay. Dropping down, I placed her hands on my shoulders and shimmied her jeans down her legs for her. Rowan's legs were super stiff, and I worried she wouldn't be able to move.

Massaging the muscles, I hoped I was doing something right. After a few minutes, she didn't seem as blue and blinked more at me. I kept rubbing her arms and legs, trying to dry up the water and putting warmth back into her body. The other girls had left, so, fortunately, it was just us for this part.

"Thank you," she whispered out after a while.

"Are you okay? What can I do?"

"This is good. Thank you," Rowan mumbled, her words difficult to get out.

I pulled her over to the couch and helped her sit down. Pacing, I tried to think about what I could do to help. This wasn't good. I didn't know if it was shock or if it was something else. Rhett had told me once about her illness, but I couldn't remember what helped as my mind spun out of control.

"What's wrong with her?" a voice asked from a doorway I hadn't noticed. Turning, I took in the guy that was leaning against the frame.

He was tall, almost eclipsing the top of it as he stood. He had dark brown hair that had a little bit of a wave to it. His stubble peppered his jaw, his stark cheekbones peeking out. He was dressed in a suit that, while fitted, didn't seem to actually *fit*. Maybe he was just uncomfortable in it? My fashion designer brain was stuck on this fact. Shaking my head, I reminded myself it wasn't important and tried to digest his words.

"I... don't know. Maybe shock? Or might be the cold water or her illness."

He immediately moved into action at my statement and began to assess her. His whole demeanor changed, almost like he'd been pretending to be the carefree guy in a suit, but now I could see genuine concern radiate through him.

"Stop. What are you doing?" I asked, realizing I was letting a stranger touch, Ro.

"I'm in med school. I can help."

Raising an eyebrow, I didn't understand why he assumed that would assuage him. He was a stranger in a place I was being held captive. This had setup written all over it. Crossing my arms, I stood in front of her.

"Listen, I know you don't know who I am, and the circumstances aren't the greatest for us to meet. But I can help, and if I do something unsavory, you have permission to kick me in the balls. Alright?"

I wanted to laugh at his comment, his easygoing nature softening me. When Rowan moaned, I jumped into action, figuring he was my best option. Moving aside, I sat next to Rowan, so he could assess her. She was staring at the wall, despondent. Taking her hand, I squeezed it as I tried to give her some of my heat.

"Ro, is it okay if he checks you out? Anything he should know?"

Slowly, she turned to me, searching my eyes, and nodded before turning back to the wall. The guy started checking her pulse and fingers that were visible.

"She's definitely in shock, and her heart rate is slow. We need to warm her up. Quick, get her out of the wet under-garments."

His face turned a cute pink at the mention of her bra and panties. He started to undo his tie, shirt, and pants, and I stared at him as he stripped down to his boxers, momentarily stunned at the golden skin in front of me. Blinking, I turned to Rowan, blocking her body with my own as I numbly unclasped her bra. Dropping it to the floor, I felt a shirt placed in my hand. Slipping it over her head, I pulled it down to cover her as I worked to get her underwear off. The shirt covered her, at least as it draped over her body.

"I'm so sorry, Rowan. I'm sorry," I murmured.

"Ssh," was all she could murmur back, stopping my apology.

Dropping her underwear on the floor, I looked up to see what the next step was. The guy watched me, concern on his face.

"You should take yours off too. You're not moving as quickly either. I'll… turn away."

He did turn, giving me his back, and slowly, I dropped the robe and took off my bra and panties. Feeling vulnerable, I snatched up the robe and tied it tight. I did feel warmer without the wet fabric clinging to me.

"Okay."

He turned at my words, assessing me this time before deciding I was okay. He kneeled back down in front of Rowan, taking her hands before looking back at me.

"Okay, we need to give her some body heat, so you on one side, and me the other, and we can wrap her in the robe too. Hopefully, it will get her blood flowing more and keep her dry. Let's wrap her hair up so it doesn't lay on her back."

Nodding, I didn't know what else to do, and this seemed logical. I went through the steps he stated and wrapped my arms around Rowan. A minute later, I felt him lay the robe across her legs, and then his arms were wrapped around both of us. His embrace was warm, and I started to feel some heat seep into my body as the shivering decreased. We all sat there for a few minutes in the quiet, soaking in the warmth our bodies were creating.

"I'm Milo, by the way," he softly offered into the quiet. His voice was soothing, feeling like honey as it wrapped around us.

"I'm Finley, and this is Rowan. Do you know where we are?"

He didn't answer for a while, and I worried I'd crossed some imaginary boundary.

"We're at a school."

Well, that was more info than I was expecting and made me hopeful that we were still at TAS.

"Do you know what's going to happen to us?"

This time it was even slower for him to respond, and I had started to nod off, exhaustion catching up with me.

"I'm afraid it's not a good answer."

"Why are you here? You don't seem like a bad guy."

I figured I might as well try to get some answers if we were going to be cuddling for warmth for the unforeseeable future.

"Ah, well, that, I'm afraid, is a complicated answer. I, like you, am here not by my choice. Tonight, is to be my *induction* into this... despicable place. My father, well, he disagrees with my career choice unless he can use it to advance his position. His boss, my uncle, sent me down here to give me a taste of what my life could be. I think... I think he was hoping you girls would sway me or something."

I digested his words, trying to calculate their value and honesty. My gut told me that Milo was truthful and his actions from moment one had been honorable; I had to trust that he wasn't that good of an actor.

"Did it?" Rowan croaked out, surprising us both.

"Not in the way they were thinking. How are you feeling?"

"Sore, but warmer. Thank… thank you."

"How did you guys get down here?"

"Down?" I questioned, picking up on the usage of the word.

"Yeah, you're underground at the school."

Rowan turned to me, our eyes communicating the hope we both felt at that statement. Needing to verify, I asked Milo a critical question. "The Aldridge School?"

"Yes, the sports one. Do you know it?"

Our bodies relaxed at the news, and tears pricked my eyes in relief.

"Yeah, we know it. I work here, and Rowan lives in town. It means they didn't take us far."

Milo seemed shocked by this news, anger filling his face. "What do you mean, you work here?"

"I'm a costume designer and work on the tech side of things for the kids and social media."

"So, you didn't agree to be here? You're not some criminal who has harmed others?"

"No."

His breathing became rapid, and he let us go as he started to pace. He yanked at his hair, mumbling under his breath. Milo was still only in his socks and boxers, making an interesting picture to watch as he paced. After a few moments, he turned, a decision on his face.

"Okay, we're getting you out of here. You need to get dressed and play along until it's time. We need to make them believe you're headed to the ceremony. I don't know what to do once we're out of here, but we'll figure that out next. I can't leave you here or allow this to happen. It's not right."

"If you can get us out of here, we have the next part handled. We can protect you, too."

"Well, it looks like I'm finally getting my wish. I'm glad I met you both, even if under these weird circumstances. Right. I'm going to grab some dry clothes. No one else has access to this room, so for now, you're safe until I return. I will be back. *I promise.*"

Milo turned and left, determination in his stride. He seemed more confident now, surer of himself than he was when he'd entered. Looking at Rowan, I knew what I needed to do. This was my chance to protect her and get us out safely. It might be the only thing that redeemed me.

# eight

. . .

## oliver

MEN DRESSED in expensive suits and tuxedos were casually scattered around the room as they drank expensive whiskey and brandy from crystal tumblers. A haze of cigar smoke lingered in the air as they puffed on the fat stogies. It resembled more of a charity gala or black-tie event than an underground meeting of a clandestine organization.

The few women that were present were formally dressed to the nines. Formal dresses of all sorts could be spotted around the room, dripping in jewels and diamonds that glittered under the lights. It was a kaleidoscope of wealth on display.

I glanced back to make sure I hadn't walked through a time warp because it felt more like I'd stepped into an alternate dimension. Though, maybe I had—one where the rules of the natural world didn't apply. The rich and powerful had a world all of their own that mere peasants and mortals wouldn't be able to comprehend. It was becoming clear how widespread and disgusting greed was in the world.

"Isn't it wonderful?" Bash asked, grabbing my shoulder like a proud dad as I took in the room.

"Yeah, it's *unbelievable*," I deadpanned.

I didn't even have to lie on that one. It was truly un-fuck-ing-believable that this was going on right under the hockey rink. How long? For what purpose? How did no one know?

Questions plagued me as they raced through my mind. Bash led me over to a table with a few other gentlemen. Uncle Jayce had run off to deal with his issue with Leon, leaving me under Bash's tutelage. My mind was so busy trying to process everything, that I missed the introductions.

"Apologies, it's my little brother's first time," Bash boasted to the table to uproarious laughter.

"Oh, I remember my first time. Just wait until the entertainment, dear boy," an older gray-haired man bragged, sloshing his drink around.

*Yeah, I didn't think we would have the same opinions about things.*

A waitress walked over, or more like sauntered, and 'waitress' was a loose term for this girl. Based on her attire, *or lack thereof*, I'd gamble she was part of the 'on' menu services. I had a weird feeling I'd entered some secret sex dungeon and was about to be initiated in the weirdest way.

"Oh, hello, *newbie*. What can I get you?" She wrapped her arm around my neck, practically placing her tits right at eye level. I had to force myself not to pull away in revulsion, and strangely, my reaction made me happy in a weird way. It proved to me how much I'd changed from knowing Sawyer. I latched on to that knowledge, knowing I'd need it to survive down here with all these sharks.

"Water will do, thank you."

She appeared disappointed by my nonreaction to her practically bare breasts in my face. They were only covered by the tiniest of nipple tassels, and it was one of those things where you tried not to stare, but like a lazy eye, it creepily followed you and made it impossible to, in fact, not stare. Turning away, I hoped my face wouldn't be too inflamed, giving away my uncomfortableness. My brother chatted with the table's occupants as I tried to gather my wits and survey the room.

There were a few areas I couldn't see, and the more I took in my surroundings, the more I didn't understand. It was cloaked in mystery and secrets with untoward promises. The area I could see the best was the open room I was currently in. It had several tables dispersed around the room. A large open space in the middle was devoid of any tables. Based on the roped-off area around it, though, it was important.

Several curtained areas in the corners were draped with fabric, hiding them from view. It both intrigued and frightened me what they felt had to be behind closed doors if girls walking around with nipple tassels and G-strings was open entertainment. I spotted a few of my co-workers, and I was surprised to see where some of them were connected.

Observing more, I began to understand the pattern based

on where the tables were located and their position. It was a ranking system within the Council itself, and you didn't mingle outside your affiliation. I recognized a few other people, but it didn't seem as if every Council member was in attendance, including the elusive Alek Hawthorne, the table at the front empty.

"Just wait for the main exhibit," Bash stated when he turned back to me, a look of glee on his face that I found disturbing.

"Oh yeah, what can I expect to see?"

"If I told you, it would spoil the surprise, Brother."

"Hmm," I mumbled, sipping my drink as I tried to hide my discomfort. I didn't think I would enjoy whatever it was as much as he expected.

"Well, can you tell me what's behind the curtains at least? Maybe I want to go."

"What's this Bash? Your brother here a rookie to the underground?" joked a rotund, red-faced man across the table.

"He's a virgin, Frank. Remember your first time?"

Unfortunately, this resulted in having them all share countless tales of their first times, giving me no information on what to actually expect as they chortled and drank around the table with their war stories. Pulling out my phone, I wondered if I could get a message off, instead I discovered no service.

"That won't work down here. They use some type of blocking technology to ensure complete confidentiality."

"Ah, yeah, sure."

Pocketing the useless brick, I grew nervous now that I didn't have a way to communicate with anyone. Finally, about an hour later, some movement started to happen, and everyone began to straighten up.

"It's starting. Pay attention, and if you see something you like, Uncle Jayce always fronts your first time."

"Where is Uncle Jayce? I thought I'd get to talk to him."

"Who knows." He shrugged, unconcerned, focused on the front. "He probably had to take care of one of the *guests* for tonight's entertainment. He'll be around," Bash replied, dismissing me with a wave of his hand.

The volume rose as a woman in a black cocktail dress walked out to the middle of the floor.

"Good evening, gentlemen and ladies. It is now time for our auction to begin. We have several commodities up for grabs tonight, so please make sure to use your keypad to put in your bid. All sales are final."

At her words, screens lit up on the tables in front of all the seats. It looked like a digital calculator and keypad.

"Whoa."

"It's only going to get better." Bash smirked, the grin filling me with discomfort. I was getting tired of his smirk, to be honest. This was why I hated surprises. I didn't like not being in on things. Anxiety built inside me, but I reminded myself I was doing this to save my family, and I needed to stay calm to do that.

"Our first item tonight, female, sixteen, brown hair, blue eyes, and hails from North Carolina, her family line is…"

When her words penetrated my mind, revulsion coated

my throat, and I had to hold in my need to vomit. *Oh, my God. This was an auction for people.* I'd heard about these things, but not like *this*. I didn't think any of us thought it would be this way. Hiding my abhorrence of the event, I pasted a smile on my face and watched men and women around the room chatter and discuss the poor teenage girl that was now on display.

I'd missed it initially, but she was standing on a raised dais, dressed in a blue evening gown, heels, and made up. There was a camera on her to give a closer inspection, and next to her picture was a profile listing her stats like she was a piece of a collection. I guess if it was an auction to them; she was just an item. She stood still, no emotion on her face at what was happening, and I had to stop myself from running up there and saving her.

They didn't give her a name, just a number, further dehumanizing her. I examined her closely to see if she was the missing girl, but I couldn't be sure. I hadn't known Jill, so she hadn't remained in my mind. I was kicking myself now for not paying closer attention.

I blinked, and they were already lowering her back into the ground. Now, I could see how it opened and the platform raised and lowered with a button the woman pressed. As she was dropped, another section began to rise. Heavens forbid these vultures had to wait for them to change out 'specimens.'

Weirdly, it was a genius method of presentation. There was no way for them to run if they had them contained in one area, and it had that whole cool factor of watching someone raised and lowered into the ground in a circular pattern. That was if it didn't make you sick just thinking about it. I needed to brush my teeth after this—my gag reflex didn't understand my need to play it cool.

In no world was this cool, though. *Ack.*

I'd spaced out through a few more people, trying not to lose it with each new level of disgust I was having thrown my way when the speaker's introduction sparked something in me.

"Better decide soon, brother. They're rounding out to the end now. All the good ones have been taken."

I deserved an award for not throwing up on people after this. Seriously, my ability to hold in my vomit was not a strength of mine, and Bash was two seconds away from me punching him in the nut sack.

"Before our final item, we will do two bids this round. We'd like to refer to this lot as an advanced unit due to the objects' age exceeding our normal commodities. Object A is twenty-two, brunette, and while not on the athletic side, appears to be in decent shape. Object B is twenty, raven hair, and I'm informed has a rather delicate immune system, so consider that."

Finley and Rowan appeared on the screen, and I was momentarily stunned to see them in this place. My heart started to race, and I knew I needed to get them out. All of these people, kids mostly, deserved to get out of this situation, but I couldn't do anything for them right now. Tapping my brother, I anxiously tried to figure out how to enter a bid.

"Bash, I made my decision. Help me."

Bash turned to me, rolling his eyes, but showed me where to put my finger for the scanner and where to enter my bid. Nerves racked me as I fumbled to enter a number, hoping I would win.

"Wow, that's an admirable bid there, brother."

Looking up, I tried to gauge his meaning, but I didn't care because I would pay whatever for them. A few minutes later, a 'sold' flashed up on the screen, and I sat back and relaxed, feeling exhausted from the adrenaline rush.

"Now what?"

"Eager are we, Oliver? Relax, you'll find out in a few minutes. There should be only one person left. Their *grand* finale. It's usually the best and most promising student here. I wonder who the honor was bestowed on this year?" he mused.

Ignoring my brother, I could only focus on the girls. My leg tapped anxiously under the table as I waited for the auction to end so I could go and claim my prize. They had to be so scared. Did the others know? I wouldn't know the answer until I could get out of here with them. I tossed back my water, trying to wet my parched throat.

Dizziness assaulted me, and I realized I wasn't breathing. Sucking in a breath, the room started to come back into focus as I slowly pulled in air. In and out, I slowly began to slow my heart. Bash slapping my shoulder had me lurching forward into the table.

"Let's go. I can't wait to see this!"

Bash's excited glee was making me ill. How could he be okay with this? I'd thought a lot of things about my brother over the years, but never this. Following him, I walked distractedly behind Bash as he led me to wherever they were held.

"Lot number?" a voice asked when we approached one of the curtains in the back. Bash turned to me, and I momentarily panicked.

"Uh, I don't know. It was the last two."

The attendant sighed before rolling her eyes and typing in a number. She handed me an iPad to scan my thumbprint again. Once it turned green, she opened a door for us to go through. Bash was skipping along like a kid on Christmas morning instead of the thirty-three-year-old he was.

Stopping in front of a room, I exhaled with relief when it opened to Rowan. Keeping my cool, I slowly walked in. She stood up at my entrance, but at my slight head shake, she held back her relief, dropping her eyes to the floor.

"What about the other one?"

"It was just this one. The other item, Object A, you were outbid on," the attendant responded in a flat tone. Fear filled me with not saving them both. Back-up plans flashed through my head on how I could fix this.

The attendant left, closing the door as she did, leaving Bash, me, and Rowan alone in the room. First, I had to get rid of my brother and then figure out how to find Finley.

"Uh, Bash. I think I can take it from here."

"Whatever you say, Brother." He saluted, spinning on his heels. "The first one is on Uncle, so use it wisely. He'll come to collect though, *don't forget*."

With those cryptic words, he exited the room, closing the

door behind him. My body lost the tension, and I rushed over to Rowan, wrapping her in a hug as I felt her body relax too.

"Where's Fin? I thought I won you both. Shit, this is bad. What do we do? How did you guys end up here? Do the others know?" I was rambling as I threw a zillion questions at her.

"I-I-," she cleared her throat, and I realized how much of an ass I'd been to start interrogating her. "I think Fin is safe. Come on. We might be able to catch them. I need to get out of here."

"You're right. Let's go. I think I need to take twenty showers."

She nodded into my hug, and I knew this experience would haunt her. Thankfully, it was soon to be over. Taking her hand, we walked out of the room back into the dimly lit hallway. There weren't any exit signs shining with arrows, so I had to look around to see if I could find a way out of this place.

Hoping that Finley was indeed safe, as Rowan suggested, I took a chance and turned left. Walking down the dark hallway, I kept Rowan under my arm as we made our way toward freedom and back to our family.

# nine

· · ·

## sawyer

"WELL, THAT WAS A TOTAL BUST," I sighed to Henry. We'd gone into the "secret club" to find it was literally a "secret clubhouse." A room used to get away from the students and have privacy. It was used for meetings apparently, but nothing tawdry or any evil masterminds in sight, and I felt weirdly disappointed. Not that I wanted to fear for my life, but the hope of finding something had been high.

Now, I just felt defeated and sad.

Henry and I headed out of the cafeteria, the weight of the Council on our shoulders, and I wondered if we even had a car here. The day was a blur at this point, with so many emotions overwhelming me, I wasn't sure what was going on. Trusting Henry had it together, I followed him as the other notable alumni led us out.

Henry was texting on his phone, so I assumed it was to either get a lift or let them know we were okay. I wasn't paying attention, so I was surprised when someone knocked into my shoulder. The back of their head looked familiar, but they were gone before I could determine who they were. Based on the hoodie, they were probably a student in a hurry to make curfew.

Henry stopped, glaring at his phone, so I absently bounced on my feet, trying to stay warm. Dress clothes and heels did not provide enough warmth in the cold Utah weather. I pulled my jacket tighter and shoved my hands into my pockets, trying to hold in the heat I was generating. My hand brushed against a piece of paper, making a weird crinkling sound. I hadn't put anything in my pockets, so I wasn't sure what the noise could be from.

Pulling it out, I was surprised to find an envelope addressed to me. That student must have put it in my pocket when he bumped into me. But why? Tearing the seal, I found myself blinking in disbelief at the familiar scrawl on the page.

*Love,*

*Would you believe I'm writing this from London? I've mailed it to a student in hopes you will actually get it and not shred it. The night you confronted me, something in me snapped, and I realized how much I was fucking things up. I know I've hurt you with my behavior, and I regret making you feel as if I didn't think you were the most precious thing in the room.*

*I know you're turning up your nose at that concept because you don't want to be seen that way, or at least the implication that* being precious makes you weak. If there was ever a person who was as far from that word as they could get, it would be you, love. So, hear me when I say you're precious because of who you are and what you've come to mean to me.

The steps I'm taking aren't going to be easy, and to do those, I'm going to be away for a while. I can't afford to lose that time with you. I already have so much to make up for, and I don't want to waste it because the next time we're face to face, I want to kiss you senseless.

Yes, love. Kiss you fucking senseless.

While I hold no guarantee that this will fix anything or absolve me of my sins, I hope it will connect me to you in a way I've been missing. You see, I've been able to charm people my whole life and use my natural skills to harbor relationships—except with you. I messed that up from moment one, and I only kept sliding backward.

Believe it or not, I think you intimidated me. Sawyer, you're beautiful in all the ways a person should be. Not just your outward appearance, but your heart and soul. It radiates through you so much that even my bloody dog saw it before I did. He's a great judge of character. He never did like the evil bitch.

Before I digress too much, I hope you accept these letters as my way of showing you my true self—my heart. Allow them to be a way to get to know me and share with you the things I haven't been able to say. I hope that by writing them down, I can put my feelings into words better, and when I see you next, time won't have been wasted.

I'm leaving London, and I hope this makes it to you in a week. I've sent it to a contact, so if someone you didn't know approached

111

*you, they were innocent. I wish you luck at the expo. I don't know what my plan will be at this point, but I will keep you abreast as long as it's safe.*

*I have acquired a significant player that will aid in our mission. Can you make sure Rhett is okay? I know things need to mend with us too, but in the meantime, can you look after him for me? I'm borrowing his moves of romance, and I hope I do it justice. You deserve nothing less.*

*Until the next time…*

*Happy Birthday, Love*

*Wholly yours*


My hands shook slightly as I digested Elias' words. He was *trying*. And I had to give him credit for the effort. The part of my heart that had hardened where Elias was concerned began to thaw, and I found myself wishing for more letters soon. I wanted to get to know *this* Elias.

"Smalls, everything okay?" Henry asked when he noticed I'd stopped, concern on his face.

"Yeah, it's fine. Sorry, just a tad emotional with everything going on."

I folded the letter delicately, treating it as the precious item it was. Putting it back in my pocket, I hoped I'd be able to keep it safe. I wouldn't admit this, but I already had plans to read it repeatedly when I was alone. I wanted to drown in each word like a love-drunk teenager.

Wetness on my cheeks surprised me. I hadn't realized I was crying, but all the emotional highs and lows from the day had caught up to me. Causally, I wiped them away, not caring that my eyes were leaking. It was a good reminder that despite all the times I felt I needed to lock away my emotions, they were still there. Tears were a reminder of our humanity.

Henry watched me but didn't press. He knew if I was ready to talk, I would. He remained quiet, offering me the space to feel without pressure to explain it. Henry always knew what I needed, even when I didn't. When I'd gathered myself, he updated me.

"Soren said our ride's almost here. They were already headed this way after my text, in case we needed a rescue." He grinned, soothing me. "They should be here," he paused, "there they are. Come on. I need to know if there are any updates on Fin."

Nodding, I grabbed Henry's hand, and we walked over to the car. The passenger door flew open before we reached the SUV, and Mateo ran to me, hugging me tight in his embrace. Henry was actually in the hug too, and I realized that Mateo had wrapped us both in his arms. Their friendship continued to grow, and it warmed my heart to see my guys building their own relationships outside of me.

"You're okay," he breathed into my hair.

"Yeah. Any word on Fin? Rowan?"

The tears I'd managed to stop started to flow again at my question. Mateo had that effect on me, I guess. He made it okay to be vulnerable, and despite Mateo's belief that he wasn't strong, he made me feel protected when I was with him. Mateo was someone who understood the darkness, and I knew he wouldn't get lost in mine.

"We've found some info, but let's get back to the house to explain. It will be easier to share there."

Henry was quiet as we headed to the car. I squeezed his hand, knowing he was worried about his sister. He pressed back but didn't look at me. I let it go, for now, knowing he was trying to hold everything together. If we didn't get them back tonight, it would be an explosion of feelings from all of us as we tried to manage our fear.

Charlie was driving the SUV, and I relaxed when I saw him, needing his strength. "Hey, Sawdust."

"Hey, old man."

My tears threatened to rise up again at his look. The ride back was quiet as we all waited to find out any information. I also had Elias' words swirling in my head, bringing up conflicting emotions. It was hard to feel happy when my friends' lives were in peril.

There were a lot of cars in the drive I didn't recognize, but they all faded into my memory as I walked into the house. Arms wrapped around me from all directions, and I wasn't sure who was hugging me, as everything was a blur of bodies.

When people pulled away, I spotted Ace standing off in the corner, watching anxiously. Realizing I needed to take care of this now, I walked over to him. He straightened when I got closer and shuffled his feet some. I hated that our relationship had come to this awkwardness.

"Hey."

"Hey."

"Listen, I know when I found out about you working for the Agency, I didn't handle it the best."

"You don't need to apologize, Sawyer. I'm sorry I didn't tell you sooner."

"No, I get it. We were just getting to know one another. Plus, I had my own secrets, and I wasn't exactly handing them out, so I understand, I do. I think when I learned about you, it was just bad timing. I'd already been slammed with new things that weekend, and I was in overload mode. You had the unfortunate timing to be the one who received all of my emotions."

"I did want to tell you, and if it matters," he said, sincerity in his voice, "I never faked our friendship; that was all real. I promise."

"I believe you, and I forgive you. Can we try being friends again? I miss you."

"I would love nothing more than that, Sawyer."

A smile graced my face, and I pulled him into a hug. It felt good to have righted this friendship. I needed people in my life, and Ace was a good person. He was doing his job, and I couldn't fault him for that. It was actually an excellent quality to have in a person.

"Okay, well, I need some answers. HQ?"

"Yeah, let's head there."

We walked over, and I noticed that most of the people from earlier were now nowhere in sight. Stepping into what felt like our second home these days, I finally registered everyone as I took in the room. Charlie was talking to Rhonda, and Isla was listening. Seeing the three-parental figures together made me happy. Now, if I could get Charlie and Aggie to meet, I think my world would be complete.

Soren had his arm around Henry, holding him to his chest as they sat against the wall, and I was glad to see Henry letting someone comfort him. Mateo was seated next to a guy I didn't recognize, focusing on a computer. Tyler spotted me standing in the doorway and came over to me, wrapping his arms tight around me.

"Hey, Ty."

"Hey, Wildcat. I'm glad you're safe."

"Any word from Ollie yet?"

"No, nothing. It's like he just disappeared off the radar. Cohen thinks his signal is being blocked, so I'm trying to reassure myself."

"He's tough, Ty," I softly reassured him. "Ollie can do this. But who's Cohen?"

"Yeah, you're right. I just… yeah." He nodded, his shoulders relaxing. "And Cohen is next to Mateo. He somehow knows Fin."

Interesting. I turned that information over in my head as I took in the rest of the room. Rhett was slumped down in a chair, the fear weighing heavily on him. My heart broke for him. Asa was next to him, an almost identical look on his face. Pulling Ty, I walked over to both of them, hoping I could provide some comfort to my brother and grumpy protector.

"Asa."

His head snapped up, and he stood, embracing me. Asa's body shook, and I tried to be the strength he needed. Numbness and the unfortunate reality that I'd been through something like this before held me together at the moment, allowing me to use that to help them. Maybe my horrible past could be used for something good for a change.

He kissed my head after a few minutes and sat back down. Ty had taken the seat next to Rhett, so I took that as my opportunity to sit in his lap again. We needed more chairs, but I didn't mind the seating arrangements when I got to sit in one of my boyfriends' laps.

Rhett pulled me close but stared at the wall despondently. Real worry sat heavily on my chest as I took in his features. Pulling his face down to mine, I searched his eyes. Pain and fear swirled as he stared back at me, and I was scared I was losing him.

"We will get them back. They're both strong. You have to hold on to that."

He stared for a while, and I wondered if he'd even heard me. Finally, he nodded and kissed me. It was full of longing, and I prayed my words would be true, or I'd never be able to forgive myself. Pulling back, he whispered, "Thank you, baby."

I wrapped my arms around his torso and laid my head against his chest, listening to his heartbeat. A few minutes later, a man I didn't know walked in. He went to the front of the room, and I figured he must be someone with the Agency. He had a kind face, and I instantly liked him.

"Okay, what do we know? Sawyer and Henry, what did you find on your tour?"

"Um, first; who are you?"

His face blossomed red at my question, and I immediately

felt bad for asking, but like, hello! I couldn't just disclose stuff after what Ashlee had shared. Speaking of, where was that girl? I looked around the room again, but I didn't see any other undercover Agency people other than Ace.

There were officially too many people with secret identities in my life. I needed to know who everyone was and their association with either organization at this point. I had too many years of living with my own secrets that it made me unable to do it anymore. When everything was a lie, nothing felt real. I was tired of living a half-life—I wanted it all now.

"Apologies. I feel like I know you from all the years Tyler has talked about you," he smiled. "I'm Brandon Mathews, I work for the Agency, and I'm Tyler's dad."

I glanced at Ty, and he was also sporting a slight blush at his dad outing him to me. Turning back, I smiled in return, happy to meet the dad of my boyfriend. When he didn't even blink at me sitting in Rhett's lap, I liked him even more.

"It was a total bust. The private tour, invitation-only thing, well, it's just a fancy room with a passcode. It was a nice little area but offered nothing on the Council unless it's some secret clubhouse they meet in or that induction comes later. No one from the Council who'd been at our table followed us there. Abernathy and Bellamy were both gone."

"Well, that's disappointing." He frowned, and I had this weird urge to want to impress him. Unfortunately, all I could muster was a responding grunt because what else was there to say? The situation was so much more than just *disappointing*.

Henry shared some other details as I wondered where

Samson, or Agent Bald-faced-liar, was. I needed to find some time to confront him about the news I'd learned. Though, knowing me, I'd probably just blurt it out when I was heated. I wasn't one to sit on information. Effective communication was going to be my new mantra.

"Cohen, any update on the computer?"

Before he could answer, the doorbell started to ring incessantly, followed by a pounding on the door. Jumping up, I took off for it as shouts of protest to wait trailed behind me. I beat everyone, and despite it probably being a stupid move, I rapidly unlocked the door, fumbling with the deadbolt before wrenching the door open.

One of the happiest sights stood before me, and I felt myself grinning from ear to ear. Ollie was holding Rowan. Delight and relief flooded my body at having them both back. Words and sound started to return, though, and I realized Ollie's face didn't match the glee I felt. Registering his comments, I finally heard what he was saying as I took in Rowan.

"Call a doctor, now. She needs help."

Rhett pushed past me as he gathered Rowan in his arms, carrying her inside. Rhonda was already on the phone, presumably calling someone to help. Anxiety returned as I realized we weren't out of the woods yet. Ollie lifted me off my feet as he wrapped me up in his arms, and I clung to him.

Tonight had been emotionally draining for us all, and I was glad to have him back safely. Looking over his shoulder, I realized Fin wasn't here.

"Ollie, where's Fin?"

He tensed before dropping me back to my feet.

"I'm sorry, Sawyer. I tried. I thought I had them both, but when I got there, she was gone. We thought she would be here already."

"What do you mean she was gone? Gone where?" Henry's question rang out from behind me, echoing my thoughts.

My momentary relief fled, and I was back to feeling panicked. Would we ever be whole again, or had the Council finally found a way to destroy me?

# ten

. . .

## rhett

SAWYER TOOK off at the sound of the doorbell, and I ran after her, worried some new threat was here. When she threw it open, I began preparing a reprimand for her in my head until I saw Ollie standing there. Shock momentarily stunned me in place until my vision took notice of the brunette under his arm, leaning heavily against him.

Rowan was barely standing, clinging to Ollie. Pushing forward, I didn't realize I'd moved Sawyer until I felt her falter; guilt gripped me, but I had to get to Rowan right then. She needed me. Taking Rowan in my arms, I heard Ollie's shouts as they penetrated the fog that had surrounded me since I'd received Soren's text.

"She needs help. Call a doctor."

"Ro? Ro? It's me. What's wrong? Where does it hurt?"

Fear of what my baby sister had suffered swirled in my head, and I worried I wouldn't be able to protect her from the trauma of her experience. The sins of the world had seeped into our sleepy town, no longer allowing it to feel safe anywhere.

"Rhett?" she mumbled, blinking at me from my arms. I placed her gently down on the couch as I examined her. Her breathing was labored, and she looked pale. Fatigue plagued her as she fell into an unconscious state, but that didn't worry me. The swollen joints and rash on her arms had me fearing the episode that was to come. Mom was by my side in an instant, someone having alerted her to Rowan's arrival.

"How is she?"

"Her breathing is labored, and her joints are swollen. The rash here is the most troublesome."

"I'm calling Dr. Martin."

I nodded, agreeing with her plan. Rowan would need to be taken in and looked at overnight. She would need fluids and some antibodies to help her, but the thing with Lupus was there wasn't a cure, and they could only manage her symptoms. Anger roared to life in me at whoever had taken her, the suffering and pain they'd caused along with the traumatic ordeal wouldn't be something she'd easily forget.

My breathing became rapid, and all the anger I'd been holding back was now on the surface. Clenching my fists, I felt my face flush, and I knew if I didn't do something, I'd hurt someone I loved. I'd already pushed Sawyer, albeit unaware, there was no telling what else I was capable of.

Standing, I began to pace, trying to calm myself but

knowing I needed to punch something. Leaning against the mantle, I pushed into it as I tried to regulate my breathing and used the force to stabilize me. It helped as I felt the hard rock dig into my palms, giving me a reprieve.

When I turned back around, I noticed the others had flowed into the living room, wanting updates. Watching Sawyer tend to Rowan, I was able to take in other details. She was wearing an evening gown I'd never seen before, making me more curious about what had been going on and where the hell they'd been.

"Ollie, where's Fin?" she asked again, smoothing Rowan's hair back. She kept looking at her, and I knew she felt guilty. I would need to remind her later she wasn't responsible for this.

"I don't know. I saw her, and I tried to get them both, but when I got there, it was just Rowan, and she said Fin was safe. So we left, and I was hoping she would be here by now," he admitted, looking around at the faces filling the room.

Half of the occupants were dressed up in suits and gowns, and the other half were in a mixture of outfits. This odd detail stuck out to me as I tried to distract myself from leaving the house and hunting down the people responsible for this. My logic wasn't wanting to listen to how idiotic that would be.

No, the protector in me wanted to make the men pay who'd deemed it okay to hurt my baby sister. I had a strong urge to burn down their villages and wreak havoc, my primal needs surfacing. I'd never believed violence solved anything. But right here, at this moment, it was what I craved, and nothing short of annihilation would satisfy my need for vengeance. They would pay for their sins.

It was Sawyer's voice that seemed to pull me back to reality as I heard the fear in her voice. "Where were they?"

"I don't even know how to explain it," Ollie started, running his hands through his auburn locks. Sitting down, he looked up at us all as he began to tell his story. "It was the most sinister place I've ever seen. There's a whole underground facility under the hockey rink. They were having an *auction*," he sneered, struggling to get out the word. I watched as he swallowed, clearing his throat, and I knew it was as we feared. "That's... where I saw them. When I realized they were up for sale, I jumped on bidding for them both. I thought I'd succeeded too, but I only found Rowan when I went to collect my prizes. I'm so sorry, Sawyer, Rey. I tried."

Ollie was distraught at the information he had to share, and while I could acknowledge the growth he'd made in expressing his emotions, all I could hear on repeat was "auction." *Rowan had almost been sold.* My emotions swirled with anger and fear, and I wasn't sure which one was winning as things began to grow fuzzy around the edges.

"Ollie, it's not your fault. You did more than any of us, and without you, Rowan wouldn't be here now. You've at least told us where they are. Now we know how to find Fin. Thank you for trying," Rey replied, the sound defeated. He appeared shell-shocked, and I wondered how much of what Ollie said he'd grasped.

I think it would be harder to let yourself entertain the

thoughts when they weren't back in front of you. If you let yourself imagine the worst, rage or paralyzing fear would take over. Neither were helpful emotions in this situation. Later, when we were facing them down—because mark my words, it was inevitable—was when that rage could be unleashed.

Rey sunk back on the couch, and I moved back over to Rowan, needing to hold her to remind me she was here. It was a little insensitive, but I knew he'd understand. I was just as worried about Fin. She was my best friend too. Picking up Rowan's hand, I tried to transfer some of my heat to her.

"Is she going to be okay?" Asa asked, looking at Rowan.

"Yeah, I think so. We just need to get her to the hospital to be watched overnight by her team. We're just waiting to hear what they want to do."

"That's good."

At Asa's words, Mom rushed back into the room with the phone still clutched in her hand.

"He said to bring her in now. He'll meet us there. Can you drive?"

Before she even finished, I had Rowan back in my arms as I headed to the garage. As the door lifted, I saw all the cars that littered our drive, making it impossible for me to get out.

"Who drives the last car?" I shouted, and then just demanded. "Keys, now."

Charlie had followed us out and tossed the keys to me, understanding on his face. I rushed to the vehicle and placed Rowan in the backseat when Sawyer hopped in with her. I smiled appreciatively at her. Mom took the passenger seat as

I rounded the car to the driver's. Just as I went to back up, a flashy sports car pulled into the driveway, blocking me in.

A grunt of frustration left me as I glared daggers at the car. I blared my horn but instantly stopped when I saw who got out. A dazed Fin, also wearing a gown, opened the door to the passenger seat, and a guy I didn't know got out of the driver's side.

"Fin!" exclaimed Sawyer as she jumped out of the back door.

I didn't know if I was angry or annoyed when the car remained there. Sawyer saw my dilemma and rushed over to the driver, communicating something to them. The guy got into the car, backing out and effectively making room for me to go finally. Sawyer looked torn as she swished her head back and forth from me to Fin. I never wanted her to feel like she had to choose, and the hospital would be a wait fest.

"Stay. I'll call you with updates," I told her. She nodded, a look of gratitude on her face before blowing me a kiss.

Sawyer ran to Fin and embraced her, and I relaxed as well in the knowledge we were all back home, safe. I backed up and headed to the hospital, and my mom gave me a reassuring smile, the relief evident on her face as well. Rowan was my focus now. I could relax fully once I knew that she would survive this. *She had to survive this.*

## rey

Anxiety wracked my body as I watched Rhett rush out the door with Rowan. Where was *my* sister? I wanted to cry and punch something. It was an odd feeling for me, as I usually internalized everything. Nothing was making sense at all. The message had them together, but now, they were separated? What the hell was going on here?

My brain was getting stuck like a loading menu that was buffering. It was the spinning wheel of death as I tried to understand all the pieces that were moving. Thoughts of never seeing Fin again were too frightening to comprehend, and I shoved them away, not allowing myself to go there.

The fact was that I didn't know how to process this. How does one even prepare for it? Maybe they taught a class during Agency orientation: When loved ones get kidnapped 101.

Now I was starting to ramble in my brain. I think Sawyer's code orange was contagious.

What Ollie had shared frightened me more than I ever knew was possible, and anytime anger would start to overtake me, I'd become overwhelmed with anxiety instead. My emotions were not cooperating or communicating with one another, and I couldn't decide what I wanted to feel. Based on what Ollie reported, the auction alone had bile rising in my throat for what my sister could potentially have gone through. Would Fin even be the same when we got her back?

I had to keep thinking she'd return to us because the thought of not getting her back was too horrible even to consider. The anger started to build again but quickly faded. I wanted to beat myself up for not being able to muster up some rage and fury, but it wasn't me, and until I had solid information, I knew I couldn't even entertain those thoughts.

I might not be responding how people assumed I should, but this was my pain, my grief, not theirs.

"Rey, we'll keep looking. Ollie saw her less than an hour ago, and she was safe, plus Rowan said she was. We have to trust that," Soren assured me, and I absently nodded.

"Yeah, you're right. I just…"

"I know."

He wrapped me up in his arms, and I let him offer me his comfort. I didn't know how I'd deal with this without him. Soren had been the rock Sawyer and I needed today. I hadn't felt like I had to do it alone or manage it by myself. There was comfort in that, knowing everything wasn't placed on me. Perhaps that was why I was able to keep the anger at bay—it was safe for me to show my vulnerability.

The door opened again, but I didn't look up. I assumed it was someone who had gone outside just returning. Maybe we should all head to the hospital and be there for Rhett. It would be better than sitting around here and feeling useless. I hated feeling helpless.

"Wow, I got kidnapped, and I don't even get a running hug. I see where I land on your concern meter," a voice complained.

Jerking my head up, I took in my sister, my eyes not believing what they were seeing. "Fin?"

"Uh, yeah. It's me, dork. You're sure making a girl feel

pretty unworthy here. I've been gone, what five hours at the most, and you've already forgotten me," she sassed, turning to Sawyer. "Better watch out Sawyer, he'll—"

I didn't let her finish the sentence as I bowled her over in my hug. I picked her up and held her to me tight. Tears ran down my cheeks, and I didn't even care. My sister was here, and she was safe. Everything would be okay now.

I felt Soren hug us from behind, Sawyer joined on the other side. For a brief second, I relished in this simple hug with people I loved. Sitting Fin down, I stared at her, unsure what to do now and needing my brain to latch onto this updated reality.

"I'm so glad you're okay. When we…" I couldn't get the words out as my lip trembled and she hugged me around my waist.

"That's better, Bro," she joked, trying to help me not feel embarrassed.

"Fin?" Asa said behind me, and I briefly berated myself for continuing to forget about him.

Stepping back, I let Asa take my sister in his arms, holding her close. Pulling Sawyer to me, I held her as Soren kept his arms around me from behind, his extra height and build offering an excellent base to lean against, his solidness grounding me. I felt as if my heart was beating again, jump-starting itself into action. The buffering wheel had finally loaded, and my brain was firing on all cylinders again.

A guy I didn't know stood back awkwardly as we all hugged caught my attention.

"Who are you?"

"Oh, me? I'm Milo. I bought your sister."

"You did what?" bellowed out of me as I stepped out of my three-person hug, gearing up to punch this dude right in the face. The anger finally had a target, and I was ready to strike.

"Hey, he didn't mean it that way," Fin protested, stepping into my path, placing a hand on my chest. "Milo *saved me*, Henry."

I registered her other hand on my arm, tugging me to look at her. Except all my fear and anger had surged up now, and I was too focused on the man in front of me.

"Henry Alexander, you look at me right now!"

Fin yanked on my arm harder this time, but I still ignored her, breathing rapidly as I tried to figure out how to punch someone. I'd never done it before, but I felt I'd watched enough TV to know. A tiny blonde barely entered my line of sight before I felt her tugging my nose, yanking me down into her face.

"Henry! Not cool. Calm yourself," she ordered, her face fierce. "He's not the enemy here. Don't go throwing around your big brother energy and doing something you'll regret later."

Smalls' words sunk in, and I relaxed with her, breathing at the same time she did. Nodding, she let go of my nose, and I stood back up.

"Sorry, it's been a bit of an evening, and unfortunately, you got to be the recipient of all the wrath I've been holding back. I guess." I shuffled on my feet, embarrassed. "I owe you a thanks for saving my sister."

He nodded and relaxed now that he wasn't going to get punched. Finley walked over to him, and I wondered what their connection was as they appeared friendly. She pulled his hand and dragged him over to introduce Asa. They awkwardly shook hands, and I couldn't take the uncomfortableness. Turning, I stalked off to HQ. I shouldn't be angry, but now that my fear had vanished, it was bubbling to the surface. Sawyer and Soren followed behind me, creating a follow the leader scenario.

Mateo and Cohen were still working on the laptop, unaware of what had taken place, unless someone had clued them in, which, in the state we were all in, doubtful.

"Hey, Rowan is headed to the hospital, and Fin should be in here in a moment."

Cohen's head snapped up at Fin's name, a look of apprehension on his face. Slowly, he lowered the laptop screen and scooted back his chair. He appeared disinterested, but I'd seen that look cross his face and knew he was worried about something despite his calm demeanor.

"Well, I guess that's my cue to leave," Cohen stated, gathering his belongings.

"I'm sorry, with all the chaos, I missed your relationship with Fin. How did—"

"*Cohen*? What are you doing here?" Fin's voice asked, uncertainty lining her tone.

He shuffled, looking all sorts of confused, embarrassed, and uncertain himself. Rubbing the back of his head, he finally pulled his shoulders back and looked at the newcomers.

"Hey, squirt. Glad to see you're safe," he faked energetically. "Time for me to go, though."

"Wait… I thought you said you were meeting Fin tonight," Mateo questioned, rising as he did, crossing his arms as he stared down the man.

"Uh, yeah, about that." He cringed.

"Meeting me? What's going on?" Fin mirrored Mateo and crossed her arms, sending death glares to the dude. I kind of felt sorry for him. No one wanted to be on the receiving end of one of those. I knew from experience.

"He—" Mateo tried again.

"*Nothing.*" He glared, cutting off Mateo. "I'm going."

Cohen tried to move around the table, but Sawyer stepped into his space and braced her hands on her hips. "I think you should have a seat." She might be tiny, but my Smalls was powerful.

"I—" before he finished, he ducked and tried to fake her out to escape around her, but she lifted her leg again in a perfect attitude move and tripped him up. People always underestimated her, and I loved watching them fall when they did.

Asa shut the door, standing in front of it so Cohen couldn't escape if he did manage to get around the girls; he was currently on the ground groaning. Fin casually walked over, blocking his prone body even more.

"Time to start talking, Cohen. Care to tell me why my dad's intern is in Utah and intermingled with my friends? Hm?"

"Intern?" I stuttered as recognition started to filter

through me, and I remembered a couple of summers ago when I'd been home and dad had some guy over for dinner one night.

I would've been about twenty. Fin had just turned eighteen and still struggled with her anger. Thankfully, she'd gotten caught a few months prior to her birthday for hacking and some other misdemeanors. Otherwise, her punishment would've held more weight than the community service and mandated therapy. Dad had sung this guy's praise, but I remembered he'd been standoffish and quiet.

"Cohen Campbell, right?" I finally recalled, putting the pieces together. He sighed, nodding as he sat up, rubbing the knee he'd fallen on.

"I can explain. I'm not the enemy. *I promise.*"

"He told me he was meeting you tonight to swap info," Mateo spit out, finally able to without interruption. Cohen dropped his head, resignation on his features.

"No, that's not true. I was meeting a contact, Chaos… but… but," she trailed off, an odd look covering her face as she tried to merge the two things.

Cohen, or I guess Chaos, waved a hand, his head still lowered into his arms on the ground.

"You're… you're fucking *Chaos*?" Fin screamed, a manic look coming over her face.

He sighed before standing, pulling himself together, and I saw the honesty reflected on his face and perhaps a little bit of relief of not having to hold in the secret.

"Yep, I'm Chaos. I didn't know you were Oblivion when we met," he pleaded. "I'd gotten a job interning for your dad that summer after college. I started to put the pieces together when your dad talked about the trouble you'd gotten into. It's why…," he stopped, looking around, "can we talk about this in private?"

"No," chorused around the room, causing his face to go red.

We all waited anxiously for him to continue, happy to endure his pain for a moment to forget ours, even if just temporarily. However, Sawyer decided to give him the benefit of the doubt.

"Actually… does it have anything to do with what happened tonight?"

Cohen looked at her and shook his head, a smidge of relief on his face.

"Okay then, well, it's really not our business. It's Fin's, and she can choose to share with us later, but it's been a hell of a day, and it's my birthday, and it's the first one since sixteen where I have friends and a brother. So, can we maybe table this, do a recap of the day, and check on Rowan?" She clasped her hands in a pleading gesture, still in her dress, and I realized how selfish we were being. This day had really gotten away from us all.

"Ah hell, sweet pea. I vote for you and Asa to get a redo of your birthday, and we celebrate it on a better day. In fact, I demand it. We will dub a different day as your birthday because this date in history is just as lousy for you both, and birthdays should be fun. So, I'm going to round-up whoever is here so we can put a lid on this day."

"Thanks, Sor. What do you think, Asa? New birthday?"

"I think that sounds like the best thing I've heard all day, Sis."

They exchanged smiles, and I was happy for them to have their bond. Soren was right. We needed to change their birthday, as it had only brought pain to them for years. Those of us in the room took seats around the table while we waited for whoever was left to come back. Milo sat at Fin's side with Asa on the other. I kept forgetting about him; he was so quiet. Cohen awkwardly sat a few seats down from them, closer to his new friend Mateo.

He had this whole bad boy vibe going on with the black jeans, dark hoodie, and tattoos I could see on his neck. Cohen even had an eyebrow ring now and was a far stretch from the endearing geeky guy I met a few years ago. That guy had idolized my father.

We'd hung out a few times while I was in town that summer and gotten along well. This Cohen... just had a whole different vibe about him. It was too late tonight to figure it out anyway, and I had a feeling he might be sticking around if the side eyes he kept throwing at my sister were any indication.

Ace, Charlie, Isla, Tyler, Ollie, and Tyler's dad walked into the room a few minutes later with Soren. Everyone took seats around the table, exhaustion evident on all of our faces. No one spoke for a minute, and I wondered who would speak up. Mateo was the first one to break the quiet, and I saw Smalls smile at his confidence.

"Well, okay, I guess if no one has anything to say, I can start?" No one interrupted him, so he continued, "Very well, let's do like a round table wrap-up? That way, we're all on the same page?"

Everyone nodded, and that was how we spent the next twenty minutes. Milo and Cohen both had looks of shock at one point, but by the end, they appeared to be invested and onboard, and I wondered if I was going to need to do the big brother thing and put the fear of God in them. Asa was a good guy, and I knew he cared for her, but if Fin was in the market to build her own harem, I would have to vet out these other two.

A wicked grin pulled across my face at the fun I could put them through. Soren saw me and shook his head, picking up on my line of thinking. Milo gulped at my look, but Cohen just smirked back and raised his eyebrow, almost like he was saying… *Bring it.*

Oh, just you wait, old friend. I'd make you earn your spot with my sister. The big brother urges in me roared to life after having her taken from me, so they'd better be glad this was all they'd have to experience tonight.

When we finally ended, I hugged Fin tight to me, not wanting to let her go. She finally agreed to stay over in Elias' room once Ty said he would sleep in Oliver's. It was a regular slumber party. I didn't invite the other guys; they could wait a day. They seemed to have gotten the hint, thankfully, as they both made awkward exits with Fin. Smalls was eyeing them all, and I watched the wheels turning in her head as well.

"It's been a day, sweet pea. Let's head to bed. Where are you sleeping tonight?" Soren asked. Smalls bit her lip as she looked around the room and landed on Mateo. I understood her reasoning. Soren and I had each other, Ty and Ollie had whatever they were, and Rhett was with Rowan, leaving Mateo alone. I got it, but after the day we'd had, I wanted to hold her just as much.

She was about to open her mouth with an answer when she looked back at me. My face must've shown my disappointment because she offered a new solution.

"What if we all have a slumber party in the media room again? I think we could use the comfort of one another tonight."

"That sounds perfect, Smalls." I grinned as agreements went around the room from the others.

"Awesome… but can we maybe bring down the mattresses this time? That floor is harder than it looks!"

We all laughed, but silently, I think we all agreed with that too. Over the next half hour, we all changed and built a massive fort bed in the media room. We put on a cheesy feel-good movie and cuddled close to the ones we loved, missing our family that wasn't here. After a day like today, where so much had been up in the air, it felt good to remember what mattered.

This life, with these people, was it for me, and I would fight whoever I needed to, to keep it. The Council had almost destroyed it tonight, and we wouldn't underestimate them. This was a war, and there would only ever be one winner. I just hoped it was us in the end.

# eleven

. . .

## sawyer

"BABY." The sound filtered through my brain. Someone was whispering to me as they shook me awake. Snuggled between two warm bodies, I couldn't recall who they were at the moment. I'd crashed once we'd all laid down, and I wasn't sure who I'd ended up wedged between.

Peeking one eye open, I made out the dark raven hair of Mateo in front of me as it curled onto his forehead. His eyes were closed, and small breaths were coming from him. The shaking started again from behind me, more insistent this time. Tilting my head, I tried to see who dared wake me this early. Well, I assumed it was early, based on the level of tiredness I felt. It was purely subjective, since the darkness of the room belied the actual time.

Rhett's head hung over me, exhaustion coating his face.

When he finally saw me peek up at him, a slight smile tilted at his lips. He wiggled a to-go cup in front of me, making me instantly forgive him for waking me. I peeled back the blanket and moved the arms off me, neither person waking at my movements. I could see Oliver was now behind me with Ty next to him. Soren and Henry were on the other side of Mateo, snuggled with one another.

Asa and Fin were still sound asleep in another corner, but I couldn't see Ace or any others, and now that I thought about it, I wasn't even sure if the rest of the people had stayed. Ever have one of those moments where you can't distinguish reality from dreams? That was how this morning felt. The events of yesterday felt so far removed from reality that they had to be a dream.

Rhett offered his free hand, helping me to balance as I stepped out of the cuddle huddle. Huh, that was kind of a cool phrase. *Cuddle huddle.* I was claiming it.

Quietly, we made our way out together and went into Rhett's room. Once the door shut, I wrapped my arms around him, realizing I never checked in last night before I fell asleep. I needed to know how Rowan was doing. I felt his body relax some in my hold, and I wanted to berate myself for forgetting about him, but the reality was that a lot of shit was going on. To top it off, it all mattered, so I couldn't fault myself or anyone else for forgetting something in the midst of things. We were all doing the best we could.

"How is she? How's Ro?"

"She's stable. They were able to get fluids into her and get some of her swelling down. It's mostly going to be rest and taking care of herself at this point."

"Oh, that's good to hear. Man, how did we get here?" I asked, pulling back a little to look up at him. "I still feel as if I'm waiting to wake up from a nightmare."

Rhett pulled me tighter, and I let him, dropping my head back to his chest, knowing he needed to feel me, to make sure I was okay as well.

"There's something I need to tell you."

"Okay, is this something I should sit down for?"

"Maybe."

Anxiety started to build, but I took in a deep breath and reminded myself who I was, who we were. *I got this.*

Sitting on the edge of the bed, I took the tumbler from him. Excitement briefly raced over me as I anticipated my first sip. I wasn't sure if it was tea or coffee, but I didn't care and would be happy with either. The aroma of a dark roast filled my nostrils as I inhaled the coffee.

"Mmm, thanks for this."

Rhett smiled, a nervous look on his face. He leaned back against his desk, shoving his hands in his pockets. His distance from me was worrisome, but I waited to hear what he had to say before I jumped to conclusions—Elias was teaching me that.

"The other night," he started, "I know you felt me tense when Agent Ballsack said we were all connected somehow," he started, staring at the floor. Rhett sighed, looking up into my eyes before he started again. "Rothchild... that's my father's family. Ryan Rothchild Turner is my father. He left when Rowan got sick, and only came back when he wanted something. But I remember meeting a Rothchild."

Rhett watched my face as he shared his story, but I displayed nothing, holding to my vow to be open and just listen.

"Granny Rothchild. I met her when I was about five. That time's all a blur since it was before Rowan was born. One summer, I spent it with her, and it was one of the best summers of my life." He smiled in remembrance. "At the end of the summer, my parents came to pick me up, and I heard fighting between my dad and Granny. I guess I repressed it or, I don't know, didn't want to believe it, but the other night I put the pieces together."

He gulped, tears brimming in his eyes, and I wanted to go to him, but I knew he needed to get this out first—it was important.

"My dad... I'm pretty sure he killed my granny. In her will, there was a letter to me. Over the years, my mom forgot about it and had put it away for me when I was older. She gave it to me yesterday and what I read, Sawyer, it's *shocking*. Granny had started to collect information on something she believed was dangerous. She knew her grandson, my dad, was after something and didn't trust him."

Rhett finally moved closer, sitting next to me on the bed. I set my coffee down, so I could turn entirely to him. He clasped my hands when I did, making me thankful they were free.

"She'd known about the Council, baby. Her research suggests it started as a way to encourage young leaders, but as a lot of things do, it became corrupt and changed. She left me an inheritance and all the information she'd collected on them. I think we might be able to use it. Granny died at the hands of my father, because he wanted something he felt was his birthright, so I'm going to use that birthright to take them down."

Blinking, I took in his expression, processing what he just said. The fear he must've felt as a little boy, to lose someone he loved like that. Rhett had always been a force to be reckoned with in just his pursuit to protect *me*. But now… they'd taken his sister and tried to sell her, in addition to killing his grandmother. He wouldn't rest until he'd avenged those things.

Rhett had always been a bear of a man, but for the first time, I saw the deadly grizzly that lived inside him too.

"Okay."

"You're not going to try to stop me?"

"No. This isn't just about me anymore. We've all lost something or someone at the hands of these people, and we all get to choose how we deal with it. As long as we do it together, we'll be unstoppable. I do have one rule, no scheming on your own or putting yourself in unnecessary danger."

He looked guilty for a second, and I knew he'd done something already.

"What did you do?"

"You're right. We need to do things together. I was just so upset yesterday after I found everything, I didn't think. I… I contacted my uncle and told him I'd learned about the Council and what it meant to be a Rothchild and that it was my turn to figure out what it meant for me."

"What did he say, Rhett?" I asked, trying to contain my frustration.

"Well, he offered to meet me when he's in town. Richard didn't make it in for the expo but he's willing to schedule some time to meet. He did give me access to the box he shares with another Council member…"

"Oh, and who would that be?" My words clipped out, but the way he was drawing this out had fear clawing at my chest.

"Abernathy."

"Ah, so you had the pleasure of meeting my sperm donor." I nodded. "So did I, last night."

"Yeah. He was an ass, but I talked to some other people in the box."

"Anyone important?" My heart had started to return to normal, but his vagueness again was making it want to jump back up into my throat.

"Yeah, I think so, but that can wait." He swallowed, licking his lips. "Sawyer, I don't want to hide things from you, so I feel I need to tell you that I saw…"

When he trailed off, I rolled my eyes, tired of the tip-toeing around things. "Saw who? Just tell me, Rhett. I can take it. It's worse not knowing."

"…Elias." Warmth filled me. He was *back*.

"Okay, isn't that good?"

"He wasn't alone in the box."

"Go on, rip that Band-Aid off." I self-deprecatingly laughed.

"He was cozy," he gritted, "with Adelaide."

Cold water rushed over me at the mention of my nemesis. But... his letter ran through my head and his statement of having to do things he might not want to. I decided to trust him. I needed to start seeing him for the man he was, instead of the villain I kept painting him as.

Elias had always been the riskiest for me to trust. I could see that now, and it was my own issue. I never felt good enough for him and like I had the most to lose by giving him a chance. It was time I took a chance on myself as well.

It wasn't fair to keep penalizing him for our first meeting. He was trying to tell me who he was, and I had to give him that opportunity. There were too many other people in my life that wanted something from me and not enough who just wanted to know me. I needed to start seeing the difference. Nodding, I kept my worries to myself.

"Anyone else?"

Rhett looked at me for a second, making sure I was okay with the news.

"A couple of people that work at Rothchild, Inc. I was able to get a feel for the dynamics there and what kind of man my uncle is. Not many knew my father, so I don't know the extent he's involved in things. Hopefully not at all. If I could get through without having to see him, that would be the best outcome. He brings nothing but heartache and broken promises every time he comes near us."

"How do you feel about it all? Your father?"

He titled his head, taking me in, and I think it was the first time he'd ever considered it or had someone ask how *he* was. Rhett was going to have to get used to others caring for him too. He wasn't alone in that department anymore.

"I had time to think about it last night at the hospital. It was shocking, but I always knew my father wasn't a good man. Learning this new information didn't change how I saw him; it only confirmed it, I guess. Having the memory of my granny back, it's bittersweet. I'm happy to remember our summer and who she was, but sad that I didn't get more time with her and that she never got to meet Rowan."

"There are too many people in our lives that have been taken in pursuit of the Council. It's time we stop it."

"Baby, it's really hot when you get all pissed off and territorial."

"Oh, how hot?" Other parts of me started to wake up from the heat in his eyes, and they were ready to have some fun.

"How about I show you instead?"

Rhett pulled his shirt off in a one-hand move I loved before he attacked me with kisses. Our tongues swirled together, racing one another to demonstrate our love. His hands started to push up my shirt, his thumbs sweeping the skin on my belly. Shivers raced up my spine at the coarseness of them. Tracing kisses down my neck, he began to suck, pushing flat against the bed.

Hovering over me, he pulled my shirt off, completely displaying my breasts to him. I'd taken off my bra last night in protest, not caring that my friends and brother were all in the room, too; my brazenness was paying off as Rhett easily took my nipple into his mouth, unencumbered by anything, his hands freely roaming my torso.

Running my hands through his hair, I tugged him to suck harder. He was a magician because as he laved me with kisses up top, he also managed to pull my sleep pants down over my ass simultaneously, surprising me when his thumb grazed my clit.

Moans erupted out of me at the feeling, and I was dazed as he moved lower. Rhett's mouth began to brush my other lips, nuzzling me as I wriggled under him. My legs fell open, offering him better access as I felt him savor me. His tongue licked up my center, his hands now bracketing my thighs as he pressed them down onto the bed, keeping me stationary.

Arching my back, I swished my head back and forth in ecstasy as he pilfered my core. Slowly, he started to run a finger up and down, coating his finger in my wetness. I could feel my excitement covering his face as he devoured me, my arousal dripping down my pussy. Without warning, he thrust a finger into my core, plunging deep as he arched it up inside me. Dragging it back out, he teased me before diving back in.

Rhett continued this madness of slow torture, and I dropped one hand down to his hair to pull, needing to have contact with him. My other hand caressed my breast, twisting my nipple in rhythm with his sucking of my clit. He pulled back, watching me as he continued to penetrate me with his finger.

"It's so fucking hot watching you touch yourself. Can you take more, baby?"

"Yeeesss," I moaned out, needing to feel myself clench around him. Instead of giving me his monster cock, he inserted a second finger, this time picking up speed. He went back to licking my clit as he plowed me with his digits.

"Fucking hell," I gasped. The sounds of my wetness squelched around his fingers as he vigorously plunged into me. Rhett gave one big lick and then pulled back, adding his thumb to my clit. He thrust his fingers deep in me, and it almost felt as fulfilling as his cock with his punishing pace. When he circled my clit, I grasped both of my breasts as I rolled my nipples between my fingers, setting off my orgasm. My climax erupted, sending stars throughout my vision as I felt my walls tighten around his fingers.

"So good, baby," Rhett cooed.

Panting, my arms fell to the sides, my body a puddle of goo from the ecstasy. Sitting up, I gave a mischievous look to my grumpy bear, spreading my legs wider. I imagined my cum evident as it glistened on me. Rhett licked his lips, and it looked like I was about to get my wish when a knock sounded on the door.

Falling back, I groaned, knowing our time was up. Happiness for the time I'd gotten to spend with him spread through me. When people were always trying to kill you and take the people you loved, you appreciated these precious moments. I would take whatever I could get with any of my guys because there would never be enough.

Rhett handed me a shirt before walking over to the door. Glancing back to make sure I was clothed, he cracked it open an inch.

"Hey, oh good, you're both here. Breakfast is ready. Though, I think I like your idea of breakfast better." Ollie chuckled, wiggling his eyebrows.

Laughing, I handed Rhett his shirt when I walked over to him. He looked down, adorably forgetting he wasn't wearing one. Chuckling, I smacked his abs, grazing his happy trail as I did. I would need to finish this later. No way my hussy vagina would be satisfied with only oral when she had a buffet of cocks to explore. Hey, she wasn't wrong.

Ollie grabbed me around the waist, lifting me as I squealed, carrying me up the stairs in his arms. Giving in, I wrapped myself around him, happy to have him home safe with me. Yesterday had been challenging and a great reminder of who we were dealing with.

It was time to show those old fuckers why we were teaching at an elite training facility. We could bend, we could dodge, and we could outmaneuver anything they threw at us. We were athletes at the top of our game and hired to teach the best. Guess we needed to remind them why we were the best.

Game faces on, bitches.

# twelve

. . .

## sawyer

"GOOD MORNING!" Finley chirped from the dining room table. I assessed her as I walked over, hugging her tight. She wore a brave face, but I needed to sit her down later and make sure she was okay. It couldn't have been easy being taken like that.

We hadn't even talked much about what they went through, just the details of the place, wanting to give them time before they were bombarded. My brother watched her closely, and I noticed he kept touching her. Almost as a reassurance to himself she existed. Mateo was busy organizing drinks at the coffee bar, so I decided to help him. Stretching up on my tiptoes, I kissed his cheek.

"Hey, cutie!"

"Good morning, Dulzura," he said, looking over at me as he smiled.

"How can I help?"

"Here, you can take the juices over. I'll grab the tea and coffee."

Nodding, I grabbed the OJ and CranApple juice and walked over to the table. I didn't make it far, though. As soon as I placed them in the middle, I was grabbed around the waist and hoisted into a lap. Nuzzling my captor's neck, I found a smiling Ollie had captured me.

"Good morning, Ollie."

"Good morning, pretty girl," he cooed as he started to kiss my collarbone.

"Mmm. Be careful what you start," I whispered.

"Oh, I can definitely finish," he teased, giving me a look. "Besides, you don't have room to talk, Miss Baring-Her-Ass to me like it's the main course for breakfast."

Oops. I'd forgotten I didn't have anything on under my oversized t-shirt. Innocently, I blinked up at him, hiding my red cheeks. He gave me a knowing grin as I felt him lengthen against me. We held each other's gaze, a million emotions flitting across our eyes as the rest of the room disappeared.

Someone placed a large platter on the table with a bang and broke us out of our stare down, causing me to jump at the noise.

"Sorry," Finley proclaimed, no hint of remorse in her tone at all. Sticking out my tongue, I was secretly grateful she'd interrupted us since we'd forgotten who was in the room. When Charlie walked in a few minutes later, my cheeks flamed brighter, and I hurriedly scooted off Ollie's lap, making a mad dash for the stairs, his chuckles trailing after me.

Pants! I needed pants pronto. It was one thing when I was just hanging out with my boyfriends, not so much with my pseudo-grandfather figure here.

Darting into my room, I pulled out the first pair of panties I saw, and grabbed a pair of leggings. Deciding to put on a bra as well, I tossed off the large t-shirt as I selected a fitted tank with a bra. Good enough. Choosing some fuzzy socks and a sweatshirt, I made my way back downstairs, forgoing my hairbrush. Some things weren't as important.

Hopping into the last sock as I turned the corner. I righted myself as I walked back into the dining room. Thankfully, no one seemed to have noticed my embarrassing exit other than Ollie, so I sat down with the others and scooped out food as it was passed around. This was some sitcom shit right here—sharing a meal with my friends and family around a table. The development of this made me grin as I passed the biscuits to Soren on my left.

It cemented how worth it this all was. If this was the end result of all the pain and suffering I'd endured in the past five years, then I was okay with that. I missed my parents every day, but they wouldn't want me to miss out on life. They'd want me to live my dreams to the fullest. Having family and friends who loved me was the best version of a life I could lead.

"Sawdust, what are these plans you have for me today?

My flight is this evening, so I need to be at the airport around 5 pm."

"That's doable. I just wanted to take you around the town and introduce you to Aggie. She's the only one you haven't met yet."

"Oh, can I come too?" Fin begged, practically bouncing in her seat.

"Of course! Whoever wants to join can. I'm sure she'd love the company."

No one else was available, but it worked out for the best, as it meant I could get Fin alone to make sure she was okay.

"This French toast is amazing! Oh my God, I think I want to eat this every day," I groaned. Soren's face tinted at my remark, or perhaps it was the noise I made. Oh well, it was the response he'd get if he kept making me orgasmic food. Agreements went around the table as we all fell into silence, enjoying our meal.

"I'm stuffed. Someone will need to roll me out of here," joked Tyler.

"That was wonderful. It makes me wish I was staying longer," Charlie said, patting his stomach.

"Well, I'll do the dishes, and then I need to take a shower. Fin, Charlie, we can leave in about an hour or so if that works for you both?"

"Yep, I'll head back to my house. Can you pick me up on the way?"

"Sure can."

"I was going to show Charlie some old footage and memorabilia, so that gives me plenty of time," Ollie said, looking at Charlie who smiled in return. He was such a geek when it came to hockey.

"Okay, well, we all have a plan." I clapped. "I'll see the rest of you later for lunch or dinner, I suppose."

Kisses went around as everyone headed off to do whatever they needed. I started on the dishes and was happy when Henry joined me. Together, we finished them in record time, and I headed up to my room to start my day.

Taking a quick shower, I rummaged through my closet when I noticed a bag poking out from under some clothes. I had a bad habit of tossing all my dirty clothes on the ground instead of in the hamper, you know, the one that was two feet away. Shoving the piles of clothes off it, I found a small gift bag that was slightly crumpled from being under everything.

Isla's mention of a gift raced through my head, and I wondered if I'd finally found it. Sitting on the floor of my closet, my hands shook as I peeked into the bag. A small navy box wrapped in a matching ribbon sat in the bag, all unassuming. Anticipation surged through me with each breath. What could she want to give *me*?

Lifting the box out of the bag, I rolled my fingers over the soft ribbon. One side was made of velvet, making it soft and smooth. The other side felt more like satin, and my fingers glided over the ribbon in a satisfying motion. I could sit here and rub this ribbon all day with the relaxation it provided. Or perhaps I was avoiding opening the box. Sucking it up, I pulled the ribbon, watching the tails fall to the side.

Slowly, I lifted the top of the box, the sides making a hiss as the air escaped between them. Perched snuggly inside was a navy-blue velvet jewelry box. Turning it over, I shook the box until it loosened, plopping into my palm. Carefully, I lifted the lid, the hinges creaking with the effort. Laying on top of a satin pillow was an antique watch.

The links in it were gold and delicate, shining in the light. The clock face was intricate, displaying the inner workings of the watch—the cogs and gears moved while the hands ticked around the face. The numbers were engraved in a fancy type-face; the brand etched into the clock itself. *Patek Philippe*, I mouthed, the word feeling awkward on my tongue. The back had an inscription, but it was in a language I was unfamiliar with.

I cautiously placed it on my wrist, the weight of the time-piece unfamiliar as it sat there. Grabbing my phone, I snapped a picture and sent it to Isla, having exchanged numbers. With great attention, I fastened the links together and put the boxes back in place, tying the ribbon back up. Placing it in my dresser, I picked up the gift bag to toss into the trash when I felt a small card inside.

My name was on the outside of it in a delicate script. Rubbing my thumb over the cursive, I felt the raised ink. The importance of having my biological mother write my name hit me in the chest, and I wasn't sure if I could read her note. The reality and fear I wouldn't be able to focus, had me opening it up. My eyes glanced over her handwriting, memo-rizing it as I absorbed the words—words that knocked into me with great astonishment and trepidation equally.

Dressing in a daze, I absorbed the words that had accom-panied Isla's gift. I pulled on some socks, not focusing on which ones or if they even matched. Sitting on my bed, I once again heard an odd noise. A crumpling sound came from under my rear, pulling me from my musings. Lucky looked up at me as well, tilting his head in a way that looked like he was asking what the noise was from. Lifting up, I found an envelope laying on my bed, wrinkled from my derriere squishing.

Today was the day to find missing packages and letters, I supposed. The handwriting was immediately familiar, and I realized it was another letter from Elias. Ripping it open in a flash, I leaned back against my pillows to devour his words.

*Love,*

*A great deal of things have changed since my last letter. By this time, you should have gotten my first letter. If not, then just know it will make sense once you do. Maybe wait to read this one until then? I doubt you'll listen to that, but I had to try. I'm going to assume you have from here. (How do you make me smile even when writing to you?)*

*I'm back in America and I've returned to my family home in Connecticut. I never liked this house; it's cold and lonely here. I never understood how a place could be warm and inviting until living with the guys at TAS. When you came along, it made it even more so. I can see that now.*

*My hands are shaking slightly as I've set something in motion. I just made a deal with my father. He thinks I'm going to take his name and join his cause finally. There's something I hadn't shared, and to be honest, I didn't understand the importance until I started to research your family history.*

*My mother was the personal assistant of my father, and they had an illicit affair. When she realized she was pregnant, my mom had seen enough of his world to know she didn't want to raise a child in it. She quit and took me to New Jersey, where we lived for four years. She was sick, though, cancer I'm told. She died and had put in her will that my biological father was Richard, so I was sent to live with him.*

*In some ways, I am grateful because he did take me in. He wasn't abusive and gave me everything I could want. He sent me to boarding school in London when I started school, and I spent most of my time there over the next fifteen years. I have three older siblings: Tomas, Harrison, and Penelope. Tomas didn't care for me, Harrison tolerated me to some degree, but Pen was my ally since we were the closest in age.*

*Why am I telling you all of this, you may be wondering? Because unfortunately, it matters. A greater deal more than I ever imagined. By now, you have probably uncovered the current members of the Council board. If you haven't, I've enclosed the picture and list of names I found. This picture is what prompted me to leave. It's what set everything into motion, outlining what I needed to do.*

*My father is Richard Fitzroy, and he and his friends have a business together. The Council is more than just a board; they make up the CEOs of the biggest industries. This part isn't public knowledge, and I expect they do it to maintain their power and anonymity. But together, the current board, who've been in control for 21 years, created EXOSIA Corp. The corporation has its hands in everything from finance, chemicals, cars, real estate, and more. Fitzroy's themselves are in banking and finance which is where I'm expected to work.*

*There is another thing my father wants me to do first.*

*He is sending me to TAS to speak with your biological father about a deal. I think there might be trouble within the ranks. I will find out more. Just know that whoever I talk to, whoever I'm with... it doesn't mean a thing. I'm playing a part. I know that trust is hard, and I hope I keep showing you that I can be worthy of it.*

*I wish I could say more, but I hope this helps.*

*I miss everyone. I miss you.*

*I hope you think of me as much as I think of you.*

*Yours Wholly.*

Looking at the picture, I was momentarily shocked as I took in the seven men that graced it. The most shocking part was that Council wasn't a term for their group, but an *acronym*—C.O.U.N.C.I.L.

What did it mean? The chapter meeting information confirmed what Samson had told us already. There were several locations of this sinister group, but the central area was TAS. The school was the starting point, just as my father had stated all those years ago.

Questions swirled in my head as I processed Elias' letter. Remembering my vow to trust him, I'd give him the space to show me who he was. He was risking his life for us; I could risk my heart. Choosing to have courage and deal with the risk of loss as it came and not in fear of it was how I wanted to live. Nothing in life was guaranteed, and playing it safe was boring.

Laying back, I held his letter to my heart, attempting to seal his words there forever. Tingles exploded as I thought of how his letters made me feel, and a giddy excitement flooded me. I suddenly found myself on pins and needles as I waited for his next one. Elias and I had our own love story to tell, and I, for one, couldn't wait to see how it all unfolded.

# thirteen

. . .

## finley

THE KNOCK on my door jolted me out of the daze I'd fallen into, and I turned to see who it was. One of my roommates was leaning against the doorframe, looking at me in concern.

"Uh, hey, Ashlee. What's up?" She regarded me for a moment before coming further into my room, shutting the door behind her. She leaned against the door, effectively blocking my escape. "Hey, so," she said, twisting her hands, hesitancy in her voice, "I know we haven't talked much, but I wanted to see how you were?"

Her question hung in the air like a delayed fart, and I scrunched up my nose in thought. What was she talking about?

"Not to be rude, but what the hell are you talking about?"

Ashlee chuckled, coming closer into my space. *Hello,*

*boundaries!* We might be housemates, but this was my room the last time I checked.

"I'm guessing no one told you I work for the Agency."

"Oh," shock resonated in me as I tried to keep my face neutral. "Nope. Can't say I've ever heard that before."

"Yeah, well, secrecy and all that." She waved her hand, rolling her eyes. "But now that the cat is out of the bag, I wanted to see how you were after the whole ordeal of last night. I was supposed to be at the house, but something else came up. My handler briefed me this morning that you'd been recovered."

Blinking in shocked astonishment at her news, I tried to put what I was feeling into words. None came to mind, and a cold realization sank over me. There was something off about what she was saying, but my own emotional turmoil was clouding everything. Shoving those memories and thoughts into a box, I pasted my "everything is fine" smile on my face before answering.

"I'm great. Yeah, nothing happened, and I'm home. So yeah, good, good."

"You just said good twice, telling me that you're probably not as good as you think."

Welp, she had me there, but I didn't want to have this conversation with her per se. Shrugging, I went back to working on the shirt I'd been unfolding and refolding for the past thirty minutes. I should probably get dressed, but I broke out into a cold sweat every time I went to get in the shower. Logically, I knew what was happening. Ignoring it meant I didn't have to acknowledge it was real.

"When I'd finished my training, one of the first missions was to infiltrate a high school. I was one of the youngest, so I fit the profile. Naively, I was pumped and full of arrogance, thinking I could do the impossible. The mission ended up more complicated than reported. The drug traffic ring proved more complex than our intel had suggested." She swallowed, her eyes falling to her hands. Her voice had a faraway quality to it, and I recognized something in it—*fear and shame.*

"I thought I could handle something on my own, but I'd been wrong. I ended up in too deep with no way out, and they assaulted me. My team pulled me out before it went too far, but is there such a thing as too far when it comes to sexual assault?" she asked, pausing in her memories. She said it all monotone, almost as if she focused on it, then the emotion would overwhelm her.

"I tried to deny what had happened to me, and I pushed it aside. My behavior turned reckless, and I found myself in situations I hadn't meant to be. Regret is a heavy emotion to carry, and I have a lot. The biggest one was not talking about how much that experience had affected me. If I can shield you from some of my bad choices, then I want to try. I'm here if you need to talk."

Ashlee stood after she finished, wiping a tear from her eye, having let herself feel it. The emotion she expressed was real, and I felt I'd seen her for who she truly was for the first time. Ashlee wasn't the preppy girl stuck up Queen Bitch's ass like I'd always assumed. I kind of liked this version of her.

"Wait," I yelped, the emotions coursing through me.

"Thank you for telling me that. I... I'm still trying to piece everything together, but I think I'll take you up on that offer later if that's okay?"

"Yeah, totally. You know where to find me."

"Cool."

"No problem, Fin." She smiled, waving bye.

"Bye."

I stared at the space she left for a few minutes, collecting my thoughts. When my phone buzzed, it startled me out of the trance. Sawyer messaged to say they'd left the house and would be here in five minutes. *Cheese on a cracker*!

Jumping up, I ran to my closet and started to piece together an outfit. Undressing, I realized I wasn't wearing a bra still.

*Oh, shit. The thumb drive.*

Racing back to my phone, I picked it up and called Milo. Thankfully, we'd exchanged numbers last night, before he'd left. Milo hadn't stayed after the recap, stating he needed to check in with his father. His phone rang a few times before going to voicemail.

"Milo, it's me, Fin. Hey, listen, I just realized I didn't have my clothes we wore to the thing, you know," my voice cracked. Clearing my throat, I restarted. "Anyways, I need them. They're like really important clothes, they um, are family jeans, yeah, passed down from mother to daughter. Kind of like the traveling pants, okay. So yeah, give me a call back because I really need to find my clothes, like all of them, bra, underwear, you know. Thanks."

Ending the call, I hung my head for being a rambling

idiot who didn't know how to leave a coherent message. He'd think I was incompetent, some dumb kid. The uneasy feeling of caring about what he thought rose in me again. Every time I thought about Milo and how he'd come to my rescue, I got butterflies. But I wasn't supposed to have butterflies for Milo. I had a boyfriend. Asa was the one for me. I just knew it.

My phone buzzed again announcing their arrival, and I flew around the room throwing on clothes, realizing I was standing in the middle of it topless. Making me so glad I hadn't accidentally face-timed him. That would've been embarrassing, or maybe my boobs would distract him from the idiotic message. I might have to do that next time.

Wait. Next time? I needed to get sexy doctor Milo out of my head.

Not even checking if my clothes matched, I shoved on some boots and headed down the stairs. Charlie and Sawyer idled in the driveway, making me feel guiltier. I didn't want her pseudo grandfather to think I was irresponsible or poor with time management.

*Why would he think about you?* My self-doubt chastised as I blasted my fake smile. Grinning wide, I opened the back door of the SUV and jumped into the fun-loving girl who had it all together.

"Have no fear, Fin is here!"

"Girl, you're so funny." Sawyer chuckled, and I felt vindicated that I'd managed to throw off any concern from them. I didn't need to think about it, and I most certainly didn't need to talk. I just needed to get through this day, then the next one, and then the next one. It might not be precisely what I'd learned in counseling, but it would be the things to save me.

My anxiety would cripple me if I let it, and I couldn't afford to be paralyzed in fear. There were too many people counting on me. I couldn't be weak. I didn't have time for that, nor the luxury of grieving or processing what had occurred last night. Making a list, I prioritized what to do.

"Fin?"

"Huh?"

Sawyer wore an expression of concern, making me wonder if she'd been saying my name a few times before I responded. Shit—get it together, girl.

"What's up?" I smiled, making sure to keep it plastered this time.

"I was just asking how you were. You know, after everything that happened last night?"

"I'm great. Just glad to be back and ready to kick some ass, uh, sorry, butt." I cringed, feeling embarrassed for cussing. My mother hated cuss words, so I simultaneously wanted to use them out of spite but felt guilty every time I did. Most of the time, I resorted to made-up or PG versions and only used the actual ones when they made the most sense.

Charlie chuckled at my retraction, and relief spread over my face even while flaming red in embarrassment.

"Yeah, I don't believe you for one second, Finley Amelia, and don't worry about offending his delicate ears. This old man drops f-bombs like they're going out of style." Sawyer smiled lovingly at Charlie, who only huffed at her as he drove.

"Okay, you got me. I'm, I don't know. I'm here and safe. So, let it be that for today, okay?"

My voice revealed more than I'd intended, but it helped my case. Sawyer gave me the reprieve and dropped it. When we pulled up to an expansive house, I blinked, having spaced out again. Taking it in, I was slack-jawed as I looked at the grounds. From the greenery to the architecture, beauty abounded around us, and I instantly knew why Sawyer loved it.

Stepping out of the car, I twirled in a circle, trying to take it all in. This was the kind of place fairytales were made of. Sawyer came up beside me and linked her arm through mine. Surprised by her touch, I jumped but tried to play it off. Cheeseballs, I was jumpy today. Sawyer leaned her head on my arm, her shorter stature putting her right below my shoulder.

"Come on, short stuff," I joked, "introduce me to Aggie."

Sawyer gave me an assessing look, knowing I'd deflected with humor, but allowed it for the time being. Her look soothed some of the rough edges I felt, and I took a breath for the first time in hours. There was something to be said about having a friend who knew you well enough that they could calm you with just their presence.

Charlie waited for us at the steps, and we made our way over to him. He patted me on the shoulder when we passed, the gesture bringing tears to my eyes. *Okay, Finley, buck up girl —there's no crying at teatime.*

"Miss Sawyer, the mistress is waiting in the parlor for your visit," a refined man stated. I wouldn't say he looked down his nose at us, but I wouldn't say he hadn't either. I wondered if they got him out of a catalog? Butlers 'R Us?

"He's chipper," I whispered to Sawyer, causing her to laugh as we walked into a formal room. A kind looking woman sat in a wingback chair, her legs crossed at the ankle. She held a delicate teacup and saucer, casually sipping tea like a proper lady.

As she noticed us, she placed it on the coffee table. A smile gracing her lips as she took us in, her love for Sawyer shining brightly. Warmth spread through my chest, and a tinge of envy at the amazing people Sawyer had collected. The past five years had been hell for me, and I would never begrudge my best friend for making something of hers. It pushed me instead to run after my own.

"You must be the amazing Finley," Aggie praised, my cheeks reddening at the compliment.

"Oh, I don't know about all that, but I could say the same about you, Aggie." She smiled at my comment before turning and taking in the man behind us.

"Aggie, I would like you to meet my Charlie," Sawyer said, introducing them to one another. They both paused, assessing one another. I smiled, finding humor in watching them.

"It's a pleasure to meet you, Aggie."

Charlie stretched out his hand, offering a greeting. It appeared they were partaking in some kind of weird old person flirtation. Aggie offered her hand, and in a smooth, debonair move, Charlie turned it, kissing the back of her hand—why the sly old fox had moves!

Sawyer stood frozen, a look of shock on her face that quickly morphed into her scheming face. *Good luck with that girl*, I thought. These two would either crash and burn all on their own or find a second happiness in one another. I rooted for the second option. The world could use more love stories.

We sat and drank our tea, Sawyer chatting with Aggie and Charlie. They both regaled us with the expo yesterday since neither Aggie nor I had been there. It was nice to hear how she and my brother had performed. The pang of why I missed it sent me into a rabbit hole of dark thoughts I'd been trying to avoid. Tuning out the conversation around me, I replayed over and over the mistakes I'd made, looking for solutions.

Similar to a coding sequence, my brain would run all the different commands across itself in quick fashion. It amplified my anxiety and need for perfection leaving me feeling like a complete dumbass. While it was helpful when hacking, it wasn't so great when it came to life.

Sawyer grabbed my hand and squeezed three times, grounding me back to the conversation. I left the graphs and flowcharts in my mind and tried to focus around me. When she tightened her hand in mine, I noticed I'd been picking my thumbnail subconsciously to the point of bleeding.

"I'm sorry, but could I use the restroom?" I interjected, standing as I tried to hide my hand.

"Oh, yes dear, the powder room is down the hall."

"Thank you."

Quickly, I made my way out of there and down the hall-way, peeking my head in each open door, looking for the "powder room." It made me laugh at the absurdity of words rich people used to describe things. You took a shit there; calling it a powder room did not change that fact. My sassiness was strong today, and I realized how much I must've shoved into the box to forget what had happened.

Finally, I found the half-bath and quickly entered it, shutting the door and world behind me. For a brief moment, I leaned back and breathed. Why was this so hard? I was back home. Nothing terrible had happened. I was safe.

So, why didn't it feel safe?

Turning on the tap, I ran my bloodied thumb under the cold water, the stinging a welcomed relief to the pain I felt internally. Without my permission, the top of the "deal with it later" box flew off, and all the feelings I'd been repressing for years flowed out, slamming me in the chest.

Gasping for air, I doubled over the sink, clutching at my chest as I managed to suck in a breath. My pocket buzzed, and I shakily reached for it, trying to retrieve it from the confines it was trapped in. Trembling hands hit the answer bar. Lifting it to my ear, I realized I'd answered a video call.

"Finley?" questioned a concerned voice.

That sound of concern was following me, and I was starting to hate it. I couldn't answer them as I raggedly took in breaths, nodding that I could hear them.

"Finley, where are you? You need to breathe. I think you're having a panic attack. Lift the camera and stare into my eyes, okay?"

Nodding without thinking, I lifted it from my ear to my face, gasping with each breath.

"*Finley*, focus on my voice. Breathe in with me, listen to what I'm saying."

Slowly, I focused on the movements he was making as I mirrored my breaths with his. Each exhale started to slow my heart and bring me back down to the present. All wrapped in the comfort of Milo's voice as it surrounded me.

"There she is." He smiled. "You had me worried there for a moment."

"Sorry," I mumbled, feeling embarrassed for the endeavor.

"Finley, you have nothing to be sorry or feel embarrassed about. Last night was scary, and you don't have to go through this alone. If you let me, I'd like to get to know you more. I know... I know you have a boyfriend. And I get it, but I think we could be friends."

I nodded before he finished because I did want to be his friend. We'd bonded through the experience, and while he hadn't gone through it like Ro and me, he knew what went on down there. I had a feeling he hadn't had an easy life at the hands of his family either. As much as everyone else outside Ollie could imagine what I'd been through, none of them would know. But Milo would.

"Did you... get my message?" I managed to get out.

"Yeah, that's why I was calling. Sorry I missed your call earlier. I was, well, it's not important. I called and found they dumped all the clothes into a bin, so I'll run and get it. Can I bring it to you?"

"Yeah, that works. I'm not at my house or even the house we were at last night, but I should be back in about an hour."

"Perfect."

He started to say something else when I heard a voice in the background calling out to him. Milo's eyes shifted to the left before returning to me. "Hey, listen, I got to go, but I'll see you in about an hour."

"Yeah, okay."

"And Finley…" he trailed off, "it was nice to see your face."

Before I could say anything, he hung up and I felt more confused than I had earlier. Milo had just flirted with me, right? But it sounded very much like a female voice in the background. Realizing I'd get no answers hiding out in the 'powder room,' I quickly washed my hands and threw some water on my face before making my way back.

Locking down my features, I put a better lid on the box and tossed it into a dark abyss, hoping it stayed there this time. *I was Finley Amelia Reyes, dammit.* I didn't have time for mental breakdowns. It could take a number for all I cared. Too much other crap had to be contended with, and first up was helping my best friend get justice for her parents.

Everything else, well, it could suck my big toe.

# fourteen

. . .

## sawyer

"THANKS FOR THE TEA, Aggie. I'll call you next week to set up another visit."

"Of course, dear. I look forward to it. You've brought a bit of spark back into my weeks with your visits."

Smiling, I hugged her before following Charlie and Fin out the door. Charlie had kissed her hand again as he said goodbye, and I wondered if there was a romance brewing. I'd never seen Charlie act this way before, so it made me curious. Fin had been quiet since she returned from the bathroom, and I knew I needed alone time with her today.

As Charlie pulled out of the driveway, I drifted off in thought as the GPS directed him to the house. This morning's letters were still buzzing through my head as I replayed their contents over and over. I needed to ask my brother if he knew anything about the watch. Twisting it on my wrist, I ran my fingers over the clock's face. It was smooth glass despite being older, and I wondered if it was some special type of glass that didn't scratch or if it had never been worn before.

The car was quiet as we drove back, all of us apparently lost in our thoughts. There were a few cars in the driveway when we approached and curiosity built about who was here. We needed a collective name for us all. Winter Soldiers? Nah, too, Marvel. Ice Pack? Maybe, though it sounded a little Mighty Ducks.

Lazily, I trudged up the stairs a million thoughts away, following Charlie and Finley. We found a few of the guys playing a video game in the living room, pausing it when they spotted us.

"Hey, sweet pea! How was your visit?" Soren beamed as he jumped up off the couch, knocking into Ollie and Mateo in the process. Some good-natured shoving went on as they all started to clamber to the floor to greet us.

Soren reached me first due to his shoving. Picking me up, he spun me in one of his patented hugs. I squealed with delight as I clung to him. He nuzzled my neck, and I felt other parts of me start to wake up. I'd be glad in a way when all of our out-of-town guests were gone—my libido would get free reign again.

"I think we need to schedule our next book club. I have many thoughts on the book and what I want to do *after*," he growled into my ear, sitting me down—damn *boy*. Struck speechless by his words, I nodded vigorously in agreement, causing him to smirk.

Mateo and Ollie greeted me just as enthusiastically, and I felt as if I'd been gone for weeks and not mere hours. My body wanted to give in to the cuddle huddle on the floor with my guys, but noticing Fin standing awkwardly to the side shuffling her feet, it was time to activate the best friend pact.

"Old man, you okay down here for a while? I need to speak with Fin." I nodded in her direction as I quietly conspired with him. He looked over, giving me a reassuring smile.

"I'll just hang here with the guys and see which one is my favorite," he boomed, causing all the guys to straighten up and fall over themselves to win the title.

Laughing, I walked off, enjoying his shenanigans with them. I'd been worried when I broke the news to him, but he'd taken it in stride, claiming I'd have more protectors this way. Throwing my arm around Finley, I directed her toward the stairs.

"Come on. It's time for some best girl time."

Fin bit her lip, nodding reluctantly, and allowed me to direct her. We climbed the steps together and, on soft footfalls, made our way into my bedroom. I moved her over to the big chair, and we both climbed in. Lucky had stayed downstairs with the guys. I didn't want to admit it, but he missed Elias. *Hell, I missed Elias.* Focusing back on my friend, I pulled her into a side hug.

"Fin, talk to me."

"I... I... don't know how Sawyer. It feels like everything is so loud, and yet nothing makes sense," she paused, picking at her nails. *"It's all my fault."*

Fin broke down into a sob as she let out the feelings over the incident. Wrapping her fully into my arms, I held her close as she sobbed. I tried to hold her together as she let out the pain and hurt she felt.

"It's okay to cry, Fin. It just means you care and feel strongly for things," I soothed. "I can't imagine what you experienced. That is yours, and only you can put words to it," I offered, remembering how frustrating it was for me when everyone kept telling me how I should feel. "You don't owe anyone an explanation or need to share it if you don't want to. You get to decide, sweetie." I kept rubbing her back as I gently rocked her. "Please hear me when I say this part. It was not your fault. Rowan wanted Rhett to make sure you knew that too."

I felt her cry harder, so we sat in the chair, curled up as I held my friend, my sister. Lucky trotted into the room after we'd been sitting there for a while. He walked over and hopped up onto the chair, pawing at us to let him in between us. It was funny enough to make us laugh, allowing him to settle between us so we could pet him. He greedily accepted all our love and affection.

Chuckling, Fin looked at me, tears in her eyes, and I saw the inner warrior peek back at me. "God, I've missed you. Thank you for being you and understanding."

"I hate that this happened to you, and part of me does feel guilty for bringing this into your life. But it's no more my fault than it's yours," I affirmed, wiping my own tears. "The Council's the one at fault. We will make them suffer for this."

"I hope so because… the things that are going on Sawyer,

they're not good. I was trying to help Jill, but I think I screwed it up. I wanted to fix it, you know, on my own, but I made it worse and involved Rowan. I don't know if I'll ever forgive myself, nor do I expect Rhett will."

"Nonsense, Fin. Rhett isn't going to blame you. Rowan is her own person, and you didn't force her to do anything. She chose to. Get that in your head, *please*."

"Ugh, you're impossible. Fine, she chose to, but it doesn't make me feel any better."

"What I want to know… just who are Cohen and Milo? Are you making your own little harem? Hmm? Do I need to talk with my brother?" I giggled.

Fin's face heated, and she tried to hide it in the cushion. Tickling her, we inadvertently jostled Lucky in the process. He gave us major attitude as he repositioned himself, huffing at us the whole time. That damn dog was so adorable with his attitude, reminding me of Elias. I understood how they got along so well now.

"Um… well, I don't even know, to be honest." She blushed. "It kind of all happened, didn't it? Chaos, or Cohen, well, I met him a few years ago when I got in trouble for hacking and other stuff. I guess I met him as Chaos first online and then as Cohen, my father's intern. Except I didn't know they were the same person. I still need to beat him up for keeping secrets."

"Are you sure he knew?"

"You know, I don't know. It looks like we do need to have a chat. We've always flirted online as our online alter egos, but I didn't take it seriously. Cohen had been quiet in person.

177

I saw him a few times that summer, but it wasn't like sparks flew. Guys weren't interested in me that way. I've kind of always been in the friend role or too nerdy to think of as sexy. Asa was the first guy to make me feel okay for being me, you know. It feels wrong to even consider other guys. Is this what you went through?"

"Yes and no. I kind of came into the house with no expectations and with an attitude of living in the moment." I laughed. "It started to turn real, though, once I got to know the guys. That was when it was hard, and I battled with myself over it. Rhett was the one who told me it was okay and that he believed it was possible for me to care for more than one person at a time."

"Always the romantic one." She grinned.

"Yeah, that he is," I sighed dreamily, setting us off into a fit of giggles.

"So, Milo? What about him?"

"I met him last night. He helped me with Rowan after the awful cold shower we were treated to, and she was having trouble moving. He was the first kind person we came into contact with, well, the only kind person down there. He saved me, Sawyer." A tear slipped down again as she relived it. "I don't want to admit it, but there's something inherently beautiful about that, you know?"

"From personal experience, my biggest advice is to talk about it. Communication and honesty is the only way forward. You might be surprised at the outcome."

"Thanks, girl. Though I kind of feel like my relationship status should wait till after all this is over. Besides, I'm kind of just getting used to one guy caring about me, but I will keep it in mind for later, definitely later." Fin laughed.

"Understandable, you gotta do what you're comfortable with and can handle. I'm here, though, anytime you want to discuss it. We need to do this more."

"Definitely. Come on. Milo is supposed to be bringing me something."

"Oh, sexy Milo is coming back? Hopefully, Asa is here too. I need to ask him something about our mother."

"It's still weird at times for me to hear you say that," Fin admitted.

"Yeah, me too," I agreed. Picking up Lucky, we made our way downstairs. It had felt good to talk to Fin, and I did feel my own experiences had helped me be there for my friend in a weird way.

The guys were setting up a buffet for lunch, and we grabbed plates of finger food as we all sat around playing video games, trading off turns. Before Fin left to talk with Asa, I remembered to ask him about the watch. He'd never seen it before, so it hadn't been much help. Fin promised to text me later to give me an update. It felt like I blinked and the afternoon had sped by, and it was time to head to the airport with Charlie. I was having a lot of mixed emotions about it.

Rhett had gotten back an hour ago after seeing his sister home. She'd improved enough to return home and was almost back to her usual self based on the video call we did. Rhett looked exhausted, so I sent him to bed despite his protests to drive us to the airport. In the end, Ollie and Tyler won the opportunity to drive us after a brutal paper, rock, scissor competition the guys did. I laughed at their ridiculousness, all wanting to be the ones to score brownie points with Charlie.

Ty and I were in the backseat, letting Charlie have the front while Ollie drove. The music played softly, Charlie and Ollie comparing hockey skates and stick brands. Ty chirped in a few times, but he mostly held my hand as we listened to them chat. I loved the bromance Ollie and Charlie had developed.

"Hey, Sawdust? I have a question for you."

"Shoot, old man. What's up?"

"I was thinking about coming back out here after I took care of some things at home with the rink. Would that be okay with you?"

Shock stunned me for a moment as I took in his words. "Um, are you doing that because you want to or because you feel like you need to?"

Charlie turned in his seat to speak to me directly. "Because I want to. The rink isn't the same without you, kid, and I want to be part of your life. You do have a lot going on here, and maybe I could be of some help with it," he admitted before a blush started to form on his cheeks. "Plus, I kind of want to see the lovely Agatha again."

"Oh, *Agatha*, is it?" I teased. "Well, in that case, I would love it. I just didn't want you to feel like you had to give up your life for me."

"Sawdust, you are my whole world. I hope you know

that. You have been for a while now, annoying attitude and all."

"Don't make me cry, old man," I sniffled, already feeling the tears welling up in my eyes. He wasn't doing much better but brushed it off.

"He can't bear to leave *me* bite-size. That's the real truth," interjected Ollie, causing us to move past the emotional part and into laughter.

"Thank you," I mouthed to him in the rearview as Charlie turned back around, surreptitiously wiping his eyes as we all tried not to notice. After his news, it wasn't as sad saying goodbye a few minutes later, knowing he'd be back soon.

"Be safe, and don't forget to use protection. Or don't. I think I might like some grandkids," he joked.

"Ha! Funny! Don't fall and break a hip because you'll have to wipe your own ass," I teased.

"See you, Sawdust."

Hugging him tightly, I breathed in his smell of cedar and flannel, and relaxed in his embrace. This man had shown me it was okay to love again after losing my parents. I didn't think I'd ever thanked him for that.

Charlie shook hands with both the guys and then lumbered off to the security line. We stood and watched him go and made sure he made it through like proud parents at a kindergarten graduation or something.

Once he was gone, Ty and Ollie both took a hand, and we walked out together, displaying our relationship proudly for all to see. Surprisingly, I found we got way more jealous stares than disgusted ones, which made me thrilled. Ollie had us singing silly songs on the way back, and I was grateful for his fun-loving personality and his ability to always make me smile.

"Thank you for saving the girls, Ollie. Whatever it is you now owe your Uncle, you don't have to pay it alone. I just want you to know that."

Ollie glanced at me, a look of amazement on his face.

"Pretty girl, you never fail to amaze me," he professed, kissing the palm he was holding.

"What about me? I'm pretty amazing too," Ty chimed in from the back.

"Well, that goes without saying, Ty. Don't be so extra!" Ollie threw back, leaving us all in a fit of hysterics. This weekend had been hard, but we'd survived it because we had done it together. We just had to keep remembering that.

# fifteen

. . .

## sawyer

FIN WAS BACK at the house when we returned, snuggled up with Asa on the couch. I hoped it meant she'd talked with him. She smiled in acknowledgment when she spotted me. The rest of the crew—Ice Breakers? TAS Crew? Names kept running through my head. I'd have to keep working on it— were spread out playing a board game.

"You're back!" exclaimed Soren.

"Yep! You'll never guess what Charlie told us." I cheesed, rubbing my hands together in glee. Of course, Ollie took it to a whole new level and the guys followed.

"He's secretly a millionaire?"

"He's the inspiration behind the grumpy old man in *Up*?"

"He's buying you a pony!"

"Oh my God, shut up! You guys are crazy." I laughed.

"No, he told me he's thinking of coming out here for a while and possibly selling the rink."

"Really? That's awesome." Grinned Henry.

"So, what are we playing?" I asked, taking a seat between Mateo and Henry.

Before anyone could answer, the doorbell rang, causing us all to groan. Here lately, nothing fun ever came from anyone ringing that doorbell. We all looked at one another, no one moving to answer it. It felt like a giant game of 'not it,' and I lost.

Sighing, I went to answer the door. Ty followed after me, probably to make sure it wasn't someone here to kidnap me. When I opened the door, the figure turned, having been looking out at the horizon.

"S—," I started, stopping myself. "Brave Heart, what can I do for you?"

"Hey, tiny dancer. I was hoping I could talk to you and Asa."

It was the first time he'd looked sincere, so I nodded and opened the door the rest of the way for him to enter.

"Oh, some kid asked me to give this to you, too," he stated as he handed me an envelope.

Noticing the handwriting immediately, I took the letter with a smile—another letter from Elias. I was starting to crave his words like an addict, wanting more and never having enough, a cheap substitute for the real thing.

"Uh, thanks."

Tyler nodded that he'd send Asa and left us to head to a private room. I navigated us away from the living room where everyone else was. I hoped to avoid disruption at the moment. Ever since learning who he was, it had brought so many questions to my mind, and I'd decided to have a confrontation with him about it in private.

My animosity had also decreased toward him, realizing I'd been putting all my anger on him when he'd been trying to help. Brave Heart made it so easy, though, when he pushed my buttons. I had a suspicion it had been on purpose. He wanted me to be fired up and go in understanding the severity of the situation, so I would take charge.

Flipping the light on in HQ, I leaned against the table; arms crossed as he shut the door behind him. I didn't know where I stood with him yet, so I would wait to see how this played out before I lowered my shields.

Clearing his throat, he leaned back against the door and looked nervous as we waited for Asa. It was the first time I'd ever seen any emotions on his face, and that realization had me dropping my own mask. Relaxing my face, I lowered my hostility and placed my arms behind me on the table as I tried to present a friendlier front.

Asa knocked a few minutes later, and Brave Heart let him in. He looked at us both, confusion on his face. Eventually, he came over and sat by me against the table as we both waited for Brave Heart to start talking. When he didn't say anything, I took pity on him and opened the floor up myself.

"What's up?"

"Hmm, well, the sarcastic ass in me wants to reply, the sky, but I'm trying not to be so confrontational today," he breathed out, fluttering air over his lips in the process as he exhaled. "There's something I need to tell you, but I don't want you to be upset, so that's why it's hard to find the right words."

"I find it's better just to say them. Perfect ones don't exist."

"Yeah, I suppose you're right. Sometimes I look at you, and it takes my breath away at the beautiful young woman you've become. I don't mean that creepily either." He chuckled.

Smiling, I encouraged him to continue, wanting to know what he was going to disclose.

"I've played a part for so long I've forgotten who I was under it. Sometimes, I wonder if I even needed to play the part. In the beginning, I accepted everything my superiors told me. Being young, I didn't know how to question things. Believe it or not, I wasn't always this way."

"I can relate to playing a part for so long you forget who you were to begin with," I admitted. "I think until I came here I'd forgotten who Sariah was. In this place, I've been able to find all the parts of me."

"I would agree with that. Not to be creepy again, but I've watched you both your whole lives. These past months, Sawyer, you've been the happiest and most free I've ever seen. This place, these people, have been good for you."

"Even if it was all orchestrated by you," I inserted, not being able to help myself.

"You make me sound like some puppet master. In reality, this place was already where everyone was headed and part of their natural progression. My part was identifying the people who I thought would be the best fit for you. I watched these guys, and I saw their bond, but more than that, I saw they were missing something. I hoped it could be you. I masterminded the housing error, but other than that, it's all been genuine, Sawyer. You could have ended up in a house with five other people who were agents or connected to the Council and still have found these guys. I know it. The connection you all have is real."

"I know it is, but thank you for saying that. It was a bit of a shock at first to feel like everything in my life had been orchestrated from birth, but I made my own decisions with the information I had every time. The Council might be responsible for killing my parents, but my choices have always been mine even if I haven't always liked my options."

"You're starting to see the big picture, aren't you?"

"Yeah, I think I am."

"And?"

"While I don't appreciate you laughing at me about taking down the Council, I get why you did. I'm just a skater. I'm not a trained agent or natural badass."

"You're still a badass, tiny dancer. Don't ever doubt that."

"Well, that might be true." I laughed, Asa, joining me as I remembered kicking Brave Heart. "But I don't stand a chance against the Council. It's bigger than I ever imagined. The part I don't get is why you brought me here now? What is it you expect me to do?"

"You already know the answer to that."

It had been the answer I expected, but as silence hung in the air, I didn't want to answer, nervous about what the outcome meant.

"The vote."

"The vote."

We stared at one another for a few minutes accepting the honesty we'd laid at one another's feet. Asa watched us bounce back and forth like a weird version of tennis, unsure what he was here for.

"Is this what you wanted to talk to us about? The vote?" Asa finally voiced.

"No, not exactly," Brave Heart started, and I realized he was going to come clean. "Did you know I went to this school? Back when it was only a school with an emphasis on sports, but not the private training center it is now."

I didn't answer, wanting him to tell us more. Asa sat quietly as well, absorbed in the story.

"Well, I did. I knew your moms, Victoria and Isla, both of them. We were all friends. I uh," he paused, collecting himself. "I grew up in a very rigid household, and we were expected to fall in line and do the family business. Believe it or not, I come from a long line of stockbrokers and accountants. There was a family firm, and we were expected to carry on the line."

"You don't give off accountant vibes," I teased.

"Definitely not." He chuckled good-naturedly. "Numbers were not my thing at all. My older brother was good at numbers, and I assumed he would fall in line just as he was expected to. When he bucked tradition and started his own business, well, it made it easier for me in a way. I just didn't realize how important the business he started would become. My brother had bigger visions than our family's lineage.

When I discovered his true purpose, it changed the course of my life, as well."

He finally walked over and sat next to me at the table. When I discovered the news the other day, I wanted to slap him and give him a piece of my mind for keeping it from me. Today though, things were different. Not only had he approached us and was being open, but the night before had put things into perspective for me.

I had to quit lashing out at the people close to me just because I could. They weren't the enemy. No, the enemies were clearly labeled in this story and the only ones who needed to suffer.

"Tiny dancer, before I even knew about you and Asa, I vowed to keep the people close to me safe. When I was eighteen, that was only about three people—Isla, Victoria, and Logan. Sometimes I wonder if I made the wrong choice leaving, but in my mind, I thought I was keeping them safe that way—keeping *her* safe."

My heart broke for him, and part of me wanted to put him out of his misery and tell him I knew, but I also wanted, *no needed*, to hear him say it.

"I uh, I found the Agency, and I left one night. I didn't know Victoria was a Draven, but when we discovered the TAS chapter's plans after an incident with Alek, we both realized we needed to do something to stop them. Victoria had been trying to separate herself from her father. He wasn't a good man and was involved in some crime in Brazil, but he did love his daughter. She never told me why he joined the Council though."

He waited a minute to see if I connected things, but other than finding out about my mom's father, I knew this info from her journals or had been able to piece it together at least. I wasn't sure if Asa had figured out who he was yet, so I waited.

"I never expected Isla to be vulnerable with me gone, and it's the biggest regret of my life because of that error in judgment. I left the love of my life open for my brother to steal."

"You're the Samson from the journals," I finally announced.

Asa tensed, connecting the dots at the name after his mom had told us the story yesterday.

"Yeah, and subsequently," he paused, "your uncle."

"Why didn't you ever say anything?" Asa asked.

"I thought it was easier to keep my distance, or maybe that was just my excuse. I see so much of your mom in you, but I also see *him* and it's a slap in my face for letting him get his claws in her."

"What does this mean now?" I wondered.

"Whatever you want it to mean. I was acting like an ass because I wanted to keep you at arm's length. I thought it would be safer that way, and maybe easier. Yesterday's events reminded me that I couldn't underestimate the Council or my brother. I don't want to have another regret in my life and not get to know you guys as more than the casual observer I've been. Plus, I'm hoping Isla might forgive me one day."

"You might have more of an uphill battle there than you think. Good luck," teased Asa and I had to agree. Isla spoke of him fondly, but I had to wonder if she knew why he'd really left and hadn't told her, that she might go all fierce kitty on him. I kind of wanted to be there for that—with popcorn.

"I know this doesn't change or make up for things, but can we maybe start over? I'd like the chance to be your uncle."

"Yeah, I'd like that." I smiled, trying to hide the tears brimming in my eyes.

"Me too," Asa agreed.

"Great. Maybe I could show you the Agency and what I do some time?"

"Yeah."

"And I'll tell your mom. I need to make it right with her."

Leaning over, I gave him a real hug, and I felt him deflate into my arms. This was right, and I knew all those times I'd survived; he had been there leading me in directions that would be safe or good for me. That counted for something.

Kissing his cheek, I left him and Asa to figure out their goodbye. I was hitting my emotional limit for the moment and needed some time to myself. Not to mention, there was a letter burning a hole in my pocket I was dying to read.

I decided to bypass the living room again, knowing if I saw them all, I'd give in to what they wanted when I needed some time alone. For five years, I'd spent practically 90% of my time alone, and now it was the opposite. As much as I liked and loved most of the people down there, I missed my quiet time.

Settling down in my favorite chair, which had quickly become my emotional reading chair, I snuggled under the blankets and waited for Lucky to jump up with me. He'd been snoozing in his bed on the floor, but at my entrance had decided he needed to be closer to me. With a new level of excitement, I opened up the letter.

*Love,*

*I saw you briefly yesterday. You and Henry were on the ice and skated beautifully together. I couldn't take my eyes off you the whole time. I wanted to run out to you afterward so that I could tell you how beautiful you'd been. Stopping myself was one of the hardest things I've had to do. Playing this role has been easier than denying myself that. I didn't think about how hard it would be being back here. Being this close to you and the guys and not being able to say anything is absolute torture.*

*I hope you are getting these letters as I expect you to. Mostly, I hope you're enjoying them and reading them. That is the only thought and hope pushing me through all this.*

*Did you ever hear how Rhett and I became friends? It's almost as good as our first meeting. Well, actually, that meeting was horrible. I hope to one day redo our first meeting. Perhaps we can pretend it is our first time and get to know one another again, anyway, back to Rhett.*

*I was placed in the house, and I arrived straight from London with all my possessions. I walked off the plane thinking I was going to be the top shit, and when I saw this beast of a man waiting for me, I almost turned around right then and went home. He barely talked, speaking primarily in grunts, and I was sure it was going to be a horrible place.*

*I probably offended him in that first meeting as well, but I couldn't tell you how now. Somehow over the next few weeks, we did manage to fall into a rhythm in the house. None of our other guys were there yet, and the guys living there at the time were more loner types. It had been called the Lone Wolf house, actually.*

*I was bored and couldn't sleep one night and found myself in the gym. I'd always been interested in fighting, but I had taken fencing at boarding school. Assuming I was tough shit anyways, I put on some gloves and started wailing on a bag, and I almost threw out my arm doing it. Rhett came in for his workout and watched me fumble about for thirty minutes before finally breaking down and speaking.*

*His first words to me other than the grunts were, "If you keep hitting the bag that way, you might as well hand over your nuts because you're leaving yourself wide open for an attack."*

*It stunned me, and I think the shock of what he said was the last straw for me that night, and I laughed. It was such a strange sound coming from me, and I realized how long it had been since I'd laughed. Rhett joined in my laughter, easing the tension around us. I told him if he knew so much about it, then he should teach me.*

*To my surprise, he shrugged his shoulders and came over and started to teach me, just like that. No negotiations, no strings, nothing from me required on his part, and it was a foreign thing to me after growing up in the world I had. I didn't know how to take it at first, and I kept trying to find ways to pay him back. I bought him some new equipment, bought him a gaming system, and even bought him some new protein blender thing that was top of the line.*

*He sent it all back and told me to stop. His friendship wasn't for sale, and all I had to do was be his friend in return. It blew my mind, but when it finally sank in that he was serious, I realized how refreshing he was. Rhett meant what he said and did what he meant. He was true to his word and had no hidden agendas.*

*After that, we started training regularly, and I found I loved it. Rhett told me I was a natural, and my extreme stubbornness and competitiveness would serve me well if I wanted to compete. It was the first time I saw a future or dream outside my family. Rhett gave me my first glimpse of hope. You gave me my second.*

*Until we meet again,*

*Wholly Yours*

Damn… whatever chance I thought I had at protecting my heart was gone. I couldn't deny it any longer. Elias had wormed his way in, and I was falling in love with the bastard. It wasn't as scary as it had been a few weeks ago. Thinking of how a perfect first meeting would be with him, I found myself walking on clouds as I fell asleep that night.

# sixteen

. . .

## tyler

THE COFFEE LEFT a bitter taste in my mouth as I swallowed it down from the cup I was holding. I wasn't a fan of coffee in general, but it seemed the thing to do in this setting. I was seated around a large conference table with several other agents, both young and old. My father was next to me as we waited for the meeting to start. It was Monday morning, but due to the alumni weekend, there weren't any school sessions today, giving us all a day to recuperate.

I had special clearance to attend this meeting due to my connection with Sawyer and my family lineage. My dad hoped it would sway me to officially commit to the Agency and take over his position when he retired. I wasn't sure I wanted it, though. I'd envisioned a life, and it didn't include being a secret agent.

Agent Dickwad finally walked in and took a seat at the head of the table. The chatter around the room died down as everyone waited to hear what he had to report. He seemed different today, not as contentious, and it made me feel uneasy at what that could mean. When people started changing their personalities, it was typically for a reason.

"What's the status of the missing girl?"

"We think we've found who initially nabbed her from a partial print left in the car. From Oliver and Samuel's reports, we've narrowed it down to a few possible buyers. The camera bug placed on Latimer's belt gave us some insight into the room. Unfortunately, it was on the back of his belt, so the angle isn't the greatest, but we could identify some people. The audio picked up a little more, and based on the descriptions of the 'lots' as they are referred to, we believe we've narrowed it down to three possibilities," an unfamiliar female agent reported.

"What is our next move?" a redheaded male asked.

Agent Shithead steepled his hands as he digested the information, leaving us all in silence as we waited for him to respond.

"Do we have locations for the three possible girls at the auction? Who purchased them?"

"Not yet. Their network is impenetrable, and we're trying to piece together the few things we've been able to gather on their database."

"Where are we with the Director?"

"The information we have on him is spotty. He's good at covering his tracks. An outside source believes they might have something for us today, so I'm waiting to hear what they have before I compile my report," my dad responded, shocking me.

I didn't realize he was investigating the ice skating program director, but I shouldn't be surprised since profiles and probability were his expertise areas. Agent Killjoy nodded, turning to the next person. Around the table, agents filled him in on the case, and I was surprised and impressed at the operation. I never knew it was this organized and complex on campus, but it shouldn't have been shocking after learning more about the Council. It would take an organized front to take them and other bad guys down.

"We need to find Jill soon, or I fear it will be too late. Locations for all the girls need to be recovered to put a stop to Latimer's trafficking ring. Compile the data from the bugs and cameras planted in the rooms of the well-known associates and get back to me. I want a follow-up in eight hours. You're dismissed."

Everyone gathered their belongings and began to leave the room. Ace caught my eye and gave me a small smile. I wasn't a big fan of his still, but for Sawyer's sake, I would try. Acknowledging him, I looked around the room at the other agents leaving. No one paid any attention to me since I was the lowest ranking person in the room. The coffee I'd been attempting to drink earlier sat on the table, mocking me. Rising, I picked up the cup and began to follow my father out of the room.

"Mathews, I wonder if I could have a word first."

We both turned, not sure who he was addressing. At our

movement, he chuckled, realizing his mistake. "The younger Mathews." He gestured back to the table. My father nodded at me as he left the room. He probably thought it was an excellent sign to meet one-on-one with the head of the department. He didn't know the things I did, though, about Agent Jerkface.

"Sir," I said, trying to hold back the sarcasm.

"Tyler, I was wondering if I could ask you some questions about Sawyer."

"You want *me* to give *you* insider information about my *girlfriend*?" I scoffed. "Yeah, no. That won't be happening. Whatever your relationship is with her, it's your job to fix it."

Crossing my arms, I stared down at the agent in front of me, not caring that he was my father's boss.

"You're right; that wasn't the right way to ask. What I mean is… well, you see, I've made a lot of mistakes in my past, and I want to do things better. Sawyer and Asa are part of that commitment. I've watched them both from afar their whole life, but I don't feel like I know them. I know their schedules, their routines, and what they eat for meals. But I don't know how they feel about things or think. I know a birthday redo is planned for this weekend, and I want to do something to make it right. Could you help me?"

Assessing his words, I looked over the man. Agent Bubblebutt appeared sincere for once.

"Perhaps. Maybe you should tell me your name, so I quit making up ones in my head unless you prefer to be called Agent Butthole. However, it does have a nice ring to it. Though, some of the ones Ollie's created are even better."

He laughed, causing me to relax. "Fair enough. You may call me Samson, only outside the Agency, of course."

"Understood. Samson," I paused knowing the name, "as in 'Samson' from the journals and dated Isla?"

"The very one."

"Does…"

"Sawyer and Asa know? Yeah, I'm not that much of an asshat to tell you a secret first. I told them yesterday, but something tells me Sawyer already knew since she didn't maim me." He chuckled.

"Yeah, that sounds about right."

"There's a little more to it than just dating Isla, though. My last name is Abernathy, making me their biological uncle." He took a breath after dropping that, "So, will you help me now?"

Momentary shock filtered through me at the news. I never would've thought he was that connected to Sawyer. Now that I knew he was related to them, I could see some similarities. I wouldn't stand in the way of Sawyer getting to know someone from her family, especially if they would be good for her.

Samson had a lot to prove and make up for, but knowing he'd spent most of his life protecting her one way or another, even if at a distance, made me respect him. We spent the next twenty minutes discussing some possible ideas for him. When I got up to leave, he clasped me on the shoulder, halting my movements.

"I know your relationship with Sawyer is unconventional, but I do approve. I watched your relationship with her in

Iowa, and I know your feelings are deep. Oddly enough, you're the one guy I know the most about because of your proximity to her the past few years. So thanks for helping me. I know I didn't make the best first impression, and that's not who I am, but it was easier to be a jerk and keep them at an arm's length."

"I can understand your reasoning, and now that your secret is out, hopefully, that will be your chance to get to know them for real. They're both worth getting to know. I think your idea for Saturday is a good first step. I guess I'll see you then," I stated as I left the room.

I was surprised to find my dad waiting for me outside the room.

"Hey, everything go okay?"

"Oh yeah. It was personal stuff."

"Good. I was nervous at first."

"Nah, it's fine. Want to grab some breakfast before you head back to the hotel?"

"Yeah, Son. That would be great."

We headed out to his car and enjoyed a large breakfast before he dropped me off at the house. I'd submitted paperwork the other day to officially transfer to live with them. Rhett had spoken with me about how he had planned to transform a second office downstairs into a room for me. It had felt nice that he wanted to make sure I had a place of my own. I felt officially embraced into the family. Using the key I was given, I let myself in the front door.

The smells that greeted me made me regret the meal I just had, but it had been good to spend some time with my dad.

He was usually so tied up in cases that he wasn't present at home. Feeling like we had something in common outside of hockey to talk about had been refreshing.

Walking into the kitchen, I found Ollie at the stove as he danced and sang to music playing from his phone. He was in his own world as he put on his performance for Sawyer, who was sitting on the counter. She smiled wide and laughed at his moves. The scene created a slew of emotions in me, and I leaned against the doorframe, watching them with a smile on my face. This was the future I wanted.

Sawyer finally spotted me, but I motioned not to say anything as I crept up behind Ollie. We were still figuring out what we were to one another and what it meant to be in a relationship. It was freeing and exciting to know our feelings were reciprocated. Walking up behind him, I grabbed his sides and started to tickle him.

"Ahhh," a high-pitched squeal left his lips, and I chuckled along with Sawyer as Ollie twisted out of my grip, tapping my nose with the spatula he held.

"No sirree!" he proclaimed as he tried to distract us from the squeal that had erupted from him moments earlier.

"Oh, is that so?"

"Ollie, I don't think I could even scream that loud," joked Sawyer, causing Ollie's cheeks to heat. His red hair wasn't doing him any favors at the moment. Deciding to help him out, I moved over to Sawyer, wrapping my arms around her waist as I settled between her legs. I quite liked having her at this level. My dirty thoughts must've been displayed on my face based on the knowing smirk she leveled at me.

"Hey Wildcat, I missed you."

"How was your meeting?"

"I have some info I can update everyone on later. But first, what are our plans for the day off? Hmm? Because I have a few suggestions," I growled.

Heat filled her eyes, and I knew she'd picked up on some of the naughtiness in my tone. She wrapped her arms around my neck, pulling me even closer to her.

"Oh? What might those be?" she whispered.

The rest of the room had faded as I focused on my girl in front of me. Dipping my head, I sealed our lips together in a searing kiss. I settled my hands on her ass and pulled her closer to me, her core hitting me right where I wanted it to. Deepening the kiss, I swirled my tongue around hers as she ran her fingers up the nape of my neck through the strands of hair. Sawyer twisted her fingers in my locks, my cock twitching as she tugged.

Her breasts rubbed against my chest as I rocked into her. I couldn't get enough friction at this angle, and I was about to move her back some more on the counter when a body lined up behind me, causing me to momentarily gasp at the feeling of the hard body. Sawyer stopped as well, our lips pulling apart as we took in a breath.

"As fucking hot as this is, breakfast will burn if you don't stop. So for the love of all crepes, can we reschedule this fuck sesh for when I don't have to pull my concentration? Please... I promise to make up for it." Ollie nipped my ear, his breath teasing my neck with his words. Despite wanting to help him out and stop, his words and hard body were not making it easy.

"That's so damn hot," moaned Sawyer, causing me to rub back against Ollie. It hadn't been intentional, but at his responding moan, I did it again, fully aware that time.

"What's smoking..." a voice trailed off, stopping when they took in the scene. The words must have reached Ollie, though, as he quickly pulled away with a curse and moved back over to the stove.

"Shit. Well, that one's all yours, Ty."

"I'll take it," I grumbled, falling into Sawyer. I would much rather trade a burnt crepe for having him against me any day. She hugged me tight and laughed at my obvious discomfort—wicked woman.

I turned once the arousal in my pants had subsided enough, and Sawyer draped her arms over my shoulders, pulling me to her as she wrapped around me like a koala backpack, but I wasn't complaining. Ollie motioned that he was finished, so I grabbed Sawyer's legs and moved away from the counter. Her squeal of glee at the movement had me smiling all the way to the table. I wasn't hungry, but I would down that burnt crepe since Ollie had made it for me.

Most of the others were around the table when we made it into the dining room. Depositing Sawyer into the chair next to me, I sat down with our rapidly growing family.

"So, I was thinking, and we need... like a name. I've been trying to come up with one on my own, but apparently, all my creative juices have fled me because all I could think up was Ice Pack, and it doesn't have the effect I'm going for," Sawyer mused.

"A what now?" Rhett asked before shoving food into his mouth.

"A group name. So I can refer to you all at once. I mean, I guess *Sawyer's boy toys* could work," she teased.

"I think you mean men, baby. There isn't anything boyish about me," Rhett retorted, giving her a heated look.

Remembering the monster he was rocking had me shifting in my chair as much as Sawyer was. The shower we'd all taken was playing on repeat in my head now. Damn, I wanted to pounce on her and find some alone time. Or maybe I could get up some courage to make a move on Ollie. The boner situation in my pants wanted some attention. Despite my internal musings, the others had continued the conversation.

"So like a group name for us in the house? Or one to include our friend group too?" Mateo enquired, seeking clarification, a thoughtful look on his face. I had a feeling he would find the perfect one for us.

"Hmm, I guess it depends on the name, maybe one, maybe both," Sawyer shrugged in response.

"Oh, what about Hot to Trot," Ollie offered.

"Except we aren't thoroughbred horses," Henry deadpanned.

"Speak for yourself. I'm quite the racehorse in bed."

"Yeah, buddy, I don't think that's something to brag about," joked Mateo causing us all to laugh uproariously.

"Oh, what about Sawyer's Sassy Molassy," Soren joked,

and we all laughed even more. A rapid succession of names started, and we lost track of who was saying what through our laughter.

"Cool team name goes here!"

"Code Orange Pack."

"Ice Ice Babies."

"Council Wreckers."

"Team Double Dips."

"Bros and One Hoe."

"One hit, Sawyer."

"Smooth Operators."

"Fam Bam."

"Hide and Seekers for Sawyer's Peepers."

"Sawyer's Sausage Fest."

"Full House."

"Polybros."

"Sharing is Caring."

"Cocked and fully loaded."

"Pokemen, because our dicks poke her?"

We all groaned at Ollie for that one.

"What about," Mateo started quietly, "the Brotherhood of Sawyer's Heart and BOSH for short?"

"It's cheesy, but it has merit. I like it." Sawyer grinned. I think she was just happy we were all taking it seriously. The silly girl still doubted our commitment to her.

"Nomination accepted."

"Seconded!"

"Third, it's official, pretty girl! Your BOSH Boys are here to stay. We should make t-shirts and stickers!"

"Ollie, your ridiculousness is one of my favorite things about you."

"What's your favorite?" He grinned wide, leaning across the table at her. "It's my dick, isn't it?"

"Nope!" She grabbed the bacon off his plate, taking a bite out of it. "It's how much bacon you give me."

The table laughed, and Ollie shared how he mistook her as a tourist the first day, and she'd taken his bacon then too. When the laughter died down, Sawyer turned to me.

"Ty, you said that you had some updates for us?"

"Oh yeah, the Agency is working on a plan to take the Director down. It's looking more like he was involved with Jill. They've narrowed it down to three possible girls that could be Jill from the auction and their locations. Though the long-term plan is to recover all the girls."

"Anything we can do?"

Before I could respond, Finley walked in, a trail of guys following her. I needed to get the scoop on that, I mused to myself.

"I might be able to shed some light on things. Though, are there any leftovers? This looks yummy!"

Everyone quietly made room at the table and handed the newcomers some plates. Cohen wasn't a stranger, having spent a few hours with everyone the other night, but Milo was a new entity we were all unsure of. Asa had a pained look on his face, and I decided to check in with my friend later. It had been a rough couple of days for him. I wanted to make sure he knew we cared as much about how this affected him too.

"What might you be able to do, Fin?" Sawyer asked once they had settled around the table.

"Well, the night, uh, it all went down. I was retrieving something from the Director's computer. Through some unfortunate circumstances, it got wet, and then I left it. Thankfully, Milo was able to retrieve it, and Cohen thinks he might be able to help me restore it."

Ah, so that explained the two mystery dudes' presence. Picking up our plates, we cleaned up breakfast and then regathered in HQ. It looked like my dick was going to have to wait a little longer before he got some relief.

# seventeen

. . .

## sawyer

A FEELING mixed with dread and apprehension filled me as I waited for everyone to file into HQ. Finley's announcement had me curious about what she needed to share. She walked to the front, commanding the attention of the room. It was a role I'd never seen her hold before, but oddly it seemed to match her perfectly. She always had this air of confidence about her, even if she didn't see it.

"So, despite being captured the other day, sorry about that, by the way," she grimaced. "I was able to retrieve this."

Finley held a flash drive up as she spoke before handing it over to Cohen. "Cohen was building me a profile of Donnelly because something never felt right about the whole scenario to me. Jill had reached out to me for help, but I didn't realize it was about Director Donnelly."

Cohen gave her a remote, and she clicked it on, lighting up one of the smart boards. Ah, so that was how it worked. The screen filled with photos, and we all quieted as we took them in. The first photos were of a young Donald Donnelly.

"Nothing of great importance, but he grew up in a middle-class family, mom and dad stayed married, and one younger brother. He started skating at a young age, and his mom supported his passion. She took him to many competitions early on and found him sponsors to help cover costs. He won several awards at the beginning of his career and was accepted into TAS on a scholarship. He went onto the Olympics but didn't place. After that, he bounced around from place to place, trying to regain his traction."

Finley clicked on a few more buttons, and a picture with an up-to-date Donnelly appeared. There were several pictures with him and younger females, and I was starting to get the feeling I had with him at the rink—the ick factor.

"At some point, he switched to pair skating and won a medal. Donnelly rode that high for a few years but never succeeded any further. After a few failed coaching attempts, he found his way here. Donnelly started as a coach and then advanced three years ago to director. Since that time, there have been rumors, but nothing that stuck."

The unease sat heavy in my gut, and I knew I'd been right. The only consolation to the whole thing would be if there was finally evidence connecting him to Jill or the Council. After everything, to get a win would make it all seem at least worth it.

"Here's what I know. Jill reached out to Oblivion, my code name on a white hacker site that helps girls who get into tricky situations." She cleared her throat, and I knew there was more to the story based on her behavior.

"She told me that her 'boyfriend' was harassing her and that she'd sent him nude pictures. She regretted it, and I have a feeling she was forced into it. Her boyfriend was using them now to blackmail her into staying in the relationship. Jill was afraid they'd leak and effectively ruin her career, so she reached out to see if there was a way to get them from his phone. "

"And you're leaning toward her boyfriend being the Director?" Soren asked.

"Yes, based on some other info I gathered. It was a burner phone listed to a random name. Why hide your information if you're not trying to hide something?"

"No reason, unless you're shady."

"Exactly, though that was rhetorical. Love the enthusiasm, babe!" Fin enthused to Asa, causing him to blush.

It made me wonder if my brother felt threatened by the other two guys having more to do with this case, not that Asa had any experience, but still, he was probably feeling useless. I could relate. The more secrets I'd learned, the more out of my depth I felt. I'd been so naive thinking I could arrive at this school and just get vengeance at the snap of my fingers. Battles weren't waged that way, and it was clear, this was a war of power and greed.

It was becoming glaringly clear Brave Heart, or Samson,

had been right, and it hurt every time I had to admit that. I was a twenty-two-year-old ice skater. I needed to accept the fact that while I was in this fight, I wasn't necessarily going to be the one to end it. I had a feeling my brother and I were feeling the same thing.

"I tracked the phone's serial number, and it was purchased at a mall kiosk with cash," Cohen piped in.

"Which leads me to the Director..." trailed Finley, glancing at Cohen.

"Nothing yet," he responded.

"Okay, so when Jill was taken, a pit formed in my stomach, and I knew I had to do something. I felt responsible like I'd aided in her kidnapping. I hoped the Director, oh wait," Finley stopped, literally facepalming her forehead, and I busted out laughing. It was such an 'us' thing. Finley laughed too as her cheeks flamed, and I finally saw her nerves shining through. She was in impress mode. The question was, was it for someone, or someones?

Looking over at her menagerie of guys, Cohen was working on the computer and oblivious to what was being said. Asa was watching her closely, never taking his eyes off her. It was clear how much he'd fallen for her now. Milo was slumped back in the chair, acting as if he didn't care as he took in the room.

They were all so different, but I saw pieces of what Fin would find attractive in each of them. She was going to need to face this at some point. Hiding her head in the sand would only last for so long and end in broken hearts. I didn't want hers or my brother's to be casualties.

"I forgot to mention why I thought he was the mystery boyfriend in the first place," she admitted, gaining some of her flow back. "In doing my due diligence, I kind of hacked into Jill's phone as well," Fin's voice went a little higher on the kind of part, and I realized I didn't know the story there. She'd only ever talked about it in riddles or vague words.

"She had her boyfriend saved as Daddy Don, and while that is cringeworthy in itself, the photos I found were worse. He was good and didn't show his face in any," she said, wrinkling up her nose.

"There was one, though," she clicked over to a new picture on the screen, "where I saw this."

It was a picture Jill took as a selfie. She was sleeping next to a male body. His face was hidden in the shot, but she hadn't been careful with the background images. On the nightstand was a picture, and while it was difficult to make out the people in it, the school emblem and class year were evident in the corner of the frame. *TAS, 96.*

"Class of 1996? But that could be a lot of people," Henry mused.

"Yes, except that laying on the nightstand along with some change, Chapstick, and a condom wrapper.." Fin full-body shuddered at that, and I was with her because ew. "...is an ID."

She zoomed in, and we all followed, almost as if getting closer physically would allow us to see it better too. Squinting because it was very unfocused this zoomed-in, I titled my head, trying to decipher what it said.

"I can't see anything," Ollie admitted.

"Yeah, well, it needs to be rendered some, but what you can see is that it's a TAS employee ID."

Fin had a smug look on her face as she proudly circled the part she wanted us all to see with the red dot clicker. She was enjoying this entirely too much. Fin apparently had a boss bitch dream. She would rock it and look killer while doing it.

"I scoured the database and yearbooks to see which staff members we have that also attended here in 1996, and that left me with three people."

Fin clicked another slide, and a picture of a woman came up, she looked vaguely familiar, and I realized she was the woman I saw in the hallway that night with Abernathy's goon.

"This is Allison Pekins, and she works in the front office admissions with student housing and staff arrangements. The second person is Bryce Hammond, who works as a custodian. He's not exactly the 'have an affair with a student' type seeing as he's married with three kids and about as attractive to a younger female as Santa Claus."

The picture on screen showed a man in his forties who had a bushy beard, kind eyes, and a potbelly. I saw her point, but no one could be counted out. She clicked on the last photo, obviously saving it for the big reveal.

"Which brings us to Donald Donnelly."

The picture was taken a few years ago, and I tried to look at it objectively. Would I have thought he was attractive as a sixteen-year-old? He had a certain older man vibe that could be considered attractive. Donald was clean-shaven, had blue eyes, and a head full of dark hair slicked back. If I looked at him objectively, he had nice features, I supposed, and was in good shape due to his fitness regimen. But knowing him, how he made me feel, and the way he leered at girls gave me the heebie-jeebies, and all I wanted to do was gag.

"I started looking into more of his history at other schools, but all I could find were some vague mentions from others about rumors over the years. They mostly revolved around him picking a girl to be his *star* for the year, and then they would always make the Olympic team. I couldn't find anything solid, so that's why I reached out to Chaos, or Cohen, to go to the places I couldn't."

"Right, so when Fin, or Oblivion, reached out, I started to dig and realized the extent of this information. It just so happens that Donnelly has an ex-wife. When I reached out, she offered to tell me everything in exchange for proof of his affairs and duplicitous nature. Donnelly had a better lawyer, probably paid for by the Council, during their court proceedings and took everything they'd built together. He threatened to make it appear she was unstable if she challenged it. In addition, she's to pay him alimony each month. Needless to say, Melinda was delighted to help in exchange for helping reverse their case."

"Wow, he's even douchier than I thought," Henry grumbled.

"Does this mean we have it then?" Rhett questioned. He'd been more withdrawn since Saturday, and I think with everything going on and Elias being gone, it was affecting him more than he realized.

"I think the profile we have on him will be enough that

the school board can no longer ignore his possible affair with a student. Despite their connection to the Council, they will have parents and the Olympics committees to answer to. The last thing they want is a scandal to shut down their money maker. We can anonymously send it with threats of going to press if not dealt with immediately."

"Okay, I like that plan. Though, I kind of wanted more to happen to him. He can't get away with these things," I griped.

"That's where the files from his computer will come into play. My white hacker friends will dismantle his entire life, and he will have nowhere to run. Arresting him will then happen quickly."

"Is it horrible of me that I'm hoping his cellmate is a big ole guy?" joked Ollie.

"No," echoed around the room, causing us all to laugh.

"It's going to be a while for this to work its magic on the corrupted files, so you all don't need to stick around. It's not all that exciting," Cohen disclosed after pushing back from the table.

His words were like a school bell going off as we all jumped up and made our way out of the room, laughing and shoving to get out first. Finley looked awkward standing up front, and I decided to help her for a moment. Grabbing my brother, I pulled him with me out the door.

"Did you need something, sis?" Asa joked. It had to be humorous—my small frame pulling his large one. Yeah, I didn't care.

"In fact, I do." He followed me up the stairs and into my room, sitting with me on the bed.

"Yes?" he said, exaggerating the word as he rolled his eyes.

Bumping his shoulder, I searched my mind for how to say this delicately, which meant I blurted it out unceremoniously. "Are you being weird about Fin's growing harem?"

Shock registered on his face at my abruptness, but all I could do was shrug my shoulders. How else do you ask your still new brother if he felt insecure about more dicks entering the relationship? Yeah, they didn't put that on a greeting card at Hallmark.

Once he recovered from my blatant question, a look of concentration covered his face. "I honestly don't know. Things have been weird since she was kidnapped."

"I think the important part of that statement is 'she was kidnapped.' You need to give her time and don't smother her. She'll talk about stuff when she's ready. Be open-minded and think about it before you go all alpha male, okay?"

"I'll try," he sighed.

Hugging him tightly, I held him to me for a few moments soaking in his warm comfort. Asa kissed my forehead before walking out of the room. Lucky trotted over to me and leaned on my legs wanting to be picked up. Pulling him to me, I cradled him and walked over to the big chair.

It had become my favorite spot. The only thing I'd been wrong on was the amount of time I got to use it. In the beginning, I assumed I would be in my room the majority of the time, continuing my loner ways. But once I met the guys and became friends with my coffee crew, the loner part of me faded into the background.

Deciding to take the alone time for the gift it was, I settled in with my Kindle to finish the book Soren and I were reading. We'd already finished the third in the Destiny Series, and were now reading the author's newest book, *Wolf Hunts*. It was more emotional as it dealt with grief, and it was hitting Soren and me in the feels. It was a safe way to process our emotions.

A knocking surprised me as I had fallen into the book world. Tyler was leaning against the door jamb, and I smiled when I took him in. He was so handsome that sometimes he took my breath away. His brown hair with the soft curls that tilted up just enough, his honey eyes that always conveyed his feelings, and his sweet smile that made me feel both desired and cherished at the same time made my insides melt.

"Hey, Wildcat. What have you been up to?"

"Fighting witches and the patriarchy." I beamed. My comment took him by surprise, and he bellowed out a laugh, bending at the waist.

"Well, Wildcat. I can say that no patriarchy stands a chance against you, nor do these witches. Now, could I possibly steal you away for a bit? I miss you."

"Of course," I chirped, putting down my Kindle. Shifting Lucky, I made room for Ty to join me in the chair. His delight at my response made my insides tingle, and I was happy to curl into his side once he sat down. Ty and I sat there talking about some funny memories for a while, relishing in one another's presence. With everything that had been going on lately, I hadn't spent enough quality time with each guy. I would need to do that this week.

"Samson told me who he was today."

"Oh, he did. What do you think?"

"At first, I was surprised. Especially when it seemed like he was pumping me for information, but once he told me his intentions, I was able to see his care for you and Asa."

"Yeah, I think so too. He wasn't all 'I know everything, listen to me' yesterday and was open about things. I think he was in a hard predicament and did the best he could with the information he had. I know he regrets leaving Isla, and he protected me when I needed it. I wish I'd known sooner, but at least I have the chance now to know him more."

"Yeah, and I do think he wants that based on what he was asking me. How do you feel about all the secrets? Charlie? The connections?"

"Had to ask a hard one, huh?" I laughed. "Well, I've accepted it for the most part. Charlie was honest with me, and I understand his position. The connection thing is weird, but talking with Samson more, I see how it wasn't a conspiracy or ploy. It just happened to be that way. Though, I won't lie that I'm looking forward to the day where my decisions and choices will be free from anything Council-related."

"Here, here." Chuckled Ty, making me vibrate with his laughter.

We cuddled in the chair with Lucky for a while longer before someone called us down for Lunch. Jumping on his back, I made Ty give me a piggyback ride down the stairs like he had this morning. Finding fun moments whenever we could was how we separated ourselves from the Council and even the Agency. We could enjoy the laughter because we all knew pain and understood the gift it was.

# eighteen

. . .

## oliver

TYLER, Sawyer, and I were cuddled up on the lounge bed, watching a movie after we'd eaten lunch. The rest of the guys had filtered off to do God knows what with their day. The movie was an action one, but, to be honest, I hadn't been paying attention to it for a while.

Sawyer was lying on my chest, and her hand was in my pocket as she wrapped around me. I thought it was odd at first, but it weirdly worked. Ty was next to me, our shoulders touching, Sawyer's lower half in his lap. He casually caressed her hip where her shirt had ridden up with his hand. Between the two of them, I'd been a little *distracted*.

"Are you even watching, Ollie?" Sawyer asked, her voice rumbling through my skin, almost like she was inside me.

"Yeah, it's great."

"Uh-huh. Can you believe that guy blew the head off the other one?"

"So badass."

At my answer, Sawyer whipped her head around, a smirk on her lips, and I knew I'd fallen into her trap, but what a place to be.

"We're watching *Mighty Ducks 2*, jerk!"

Looking up to the screen, I realized she was right. When did the movie switch to this one? A young Joshua Jackson was on screen making an epic speech.

"Huh. I thought we were watching that superhero one. When did we switch?" I scrunched my nose up in thought, trying to remember how long we'd been down here. Was I that out of it?

"You know what his punishment should be, Wildcat?"

"Oh, I definitely agree."

Sawyer lifted completely off us and was poised between us on her knees, a look of mischief alight on her face. Tyler propped himself up on one elbow, his expression mirroring hers. A feeling of jealousy briefly flitted through my mind at their shared history and ability to communicate so effortlessly. Pushing that aside, I focused on the now and the future we had before us.

"Why do I get the feeling I'm not going to like the look on your faces?" The skepticism was heavy in my words as I debated my next move. Remembering the earlier tickle catastrophe, I rolled over and jumped up, sprinting for the door before they could attack. I could hear them scrambling behind me, but I had one advantage over them—I knew this house better than they did.

Darting into the storage room, I quickly locked the door before looking around for a place to hide if the lock didn't stop them. I doubted they'd even find this room, but maybe I wasn't as quick as I thought. I hoped my quick thinking would've left them stunned and confused for a few seconds, giving me the upper hand.

Glancing around the room, I found a bunch of boxes that had been shoved down there. My curious nature got the best of me, and I started to peek inside of them. At first, it didn't make sense, but as I sifted through it more, a wide grin spread across my face. Oh, this was going to be epic.

Grabbing one of the items out of the box, I crept to the door and unlocked it. I squatted in position and then shoved something over to make a loud noise to draw them. Thankfully, they were still downstairs, and a few seconds later, they both busted through the door.

"Come and take your pun—"

Before Sawyer could finish her sentence, I blasted them both with the silly string canisters I'd found. Her squeak as she was hit with the cold pink stuff was hilarious and worth them finding me. Tyler laughed as I covered him in it as well, and Sawyer tried to protect herself by doing a funny pose. Her knee was up, and her hands outstretched as she attempted to shove it away from her.

The canisters ran empty after a minute, and they were both covered head to toe in the stuff, and I couldn't hold my laughter. Grabbing my phone, I started to snap pictures of them. They looked like fluorescent swamp monsters. Once

Sawyer realized I was taking them, she ran for me. The room didn't have much open space, so I had nowhere to run. I immediately realized my error in judgment but couldn't do anything about it. Oh well, worth it.

"Oh, you think this is funny, Ollie Bear?"

She tackled me to the ground, rubbing her body all over me to transfer the silly string. Her hands started to tickle me, and I curled up in a ball as more squeals left my mouth.

"Time to face the consequences."

Ty joined her on the floor, and soon we were a rolling ball of silly string bodies as they tickled, and I tried to get away. I couldn't even tickle them back because I was crazy ticklish, so I gave in and curled into a ball and tried not to pee myself. It wasn't my finest moment of masculinity as I mimicked a hyena.

"I yield, I yield," I finally managed to whisper through my screams, hoping it would stop the torture. Sawyer had straddled me to hold me in place so I couldn't curl up, and Ty moved overhead, holding my arms down. I was effectively restrained and had no chance of escape.

"What do you yield?" the pink pixie asked, a fierce look of determination on her face.

"Sawyer and Ty are the coolest, and I shall never dare to stare at them instead of watching a movie ever again!"

"Wait, you weren't watching the movie because you were watching us?" Sawyer tilted her head, confusion now lined her brow.

"Uh yeah. You're both very distracting—especially when

you're both touching me. I was focused on your breathing and the feeling of your heartbeats."

"I think that's the most moronic, yet sweetest thing you've ever said."

Before I could retort back, Sawyer crashed her lips to mine. My arms were released, and I felt Ty move around to my side. I was soon lost in her kiss as we ravished one another. Sawyer was already straddling me, putting her in the perfect place. She started to rock against me as she threaded her fingers through my hair. I lifted my hands to her hips and helped her press into me.

I'd lost Tyler in the maddening sensations I was experiencing, so when Sawyer released my hair for a second and sat up, I was confused why she had. When I opened my eyes, Tyler lifted her shirt off her and then took his own kiss. The silly string fell around them as they devoured one another. He'd already taken his shirt off along with his pants and kneeled next to me in only his boxer briefs.

My eyes zeroed in on the hard length that stood out against the tight fabric, highlighting his arousal. It was a beacon calling to me, and I tentatively ran my hand up his leg to see if he would stop me. Everything was so new, and I hadn't quite figured out what was allowed and what wasn't. When Ty didn't pull away, I kept going until I grazed my hand lightly over his hardened cock.

His groan into Sawyer's mouth had me biting back a moan of my own as I pressed my hand into him more. A thrill ran through me at feeling him twitch beneath my hand, and I realized I wanted more. My desire increased tenfold at giving in, and I rocked up into Sawyer, wanting to feel them both at the same time.

Sitting up, I yanked my shirt over my head and helped Ty unclasp Sawyer's bra. Watching them kiss one another was one of the hottest things. Each time their lips touched, it was like they fell into their own little world. To be a witness to it was both a privilege and curse because it turned me on to watch the magic unfold, but it only made me want them both more. Imagining breaking their kiss hurt, so I started kissing Sawyer's shoulders and rubbed my thumbs over her pert nipples.

Sawyer's moan encouraged me, and I claimed her nipple as mine. She began to rock into me more, the angle even better than before. My sweats tented with each slide of her core against me, making my cock that much harder. Cupping her ass, my fingertips bit into her skin, grabbing the flesh. For a few seconds, I massaged her luscious ass in my hands before reaching up to the waistband and shoving the leggings, along with her panties, over her butt. Sawyer lifted herself some, and I was able to push them down more, giving me access to her core.

She was spread wide over me now, almost immobile by the pants around her thighs. This height provided perfect access to go in for the cream I wanted. Tyler pulled back from their kiss as I dived in. He watched me lick up her seam in one long movement. Sawyer grabbed my hair now that her hands were free, pulling herself closer to me. Being the good teammate he was, Ty used her distraction to pull her pants the rest of the way off.

Suspended in the air, I took her knee and placed it over my shoulder, opening her up wider. Sawyer's back arched back as I devoured her in long, slow licks. I started to push my finger in as I focused on her magic button with my tongue. Applying pressure, I began to stroke it with the tip as I thrust my finger in and out.

Peering up, I saw Tyler had moved behind Sawyer. Her head laid on his shoulder, thrown back in ecstasy as she ground into my face. Ty was watching me as he cupped her breasts, flicking her nipples between his fingers. His eyes blazed with a fire of the eternal sun, or whatever the saying was. I could feel the heat from them as he watched me tongue fuck our girl between us.

Feeling fueled by my passion, I drifted my hand back from her pussy and found the treasure I sought. Tyler's cock was now free, and I came into contact with the steel rod wedged between Sawyer's ass cheeks. Gripping his length, I watched as his eyes rolled back at the sensation, and a feeling of pride filled me at his reaction. He liked it and wanted more. I found myself wanting more too.

Thrusting two fingers into Sawyer, I stroked his cock underneath, rubbing it between her cheeks. Their moans encouraged me, and I found myself wanting to see them come undone. I rubbed my thumb over the tip of Ty's cock, feeling the pre-cum that had gathered. Spreading it, I started to stroke him with more vitality, gripping him tight. They were both lost to feelings of ecstasy as I brought them to the brink of an orgasm. Moans infused the room with sound, making it obvious we were enjoying ourselves down here.

Not able to stand it any longer, I pulled my fingers from Sawyer's pussy and pushed my straining waistband down, allowing my cock to pop free from its restraints. In a move I wasn't sure how I managed, I lowered Sawyer down onto my erect dick in one swift movement. Her moan of pleasure covered the squeal of surprise she'd started to let out at the change in gravity. We moved together, creating a rhythm of epic proportions.

Tyler moved to the side, and Sawyer licked up the base of his dick. I watched, intrigued as she sucked him into her mouth, and I struggled not to combust from the erotic picture we made. Taking her ass back into my hands, I spread her cheeks wide as I began to thrust up at an unrelenting pace. Using my strength, I pulled her down onto me just as powerfully.

"Yes, Ollie, fuck," she moaned before taking Ty back down her throat. She began to hum around him with her moan, and it set him off as he detonated a few minutes later.

"Fucking hell, Wildcat."

Sawyer licked her lips as she gave him her seductive eyes, and his dick started to get hard again at the gesture. Focusing my attention back on Sawyer, she turned and kissed me thoroughly, swirling her tongue around with mine, sharing the cum flavored kiss. Pounding up into her, I was unrelenting until we were both screaming out in pleasure.

"Yes, Sawyer, fuck, fuck, you feel so good. Come for me, sweetie."

"God, I'm so close, so close, Ollie."

It didn't take long before I felt her walls tighten around

my cock, and my dick began to spasm inside her. Holding her to me as the sensations blasted through my body, I jerked up as ropes of cum left me.

We stayed entangled together, catching our breaths before I fell back to the ground next to Ty. The three of us laid there for a few minutes, the silence comforting as our breaths filled the space—a sense of satisfaction coated all of us as we melted into one another.

Five minutes passed before Sawyer spoke. "What is all this stuff anyway?"

For some reason, that struck me as funny and caused me to laugh loudly, clutching my stomach in the process. When I returned to the present, it was to find both Sawyer and Tyler looking at me oddly on their elbows.

"Sorry, I don't know why that was funny, other than it just was." Shrugging, I carried on. "It's random things mostly, but what I found of interest was the random odds and ends from our prank wars over the past years."

Sawyer's eyes lit up, and I could see the plans already forming in her mind.

"I know what we need to do," she stated proudly, getting up and dressing. Ty and I watched her from our position, in no rush to get dressed ourselves. When Sawyer realized we weren't joining her, she turned and placed her hands on her hips. It was a look meant to be challenging but only made her cuter in the end—my bite-sized pixie.

"Wildcat, what is it we need to do?"

"Isn't it obvious?"

When neither of us responded, she rolled her eyes, giving in.

"We're going to start a prank war."

The smugness was hot. Looking at Ty, we grinned at one another before jumping up and throwing our clothes on as well. This would be epic and fun, something we could all use. Sawyer was a fucking genius, but I wouldn't admit it to her. I didn't need her ego getting out of hand after all. I was kind of bummed I hadn't thought of it myself.

Once we were clothed, we started rummaging through the boxes and discussing different ideas we could try. Sawyer ran upstairs to grab a notebook at one point, and then we started listing out all of our thoughts and finding the corresponding items needed. We had almost everything and only needed a few more things from the kitchen or town.

Outlining our first prank, we broke apart as we divided the setup. Smiles were plastered on all of our faces as we headed into battle. This might be wartime, but the only casualty here was hopelessness.

# nineteen

. . .

## sawyer

LAUGHING, Ollie, Ty, and I ran into my room breathless and collapsed onto the floor in a giggling heap. We had just finished aluminum foiling the entire fitness room. Initially, we'd thought about foiling someone's room, but the effort and amount of foil needed felt excessive. We wanted to prank but were conscientious of our time. We were well-balanced time management athletes, after all.

"Oh my goodness, I'm dying. Who do you think will be the first one to find it?" Ty asked.

"Rhett," both Ollie and I said together, causing us to laugh more.

"Let's connect the camera and watch," Ollie suggested.

Moving off the floor, they headed for HQ to view from the laptop. Ollie had some cameras leftover from his "sting operation," as he was now calling it. I didn't think the Agency wanted him using them this way, but I also didn't really care. It would be funny, and that was starting to rank high on my priority list.

Thinking about the person who'd be compiling all the feeds had me laughing again. It was sure to be an entertaining day for them when they got to ours.

Standing, I spotted a white blotch on my purple bedspread. When my brain processed the shape, I knew it had to be another letter. Making a quick excuse, I told the guys I'd meet them down there in a bit.

I didn't want to admit I'd been waiting all day for it, having gotten accustomed to receiving them daily. I was a bit anxious to read this one after the things he shared in his last one. Each letter drew me closer and closer to the man Elias was, and I liked getting to know these layers of him.

Opening the seal, I laid down on my stomach, resting on my elbows and kicking my feet in the air. For a second, I laughed at how girly I was acting, like a regular Sandy Dee from *Grease*. I guess Elias brought out the feminine side in me.

*Love,*

*I hope by now you've started to get to know me for the person I am. God, I hope you're reading these. As sad as it might sound, they are the one thing giving me courage that the future I want will be there at the end of this. If you haven't heard by now, I'm here with Voldemort. Not by choice, mind you. Every second in her presence is excruciating. I'm talking about nails on a chalk-board, excruciating.*

*I'm gathering information, and I hope to return to our family soon—to you, Rhett, Lucky, and the guys. It's the only thing keeping me here, knowing I'm helping to keep you all safe. So far, I've gathered there will be something big at the National Team qualifications. There's a competition coming up and a meeting of the Council will take place. I have a feeling it will be in regards to the vote. It all feels connected. I'm still putting the pieces together, and I'd like your help. Hopefully, between us, we can find a way into the event and discover its importance.*

*So far, I've told you about my childhood, my mother, and how I met Rhett. In this letter, I wanted to tell you about my history with Voldemort and how I got engaged to the Ice Princess herself. After a comment my father said a week ago, I don't think it was a coincidence. There was something in it for my family. I'm realizing that anything to do with my family and TAS has to be Council-related. Which only makes me feel even more used. But I digress...*

*I'd started at TAS four years ago, and believe it or not, my dating history had been relatively limited. I'd dated a few girls at Oxford, but I'd been focused on my studies, so nothing serious ever developed. Once I was in grad school, my family started setting me up with ladies they thought were suitable matches. Function after function, I was expected to attend and host these ladies. Eventually, I put a stop to it and made my belief clear on arrangements such as those.*

*My father apologized, and I thought that was it. For the rest of my time there, I didn't have any surprise dates or daughters I had* to 'host.' I think he was just waiting to find the perfect situation to formulate the outcome he desired, and he went about doing it in a way I'd never expect. He made it appear natural.

I was traveling with a few students over the summer who needed some tutoring while competing. At one of the competitions, I met Adelaide in a bar. I had no idea who she was at the time. I didn't know she was an ice skater, didn't know she was my boss' daughter, and didn't know she was pretending to be the perfect girl. I'm embarrassed to admit I fell into bed with her that first night.

Looking back, I can see the play-acting and all the cleverly staged answers she gave on certain topics. She'd been primed to interest and seduce me. Sad to say, it worked. I was clueless the whole time and dismissed any red flags because I was so enamored of her or who she was pretending to be.

I'm not trying to get a woe-is-me response. I just want to explain how I could end up with someone of her nature. For two months, we met and dated in secret. At the end of the summer, she told me she'd gotten a job at the school and admitted she was an Aldridge. I was angry initially, but she convinced me with some brilliant lie about how it was refreshing not to be known for her family due to the fame, and it resonated with me. I'd started to use my mother's last name for the same reason. Ultimately, I bought it because I wanted to. It felt nice to be liked and wanted for me.

When she arrived on campus, things were great at first. However, her true colors naturally began peeking through. First, it was the Ashleys she recruited to be her minions. Next, it was her hitting on my roommates, and lastly, it was the rumors I heard from the students of her bullying nature. I overheard her *berating a student, and I couldn't take it anymore. I was going to break up with her. It was Christmas break, and I thought it would be a good time since we'd be off for a few weeks to let the gossip die down before school resumed.*

*Except, she'd anticipated it.*

*Just as I was about to start listing all the ways we weren't suitable for one another, she apologized and confessed she struggled with acclimating to a real job and the pressure of her parents being the bosses. I can see now how it was all shite, but she used tears and her body to sway me at the time. She came home with me that Christmas, and somehow I'd proposed before the break was over. I don't even remember having wanted to, much less doing it.*

*I think I was drugged or smashed because I don't remember the proposal at all, love. I woke up on boxing day with a killer headache and little memory after Christmas dinner. Yet, here Adelaide was with my family's ring on her finger, acting all loved up with me. To this day, I don't know if I said the words or if she schemed it with my family to make me believe it happened. It's hard now to even imagine myself getting down on one knee for her.*

*When we returned to campus, life was normal again, and I tried to put it out of my mind that we were engaged. She kept insisting we set a date and meet with wedding planners. I buried myself in more work and started training harder with Rhett. I hid this part of my life from her, and it was the only place I felt free. I didn't want her to ruin it. Looking back, I was dreading everything about the engagement long before I discovered her cheating. It was just the first excuse I had to call it off.*

*As you can imagine, things didn't go well from there. I thought I was classy by not telling everyone about her misconduct, that I was saving her name. For a year after, she received sympathy from everyone on campus and in the media. Yet, she sent me harassing texts constantly and continued to proposition all my roommates. It was during this time I adopted Lucky. The family that had him couldn't keep him any longer because they were moving away. They had posted something around campus to see if anyone was interested.*

*It was love at first huff with him. His attitude and flair for life gave me hope. He was stubborn and prissy, and I recognized myself in him. Lucky pulled me out of my depression because I had to take care of someone else. It was him and the guys that saved me from myself last year.*

*It's clear you needed him as well, and he loves you like something I've never seen before. Some days I wonder if the family was real and if Lucky wasn't always meant to be with us. It feels like he was trained to be the dog we all needed. We're all the lucky ones, really. I miss him. Give him an extra cuddle for me.*

*Oddly enough, his adoption day is coming up. I've ordered him something I had custom-made at the local pet shop. Could you pick it up and give it to him? His adoption day is the 15th. I'm sorry I didn't mention it sooner. With everything that has been going on, it slipped my mind until I saw the calendar reminder.*

*I hope none of this information paints me in a worse light in your eyes. I felt I needed to explain. I'm not trying to make excuses. I chose to date her, I decided to stay with her after the red flags, and I'd committed to remaining engaged even if I wasn't feeling it. I own that. I invited the poison into my life and then* wondered why everyone around me was getting sick. It's insane how much I ignored.

At first, I was bitter and angry about the break-up. I thought it was real or had convinced myself at least that it was. I stewed in my hatred, and I became a miserable person and made women the enemy. It doesn't excuse my first meeting with you, but it was how I'd come to be that man. You should've done more than slap me. I was a tool.

No matter how I was feeling, I didn't have the right to say any of it. It was wrong, and the dressing-down you gave me was exactly what I needed. It pulled me out of my own arse and woke me up. I'd been sleepwalking through life and hating everything. The slap jolted me into seeing what was real—you.

Sawyer love, you've always shined brighter than anyone else in the room. You pull us all to you with your fire and light. Your strength is evident in everything you do. You stand up for what you believe, and you protect your friends. You love hard, and you have such an amazing heart. I knew I was in trouble that first day; I just didn't realize the impact it would have on my life.

Like a whipping wind, you cleared my eyes of the sand and fog and showed me what was real. Despite our tumultuous past, there have been genuine moments with us as well. Those are the things sustaining me and pushing me forward to have more. To trust that it can be.

The heat I feel for you, and the emotions you draw from me are more significant than anything I ever felt for Adelaide. I can see that and understand the difference. The real thing is worth waiting for.

You, my love, are the real thing.

*I will keep writing letters until I can convince you we could*
*have a shot at something real together.*
*As always,*
*Wholly Yours, love.*

Elias continued to slay me with his words. While it hadn't been fun reading about his relationship with Queen Bitch. It did make me feel slightly better. At least she wasn't what he was after. It sounded like it had been some elaborate scheme too. In a way, I felt sorry for him for being deceived by his family. But I knew he wouldn't want that, so I pushed it aside. He'd been right that he'd made his choices and had to suffer the consequences.

Petting the fluff ball beside me, I sat up and thought about how everything had fallen into place. I was thrilled he'd told me the date and story of Lucky's adoption. I would need to visit the pet shop and pick him up a gift too. Crazy themes for doggie birthday parties and images of all the fun I could have started to build in my head. It was in this peaceful state that I was attacked moments later by a deluge of water.

Screeching, I jumped off the bed, dislodging Lucky as I went. Thankfully, I'd put the letter down, so it hadn't become a dripping wet mess. The same couldn't be said about my clothes and hair as water rolled down my body. Peeking up through the wet strands, I glared at the laughing boy who was about to die.

"What. Have. You. Done?" I screamed. He didn't even have the decency to look apologetic.

"It's war, sweet pea!"

"Oh, you're dead, Sor! Dead!"

I might have been a little hysterical, but when I was planning doggie birthdays and feeling all loved up from Elias' words, the last thing I wanted was to be drenched in freezing water. Taking off at a charge, I surprised Soren, who continued to laugh at me and tackled him to the ground. Straddling his waist, I started to fake punch him as I rained down comments.

"This is uncool. I can't believe you. Ice cold water, really? I'm going to get you back for this. Just you wait!"

He'd curled up into a fetal position, laughing while he staved off my smacks. Grabbing the Super Soaker he'd dropped, I picked it up and pumped it before letting a spray of water fly. At this proximity, it probably stung a bit. Now, I was the one laughing, and I cackled with glee at his squeals. When it ran out of water, Soren lowered his hands, a massive grin on his face looking up at me.

"I concede. But you have to admit that was fun."

"Maybe a little."

"Now, who are we getting next?"

A smile grew on my face as I thought of our next victim. Climbing off, we headed into the bathroom to refill the water barrel. Surprising Rhett a few moments later, I had to admit it was fun being on the opposite end of the cold water.

Rhett gave me a look as he stood dripping water, and I dropped the gun like a dumbass and took off running, slipping and sliding on the hardwood floors as I went, leaving wet footprints in my wake. It wasn't the wisest decision, but it was fun. We spent the next hour chasing one another around the house with the water gun, and by the time it was all said and done, no one had escaped a Super Soaker bath.

The next hour was spent walking through the house mopping up our mess, which admittedly wasn't as fun, but hey, if you're going to play, you gotta be able to pay. Or some-thing responsible sounding like that. Once we'd used all the available towels in the house, we started laundry, and I admittedly was rethinking some of the pranks Ollie and Ty had suggested earlier. Clean-up was not as fun as set-up.

The doorbell rang, our dinner arriving. We'd voted to order Chinese food since we'd spent the late afternoon in a water fight. Sitting quietly around the living room, we ate our food, and it was a blissful, pleasant evening just being us.

"Despite the ice-cold water, that was a fun afternoon," Henry acknowledged. Nods and sounds of agreement echoed through the room around mouthfuls of rice and noodles.

"You know what this means, though, don't you?" Rhett asked, a look of mischievousness on his face.

"What does it mean?"

"Prank War 2020 has started."

"Oh, that sounds ominous," I said, looking around nervously.

"Only one team will come out the victor."

"Teams? And, um, are there rules to this?" I was starting to think I might've gotten in over my head. The guys all looked suspiciously thrilled about something, excluding Mateo. He looked about as deer in the headlights as I did.

"Don't kill anyone. Don't ruin anything. Don't mess up anyone's job."

"And teams, since you three started it, you can be together and have Mateo."

"Well, that leaves a lot unsaid," I mumbled, anxiety starting to coat my skin. Mateo winked at me, and I realized we just might have a secret weapon.

"May the odds be ever in your favor. No man, or woman, is safe."

Well, that got intense—let the pranks begin.

# twenty

. . .

## elias

FOR THREE DAYS, I'd dealt with Adelaide, and I was at my wit's end. I'd begun to worry she had a delusional personality disorder. No matter how many times I informed her I didn't like her, much less wanted to rekindle our relationship, she conveniently ignored it. I would rather contract leprosy than kiss her, and yet, she repeatedly threw herself at me. Perhaps I should try a different language since she couldn't comprehend English. Unfortunately, I wasn't fluent in bitch, so I doubt it would be any better.

Dismissing another one of her calls, I returned to my journal, where I kept my notes. I used the key Victoria had created, making my notes now undecipherable. After decoding her messages, I'd been able to memorize the pattern and learn to use it for myself. Taking these precautions made the most sense, considering I didn't trust anyone around me momentarily.

My father was still under the impression I was here to broker a deal with Abernathy. A small faction on the Council wanted a new leader, and a coup was in the works to dethrone Hawthorne. From what I'd gathered, Abernathy, Latimer, and Draven had always been on one side of the equation, with Rothchild, Bellamy, and Fitzroy on the other. Hawthorne had commanded control from the beginning, and since the others couldn't sway one seat, the head stayed.

Bellamy felt he'd finally gotten to Abernathy, but I wasn't sure how accurate the information was. Because it seemed contrived and like there was more to the story. I was starting to formulate Sawyer's importance, and if my suspicions were correct, it didn't bode well. Not now with how much turmoil there currently was among the seven.

A knock at the door broke my thoughts, and I placed my teacup on the table and headed to the door. I'd visited my favorite tea store while in London, and I'd been enjoying it ever since. I couldn't wait to share it with Sawyer. It was one of the things pushing me to keep going despite the separation. Peering through the peephole, I was surprised by who I found on the other side.

Throwing open the door, I greeted him. "Rhett! Uh, hey, come in."

Quickly, I moved back to let him enter, hoping he hadn't been seen. He walked in silently, light on his feet, moving with the shadows. The idiocy of attempting to hide from this man, my best friend, hit me. I couldn't hide from him, not in the same town anyway, and not when he knew this town better than any of us.

"Smart using an Airbnb, but when I couldn't find you at the hotels, I only needed to figure out who was out of town," Rhett explained without me even having to ask.

Yep, more brilliant than anyone ever gave him credit for. "I'm sorry, mate. I wanted to reach out. I figured it was too risky, and I was trying to minimize the blowback. It's probably even too risky to be here now. Adelaide is always popping by even when I send her away," I apologized, exhaustion heavy in my tone.

"I needed to talk to you."

Accepting his words, I nodded and directed us to go into the living room. We both took seats on the sofa and silently stared at one another for a few moments. His hair looked longer, and he hadn't shaved in a few days making his stubble stand out more along his jaw. I could see the weariness around his eyes and knew this week had to be wearing on him. Rhett took care of everyone else to the point of forgoing his own health.

"I wanted to thank you," he started, shocking me with his opening. I'd been prepared for him to shout or scold me. I deserved it, honestly. Rhett observed his hands clasped in front of him, head low.

"I'm not sure what for," I admitted.

His head lifted at my statement, and I could glimpse tears brimming in his eyes as he began to talk. "I know it was you who paid for Rowan's hospital stay. She was provided a private room and tended to straight away. She's been treated there her whole life and has never been admitted that quickly. I tried to figure it out at first, but when Sawyer told me you reached out to her, I knew."

Silently, I nodded, not sure how to answer. I wouldn't lie, but praise for doing what was right didn't feel acceptable, either. "I wanted to help. Rowan shouldn't be punished for something that wasn't her fault. I couldn't help with the search or keeping her out of it, but I could do that."

"I still want to thank you, Elias. It meant a lot to my mom and me."

"Of course, Rhett. You're my brother, and I care for you. Rowan is important to you, and therefore, she's important to me."

He nodded, swallowing before something shifted in his eyes before he took a deep breath. "I needed to get that out of the way first because I didn't want to dismiss your generosity. But you need to hear how *fucking pissed* I am at you, too."

Rhett's anger surfaced and took me by surprise. I never considered he'd care this much. Gulping, I held his eyes, not hiding away from the emotions he was sharing. Rhett's bravery deserved respect and my own vulnerability to witness it.

"I'm sorry. I didn't realize you'd care so much."

"That's your first mistake. *You didn't realize.* Mateo worried so much about you that day, having noticed your withdrawal and thought you'd harmed yourself. Did you realize that? Or how about Sawyer, who internalized her emotions to the point she almost inadvertently handed herself over to the enemy by walking miles in the snow?"

He was breathing hard, and I watched as he tried to hold it together. I'd never had anyone care this much, and I found it hard to accept. Mateo had been that worried? Sawyer was that upset? Thoughts swirled, and denial was rising to my tongue.

"And what about me? You're *supposed* best friend who'd just shared a fucking intimate moment with you, and then you bolted? Even before you physically left, you'd checked out days before that. Every single person in my life has left me, and then," he sucked in a breath, "*you* did too."

"Fuck, Rhett. I royally screwed up," I pleaded. "You're right. I didn't think about how anyone would respond. I never thought anyone would care. I can't say I'm sorry enough, and I know it doesn't mean anything when it's just words, but I never meant to do any of that. I honestly thought you'd get my letter and understand. "

"Yeah, well, we didn't find your letters until Sunday morning, so we spent all of Saturday thinking you'd abandoned us."

"Bloody hell, mate. I wish I could go back and redo it all. I'd never wanted to make any of you feel that way. I was trying to protect you all. I was trying—"

"To do it all on your own. It's fucking stupid, and you know it."

Hanging my head, I breathed in deep. I hadn't meant for things to get this out of control, this messy. My intentions had been noble, or at least I'd assumed. Instead, I left them vulnerable. Swallowing my pride, I lifted my head, knowing what I needed to do, to say.

"You're right, Rhett. I was wrong. We're a family, and we talk about things. I took that choice away from you, and that wasn't fair. I can't do that if we're all meant to trust one another. I let my own feelings and confusion cloud my judgment, and in doing so, I put everyone at risk. I would never purposefully do that. You guys are the one thing pushing me to take the risk, to sacrifice myself if it keeps you all safe."

"You shouldn't need to sacrifice yourself for the good of others. *We all matter.* We all get a voice. You stated you wanted to make yourself worthy, but you've always been worthy. You don't have to earn our love or respect. You have it."

"I…" Swallowing, I tried to accept his words. No one had ever told me that before, and my first reaction was to deny it. Except I knew Rhett. He wasn't one to toss out words, and most of all, he wasn't a liar. "It's hard to believe I am when I've grown up believing something different my whole life. But… I want to."

"Elias, we all have things we struggle with. None of us are perfect, but somehow together, we all fit. We need you, man. Things have been off without you because there's a gaping hole where you're meant to be. No one else can fill it." His tone was gentle and full of unsaid emotion. "Please, let me in. You're my best friend, and I need you in my life."

Nodding, I didn't notice my tears were falling until I felt them hit my hands. Touching them, I studied them in amazement. For so long, I assumed I didn't have real emotions, that I'd been too damaged to care for someone. These tears proved otherwise. These saltwater drops showed me an open heart leaking through my eyeballs. They signified grace and joy were possible. Mostly they expressed how I could love people with all my heart and have it returned.

Rhett pulled me into a hug, and we cried together unashamedly. I felt like a new person when we pulled back. We sat and talked for another hour about everything that had happened since I left, and I shared my plans. He appeared nervous but trusted my knowledge of this world and understood what I had to do. Rhett disclosed what he'd found from his grandmother, and it helped click together some pieces for me.

The information he had on the Council extended back years and could be the piece my benefactor needed to secure their arrest. Rhett looked relieved when I suggested taking it off his hands and admitted he had no idea where to start with it all.

"Do you think I should meet with my uncle?"

"I think that's something you have to answer for yourself. Do you want to meet with him to get answers on your family line? Or is it more of a personal vendetta that might result in tipping your hand? I think the why is the thing that you have to ask yourself. My two cents, I don't think there is anything you can gain from Richard we don't already know. There are already a lot of pieces on the board. Let yourself remove this one."

"Yeah, I think you're right. The day I remembered, I'd been filled with this need to do something, but after Rowan was taken, it left me in a way. Rash decisions don't seem to be the best things for me."

When the conversation came to a lull, I pulled the Band-Aid and found the courage to ask what I'd been too scared to voice—Sawyer.

"So, she's been getting my letters, then?"

"Yeah. I think she's only told me so far."

"Does that mean," I inhaled, "she's reading them?"

"You're an even bigger idiot than before, Elias, if you think Sawyer doesn't have feelings for you. She was scared, and you're intimidating with your big brain and posh attitude," he joked. "The fact I see her floating around with a smile on her face after reading a letter tells me they're working. I'd keep doing whatever you're doing. I like that you're romancing her like a long-lost love with letters, it's romantic as shit, and I approve."

"Well, that means something coming from you, the true romantic."

Rhett stood and started for the door. "I'll let you know if I find anything. I just ask that you try not to stay away too long. We all need you, bro."

"Deal." I hugged him again, and when he went to reach for the door, I blurted the last thing that had plagued me. "Are we going to talk about our time in the fitness room?"

"Did you enjoy it?" I nodded my answer. "Then, what's there to talk about? We'll figure it out like we do everything else—together. It's not something we need to figure out immediately or label. We care for her, we care for each other, and we enjoyed our shared time," he shrugged, with no embarrassment or shame.

"You make it sound so simple."

"Why shouldn't it be?"

I guess he had a point. It was only problematic if we made it so. Hugging him tightly one last time, I realized how much I missed genuine affection. We said our goodbyes at last, and he slipped off into the night.

As risky as it was for him to be here, I was glad he'd found me. I'd needed to see him, and it helped ease my anxiety. The information I'd gained would be paramount in the days to come. The biggest revelation, I wasn't alone in this.

The phone ringing woke me a few hours later. Reaching for it on my nightstand, I didn't think to check the caller ID before answering it in my sleepy state.

"Hello?"

"Elias, sorry to wake you. I forget about the time difference."

"No need for apologies, Mr. Hawthorne. How can I help you?"

"I got your message last night. I'm flying to the States. I'll meet up with you later this week. Do you think you can stall Abernathy and your father so you can remain in Utah?"

"I think I can do that."

"Good. Very good. I'll see you soon then."

The phone clicked before I could respond, and I was left with silence in my ear. Glancing at the clock, I saw it was 5:30 am here. I decided to go ahead and get up. After Rhett's visit, my brain was in full problem-solving mode, and I'd decided to make a bold move with Sawyer. It was time.

Grabbing my pen and stationary, I sat down and poured my heart into the most vulnerable and open letter yet. I poured myself into every word, and I hoped it would be met with the same openness. This one was it. The last love letter I would send. It was all or nothing from this point onward.

Sealing the heavy cardstock closed, I wrote her name across the front. I set it aside to pass on to Josh later. He'd been helping me deliver them or having some of his friends assist. I was going to need to write that kid a glowing recommendation for all the effort he'd put into this.

Just as I was starting my coffee, my phone rang, and this time, I checked the caller ID—my father. Exhaling, I slowed my heart to help me stay focused on the part I needed to play.

"Father. How can I help you this morning?"

"Elias. What's the update with Abernathy?"

"We're meeting today for lunch. He's close to swaying his vote. I've uncovered some other information, and I believe I will be able to sway Draven too."

"Hmm, don't be getting too big for your britches, boy. If you go flapping your jaws to everyone, we won't have the advantage. Stick to the plan. I've been working on Abernathy for years. This isn't something you can swoop in and solve with one *lunch*."

"Understood, sir. I will report back once I've had my lunch with Abernathy."

"Good. Elias, I don't mean to be harsh. I do appreciate the zeal. I've not seen it in you in the past, and it's rewarding to watch you flourish. To finally have you take up your mantle in the family. I'm proud, Son."

The words I'd been waiting my whole life to hear had finally been spoken, and yet, they felt flat. Everything Rhett had said yesterday clicked. I didn't need my father's approval because I had it from seven people who knew the real me and cared for me. My father only approved of a person who didn't exist.

"Thank you, Father. That means a lot."

"Don't let me down, Son. I'll see you at the end of the week?"

"That should be enough time to secure Abernathy."

"I will schedule the plane to retrieve you on Friday then. I look forward to your report."

Before I could respond, the call clicked off. What was it with entitled CEOs not even saying goodbye before ending a call? Was that not commonplace anymore? I was thankful I wouldn't have to enter that world.

Once I double-crossed my family, I would be cut off permanently. It didn't scare me as much as it once had. I'd never wanted the same future, but I'd been nervous about making a name for myself on my own and not having my father's inheritance to fall back on. I didn't need it, though. Money wasn't everything, and I had people in my life that were worth far more than the millions in my trust fund.

Straightening my tie, I grabbed my satchel and suit jacket before heading out the door. My father thought he was secure in his position and that he'd seen all of his enemies coming.

He didn't expect me, wouldn't expect me. It was one of

the trickiest chess moves in the game—the concealed attack—but one of the most lethal.

While he was building his defenses against his perceived enemies on the board, I'd moved into position, ready to strike. This time, the trap was mine, and I would secure his queen. Abernathy would be mine, and he would pay for the harm he cost his daughter. Because in the end, only one queen could stand, and Sawyer Sullivan was the only queen that mattered.

# twenty-one

. . .

## sawyer

"SSH, he's going to hear you!" squeaked out from behind me.

Rolling my eyes, I kept moving forward as I army-crawled toward Rhett's door. Our team was striking against Rhett while he was out. We'd been meeting all week and had set up a few minor pranks. Our strategy was to lull them into a false sense of security before we struck gold.

Strike hot and quick was our motto and subsequently our team name—Hot to Trot.

Ollie had gotten his racehorse name after all. He'd given us all BOSH shirts after they arrived in the mail, and now it appeared I was about to be given another one. It was cute in an adorable nerdy way, and he seemed to have found a new hobby making t-shirts. The BOSH one had a heart with wings on it and the letters BOSH on the front. It said, "When love takes flight, anything is possible." It was cheesy as hell, but it had made me blush and subsequently hug him hard.

I had no clue how serious they took these games. The rules had been simple enough, but the point system made calculus seem easy. I'd be more impressed if we weren't currently at the bottom of the board. Pranks were weighted based on level of skill, surprise, reaction, and any damage took points away. It was refreshing they weren't about destroying one another in the name of fun.

"Are you there yet? I can't see your tiny frame," whisper-shouted Ollie.

"Now, who needs to be quiet?" I mumbled.

I finally made it to Rhett's door and placed the tiny camera we had under it. We'd fastened it to a bendy stick so we could see into his room. Slowly, I pushed it under the crack and watched from the screen on my phone. The room started to come into focus, and I made out his furniture. From the angle, I couldn't tell if he was in his bed or not since it was higher up. He'd said he was going out, but we couldn't assume the intel was correct, so countermeasures were needed. At no sign of movement, I sighed and crept up to my knees, slowly turning the doorknob.

It released with a small click, and I waited to see if he would stir. When nothing happened in the room, I lightly pushed it open further. The guys had voted for me to check his room, stating he'd be less likely to yell at me if I was caught. The level of fear they held for Rhett always made me chuckle, but I didn't like being the sacrificial lamb either.

They finally convinced me by stating I could take my clothes off and distract him. It was a lowball tactic, but I wasn't above using my womanly wiles if it worked.

It was in moments like these where I was continually proven how different our group relationship was. They weren't upset about me sexing up Rhett; hell, they encouraged it. I was one lucky hussy, that was for damn sure.

Once I had the door open, I squeezed through the gap and looked around the room. I brought the camera to eye level so they could view what I could see. After a full sweep, it was obvious he wasn't here and our intel was correct. Relaxing, I sent a text stating it was all clear.

Mere seconds later, the door opened further, and Ollie and Ty entered. Mateo was on lookout duty for this one. Together, we got to work and started turning his furniture backward. I even swapped some of the drawers so his underwear would be in the wrong spot. Ollie was going to try to flip his mattress and hang something in his shower, but I didn't have high hopes for it.

Elias would've been the perfect target for this one with his meticulousness, but Rhett was by far the second-best choice. He was organized and didn't hoard things. As much as I loved Henry, his room was a mess and a hazard to navigate. Soren's was neater, but he had the most random things that it would take decades just to get it all. Plus, neither of them would care as much.

No, Rhett was the best bet. A bonus was his room being separated from the others, allowing us the greatest opportunity at not being overheard. He'd mentioned he was staying at his mom's tonight to spend some time with his sister, but it was said somewhat suspiciously, making me unsure if it was a trap or factual information. I guess it was good to know even in prank wars; he was honest with me.

After about twenty minutes, we'd gone through his closet and changed all his shoes, and tied them to the wrong pair. We mixed all his clothes on the hangers and hung half of them in the shower. His dresser, desk, and nightstands were now facing the wall, and his mattress was turned upside down. The funniest thing about this prank were the still shots of his furniture taped to the front to give the impression at first glance that everything was the same.

Thoughts of him trying to open a drawer that wasn't there and looking at his hand like he'd gone through the wood had me rolling around on the floor for a good five minutes. When I went to flip his easel, a picture poked out of a sketchbook. Carefully, I lifted the edge and studied it. It was breathtaking. Rhett had several silhouettes of me on one page like he practiced getting my essence right and then had drawn it full scale.

The beauty he saw in me was almost tangible. His skill jumped off the page with the shading and contours, and I could almost touch it. That was how real it looked.

"Whoa, Wildcat, that's amazing."

"Right? I... I just... yeah, no words."

Tyler smiled and pulled me into a side hug, wrapping his arm around me. I saw another thicker book hiding, and I opened it as well. I was amazed to find a book Rhett appeared to be working on. A noise had me jumping, and I placed the drawings back. I felt bad now for snooping on his private things, and they were too precious to do anything to them.

Jumping back, I saw that Ollie had been the one to make the noise, a guilty look on his face as he held a picture frame in his hands that had fallen and broken. "Oops, I'll replace it. He'll never know. I think that's everything else. Let's take pics," Ollie said as he carefully set the frame back down. It was of a young Rhett and an older woman, and I knew it had to be Granny Rothy. I would make sure it was replaced knowing the history there.

Getting close, we laughed and took silly poses around his room before we set the camera up on the ledge of his door frame, hoping it would catch his reaction. The camera didn't record unless you were active in the app. That way it wouldn't run out of batteries, but we had to be vigilant on watching for when he returned home too.

Giggling, we quietly tiptoed out of the door, falling back into our spy mode. I was even decked out in all black to get into character. The prank war had been a great escape from the Council and all the family bullshit drama that went with it. The last few days had felt like it had when I first arrived, minus the not knowing if I could trust people thing.

Racing up the stairs, we found Mateo as we rounded the corner. Grabbing his hand, I pulled him along with us. Our laughter grew the further we got away from Rhett's room, and I wasn't sure how much longer we would last before we collapsed into hysterics.

"Dulzura." My sweet guy beamed at me as we ran.

Smiling, I pulled him more, and we finally made it up the stairs and into my room before the other team caught us. Once the door was shut, I fell onto the floor, rolling in laughter, unable to hold it anymore. The guys joined me, and we fell into a contagious laughing train, unable to stop. What had to be at least five minutes later, we managed to get our laughs to the quiet wheezing ones and calm ourselves.

"Oh, my goodness, that was the best," Ty said breathlessly.

"Gah, I can't wait to see his face. It's going to be classic."

"Yeah, you guys might want to bunk in here tonight. Safety in numbers," I joked. I just wanted a massive cuddle nest, and it was an easy excuse.

"You can just ask us to stay over, Dulzura, if that's what you want."

Well, damn. I guess I wasn't as sly as I thought. Slapping Mateo on his stomach in jest, I rolled over onto mine to get up. From this position, I was now facing the wall and noticed Lucky's bed was empty. He was usually in here, so not finding him in my room was odd.

"Wait, where's Lucky?"

The guys sat up and turned as well, looking to where I'd been. "Gee, thanks, guys. I'm so glad you don't trust my ability to know if my dog is here or not."

Standing, I walked over to my bed and looked under it, opened the closet and bathroom doors, but still, he wasn't anywhere to be found.

"He's probably just with one of the other guys. Do you really want to go and knock and ask them? They'd probably wonder more about why you're up at 2 am. Come on, he couldn't have gotten far, and it will be easier to find him in the morning. Let's get some sleep."

Ollie's words made sense, but I didn't necessarily like them. Almost every night since I'd arrived, Lucky had slept with me or in my room. It felt unnatural now not having him here. Quietly, I got ready for bed and climbed into the middle. I'd gotten my wish to have a massive cuddle huddle, but now it didn't feel as fun. Ty's arms wrapped around me from behind, pulling me closer to him.

"It will be okay, Wildcat. Try to get some sleep, okay?"

Nodding, I closed my eyes, but I couldn't stop the dreams of flying dogs with aluminum foil hats wearing backward pants toting water guns.

Whimpering woke me a few hours later, and I crawled over the half-naked guys to get out of the bed. Opening my door, I looked down to find a very distraught dog. Lucky shook as he stood dripping water on the carpet, looking pitiful. Cradling him, I carried him into the bathroom to get him dry. Cooing nonsense at him, I dried his fur and tried to reassure him.

"Sawyer, everything okay?" a sleepy Mateo asked through the crack in the door.

"Yeah, it's fine. You can come in if you want. I found a wet dog."

The door opened slowly as his eyes adjusted to the dim light. Mateo's eyes were squinted, either from the light or not having his glasses on. His scrunched-up face was cute, and I couldn't help but stare as he made his way over. He also happened to be shirtless and rocking some low-hung boxers. Lucky whimpered, and I remembered who I was supposed to be focused on, not my sexy, sweet boyfriend.

Focusing back on my dog, I ran the towel over his fur. I was sitting on the bathroom floor with Lucky between my legs and realized I would need the hairdryer. The dog had a lot of hair! Elias had given me a ten-minute lecture one night on the maintenance and difference between dog hair and fur.

"Ah, guess you found him then?"

"More like he found us. It looks like he was out in the rain. I don't know how he got back in or out even, but I'm glad he is."

Mateo joined me on the floor, and I kept making cooing sounds to the dog as I dried him. Lucky seemed much happier now that he was getting attention. Turning on the hairdryer, I kept it low as I moved it around. Once he mainly looked back to normal, I scooped him up into my arms. When I began to stand, I lost my balance and tipped over due to the disproportionate weight, landing right in Mateo's lap.

"Well, hello, Dulzura," he purred, lighting a fire in me. He steadied me as I started to stand again. "You don't have to throw yourself at me. I'm already head over heels for you."

Mateo's words stunned me, and I stopped mid-movement and stared at my beautiful, sweet boy. Without thinking, I leaned down and kissed his lips. Lucky didn't like the position and started to wiggle out of my arms. Setting him down on the ground, I used my now free hands to wrap around Mateo's neck, pulling my body closer to his.

Mateo kissed me back enthusiastically and gripped my ass as he pulled me closer. He'd gotten more comfortable making moves and touching me over the past six weeks, and I loved the confidence I saw shining through. Sliding forward, I found myself straddling him and in a much better position, to be honest.

"Dulzura, I want you so bad. *Fuck*," he groaned, the sound vibrating in my chest.

His cussing made me feel a flutter below, and when he used it in combination with my nickname, I couldn't help the body roll I did, causing us to fall backward onto the soft rug. Smiling, I sat up and yanked my top off my head quickly, not wanting it between us any longer. The benefit of sexy times while sleeping was less clothes to remove.

"Is it normal to be speechless every time I see you naked?" Mateo whispered.

My cheeks heated at his words. Mateo disarmed me in the best ways every time. "I could say the same about you," I purred, rubbing my hands up his naked chest. His abs were on display, his pecs defined, and I lost myself for a minute as I traced them. Mateo's frame was slighter, but he was just as muscular as the other guys.

Before I could get too lost in my tracing, Mateo moved and conquered my mouth in a sweet yet powerful kiss. My nipples rubbed against the pecs I'd been caressing, and the sensual touch was turning me on. Rocking back, I felt myself wanting more and more with Mateo. We'd gone further over the time we'd been together, but we hadn't taken that last step yet. I felt since it was his first, he got to decide when he was ready.

"Sawyer, my Dulzura, I..."

"Ssh, it's okay," I cut him off, not wanting him to feel pressured. I continued rocking myself on his hard cock. The angle was perfect, and I was on my way to orgasming.

"No, that wasn't what I was going to say," Mateo said, stopping my hips with his grip. Pulling back from the lust driving me, I traced his face with my hands as I tried to understand what was wrong.

"Okay. I'm sorry, I didn't mean to cut you off. I just... didn't want you to feel pressured for something, that's all."

"Well, I think you need to let me decide and speak for myself."

Grabbing his cheeks, I raked my fingertips into his hair as I stared into his soothing blue eyes. "You're right. You're absolutely right. What did you want to tell me, Mateo?"

"I was going to say," he swallowed, "that Sawyer, my Dulzura, you're the most amazing person I've ever met, and I love you."

Tears sprang to my eyes as I focused on him. "You do?"

"Yeah, I do. So much." He smiled. "I didn't know I could love someone this way, you know. I knew I would find new experiences coming here, but you've been the biggest surprise of all, and I'm so happy our paths crossed."

"And me being with everyone doesn't bother you?"

"No, not one bit. I choose who I let into my life, and I've

never been happier or more accepted than I have in this house. Your beautiful spirit called to my brokenness, and nothing was going to stop that from happening. I believe no matter how we met, you and I would've always ended here."

"And where is here?" I asked with a grin, wanting to hear him repeat it.

"In love, Dulzura, in love."

Pulling back, I couldn't help but poke at the sweetest boy I'd ever met. "I'm pretty sure you're the only one who said it so far."

"Perhaps, but I know you do."

"Oh, how do you know?"

"The same way I know I loved you. Thinking of you without me just doesn't work. You're the milk to my cookies, the jelly to my peanut butter, and the heart to my life. I need you, and you need me. It's simple, really. Once I realized that, nothing else mattered. I love you, Sawyer, and I'm not going anywhere. So, you might as well get used to it."

Smiling wide, I let all my shields fall away, allowing him to see me with 100% authenticity. "My sweet Mateo, I think all those Disney movies have made you a romantic. That was one of the most beautiful things anyone has ever said to me. And… you're right," I inhaled, "I do love you, so much."

Sealing my lips to his, our frenzied passion resumed as we relished in the love shared between us. Mateo stood from his sitting position in an impressive move, and I wrapped my legs around him as he lifted me by the ass.

"Where are we going?" I squeaked, the movement jolting me unprepared.

"To my bed. I didn't envision losing my virginity or making love to you for the first time on the bathroom floor." He smirked, making me wetter.

"Well, then onward. What are you waiting for?"

Laughing quietly as to not wake Ty and Ollie, he carried me out of there and into his room before either of us could say anything else. My back hit the mattress a moment later, and neither of us waited any longer to fuse our lips back together. Mateo's kisses were as sweet as he was. It was almost as if I could taste his hope with each peck. His tongue swept out and licked between the seam of my lips, and I opened greedily for more of him.

Moving my hands over his back, I caressed his smooth skin as his muscles flexed beneath my touch. My hands drifted lower, and I pushed the band of his boxers over his ass, cupping it as I did. The moan he released into my mouth was pornographic, and it unleashed a side of Mateo I'd never witnessed before. His hand drifted down my body with a confidence I'd never felt. As I rocked into him, his fingers found my clit, and I was so close to detonating that I found myself returning his moan.

Releasing his mouth, I tossed my head back, the moan pouring out of me so loud I was sure to have shaken the walls with the force of my pleasure. Mateo put his confidence to use and plunged his fingers into my dripping wet pussy, causing me to tighten around him as my orgasm slammed into me.

"Fuck, Mateo. Oh my God, yes, yes, yes," I chanted as nonsensical words started to flow out of my mouth.

"The fact I made you this wet is the biggest confidence booster you could ever give me, Dulzura."

Groaning in response, I arched my neck so he could place kisses there, finding it was a spot that made my toes curl. When he found the sensitive spot, my back arched, and I felt my eyes roll back into my head from the sensation. Kicking off his boxers the rest of the way, Mateo looked down at me laid out on his bed. My body was flushed from pleasure, and my nipples peaked from the exquisite torture they experienced against his chest.

"Every day, I wonder when I'm going to wake up and realize this is all a dream. But I'm living the dream, and I don't ever have to wake up from it. You are the dream I didn't know I wanted to dream."

"For someone who barely spoke when we first met, you sure have a way with words, handsome."

"You make it easy. I just have to speak my heart."

"I love you," I breathed as I was overcome with emotion.

"And I love you."

"Are you sure?" I asked one more time, and he nodded.

Mateo looked down, and I saw his swallow as he lined his dick up with my entrance. Slowly, he started to push in as I pulled my legs tighter around him. Once he was fully seated, he froze over the top of me, and for a moment, I was scared he regretted it.

"Are you okay?" I asked, trying not to move, despite my body yearning for it.

"Mmhm," he said, breathing deeply through his mouth.

Grabbing his face, I pulled him down to me until our noses touched.

"Hey, just stay right here with me. Okay, it's just you and me. When you're ready, just start to move like your body wants. Just follow your instincts, and if it's over quick, it just means we get more practice."

"I... I don't know if I can move."

"Okay, don't focus on what you're supposed to do; just focus on me. Focus on my voice. Now tell me, how do you feel inside of me? Just think about the feeling."

Mateo swallowed before answering, and I could see the strain he was under, "You feel warm and wet, and oh so tight. It's one of the best things I've ever felt," he admitted, his cheeks going a little red.

"You feel perfect too, Mateo. Do you want me to help, or do you need to do this?"

"I can do it. I want to do it."

Nodding, I kissed him, trying to bring us back into the moment and not letting him sink into his fear of whatever was stopping him. Based on what I knew about him, I imagined he was putting a tremendous amount of performance pressure on himself that was unnecessary. Slowly, he started to relax, and I didn't realize how tight his body had been until I felt it loosen.

Grabbing his ass again, I slowly began to move my hands all over him, hoping to entice him to follow his body's wants. As I drifted down more, I cupped his rock-hard buns and squeezed, remembering the response I'd gotten last time.

Mateo's kisses became more passionate as he slowly started to push into me.

As he moved, I encouraged him more with my feet as I pulled him tight to me. Once he had the shallow thrusts down, he pulled back and slowly drew in and out of me with deeper thrusts. Despite it being his first time, he was picking up on the rhythm of our bodies and how we moved with one another.

Staring into his eyes, I saw the moment he thoroughly let go and gave in to himself. With two deep thrusts, I felt Mateo tighten and hold me as he emptied inside of me. I didn't come that time, but it hadn't been about me. I wanted Mateo to get comfortable with himself and with me so he could let go when we made love. Watching him had been orgasmic in itself.

As he laid panting beside me, I kissed his cheek before cleaning myself up. Wrapping myself around him, I stroked his cheek as I peered into his eyes. This boy, *well man*, loved me, and while I might not feel worthy of that love all the time, I knew to have earned it at all was one of the most precious gifts in the universe.

We fell asleep naked, wrapped up around one another, and not even a prank would've gotten me out of his bed. Mateo and I were milk and cookies, sweet and satisfying, and I couldn't wait to have more.

# twenty-two

. . .

## rhett

LIFE FELT as if someone had turned it up to turbo speed the past week. Every time I started to handle one thing, I was smacked in the face with another. Things were feeling more stable now since my conversation with Elias. I guess it felt like I had my best friend back in my corner, or perhaps it was just feeling one step closer to finding a resolution. Either way, I was feeling lighter than I had in days.

I'd stayed at the B&B last night after my visit with Elias. Mom had some chores for me. She'd wanted me to change out the smoke detector batteries. She joked I didn't even need a ladder, so I should do her a solid for pushing me out and using my height for good. I didn't mind, though. I would help her with whatever she needed. My mom was one of a kind.

"Mom, I'm headed out. Call me if you need anything else."

"Bye, Son, make sure to bring your pretty girlfriend again for dinner. Hell, bring the whole BOSH crew along."

"Did you just say *Hell*, mom?" I stood stunned in the doorway, blinking, never having heard her say a cuss word before.

"Yep, and I can say damn, shit, and fuck, too."

Rhonda Taylor stood proudly with her hands on her hips, daring me to say something. Raising my hands, I smiled and backed out the door slowly, not wanting to set off the mama bear.

"Okay, okay," I teased, "you're right. You *can* say those. It just took me by surprise. Thanks for keeping me on my toes. Bye, *Mom*."

She stuck her tongue out at me, and all I could do was shake my head. She'd been hanging out with Sawyer and Finley, by the looks of it. I seemed to collect sassy women in my life, but considering they were the best women I knew, I guess that wasn't such a bad thing. Heading to my SUV, I felt the smile still on my face. It had started to become a more permanent look for me. They wouldn't be able to call me grumpy here soon.

Laughing at my stupid joke, I drove home, hoping to find some time to see my girl today. Between my schedule, hers, and just general life stuff, time felt limited at the moment. If I hadn't known I was in love with her weeks ago; I definitely would by now.

Sawyer was the first person I thought of when something

good or bad happened. She was the one I wanted to share everything with. The number of times I pulled my phone out to text her a random thing was surprising. I hated texting, but with Sawyer, I could send her a million a day and still feel I had things I'd want to send.

The house looked quiet as I pulled up, and I wondered if anyone was still home. It was early Wednesday morning, and I wasn't familiar with everyone's schedule anymore. Elias had tried to get us to do some group calendar thing. It'd seemed dumb at the time, but now with Sawyer and our group, it made more sense.

I hesitated as I opened the front door, wondering if I would find myself a victim of a prank. Team Hot to Trot wasn't as skilled as Ready to Rumble in their approach yet, so anything was expected from them. They had tried to get me the other day with something over the door, but I saw it before I entered and disabled it. We hadn't even pulled out our big gun pranks yet, and we were already smoking them. When Elias returned, we would be unstoppable. Elias was the true prank champion.

Everything appeared safe as I entered, and I used my unannounced arrival to my advantage by creeping in and seeing if I could catch anyone or hear something. As I made my way through the house, though, all I was met with was silence. Assuming they were all gone, I decided to grab a shower and get started on my day.

Opening my door, I hadn't expected to find it the way I did. Spinning around, I took in their handy work. How they'd gotten my chairs to stand like that was a true masterpiece. Opening my drawer, I swiped through the handle until I realized what was going on. Looking closer at everything, I finally understood what they'd done.

The chairs had been a diversion to distract me from the true genius of their prank. Dropping my head to my hands, I stood there and laughed for a solid minute before gathering myself and taking a video of my room. Sending it to the group chat, I updated their score, and they were now only one point below us. This had been a good one and completely caught me off guard. When I opened my closet, I was even more impressed. Everywhere I turned, I kept finding hidden treasures of laughter.

As soon as the text had been sent, my phone started blowing up with responses.

**Soren:** Oh man, that's hilarious.

**Baby:** Ah shucks! I wanted to see your face.

**Ollie**: Did you cuss? LMAO

**Rey:** How long did that take you?

**Ty:** Surprisingly, not that long. Sawyer doing an army crawl down the hallway was the real treat.

**Mateo:** I missed that! Someone else is on the lookout next time.

**Ollie:** Don't worry, I took a picture.

**Baby:** You did not!

**Ollie:** It's like you don't even know me, pretty girl!

**Rhett:** I didn't cuss, but my mom did when I left today. That threw me.

**Ollie:** No way! What did she say? I'm so curious now. I think my face would get stuck.

**Rhett:** That makes no sense.

**Ollie:** It makes total sense.

**Soren:** Yeah, I have to agree with Ollie. His face would get stuck.

**Rhett:** You guys are nuts.

**Rey:** Well, are you going to tell us?

**Rhett:** Why is it so important?

**Baby:** It's just one of those things you don't expect. I think it's a bit of morbid curiosity. Like if we saw Santa in a bikini, or you eating a whole cheesecake. It's just out of the norm and would make you take a second look.

**Ollie:** Santa in a bikini isn't something I particularly want to see, babe.

**Baby:** It's a metaphor, Ollie.

**Ty:** Sawyer explained it better, Ollie.

**Ollie:** No fair!

**Rhett:** Okay, geesh, you gossiping gooses, first she said hell, and then she said shit, damn, and fuck. I think my mom has been hanging out with Sawyer and Fin too much because she also stuck her tongue out at me.

**Baby:** Yes! We are the best! Though, I don't think you meant that as a compliment.

**Rey:** Oh, I'm so telling Fin.

**Ollie:** Are you saying they have potty mouths?

**Rhett:** I'm not saying anything. This is why I don't like text conversations. Everything gets twisted.

**Soren:** Only if you say twisty things, grump.

**Soren:** Speaking of, I heard Lucky at the front door this morning soaking wet all curled up. I let him back in but he ran before I could grab him.

**Baby:** Oh poor guy! He came to me and I dried him. We've gotta be better about watching him or Elias will revoke my rights!

Shoving my phone back in my pocket, I ignored it when it continued to vibrate. I didn't like having to try to keep all the threads together in a group conversation. Texting Sawyer was easier. Everything was contained, and there wasn't as big of a margin for error. Heading to the bathroom, I hoped the clothes I grabbed matched since they were upside down and inside out. However, when I got to my shower, it was a clothing rack as well. Chuckling, I took it all down and hoped that was the last of the surprises.

It was early afternoon, and I was waiting outside the skating rink to catch Sawyer after her lesson. After my shower, I'd looked at the messages and hadn't missed anything important. Mostly them continuing to give me grief and then apologizing when I didn't answer back. I sent Sawyer a separate message saying I wasn't upset and hadn't meant for it to sound like I was saying mean things about her. She replied immediately, and I was glad things were clear between us again.

Everything felt right in my world, and I was learning to accept them day by day. Rowan was doing better after her flare-up and was almost back to her usual level of activity. Elias wasn't ignoring me anymore, and we'd cleared the air on a lot of things between us. And mostly, Sawyer loved me. That made every day better.

"Hey, stranger, what brings you to these parts of town?" Sawyer drawled in a fake western accent.

"That was the worst accent I've ever heard."

"Ah, but it made you smile, so it's still a win in my book." She wrapped her arms around me, and I did smile.

"Is that so? What else is a win in Sawyer's book?"

"Oh, lots of things, most of which I can't mention here, or I'll get us in trouble."

"I think I'm going to need to hear this list."

"I will be more than glad to share it with you." She chuckled.

"Are you doing anything now? I was hoping to get some time with you."

"Actually, maybe you could help me out. Elias told me that Lucky's adoption day is this week and that he had a gift he needed me to pick up at the store. He asked if I would do it, and I wanted to get Lucky something as well. Do you think you could take me into town and help me with that?"

"Baby, we could be scooping up horse manure, and I'd still want to do it with you." I grinned.

Sawyer scrunched up her nose at the thought of horseshit, but I was serious. I was in this for all things—good and bad.

"Well, that's a vivid image, but I don't think this will be as painful. Thanks, grump." She beamed. Leaning down, I kissed her softly on the lips.

"So, how did he propose?" a voice loudly asked over Sawyer's shoulder.

Looking up, I saw Adelaide and one of her Ashley cronies. The bitch looked right at me as she said the next part, intentionally doing it to strike at the girl in my arms. I felt Sawyer tense at the question, but I held her to me, not wanting Adelaide to get the reaction she wanted.

"He did it after our sex marathon. Elias told me he was so happy to be back with a real woman instead of a slut. He got down on one knee right there and told me he'd been a fool and for me to please take him back. Of course, I couldn't say no to that. It's love after all," she boasted, flashing a massive diamond on her finger.

The shock of her words caused me to loosen my hold on Sawyer, so when Adelaide was finished, Sawyer turned and addressed her. I tensed, worried things were about to escalate.

"Congratulations on your engagement. Best wishes for you and the groom."

I'd barely digested the words when I felt her pulling my hand to follow. Adelaide had about the same look on her face as mine, and I quickly schooled my features when we passed. When we were a safe distance away, Sawyer turned to me.

"Where are you parked?"

Confusedly, I examined her, trying to solve the puzzle before me. "You're not upset."

"Why would I be?"

"Because of what that bitch just said back there... about Elias."

Scoffing, Sawyer rolled her eyes and started pulling me again. "First, why is she bragging about a proposal after sex? She's clearly making it up. Elias would never do something so last minute or spontaneous. So she's either lying, it's fake on Elias' part, or he's gone insane. Second, I'm not going to believe a damn word out of her mouth. She's a manipulator and a people user. I trust Elias. He's on his mission, whatever that is, and I know he isn't back with her. No way."

Shaking her head, Sawyer kept walking, pulling me despite not knowing what direction to go. Once I'd regained my composure, I directed her to the right where I was parked. Sawyer relaxed as she let me take control, and I realized how much she and Elias had changed. They weren't jumping to conclusions about things, and were giving one another the benefit of the doubt.

There was hope for them yet.

I didn't doubt they both cared for one another. It was clear to everyone they wanted to tear the clothes off each other and fuck until they couldn't breathe. That was passion and chemistry. The true test would be if they were willing to drop those walls to let one another in. It looked like they'd finally found a way. Happiness bubbled up in me, and I recognized the relief I felt at that thought. I wouldn't have to choose between my best friend or girlfriend, and neither would they.

As we got up to the SUV, I hoisted Sawyer up by her thighs in a sweeping move and pushed her back up against the door. Slamming my mouth down on hers, I devoured her as I expressed all the things I couldn't say at the moment. There were some things romance movies didn't prepare you for—vulnerability.

"Whatever I did to deserve that, can I do it again later without my clothes? Because damn, that was one hot kiss."

"You were just you, baby."

"Well, that's simple then."

"Yeah, simple."

"Why do I feel like that has a different meaning?"

"Because nothing with you is simple, and yet it is… simple."

"That makes no sense whatsoever."

"It makes perfect sense. Just like our family does."

"Yeah?"

"Yeah."

"Okay, I'm good with that."

"Good. Now, let's go and see how we can spoil our furbaby."

"Ah, you just called Lucky your furbaby."

"If he's yours, then he's mine. That's how this works from here on out. You and I are endgame."

"Did you steal that from Marvel?"

"Hey, I blame you. You're the one who made us have that Marvel movie marathon. You're just as guilty."

"I'll allow it," she grinned, "because I agree."

Shaking my head at her cuteness, I dropped her back to

the ground and opened the door for her. Getting into my seat, I drove us to our town's one pet store—Happy Paws. We walked in, hand in hand, and I had to admit I enjoyed these simple moments together. The blissful domesticated life was severely underrated.

The bell over the door chimed as we walked in. The unmistakable dog and cat smell hit me as we entered, and I wondered how someone worked there all the time with it. Dogs barked in a cacophony of sounds that would drive me crazy, but I guess you had to love dogs to work here.

Sawyer walked over to the girl at the counter, a big smile on her face as she took in all the dog and cat items. I could tell already she wanted to buy everything.

"Hello, welcome to Happy Paws! I'm Megan. How can I help you today?"

"Hi, Megan! So first, I'm supposed to pick up an order for a friend, and then I need help finding the perfect gift."

"Of course, what's the name for the pickup?"

"It might be under Elias Turner or Lucky? I'm not sure, actually. He just told me it was here."

"Oh yes, I know what you're talking about! Just a second, and I'll grab that for you. It turned out so cute! You're going to love it."

"Oh yay! I can't wait to see it."

Sawyer started meandering around the rows of chew toys and doggie clothes when the store clerk walked away. Her excitement was adorable to watch as she picked up tiny sweaters and things. She caught me leaning against the aisle, watching her at one point, and stuck her tongue out at my smirk. It proved my point earlier about my mom, but it only made me happier to see them bonding.

"What do you think? A little sweater that says 'Ruff-a-sorus' or, a little figure skate chew toy?"

"Baby, I think—"

"You're right. I should just get both!"

I shook my head at her because what else was there to do? Sawyer brought her purchases over to the counter just as Megan returned.

"Oh, good. You found something. Those are both adorable. You sure have one lucky puppy!"

"Huh, that's funny because his name is Lucky!"

"Ah, yeah, that's right! That's the cutest," gushed Megan. "Here's the custom order. It's this super cute leather collar with his name embroidered on it. Duh, me."

"That's awesome. He's going to have the best little day!"

"Okay, here are your purchases. Thanks for choosing Happy Paws!"

"Thanks for your help, Megan. You've been so kind. Bye!"

Sawyer was all smiles as we walked back out to the car, and she was even swinging our hands as we went. I was so caught up in the moment I didn't notice the car that had blocked the aisle to where we'd parked. As we approached, two guys in combat gear stepped out, stopping us. Sawyer tensed at the sight of them, and I immediately went on high alert. A car door opened, and a man in a suit approached us. The way she squeezed my hand alerted me that she knew this man somehow.

"Well, if it isn't, little Sariah Brennon, all grown up. My, my, what a stunning woman you've become. Just think of all the years we could've had together."

"You're mistaken. My name is Sawyer Sullivan."

"Yes, that is what your ID states, but we both know that's a lie. In fact, even Sariah isn't real, now is it? It seems you have a very sordid past Ms. Abernathy."

"That's not my name," she stated through her teeth, her breathing starting to rise as her anger took over. I couldn't take it anymore and moved in front of her.

"I'm sorry. I didn't catch your name?"

My question distracted his obsessive gaze on Sawyer, and he moved it toward me. He took in my stance and height, and a flicker of recognition crossed his eyes.

"Apologies, how rude of me. I'm Leon Rojas, and your girlfriend and I go *way back*."

"Interesting, because it doesn't seem like she knows you. Say, didn't I see you the other day at the Alumni skate? Yes, I do believe I did when I was in Abernathy's booth." Leon swallowed at the mention of seeing him. He hadn't expected me to be of any importance. It seems his employer didn't have all the names on the board. "You might know my family, Rothchild?"

At the mention of my father's last name, a panicked look crossed his face for a split second before he wiped it clean. However, it gave us the advantage I hoped it would, and he started to backpedal.

"I don't recall seeing you, but maybe you're right. Ms. Sullivan, it appears I'm mistaken. Sorry for the inconvenience."

He turned on his heels, sliding into his car faster than we could respond. Just as quickly as they'd appeared, they were gone.

"Leave it to fucking R to rain on my parade. It's like the Council knows the moment I'm happy and go, nope, that can't be, let's go and fuck things up!"

"Baby," I started, but Sawyer continued to rant, not hearing my words.

"Seriously, why do they—"

Grabbing her, I hoisted her over my shoulder in a fireman's carry and continued to the car. I'd always wanted to make that move actually, so when the opportunity presented itself, I couldn't help it.

"Rhett! Put me down!"

"Nope."

"Rhett!"

"Sorry, baby, I'm living out a fantasy right now. So, you're just going to have to play along."

"But—"

"Nope."

Sawyer gave in as I finished our trek to the car, and I couldn't help but smile. The Council had tried to make a play, and they'd failed. It only proved we could do this. We could take on the Council and survive. It was no longer a matter of winning; it was a matter of surviving. I didn't need to win, but I needed us all to live.

"Okay, baby," I started as I slid her down my front, "you know what we need to do now?"

"No," she pouted, crossing her arms.

"Well, first, none of that," I pushed her lip up, "and second, I think this calls for ice cream."

At my mention of ice cream, she quit trying to fight me and regarded me with a serious expression. "Can I get two scoops?"

"Baby, you can get as many scoops as you want, plus sprinkles. Hell, you can have the whole kit and kaboodle for all I care!" I laughed.

"Well, when you put it that way, what are we waiting for? Let's go! This girl needs some cookie dough, and oh, I wonder if they have…"

Her ice cream order trailed off as she got into the car with her purchases, and I laughed the whole way around to my door. This girl, I'd give her the moon if she wanted it. Now that I'd found my tribe, nothing would stand in the way. *Nothing.*

# twenty-three

. . .

## sawyer

THE SMELL of popcorn hit me as we made our way through the hockey stadium, making my mouth water. The line was long, though, so I just stared longingly at it. Concession stand popcorn was the bomb, but I didn't want to wait in that line for it. Sighing, I kept walking toward our section, occasionally looking back, hoping the line would change. Asa had offered us the box, but with the possibility of his dad, correction, *our* dad being in town, I didn't want to chance it.

If I could go without seeing him again for the rest of my life, I'd be happy. Sharing a dinner with him the other night had been torture. The man had ruined my appetite, and I didn't get to eat dessert. Anyone who ruined dessert was a toxic waste dump and shouldn't be allowed in your life—point-blank. *Desserts were sacred.*

"I see you looking at the concession stand like it's your long-lost lover. You want popcorn, don't you?" Henry teased.

"It's fine. The line is too long."

"Smalls, you're too cute. I can see the drool already hanging off your lip. I'll grab some as long as you save me a spot. I need some cuddling with my girl today," he whispered before turning toward the tantalizing smell of butter. A girly sigh left me this time as I watched him walk away. Some days, I just basked in the glow of happiness that this was my life.

"Come on, sweet pea, let's grab seats before they're overrun with students."

Soren wrapped his arm around my waist and pulled me along. Mateo and Fin had stopped at the entrance to our section to wait for us. Sighing again, I rested my head on Soren's chest as he pulled me along, chuckling.

"I know. He's the real dreamboat," Soren sighed along with me, causing me to join him in giggling.

"You guys are amazing together. I'm glad you found one another and still have room for me," I disclosed unconsciously. Soren stopped and motioned for Fin and Mateo to go on ahead.

"Hey, what's this about? Have we made you feel left out or something?"

"No, not at all. The opposite. I'm just happy for you both too. Obviously, I'm most happy for me because I get you guys separately and together, and like, hot damn, but I'm also happy you have that with one another. Besides being hot as fuck, I know you love each other, and that's special. The world needs more love, that's all."

"Well, that was an eloquently awkward declaration there, sweet pea." Soren laughed.

Sticking my tongue out, I caught myself and realized Rhett might be right. I was a bad influence. Oh well, not much could be done now. I would embrace my signature move! Grabbing Soren's hand, I pulled him with urgency to our seats, dodging fans and families as I went. It wasn't to hide my ever-increasing red cheeks at all—nope, not at all.

My diversion failed based on the laughing boy trailing behind me. Darn it. I might not be as eloquent as others or have the best words when it came to expressing myself, but I was open and honest with them, and that was a win in my book.

Before I could head down the tunnel to our section, Soren yanked my hand to pull me back towards him and spun me until my back was against the wall. Quicker than I could stop it, he had me bracketed against the cold stone by both his arms, towering over me with a predatory look on his face.

"I wasn't making fun of you, Sawyer. I think what you said was beautiful. Thank you for saying it. I'm glad we found each other too and that it brought you into our lives. We wouldn't be as amazing as we are without all of us. I hope you know that. We work because it *is* all of us, not individual pieces. I love our moments together and our moments alone. You don't see how amazing you are, and I just want you to know. You're the heart of everything, sweet pea. I love you."

He kissed me suddenly, and I melted under his lips. It

wasn't wise to be making out like this so publicly, but Soren and I had a thing for ice rink walls, it seemed. Something hit the side of my head right before I was about to jump up and wrap my legs around Soren. Pulling back from the kiss, I turned to look at what or who had just hit me.

Henry stood with a bucket of popcorn in one hand and a giant drink in the other. His smirk was hot, and I licked my lips as I took in the sexy package he was.

"I'm scared to ask if that look is for me or the popcorn, but since we're in public, where we work, how about we save this for later? Besides, the game is about to start, and I know how you get about your hockey."

His words had me sobering, and I ducked under Soren's arm and raced the rest of the way through the tunnel to our seats. Climbing up the stands, I found Fin and Mateo a few rows up and climbed over a couple people to get to them.

"Well, that was a bizarre way to get here, girl."

"How else was I supposed to?"

Fin pointed a finger in Soren and Henry's direction, who were stopped on the staircase to her left. Soren held his middle as he bent over and laughed, and Henry looked moments away from spilling my popcorn on the floor.

"Oh."

Okay, so maybe there was an actual staircase to the seats, but I'd gotten here much quicker even if I did climb over people. There was something to be said for ingenuity. Crossing my arms, I turned back to the ice, attempting to tune out their laughter at my expense and focus on the game. It was hockey time.

Finally, the guys had a home game that didn't interfere with classes or training, and I'd made sure to be here. Rhett had something he couldn't get out of, but the rest of the crew had succumbed to my demands. Granted, it had only really been Mateo, Henry, and Soren I had to convince. Fin had already planned to be here in support of Asa.

Henry sat down next to me a few seconds later and offered me the popcorn. I gladly took it, even if it was a peace offering for laughing at me. I watched the students finish their drills as I shoveled the buttery goodness into my mouth. Henry had salted it and drenched it in butter in the perfect proportions. I knew all those times going to the movies and teaching him my method would pay off someday.

I felt Fin tense up next to me, pulling my concentration to her. She was staring at the bottom of the stairs at someone. Titling my head around a few people, I was able to make out Milo. He was staring back at her, but she had directed her gaze solely on the ice at this point and was doing her best to avoid eye contact. Elbowing her, I pulled her attention to me.

"You wanna talk about whatever all that is?"

"It's nothing."

"Uh-huh. I'm guessing either the talk with my brother didn't go well or hasn't happened yet because that," I nodded in the direction of Milo, "isn't *nothing*. You gotta deal with this girl before it deals with you."

"Sawyer, please. Not now."

The exhaustion and pain I heard in her voice were the only things that stopped me from pressing her. The whistle and bell going off to start the game had nothing to do with it —nope, none.

"Okay, I'll drop it for now, but we will be talking about this. Understand?"

Fin glared at me, but it was a good sign. A pissed Fin was better than a sad Fin.

"Fine. Now, can we watch the game? And I want some popcorn."

She grabbed a handful of the fluffy kernels before I had time to pull it back. The triumph on her face had me relaxing, but I did make sure to move the bucket closer to Henry, you know, just for safekeeping. I wouldn't say I had a protective arm around it or anything, but I wouldn't say I didn't either. Nobody better mess with my popcorn!

"Wow! I'm so impressed with how well they played. I would never think they were high school kids. I don't know why I'm shocked. I skate with girls every day that are just as amazing, but hockey is just *hockey*," I gushed to whoever would listen to me as we walked out of the stadium. Thankfully, they all indulged me in my ramble. We rounded a corner, and I bumped into a man due to my hockey worship distraction.

"Oh, sorry, sir, I didn't..." the words trailed off as I took in the vaguely familiar man before me.

His hair was more strawberry blonde than red and had a slight curl to the ends. He was dressed oddly for a hockey game in a suit and overcoat. The sneer on his face at our disruption of his passage was more than enough to know how he felt about me, but it was the coldness in his familiar hazel eyes that had me sucking in a breath.

"Watch it, *little girl*," he bit out before moving on with his companion.

A breath escaped me, and I clutched my chest as I regained my surroundings. A hand on my back directed me out of the passerby's flow and down a dark corridor before stopping in front of a door. I couldn't hear anything outside the ringing and pounding of my heart in my ears. My vision was tunneling at the edges as bright spots floated in and out of sight. I held onto the arm beside me as I put one foot in front of the other into the room. It was the only thing I could concentrate on.

Arms wrapped around me from behind, pulling me into a chest as someone dropped down to my level in front. Hands cupped my cheeks, and I stared into the calming blue eyes of my sweet boy. Mateo stared back with concern on his face. His sense of calm filtered through me, and I grabbed onto his presence as the grounding force he was.

"Hey, Dulzura, you're safe."

Nodding, I leaned into his touch, feeling his comfort. A kiss on my neck reminded me of the arms from behind. Tilting my head up, I found Soren's face nestled in my neck. My cuddle monkey watched me with soft eyes as I patted his hair. No one let go, and I didn't try to move away. I wanted to remain in their grasp for a few more minutes.

"I'm okay, now. Did…" I started but stopped to swallow, "did any of you recognize him?"

"It was Latimer, wasn't it?" Henry said from the side. Turning, I found him close, and I reached out a hand, needing to feel him as well. Nodding, I squeezed at the words.

The man who had wanted me to grow up in a good home to later "break me" at sixteen had just bumped into me and hadn't even realized it. I was such a nonfactor in his life he didn't even recognize the girl who had gotten away was right under his nose. And yet, he had shaped every moment of mine. Strange how inconsequential you could feel to someone who had the power to alter your entire life.

*I was nothing to him.*

But I wasn't nothing.

If anything, it strengthened my resolve to stop the Council vote and shut them down. No one should ever feel like they weren't enough or that their life didn't matter. These men were sitting around in their ivory towers and playing with our lives, and they didn't even know who we were.

There was a level of freedom in that knowledge. I'd always felt there was a target on my back, but evidently, I wasn't as meaningful or memorable as I believed if Jayce Latimer himself could literally bump into me and keep walking.

"Let's get out of here. I just want to go home and be with you all."

"Sounds good, Dulzura. I think we could convince them to take a night off from pranks and just enjoy a movie night." Mateo smiled at me, calming my nerves.

"Wait a minute there, I don't know about all that," Soren joked, "calling a truce is a big deal. You're gonna need more votes."

"How about we call a truce, or no one gets to see my boobs for a week? I need my guys without any anxiety that something will jump out at me around every corner. I can't wait until this week is over," I groaned. "It's been fun, don't get me wrong, but a girl needs to feel like she can walk down the hall without worrying if she's going to pee herself!"

Chuckling, the guys all agreed with me, and we headed out of the room we'd stowed away in. "Where's Fin?" I asked once I realized she wasn't with us.

"She went ahead to meet up with Asa. And before you give me that look, she ran into Ace, and they went together," Henry reported.

Dropping the eye glare I'd been preparing, I stuck out my tongue, going with my patented Sawyer response. I kept walking on a mission until I realized I had no clue where we were. Stopping, I spun around for a second to see if I could figure it out. The guys stood and watched me, offering no assistance as they smiled at me.

"I'm glad I can be your entertainment," I huffed, parking my hands on my hips. Blowing out a breath, I tapped my foot as I waited for one of them to tell me where the hell we were. Mateo caved first, my sweet boy for the win, and walked over to me and took my hand.

"This way, Dulzura, and I'm sorry. You're just too cute sometimes when you go all mama bear and then look like a lost little puppy. Seeing both sides of you at once just makes me happy."

"Well, as long as it's happiness and not laughter at my expense, I can handle it."

Mateo squeezed my hand and led me out of the dark hallway. Ever since our night together, he'd been confident about initiating intimate gestures in front of the others. He kept making me feel all gooey to see the strong man he was emerging as. Once we made it out to the common area, I was amazed at how far down there we'd been. During my panic, I hadn't realized the distance we'd walked.

The arena was practically empty by this point, and only a few parents, alumni, and spectators littered the space, waiting for the players to emerge. The game had been a lot of fun, and it was nice to see our team win. Ollie and Ty were going to be in great moods this evening. Both of the JV and Varsity teams were currently on a winning streak, and it was the first one in the school's history. I was excited for them to break some records.

Pushing on the metal bar, I walked outside into the cold. I'd barely walked through when a snowball smacked me in the face. Freezing, I stood there stunned for a moment as the wetness dripped down my cheeks. Swiping it off, I opened my eyes to see who had fired it.

Mateo's back was in front of me, and I assumed he'd moved there after the attack. A warmth spread across my chest at his protective gesture, but I wouldn't let him do this alone. I'd been the target, so I wanted to face whoever had felt it okay to throw something at me. Moving him aside, I wasn't shocked when I found Adelaide and two of her alphabet minions standing there. I'd noticed Ash hadn't been hanging around her as much and hoped she'd finally dropped the act. Henry and Soren came to my other side as I took in the three girls.

"Oops, it slipped."

"Really? You're stooping to throwing snowballs at my face? And you can't even own up to it? How juvenile."

"I don't know what you're talking about. It was clearly an accident. If your fat face got in the way, well, that's on you. Anyway, I don't have time to deal with you. I have to go meet my fiancé."

Adelaide turned, tossing her hair in a perfectly crafted move as she went. Mateo grabbed a heap of snow and went to throw it at her in return, but I placed my hand on his arm, stopping him.

"Don't. She's not worth it. Knowing her, she has someone waiting to capture it, and then we'd end up in trouble. We have to be more calculated to take her down. Besides, she's just not worth it right now. I love that you're willing to do it, though."

Leaning up, I kissed his cheek, a blush starting to form on it at my appraisal. "Come on. My pajamas are calling my name."

I took a step, pulling Mateo with me, but I felt another snowball hit me from behind before we got two feet. One hit Mateo this time as well, and we both turned to see who had thrown them. I would need a snowsuit at this rate if I was to get attacked at every turn.

A snickering Ollie and Ty caught my attention as Soren and Henry stood off to the side, watching the interaction play out. Obviously, they didn't know about the snowball I'd just received, but the timing wasn't the best. Dropping Mateo's hand, I dove for the pile of snow on my right and frantically grabbed some up. The guys reacted a few seconds later and started doing the same.

I wasn't making snowballs, though.

While they were all busy making their arsenal, I tackled Ollie and shoved snow down the back of his coat. The high-pitched squeal he let out as the cold snow hit his bare skin was everything.

# twenty-four

. . .

## sawyer

THE MUSIC BLARED through the room as I finished up my dance class. Ever since my impromptu 'dance it out' session, everyone had been eager for it to return. So now, the last fifteen minutes were dubbed as 'dance it out' time. I had to say; it had become my favorite part of the class too. It was cathartic and a bit therapeutic to just dance your emotions out. The music stopped, and everyone was left panting and dripping sweat, but smiles graced each person's face.

"Great class, everyone. See you in two days!"

Various things were called back as everyone grabbed their bags, downed water, and wiped the sweat off themselves. My co-instructor, Chris, smirked at me as he approached.

"Despite Adelaide's attempts, you've won all the kids over to your side, you know?"

Looking at him strangely, I was trying to figure out what Chris was saying. My confusion must've been evident because he laughed, shaking his head.

"You didn't know?"

"Know what?"

"Adelaide has been campaigning to have you fired since you got here. She was telling all the students how inferior you were and not to listen to you. She's also tried to poison all the instructors against you."

"So why don't you hate me? Make it harder for me?"

"I like to think of myself as a freethinker, and I've been sick of her bullshit for years. I was excited to see this girl who had shaken the queen to her core so much she was actively rooting for you to fail."

"Thanks, I think." I laughed.

"Don't mention it." He laughed with me. "So, listen…"

I had a weird feeling in my stomach now at his words; shit, was he going to ask me out?

"I was wondering if—"

"I have six boyfriends!" I blurted.

Chris looked at me oddly as he finished his sentence. "—you could cover for me on Friday? Wait, did you think I was asking you out?"

My face flamed as his words sank in. "Um, sorry. Yes, absolutely, what class?" My words rushed out quickly as I tried to cover up my embarrassment and code orange moment. His face was still in a scrunched-up question, like he'd gotten stuck on what I blurted and couldn't move past it. Picking up my bag, I bolted for the door, waving over my shoulder, figuring I could get the details later. As I crossed the door, I swear I heard him finally say, "... six boyfriends!"

Cringing, I raced down the stairs, only dressed in my dance attire, and exited the building, realizing the stupidity of my rashness. Dropping my stuff to the ground, I quickly pulled out a hoodie, joggers, socks, and boots from my bag and dressed in the parking lot. It was pathetic, but it was preferable to staying in that dance studio for one more second. With my butt in the air, I should've known it would only lead to more embarrassment for me.

"Well, well, look at what we have here, ladies. It's Slutyer."

Tensing, I took a deep breath before uprighting myself and turning. Bitchelaide and her minions stood in a classic mean girl stance circa *Heathers*. It took me a moment to gather myself from laughing at the absurdity that was Queen Bitch. I wondered if they practiced it or if mean girls just naturally knew how to stand in formation?

"Wow, you're more of a slut than I ever knew if you have to get dressed outside. What, did one of your liaisons get interrupted? I can't wait to post this all over."

As she said that, I noticed the others recording me on their phones. Seriously, technology was evil sometimes. Rolling my eyes, I continued to get dressed so I could save myself some embarrassment along with not freezing to death. Turning my back, I crouched down to zip my bag closed. Once everything was good, I strode off without even answering her. Bitchelaide thought she was tough shit, but after dealing with the Council, she was just a gnat—annoying and harmless.

Before I was even halfway home, my phone pinged with a new notification. Pulling it out of my pocket, I braced myself for whatever she'd posted because it could only be from her.

*Slutyer leaves no man untouched. Guard your men, ladies, or she'll snatch them! Thank God my Eli got away from her gaping cunt.*

Her words stung even if I didn't want them to. I knew people would talk about me and call me a slut, but seeing it written was real. Clicking on the dots next to the picture, I reported it against community standards and then closed my phone. Nothing else I could do, or I guess, nothing else I was willing to do.

I saw a few kids huddled over their phones as I passed, but I ignored it as I continued my journey home. Before I was out of the quad area, a student I recognized was sitting alone on a bench. When he saw me, he stood up and waited for me to get closer. He gave an awkward wave when I was almost to him, and I waved back, unsure what the protocol here was.

"Hey, do I know… you?"

"Hi, um, sorta. Here."

Quickly, he shoved a black envelope into my hands and walked off. Looking down, I took in the delicate way my name was written in gold across the front. *Elias.* I hadn't heard from him in a few days, and I realized I missed his letters. Deciding I didn't want to wait until I was home, I sat down on the bench the kid had vacated.

Flipping it over, I peeled away the flap and pulled out the heavy card stock. It was an elegant cream with gold filigree over the front that encapsulated the letter E. It must've been some of his personalized stationery. The attention to detail in this letter had my heart rate picking up. This one was different. I could feel it.

Opening the card, I was surprised when a keycard fell into my lap. Picking it up, I took in the name of the hotel. Was this? Sucking in a breath, I tightened my grip around it as I read the card.

*Love,*

*My time here is running out, and soon I'll need to make a move. I have a selfish request... would you meet with me? Part of my fear stems from thoughts that you haven't read my letters and don't know the truth, despite Rhett telling me you have. The other part fears that you have read them and you don't care what they say... that your mind's made up about me and I lost my chance that first night in the kitchen.*

*I think I just need to know. Before I head into the next phase, I need to know where I stand with you. Please, if I mean anything, even just a friend, would you meet me? I'm begging, and I'm not too proud to say that. I've been feeling lost, unsure, and I think if I saw you, it would give me the strength I need to finish this if I knew.*

*My biggest vulnerability is the fear that I won't be enough, and I've been striving my whole life to prove I am to my father, siblings, teachers, peers, and even girls. I'm scared, Sawyer. But*

*I'm trying to be brave and share these things with you that I've hidden. I want you to know my heart and the man I hope to be.*

*The card enclosed is for a hotel room a town over. I have an Airbnb here, but it might be compromised, and I don't trust any of the places in town outside of Rhett's mom's. Unfortunately, it's booked and probably still too risky. I'm hoping a town away will be secretive enough. If you don't show, I guess I'll have my answer. I won't bother you anymore after today.*

*Wholly Yours*

Flipping the card over, he'd written a date, time, and room number. It looked like I had a decision to make. Standing, I started my journey back home at the same pace I'd been going. My feet had a mind of their own, though, because without realizing it, I started running.

My bag smacked against my leg with each stride, but I didn't care. I needed to get home. *I needed to get to Elias.*

My knee tapped with nervous energy as I waited for the bus. I decided it would be the easiest, and that way, none of the guys would know where I was either in case any of us were being watched. I'd taken two different Ubers, one bus, and walked a good portion before I felt I was safe to go to my final location. It might've been extreme, but extreme caution always won out in my book when lives were on the line.

Falling back into that mindset had been odd. That, to me,

was a good indication I'd changed since being here. Before TAS, I wouldn't have thought twice about the measures I'd taken or the fact I hadn't told anyone where I was. I even took out my sim card so I couldn't be tracked and had a burner phone.

I left a note for Rhett, figuring he would be the only one who wouldn't freak out. Well, that wasn't right. Rhett was the most likely to freak out in his need to take care and protect everyone, but he was my best option at explaining my desire to see Elias. He'd tracked him down already and would understand. Plus, the other guys didn't know about his letter writing. I hadn't meant to keep it a secret; it was just in the chaos of those first few days, it hadn't seemed important. It was a lame excuse, but it was all I had, and I was clinging to it with everything I had.

The bus rolled up, and I climbed on after depositing the correct change. Taking a seat in the middle, I pulled my hat down more to hide my face. I was too good at this. I didn't know if it was a good thing or not anymore. At one time, it had kept me alive; now, it was helping me hide from people I cared about. I wasn't stupid. I knew even if the Council wasn't tracking me, the Agency was. I couldn't have them following me either.

So, incognito Sawyer had come out to play.

Fifteen minutes later, the bus pulled to a stop in a moderate-sized town about thirty minutes south of Oak Crest Peak.

A few people got off ahead of me, and I followed them, blending in with their group. Avoiding cameras, I made my way to a cafe across the street. Stepping inside, I pulled out my phone to look up the directions from here. It was about a five-minute drive or thirty-minute walk. Ordering a tea to go, I decided to take a taxi. It was a bit risky, but I didn't want to show up all sweaty.

Stepping into the bathroom, I pulled the hat off and gave myself a quick look over. Despite my three-hour journey, I still looked okay. Putting the cap back on, I retrieved my tea as I waited for my ride. The car pulled up a few minutes later, and I hopped in. The driver smiled politely but kept the chitchat to a minimum, much to my delight.

The hotel we pulled up to was luxurious, and I took it in as I stepped out of my ride. I decided to pop into the bathroom again and do a better touch-up of myself. Finger combing my hair, I spritzed some dry shampoo on the parts that the hat had flattened. Whoever had created that shit was a fucking genius! It was truly a girl's best friend.

Pulling out my body spray, I squirted it on as I danced around in the cloud of fragrance. I didn't know why I always did, but ever since I was small, I had started doing it, and it stuck. You could change your outward appearance all you wanted, but memories and customs were the hardest to ignore.

Straightening my top, I twisted side to side as I took in my outfit. I hadn't known what to wear, and since I couldn't exactly ask Fin for advice, I had gone with a simple dress and leggings. And boots, I couldn't forget my killer boots.

Feeling put together, I grabbed my small bag of essentials and took a deep breath. It was now or never. I'd been debating for the past three hours what to do when I saw him.

Would I kiss him? Would he kiss me? What if it was only in his letters and that magic was gone in person? Was I presumptuous thinking he wanted more?

Over and over, I debated with myself into a circle, so much so that I no longer even knew where I stood with myself. I was hoping it would just be one of those natural things, and everything else would fall into place. Yeah, nothing was ever that simple with me. Nothing.

Bracing myself, I lifted my fist and knocked on room 1213.

# twenty-five

. . .

## elias

THE WEEK FLEW by in a flurry of meetings and stiff dinners full of the typical stuffiness I loathed. The boringness of it had surprised me, and it only reiterated the impact Sawyer and the guys had on me. Real connections were worth a million five-course meals, fancy suits, and exotic vacations. I realized if you didn't have people to share those things with, they were just things. *Life was more than things.*

When I finally had some moves in place, I knew it was time to send my last letter, the one I wrote the day after Rhett visited. I needed to know if things had changed. If she felt differently about me or if I was doomed to be on the outside looking in for the rest of my life. Regardless of how she felt, I would protect her and the guys. That wasn't the question. But if the worst happened, and I didn't make it out of this, I couldn't leave it without knowing the only truth that mattered.

A few hours ago, the text came through from Josh. He'd successfully delivered the card to Sawyer in person—now I waited. *Bloody hell, waiting sucked*. I'd already paced the length of the room enough to carve a path into the carpet. Nothing on the telly kept my attention, and if I unbuttoned and buttoned my jacket anymore, I was sure to pop the damn things off.

The time for her to crush my heart or set it free was finally here. I'd like to lie and say I wasn't standing at the door peering out the peephole ten minutes before, but I couldn't. When the lift dinged, I glued my eye to the door to see if it was finally her. My hands shook, and I was certain to be a sweaty mess. The first couple of people off had my heart dropping all the way to the ground floor. I was beginning to believe my evening would end with a giant dessert from room service—nothing drowned your misery better than rich, velvety cheesecake.

When the lift dinged again, I waited with bated breath. It was a few seconds before the person stepped off, and I'd been worried it was empty. *But then I saw her*. Golden hair and curves I wanted to touch appeared in the hall.

Sucking in a breath, I watched while Sawyer fidgeted as she walked down the hallway. She was glancing at the numbers on the doors as she went until she realized it was the one directly at the end of the hallway. Sawyer took a deep breath, fortifying herself, and then with her shoulders back, head up, she made the last few steps to the door.

She looked beautiful, and I was momentarily transfixed by her. She still had her coat on due to the weather, so I couldn't see what she was wearing, but her hair was down, flowing around her shoulders. The boots she had on drew my eyes as they reached up her legs and hid under her coat. Swallowing at the thought of following them, I tried to slow my racing heart. I couldn't get ahead of myself.

Thoughts of doubt formed and ran through my head that maybe she was here to tell me to go to Hell or that she had plans later with one of the guys and was turning me down gently. I couldn't believe yet she cared, that she might feel a fraction of what I'd come to feel for her. This stupor had me frozen in my mind, missing her reaching the door.

Her gentle knock jolted me forward, hitting my head against the door. "Ow," I muttered, rubbing the area.

"Elias?"

Her soft voice asked, and I realized she'd heard me hit the door. Fuck! What great impressions I kept making. Suddenly, I realized standing there immobile was worse; quickly, I yanked the door open and came face to face with the girl of my dreams.

"Hey," she greeted, a soft smile on her lips.

"You came."

"Of course. Can I come in?"

"Yes, of course. Shit, I'm already messing this all up." Stepping back, I reprimanded myself to pull my shit together when her sweet giggle flowed into the room, and I wondered if that was the most perfect sound in the world. It settled something in me, and my heart started to race for an entirely different reason.

"Elias, I don't think we can mess this up any more than we already have. It's okay."

"I guess when you look at it like that, you're not wrong."

Smiling, I closed the door and locked it once she had stepped past me. I watched her take in the room as I stood back. It wasn't the grandest place, but it was a suite with a separate kitchen, television area, and separate bedrooms. I hadn't wanted it to seem like this was about sex, so having more to the room than beds felt important. As she looked at everything and ran her hands over the furniture, I was glad I'd made an effort.

Adelaide had never appreciated things like this. She expected them. Life with her had always been about what I could give her, and there was no reciprocation or appreciation. How I'd let myself be fooled for so long still baffled me, but it was behind me, and I didn't want to waste a single second more on her. Following Sawyer in, I stopped at the kitchen and leaned back against the counter, my hands in my pocket as she finished checking out her surroundings.

Sawyer turned and found me, and another smile spread across her lips. My heart picked up speed at her simple smile. *She was here.* Sawyer was here, and she seemed happy about it. That had to be good, right?

"I'm glad you came."

"Were you worried I wouldn't?"

"Yes, actually." I nodded, boring my eyes into hers. "I

thought I'd ruined any chance with you, and you wouldn't even read my letters."

"Well, now that I'm here, what do you think?"

"I'm still worried it's not what I want it to mean."

"Well, what do you want it to mean?" She grinned, moving closer to me.

"What is this? You're answering everything with a question," I teased.

Sawyer let out a throaty chuckle, and I felt my dick respond to the sound. "I guess I've been around the Agency people too much recently. Sorry, I didn't mean to be cagey. And I think I owe you an apology as well. You gave me one in your letters, and it was breathtaking. I'm not as eloquent with words, but I regret my behavior as well towards you. You were a dick, but I didn't have to direct all my hatred toward men at you that morning."

"Honestly, I didn't even care. Your fire awoke something up in me."

"Oh?" she purred, moving closer. "Well, I still want to say it. I'm sorry, Elias," she paused, almost like she was gathering herself. "Your letters... Well, they were beautiful. Thank you for sharing your true self with me." Sawyer was standing directly in front of me now, I could smell her pomegranate scent, and it filled my veins. In a voice I'd never heard from her before, she asked a question. "What did you want me being here to mean?"

Cautiously, I took my hand out of my pocket and placed it on her cheek. She didn't move away from the contact; in fact, she leaned into it. My fingers sank into her hair, and my thumb caressed the cheek it was resting on. Her eyes closed at the move, and I watched her relax completely into my touch.

"I hoped it wasn't too late for us to write our love story. I dreamed you would show up, and I would be able to feel our connection, to see it wasn't one-sided."

"And now?" she breathed, her eyes fluttering open. "Do you feel it? Is it how you dreamed?"

"Oh love, my dreams are poor imitations of reality. You are everything I never believed I could have. Having you here, touching you, has exceeded anything I could ever imagine. Sawyer love, if you couldn't tell from my words just how much I care about you, let me make it clear."

Taking a breath, I gazed into her eyes as I dropped all my walls and bared my soul to her. This was it, the one moment in my life that would mean everything. If there was ever a time to be completely vulnerable, it was now.

"When I saw you in the kitchen the first time, I thought I was seeing things. This beautiful Goddess was holding my dog. For a moment, I was stunned by the picture it presented to me, and I had a flash of what life could be like if you were mine. My twisted soul saw that as an attack. Making me want something I knew I didn't *deserve*."

Sucking in a breath, I placed my other hand on her neck, wrapping it in her long strands. "Mostly, I was jealous. Why did some other guy get to have you if I couldn't? The fear and longing twisted into self-loathing, and I projected it onto you. I made you into the thing I hated because I couldn't admit the truth."

A tear rolled down her cheek, and I brushed it aside. Tears were brimming in my own eyes, but I let them fall, not hiding who I was anymore.

"Your beauty and kindness captured my attention, but your heart and brain made me fall in love with you. Sawyer, love, you are the happy ending I was too scared to want, too afraid to admit, and too damaged to trust myself not to screw up. Jokes on me since I did that all on my own."

"Elias—"

Placing my finger on her lips, I halted her words. "Ssh, love. I need to finish this. When you started to date the other guys, I had front-row seats to see how this could work. I had to get out of my own way first, and well, I'm stubborn. But I'm here now, a broken man in most aspects, but a man who finally understands."

"What do you understand?" Sawyer's brow wrinkled, and her nose scrunched up, creating the cutest face. Grinning, I soaked in the sunshine she had to offer my darkness.

"That life isn't about doing everything perfectly. It's not about living a perfectly staged life. *Life is about love, and love is messy.* I want to roll around in the shit with you and the guys because when I'm with you, it's worth it. It doesn't matter that it's shit; it matters that we do it together. You showed me that all my broken pieces have a purpose, a home. *Sawyer, you are my home.*"

"Elias," she whispered, "will you shut up and kiss me now?"

Shock and fear I'd heard her wrong climbed my throat for a split second. But as Sawyer smiled, I couldn't help but match it. I hadn't imagined her words. Leaning in, I placed my lips gently against hers and sealed our souls together. My lips felt numb, and tingles raced through my body. No kiss had ever felt this monumental. Pulling back, I stared down into her eyes, wondering if she felt the same.

"Wow," Sawyer mumbled, and I started to relax in the knowledge we were in this together.

"As much as I wish we could redo things in the beginning, I don't know if we would've gotten to the same place," she admitted, her breath tickling my face. "Elias, I need you to know one thing. *You're not broken.* You're a part of the puzzle that makes BOSH. And though I've never been referred to as shit before." She smiled. "I like the concept. I'm glad I got to know the real you through your letters because it let me see the heart of who you are without our walls screwing it up."

Taking a breath, I watched as Sawyer fought against her own fears. "I realized I'd pushed so hard against you because you've always been the riskiest option for me."

"How so?"

"Because we are alike in so many ways, and you had the most power to break my heart."

"And did I?" I asked hesitantly.

"No, not at all. You showed me it was safe to be vulnerable through your own vulnerability. I fell irrevocably in love with you, Elias, through your words because it wasn't just words on paper. It was your heart."

"You love me?"

"Yes. I love you, Elias, you pretentious snob." She smiled wider, making everything feel right.

"Hey!"

"You can deny it all you want, but we both know it's true, and I don't care though, because it's you."

"It's a good thing you're so cute."

"I think your mouth has done enough talking for the night. How about you work it out another way?"

"Oh?" I asked, my voice husky. "What do you have in mind?"

Sawyer stepped back, my hands dropping away as she did. I missed the contact and thought perhaps I'd misread her statement at the loss of connection. With a smirk, she let the sash around her waist fall open and unzipped her coat. I felt like an ass when I realized she still had it on and how un-hostly I'd been the second she walked through that door.

As her outer layer fell away, I sucked in a breath at the beauty before me. Sawyer had on a tight dress that hugged her body, showcasing all of her curves. My hands yearned to travel over her body and to feel her beneath my palms. She folded her jacket over a chair and turned fully to me, and my mind faltered. Suddenly, I was glad I hadn't been a proper host because I doubt I'd have gotten through anything I said moments ago.

"*Fuck*, love."

"Yeah?" she asked shyly, and I wanted to take that look off her face. Sawyer should never feel anything other than the beautiful Goddess she was. It would be my mission to make sure she embraced every inch of herself.

Stepping forward, I grabbed her face and smashed my lips to hers. Sawyer's body melded to my front, and the passion and tension that had always been between us erupted in a fiery blaze. Grabbing her thighs, I lifted her, and she wrapped her legs around me as our tongues danced.

Her hands were woven in my hair, and it was exquisite torture as she pulled at the strands. Turning, I slowly made my way through the room as I tried to remember where the bed was located. Eventually, a wall came into view, and I pushed her up against it. We broke apart our kiss, and I traveled down her neck as she threw her head back with a moan. Her skin was soft and tasted as sweet as I'd imagined. Rubbing my nose over her pulse, I felt it race.

The feel of her legs around me had all my fantasies coming to life as she bucked up into me. Ever since the moment I watched her and Rhett together, I couldn't get her body out of my head. Their sexual escapades had spurred on several fantasies since then, including all three of us. Pulling back, I wanted to make sure we were both on the same page before I dived into the part of me I thought I had to hide.

"Love, I want you more than anything. I want to feel your hot pussy wrapped around my cock. But I won't go too far if you're not ready. I know we just had our first kiss. This isn't something I want to screw up."

"Elias, we've been tip-toeing around one another for over a month with foreplay and denying our inevitable combustion. There isn't anything holding me back now. My heart, body, and mind are yours. *I'm yours.*"

"And you said you weren't good with words."

Smiling, I turned us away from the wall and found the door that led to the king-size bed. Laying her back, I watched her reaction as I loosened my tie and tossed it aside. Sawyer rose to her knees, and I was captivated as she moved her hair to one shoulder and reached back to unzip her dress. The eroticism of the move wasn't lost on me as she lowered the fabric. My fingers slowly unbuttoned my shirt as I devoured every inch of her skin she presented.

Tossing my jacket and shirt aside, I stood before her, partially dressed, but focused on her as the dress fell away. Her breasts on display, I consumed them with my eyes. She sat back and pulled the dress away from her. I grabbed it and laid it across the back of a chair with my clothes, hoping it would keep it wrinkle-free. When I turned back around, she had a secretive smile on her face for me.

"What?"

"It's just sweet and thoughtful for you to do that. It's a side of you I never thought about." She shrugged. I stopped and considered it. Sawyer's words made sense, and I suppose I had gone out of my way not to be friendly around her so she wouldn't see my true feelings.

"Well, love, get used to it because I plan to spoil you and shower you with so much affection you never doubt my feelings for you."

"I can't wait," she beamed, falling back onto the bed. She unzipped one boot, watching as I pulled my pants down. We were in a stare-off with one another as we undressed. My focus entirely on her; I didn't know how she made taking off her boots one of the sexiest things I'd ever witnessed. Toeing off my shoes and socks, I watched from the end of the bed as she tossed her other boot off.

We were both only in our underwear, and I licked my lips as I took her in without any guilt. My feelings had been all over the place in the fitness room, but now I could drink my fill as long as I wanted. Yanking her by the hips to me, I dragged her panties down her legs slowly, never taking my eyes off hers as I did. I tossed them over my shoulder once I had them off, and shoved my boxers down before climbing onto the bed.

Like a predator, I crawled to my prey as I took her in. Sawyer's breathing hitched at my look, and I could see her taking in deep breaths as she watched me move closer. My earlier ministrations with her underwear had her leaned back on her elbows, her legs bent and open, offering me a splendid view. Her wetness coated her pussy lips, and as I got closer, I couldn't stop myself from leaning down and licking straight up her seam.

Sawyer moaned and bucked her hips up, forcing me to grab them to hold her still. Peering up over her mound, I licked my lips as she watched. Her eyes dilated more at the gesture, and the deviant part of me I thought I had to hide decided to come out and play. I dipped my finger into her and slowly pulled it back out. Sucking it down, I maintained eye contact as I twirled it around my tongue.

"Mmm, love, you taste divine. I can't wait to have my fill."

Snatching her hips down closer, I feasted on her wet pussy as she thrashed around on the bed. Pinning her legs, I held her still, torturing her with my tongue. When I began to feel her tighten around my fingers, I pulled back and placed tiny kisses over her stomach. Her huff of annoyance told me how she felt with my edging, but I didn't care. Right now was our time, and I planned to make up for the weeks of missed opportunities.

*Sawyer Sullivan was about to be owned.*

# twenty-six

· · ·

## sawyer

ELIAS PULLED AWAY from my core, and I wanted to scream at him. Instead, whimpers fell from my lips as I withered in unreleased ecstasy. I was getting ready to tell him where to shove it when he pulled my thighs closer, braced my knees over his shoulder, and speared me with his cock in one fell swoop. My mouth was stuck open mid-rant, allowing a loud moan to escape instead.

"Fuuucckk," I groaned as he started to thrust hard into me. I realized my eyes had closed, rolling to the back of my head with the force. Opening them, I found the beautiful God that was Elias above me. His tattooed chest and arms were on display as he held my legs tight to him, wanting every inch possible. His whiskey eyes were lit with a level of passion I'd never seen from him before, and it almost looked like they were on fire with how they glowed.

"Love, you feel better than I imagined wrapped around me. When I watched you and Rhett, all I could think about was being inside you. I wanted to pump you up and down on my cock while he watched. If you only knew all the dirty things I wanted to do to you."

Elias leaned down further, kissing me full of passion as he swirled his tongue around with mine. He kissed with his whole mouth and body, and no part of him felt left out as he ravaged my mouth. His hands felt like they were everywhere at once, and I knew it was an aftereffect of the sensations he'd built in me and then edged me to my orgasm. My body felt supercharged with a million tiny pleasure centers covering it.

I roamed my hands over his pecs and abs as I tried to commit them to memory, wanting never to forget the feel of him. It was like we couldn't stop touching one another for fear this was a dream, and the moment we stopped, we would wake up and be alone. With the way he was thrusting into me, there was no way my imagination could make up how decadent his cock would feel. Elias fucked unlike anyone I'd been with before.

He was a man possessed by desire, and I wanted it all. To be on the receiving end of it was mind-blowing. Elias pulled back from the kiss and grabbed my hips as he started to piston even deeper. My ankles rested on his shoulders as he held them together with his arms, creating more tightness between us. My hands grabbed onto the covers beside me in a desperate attempt to ground myself as my eyes rolled back and my orgasm slammed into me. Waves of pleasure washed through my body as he kept his pace.

"Fuck, Elias, oh my God, that feels so good. Don't stop, don't ever stop," I managed to mumble out.

"Never."

Elias started to pump into me at a pace I didn't think possible, and I swear I felt his cock hit my cervix. He was so deep in me, and I felt as if we were connected in a whole new way. At this moment, no lies or secrets were between us. In this room together, we were just Elias and Sawyer.

As the sound of skin slapping skin amplified around my moans, he dropped my legs and kissed me again. For some reason, my eyes stayed open during it, and I watched as the always perfect and put-together man fell apart inside me.

His release was beautiful as he pumped into me and held my eyes, intimacy ringing through each movement. Elias' emotions were clear on his face, and there was no doubt of his love for me. It was the freest I'd ever seen him, and it was heartbreakingly beautiful in the purest form.

"When I think about how much time we missed doing that, I want to go back and punch myself," I joked.

Elias smiled, and I swear I heard angels weeping at the sight of it. "It just means we get to make up for it now. Don't get too comfortable, love. I plan to have you on your knees with my cock deep in you again real soon."

My whole body tightened at his words, and I felt my walls squeeze his still hard cock. "Fuck, love. It might be sooner than later if you keep doing that."

The unspoken dare in his voice had my adrenaline pumping, and I found myself tightening my muscles voluntarily this time. "Whatever do you mean?" I asked innocently, all the while flexing and unflexing. *Thank you, Kegel exercises.*

Elias couldn't even speak as he moaned around the spasms, his cock still sensitive from his orgasm. I went to do it again but found myself being flipped, and my legs spread before I knew what was happening. Bracing myself against the headboard, I pushed back as he started to pound into me from behind.

"Two can play that game, love," came his husky voice.

Elias gripped my front with his arms and fucking owned me. One arm wrapped around me, snaking up to my throat as he lightly grasped it in his palm. The other dropped to cup my pussy and started to palm my clit. Pushing back against him with my hands on the headboard, I gave in to the sensations and surrendered my body to him.

"Yes, yes, yes. Fuck, you fuck me so good," I chanted, not even sure how to form words after a while as the sensations bombarded me.

Dropping my head back onto his shoulder, I peered into his eyes at this angle. Elias watched me with unadulterated possession and tenderness. Something on my face made him soften a little, and he lowered his mouth to mine and pecked my lips softly.

It was an odd experience. I felt the intense passion and force as he plundered into me from behind, owning my body as he held me by the throat and my clit. And yet, his eyes were reverent and his kiss adoring. My body was vulnerable to him, and his cock kept an unrelenting pace in and out of me. The kiss' sweetness and softness melted me entirely into him, giving him complete access to my body, heart, and mind.

This time, when I came around his cock, I felt him follow me. My body rippled with pleasure as it traveled from head to toe and sent me headfirst into ultimate bliss. I blinked my eyes open and found him watching me. We were lying on the bed now, me spooning in his arms. He leaned over me, just watching as I returned back to reality.

"*Wow*, again."

"Yeah, though, to be fair, you tempted the devil with that one."

"If that's what temptation feels like, sign me up."

"Do you think you have what it takes to tango with the devil, love?"

Turning, I ran my hands over his chest, tracing the tattoos I could see. The dragon was the largest one and took up most of his side. "You're not the devil, Elias. You might have some darkness in you or broken pieces, as you like to say, but you're not evil." Lifting my head, I held his eyes as I continued. "We all have things we carry, that we hide away from the world. It doesn't make us less than or unworthy."

Blushing, I tried to hide how fiercely protective I felt of him now and how much I wanted him to see himself for the wonderful man he was. Elias pulled me closer and draped my leg over him. I hadn't expected him to be so tactile and almost possessive in how he claimed my body. It didn't feel like he wanted to control me, more so that he needed to touch me, feel me, and demonstrate how he felt nonstop.

"Thanks, love. I'm starting to believe it. You make me want to."

Dropping my eyes back to his chest, my finger continued to run small patterns on his pec. "I read the letter you sent Rhett. He couldn't, so I read it out loud for him. So, I heard the things you said about feeling like you needed to be worthy, that you had to prove you were a great man, and I just wanted you to know that you already are." Raising my eyes, I found his eyes swimming with emotions.

"I think it was why I was so angry at you. I saw the man you were and how you loved your housemates, and I wanted to be part of that. And then when you dismissed yourself from the equation, I wanted to shake you and yell and scream at you, but my stubbornness got in the way."

"Love, I was a bloody fool and stuck in my own way. Hearing you say those words, though, that I am worthy... it's made me want to believe it. You make me believe I can be."

We laid together, listening to our heartbeats and breaths, no other words needed. A while later, he broke the silence with a question I hadn't expected.

"What the hell is *BOSH*?"

Laughing, I shared with him all the terrible names the guys had offered and how Mateo had surprised us all with BOSH.

"I like it. I'm glad I get to be part of BOSH." He kissed my nose and pulled me tighter to him, and I fell asleep on his chest, feeling my world was complete.

Elias and my time in our cocoon ended sooner than I wanted. I found the man insatiable as we spent more time than not naked and entwined around one another. I was spreading cream cheese on a bagel when a knock sounded at the door the following morning. Elias put down his paper, he was like an old man reading it while he drank his coffee, and it was too cute to tease him about it. He dropped a kiss on my forehead as he passed, and I tried not to swoon into a pile of goo at the gesture.

Since we had laid our souls bare to one another, the intimacy had grown exponentially between us. His letters having played a significant part in that, allowing me to see him without either of our stubborn pride getting in the way.

The dark rumble of my grump from the door had me leaping off the stool and racing to him. Before Rhett had time to react, I leapt for him and wrapped myself around him as I placed kisses all over his face. My grumpy love was accustomed to catching me at this point, so I didn't have any repeats of the failed bounce like I did from our first time together. Despite that experience, I couldn't seem to stop leaping into his arms. There was something about the tall man that made you want to throw yourself at him. At least, that was what I told myself.

"Hi," I beamed after I'd placed a million kisses.

"Hey baby, it seems you missed me."

"Yup." I grinned, only able to get out one-worded answers, apparently.

Chuckling, Rhett carried me over to the couch and sat down, as usual, with me in his lap; I squeezed him tight, trying to soak up all of his Rhettness. Once I had my fill, I turned on his lap and found Elias. He was watching us from the bar, the same pose as yesterday. Some of his mask was back in place, and I realized he was nervous. Elias hadn't been with Rhett and me since our time in the gym, and while we had moved past that, I think he was worried about it.

Tilting my head, I motioned him to the other side of the couch. The corner of his lips lifted in a small smile, and he nodded before making his way over and sitting down. As soon as his butt hit the sofa, I plopped my legs in his lap and leaned back against Rhett's chest. *Now, this was nice.* Rhett's vibrating chest clued me in on the fact I had said the last part out loud. Oops.

"I guess you two made up?"

"So many times." I grinned and wiggled a little on his lap. His answering moan had me flashing back to our last time together, and I instantly became aroused and shifted my legs to get some friction. Wearing Elias' shirt and some knee-high socks, it wasn't hard to figure out what I was doing. Elias wrapped his hands around my ankles, stopping my movement.

"Sawyer, love, as much as I want to go where your mind is, there's a reason for Rhett being here that doesn't involve us all naked."

At Elias' word, I felt Rhett start to harden more beneath

me, and it was a downward battle to stop myself. However, Elias' serious look had me focusing on him, and I nodded. "Okay, why did you ask him here?"

"I have a plan to take down Director Donnelly, and you two are part of it."

That stopped my movement, and I focused on what he was saying. "Go on," I encouraged, excited to hear how we could make the scumbag in charge pay for all the young women and men he'd manipulated.

Chaos, or Cohen, had come to us earlier in the week with some news. He'd found information regarding the dalliance with Jill on the flash drive and that Donnelly had been black-mailing Phil as well. The whole scandal was twisted, but the water damage had corrupted most of the files. It was all technological mumbo jumbo I didn't understand.

Donnelly had been placed on leave while the school board investigated after the few things recovered had been sent to the board and the national skating council. At least in this instance, the school board and skating council proved to be helpful in making sure specific actions were taken against Donnelly.

"First, you will ask for a meeting, claiming you have evidence that will free him. He's been hard to get in touch with, but he does seem to have a fixation on you based on your reports, so I think you would be able to sway him. Then, we lead him into a trap."

As Elias explained the rest of the plan and how Rhett fit in, I began to grow excited for an entirely different reason. This could work and be the first sign of justice we got for the damage we'd suffered. Donnelly might not be connected directly to my parents, but he'd harmed impressionable youths and used his position in disgusting ways. His connection to the Council was the icing on my kick-butt cake. His dismissal would hopefully weaken them and expose their underbelly. It was time to strike, and I was ready.

After our discussion, we watched a movie and ordered room service. I texted the guys from Rhett's phone and felt bad for ignoring them all, but Elias and I had needed this time to ourselves to find our way to one another. I stayed between them all afternoon and rotated laps. Despite my earlier brazenness, nothing else occurred between the three of us, and when Rhett and I left, I kissed Elias with everything I had, hoping it would bring him back to me quickly.

# twenty-seven

· · ·

## tyler

AFTER SAWYER'S message about a plan for the Director, she called on the burner phone and told me some key points to inform Samson. I was to meet up with him now since I had Agency clearance. Even though I knew he was her uncle now, I still kind of wanted to punch him at times. I should probably work on that, because I planned to be in her life moving forward.

The security to get into the complex was intense, and I kept forgetting the time it added to my arrival time. I was running late, and the elevator line was long. Deciding to take the stairs, I hoofed it up two at a time. I hadn't expected to come upon a hushed conversation a few floors up. Quietly, I edged my way to see if I could hear better and perhaps see who it was. Based on the whisper shouts I could make out, it didn't sound like a friendly conversation.

"You said if I did one thing, I was clear. I'm out. You keep pushing for more, and it's going to get us caught!"

"You mean you?"

"We both know I'm not the only guilty one here!"

"Maybe not, but you're the only one with their finger-prints on the evidence."

"What? That's impossible. I didn't even handle it."

"Doesn't matter. The Agency knows there's a mole. It only takes suspicion or doubt for them to start thinking it's you."

"But it's not me! It's you. You did this on purpose! You framed me!"

"I don't remember having to force you."

"That's because you lied to me! You told me it was for something else. You've been planning this from the begin-ning, haven't you? Oh, man, this is bad. This is so bad. I can't go to jail. I'll never survive."

"Calm yourself, Constance. It doesn't have to go in that direction. You just need to do one more thing for me."

"No, this is how it starts. I do one thing, and then you have me on two. I'll just turn myself in."

"Ah ah ah, that wouldn't be wise. Think of your daughter. What do you think will happen to her? Hmm? Besides, I already have her. I hoped it wouldn't come to this, but she gets a bullet if you don't follow through. Do we have an understanding?"

"Yes."

I could hear her fear as they said the last part, tears being held back. Leaning forward, I tried to get a glimpse of the two, but all I could see were their shoes. The door to the floor I was on opened, almost smacking me in the head.

"Oh hey, sorry, didn't mean to almost hit you there," the man apologized, but fear-filled me as I darted off the floor the door had opened on. I prayed the people above us hadn't seen me. I had a feeling I wouldn't survive if they had.

Panting, I ran down the hall and hid in a restroom stall for ten minutes. Once my heart rate had decreased, I snuck out of the bathroom and headed to the elevators for the rest of the way, not willing to risk it. They might be lying in wait for me in the stairwell.

When I finally knocked on Samson's door, I was officially thirty minutes late. His scowl as he answered told me how he felt about it too. I kept my mouth shut and watched as he closed the door. He leaned back against it, crossing his arms as he stared at me.

"Weren't you the one who called this meeting, Tyler? And yet, you have the gall to be late? *Really late.*"

Picking up a pad of paper on his desk, I wrote out a message. *When was the last time you did a sweep?*

Samson saw my note and walked over, concern showing on his face. "An hour ago, why?"

Writing out again, *no one else has been here since?*

"No, just me."

Relaxing, I sat in the chair and motioned for him to take his seat.

"First, I was coming to update you on a plan for Donnelly.

But on my way here, I overheard something in the stairwell. That's what took so long, well that, and the security."

"I'm listening," he responded, his scowl dropping, and he relaxed back in his seat.

"There's a mole, but the person about to be identified was doing it for what they thought was an Agency task, but now, they're being blackmailed if they don't do something else."

"Did you recognize who they were?"

"No, I couldn't get a good look before someone interrupted. But I did hear the name Constance and see their shoes."

"Their shoes?"

"Yeah. They were very *unique*," I hedged, "you should be able to identify them, but I don't know if they were the mole's or the innocent's. It sounded like Constance was the one being framed, something about her daughter."

"Well, let's start there, and we can figure the rest out. Thank you for bringing it to my attention. Now, you said there's a plan?"

"Elias contacted Sawyer and figured out a way to get the Director out of hiding and connect it to the Council."

Samson listened as I shared with him the few things Sawyer had told me when she called earlier. They'd been hush-hush on most of the details, in case our phones were tapped. It was the most spy stuff I'd done in a while, and it had my blood pumping. I didn't think I wanted to live this life, but with Sawyer, it was fun. It might be a conversation to have after we weren't trying to save her life.

"I'll get you guys whatever you need. Just tell me when."

Samson nodded, on board. "Thanks for including me, Ty. Now, what were these shoes you saw?"

"Um, well, I'm not an expert, but they were quite ugly, but they had those red soles, so I know from Fin they're expensive. They were bright orange. I'm talking almost neon. I doubt many women are wearing them today."

Samson nodded, a look of recognition on his face at my statement. Using the time range I'd been in the stairwell, they could watch and pinpoint their companion as well. Technology was amazing, and I tried to remember that as I went back through security to ensure I wasn't leaving with anything classified. The next time, Samson was meeting *me* because this was ridiculous.

Asa and Ollie were on the ice with the senior-level hockey guys when I made it to the rink. The slap of the sticks was a soothing balm to my frayed nerves. Leaning against the rails, I watched as Ollie skated around the players, demonstrating a skill. He was magnificent on the ice and had a genuine love for the sport. He was one of those people who was blessed with talent and passion.

At the whistle, the players demonstrated what he'd shown them, and I watched as one of the left-wing players stole the puck and blasted the guy into the boards. Cringing for him, I headed to the locker rooms to get in some weight training before the junior guys arrived in about an hour.

I was on my second set of weights when I heard the door crash against the wall, followed by cursing. Setting them back into place, I wiped the sweat off my face as I headed to see who it was. It had to be one of the other instructors because I was on the staff side of the locker room, and practice still had about twenty minutes left. When I turned the corner and found Asa sitting with his head braced in his hands, mumbling under his breath.

"You okay, man?" He jumped at my voice and lifted his head to meet my eyes. Walking closer, I could see the stress and possibly fear warring in his eyes.

"Asa? Is everything okay? Is it Sawyer?"

"Sawyer's fine. This is… Fin, and my *dad*."

"Want to talk about it? I'm a good listener and an outside party, so I've got no allegiance to either."

"Except that you date my sister."

"Well, we can pretend that part doesn't exist at the moment. I just met Fin, though, so I wouldn't feel loyal to her over you, is what I'm saying. Not that I'm not loyal to all of us, I just meant—"

"Okay, dude." He chuckled. "I get it. And I guess you're right. You weren't friends with her like all the other guys. It's just, ever since she returned from being taken, she's been different. She's distant, and I get that she went through something traumatic; I just want to be there for her. But she won't talk to me about it. I'm not blind either," he grumbled. "I can see there's something between her and another guy, but she keeps telling me that everything is *fine*. Things are so far from fine. I'm about to shout if I hear that word again!"

"Okay, okay. I can hear how stressed you are, and it's going to make you explode if you don't do something about it. Tell me the father part, and we can figure something out."

"My father is a whole other bag of worms. I don't think there's anything to be done about him yet. He's just pushing me to take some responsibility, not knowing that I know what a huge asshole and slimeball he is, so I've just been pushing him off, and he's getting pushier. He wants to have dinner with me before he leaves town."

"Fucking hell, dude. That sucks."

"Hence, my frustration now."

"But why now? Did something happen to set you off out there?"

"Ah, yeah." He grimaced. "I might've been taking it out on the kids. Ollie sent me to cool off. I was yelling and cursing at him for it, but he had every right. I hate that I'm letting it get to me that much. I guess I hadn't realized how much I was bottling up, but I got my father's text right before practice started."

"Hey, it happens to all of us. And usually, hockey is a great place to exorcise your demons, but it's usually better if it's not directed at the teens," I teased. "So, Fin... I think you have to let her come to you when she's ready. You can't force someone to deal with their trauma if that's what's going on."

"Yeah, you're right, and I know that," Asa twisted the towel in his hands, frustration leaking out of him. "I hate the whole inactive part. I'm a doer, I like to *do*, and this is driving me crazy because I can't fix it."

"Maybe all you need to do to 'fix it' is be there. Quit

339

pushing and listen to what she wants. She's telling you with her actions. You just need to drop your own agenda first to hear it."

"Huh, I never thought about it like that," he admitted, some of his anger leaving him. "But... What about the other stuff?"

"You mean her potential feelings for someone else?"

"Yeah, how do you deal with that? I never really had to think about it because once I knew Sawyer was my sister, she was already with the guys at the house, so I accepted it as it was. Now, I'm wondering how to make it fit with my world, and I feel like I'm missing a lot of pieces."

"And I might not have the ones you want." I laughed. "Sawyer and I had a very different start than anyone else. She was so different in high school than she is now, and at the time, the only thing she could do was a 'friends with benefits' relationship with me and another friend." I blushed, admitting that to her brother. "Now, I understand why, but back' then, I was a teen who just saw a girl who was my friend and easy sex. Sorry, no disrespect."

"None taken. It's weird to hear about a life you weren't part of, you know?"

"Yeah, I get that. It wasn't until a year into our arrangement that I started to develop deeper feelings. She wasn't ready for more back then. My relationship with Sawyer has always had more than one person in it. And I guess when I realized I was kind of in love with two people myself, I could understand where she was coming from. Love isn't limited, and as long as everyone is upfront about their feelings and where they stand, why can't you all be together?"

He tilted his head, a look of contemplation on his face. "You've given me a lot of things to think about that I hadn't considered. I guess this was a good idea, to, you know, talk," he admitted. "Thanks, Ty."

"Anytime, man. I hope to be in your life, you know. So, if you ever need anything or want to talk again, I'm here."

"I'd like that."

Asa got up, and I realized it was getting closer to my class time, so I cleaned up the area I'd been in and got dressed in my gear for practice. Ollie caught me as I was lacing up my skates.

"Hey, boyfriend!"

"Hey, Ols. Are we labeling each other now? Do we have pet names?" I chuckled, bent over to finish my knot.

"Um, of course," he scoffed, a grin on his face. "We are so *that* couple!"

"If you say so, poo bear," I teased. Ollie laughed, and I still found myself amazed at the lightness and joy I found with him now.

"How was practice?"

"Good. They're making progress with the slapshot."

"Yeah, I got to admire you while you went over that. You're so hot on the ice," I flirted, standing up. My skates gave me a few more inches, making my height the same as his. Standing in his space, he pushed me against the locker, catching me off guard.

"Oh, yeah. Tell me more about that?"

My heart raced, and my blood pumped toward my cock in rapid succession. It pressed against my cup as I got hard, and it was a pain I hadn't expected. At my wince, Ollie pulled back, concern on his face.

"What? What is it?"

"Just you being too hot. Fuck! Getting hard in a jockey cup, don't recommend it!" I groaned as I tried to think of things to take my mind off of it. Ollie laughed boisterously, and I decided to remove myself from the temptation. Muttering under my breath, I flipped him off over my shoulder, making my way out to the ice.

"Ah, don't be that way, muffin!"

"Ha, ha. See you later, troublemaker."

His laughter followed me out the door, and despite the temporary pain I'd felt, I couldn't help the smile that graced my lips as I skated onto the ice. Ollie was definitely a troublemaker, but he was my troublemaker, and I could live with that.

# twenty-eight

. . .

## rey

HUMMING, I strummed out a few more chords on the guitar as I tried to work out the key change and chord progression I was going for. I'd been working on a surprise for Sawyer's birthday, and since we didn't get to celebrate it last week, I was looking forward to the redo to share it with her. I was shitting myself, no doubt about that, but I was also weirdly enjoying it.

Scribbling something in my notebook, a knock at the door stole my attention. Setting my guitar on my bed, I got up to answer the door. I'd shut it so Sawyer wouldn't hear what I was up to. I wanted to surprise her, and so far I'd been able to keep it under wraps. Their party was tomorrow night, so I was in the home stretch.

Opening the door, I found a grinning Soren on the other

side. "Well, hello, handsome," he cooed. No matter how many times he flirted with me, I found myself still blushing. Soren noticed, and it only made his smile amp up.

"Hey, back. What's up, Sor?"

"Well, I had some free time and thought I'd come to bug you." He grinned at me.

Opening my door wider, I happily let him enter. "Be my guest."

Soren passed me and very casually grazed my crotch as he walked by. My cock woke up and took notice of the touch. Once I understood I needed a deep connection to be sexual with someone, it was crazy how much my sexual appetite had increased. I'd always felt strange as a teen when all my peers were comparing their conquests, and I had no interest. At first, I'd assumed it was just because I missed Sawyer, but I found little to no regard for the act with each passing year.

At one point, I assumed I was defective, so after getting drunk at a party, I lost my virginity, fumbling around in the back of a Volkswagen. There'd been only two other times, and neither had been enjoyable. That wasn't how it was with Soren and Sawyer. With them, I became a sex-crazed teen, just like all my peers had been. It was a relief in a way to know I wasn't defective or malfunctioning.

Soren dropped down onto the bed, careful not to shake my guitar. He made himself at home, leaning back against my pillows, his arms behind his head in his classic pose. Soren's long locks fanned out around him, and his shirt lifted some. I swear the man was always tempting me with his abs and golden happy trail. Licking my lips, I caught his smirk out of the corner of my eye and knew I'd been right.

*Soren Stryker was a fucking tease.*

Ignoring my arousal, I sat back on the corner of the bed and picked up my guitar. Ever since he'd heard me play, I'd felt more comfortable playing around him. Strumming the chords, I fell into a trance and lost myself to the music. When I came to the end of the song, I felt his arms wrap around me from behind, his head dropping down on my shoulder as he kissed my cheek.

"That was beautiful, Rey."

Turning slightly, I caught his eyes as I spoke, "Yeah? I'm going to play it for Smalls on her birthday."

"She's going to love it."

"Thanks."

"Of course, though, I should be thanking you since you played that for me."

Laughing, I turned back and managed to get my guitar put in the case, despite Soren continuing to hold on to me. It was like having an overly large koala on my back. Once it was secured, I threw my weight back, making him land on the bed with me on top of him now. I felt like a turtle in his shell; chuckles erupted out of us both at the position.

"You're incorrigible."

"Maybe, but you love it." He grinned more, effectively melting my heart in the process. Turning sideways, I shifted off him so I could see him better. His hand fell to my hip, and I brushed his hair out of his face.

"Some days, I wonder what I did to get so lucky to find you," I whispered.

"Nothing."

"Huh?" My face screwed up at his answer. Soren laughed and finally took pity on me.

"Us finding one another has nothing to do with luck. It doesn't work that way. We found one another because we chose to. We make our own luck, Rey."

"What about soulmates? Do you not believe in those?"

"Not in the sense you're meaning. Basically, I don't think things are out of our control. People come into your life and what they mean to you is up to you. Being vulnerable and opening your life to someone is hard… scary. Taking that risk and choosing to be open to the possibility it might work or it might not, that's all on you. You're my soulmate in the sense that my heart latched onto you and didn't want to let go. You fit me in ways I never knew possible. Add in Sawyer, and I feel like my heart is the fullest it's ever been. My life is better because you two are in it, but it had nothing to do with luck. It had everything to do with trust and courage. That's what love is at the end of the day. Trusting someone with the most precious thing you have and being brave enough to leave it with them."

"I guess I never thought about it that way, but I like how you see it. It means my fate is up to me, and I'd choose you a hundred times over."

"Ditto, babe, ditto."

Smiling, I laid my head on his chest, and we somehow fell asleep in one another's arms.

The first thing I noticed was the cold. The second was the odd texture, and the third was the smell. Peeking open my eyes, bright pink lines met me. What the hell?

Sitting up quickly, I found the pink stuff coating my entire body. Looking over at Soren, I found him covered as well, but his was green. *We'd been silly-stringed.* Giggling had me turning as a flash of a camera went off, blinding me for a minute. When a blond head raced out of the room, I reacted and took off after her.

When I got out in the hall, though, I couldn't figure out which direction she'd gone. Checking her room first, I wasn't surprised when I didn't find her in there. It was the most obvious choice, and Smalls wouldn't have headed there. Trying Soren's room next, I was met with another empty space.

Deciding to try all the rooms, I started going into them all, trailing pink silly strings as I went. When I got to Ollie's room, I still hadn't found her. I started to wonder if I was going crazy and had only imagined her. Rubbing the back of my head, I decided I must've missed her in one of the rooms. Stepping into the hallway, my phone vibrated and halted my search.

The group text had a picture of Soren and I covered in silly string, and then one of me waking up looking at the stuff oddly. Rhett responded immediately, rewarding them points, and I was surprised to see we were now only ahead of them by five points. *Shit*! We had a week left in the prank war, and we needed to do something epic to win.

Before I could plot more revenge, another text came in asking everyone to meet in HQ. Stomping back to my room, I flung off the silly string and woke up a disgruntled Soren. When he spotted the silly string, he released a loud laugh, and my bad mood could only handle so much pouting. Soren continued to laugh and give them credit, and I had to admit, it was funny. Smiling finally, I shook my head and picked off the last of the pink stuff.

Smalls thought she was exempt from the pranks because she was our girlfriend. I think I needed to show her how equal we all were. Thinking of ideas for my girl, a pep filled my step, and I joined Soren as we headed downstairs. Oh, this was going to be fun.

We walked into the room a few minutes later, and everyone laughed when they saw us. I guess I hadn't been the greatest at getting all the pink strings out of my hair. Smalls was almost out of her chair from laughing so hard. Walking over to her, I shook my head and tried to drop as much onto her as I could. Soren sauntered in without a care in the world, picked her up, and sat back in the chair with her in his lap. He nuzzled into her neck, and I watched as she melted into him.

Well, fuck. That was definitely a better move. All hail Sor and his lackadaisicalness. Laughing, I took the seat a few over between Mateo and Tyler. Mateo smiled at me, and I remembered my promise to include him more. He'd be a loner if we let him, and I didn't want him to feel that way. He was weirdly the odd man out with everyone else having a guy best friend counterpart. Sometimes it sucked being the last to arrive. Well, screw that. He could be my best friend too. I was going to be polyfriendous.

Feeling happy with my decision, I hadn't noticed everyone was looking at me. A squish ball hit me upside the head, and I turned to see who'd thrown it. Ollie had a look of innocence that screamed guilt. Picking it up, I threw it back at him, catching him off guard. Our playing around was too much for Rhett, and he leaned over and grabbed the ball from Ollie before he could retaliate.

"Guys, come on. Focus. We need to finalize our plan for Director Dickhead."

"Finalize? Meaning there's a plan already?" I asked, feeling a little left out.

"Uh, yeah. Elias has a plan." Sawyer blushed.

I couldn't help the smile that spread across my face at her blush. I guess they'd patched things up. The woots that followed from Ollie only made her crimson more pronounced, and when he started singing *"Elias and Sawyer sitting in a tree,"* she covered her face into Soren's arms. Even Rhett didn't redirect Ollie that time. Elias was our brother, and I was glad they'd found their way to each other. I was still pissed at him for leaving the way he had, and he would need to grovel, but at this moment, I could be happy for two people I cared about.

Sawyer picked her head up, and the confident girl she'd become shone through, "Yes, okay. Elias and I don't hate each other anymore, and we screwed our brains out. There, can we move on now? I'd like to take Donnelly down."

"What's Elias' plan?" Mateo asked in an attempt to move the conversation along. Sawyer smiled gratefully at him before responding.

"It's simple, and that's what makes it so brilliant, but it will include all of you."

As Sawyer detailed out the plan Elias had made, Tyler added the parts he'd gotten from Samson as well. Rhett highlighted the different roles we'd all need to play, and I couldn't find any fault in it. It seemed too simple to work. But maybe there was credence in the whole K.I.S.S. concept; *keep it simple stupid.* Complicated things made things too complex and more likely to fail.

"When are we putting this into play?" Soren asked.

"Tonight."

"Tonight? Okay… Well, that puts things into perspective. Anyone else getting sweaty?" I asked, clearing my throat.

"It's now or never, champ." Smalls grinned.

Laughing awkwardly, I got up with the rest of them and headed to get ready. It seemed we had a Director to take down tonight. Mateo clapped me on my shoulder, and I realized he was the one comforting me this time. Smiling, I thanked him and channeled his calmness. We could do this. We were BOSH, after all.

# twenty-nine

. . .

## sawyer

I WAS NERVOUS, but I didn't want the guys to know. If I showed my true feelings, it would make them worry more, and I couldn't have that. I finally felt I was getting somewhere, that I would get justice for all the atrocities that had occurred in my life. I needed this more than I realized. It was time.

Taking a deep breath, I walked up to the room Donald Donnelly was staying in. Once the committee had put him on suspended leave under further investigation, he'd vanished. We hadn't heard from his ex-wife either, who was hiding out of the public eye. With Chaos, or Cohen's, help, we'd been able to track Donald to a crappy motel a few towns over.

The eerie similarity to my adventures the day before to meet Elias didn't escape me, but this place was no five-star resort. In fact, one of the Yelp reviews had said, *"This is the worst place I've ever stayed. Nightmares have nightmares of this place."* I'd need a full-body scrub down just to wash off the filth when I left here.

Room 3C loomed before me, and I raised my shaky hand to knock. *"You got this baby,"* Rhett's voice boomed in my ear, causing me to jump. I'd temporarily forgotten they were there. Clutching my hand to my chest, I heard a few of the guys chuckle through the earpiece. Flipping them off over my shoulder, it had at least taken off the layer of fear. Embracing my sassy pants, it was time to kick some butt.

*Knock, Knock.*

The sound echoed back to me in the quiet space, and I wondered if we'd gotten it wrong. Maybe this wasn't the place? I was just about to leave when the door opened a crack, and an eye peered back at me.

"Director Donnelly?"

"Sawyer? Is that you?"

"Yeah, it's me, Director. Can I, um, come in for a minute?"

"Now isn't the best time, Sawyer." He started to shut the door, and I panicked. I couldn't lose my opportunity.

"Wait! Please, I need help, and I didn't know who I could talk to about it. You've always been so nice to me." My lip trembled, hoping to sway him. I cast my eyes down, fidgeting. "I just thought… But you're right. It's not a good time. I'll just go."

Mustering up some fake tears, I made my voice wobble as I turned around to leave. I hoped he'd take the bait and drop his guard. The door shut as I took a step away, and I feared

I'd lost him. A minute later, the sound of the chain being released sounded, and as I took another step, the door opened.

I was halfway to the stairs, so I kept my head down, hair in my face to give the illusion I was still crying.

"Sawyer, wait. You can come in."

Hiding my smile, I slowly turned and walked toward him, shuffling my feet as I went. Keeping my head down, I sold my story. This time when Rhett spoke into my ear, I didn't jump. *"Good job, baby. Keep going. We're all here with you."*

I had a tiny camera and earbud on me so they could hear and see what was happening. A few of them were in a room close by, and the others in a vehicle ready to go if we needed to hightail it out of here. I was confident it was the only reason why Rhett wasn't freaking out about sending me in with a child molester.

Elias' plan had been simple—use Donnelly's weakness against him. While I wasn't an underage student, I had the vulnerability aspect he preyed on. It was our 'in' to get the info we needed to cripple him and the Council.

"Sawyer, is everything okay?"

He touched my arm as I walked through the door, and I held back the involuntary flinch his touch produced. He needed to believe my interest, or he'd clam up before it even started.

"I just, I…" The tears started to fall again, and I was amazed at my ability to pull it off. Maybe all the shit I'd been through was good for something—instant tears.

He pulled me into a hug, and I counted to five before pulling away. Mostly because I needed the camera to see him, but selfishly, I didn't want to be touched by him. If the Almond Joy I felt pressing against my middle was any indication, Donnelly was aroused by the thrill of manipulating me. He was truly vile.

I bit the inside of my cheek to keep the bile back. Perched on the end of the bed, I hoped it would give me enough space away. *These clothes would need to be burned later.* It wasn't even from the bed bug reports this place had or the nastiness I could see on his sheets. No, it was having to be in his presence.

Folding my hands in my lap, I tried to focus on the words I needed to utter. The guys went quiet thankfully, I didn't know if I could tune them out otherwise.

"I hope you don't mind me showing up. I had a friend trace you. I know that was wrong, but I think you're the only one who will understand," I admitted sheepishly.

*"Good Sawyer, pull him into a false sense of security and feed his ego. You're doing great, Wildcat."*

Donnelly sat down next to me, and I tried to keep my body turned so he couldn't touch me. How had he lured teens in? He was such a creep and gave me that instant ew vibe. Donnelly placed his hand on my knee, and I started breathing deeply to not panic. I could hear Mateo's soft reassurance in the background, helping me count my breaths, and it soothed me.

Once my heart was calmer, I looked up at him. "Jill, she

—" but before I could finish, he pulled his hand back, shutting down.

"I don't know what you're talking about. I think you should leave. This was a mistake."

Shit! Shit! Shit!

"No, please, I didn't mean it that way. Just that she told me you were a good listener, that you *helped* her. I know you're not what they're saying. You're a good man, and you were just helping. Right?"

Have you ever had one of those moments where you have no idea how you did something?

On the ice, I knew this feeling well. Sometimes you had to shut your brain off to perform the jumps and rely on your muscle memory to carry you through. Otherwise, you'd terrify yourself with all the horrible ways it could go wrong. At that moment, in his room, my brain did something similar. I jumped into crisis mode, and my mouth did the talking. Fortunately, it seemed to have worked because he sat back down, even if it was further away. Swallowing, I tried to keep my panic at bay to avoid ruining my shot.

"You're right. I am a good man, and these allegations against me are false," he spewed.

His anger was right on the surface now, and I needed to wade through this delicately. I couldn't afford for him to withdraw again or, worse, pop off the handle and do something to me. The guys would be inside this room within two seconds if I were to get hurt again, still angry from the last time he left bruises on me. The knowledge they were near eased me, and I focused back on the task at hand.

"There are already students arguing for your return. You'll see. I'm sure you'll be back within the week."

"Humph. It serves them right to allow these outrageous claims against me. Maybe I won't even return unless they double my salary."

He smiled vindictively at the thought, and I was thankful for the knowledge he wouldn't be returning to campus, much less with a salary increase. The man was a deluded narcissist if he believed he was getting a fucking promotion after this!

Nodding along with him, I found it easier to agree if I didn't have to say the words. He seemed to come out of his overinflated stupor and remember I was there. A salacious smile appeared, and I gulped, trying to stay focused on the task at hand.

"So Sawyer, did Jill say anything else? Did she talk about the special lessons we had?"

"Um, no. What kind of lessons?" I gave my most innocent look, blinking up at him, giving the picture of a desperate girl.

"Tell me your problems, Sawyer, and I'll see if I can help."

Falling into the topics I'd practiced earlier, I told him about finding I had a twin and meeting my biological mother, but now, I was confused and there'd been a big fight between my brother and me. I rambled on and on with my sob story, hoping to pull him into my web.

His hand kept creeping up my leg, and if he moved it any higher, I didn't know if I'd be able to stay in character. I wanted him to go down, but I had no intention of becoming another of his statistics in the process. Shifting a little to cross my legs, I moved over, so his hand fell away naturally.

"I just don't know what to do, Director," I finished, looking up at him as if he had the answer.

"Wow, Sawyer, I had no idea. You must feel very alone."

Again, he moved closer, and I had to keep breathing not to give him a good throat punch. I needed to move this along before I found myself in a position I didn't want to be. Standing up, I started pacing, pretending I was anxious. Scratch that; I was fucking anxious! I didn't have to pretend— bloody hell. Ah, shit, I was spiraling! I was starting to sound like Elias in my head. His cum had penetrated my brain, slowly turning me British!

My breathing picked up, and I started to see dark spots at the corners of my eyes. No! I couldn't pass out. That would be the worst possible choice. Mateo's voice came through to me finally, well all the guys were shouting at me, but I heard him and listened.

*"Dulzura, it's okay. You're doing great. Just breathe. In and out slowly. Focus on what you're there to do."*

Slowly, I found my heart rate as I paced the room. Thankfully, Donnelly hadn't moved while I was panicking other than to sit back and lounge on the bed. I think he was trying to seem more inviting? Sexy? I tried not to focus on his reason and was happy he hadn't tried to approach me.

"Thank you," I mumbled, hoping the guys knew it was for them, comforted when they calmed down.

"I do feel alone, and there's just so much *pressure*. Jill, she um, she said that you knew people. That you could get me in touch with someone who makes all my dreams come true?"

"I could do that. I didn't realize you were so close to Jill, though."

Donnelly sat up, an indecipherable look crossing his face. Shit, shit! Thinking fast, I answered without thinking, "Oh yeah, she's one of my boyfriend's students, so I saw her a lot. Do you know where she is?"

He sat up and closed off, and I knew I'd just overplayed my hand.

"You know what, I think it's time you left."

"I'm sorry, Donald," I squeaked, hoping his name would make him more comfortable again. "I didn't mean to ask that. It's just all jumbled in my head. I fought with Henry today on top of all the things I already told you, and I'm just going out of my mind."

Donald softened a little, but was still suspicious. Sitting back on the bed, I tried to keep my distance but hopefully get him back to the safe spot where he'd confess something. "Do you think you could, um, you know, *help me*?"

He watched me, and I hoped I hadn't blown it. Biting my lip, I fidgeted with my hands and awaited my fate. I didn't have to fake the anxiety this time either. Everything was on the line here. This was the moment that would either propel me forward or send me crashing to the floor, mainly because if he touched me again, one of our asses was going on the floor.

"Let's say I did have someone I could connect you with. That could help make all your Olympic dreams come true.

What would you be willing to do for me?" He scooted closer, closing me in on the bed with his arm behind me. Donald brushed some hair behind my ear, and I couldn't control my body from tensing at his touch.

"Um, anything?" I hedged. He trailed his finger down my neck, and my body shuddered again, and a whimper followed. I could hear the guys screaming at me to just get out of there, to save myself, and we'd find another way. But I was so close, I could feel it. I just needed to push myself a little.

"Ssh, Sawyer, just relax. If you want the things I did for Jill, you need to be a good girl like her. Did she tell you all the naughty things she let me do. Fuck, that girl was dirty."

I ignored his words and focused on him finally admitting to his relationship with Jill. "I miss her. I just wish I knew if she was okay, you know."

Donald looked at me, and I gave my best naive eyes with some tears. It must've worked because he spilled *everything*.

"I could take you to her," he tried to move toward my neck again. I couldn't take it again, so I faked a sneeze. I almost head-butted him in the process, but thankfully he'd been quick enough to get out of the way. Keeping my hands over my nose, I mumbled through them, "Could you get me something to blow my nose? Some toilet paper?"

He looked annoyed at the request but rolled his eyes, getting off the bed and heading into the tiny bathroom further into the room. As soon as he was out of sight, I grabbed the phone I'd seen on the nightstand and replaced it with the clone one I had in my pocket. Mateo had tried to tell me how it worked, picking up the signals or something the moment I was in proximity of it, but it all sounded about as exciting as theoretical physics.

Sitting back on the bed, I mumbled the code word, "armadillo," and attempted to slow my heart thumping in my ears. Just as he walked back out with one square of fucking toilet paper, my phone rang in my pants pocket, right on cue.

Jumping up, I acted surprised as I grabbed the ringing device, careful to grab the right one and not give away our ploy. "Hello?"

"Hey, Smalls, you're doing great. Now just walk to the door, fake an excuse, and if he doesn't let you out, Rhett's standing there to bust it down. He won't be touching you again."

The steel in Henry's words had my blood rushing for an entirely different reason now. Hiding my blush in my hands, I turned back to Donnelly with the phone still on my ear and made an excuse.

"Um, thanks, Donald. I've got to go, emergency. But I'll be in touch to talk about that thing. Thanks for the talk," I rambled, walking backward to the door. It helped that I knew Rhett was there, but if he busted in here, then the whole thing would be for nothing.

Donnelly looked at me oddly, but didn't stop me from leaving. When I was far enough away, I turned and headed for my escape. Placing the last bug on the wall, it was so small it blended into the wallpaper. I opened the door and flew out as quickly as possible without being suspicious. As soon as I turned the corner, Rhett had me in his arms. I hugged him tightly as if my life depended on it and wrapped my legs around him, thankful when he carried me down the backstairs out of view.

"Ssh, you did it, baby. You did it. You're safe now."

My whole body was shaking as the adrenaline left me, and I hung on to my teddy bear as he carried me to the rest of the guys.

As much as I couldn't wait to wash Donnelly off me and burn these clothes, I felt accomplished in the fact I'd planted the phone and got him to confess on camera. If he contacted anyone about Jill or the Council, we'd know, and we could shut them down for good and hopefully get a location.

Elias told me Donnelly was just a pawn, and we would use him against the Council in the same way they had used him—by distracting them from our real goal. I didn't understand his chess metaphors, but I trusted Elias, and my knight was about to capture the king.

# thirty

. . .

## sawyer

AN EMERGENCY MEETING was called for the ice skating program on Saturday morning to discuss who would be stepping in as director while Donnelly was under investigation. I feared Queen Bitch herself would be put in charge and further make my life Hell. At least this time, Henry would be attending the meeting with me, and I hoped not to inadvertently challenge anyone. We were both barely awake after our late-night caper. Regardless, it felt amazing going to sleep, knowing we were making moves.

The Agency monitored the clone phone and video camera and already had some good leads and evidence for our case. Donnelly wasn't a significant player, but he would lead us to others. He was the most accessible link and the most disposable player in this whole thing. I still got body chills every time I thought of his hand on me. The shower I'd taken last night had been scalding, and I'd scrubbed every inch of my skin to rid myself of his filth.

Ollie and Tyler had been all too willing to help me forget as well. Now that I thought about it, that was why I was so tired. Ollie and Ty were still snoozing away in my bed, and I had toothpicks prying my eyes open. At 8:00 am on the dot, Adelaide, her father, and a woman who looked familiar walked in. Based on the scowl Bitchelaide wore, I was hopeful her displeasure meant she wasn't taking over.

"Thank you all for making it this morning. Since the Olympic committee is reviewing Director Donnelly's case, we've hired an interim director. Thankfully, a good friend had some free time and accepted my offer to come and lead the program. Please welcome Madelyn Lott, alumni of TAS and coach to many Olympic medalists. I'll leave you to get acquainted."

Mr. Aldridge left after that, and Adelaide hunched down into a chair at the front. She looked like a two-year-old who hadn't gotten her way and was now sulking in the corner. It was hilarious and so not becoming. A few of the other female skaters turned away from her, not wanting to be associated with Adelaide in front of the new director.

I didn't know if his hiring a woman was strategic on the tail of a scandal or if it was a matter of circumstance, either way, I was glad it was a woman. The room stared at her as we waited for her to speak, hopeful she would move us in the direction we needed.

"Well, hello, everyone," she started, walking around the

room. "Like, Dimitry stated, thank you for being up this early on a Saturday for a meeting. I wanted to get a head start on the week with everything going on. So I'll introduce myself some more, and then I want to hear from you all and what you'd like to see done differently in the program."

Some murmurs started around the room but quieted down as she began to talk again. The other instructors seemed relieved to have her, and it looked like Adelaide's reign of terror might be ending.

"I attended TAS as part of the 1999 graduating class and went on to the Olympics. Sadly, I didn't medal that year, but I've trained several Olympians in ice dancing and figure skating since then. I'm currently recovering from knee replacement surgery, so I didn't have any current trainees, which seemed to work perfectly for me to step in here. Now, let's go around the room, and you can tell me about yourself."

While it was one of those annoying ice breaker things, I didn't hate it as much this time because Adelaide's discomfort far outweighed my own. Her face seemed to get madder with each word Madelyn said, and I hoped her head would explode for real this time.

When I heard Henry's voice next to me, I focused back on the room. He finished by saying he enjoyed the switch to ice dancing with me, and I noticed Madelyn's eyes start to take an interest in him. Henry had his arm on the back of my chair, so I stared down the Director to make sure she wasn't macking on my boyfriend; he squeezed my shoulder when it was my turn.

"Oh, hi, I'm Sawyer Sullivan. I'm new this year, and I've

trained in figure skating, pairs, and now ice dancing. I teach the junior level girls and guys, and dance two days a week."

Stopping myself from spilling all my secrets, I kept it simple, not wanting to share my story with all these people in the room. Queen Bitch glared at me as I spoke, and I wondered what I'd done now. Once everyone had gone around the room, Madelyn went over some things she was changing and what our stance would be to the students as the scandal continued to unfold.

At an hour, she dismissed us, stating she wanted to make meetings a regular thing, so to make sure to check our emails for the next one. Perfect, because I didn't have a million other things to do; attending these meetings were also now on my plate. I needed some of my personal drama to resolve so I could enjoy my job.

As Henry and I gathered our stuff, I was surprised when I found Madelyn waiting at the front for us. "I was wondering if I could talk to both of you really quick?"

Glancing at Henry, I raised my eyebrow to see what he wanted to do, not that we had a choice.

"Yeah, sure," Henry answered for the both of us. Lacing his fingers through mine and making me smile. I loved how he made it known we were together, even if she wasn't trying to steal him from me. When we got to her office, the window blinds were open, and sunlight streamed in, making the place feel more inviting than it ever had. Boxes covered the floor on one side, and it looked like some were hers and someone else was packing up Donnelly's possessions. He'd left in such a hurry; he hadn't had time to clean out his office. I suppose the fact they were packing him up meant the school wasn't expecting him to return.

Madelyn leaned back on her desk, no seating available in the chaos. Henry and I stood as we waited to see what she wanted.

"When you said your name, I realized you were the skaters I watched last weekend," she paused. "And, well, I was impressed. How long have you been ice dancing?"

Stunned silent, I stood there gaping at the woman. I'd assumed she wanted to berate us for something or even that she'd heard horrible things from Bitchalide. I wasn't expecting her to take an *interest*.

"We've only been ice dancing for a few weeks, actually," Henry said. It was a good thing since I appeared to have lost all my words.

"Really? But you were excellent. Some of the best partnering I've ever seen."

"Oh well, we've been skating as partners since we've been able to skate," Henry beamed. His assurance in us had my stupor breaking, and I smiled back at him.

"Then why did you stop?" Madelyn asked.

"That's a long story, but the easy version. I got injured at 15 and wasn't able to skate at the same level. When we reunited here, we thought it would be fun to skate in the expo together."

"You did that level just for fun?"

If I ever wanted to know what incredulous looked like, it was Madelyn's face right now.

"Uh, yeah? Was it that bad?"

"No, no, quite the opposite. I need to sit down. Shit, I already am. I mean," Madelyn fumbled for her words, and it made me like her more. Softening my shell, I smiled at her, hoping it would help her settle whatever she was trying to say.

"The level of difficulty you guys managed in that 'fun skate' is comparable to some of the top ice dancing couples right now. You know Charlie and Meryl? Scott and Tessa? You're almost at their level."

Now it was my turn to stare at her as if she'd lost her ever-loving mind. "What are you saying exactly?" I hedged.

"Well, I was going to encourage you both to join one of the local competitions in a month, but now," she stuttered, "now I want to coach you guys and take you to the Olympics!"

Henry and I looked at each other, not sure what to say. I glanced back at Madelyn, wondering if this was all a long ploy? Was Adelaide going to pop out and crush our dreams? Was this the Council's way of getting to us?

"The Olympics? Is this a joke? Did Bitchelaide put you up to this? Where's the hidden camera?"

Dropping Henry's hand, I started to look around, trying to see if I could find something. This was beyond cruel. In my desperation to prove her ploy, I didn't hear anything she said or Henry as he tried to grab my attention. Arms wrapped around me from behind, and I stopped my search. Dropping his head, he whispered in my ear, "It's not a joke, Smalls. It's *okay* to be hopeful."

Turning in his embrace, I hugged him and held onto him

for a minute. I needed to soak in his love and encouragement. What did this mean? Looking up, I met his eyes and asked the question that was racing through my mind. "But is that what you want? I thought music was the dream?"

"Smalls, you're the dream, the fantasy, and the reality. Skating without you by my side never had the appeal, and I tried to force it as long as I could, but I never found the thing you and I have—love. Music will always be there. But this could be our chance to make our teen dreams come true. We could do this together. I'd like to try."

Tears pricked my eyes, and I admired Madelyn for giving us this space to talk it out. She didn't interrupt the moment, and I was grateful. Nodding, I bit my lip to keep the tears at bay, but one escaped anyway. Henry wiped it away, and a laugh escaped me at his gesture.

"We're going to do this? We're going to try for the Olympics?" I laughed out almost hysterically.

"Yeah, I think so," he said, beaming at me.

Squeezing him tight, I turned back to the woman I'd been rude to and found her smiling genuinely at us. "Sorry, it's just… yeah."

"No apologies needed. I get it. Sometimes it's hard to trust the good when all you've had is bad. I promise I'm not yanking your chain or filling you with false promises. I'm the real deal, and I think you guys have what it takes."

"Then let's do this."

We delved into a training schedule that would work around our classes, and Madelyn even took a few of them off our programs to help free up time. Since there were so many coaches, it wasn't a hardship to add a few people to others, especially when I found out that Henry and I were teaching more than any other instructor! Henry was aware since he took on extra ones to help keep him distracted, but I'd been hoodwinked by the recruiter and had agreed to do twice as many. It had Adelaide written all over it. She just had to be behind this somehow.

"Well, I look forward to seeing you two tomorrow morning then. We have a lot to cover in the next month."

We walked out of the office, kind of stunned but mostly overjoyed. Henry and I… we had a second chance, and that meant everything.

Brushing my hair, I almost wanted to bail on the party tonight. I knew it was a big deal to Fin to do this right for Asa and me, but after the past week, *I was exhausted*. I'd done some core training with Rhett when I'd gotten back from the rink, and now every muscle in my body was yelling at me. The man knew his shit, but I hated him at the moment.

When he was in his fitness instructor mode, he was impossible to crack. I even flashed him a boob at one point to get him to stop, and he only lifted his eyebrow and added ten more rounds, the fucker! I stopped after that, not wanting to pay the consequences if it didn't work. I wanted a second round of our fitness sexcapades, but it didn't seem like it would be happening anytime soon.

Henry had shared the news with everyone, and it had become the guys' mission to get us Olympic ready. Even Ollie was serious and had called a cease-fire for the prank war in reverence for the party tonight. So after a grueling afternoon with no sexy times, I was struggling to lift my hairbrush to my head.

A knock on the door preceded it opening, and I glared at Fin as she entered, an innocent expression on her face. If she thought that was a knock, the girl had another thing to learn. If I was in here having sex, there was no way I'd hear that or have time to cover myself. I couldn't wait for the day it was Henry and me. Maybe then she'd be scarred enough to learn a proper knock.

"What?" She grinned. "I totally knocked."

Rolling my eyes at her, I continued to brush my hair in the most painful exercise known to man. Thankfully, Fin took pity on me and came over and took charge. Within minutes, she had my hair pulled back in some crazy cool braid, and I decided she should always do my hair. It looked better when she did it anyway. Handing her my makeup bag, I batted my eyes at her, pleading.

"Like I'd let you leave having done your own makeup, bish!"

"Hey, if it means you do mine for me, I'll always suck at it!"

"Whatever, girl." Fin laughed.

It was the happiest I'd seen her in a while. It'd only been a week since the whole ordeal, but it felt longer.

Kris Butler

"Are you doing okay? You know, with the whole week anniversary of it?"

"Is that a thing? Because I don't want it to be a thing," Fin grimaced. "I'm doing... okay. Some days I have nightmares about it, and others, I'm flooded with a huge amount of guilt and remorse. I live in a constant state of hating myself and being happy to be back. It's exhausting, actually."

Once she started talking, she opened the floodgates and finally poured her heart out to me.

"Hey, it's okay to feel all of that, you know. There isn't a guidebook on how to deal with being drugged and almost sold into sex slavery. If you find one, though, can I borrow it?"

"Huh, I guess we do both have that in common now. Not something I wanted to share, though. Flaming donkey balls, how did we end up in a life where that was normal?"

"Genetics?" I joked, trying to lighten the dark mood that had settled.

"Yeah, maybe. Things are just; I don't know. It's like my heart and brain can't figure out what they want to feel anymore, and it's never the same thing. Part of me hates myself for ruining everything. I think... I'm worried I screwed it up with Asa. I don't know how to talk to him about it though."

A tear fell down her cheek, and I pulled my friend into my arms. "Hey, it's okay. I think in these circumstances, every-thing you're feeling is natural. And there isn't a right or wrong way to share how you're feeling. Asa just wants to help. I think he feels helpless in a way. Milo and Cohen

372

appeared on the scene that night and saved the day. I saw him, Fin, he was worried for you. He was scared he'd lost you. So, maybe take that in and see that while it might feel overbearing or suffocating, he's telling you how he feels. You guys need to have that talk I keep telling you to have. Just be open and honest, and lay it all out there."

"I'm scared too. I get that he wants to show me he's okay with things, but sometimes I find him watching me, and I wonder if he wishes he hadn't asked me out. That I'm too much and not worth the effort," Fin cried.

Rubbing her back, I tried to comfort my best friend. Traumatic experiences didn't make sense, and everyone experienced them differently. After a few minutes, she pulled away and grabbed a Kleenex off the vanity.

"The worst part though, Sawyer, outside the being drugged part and pulling Rowan into it, *I liked it*. I had fun! What does that say about me? Breaking into the office, outsmarting him, and escaping later with Milo... I enjoyed it. It was the most fun I'd had in a long time. What does that mean? Am I crazy?"

Fin's lip trembled, and I could see another meltdown on the horizon.

"Finley Amelia Reyes! You are one of the bravest, smartest, and most amazing people I know. You enjoying the spy crazy stuff isn't any weirder than me throwing my body through the air and landing with tiny blades on ice. We all have things that set our souls on fire, and it doesn't have to make sense to anyone but you. It doesn't sound that far out there from the Finley I knew as a kid, either. You always wanted to be a spy kid, after all. Maybe talk to Samson." I shrugged.

"You don't think it's stupid?"

"Not at all. I think it's great, babe! And I can't stress this enough, *talk to Asa*!"

Laughing, she nodded. "I know, I know. Ugh, I just get all confused and doubt myself and then think he won't want to hear it."

"Lies, all lies! If you don't, I'll have to take a move out of your playbook and lock you two in a room together until you do."

"You wouldn't!"

"How many times did you do that to Henry and me? You're so owed a few!"

"Okay, that might be fair. You were a stubborn preteen, though."

"Yeah, yeah. Now, are you going to help me pick out something to wear or trust me not to mess up the hair and makeup effect?"

"Hell no. Sit back, and I'll make you pretty!"

"You're the best, Fin."

"Back at ya, sis!"

Laughing, I watched as she browsed my clothes, and I waited for her to do her magic. Fin didn't see all the great talents she possessed. She was versatile, and I bet she'd be a great addition to any program. When she turned around with a dress I didn't remember putting in there, I shrugged, and she skipped over, bringing it to me.

"This is gorgeous! When did you get this?"

"No clue. I didn't buy it."

Looking at the hanger, I saw a note hanging down from the tag.

*Happy Birthday, Love.*
*I can't wait to see you in this and then take it off you.*
*-Wholly Yours*

"Damn, that's hot!" Fin exclaimed, fanning herself. I couldn't disagree. Slipping on the iridescent dress, I couldn't hide my inflamed cheeks. The material was like silk as it kissed my skin and changed colors in the light. The sleeves were see-through and capped at my wrists. It had a full skirt, and I felt like a modern-day princess as I twirled in it. Fin handed me some shoes that went with it, and then I did feel like Cinderella. You know, if she had seven boyfriends. Maybe I was more like Snow White?

Suddenly, I was looking forward to this party, hoping my missing prince would be there. Elias kept surprising me in the best ways, and it was hard even to imagine the Elias I met in September. This man oozed sin in all the best ways—with sincerity and sinful sensations.

# thirty-one

. . .

## soren

REY and I'd left early to ensure the private room Fin had reserved met her decorating standards. Why she put us in charge was the question of the hour as we tried to hang the last of the streamers. Seriously, girls were amazing with this craft shit! I couldn't for the life of me figure out how to make it do the curlycue thing Fin wanted. I was about to throw down with some ribbon.

"Fuck!"

Rey's shout echoed around the enclosed space, and I couldn't help but laugh as one of the posters he'd hung moments ago crashed to the floor. That was it. Women were officially *otherworldly*. There was no doubt in my mind. How else did someone decorate a room with flawless precision? *Woman magic*.

"Just shove it under a table or something. Sawyer won't even notice, and Asa won't care," I mumbled as I placed the last centerpiece. It had seemed simple when Fin had gone over the last-minute details to do while she *rescued Sawyer from a clothing disaster.* But as we struggled to get anything to cooperate, I wondered if we were this incompetent at life?

Stepping back slowly, my hands braced out in front of me; I moved away from the centerpiece like it was a wild animal. The paper cuts on my fingers could attest it was. When nothing fell over, I exhaled in relief. They needed to get here soon while everything was still standing. I didn't have much faith in the shelf life of our attempts.

"Rey babe, just walk away slowly and don't touch anything else."

"Easy for you to say," he mumbled.

Turning, I found my boyfriend in some Twister pose as he tried to hold two things on the wall with his butt and one hand, a set of balloons with his foot, and a wobbling centerpiece with his outstretched hand. I couldn't help it, and I burst out laughing at his predicament. Snapping a quick picture, I took pity on him and helped him get untangled.

"Thank you. My ass was starting to go numb holding that so tightly to the wall."

"Good thing you have buns of steel."

"It's a good thing you're both cute," we heard from the doorway.

"Ew, and that isn't going to save them from me!" Fin retorted back.

In the doorway stood most of the BOSH crew watching us

with grins on their faces. Fin was tapping her foot, arms crossed, a frown in place. She was clearly not impressed with our decorating skills. Hopefully, she'd never ask us to do this again. Give me ice or transportation duty any day of the week over decorating! With a sheepish smile, I shrugged and set the items I'd taken from Rey down before running to my sweet pea.

Sawyer looked stunning in a dress that seemed to transform colors with the light. It looked like a rainbow and a piece of ice had a baby. Picking her up, I ignored Fin's protests about wrinkling the fabric and swung my girl around. Sawyer's glee every time I did this was what always had me going back for more. Squeezing her tight to me, I kissed her quickly before setting her down.

"Stay with us tonight?" I whispered. Sawyer nodded, a smile lifting her lips before she began greeting the other guests who were now arriving. Charlie and Aggie looked to have arrived together, and I smiled at what that might mean. He'd just flown back in this morning and Sawyer ran to give them both a hug. It made me happy to see her embracing everyone. Heading back over to Rey, I jumped in to save him from the tongue lashing Fin was bestowing upon him.

"Seriously, Henry! I only asked you to do the basics, and you couldn't even get that right!"

"Whoa, there, little Reyes! We tried, okay. We just don't possess the woman voodoo magic you do. I hereby declare you Queen Supreme of all things!"

Thankfully, my comments helped ease some of the tension

from Fin and reduced her anger at her brother. She slumped a little and exhaled, clearly showing her stress.

"Fine. You're right. I am the best. Just go back and make sure everyone has drinks or something. I'll fix this." She waved her hands over the centerpiece disasters.

Hearing the dismissal given to us, I grabbed Rey's hand and pulled him quickly with me. Ice duty, here I come! I'd totally rock the shit out of this task.

"Is it me, or was Fin more Fin-esque back there about things? I'm worried she's falling back into how she was that one summer…"

Henry trailed off, biting his lip as he turned to watch his sister. She was alone working on the picture collages she'd made for the centerpieces, as everyone else laughed and joked in the front of the room. Asa was with Sawyer and their mom, and I could see him glancing back there every now and then, a concerned look on his face as well. She was more worried about the details than she was with being with her friends and enjoying it.

"You might be on to something. Asa looks especially perplexed as well. Leave it for now, nothing you can do at a birthday party for your girlfriend and her twin brother. Besides, you need to warm up. I'll cover drinks while you do that."

"Shit, is it time already? Thanks, Sor. I'll make it up to you later tonight."

"Don't make promises if you don't intend to keep them," I teased.

"Oh, I intend, I intend."

Henry licked his lips as he walked backward from me, and it was one of the hottest things I'd ever seen. Fucking hell, now I was about to be sporting some major wood in a room full of people. Discreetly, I shifted myself as I walked over to check on the ice. Leaning back against the wall, I watched everyone interact with each other.

It was nice to sit back for a moment and people watch. Usually, I was in the thick of everything, and I didn't get this view of things. Rhett was quietly standing with a drink in his hand, his arms crossed as he listened to his mom talk with Rowan. His eyes watched Sawyer's every move, and even though he wasn't smiling, his eyes were alive with love, lust, and protectiveness. We were all lucky to have Rhett in our corner.

Ollie and Ty were tossing popcorn into the air and seeing who could catch the most pieces. Sawyer cheered them on as they raced one another to get the most before the time ran out. Mateo was holding Sawyer's hand, and I smiled at how much he'd come out of his shell. He was such a beautiful soul, and I loved what he added to our family, our brotherhood.

Asa and Isla walked over and joined Charlie and Aggie, and I watched as Rowan headed in Fin's direction to ask if she needed help. Fin lessened some of her anger when she approached and accepted. They'd grown closer since last week, and though it didn't seem any of the Taylors held Fin responsible, it was clear Fin did. The guilt sat heavily on her shoulders, and I wondered if it was all that was bothering her. Henry was correct; something was going on there.

"Psst."

Turning at the sound, I found Henry with his head peeking through the door to my left. Walking over, I saw him with his guitar and knew it was time. Winking at him, I walked to the lights and switched them from the overhead ones to the soft lanterns. Everyone turned when I did, and I smiled and nodded to the front of the room.

Henry had moved into position behind the microphone and shyly positioned his guitar as he took a steadying breath. His hands were shaking as he adjusted the microphone, and I tried to give him my confidence to trust in himself. Once he had it in place, he spoke into it.

"Um, hi. Everyone, I'm Henry or Rey, depending on who you asked." He chuckled. "Man, I'm nervous, uh. I didn't expect to feel this nervous." Clearing his throat, he tried to focus on the birthday girl. "A passion of mine that's kind of been a secret is that I love to write songs and play the guitar. I, uh, don't like to play in front of people, but since it's a birthday surprise for the girl I love, and well, her twin brother. Sorry, Asa, I'm just not there with you yet," he joked, causing everyone to laugh. It seemed to help ease some of his nerves, and he relaxed more into his stance.

"No hard feelings, bro. But next year, I expect a love song," Asa yelled from the crowd. Everyone laughed more, and it appeared to be the last bit of courage Rey needed.

"You got it, man. Since it's Sawyer's birthday redo, I thought I'd be brave and share this song with all of you. This is for you, Smalls. I love you."

"Awww," could be heard from the women in the room as Henry started to strum his guitar.

I watched Sawyer as Henry sang about first loves and kisses, and if I hadn't already been in love with them both, I'd be jealous of the love they shared. It was pure love built on childhood dreams and innocence. It was the best kind of puppy love that transformed into the real deal. I could almost see hearts coming out of Sawyer's eyes, and as I listened to his soulful voice and watched her glee, I fell in love with them both even more.

"You know, I didn't think it was possible, but you guys make it look easy. The love you both have for that girl is palpable. It's so thick you can see it in the air and feel it around you. I won't say I don't worry because I do. Sawyer became my whole world unexpectedly, and I'd do anything for that girl. But I can see that she's also yours, so I'll let her go and entrust her care to you lot, this *brotherhood*. What is it you're calling yourselves?"

Emotion was thick in my throat as Charlie spoke to me. I almost couldn't get the words out. "Um, BOSH, sir."

"Now, Soren. I thought we already talked about this sir business. Charlie will do. BOSH, that's right. Well, I know it's probably not traditional to do it this way, but I know how fleeting time is better than anyone, and when love knocks on your door, you don't tell it to go away or that you're too busy. Love doesn't work on your schedule," Charlie paused for a second, and it seemed he glanced at Aggie as he spoke the last part. A small smile graced his face, and it changed his whole persona. I could see the man that Sawyer loved dearly under the gruff exterior. It was almost like seeing Rhett in the future, though hopefully, with all of us, we'd keep Rhett from hardening himself.

"What I'm failing to make clear is that if you all, *BOSH*, are serious and want to make it more, you have my blessing. I know most of you are still young and figuring out what you want to do with your life, but if you take any advice from an old fart like me, it's not to waste it. I spent so many years chasing what I thought made me happy while the love of my life waited for me at home. To return years later and only get five more with her. I wouldn't trade those for anything, but a day doesn't go by that I don't think about what it might've been like if I'd realized the only thing that would make me happy was me and not chasing ghosts. Well, I think that's the most I've said all year, so I'll leave you be. Just pass my message on, will you?"

"Of course, Charlie. And thank you, we do all love her, and I know for Henry and me at least, we plan to have a future with her in it, whatever that looks like."

"I'm happy to hear that, Son."

He awkwardly squeezed my shoulder and walked back over to Aggie. Henry had finished on stage, and now Ace and Sawyer were doing a karaoke number. I hadn't even noticed him enter, so absorbed in my conversation with Charlie.

His words shocked me, but in a way, I also got it. Life wasn't guaranteed, and as much as we liked to think we were invincible, there were things out there that didn't care. On top of that, we still had the Council to contend with, and if they'd proved anything, it was that they only cared about themselves. They'd go to whatever extremes necessary if it meant they got what they wanted.

Watching the family I'd made for myself dance and laugh; I made a new vow. Years ago, I'd quit to save myself. Now, I'd take up whatever arms I needed to save them. Everyone in this room mattered to me in more ways than I'd ever thought possible.

The Council destroyed people's lives for material things and power. They were fools if they didn't realize the greatest power of all was love. There was nothing of greater value in the world than to be loved.

They might have private jets, personal chefs, and thousand-dollar suits. They could get anything they desired and be on a first-name basis with the president. They might even have access to all the diamonds in the world, but it didn't matter.

We had Sawyer's smile and heart, Rhett's protectiveness, Ollie's laugh, Ty's kindness, Mateo's solid assurance, Rey's passion, Elias's courage, and my promise.

Nothing else compared. *Nothing.*

# thirty-two

. . .

**sawyer**

THE NIGHT HAD BEEN AMAZING SO FAR as I danced away and sang karaoke with my friends and family. Fin had outdone herself, and I could see touches of her love everywhere. When she had time to print and make photo centerpieces was beyond me. The woman was fucking Superwoman with her level of organization and crafting.

"Cake time!"

The remake of the song "Colorblind" I'd been dancing to with Mateo had come to an end, and I lifted my head to see who'd promised cake. Mateo had been watching me and laughed at my reaction.

"Are you excited about cake, Dulzura?"

"Uh, yeah," I deadpanned, smiling big. Tonight was going

so well, and I tried not to think about the chaos we were then due. And not the hacker we'd come to like.

A few seconds later, Fin walked through the doors, a cake with candles lit in front of her face. Skipping over, I grabbed Asa's hand as I passed and pulled him along with me. Like a brother, he shook his head and smiled at my silliness. Stopping in front of the cake, I waited for the song to die down before turning to my brother to blow the candles out together. He nodded when he caught my eyes, and we turned back to the cake and blew simultaneously, doing an awesome twin thing.

Cheering and laughter rang out around the room, and when the candles relit, I knew Fin had tricked us. Her devious grin only solidified her blame.

"Really, Fin?" I laughed, plopping my hands on my waist as I fake glared at her.

"What? I'm honestly surprised! I thought you had enough hot air up in that head of yours."

She couldn't hold her innocence any longer, not that she'd tried too hard to begin with, and almost dropped the cake as she bent over laughing. Asa, thankfully, thought to grab it and handed it off to his mom, err, our mom. I was trying to get better at calling her mom; my brain just hadn't caught up yet. Isla was holding the cake, about to ask what we wanted to do with the still flaming candles, when the door opened again.

I looked at the sound, hoping it was Elias, but instead, it was one of the last people I'd want to see here—Adelaide and her remaining Alphabets.

"Well, well, well, look at what I found," she sneered.

"I'm sorry, I didn't realize we were missing. Can I help you find your way out now?"

One of the Ashley's laughed at my comment, and I realized Adelaide was down to two. Was the QB losing her minions? She didn't like the laugh and shot, whichever Ashley it was, a nasty look. Instead of leaving like she should've, Bitchalide opened her damn mouth *again*.

"Oh, were you not able to blow out your candles, Slutyer? I thought for sure a whore like you would be amazing at blowing, but I guess you don't get enough practice when you're always on your back."

Before I could even think of a response, the most amazing thing happened. Isla had been taking the candles out while QB flapped her gums. She'd started to cut the cake into slices, but when she heard Adelaide's words, I guess her mom instinct took over. Isla turned and launched a piece of cake at her in a rather amazing throw. It hit the Ice Princess square in the face, and for a brief second, there was absolute quiet as we all stood in shock.

The Queen Bitch didn't appear to know how to handle it either and stood frozen as icing dripped down her face in purple and blue streaks. Once it registered, a shriek higher than Ollie's unleashed from her throat and rang out through the room. The girl had some pipes on her. We had to cover our ears to stop some of the violence she was perpetrating on them.

"Why, you little *bitch*!"

"I think you should leave Adelaide. You weren't invited, and I won't stand for you talking to anyone in that manner."

His presence coated me and eased the sharpness of her voice, and I knew Elias was finally *home*. Peeking around the dripping cake drama queen, I found it impossible not to look on with love at my knight. I didn't think and just reacted. Walking with confidence, I strode up to him and pulled on his tie, bringing him to my level. His eyes searched mine, and I closed the space and kissed him for all to see. Life was better when there wasn't any space between us.

Elias' arms wrapped around me and pulled me into him. He was finally here, and now my world was complete. Outside of Bitchalide and her minions, every person I loved was here tonight in this room, and Elias made us whole. His tongue sent shivers down my spine as he claimed me in front of everyone. Pulling back, I smiled at him, not caring what everyone else thought.

"You came."

"I did."

"You bought me a dress."

"I did."

"What now?"

Smiling, he moved a piece of hair out of my eyes before answering. "Whatever we want."

"And if I want you back with us?"

"Then I'm back."

"Good. Rhett's getting a little lonely, and he's been taking his aggression out on me in the training room..."

At my mention of Rhett and the training room, both of our

eyes became heated, and I lost track of where I was going when I started.

"Oh, *love*, I can't wait to see where your brain goes with that, but *later*. I need to finish taking out the trash."

Kissing me on my nose, he let me go and walked over to Queen Bitch. She was still stomping and screaming for someone to do something for her. Staying back, I crossed my arms over my chest and debated which was funnier. Adelaide covered in icing, stomping around like a two-year-old, or the fact that no one, not even the Alphabets, offered her help.

Elias handed her a napkin and then directed her back toward the direction of the door. She was ranting and raving the whole way, and I couldn't make out everything she was saying. When she said something he disagreed with, his voice rose for us all to hear.

"You do whatever you feel is necessary, Adelaide. You knew our date the other night was fake and a means to an end to get a seat with Abernathy, so you can spew whatever lie you want, but no one will believe you. Maybe you should try being nicer to people next time?"

Before she could respond, he pushed her by her elbow the rest of the way out of the room and shut the door behind her. How she thought it was okay to just walk into a private space like she owned the place was beyond my comprehension, but I suppose entitlement didn't make sense to begin with.

"Well done, Ms. Walsh!" Ollie chuckled. "Even if it was a waste of a perfect piece of cake."

The tension dissolved into laughter, and I smiled at my fun-loving boyfriend. It was nice to see Ollie using his charm and big mouth for a good purpose. After Bitchalide had gone, I turned to the Alphabets, who were standing back, shyly. I observed them and decided I didn't care as long as they didn't cause problems.

"Don't be a bitch, and you're cool with me," I volleyed and turned to grab some cake.

Soren was already standing, waiting to hand me a piece, and I almost jumped on him when he did. I would've been crabby if I hadn't gotten any. Moaning as I took a bite, I inhaled the frosty deliciousness. Arms wrapped around me, and Soren whispered in my ear, "I can't wait to find all the ways to get that sound out of you."

I almost choked on the cake, which would've been a crime two times over. One for wasting good cake, and two for not getting to do what Soren promised. Grabbing a drink off the table, I swallowed it down to clear my throat. Once I could breathe cake-free again, I glared at Soren, who was chuckling at my reaction.

Deciding to find Ollie and compliment him on his amazing creation, I stuck my tongue out and turned on my heels, making the dress spin out around me. I felt the fabric against my skin and smiled at how smooth it felt. Ollie was talking with Ty and Charlie. Making my way over, I noticed Elias had joined Rhett against the wall. It was good to see them together again.

Ace and Chloe were being friendly with the Ashley's, and I realized I'd need to learn which was which if they decided not to be bitches anymore. I vaguely remembered Ace telling me one of them was a bobsledder and Chloe's roommate, so I guess it made sense they'd be somewhat on good terms. Asa, Isla, and Fin sat at a table with Rowan, Rhonda, and Henry as they all ate cake and laughed at some story Rhonda was sharing.

"Happy Birthday, bite-size!"

Rolling my eyes playfully, I wouldn't let Ollie know that despite the amount of grief I gave him, I didn't hate the name anymore. He'd given it to me, so of course, I liked it.

"Thank you, Ollie. You outdid yourself on the cake. I just wanted to come over and congratulate you on it."

"Well, I know a way you can thank me," he started until he realized Charlie was there and quickly changed his tone.

"Oh, how is that?" I teased, his ears turning red.

"You know, by um, helping me clean the dishes when we get home."

"Uh-huh. Yeah, sure, I can do that."

Before I could say anything else, Fin made another announcement. I swear that girl was everywhere today. "Present time!" she shouted.

I hadn't been expecting gifts. It wasn't something I'd done in the past five years, so a feeling of bittersweet happiness filled me. It was nice to celebrate for once, but it also highlighted my parents being gone. I couldn't let that hold me back. New memories would never be made if I didn't at least try. If I got to share them with my brother and family now, it would be worth a few moments of sadness.

Being the center of attention was strange when I wasn't on the ice, but it wasn't too awkward since it was people I was familiar with and loved. At least, that was how I felt about it.

As I took a seat at one of the tables, Fin started piling things in front of me. Seriously, what was I going to do with all of these things? I think Mateo could see my eyes bugging out of my head and came over to help me.

"Here, Dulzura, this one is from me."

Mateo handed me a medium-sized box wrapped in blue paper. Smiling softly, I unwrapped the gift and found a sweatshirt inside. Pulling it out, a smile spread across my face. *"Forget glass slippers. This Princess wears ice skates."*

Kissing him quickly, I pulled back to tell him how much I loved it. "This is perfect. Thank you."

His smile helped me not feel put on the spot. I could enjoy getting gifts if I got to see his joy as well. Soren handed me a gift next, and so went the next half hour as I unwrapped what felt like a million gifts from my friends and family. Asa had opened his presents as well, but it was apparent I had the most, and while I felt terrible about it, I did have seven boyfriends, so there was bound to be a discrepancy.

In the end, I came away with a signed paperback from Soren of the first book we read together, *Destiny Awakened*. A sketch of me with a few of the guys from when we'd gone skiing from Rhett, new tea bags and a mug that said, *"I like my tea how I like my men, HOT,"* from Ollie, and a baby Yoda blanket and socks from Ty.

The blanket said, *"feed me snacks and tell me I'm pretty,"* and I wanted to feel attacked by it, but it was too damn accurate to get upset over. Not to mention it was hella soft. I kept rubbing my face against it after I'd opened it.

Fin and Asa gave me some earrings, Chloe a gift card to

the coffee shop, Ace a lift pass to take me out bobsledding one day, and Rhonda and Rowan got me a leather journal and some awesome journaling pens. For not expecting gifts, I felt truly blessed to receive what I had.

Charlie handed me a bag but told me to wait. Aggie nodded, and I had a feeling she'd helped with it. I tucked it away, not emotionally ready to open it in front of others. I hadn't expected anything from him other than his visit, so I was curious to see what his gift was. We hadn't ever made a big deal out of birthdays before.

Isla had been pleased to see me wearing the watch, and it felt nice to feel connected to her family line, like maybe I wasn't so alone in the world anymore, even if I wasn't ready to deal with the contents of the letter she'd written me. Thinking of it now, though, I knew I couldn't put it off much longer. I would need to face up to it. At the thought of facing things, I realized I'd forgotten one person—Samson.

He'd texted earlier and said he wasn't ready to face Isla yet, but that he would make it up to me in a big way. It stung, but I understood more than I wanted to admit. I walked away from Henry all those years ago in an attempt to protect him, and if it had been for over twenty years, I think it would've been hard to face him. So, for now, I'd give him time, but I wouldn't let him get away with it forever. I wanted both of them in my life, and that meant not keeping secrets.

Things started to wind down after that, and the sugar crash was coming. We packed up all the gifts, took down the decorations, and picked up our trash. I wasn't leaving Fin to handle it, despite her many attempts to push me out of the room. When I didn't listen, the glare she sent me was cute, like she thought it would deter me. Too bad, Finikins! Blowing her a kiss, my stubbornness won out, and we managed to get the room back to order in ten minutes.

As we finished up, Elias approached and asked if I'd stay back for a moment. He wanted to give me a ride back to the house. I was about to decline and tell him Soren had already asked me when he interrupted.

"I know you're already spoken for tonight. I just wanted to show you something."

"Then I'd love to."

My words acted like a trigger for the events that unfolded. The lights went out and fairy lights lit up the room. I hadn't noticed them before, but they hung across the beams, their white light cast a soft glow across the room. Romantic music began to play over the speakers, and I recognized it as "Arms" by Christina Perri.

"Can I have this dance?"

Blushing hardcore, I placed my hand in his, and he pulled me into his arms as he began to dance me around the room. Staring into his eyes, everything faded, and it was him and me as we let the words of the song sink into us. When the song was over, it felt like I'd been transported to a different place.

"Happy Birthday, love."

"Thank you, Elias."

The kiss of a thousand fires was placed on my lips, and I was glad his arms were around me, as the song echoed in my head, *"you put your arms around me, and I'm home."* Elias was showing me he was home and committed to our family. It was everything I could want.

It was quiet as we drove back to the house. We were in an expensive sports car that probably cost way too much. The leather was soft against my legs, and the seat warmer kept my bum nice and toasty, so I wasn't complaining. Elias' hand on my leg didn't hurt either.

"It was good to see you with everyone. We've missed you," I admitted.

"I missed you all too. I'm glad to be back as well. My father isn't happy about it, but we'll deal with it."

"Exactly. *We*! Don't go and try to be a hero alone again. We do this together."

"Yes, love. *Together*."

"Don't think you can get out of things just because you sound cute when you say it," I teased.

"Oh, just cute? What about *sexy*?"

His hand on my leg shifted up, and I sucked in a breath.

"Oh, you better keep your eyes on the road, mister!"

I tried to sound funny, but I was a little nervous. Cars still terrified me with my track record. Add in it being late at night, dark, and somewhat snowy conditions, and my heart was racing for an entirely different reason now. Elias must have heard the genuine fear and slowed down, not that he'd been driving fast to begin with.

"I'm sorry, Sawyer. I didn't mean to scare you."

"It's okay, just, you know, bad track record with cars."

"Yeah, I should've realized. I never want you to feel unsafe or ashamed about feeling scared."

"You don't. It wasn't you. I promise."

Turning to him, I squeezed the hand he moved back to the shifter. He pulled into the driveway a few minutes later, and we entered the house together. Lucky went crazy when he saw us both, running on the hardwood floors in all directions because he couldn't get traction fast enough to get to us. He wouldn't stop barking either to get our attention until we were both on the floor petting him simultaneously. He was in a rare frenzy as he licked Elias all over, smelling him like he was trying to figure out where he'd been.

"See, it's official. Lucky doesn't want you to leave either," I beamed.

"Well, what Lucky says, goes."

Lucky finally calmed down, and Elias was able to take in his collar and the sweater he was wearing.

"What on earth?" Elias questioned, picking him up and looking at the dragon on the back.

"What? He gets cold!" I protested. Elias rolled his eyes, but smiled all the same.

"You better be glad I love you, Sawyer, because *my dog* doesn't wear clothes."

"Well, it's a good thing he's *our dog* then."

Sealing my statement with a kiss, I grinned as we stood. We walked into the living room and found the guys playing their game. Elias walked over and cleared his throat, and the guys paused it when they saw him.

Holding Lucky in my arms, I walked over to the space between Soren and Ollie and curled up between them, kicking my heels to the floor. They both snuggled into me, and I was the filling in a funny boy sandwich. Sighing, I patted Lucky as I took in their affection. Sometimes, it was good to be me.

"I just wanted to apologize for how I left things. I didn't think about how it might seem, and for that, I'm sorry. I've already apologized to Rhett and Sawyer, but Mateo, I feel like I owe you one as well. Really, to all of you."

Elias seemed a bit flustered as he undid his tie. "I'm kind of shit at apologizing, I've found. I was taught not to do it, that it's a weakness. But that's wrong. I love you guys, and I'm sorry my actions hurt you. I didn't intend for that, and I take responsibility for not thinking it through. I hope you can forgive me and know that the past few weeks have been Hell without you all. I'll grovel, plead, whatever it takes, just know that," he cleared his throat, "you're my family, and I love you all."

It was quiet for a second as everyone let the words hang in the air before Mateo spoke up.

"You're forgiven, just don't get in the habit of thinking you can do it all on your own," Mateo answered firmly. It was kind of sexy seeing Mateo stand up to Elias and not letting him off the hook with an "it's okay."

"Yeah, someone reminded me of that tonight." He smiled at me.

"Well, okay, now that you've got your head out of your ass, get over here and help me kick Ollie's butt," Henry retorted, holding out a controller for Elias.

Ollie snorted at Henry but shifted me into his lap more so Elias had enough room on the couch. And that was how we spent the next few hours as they traded turns playing and cradling me in their laps. BOSH was back together, and I couldn't think of any better way to spend my evening.

Before it got too late, Soren conceded his turn and gave me some very sexy bedroom eyes that promised me all the things he said earlier. My lady parts woke up at the suggestion, my hussy vagina entirely in charge, and it was a race to see who could make it up the stairs the fastest.

# thirty-three

. . .

## sawyer

HALFWAY UP THE STAIRS, Soren grabbed me from behind and twisted me over his shoulder in a fireman's carry. Giggles erupted out of me as I hung upside down. I felt kind of bad that I was wearing the dress Elias had wanted to take off me, but Soren's hands moved up the back of my thighs, and the guilt fled.

Choosing who to spend my time with would always be difficult when I had so many amazing men in my life, but my promise to myself and them was always to be present with the person I was with. It was the only way I could promise to give them everything. *When I was with them, they got all of me.*

Besides, there wasn't any rule that said I couldn't put the dress back on for Elias to take off me later.

Soren took a detour to my bathroom, and I was confused

for a moment when we bypassed my bed. Then I smelled the lavender and saw the candles burning. I had a feeling this had been planned. Setting me down on my feet, he smiled before turning me around. Henry sat on the edge of the ginormous tub filled with bubbles.

"Fancy taking a bath with me?"

Tipping my head back, I looked at Soren upside down. "Are you joining too?"

"Of course, sweet pea." *Man, his grin was killer.*

Soren slowly lowered the zipper, and I shimmied out of the beautiful dress. Carefully, I placed it on the counter before shedding my undergarments. Soren and Henry both watched me with hooded eyes as I bared my body to them. Smiling, I walked closer to the tub and took Henry's hand as he helped me step into the warm water.

The bubbles kissed my skin as I sank into the water. It smelled delightful, and the oils in the tub were already making my skin feel soft as they nourished my body. A soft sigh escaped me when I was fully submerged under the soothing water. Glancing at my boys, they were frozen still as they watched me. I found it funny they were so enchanted by the simple act of getting into bathwater.

"Well, are you going to join me? Or do I have to do it by myself?"

My question was the firing gun they needed to start shedding clothes in a race to join me in the water. Soren beat out Henry solely because he only had on a t-shirt and jeans. His whole commando thing worked in his favor. His pierced cock sprang forward as they lowered, and I couldn't help but lick my lips. Henry got distracted in shedding his jeans as he watched me eye Soren's dick, getting lost in his own haze of desire.

It turned me on so much, watching their passion and desire for one another. Soren stepped into the water and gathered me up into his arms. The tub was a small pool and could fit four of my giant boyfriends with no issue. Henry blinked, his trance breaking, and resumed taking off his pants and boxers. He almost fell into the water as he pulled off his socks, and I wanted to laugh, but I was too transfixed by his bouncing cock. The dripping head called to me, and before he could step in, I knelt and kissed it.

Henry froze where he was, one foot in the tub and the other still on the bathroom tile. At his cessation of movement, I took him in my mouth further and sucked him down. Soren and Henry both groaned at the action, spurring me on. Henry gently placed his hands on my head, and I realized my hair was still twisted up in the braid crown Fin had given me.

Twirling my tongue around his shaft, I lifted a hand to pump the base. Slowly, I sucked his cock deep in my throat, twisting my hand at the bottom. Hands roamed me from behind, and I felt the water shift around me as Soren moved. Kisses fell on my shoulder and neck before he whispered in my ear, "Suck our lover's cock down. Show him how much we love him."

Hearing Soren made me moan around Henry's dick, and the vibrations increased his pleasure. It was becoming harder to focus as Soren's slick hands moved over me. Grazing my breast and pulling at my nipple, he teased my entrance and rounded my ass before returning to my stomach. He was painting me with his hands and driving my desire higher with each caress.

I must've stopped my movements, distracted by my own pleasure, and I was caught off guard when Henry started to thrust into my mouth and remembered I was supposed to be sucking. Working together, I was soon deep-throating Henry as Soren's hand finally dipped into me, making me almost lose my hold over my concentration. When I felt Sor's dick nudge up against my ass, I couldn't hold the moan back any longer.

With a pop, I let go of Henry and threw my head back onto Soren's shoulder, and gave in to the sensations coursing through me. His fingers pumped into my core, his piercings rubbing against my rosette. Henry bent down to kiss me, his tongue and hands a frenzy of activity as I lit up like the fourth of July and detonated. As I orgasmed, they moved, and when I came back to reality, I found myself cradled in Soren's arms with Henry looking at me from across us in the water now.

"Are you ready for more, Sawyer?"

Nodding, I pulled Soren's head down and kissed him. His kisses made my toes curl with how passionately he took my mouth. Soren Stryker kissed with all the intensity he did everything with. He lifted me up and slowly sank me onto his cock. It felt so tight from this angle, and his piercing rubbed against me in new places.

"Fuck, Sor," I whimpered, consumed by pleasure. Henry moved in front of us, and I found him standing with his cock in hand as he watched. The water moved around us, and I knew we wouldn't be able to get too crazy in here, or the bathroom would be flooded. Soren moved me slowly, in little spurts as he watched Henry. Deciding I wanted to feel both my men around me, I braced my hands against the side of the tub and maneuvered myself. Of course, the action felt amazing, and I had to pump myself a few times before pulling entirely off him. It was only reasonable.

Soren groaned when his cock was free of me, and I heard it slap the water. I almost turned back and said, "fuck the bed," but I wanted both my boyfriends and the tub was only going to make it dangerous. *I wanted to be wet, not the floor.* Henry looked at me curiously as I stepped out and grabbed a towel off the counter. Once I was dried, I dropped it on the floor and turned, walking on my tiptoes.

"What are you waiting for, boys? Come and catch me!"

Darting off, I attempted to be sexy as the sound of splashing was heard behind me. I would need to check my priorities next time I decided to be seductive because somehow, I'd completely forgotten they were in the water. Water sloshed everywhere as they raced to get out of the tub. I tried not to cringe at the amount that had to be on the floor. This was what I'd tried to avoid!

When I heard their feet hitting the tile, I ran and vaulted myself into the bed. The grunt that sounded below me took me by surprise, quickly followed by a groan and not the good kind. Scrambling off whoever I'd just nailed in the gonads, I raised my fists to fight them.

I might be naked, and I might be small, but I was scrappy.

I'd do my damndest to take whoever this was out, even if I had to do it with my boobs swinging. Well, I mean, they weren't that *big*. Maybe I could poke them out with a nipple to the eye? Weaponize your breasts, girls! You never know when you might be in a pinch and need to get out of a situation, and the only thing that would save you was your nipple.

"You picked the wrong time to try and take me, buddy! I'll break your face, and then my boyfriends will too!" I proclaimed, standing with my fists raised.

About this time, Soren and Henry were fighting to get through the doorway of the bathroom. They looked up when they heard me and found me in my fighting stance, butt naked and a squirming humanoid shape in the bed.

"You got two seconds before I karate chop your balls! One, two—"

"Sawyer, wait!" shrieked a high-pitched voice that sounded vaguely like Mateo.

At his shout, Mateo finally freed himself from the covers of doom he'd been tangled up in, a look of panic on his face.

"Oh, for the love of orange soda! I almost killed you with my nipple!"

Dropping my hands, I collapsed to my knees on the ground, exhaustion plaguing me as the adrenaline ran out. When Ollie and Ty ran into the room a second later with startled looks, I gave up and just laid back starfish style on the carpet.

*This was where I died, naked and all.*

I didn't know who started laughing first, and I hated them all at this point anyway. This was the issue with too many boyfriends. When they all ganged up on you, you were outnumbered!

"I can't believe you almost karate chopped poor Mateo's balls!" snorted Ollie.

Flipping him off, I laid there hoping they would all get incredibly hard boners from my naked body and wouldn't have any help from me taking care of it.

"I can't believe she was going to fight him nude! And with her nipple," Ty chortled out.

They were both bent over laughing, and I'd had enough of the ridicule. I'd been ready to take some Council ass down! Sitting up, I crossed my arms over my breasts and leveled them with my glare. "Well, believe it when I say you won't be getting any nipple action anytime soon!" That shut them up and I felt vindicated for a whole thirty seconds. Mateo kneeled beside me, handing me a top.

"It seems I'm always getting you into topless situations, Dulzura." He smiled his sweet smile, and I couldn't be mad anymore. "I'm sorry I scared you. I didn't realize you were with Soren. I mean, I guess I should've, but well, yeah. I heard the bathwater and thought I'd wait for you, but I must've fallen asleep. I feel terrible about it all."

How were you supposed to be mad at that? Short answer, you couldn't.

Pulling him into my arms, I hugged him tight to me. The world needed more men like Mateo. He lifted me into his arms and placed me on the bed, tucking me under the covers. The exhaustion was heavy now, and I no longer had sex on my mind. Ollie and Ty walked over once I was settled under the covers.

"We're sorry, pretty girl. We didn't mean to laugh at you or hurt your feelings. You're just naturally funny, and it makes me smile. That's all. Own it."

"Thanks, Ollie. I'll try to."

I leaned up and captured his lips quickly. I wasn't mad at him. In retrospect, it was funny. I'd just had the energy rush out when I thought I was fighting for my life. We needed more laughing moments, and he was right; *I was hilarious.*

"Love you, Wildcat," Ty whispered, kissing my cheek. Grabbing his shirt, I pulled him down to my lips, not wanting him to leave without a proper kiss.

"Love you, Ty."

He looked relieved by my action, and I was glad I'd given in. They moved away, and I found Henry and Soren semi-dressed in shirts and boxers standing at the foot of my bed, looking torn. It struck my tired brain at the oddness, but I guess Soren did own boxers after all.

"You don't have to leave."

They nodded and took their shirts back off. I realized Mateo was still holding my hand, and I knew I wanted him to stay too.

"Would you stay too, Mateo?"

Henry and Soren had been making their way around my bed to bracket me, but at my question, they paused to see what Mateo would say. He looked at them, and Henry seemed to understand what he was asking. "It's cool with us if you stay, man."

Mateo smiled, and I realized how important that had been for him. He needed to feel included with the guys and not on the outside like he'd felt his whole life. Smiling wide myself, I scooted back so he could slide in next to me, with Henry and Soren behind me. Henry spooned me, and I felt Soren's arms wrap around us both.

Well, the evening had gone from one extreme to the next. I would never be upset about ending it in the arms of my lovers. At this rate, I would need a giant bed. There was no way Rhett could fit into a bed with anyone else, that mountain was *all man*, and I loved climbing him like my own personal jungle gym. My thoughts trailed off and fatigue took me under, falling asleep quickly.

A few hours later, I was dreaming. I knew I was. It was the only explanation of how I was in the same room with both Isla and Victoria. They were arguing, and I didn't know what it meant. Moving closer, I realized that they couldn't see me, so I moved up to them to hear.

*"You need to tell her!" Victoria exclaimed.*

*"Why? What good would it do now? I just got her back. I don't want to lose her again."* Tears fell down Isla's cheeks, and I wanted to comfort her and tell her I was right here! I hadn't gone anywhere, and I wanted to get to know her too. But it all fell on deaf ears as my words stayed stuck in my throat.

*"Keeping it from her only hurts her more. You know this. Think about how you felt when you found out."*

*"I know, okay!"* Isla turned her back to Victoria. *I watched as she put a hand on her back.*

*"They will come for her. If she's not prepared, you will lose her. Tell her about the order. Do it before it's too late."*

On that cryptic note, the dream disappeared, and I woke up. Sitting up in bed, I was surprised to see it was still dark outside. All three men were still asleep, so I scooted over Mateo to get out of the bed. I knew the dream hadn't been a vision or real. *Victoria was dead.* I knew this. But my brain was trying to make me remember something.

A week ago, I'd read Isla's note, and I'd shoved it into a corner of my mind, not ready to deal with it. Earlier tonight, I knew my expiration date was coming to a close. It seemed my brain was telling me time was up now. Opening my closet, I shut the door behind me quietly and flipped on the light as I made my way to the top drawer of the dresser.

Opening it, I found the box and letter exactly where I'd put them. Taking a breath, I picked up the card and opened it again. Sitting on the floor, I read the words I needed to hear— no more hiding.

*Sawyer,*

*I still find it hard some days to believe you're here. When they told me my baby girl hadn't made it, part of me died that day. I tried to be a good mother for Asa, but I know I let him down at times. It was hard to look at him and not remember what he was meant to be—a twin.*

*A deeper part of me was glad you were gone. Hear me out before you get outraged. I was glad because it meant I wouldn't have to pass on my family's horrible tradition to my daughter, to my innocent baby girl whose only crime was being born into this family.*

*I don't want to tell you this. I wish I could keep it from you, but it's all so clear now. My grief had clouded me and made me blind to the signs, to the truth. By now, you've learned about the Council and how your father, Orson, orchestrated for you to be given to a vile man, Jayce Latimer. Fate was looking out for you, though, and placed you with my dear friend Victoria.*

*When you told me she was your adoptive mother, some of my shame fell away because I knew she would've loved you as her own. I'm thankful to her and Bryan, or Scott, for loving you and keeping you safe, for giving their lives for you.*

*It wasn't by chance that I ended up with Orson. I see that now. I'd always wanted to believe I wasn't that naive, but it was a setup from the start. I want to hope that Samson wasn't part of it, but where the Abernathy's are concerned, it's rare that anything had a good intention. The only ones I'd ever liked in that wretched family were Samson and Gertie, their mother. She was too kind for this world.*

*Time to talk about my family then. The Walsh's hail from Ireland and were livestock breeders. Somewhere in our family history, a deal was struck, and our family became a tógálaí slíocht to the Council, which loosely translates to offspring builder. It's as creepy as it sounds. When my progeny "died" and I'd fulfilled my duty of producing an heir for the Council, I was clued into what our family had become. My whole life, it had been hidden from me, and I was made to believe otherwise.*

*I don't want that for you, my darling. Mostly because I just got you back, and I don't want to lose you. But also because I think you're in a position to stop it. I hate to put that pressure on you. But I think it was why they took you as a baby.*

*I have to assume they wanted to keep you close, groom you, and then break you. They could turn you into their perfect weapon of seduction and power. It sickens me, but I believe they wanted to groom you to bed all the heirs (excluding your brother) and produce the ideal replacements ensuring the current seven remained in power forever.*

*Now that they know you're alive, I'm fearful of what my family might do.*

*They will come for you if they haven't already and aid the Council in their pursuit. They take their lineage seriously, and they will want to regain that power. While I'm not the only Walsh, I've been the only one to bear a female in over twenty years. To find you now, at childbearing age, they will be chomping at the bit.*

*I wish I was brave enough to tell you this face to face. I hate that it's in a card I had Asa give you. I'm not as courageous as you, but I want to be. I can see how much stronger you are, darling. So while I hate this for you and wish I could take it from you, I know you are the one meant to stop it.*

*You're so strong, Sawyer, and you've built yourself a family. You've surrounded yourself with love. They won't be able to break you like they broke me.*

*The only help I can offer is the watch. It's important. I can't tell you more, but it's a deal I made back when I still believed in something. Back when I thought I could make a difference. Please, keep it on you at all times. When you need it, you will know.*

*Keep your eyes open and your loved ones close. When I met you, I saw how much stronger you were, stronger than me. I hope you will forgive my cowardice because I want to get to know you. I would like to be in your life.*

*I'll wait for you to reach out and let me know if you're willing to give me a chance. I couldn't take it if I got close and then lost you. I knew I had to tell you now. You inspired me to be brave.*

*Above all, I hope you know that you and Asa are my greatest achievements.*

*I love you, my darling girl.*

*Isla*

Before crawling back into bed, I decided to open Charlie's gift. Pulling the weighted box out of the gift bag, I still had no clue what it could be. Opening it, I gasped as I took it in. The silver frame glistened in the dim light, and while it was gorgeous and one of the prettiest frames I'd ever seen, it was the engraving and picture that brought tears to my eyes.

Tucked inside was a picture of Charlie and me hugging last week someone had snapped. Despite not seeing our eyes, the love and connection shone through our bodies as we held one another. On a small plaque below the picture, the following was engraved: *To my Granddaughter.*

The old fart had officially made me cry.

Once I dried my tears, I snuggled close to my guys as I thought over everything. I had to tell them. I couldn't hide from it anymore. She was right. I was strong and brave, and I had these men in my corner. It wasn't fair, but I would fight this battle because I could. I had something to fight for, and that made me dangerous.

Latimer might've thought he was building me up to make it more fun to break, but he screwed up. By giving me loving parents, I learned what unconditional love felt like. No matter how much I doubted things at times, I never doubted their love for me.

Love would be my weapon, and I would destroy the evil the Council represented. They could huff, they could puff, but they wouldn't be blowing this house down.

Besides, I now had weapons of mass destruction—nipple guns.

# thirty-four

· · ·

## mateo

SOFT SNORES GREETED me as the sun started to peek through the curtains. Squinting my eyes, I found a blurry Sawyer still asleep in front of me. She looked so peaceful, and I stared at her for a moment, just watching her. I hadn't meant to cause a ruckus last night when I surprised Sawyer. In fact, I berated myself pretty hard for not realizing she'd come up here for some sexy fun time with Soren and Rey.

"I can hear you thinking all the way over there," Rey whispered, and I lifted my head slightly to see an even blurrier figure with one eye open. Sheepishly, I smiled and shrugged. I was a thinker, and admonishing myself was kind of my thing. Guess I should get a new hobby.

"I just feel bad about how things ended last night," I mumbled.

Rey opened both of his eyes at my words, and with a devilish smirk, moved the hair away from Sawyer's neck. "No time like the present to make up for it," he rasped, kissing her.

I stared blankly, unsure how I felt. Things with Sawyer and I had progressed, and I felt comfortable with where things were with us. Did that mean I was ready for more? I watched transfixed as he trailed kisses down her throat to her collarbone, and I found myself not caring. My dick certainly didn't, as it started to get hard at the sight. Sawyer moaned and moved her hips, and my body decided for me.

When Rey's lips landed on her shoulder, he pulled the shirt down, swirling his tongue around the exposed area. Sawyer was still asleep, but her tiny moans and movements told me she wouldn't be for much longer.

"Help me with her shirt," he whispered, and I hesitantly lifted the hem up. I watched her face the whole time to see if she didn't want me to. Sawyer moved more toward me, and I took it as a sign to keep going. When it reached her head, Rey moved her hair out of the way and skillfully pulled the shirt over. She laid half in my arms and his, and I gazed lovingly at my beautiful girlfriend. Licking my lips, I met Rey's again as he watched me wrestle with indecision.

"If you're not ready, we can stop," he assured me, finalizing my decision to dive in. He was comfortable with me here, and it wasn't a pity thing. Feeling part of it made me quiet the thoughts in my head.

"No, I'm ready."

Rey nodded and let me decide where I wanted to start.

Dropping to her breasts, I swirled my tongue around her nipple, the one she said would've killed me last night. *If I had to go by Sawyer's nipples, at least I'd die happy.*

Moving my hands up her body, I roamed her skin as I left kisses on her breast. I sucked more of her into my mouth, her moan sounding louder, and with a little gasp, I knew she'd finally woken up.

"I thought I was dreaming," she breathed, "this is better than any alarm clock."

Continuing my journey, I occasionally would encounter Rey's hands as we both mapped out her body. It startled me the first time, but it wasn't weird. We were Sawyer's octopus lover, each of us a moving part, and I was running into another tentacle. Gliding up to her mouth, I took her in a kiss that left us both gasping for air. Sawyer continued to rock into my very hard cock with each roll of her hips, and I had to agree—this was hands down the best way to wake up.

When I heard Rey groan a second later, I assumed the last member of our sleepover was awake. Sawyer's hands began to roam my body, and when she slid her hand into my boxers, I joined the room as I cursed out in pleasure.

"Shit, Dulzura, that feels good."

"Why is that kind of hot hearing him cuss?" I heard Soren whisper to Rey.

"Shut up and kiss me, you weirdo."

Sawyer trailed kisses down my chest, and I opened my eyes and found Soren and Rey tangled with one another. Rey's head was tilted back to kiss Soren over his shoulder, who had moved up to lean over him. As my eyes traveled down, I found Soren's hand gripping Rey's cock. I'd never seen guys passionately kiss before or even being sexual with one another. It wasn't awkward like I'd imagined. I saw two people in love, and there was nothing odd about it. It was beautiful, actually.

Sawyer freed my cock, wrapping her mouth around me. Falling onto my back, I succumbed to the sensational pleasure coursing through my body. When I couldn't take it anymore without fear of coming down her throat, I pulled her to me. Kissing one another, I wrapped my arms around her and pulled her close. Some days, I felt I'd never be able to get close enough to her.

Sawyer lifted her leg over my hip, and I used it to pull her even more. Staring into one another's eyes, I slipped into her. Every time I felt Sawyer's pussy, I wondered how I would breathe past the next second. She was incredibly wet, and I had no issues plunging into her. I held her close to me for a moment as I breathed through the temptation to fuck her into oblivion. Mostly because I would detonate in two seconds if I gave in to the need.

When I had everything under control, I began to move. I'd never been in this position before with us both on our sides. It was intimate, and I slid differently. Tangling my fingers in her hair, I held her gaze as I rocked forward, and I felt her meet me. With my other hand, I palmed her ass and assisted in propelling her forward onto my cock.

Despite Rey and Soren being on the other side of the bed, I didn't even know it in this second. My world was in Sawyer's eyes, and that was all that fit. Kissing her, I slowed my pace, wanting to treasure every second with her as if it were my last. Maybe it was my inexperience, but it felt like sex would disappear in a blink just as I discovered how amazing it was.

When I felt Sawyer begin to tighten around me, I knew I didn't have much longer either. Battling with her tongue, I swirled around hers as I plunged quicker into her. Moans echoed around the room, adding to our heightened arousal. Lifting her leg by the knee, I thrust forward hard and fast until I felt my balls tighten, holding her as my orgasm overtook me. Sawyer spasmed around me, and a sense of accomplishment filled me.

Pulling out, I fell to my back as my heart settled back to normal and my breathing evened out. Sawyer's hand was tracing circles on my chest as she enjoyed her orgasmic bliss until she was pulled back into another body. I laid there and watched as Henry took her, Sawyer surrendering to him.

It was different from how we were together, but I liked it. For once, I wasn't comparing myself to others, but seeing how authentic this type of relationship could be. Sex with me should be different, and I liked that I could tell. As I watched the three of them together, I couldn't deny it was hot as fuck. It wasn't because I was attracted to Rey or Soren. Sawyer's pleasure was written all over her face, and I found that sexy.

She looked over and found me watching them. With a beckoning of her finger, she pulled me into their embrace. I didn't know what to do with my hands or legs, but I stopped worrying about it because I didn't think it actually mattered. Somehow, Sawyer had convinced my cock to wake up again, and when she wrapped her hand around me and stroked me in rhythm with Rey and Soren's thrusts, I found myself hard as steel.

Kissing her, I relished the freedom in this relationship and the trust we all had for one another. It was beautiful when you thought about it. At the pace she was stroking my dick, I didn't last long, still sensitive from the last one. Our combined cum had given her a sticky lubricant to use. This time when I came, my eyes rolled to the back of my head, and I moaned loudly.

"Fuck, Dulzura."

"Yes, yes, yes," she moaned, and I heard the slapping of skin as they all quickened their pace and seemed to cum together. Dropping my head, I laid there naked, cum on my stomach, my girl in my arms and two of my friends on the other side of her, and I realized how happy I was.

"I'm happy."

"I'll say," teased Soren, which was followed by an "Ow" when Rey's slap landed.

"I'm glad, Mateo. You feeling okay with everything?" I heard Rey ask quietly.

"Good, and weird. Mostly because it took me a moment to realize what I was feeling, and not to get into how messed up that is, I'll just say thanks for making me feel included."

"I'm happy, too," Sawyer responded, kissing me on the nose.

"Oh, I'm definitely happy." Soren chuckled.

"Oh my God, Soren! You're hanging out with Ollie too much." Sawyer laughed.

"Well, this asshole aside, I'm happy too, and I love our family—BOSH."

"BOSH," we all said together. We laid there for a while, enjoying the freedom of being completely open and free. I guess once people saw you naked and your orgasm face, there wasn't much else to hide. When an alarm went off at 7:30 am, Sawyer and Rey groaned, knowing they had practice.

We all got up and headed in different directions for showers. Before I left the room, Sawyer grabbed my arm.

"You're really okay with that? I know that's very new to what we've done so far?"

"Yes, Dulzura. I'm good. Now go and kick some ice skating butt."

"Okay."

After my shower, I dressed in some black joggers and a long sleeve shirt. It was from one of my old sponsors, but it was worn and comfortable, perfect for a Sunday. Taking my phone from the charger, I was confused when I saw messages from an unknown number.

**Unknown:** Hey Teo, it's been a while. How are you?
**Unknown:** Listen, I know this won't make sense, but can we meet? I'll be at TAS on Sunday afternoon.
**Unknown:** If you're interested, meet me at this coffee shop
**Unknown:** Hope to see you, old friend

Dropping the phone onto the bed, a cold chill washed

over me.

My leg was bouncing as I waited at a table in the coffee shop. It might've been due to the three coffees I'd drunk while waiting, but I doubt it. Rhett had insisted on getting here early to "stake out the place." As soon as I'd gotten over my shock, I'd told the guys at the house. Sawyer and Rey were finishing up practice, so Soren went to pick them up.

Ty, Ollie, and Rhett were staged around the coffee shop with me. Elias had a meeting and said he'd catch up with us later. We hadn't told anyone else because we weren't sure what this was about yet. It was too random not to be connected to Sawyer or the Council, though. Just as I was about to get another drink, the door chimed, and in walked a face I never thought I'd see again. Standing, I waved as he made his way over.

"Teo! How are you, man?" my once only friend went in to hug me, and I awkwardly patted him as he did.

"Samuel. Hey, um, I'm good. What brings you to Oak Crest?"

Blowing out air, he ruffled his shaggy hair before responding, "Let's grab a drink first. Do you want anything?"

Shaking my head no, I sat back down. Earlier I'd drunk them to pass the time, and I felt guilty sitting at a table for so long if I wasn't contributing to their income in some way, so I'd gone a little overboard. Now, my throat was parched, unsure how to take Samuel being here, but I didn't want to risk any more liquid.

Sam returned a few minutes later with a cup and sat down across from me. He smiled, and while it seemed friendly, I could see a tightness there too. The last time we'd seen each other hadn't ended the best.

*"Sam, you don't understand! I don't want to do what you're asking me. I don't even want to ski. I hate it. They make me hate it."*

*"Teo, you can't stop. You can't give up. Not after everything my parents have done for you. Not after everything I've done for you!"*

*"What are you talking about?"*

*"Do you think it was just 'lucky' those sponsors found you? That you won scholarships and I had extra equipment?"*

*"I," shaking my head, I didn't want to think about it. "No, I—"*

*"Stop lying to yourself. My parents did all that for you. They invested in you more than they did me. They believe in you. You've stolen my parent's love and affection for the past ten years, the least you can do is honor their dream."*

*Tears were in his eyes, and I stood there, shocked. I hadn't realized. I hadn't known. Was he right, though? Was I blind to it or had I just chosen to be?*

*"I'm sorry, I..."*

*"I know, man, I know. I just need you to do this for me. It will make everything right. Please, as my friend."*

*He handed me a chip and asked me to place it on her phone*

*when she wasn't looking. Dread filled me, but I guess I owed him if what he was saying was true.*

*"Okay. If that's what you need."*

*Samuel nodded, relief filling him at me giving in. Later that day, I placed the chip onto the back of her phone, putting her case back in place. The guilt ate at me, combining with my self-hatred. I skied for another year before it all became too much, and I recklessly tried to find a way out.*

"Listen, I'm sorry about how things went down last time. I never should've asked you to plant that chip. It was stupid and reckless. I was in a bad place back then, and I took it out on you. You didn't deserve that. I'm sorry, man."

"Thank you for saying that, but what I never understood was why? Why did you tell me those things and have me do that?"

Blowing out another breath, he took a gulp down before responding. "That's a long story, and I'm not sure I want to travel down memory lane today. I started seeing a therapist, though. I was messed up back then and took out my insecurity on you. I thought if I knew how to show Caitlynn I was perfect for her, then she'd fall in love with me. Like I said, *dumb.*"

"I mean, it was a little more than that, though, wasn't it?"

Samuel had wanted my help to place a chip on Caitlynn Storm's phone. She was on the ski team with us at the time. It had ended up being a big scandal, and she'd quit. I'd always felt bad for stealing her phone. His parents had gotten the charges dropped, but he had to leave the ski team. This was the first time we'd talked since he'd blamed me for getting caught. When they'd asked me if I knew anything, I'd been honest. The fear of disappointing adults was ingrained in me from my own parents, so I hadn't stood a chance.

"Yeah, well, it's all in the past. I worked through it, and I promise I'm not doing any of that anymore."

"Okay," I drawled, "why are you here then? I have to admit I was shocked to get your text. I didn't even have you on my phone."

"Yeah, I wondered about that but figured I was the only one who called you Teo," he admitted.

"Yeah, outside my family."

"How is your family?"

"Oh, um, good. Hugo is finishing up his surgery residency, and Isabella is in her last year of law school. So you know, successful as usual."

"I bet your parents are happy."

"Uh-huh."

"I'm guessing they're still the same."

"Yup, and so thrilled with my current career trajectory. But I don't care anymore. I realized life wasn't worth living if I was doing it only for them."

"I'm happy to hear you've found that place. And well, I'm sorry to hear about you stopping skiing, but also not surprised. I shouldn't have pushed you to continue all those years ago. I felt responsible for your accident by throwing all that guilt on you. It wasn't fair of me. I was messed up. My parents had told me a family secret and were disappointed in my skiing prowess, and I took it out on you."

425

"As much as I appreciate you saying that, one thing I learned in my own therapy," I smiled, pausing, "was my choices are my own. I could've walked away at any time. I could've told my parents no. There were a million things I could've done differently, but I didn't. And while that night stuck with me, and it was uncool of you to drop all that on me, I never blamed you."

Taking a deep breath, I sat up in my seat before continuing. "Sam, you were the only friend I had, my best friend. Your family was good to me and believed in me when mine didn't. Whether that was for nefarious reasons or not, it didn't matter. I found something I loved through our friendship and had opportunities I wouldn't have any other way open for me. I don't hate skiing. I never did."

"So, why did you do it then?"

"Because at the time, I couldn't see any other way out. It was wrong, and I see that now, but I was drowning. I couldn't deal with the pressure or the stress, and I should've asked for help sooner. That's on me as much as it sucks to admit, but I've learned how to stand up for myself. Most importantly, I've been able to become my own person outside of skiing, outside of my parents. Once I was able to get out from under that environment, I was able to see how much I love skiing again."

He observed me for a minute before saying anything. "You're different now, you know?"

"Yeah? I feel different. Stronger."

"I can tell. Maybe I should see *your* therapist."

"I can get you her number." I laughed. "But what made

the difference for me was finding people who care, support, and accept me as I am. My friends have taught me I'm strong as who I am, and I really like me."

"Any chance I could be included back in that category again?" he asked hesitantly.

I didn't need to think about it. If Sam wanted to be friends again, who was I to tell him no? We all needed people to accept us and show us the way sometimes. I could be that for him just as BOSH had been for me.

"Sam, you never left. You're my friend for life. You just had to see it for yourself."

"I *really* like this Teo."

"Good, me too."

"Are your friends here?"

"Yeah, um, actually." I blushed. "Some of them are in this shop right now."

He looked stunned for a minute at my honesty, but then a wide grin spread across his face. "Well, tell them to come over. I want to meet these people that you hold dear."

Nodding, I glanced at Rhett and motioned for him to join us. He casually set the magazine down that he'd been fake reading and walked over, sitting next to me. His frame took up the whole area, and I swear Sam swallowed when he took in the mountain of a man.

"Sam, this is Rhett, one of my roommates and friends. Rhett, this is Sam."

Rhett nodded in his usual way, assessing the situation. "Is that the only reason you're here? To make amends?" Rhett asked, putting it all out there on the table. I forgot how much I appreciated that about him.

Sam looked shocked for a second until he straightened and nodded, accepting that we clearly knew something.

"I don't know how you know, but maybe I should. I've heard rumors, but I didn't know if they were true or not. That day, I was talking about the one where I felt my world was turned upside down and led me to do something reckless?"

I nodded at the rhetorical question.

"Well, that was the day I learned my whole life had been scripted. I was meant to be some big ski legend to further our family legacy. But it wasn't in the way I thought. My family was tied to an organization known as the Council."

When neither of us asked who, he nodded to himself, accepting he'd been right.

"Okay, I guess that answers whether or not you've heard of them. Teo, we were both pawns in their bigger plan. When I got in trouble, I was sent to a place that was meant to rehabilitate me. I didn't want to do the things my father was telling me, and my stupid recklessness with Caitlynn only ended in failure and embarrassment."

"That was a Council test?"

"Yeah, an initiation of sorts, but not only did I fail, but I involved a non-member. So I was sent to a place meant to indoctrinate me more into the Council way of thinking when—"

"You met Mr. Hawthorne," Elias interrupted. We all turned and looked up at him. Shock was on Sam's face and probably mine as well at Elias' proclamation.

"Yeah, how did you know?"

"Not here. Come, let's head back to the house. Soren's bringing Sawyer and Rey there."

Not even questioning it, I got up and followed Elias. When I didn't find Sam next to me, I turned, and he was still at the table.

"Sam, trust me, okay? These are my friends, and we protect our own."

"Okay, Teo. I trust you."

Somehow, my past, present, and future were intersecting and weaving together in ways I'd never considered. The part of me that freaked out at new information wanted to fall into the hole of doubt and question everything. The stronger part, the one I'd come to like, was telling me to trust in my friends, in BOSH.

It didn't matter how we got here; it only mattered that we were here together. We would unlock this puzzle as one. As weird as the meeting with Sam had gone, it was nice knowing I had my friend back, and perhaps, all the tension in the past could be placed on the Council.

Every time we turned around, they were there, and I was starting to get sick of it. But nothing they did seemed to work when it came to our bonds. They could fracture us all they wanted, but we would come back stronger every time. The Council might be termites around every corner and into everything, destroying the structure from the inside out. But we'd be cockroaches, always finding a way to survive.

Though, I think I'd keep that analogy to myself. I doubt my Dulzura wanted to be referred to as a cockroach.

# thirty-five

. . .

## sawyer

MADELYN WAS A FUCKING BEAST, and I could already see the improvements she was making in our skating. Sweat dripped from me, as I bent over on my knees and tried to regain my breath. We'd been at it for four hours, and I was exhausted. My legs and arms felt like jelly, and all I wanted to do was soak in a hot tub or sauna. Even thoughts of Henry and my last visit did nothing for me below.

I was that pooped.

"Good progress, guys. I think if we change out a few things in your routine for higher points, you guys will easily take it."

Excitement bubbled to the top of me, and I couldn't help the glee that escaped. For so long, it had been a dream I'd lost and never thought I'd get back. Now it was within my reach, and I almost didn't know if I could trust it.

Henry and I skated off the ice together and found Soren in the bleachers, smiling at us. I loved when the guys stayed to watch, even if I didn't always notice them when we were skating. It was a good thing, I guess. When Henry and I skated, we entered into our own world. It had always been that way. Outside distractions melted away, giving us an edge over our competition.

"Hey, cuties. You guys are fire!"

"Thanks, Sor."

"So… Rhett messaged and wanted us to meet at the house."

"Did Mateo's meeting go okay?"

"I don't know. I think that's what it's about. He just said to come to the house, as that's where they were headed."

"Okay, well, I need a quick rinse, and then we can head out."

Henry and I headed to the locker room, both jumping into the shower to rinse off the sweat, but didn't stay long enough to enjoy it. Redressing, we were both quiet, and thoughts about what this could be swirled in my mind.

"I'm glad things went okay this morning," Henry stated, breaking the silence.

Glancing over my shoulder, I found him looking at me as I pulled on my socks. "Were you worried? Was that something you didn't want to do?" Worry filled me as I thought I'd pushed them into something.

"No, I wasn't worried, Smalls. So stop the freak-out. I

hadn't thought I'd want to open, well, I mean," he blushed. "I hadn't thought I'd want anyone else with us because things with Sor were still so new, but that's solid, and I'm comfortable with how I feel about you both. Mateo fit naturally, and it wasn't about *being* with him. It was about us all being with you *together*. I don't want to be with anyone else sexually. But sharing it with him felt right. I don't know if I'd want to do that with everyone, but Mateo's become a good friend, and yeah, I dunno how to say this without sounding lovey."

Chuckling, I stood and kissed his cheek. "Henry Reyes, you're the sweetest you know?" Wrapping my arms around him, I hugged the boy who had a heart of gold and had made room for another lost soul. "Come on, let's get out of here. One, I'm starved, and two, I'm dying to know what's going on."

"Oh! Maybe we can talk Sor into making us tacos!"

"You're a freaking genius!"

Laughing, we grabbed our things and headed out. Sor was against the wall like he had been the first time I caught him here. The boy knew how to make holding up a wall look hella sexy. Grinning, I dropped my bag, hoping Henry would pick it up, and jumped into Soren's arms. "Carry me, I'm pooped," I fake whined.

"You're ridiculous, but because I happen to like carrying you, I'll allow it."

Soren twisted me around, so I was on his back, and I laughed as he acted like a racehorse and booked it out of the rink. Unfortunately, almost as if Queen Bee could smell my happiness, she buzzed around and waited to sting. Our trio came to a stop outside as we faced off with her.

"Really, Adelaide, haven't we gotten past these childish games yet? I'm exhausted and want to go home."

"We'll be past them when you stop taking EVERYTHING from me!" she bellowed.

"Whoa, girl. I think you need to dial it back and take a look at your priorities. I'm not taking *anything* from you."

"You took Elias, you took skating, and now you're taking my spot with this coach!"

"Hey, listen, that's between you and Madelyn, and well, Elias, too. You cheated on him, so I think that's on you. As for skating, I'm not even in singles anymore. The way you're constantly stalking me, though, I'm starting to think you're obsessed with me."

"Like I would ever care about poor little Abernathy *trash*. You're nothing but a vessel for them, and you're already falling into their laps, spreading your legs for all these men. You're a slut for the Council, and you're too stupid even to see it. You think you're so smart, but you're not. You'll never get anything past them. They have spies everywhere, even in your own midst. Do us all a favor and fucking leave!"

She turned and walked away, and I wondered what her purpose had been. Nothing she said mattered. I knew it all already, and she was dead wrong.

"Well, she was fucking lovely as usual," scoffed Henry, causing Soren and I to bellow out a laugh. Ready to get home, I focused back on what was important.

"Giddy up, horsey! I want tacos!"

We galloped off and headed to the house. It wasn't until we walked into it, I realized how differently I'd handled the encounter. The first time she'd thrown shade at me, I'd reacted and attacked right back. Now, it rolled off like water off a duck's back and didn't even penetrate. I knew the guys had helped, fortifying me in ways, but it was also me. I'd kicked her out of my headspace, no longer letting her, or the lies she spewed take up rent there. It was freeing realizing I'd done that myself. Pure strength generated in me, and I felt like a new person.

"Hey, Mateo," I greeted when we walked into the room. I noticed a new person next to him and smiled sweetly, figuring it was his friend. Bending down, I kissed Mateo, and he responded in kind. When I pulled back, something different was in his eyes as well. It looked like we had both shed some demons today.

"Hey, I'm Sawyer," I said to the mystery guest.

"I'm Samuel Walker. Nice to meet you, Sawyer." He grinned, sitting up.

Looking around the table, I didn't see any empty chairs. When Rhett noticed, he pushed back from the table and offered me his leg. However, on my way over to him, arms wrapped around me and pulled me into a different seat. Looking up at who'd snagged me, I found Elias.

"Hey." I blushed, still not used to not fighting with him.

"Love." He grinned, dropping a kiss to my lips before turning serious.

"I'll catch everyone up real quick. I had a meeting with my confidant, our benefactor, and he told me he was sending us help. When I figured out he meant Samuel, I headed to the coffee shop and happened to intercept them before too much was spilled and reported back to the Council."

"We swept for bugs, though. It was clean," Ty argued.

"I'm sure it was, but technology cannot account for humans."

"You mean there was someone there who was listening for the Council?" I questioned.

"Exactly."

"But who? There was hardly anyone there today."

"But there's always at least one person there. Quietly observing and wouldn't be thought weird if he was moving around and listening…" I trailed off.

"I'm guessing you put the pieces together?" Elias offered kindly.

"Yeah." Closing my eyes, I wondered how I could be so dumb.

"Can someone share for the rest of the room?" Ollie quipped.

"The barista," Mateo and I said at the same time.

Smiling at our commonality, I tried to let it go how often I'd dropped my shield around him and ignored my internal warning system.

"Though, we believe he doesn't know who he's reporting to. According to surveillance, it seems a man came into the shop a few days after your first visit and offered him money to report back to him on any information he could. We think it's the same man from the stolen van that ran you off the road."

Once I'd pulled my head out of my ass last week, I'd remembered Ace handing me something the night all shit had broken loose. It was a USB drive with security footage of the parking lot where the school vehicles were kept. When I'd remembered it had a school tag on it, the search had been easy to figure out which ones had been checked out.

Ace had tried to give it to me as a gift to help, knowing the Agency wasn't as concerned about it. I saw it for what it was and thanked him. He did care about our friendship and, despite not telling me his real identity, had been honest with me. When I took into account that my identity was also hidden, well, yeah. I'd gotten over my anger rather quickly.

"The piece I hadn't expected to find, though, was that while you thought Aggie might have some connection to the Council or Agency, she's clean. She's been involved in some way or another with people, but never a member of either. She's kind of like Switzerland, always toeing the party line and staying neutral."

Relief settled in me. I'd hoped she wasn't on the wrong side of this for Rhett and me, but mainly for Charlie. I could tell he was smitten with her, and it would've crushed him if she hadn't been who she'd said all along. I'd asked Chaos to run a background check for me. He was coming in handy, and I hoped Fin figured all that out soon. I was rooting for him.

"What was interesting, though, was that while Aggie was clear, we discovered that her butler, Alfred, wasn't."

Turning, I looked at Elias in shock. "Tell me. If he's dangerous, we need to get her out of that house now!"

"Don't you know I would've already done that if he was," he replied softly. Melting my heart one gesture at a time.

"Oh."

"Yeah, oh." Elias chuckled. It was such an odd sound from him but soothing, nonetheless.

"He's not connected to the Agency or Council, but he isn't who he appears to be either. He's good, *real good* at covering his tracks. From what I can tell, he's part of an order that has worked for Aggie's family for centuries. Maybe it's how they've kept out of the Council hold by having their own protection. He's retired now, but I have a feeling he's why the ambulance reached you so quickly that day. He saw the brake fluid puddle from your Vespa and called it in. The car that witnessed it was more organized than any normal bystander would've been. They had pictures, license plate numbers, and descriptions. I think they were there to protect you so the attackers couldn't abduct you once they ran you off the road. In connection with the ambulance arriving so quickly, it's the only explanation I can think of. Add in the fact that the witnesses have disappeared, and I'd say it was at the hands of this secret order."

"Wow, I feel bad now for thinking he was part of my accident. Guess I owe him a big thanks next time he throws me his usual shade," I mumbled, not happy I owed the snooty butler gratitude.

"Which brings us back to how all this connects to today. Samuel works for my contact and is a double agent. He's in the Council, but actually working for Mr. Hawthorne."

"What the fuck!" I shouted, turning to glare at Elias. His

smirk was not becoming, and I was about to knock it off his face.

"Ah, so you know my name, Sawyer?" a voice from the middle of the room asked.

"Why is that so creepy?" muttered Mateo, and I had to agree. It was like fucking *Charlie's Angels* up in here, and I didn't like it. Was Bosley going to walk up in here next?

A screen began to lower from the ceiling, and I felt like I knew nothing anymore. Had this always been here? Was this a prank? Did I hit my head harder than I thought?

Once it was down, it flicked on, and a beautiful man filled it. He was a clean-shaven man in his forties, with white blonde hair, and crystal blue eyes. He was dressed in an expensive navy suit and had a kind smile. I wasn't expecting him to look like that, nor to be showing kindness. The head of the fucking Council, Alek Hawthorne, was on the screen in the middle of the room and had been listening to who knows what in here.

"You have a lot of explaining to do," I seethed at Elias.

"Trust love. I would never put you in danger."

At his confession, I took some deep breaths, trying to regulate myself. I knew this; he was right. I had to trust this wasn't a gigantic fucking trap.

"Fine." I pouted, turning back to the grinning man on screen.

"You're so like your mother. Even though she didn't birth you, I can see her personality shining through you," Mr. Hawthorne said softly, a look of forlorn sadness coating him. Clearing his throat, he turned to Samuel and greeted him.

"Samuel, good to see you. Thank you for reaching out to Mateo. I'm glad we're all able to connect now. I apologize for the secrecy and for not revealing myself sooner. I'd asked Elias to wait until the right time, knowing the more people who knew then the likelihood it gets back to the Council. The longer I'm hidden, the more I can do."

The guys all looked at him with hesitancy in their eyes as well, and I knew that no one would buy into this unless I did. The simple fact was, I did trust Elias. Not even Adelaide could make me doubt him. If he trusted this man, then I would too.

"What can you tell us?" I offered when everyone remained quiet.

He smiled at me, almost like he was thankful for the lead-in. "You will be getting a call in about thirty minutes that they've located a possible location for Jill. Your friend Fin has been working at the Agency all day assisting them. She's a smart one, that girl."

"Yeah, she is. What does that mean? Is Donnelly done? Can we help?" Henry questioned, perking up when his sister was mentioned.

"Donnelly will be finding himself in particularly hot water Monday morning. As for Jill, it's out of my jurisdiction. I cannot reveal myself to the Agency, so that will be something to discuss with your uncle, Samson. I have a hard time believing he will put you in harm's way, considering he's spent his life protecting you, sacrificing his greatest love to do it."

"You know my uncle?"

"I do. We went to school together and were friends at one time. In the end, we chose different paths."

"You mean you chose the *Council*," mumbled Ollie.

Mr. Hawthorne didn't confirm, but I saw a slight tilt of his lip that vaguely reminded me of Elias. It must've been where he'd learned it.

"How do you two know each other?" I asked, looking between them.

"I met Mr. Hawthorne when I was in boarding school. I didn't know who he was at the time, but he became a mentor to me and, later when I was at Oxford, a trusted ally. I hadn't seen him in a few years, but he was who I went to meet in London."

"So, what is Samuel here for?" Mateo asked, looking at his friend.

"My family has business with the Bellamy's and an in with them. I'm going to use my connection to find out information on the vote coming up. That's your plan, yes? To stop the vote?"

Samuel looked at us, and I nodded, focusing on Hawthorne. "Yes, I want to take men like *you* out of power, men like my *father*. I can't dismantle the Council. I'm just an ice skater, but if I can do something to stop them from continuing their reign, I want to try. Whatever the Agency does from there is up to them. I have bigger dreams than this place, than this organization."

Mr. Hawthorne smirked again, and it was almost as if he got off on me defying him, a hint of admiration in his eyes as well. I didn't need another Brave Heart in my life, so I wasn't going to touch whatever was going on there.

"Very well stated, Ms. Sullivan. Now, I must be off. It was lovely meeting all of you, and next time, I hope it's in person. If there aren't any other questions?"

He paused but didn't appear to think anyone would ask, a mere courtesy to offer, but expected to decline. Except he hadn't factored in one person who didn't care about those things—Rhett.

"Why help us? Why go against the Council like this?"

I turned and took in his posture. He was having a hard time understanding this man's reason, and everything in him was telling him not to. The fact that Elias did was the only thing keeping him in that chair and listening. After what he said to me about his father and grandmother, I think Rhett was attributing this man—the Council's leader—as partially responsible for her death. I didn't blame him. It was hard to swallow. I didn't want to believe it either. I remembered Victoria's journals and how Alek had basically stalked her.

Alek looked right at me when he said the next part, eerily quoting back something I'd said before. "Because it's time for old white men in a tower to quit ruling the world. Because I know what it's like to sit on the sidelines while everything you love is taken from you. Because I hope and pray for a better future. But mostly, because long ago, I'd loved a girl. She asked me for help once, and I hadn't been able to. But now, I can protect her daughter, and that feels just as important."

He paused, leveling me with that gaze again, holding

more affection than I wanted to acknowledge. If Alek Hawthorne was good in the world, then nothing else made sense to me.

"It's time, Ms. Sullivan. They need to know the real reason your father gave you to Latimer, what your family name means. Until next time."

Before I could yell at him for outing me like that, the screen clicked off and raised back into the ceiling like a phantom ghost. Everyone turned and looked at me, a question on their face. Elias tipped my head up to meet his eyes. "Love, something you feel like sharing?"

Well, shit. I didn't think I was going to be getting my tacos anytime soon—nothing like big-ass bombs being dropped to ruin a meal. Now, I had another reason to hate Alek fucking Hawthorne.

# thirty-six

. . .

**sawyer**

"MAN, I'm starved. How about we get some food? Anybody?" When they all continued to stare, I dropped my head. "Can't blame a girl for trying," I mumbled.

"What does Hawthorne mean, baby?"

It was the fear and hint of sadness that did it. Raising my eyes, I sighed as I shared the most disgusting truth I'd learned.

"I only faced it this morning and planned to share it with you this evening, just so you know. Come on, food always makes things better, and *margaritas*," I quipped, feeling sullen about being called out by Hawthorne.

"Sweet pea, I'll make you all the tacos you want if you just talk with us."

"Now, that's a reward I can get behind! Though, no one

may have an appetite after this. Man, this is going to ruin tacos! Nope, I refuse! Tacos are sacred and my love language! Tacos before information. That's my final demand."

Crossing my arms, I planned to out stubborn them on this one.

"There are other ways to get information out of you, love," purred Elias' deep voice behind me, his hands rubbing up and down my legs. I almost gave in to the pleasure until I remembered Sam. Yep, that was a double nope. Standing quickly, I jogged backward as I addressed the guys.

"Seriously, I'm like super starved. I'm not trying to avoid it. I just know once I drop this, the last thing anyone will want is tacos, and I need them more than I need air at the moment. So... I'm going to go and make some, yeah."

Twisting on the balls of my feet, I sprinted out of HQ and slid on the floor like a pro into the kitchen. Pulling out ingredients, I got to work as the guys grumpily traipsed in. Soren eventually gave in and came over to help me. The other guys realized I wasn't joking and started to get everything else set up, and we had food ready in fifteen minutes. It was rather impressive teamwork, and my stomach was about to be really happy.

Loading up a plate, I inhaled three tacos before sitting back, a happy smile on my face.

"Okay, that was impressive. I kind of see why they all have stars in their eyes," Sam flirted.

"Dude, just don't." Mateo laughed, slapping his friend on his back.

"What? She's hot. I'm just commenting."

Rolling my eyes, I ignored them and prepared to say out loud the horrible truth I needed to share as I stared at my now empty plate.

"My family, Isla's side, made a deal with the Council years ago, like hundreds. Apparently, they were breeders in Ireland, and when the Council had a problem, they gave them a solution."

Lifting my eyes, I focused on the pair across from me —Soren.

"What's the greatest power of all?" I asked, but no one answered. Now that I was talking, they didn't want me to stop. "Immortality."

"But that doesn't make sense. This isn't a supernatural novel where that exists," Mateo scoffed.

"How do you live forever in a world where everyone dies?"

Soren held my gaze, and understanding lit in them. "Lineage," he whispered.

Nodding, I looked around the table at everyone. "My family became a *tógálaí sliocht* to the Council, which loosely translates to *offspring builder*."

"You're shitting me. Is this your last prank? Wait, I'm on your team," Ollie bemused, confusion apparent in his brow.

"I wish I was joking. The women in my family became promised to the Council, and a level of prestige was bestowed on them. It's doubtful we're the only ones. I don't see them being a one-business organization. They probably have little breeder farms all over." I shuddered.

"So you were given to the Council to be their baby-making machine?" Henry puzzled out, a look of disgust and horror on his face.

"It's a little worse, actually. Isla believes that I was to be groomed to be the perfect Council *slut*. Opening my legs for all the men and then producing heirs... with their heirs."

I tried not to look around the table at the men who this would've impacted. The chair smashing against the wall shocked me, and I jumped, looking up to see Ollie standing. He was having a hard time breathing as he processed things.

"So what you're saying is that my uncle wanted to basically brainwash you to be a Council whore, and then fuck you? Once he had his jollies, he then wanted to impregnate you with mine or one of my brother's sperm?"

"Yeah, that sounds about right. Me being from the Walsh and Abernathy lines made me the perfect *tógálaí slíocht* royalty. I had Council and Breeder blood. I was the perfect solution for them to live on forever through their lineage they would groom in mini versions of themselves."

"That's... Actually, I have no words," Ty mumbled. He stood, going over to comfort Ollie, who was leaning against the wall, his head banging lightly against the wall. When he passed Rhett, I realized how quiet he was being. He sat frozen, his head down as I disclosed the info I'd learned. "Grump?"

He looked up at my name for him, and the tears in his eyes broke me. Getting up, I walked over to him and climbed into his lap. Rhett wrapped his arms tight around me, his head falling into my hair as he held me.

"How can I protect you from so many enemies?" he finally admitted, his worry evident in his eyes.

"That's the beauty of this, Rhett," Mateo answered softly, "you don't have to do this alone. Plus, Sawyer's the strongest person I know."

Smiling at my sweet guy, I kept rubbing the back of Rhett's head in a soothing gesture. Seeing my strong mountain so shattered reminded me how much we all felt. This wasn't a casual thing or us just playing house. We'd found something real amidst the deception and lies against the world, telling us it wasn't worth it.

"Was that what Adelaide was implying outside the rink today?" Henry asked, having connected the dots.

"Yeah, I think so. I'm guessing someone's told her or alluded to it, but she doesn't understand the power that gave me, being their 'slut.' I'm coveted for my vagina. Who knew!" I joked.

"Well, I always said you had a magic p—"

Ollie stopped mid-sentence, remembering we weren't alone. He'd calmed down when Ty had soothed him and seemed like he was trying to joke his way back to himself.

Clearing my throat, I turned to our guest. Samuel sat quietly, watching us as we interacted and discussed this news. "Did you know? Did Hawthorne tell you?"

"No, I didn't know. My family's connected to the Council but not high in the organization. I'm guessing that secret is well kept amongst the seven."

Nodding, it made sense and how Mr. Hawthorne knew.

"What does this mean now?"

"Who the hell knows." I shrugged. "It doesn't change anything for me. I'm not going to be who they want. They try to take me, and I'll throat punch them. I've faced down spiteful prima donna ice skaters my whole life. These old guys ain't got nothing on them. They can try, but I don't break that easily."

"I think we need to share with Samson and make sure you're not unguarded. I have a bad feeling they're going to snatch you the moment you're alone," Henry admitted.

I nodded, knowing some of his fear from losing me last time had to be resurfacing.

"We need to do more. I need to call my uncle and make more moves," Ollie demanded.

"No, we need to wait. Donnelly first, and then we move in on Abernathy and Latimer. Not before, or we risk losing everything. Tell me you'll listen, Ollie."

Elias was staring at him, waiting to hear him say it. "Okay, okay, I'll wait. But I need to do something."

"Well, I'd like nothing more than to have a veg movie night with all of you."

"Yeah, I guess I could be persuaded." Ollie smiled. His smile set my butterflies into flight.

Samuel left shortly after dinner, promising to get in touch with Mateo once he had his orders from Hawthorne or if he heard anything from the Council.

We cleaned up our meal, and all changed into our comfy clothes. Even Elias was in a comfortable pair of gray sweat "lounge" pants, as he called them. I was not ashamed to admit the puddle of drool that fell from my mouth when he'd walked in. Fucking hell, gray sweats were criminal. Especially when I could see his cock outlined as he sat down and all I could do was picture the beautiful, tattooed beast. I must've been licking my lips a little too much because Ollie leaned over and shut my jaw.

I didn't even care.

I fell asleep in a massive cuddle huddle somewhere between Civil War and Infinity War. We'd been making headway on our Marvel marathon. I awoke on Ty's chest with Soren behind me. Soft snores filled the room, and I couldn't have been happier as I drifted back to sleep.

"Samson! I'm serious. Don't cut us out, not now!"

I was on the verge of stomping my foot or even throat punching him again if he didn't remove the stick up his ass.

"Hell, no, tiny dancer. The Agency has it under control. You will only get in the way. We got the info we needed, and we're going. You're not trained for this."

"Ugh, you're so infuriating. Fine, but I want to be with the people in the van or whatever. I want to be a friendly face for that girl when she's pulled out. Jill doesn't know any of you, and after the horror she's witnessed this week, she's not going to want to be surrounded by strangers. *Please*, at least give me that."

I didn't like begging, but this wasn't about me. Henry stood behind me in support, wanting the same. He was letting me talk, knowing I had the best opportunity to convince Samson. The call had come in last night like Hawthorne had said it would, but what we hadn't expected was to be kept out of it. My anger was starting to rise again.

"If I agree, will you leave me alone?" he groaned, finally giving in to my begging.

"Yes!"

"Fine. You can be with the recovery team. Do not, and I'm serious about this, Sawyer, get out of the van for any reason other than it's on fire or being shot at. Do you understand?"

"Yes, geesh." I held my hands up in protest. "And I find it insulting you have to clarify, like I wouldn't know to get out of the van for those reasons," I huffed, crossing my arms now in indignation.

"Well, I can picture a scenario where your stubbornness wins out, and you'd be all like, '*But Samson, you said not to get out of the van,*' and I don't have time today to deal with that." He did a little hand wave thing like he was trying to be a girl, his voice going up an octave. I didn't want to admit it was fairly spot-on.

"Well… *whatever.*"

The smile on his face made me want to smack it off, but he hadn't been wrong, so I couldn't be mad at him. Instead, I focused on the fact he knew me that well. The past five years had felt so lonely, but he'd been there the whole time. In a move that surprised us both, I leaned forward and wrapped my arms around his neck. It was a little awkward from his seated position, but I held him to me all the same.

"I'm scared to ask what that was for," he muttered.

"I know I'm a smartass the majority of the time, but I do love you and your snarky self."

"I love you too, kid."

He turned and hugged me properly, and I felt the last shell of my hardness fall off. The loneliness had been hard, but it led me here, and despite my parents dying, I wouldn't want to be anywhere else. *I belonged here.*

"Well, okay. That's about as much lovey-dovey shit as I can do in one day, so here, go and see Raquel and she'll let you in on the recovery team. I'm assuming that includes your shadow there?"

Nodding, I let go of him and moved back. "Yep. Package deal." I smiled. "Better get used to it."

Shaking his head, Samson grinned. "Nothing with you is ever boring."

Henry grabbed my hand, and we started out the door. Stopping halfway through, I turned back to Samson. "Don't think I've forgotten about you coming clean to Isla. She deserves to know the truth."

Resignation filled his features, and he nodded, "Set up a dinner, and I'll be there."

"Thank you."

Nodding again, he turned back to his desk, but I didn't miss the hint of fear and sadness that filled his features. I'd never not be thankful for his role in my life. He'd saved me more times than I'd like to think about. I just hated that it had cost him love and happiness. If I could help repair that, then I wouldn't feel so guilty.

So many people had sacrificed themselves to keep me

safe, and not even in a self-deprecating way did I feel it was worth it. My life wasn't any more valuable than all those that had died. I wanted to live a life that honored their sacrifice by living with no regrets.

"That was kind of sweet, Smalls."

"Shut it." I laughed.

We walked through the halls of the Agency building. Ty hadn't been lying about how awful it was to get into this place. I guess it was reassuring that they were a secure place, but it was annoying when I just wanted to talk to Samson... *my uncle.* I suppose I should start calling him that. He'd outgrown Brave Heart, and it didn't feel right calling him Agent B even if the nickname game the guys had going was hilariously fun. It was too impersonal for me now.

We came to a stop in front of the room he'd directed us to. Knocking, I waited for them to answer, some apprehension filling my gut. This would be the first person in this place I'd interacted with that wasn't someone I knew. The door opened, and an attractive young woman stood before us. Her look was disinterested as she scanned her eyes over me.

"Yes?" she drawled, her Brazilian accent thick.

"Um, hi. I'm Sawyer. Samson sent us here to talk to Raquel."

She didn't say anything but opened the door; her nose turned up. The woman, who I assumed was Raquel, went back to the table she was working on and finished assembling a med kit. Henry and I looked at one another before walking in. Looking around at the various things splayed across the room, I was curious what all was here. It was like a spy kit room. I bet this would be like catnip for Fin.

"Don't touch anything," boomed a voice, causing me to pull my hand back from the device I was about to check out.

"Sorry."

Cringing, I turned away from the cool gadgets and shrugged at Henry, who was silently laughing at me for getting caught. Trying to keep my hands to my sides, I focused on what she was doing. When it looked like I might bust out of my skin, Henry came over and wrapped his arms around me from behind to assist.

"Smalls, you have disaster written all over you in this room. I don't even think code orange would cover the magnitude of pain your oops moment would cause," he laughed.

"Well," I started, but when I couldn't argue with him, I shrugged again. "I'm not going to apologize for being curious."

"There's curiosity, and then there's *Sawyerosity*."

"I like when you make words up for me."

"Well, it's easy to do." He grinned down at me. Smiling upside down, I was about to reach up on my tiptoes when a gagging sound interrupted us.

"If you two are done making me hurl, it's time to go," Raquel ordered, walking out the door. She didn't even wait to see if we'd follow.

"I don't think she likes me."

"Don't take it personally. She doesn't like most people," a familiar voice said when we stepped out.

"Fin!" I shrieked, pulling her into a hug. "Bish, where have you been? I miss you!"

"Cohen and I've been helping on a temporary basis," she rolled her eyes, but I couldn't help but catch the spark and blush. "We cracked something today on Donnelly's phone, but I'll catch you up later. If you're going with Recovery, you better hurry," she nodded.

I caught sight of Raquel stepping into the elevator down the hall, and she didn't seem the type to hold it for someone. Releasing Fin, Henry gave her a shoulder pat, and we booked it the short distance. The elevator was closing when we approached, so I shoved my bag into the space to trigger the motion sensor. I had a fear of actually putting my body parts in the space, so if that had been our only option, we'd be taking the stairs.

It would be my luck when that sensor thing failed, my arm or leg would be in between it getting sliced in half. No, thanks! I liked all my body parts just as they were—solid.

Raquel didn't appear happy we'd made it, if the huff of annoyance she gave us was anything to go by. I didn't care. She had no importance in my life, and as long as she took us to Jill, our interaction would be minimal. When a few other people got on further down, I saw her personality change. It was probably the hot guy she was making eyes at, but I'd learned not to assume.

The elevator opened up into an underground parking garage, and we had to, well, *I* had to, hurry to keep up with the long legged Goddess. *Seriously*! Girls with long legs didn't understand how hard it was to keep up with people. My strides were two to one of hers, and that was putting it nicely. By the time we made it to the van parked ten rows over, I was panting. A few more people were loading it when we got there, but they didn't say anything to us either. Guess no one wanted us here.

"Back row. Don't talk, don't ask questions, and try not to breathe."

"She's a fucking delight," I grumbled, forgetting my earlier words not to care. Henry laughed, helping me into the van. Before we even had our seat belts buckled, they were taking off at breakneck speeds. Grabbing his hand, I sent a text to the guys to let them know we were en route.

For Jill's sake, I hoped we weren't too late.

# thirty-seven

. . .

## rey

SAWYER HELD my hand tight as we careened around the curvy road. For being the recovery crew, I'd assumed we would be a little more discreet. With the way this guy was driving, I didn't understand how every cop in the city wasn't on our tail.

"Disabled the cameras and lights," the guy sitting next to me said. Turning, I raised my eyebrow in question, not sure what he was referring to.

"I could see you wondering how we got away with driving *Fast and Furious* style. Back at the Agency, they've disabled the traffic cams and switched the lights to give us a green passage."

"Huh. Makes sense."

He laughed, clearly understanding how non-impressed I

was about the revelation. My sister was a hacker; nothing surprised me. We pulled up to an area outside of the main town about thirty minutes later. And like my seat guest had stated, no cops nor red lights the whole way. The area was dark and sketchy, abandoned trash and junk scattered around. There looked to be a congregation of warehouses in the distance, with none looking any better than the other.

"This is where she's been held?" Sawyer gasped, fear evident.

"No, this is where they moved her today. From what we can tell, she'd been at her buyer's place for the past week. We sent a message to the buyer from Donnelly's number saying that we'd discovered it and were closing in on the location. They moved here this morning. They had vans going to three different places, so we had to wait to determine the real one," my chatty seatmate answered.

Raquel glared from the passenger seat but didn't say anything to him. The van rolled to a stop, and we all sat quietly as the driver took out some binoculars and scanned the area.

"Clear," he relayed, and then everyone moved in a synchronization most skaters hadn't perfected.

"Stay here with Raquel. We'll be back."

Snorting, because, *hello Terminator*, we sat back to wait. After an hour of waiting, Sawyer was going crazy, and I wasn't far behind her. Raquel had moved up to the driver's seat, either to be ready to take off if needed or put as much distance as possible between us. I hadn't ruled out the last one. Every time Sawyer moved or went to ask me something, she sent her a death glare.

Smalls was two seconds away from a proper toddler meltdown when Raquel's voice broke the silence.

"We have movement. Get down and don't move. I can't be sure it's our guys at this distance."

Smalls and I ducked down into the space between the seats as we waited to see if it would be the Agency or Council who found us. When the doors ripped open five minutes later, we had our answers. Shouts of emergency were given as we took in the crew.

"Go! Go! Go!"

Raquel spun in the driver's seat and took the brake off before flooring the van into reverse. Whipping it around, I wondered if she had been in *Fast and the Furious* with this level of driving.

"What happened?" she shouted as she weaved through the dark maze of warehouses and clutter.

"It was a trap, or they'd been tipped off, but the girl wasn't there. Just a note and a bunch of guys waiting to light us up. We barely got out of there. The backup team is with them. This place will be a war zone in thirty minutes."

"What did the note say?"

*"Bring us the one we want, and she's yours. Try to retrieve her again, and she's dead."*

"Well, that's just fucking fantastic," I muttered.

Sawyer had a combined look of fear and disgust on her face. It was obvious who they wanted—her.

"Hey, it's not your fault, okay? We'll still get them."

"You can't promise that," Sawyer mumbled, wrapping her arms around herself. We were back at the house. Samson had sent us home, a look of sadness on his face when he saw Sawyer. She blamed herself, and I had a horrible feeling she was debating doing what they wanted. None of the guys would go for it. Keeping watch of Smalls just moved to the top of my list to ensure she didn't do anything impulsive.

"Knock, knock," Soren greeted, smiling softly at our girl.

"Hey, Sor."

"You have a visitor, sweet pea, and I don't think you want them to visit you here, like this." He grinned, his eyes dropping.

Sawyer looked down at what she was wearing. We'd come back to the house and changed and had been lying on my bed watching Netflix, too disappointed to do anything else. We'd had another training session with Madelyn this morning on top of teaching, so my muscles were screaming at me.

"Yeah, okay."

Smalls got up and walked across the hall to her room, shutting the door as she did.

"She going to be okay?"

"Yeah, I think it's just the letdown of the build-up at feeling like we were going to do something good."

"Hope so. I don't want her to slip back into that state she was in."

"She won't," I affirmed, getting up off the bed, "she's got all of us." Wrapping my arms around his waist, I kissed him on the neck and licked at the goosebumps that broke the skin.

Sawyer's door opened, and I lifted my eyes to her. She stopped for a moment, a smile gracing her lips at our posture.

"Just when I think you two can't get any hotter, you go and do *this*," she said, motioning with her hand.

"Well, if it gets a smile from you," Soren beamed, "I'll do it every day. You ready to face the music, sweet pea?"

He held out his hand for her, and I let go of his waist and grabbed his other hand. As a unit, we made our way down the stairs. I didn't know who would be at our house on a Monday, but I guessed Samson, Charlie, or even Asa from Soren's comments.

Charlie and Aggie sat on the couch, hands clasped together. They both looked up as we entered, happiness dripping from them. Sawyer dropped our hands and ran to the old man when she saw him.

"Charlie, what are you doing here? I'm pretty sure I remember taking you to the airport Sunday after the party."

"Ah, you did," he replied, hugging her close, "and then I got back to Iowa and the rink. To be honest, I hated it. It was lonely and quiet. You weren't there to annoy me, and everywhere I looked, I just saw problems. I realized it was time. I was holding onto the rink for sentimental purposes, but I didn't love it anymore. So, I called an old friend and sold it.

I'll finalize everything else tomorrow when they fax the forms over."

"What? Are you kidding? What does this mean?"

"Slow down, Sawdust." He grinned, clearly having shed some grief and pain over the past week. "I want to have more freedom to do things. I thought just visiting now and then would be enough, but it wasn't. I want to be part of your life, and that right now is here, so I want to be here. I've also become quite smitten with this woman too, so, if you're okay with it, I'd like to be a more significant presence."

"Always, old man."

Soren wrapped an arm around me, and I didn't even try to hide my tears. Sawyer had so many people in her life that loved her. She deserved it all.

"I think this calls for dessert! Surprisingly, we still have some leftover cake."

"Oh, that sounds wonderful," Aggie beamed, a blush to her cheeks as well from Charlie's comments.

I had a fleeting moment of fear as we headed into the kitchen. Soren and I looked at one another, but didn't stop the events that unfolded. Standing back, *out of range,* we watched in trepidation as the three of them became covered with whip topping.

"What did you do? Henry! Soren! Oh my God, I'm going to kill you. This is so against the rules."

"Technically, it's not." I cringed. I'd known it would be a stretch, but it had seemed funny at the time, assuming it would be Ollie.

Instead, Charlie, Sawyer, and Aggie stood in the kitchen,

the fridge open and covered in whip cream. Charlie licked his lips, grinning at the flavor. Aggie was shocked, standing with her hands out as she took in the state of herself.

When she let out a boisterous laugh, the rest of us relaxed, soon following her. When Sawyer skated over to us on her sock feet, I didn't even try to get out of her way as she hugged me, wiping the white stuff all over me in the process. Soren bent down, licking a long lick up her face and my chest.

"Mmm, yum." He grinned.

Rhett came around the corner, his eyes wide when he took in the scene. "Um, I'm innocent!" he declared, stepping back with his hands raised high. Aggie laughed more, pointing the finger at him.

"Oh, I don't know about that, Rhett. I'm sure you had something to do with this."

"No, ma'am. *Never*!"

The stricken look on his face was too much for the rest of us, and we burst out laughing.

"It was Soren and me. We're responsible and could've stopped it, but we didn't. So be mad at us if you're mad at anyone."

"Nah, this was a hoot! It only affirms my choice in moving." Charlie grinned, his whole face changing.

"Well, good!" Relief settled in me for a moment until his grin turned dangerous.

"But don't think I won't get my revenge."

*Well, fuck.*

Once we were all cleaned and dry from the whipped

cream, Rhett deducted a point from the overall standings for our team because it had gone against the family rules and involved other people. I didn't care by the end because we'd had so much fun laughing it had been worth it. Ollie was mad he hadn't gotten to lick it off Sawyer. I wouldn't lie; that had been our initial intention.

"There are only four days left in the prank war."

"We're going to need to up the ante. I think we need to hit Mateo." Soren cringed.

"No, too obvious. We need to get either Sawyer or Ty."

"Why them?" Soren asked. We were lying in his bed, facing one another as we talked. It was late, the house quiet.

"Sawyer because everyone will think we let her off the hook, and Ty because he could use a little 'welcome to the family' initiation."

"Your idea does have merit."

"Let's brainstorm in the morning. I'm exhausted."

"Night, Reybae."

Laughing, I pulled him close, placing a kiss on his chest. "Night, Sorbet," and then groaned. "Shit, we're *that couple* now, aren't we?"

"If you mean only the best kind, then yes, yes, we are."

"You're a dork, Soren Stryker, but I love it about you."

"Good, now sleep."

I laid on his chest, his heartbeat lulling me into a sweet slumber.

Over the next few days, the prank war battle continued on strong. Ollie got Soren with an air horn attached to the wall, so when he opened the door, it sounded, nearly causing Sor to pee his pants. We got Ty and Ollie by filling their cars full of popcorn. Ollie just started eating it and didn't care, making it lose its effect. Sawyer got Rhett by turning off the water while he was in the shower, making him have to chase her to turn it back on. However, the sexy sounds they made moments later had me feeling like they both won in that situation. Mateo surprised us the most.

On Thursday, I walked into my room from the bathroom and found it covered entirely in pictures of Nicolas Cage. He was *everywhere*. I stood there, shocked for a good ten minutes, before I clapped, offering the genius who'd spent the time doing it their proper due. Mateo and Sawyer fell through the door, having been waiting in the hallway to hear my reaction.

Today was Friday and the last day of the prank-off. We planned to announce the winners on Saturday. There still hadn't been any word on Jill, and each day I caught Sawyer looking more and more forlorn. Our training was going strong, and with the competition in four weeks, we would have to keep pushing. I could already feel the changes, how much stronger we were becoming. With our hectic schedule between teaching, training, and evil organization takedowns, the prank war had been a nice escape.

For our final prank, we'd planned to use their weakness against them. *Food*. Soren made caramel apples, well, actually, caramel onions that only resembled apples. It wasn't the fanciest, but it would give us points for creativity, I hoped. It was hard to think of things that weren't destructive after a while.

When I couldn't find any underwear after I got out of the shower, I knew someone had attacked. Instead of boxer briefs in my drawer, I only had Sawyer's nerdy panties to choose from. Figuring I had two options since I was running late, I decided to bite the bullet and wear them since commando was more Soren's style. Maybe I could get some points for not letting it affect me? Picking out a pair of Harry Potter undies that looked similar to men's boxers, I slipped them on before throwing on my pants. Besides my junk wanting to slip out the front, they weren't horrible.

Jogging down the stairs, I almost tripped over Lucky, who was at the foot of the stairs. Skirting around him, I wasn't paying attention when I stepped on the rug. A million pops went off, and I jumped, shrieking and spinning to see where the sound came from. With each step, the sounds continued, and I ducked for cover, fearing someone was shooting me.

Breathing heavily, I laid as still as possible, my head covered as I tried to figure out what to do. Lucky trotted over to me, and the pop sounded off again. That was when I realized it was *under* the rug. Lifting it, I found bubble wrap.

"What the hell?" Laugher behind the couch gave away Ollie and Sawyer as they rolled out from behind their hiding place.

"Oh my goodness, your face. Nice panties, man! I didn't think you had it in you," Ollie giggled through several breaths. Sawyer couldn't even get out words, she'd entered the silent laughter phase, and tears streamed down her face.

Shaking my head, I grinned, tipped my hat to them, and rolled off the offensive rug. I could go my whole life not hearing that sound again.

"That," panted Sawyer, "was... for... the... cream cheese... deodorant."

Smalls finally sat up, wiping tears from her eyes. I grinned manically wide because, yeah, *that had been fucking hilarious.* She did smell extra sweet that day, so I didn't know why she was so upset.

"Fair play," I admit, "and Ollie, the underwear thing, pretty funny. These are more comfortable than I expected."

"Wait, what?" Sawyer turned to Ollie, smacking him on the arm. "Did you put my underwear in his drawer? You didn't say it was going to be *mine.*"

As much as I enjoyed Ollie getting in trouble, I was running even later now. Bidding them goodbye, I could tell they wouldn't be fighting much longer if the tackle Ollie performed was any indication. Stepping outside, I was about to jump in my car when my name was called out.

Turning at the sound, I found my father leaning against a car at the end of the driveway.

"Son, we need to talk."

It didn't look like I was going to make it to class today, after all.

# thirty-eight

· · ·

## samson

MY HEAD WAS POUNDING, and no amount of Advil was going to help. The Agency rot ran deeper than I'd known, entrenched in a sea of corruption and deceit. I was at the point where I no longer felt confident it could be eradicated. Ty's information had given me the piece I'd been missing. Only one person in the Agency wore shoes that hideous —Rachel Brooks.

*Co-Director of Operations, Rachel Brooks*, second in command.

Once I tugged on the string with the help of Cohen and Fin, we'd found a whole mess of conspiracy dating back from the very beginning. The Agency had been established to stop evil in the world, to find ways around corrupt governments, and protect the innocent. The majority of the Agency's time and resources revolved around the Council, and most people joined to stand against them. We'd been so clouded by ideals that we hadn't seen the ruse for what it was.

It's no wonder nothing had ever stuck—they'd always had an inside man.

My life goal had been to stop the Council and protect the ones I loved. I'd sacrificed my freedom, my future, and my heart in pursuit of this. I'd always felt it was worth it, and on those nights where I laid in a crappy motel room alone, it comforted me to know I was on the right side. And now... was my whole life a waste? Had I only been fighting against myself this entire time? It felt hopeless.

My foundation had been shaken to the core, and I no longer knew what to believe. What was even true any more?

Studying a confirmed list of fifty names connected to the Council over the past five years left me infuriated. That was right, fifty people in five years. The names for the fifty years since the inception of the Agency, I feared, would be in the thousands.

The only saving grace was it appeared Ty's dad, Brandon, was clear, so at least I didn't have to drop that bomb to either him or Sawyer. I didn't have it in me to crush her again. It had also been enlightening to learn my mentee, Ace, wasn't a Council pawn. The people I could trust were dwindling, so it was comforting to know the closest to me were true.

Acting like a jackass, I'd tried to keep my walls up and not let the hard things affect me. But Sawyer had become my whole world. The guilt from not being as close to Asa sat heavy in my chest, but once he'd quit going to Orson's, he'd been safe. He had Isla and didn't need my protection, and part of me was relieved I didn't have to see her as often. Even from afar, it was painful to watch the woman I loved living a life without me.

Sawyer was the cute puppy you couldn't help but take home. She would wreck your home when you got there, but you'd smile and keep asking for more. I'd been captured by her the moment her green eyes had landed on me. She was the daughter Isla should've had with me—not Orson.

My phone ringing had me shutting the file Cohen had given me a few hours earlier. I needed to shred it so I could be sure no one would find it. If this information got in the wrong hands, things could go horribly downhill quickly. There were still good people here that would be collateral damage if that happened.

"Yes?"

"That's seriously how you answer the phone?" Sawyer's musical voice floated over the line.

"How else would I?"

It came out gruffer than I intended. I wasn't angry with her; it was just hard to turn it off at times. Especially the more time I spent in the office. I preferred to be in the field over stuck behind a desk any day.

"Hello? How can I help you? Why yes, I would like to speak with you? How might I be of service, your Majesty? You know, just a few options." She laughed, the tone floating across the receiver.

"I'll try that next time."

"I'm sure you will. So listen, I think it's time."

"I have no idea what you're referring to."

"*Bullshit.* And it is. I will drag you there myself if you don't. Isla is coming back to town tonight. I need to talk with her about that stuff I told you, and I want you there... *Please*, Samson?"

Of course, she had to go and use her soft voice on me. I could never say no to it when she was four, and it seemed I couldn't now either.

"Ugh, fine."

"Don't sound so thrilled now."

"I'm not. I'm... *terrified.*"

"I'll be there. You can yell at me later if it goes horrifically wrong, but I think she might surprise you. When I first met her, I thought she was the perfect combination of strong and classy. She wants to join our fight, and I can't see that happening without *you.*"

"I know. It's time, I just, what if... What if she hates me?"

"Then she hates you. It'll suck, but you'll have your answer. Then you can do whatever the hell you want. Maybe finally move on if you need to. I know you still love her. Otherwise, you wouldn't be dragging your feet."

"Humph. Is that so?"

"Yeah. Even though we're just getting to know one another officially, I do know you. You're my Brave Heart, my first hero, and I just want you to get your love story, your happy ending, if you can."

Not wanting to admit her words got to me, I cleared my throat to get the frog out of it. "Thanks, tiny dancer. But I already got my happy ending the day I met your bratty ass."

"Ah, Samson, getting all emotional on me. I wish I were there to hug you and record this for prosperity. Then I could watch it when I'm mad or angry." She laughed again, soothing my nerves.

"And yet you wonder why I'm such an ass to you all the time."

"Your assholery is how you say, 'I love you' dork."

She had me there.

"Fine, where's this dinner?"

"I'll text you the address. 7 pm. Don't be late, or I'll just track you down."

"Sad part, I know you're being honest."

"I'm always honest!"

"Uh-huh."

"Bye, Uncle Sam. Yeah, no. I don't think I can do that. Sounds too weird. I'll just stick to Samson."

"And you wonder why I don't answer your calls," I mocked, "be safe, tiny dancer."

After hanging up with Sawyer, I felt a smidge better. Sawyer was the type of person that made you hope.

The knock on my door a few hours later broke my stare down with the computer screen. I'd looked at the data collected from Donnelly's phone, trying to find a common factor with the Council. So far, I couldn't pinpoint anything substantial. There was enough to lock Donnelly away for life, but nothing to tell us where Jill was or who'd tipped them off.

Looking up at the open door, I found Henry and his father, David, standing there. David wasn't scheduled to be at this location. Confusion lined my brow, and I lifted my eyebrows at them. This had debacle written all over it. Motioning to them, they entered and shut the door. The action of the door closing had me focusing even more. David took a seat, his complexion pale, while Henry wore a blank expression. I didn't know if it was from practice or if the reason they were here had shaken him to his core.

"What can I do for you, gentlemen?"

"My dad has something to tell you, but we need to wait for Fin."

Nodding, I was preparing to ask when she'd be here when a knock followed by the door opening answered it.

"What's up?" She smiled, taking in the room. When she saw her dad, her facial features changed.

"Dad! What are you doing here?" She moved toward him and hugged her dad. I watched as he held her tight, his movements shaky as he did.

"Let's all sit, and I'll explain."

"Okay, David, what's going on?"

"One second, Sir. Finley, do you have the gift I sent you?" She nodded, her brow creasing. "Perfect, my brilliant girl."

We watched as she pulled out a locket from around her neck, and looked back at David, a question in her eyes.

"If you click the side twice, it will scan the room."

"What's that have to do with anything? I have it done routinely every day," I inserted.

"Not like the one Fin has. It's my own prototype with her help, though unbeknownst to her," he added as she started to protest. "It's not on the market and is above anything out there. It will only take a few seconds."

We all waited, and a few seconds later, it beeped and glowed blue for a second before returning its appearance to the indiscreet locket. It was the most disguisable device I'd ever seen and probably the quickest. This would be a significant development. Except, I didn't know if I could trust the Agency to have it.

"That's fascinating, but I doubt you've flown all the way here to do a demonstration." David sobered and focused back on me.

"Dad, it's time. You need to tell someone else. You can't do this on your own. Not anymore," Henry encouraged his father.

"I'm only here because both my children say I can trust you and that you're not secretly working for the Council. I discovered who you were many years ago, Mr. Abernathy. When Sofia told me the Council was back and they were blackmailing her, we tried to help the Brennon's escape. But there's a mole here, a few, I believe. When I told my supervisor, she acted like it didn't matter but would take care of it. So imagine my surprise when the Council was still threatening us, and the Agency hadn't done anything to help them."

"You knew? This whole time?" Fin asked, anger heating her voice.

"Yes, Fin, and I'm sorry we didn't tell you. I love your mother, and she fell in love with me. I wasn't a mark anymore, and we hoped to have hidden from the Council. But either from the skating coverage or someone in the Agency, they still found us. We told Kyla and Scott and contacted Mr. Abernathy here to meet with them."

"You were the one who sent me the urgent message," I mumbled. I'd always wondered how I missed the danger. But it was starting to make more sense. I'd been sent away the day before out of the blue. The location I'd been given was a bust, and on my way back, I'd gotten an encrypted message that things weren't safe and to meet Scott in Iowa.

"Yes, I hoped your honor was good. Scott believed in you, so I trusted your judgment. Much help it was, though, as they died the next night. I always blamed you, thinking you'd set them up."

"No, it wasn't me. I was still technically on assignment and hadn't told anyone I was there that night or where I was headed. So, someone else knew and tipped them off."

"Mom wasn't the one who turned over Sawyer? She's not stealing from a foundation?" Fin asked, emotion thick in her voice.

"No, sweetie. I told my supervisor everything years before. Your mother and I were working to protect them. I'd met Victoria at a work thing when she'd visited her dad. She knew I was with the Agency, so when she and Brent needed to flee Latimer's company, we helped her. Your mother isn't a bad person. I promise."

Fin nodded, tears in her eyes, and I wondered how much of what we believed was even true.

"What are they demanding?"

"This time, it's more than Sawyer they want," he paused, fear heavy. "They want all the kids. They're threatening to kill them."

It was silent as we all let the information settle.

"How do we stop them?" Fin asked, determination in her voice.

An idea began to form in my head, and I wondered if I was simply crazy or grasping at straws. I didn't think it mattered at this point. We either would be successful in our takeover, or we'd all failed. This was my final Hail Mary.

"Who's your supervisor?"

"Rachel Brooks."

I'd already changed my outfit three times. The concept of nervousness had gone out the window two shirts ago. I think it was time I owned up to the fact I was terrified. Watching Isla from the shadows over the years had been tortuous and riveting. It fed the part of me that needed to know how she was doing, even if it hurt.

It was a bonus when I checked on Asa, and she always appeared content. I hadn't wanted to ruin her life, so I stayed back. After a while, it became easier just to stay hidden. And when a certain amount of time had passed, it didn't feel as if anything could repair the time lost. I watched her date a few men, but nothing developed. Part of me held onto the hope it was because she still thought of me. I didn't want to admit it was because I still thought of her.

Isla had been my everything, and when my mother told me about our family involvement with the Council, I couldn't sully the person she was with that danger. There wasn't a version of my life where I got Isla and kept her safe that I could fathom at eighteen.

I wanted better for her life, and I thought by leaving, I could protect her. I understood now how it was a young fool's misplaced hope. The world was bigger than her and me, even if she had been mine. When Sawyer told me the Walsh history, I felt sick. Apparently, Isla hadn't found out until she was already married to Orson, and when she threatened to divorce him, her mother had blackmailed her into staying. It didn't surprise me that Orson and my father were in on some arranged marriage breeding contract. *It should've, but it didn't.*

Sticking with the gray slacks and navy dress shirt I had on, I headed to the restaurant. Ace was my outside eyes this evening while I was unavailable. I didn't trust either organization not to follow Sawyer or Isla, and with my presence added, it would be a perfect chance for them to strike. I had a team of people I could vouch for on standby. I wasn't taking any chances anymore.

The restaurant was elegant, and as I walked up to the hostess stand, my heart rate skyrocketed. Christ, I hadn't been this anxious since my first date. Fuck, that had been one of the scariest moments of my life. Isla was even more beautiful now, and unlike last time, I wasn't sure of the reception I was about to receive.

Sawyer saw me and walked over, wanting to walk in with me to lessen the awkwardness. I didn't have the heart to tell her it was going to be uncomfortable, no matter what.

"Look at you, Samson. You clean up nice."

"Well, when I have a reason to, I do know how to present myself." Fuck, I was already confrontational, dialing it down a notch; I tried again. "I mean, thank you. I'm nervous."

"You're going to be fine. This will be good. I mean, you might end up with food on you at the end, but it's going to be good. Time to step out of the shadows."

"You're smart when you want to be, tiny dancer."

"Yeah, Yeah. I know," she sassed, rolling her eyes. "Come on, no time like the present."

Taking my arm, she wrapped hers in the crook and led me to the table. Isla and Asa were in a conversation, so I had the opportunity to take her in uninterrupted. I sounded like a sap, but damn, I swear my heart burst into a million butterflies when I took her in. All these years, I never let myself fully see her because I knew I was a weak man, and if I ever found myself in the same room as her, I'd cave.

Being here now, a short distance away from her, I knew I'd been right. I could smell her perfume from here, the same she'd worn then. *Chanel*. It was the only one I knew the name of because of her. Her blonde hair, the same golden hue as Sawyer's, glowed under the lights, and her soft skin shimmered. Isla had aged well, and she was more beautiful than ever.

"Isla, Mom. There's someone who owes you an explanation," Sawyer announced. I didn't hear the rest because, at Sawyer's address, she'd turned and locked her eyes on me.

At first, they'd gone wide, shock filling them before tears started to build. Dropping Sawyer's arm, I rushed to her side and cradled her in my arms. I'd been so stupid all these years, *such a fool*. The longer I'd stayed away, the easier it was to lie to myself.

"Samson? Is it really you?" Pulling back from holding her, I held her cheeks in my hands.

"Yes, *Issa*, it's me." The endearment fell from my lips before I could stop it, the emotion heavy in my words. "I'm so sorry. I thought I was protecting you. I'm—"

"I want to hate you for leaving me, *but I can't*. So just shut up and kiss me, you big fool."

Studying the woman I would gladly sacrifice anything for; I almost didn't believe her words. Lowering my lips to hers, I pressed softly, wanting to remember how they felt.

"Okay, so this is way weirder than I thought, so how about you two pull yourselves apart for long enough to eat dinner, and then Asa and I will leave you to it. I'd leave now, but I've already ordered, and I'm starving. So, you'll just have to endure for like an hour," Sawyer enthused beside me.

Laughing, I turned to my tiny spitfire. "Thank you for forcing me, tiny dancer."

"You're welcome, ya meanie."

Isla laughed at our exchange, and it felt like I finally had the family I'd always been envious of Orson over. Asa scooted over next to Sawyer, allowing Isla and I to sit next to one another. It was thoughtful on his part, and I nodded my thanks.

"Wait, you two know each other?" Isla questioned, looking between Sawyer and me.

"Yep. I didn't realize he was the same 'Samson' until our birthday. He was Brave Heart to me for the longest time. My imaginary friend who slew dragons with me, and then my invisible hero saving me time and time again from death."

"You've been watching over her this whole time?"

"I felt responsible in the beginning, but once I looked into her eyes, I was hooked." I smiled at the girl in question. "Plus, I'd promised my mother I wouldn't let another female become trapped. I always assumed she meant in the Abernathy family or, even broadly, the Council. But I'm wondering if she knew about your family lineage. I think she wanted me to keep her from that fate."

"You did that for me? But you left, I thought…."

"Ssh, we have plenty of time for questions later. Let's not focus on the details now. Just know I never stopped loving you and only left because I thought it would keep you safe. I've regretted that decision every day, but I don't regret watching out for them."

"I think they're going to start kissing again," Sawyer whispered to Asa, stopping us from falling into the embrace.

"Tiny dancer, don't think I won't repay you for this!"

"Oh, that's so sweet! I have an Amazon Wishlist if you need ideas."

Asa laughed first, followed by Isla, and I couldn't hold mine in either. Shaking my head, I raised my eyebrow at Sawyer, but she only smiled wider, knowing she had me. I'd been a fool keeping love and relationships at arm's length. It might've made me a better agent, but it had made me a bitter man. Family and love were the pillars that kept you rooted in hope. They were the things the Council and the Agency didn't understand.

Power was a powder keg waiting to explode, leaving no witnesses, for there could only be one ruler when power was the end goal. But love encompassed all and made you believe in the impossible. Love gave you something to fight for, die for, and live for. There was nothing else stronger when it came down to it. Power might give you the physical ability to do something, but love gave you the emotional capacity to be something.

I hated that it took me that long to figure it out. But I was here now, and nothing, not my brother, not my fear, and not even the Council could stop me.

There were a lot of moving parts, and the Council and Agency had been playing the game longer. I couldn't wait to shake it up.

# thirty-nine

· · ·

## sawyer

HUGGING SAMSON TIGHT, I held on for a few seconds to convince myself this was real. It was beginning to feel like I had a mom and dad again. It was odd to think that, and a small part of me felt guilty for it, but I also knew my parents would want me to be loved and cherished. They would always be my parents, the ones who protected, raised, and in the end, saved my life. Nothing would ever change that or replace the life we had together. And yet, to ignore the bonds I was building with Isla and Samson would be just as much of a disservice to my parents' memory.

"Thanks, tiny dancer."

Samson's voice was filled with emotion, and it was like I was seeing *him* for the first time, the real man behind the shield he bore. He kissed my forehead and moved to shake hands with Asa.

Isla pulled me into a hug next. She clung to me just as hard as I had to my uncle. "It's not a dream," I whispered, hearing her chuckle before pulling back.

"My beautiful girl, I'm so thankful for you. I'm glad that you don't hate me for writing our family history in a letter. I didn't know how to tell you. I hadn't thought about it for over twenty years, and the first time I saw you, I didn't feel anything other than bliss. After I started thinking about the things you said and how the Council connected to Abernathy. I knew. I knew I had to tell you the real reason."

"I understand. I do. And I don't blame you," I paused, collecting myself. She was gripping my hands, tears brimming in her eyes. "You didn't ask to be a baby-making machine any more than I did. The fact you told me before I was carted off to some rich husband like a broodmare tells me where you stand on the matter. I guess," I swallowed, collecting my words as I tried to figure out how to word the next part. "I guess what I need to know is where you stand on the side of getting justice. Do you want there to be some?"

"They're not my family. I may bear their name, but I don't align with their beliefs. We've had our choices taken from us far too much, so if that means changing my name, I will. If that means revealing what they've been doing this whole time, then I'm okay with that too. I'm going to take a page out of my daughter's handbook." She smiled, nodding to me. Something about hearing her say daughter healed a piece of me. "I'm going to build the family I want. Starting with the three people right here."

A tear fell down my cheek, and I beamed back at the woman who was quickly becoming my mom. "I'm glad to hear that... *Mom*."

"Oh, darling," she cried, pulling me back into her embrace.

We held one another, and I had a sense of presence with us as we strengthened our connection. It felt like my mother, Victoria, was here at this moment with us, wrapping her arms around us too and fusing our bond together. Pulling back, we wiped one another's tears and laughed at the gesture. We were getting there. It would take time to have the shared memories and moments together, but I knew it was possible, and that was the greatest thing of all—hope.

Asa and I left them to their reunion and headed out together. It was nice spending time with just him. He was my twin, my counterpart and I wanted to be closer to him too. An idea popped into my head, and I decided to run with it.

"Hey! I have an idea. How do you feel about getting some ice cream and coming up with the ultimate prank on all the guys? They're having some manly bonding time at the house, and we're supposed to announce the winner when I get home. They'd never see it coming. Come on," I knocked into his side with my shoulder since I couldn't reach him, "what do you say?"

Asa turned to me, a broad grin on his face. "I think that sounds like an amazingly epic plan, Sis! I know just the place to get ice cream too. There's this cutesy one I've always thought sounded cool."

Heading to his Jeep, we jumped in and headed to an ice cream shop. It was adorable with its mom-and-pop decor, and I wanted to live in it. The door chimed a little ditty when we entered, bringing a bright smile to my face. This place was a childhood dream wrapped up in cotton candy with a chocolate outer shell.

"Well, hello, dearies. How can we help you at Ice Dreams?" the cheerful woman behind the counter asked. She was decked out in all pink and had on a tutu, flamingo leggings, and a 'kiss me, I'm sweet' shirt. On her head, she wore a unicorn headband with her rainbow hair in pigtails. I fucking loved it.

"First, love the whole thing you have going on here! You look absolutely fabulous."

"I do, don't I?" she beamed, doing a little twirl.

"Love it!" I cheered. "This is my first time here. What do you recommend?"

"Oh, Ice Dream virgins are my favorite. I have a little test I like to do. Care to play?"

"Abso-freakin-lutely!" Asa laughed at my enthusiasm, but let me continue. "This is my brother. He wants to play too," I inserted, before he could say no. Sticking my tongue out at him, I couldn't help the laugh when he rolled his eyes back. We were already acting like siblings. I guess this was a good idea.

"Okay, are you ready?" the dancing unicorn asked.

"Yes!" I answered for both of us.

"Answer these without thinking about them. Understand?" We nodded, and I was eager to hear what she had to ask.

"First question, if you had to pick between only having chocolate for the rest of your life, or having any flavor you wanted, but only once a month. Which would you choose?"

"Chocolate," Asa answered, just as I said, "Any flavor."

The unicorn nodded before continuing, "Which would you rather do, jump out of an airplane, bungee jump off a bridge, or repel down a 10ft rock wall?"

We both took a second, and when we didn't answer right away, she cleared her throat, giving us a look. Opening my mouth, I let my subconscious answer, "Bridge." Asa responded with "Plane," surprising us both. The dancing unicorn smiled a smile that hinted at knowing something we didn't before continuing.

"Okay, the last question, are you ready to have your minds blown?" Nodding, we both looked at each other, waiting to see what she'd ask this time.

"If you had a bag of candy and you came upon someone who didn't, would you share some of yours or keep it to yourselves?"

"Share," we both said quickly. The dancing unicorn nodded and went back to make us whatever ice cream concoction she figured out. Asa shrugged and moved down to the register to wait. When she came back with two cups a few minutes later, I was excited to see what her test had revealed in the form of ice cream.

"For our lovely pixie mixie, we have two scoops of cake

mix ice cream, mixed with Reese's cup, with chocolate drizzle and peanut butter chips on top, and half of a banana for our unicorn horn."

She presented me with the massive waffle bowl, and I stared in wonder. It was the most beautiful thing I'd ever seen. Carefully pulling it toward me, I took a bite and almost died on the spot. *It was perfect.*

"Oh, man. That is good!" I exclaimed around a mouthful of ice cream nirvana. "You're amazing!" She smiled at my compliment before handing Asa his.

"And for our handsome, noble prince, we have two scoops of mint chocolate chip in a dipped waffle bowl with just a touch of Irish coffee drizzle and white chocolate shavings."

Asa's eyes were huge as he took in the ice cream creation. I watched as he took a bite, uncertainty on his face. When the mix hit his tongue, his eyes rolled back, and a look of contentment covered his face. Laughing, I tried to sneak a scoop, but even with his eyes closed as he savored his bite, he moved his bowl out of my reach.

"That's so mean!"

"Nope. You have your own," he cheesed to me. It was the most carefree I'd ever seen him, and I realized how special this place was. It had to be magical. Maybe she was a real unicorn? I was happy he'd brought me here.

"Okay, spill, dancing unicorn! How did you do that?" I asked with exuberance, slightly bouncing on my toes.

"You see, I've found most people can be summed up into three characteristics when it comes to ice cream. The first question gauges your level of spontaneity and impulse. Are you someone," she pointed to me, "who likes spontaneity and variety even if that means limited access. Or," pointing to Asa, "one who likes stability and comfort but doesn't get bored easily."

"Humph, I guess that does make sense," I pondered, turning to my brother, who nodded along.

"The second one determines your level of adventure. Are you more likely to stay in your comfort zone, be risky within reason," she lifted her eyes to me at that one, "or surprise us all and like a little danger." She winked. "You flipped what I'd initially thought with that answer," she professed to Asa. "Adding the topping and a somewhat exotic flavor to your creation."

"I never would've thought to try this. I do love mint chocolate chip, so you were spot on there."

"Yeah, I can get a sense of most people's ice cream foundation based on their personality after years of practice. It's the level of creativity that varies."

"So, what's the last question about?"

"Ah, well, you see, that's what we like to call in the biz 'the real question,' the factor that matters the most," she paused, leaning in like she was telling us the world's greatest secret. She had us on the edge of our ice cream stools as we waited with bated breath. When it looked like we would explode if we didn't know, she finally caved.

"Cone or bowl." She laughed, the sound boisterous making me like her even more. "Those who are good with sharing often opt for a bowl, whereas those who don't want a cone. Then there's the odd caveat of those who are messy and need a bowl. Either way, I usually guess right," she winked.

"Wow, that's like the coolest ice cream magic trick ever! I can't wait to bring the guys here."

"Well, I hope you do, sugar. You're the cutest, and I think I'm even going to name that ice cream combination the 'pixie mixie' after you."

"That's the coolest thing ever! Asa, I'm going to be an ice cream!"

I patted his arm enthusiastically, causing him to roll his eyes again. The dancing unicorn left us after that to finish our ice cream. Before I knew it, I was scraping the bowl clean. The most impressive part of it all, I hadn't gotten brain freeze once. It was decided, this place was magic. Tossing our garbage, we said goodbye and headed back out into the night.

The ride back was quiet as our ice cream settled. It was an enjoyable quiet, though, and I found myself relaxed in our sibling bubble. When we pulled up to the house, I paused before opening the door. Turning, Asa lifted a brow, curious to what had stopped me.

"Thank you. I enjoyed this. Would you want to do this more often? Maybe have a sibling dinner or something each week? Just the two of us? I feel like I've missed so much, and I want to get to know you, like really know you, outside of our other friendships and relationships. Does that sound dumb or even make sense?"

"I think it sounds like a great idea, and I'd like it a lot."

Hugging him, I felt better as I exited the Jeep. Waving, I

jogged up the steps and headed inside, forgetting all about our prank plan. I was high on sugar and sibling bonding. The house was quiet when I entered, so I headed to the movie room, figuring they'd be there. Deciding to have some fun with them, I kicked off my shoes and tiptoed down the stairs. Lucky had to be either with them or upstairs asleep, making this even more accessible.

I'd expected to find them watching a movie or having a video game battle. What I hadn't anticipated was to walk in and see them all bare-chested, sitting in a circle. Soft classical music played, and all their focus was on the easel in front of them. Once I got over my drool fest, I could see they were painting. It reminded me of one of those wine and canvas things where you drank yourself silly on expensive glasses of crappy wine and tried to recreate a picture an instructor led.

In this scenario, it seemed Rhett was the teacher, and all the guys listened carefully as he told them which paint to dip their brushes into lightly. I was so stunned and *abnotized*, I'd forgotten my initial reason for sneaking. Scanning the rest of the room, I found a table with snacks and drinks. I was beyond impressed with their dude night provisions. Smiling, I was kind of turned on that my guys were above the typical beer and smashing of heads dude nights.

I stood watching them, leaning against the doorjamb for about five minutes before anyone noticed me. It was interesting to see them interact with one another without me. While Ty and Ollie tended to hang with one another in a big group setting, I found them intermixed when it was just the guys. Elias was next to Ty, and I watched them talking about something and laughing. It was a strange sight, but I liked it.

Mateo was sitting next to Ollie and Henry, and Soren was on the other side of Elias, with Rhett in the center. It seemed BOSH was stronger than ever, and I couldn't be happier. It was Elias who spotted me, ever the observant one. He winked, a wicked smile on his face, and I wondered what mischief he was up to. Elias stretched dramatically and made a big show of it. I held in my giggle, not knowing what he'd planned.

"Well, guys, I think my masterpiece is finished, and I'm *knackered*. Gonna head to bed."

The guys turned to look at him, not understanding his claim but accepting it all the same. He walked over to Rhett and whispered something before heading out of the room. I scooted back into the shadows in case anyone looked my way. When he got to the door, he grabbed my hand and pulled me with him. I went to ask a question when he hushed me with a finger over my lips. My tongue snuck out and licked him, heat lighting up his eyes. Elias tugged me into Rhett's room and had me in his arms in a matter of seconds.

"Oh, love, you're being naughty spying on us like that. What were you hoping to find, hm? Did you think we'd be talking about you? Or perhaps doing something more *delicious*?"

Elias licked up my neck, and my words got stuck in my throat, only a moan escaping. "I-I-I-I don't know," I finally finished. Elias lifted me onto Rhett's dresser, bringing me closer in range.

"Oh, I think you do, love," he whispered with a tug on my ear. Words fled me, and all I could focus on was the feel of him pressed against me. Running my hands over his sculpted shoulders, I ran my fingers through his floppy hair, wanting to mess it up. Disheveling my proper boyfriend up a bit made my lady parts sing.

"I have to admit, my mind went places when I saw all of your abs on display. Painting, though, wasn't it." Chuckling into my neck, he placed kisses in my favorite spot, and I felt the vibrations all the way to my toes.

"I think you have a guy kissing guy kink, love."

"I mean…" I shrugged. "If that's what you want to call it. I just think it's hot," I panted.

"The sounds you make drive me *wild*."

Yanking my hips, he pulled me closer to him, hitting my clit with his hard dick. My dress was shoved up, and I was thankful for the access as I felt him rub up against me.

"Fuck, Elias. That feels so good."

"You know what I love about you, Sawyer?"

"Hmm, my brain?"

"Yes, most definitely," he breathed, sucking on my skin. "But never once have you shortened my name or called me Eli."

"Well, yeah. You don't like it. Why would I?"

"It's just that most people do what they want to do, and even when we hated each other, you still didn't do it."

"I guess I understand the importance of a name, Elias. I've had three after all," I grinned. "But I remember you introducing yourself to Mateo. Even though you'd been an ass to me, I heard what you said."

"What did I say?" he asked, a look of vulnerability on his face.

"You said, and I quote," I imitated in my best British accent, "my name is Elias, mate. Don't call me Eli. I won't answer it unless you want a punch in the face," I finished, laughing.

Elias joined in with me, shaking his head. "Wow, I was such a wanker."

"I mean, yeah. But you're mine," I said sincerely, kissing his nose. "I asked Rhett later why you said that to Mateo, and he told me that not only did Queen Bitch call you that after you told her not to, but that all the boys in boarding school use to make fun of you by saying 'E-lies' because they didn't believe you were who you said you were."

"Yeah, being called a liar each time someone calls your name didn't make it my favorite. Plus, my mom gave me the name Elias, and it was the last thing I could hold on to of hers." Elias' vulnerability blazed in his eyes, tears coating them. I loved how unafraid he was now to show me his soft-ness. It was hands down one of the sexiest things I'd ever witnessed.

I brushed his cheek with my thumb, tracing around his lips. My hands didn't want to stop, afraid they wouldn't get another chance to touch him so openly.

"You know, I like that."

"Like what?"

"When you called me yours."

"Well, you did sign all your letters, wholly yours, so I'm just claiming it," I beamed.

"You can claim me everywhere and however you like, Sawyer Sullivan. I am yours, wholly."

Just what the fuck are you supposed to do when a man says that to you? Kiss the ever-loving daylights out of him first, and then fuck his brains out, of course.

# forty

. . .

## elias

THE HEAT in Sawyer's eye lit to an inferno, and she pulled me to her, tugging at the strands of my hair as she did. Our mouths crashed together, seeking one another to extinguish the flames licking our skin. It was a burn I accepted gladly as I pushed myself closer to her. My cock was straining, tenting my lounge pants as it sought its perfect fit. Nudging her core, I debated pressing in, *my clothes be damned*, but I needed to feel her wrapped around me.

Sawyer must've felt the same because, within seconds, she'd pushed my pants down with her heels and rocked against me. With my pants lower on my ass, my dick sprung free of its confines and nudged her pantie-clad pussy. Whimpers fell from Sawyer's lips, and I devoured them with my tongue, capturing them to keep. I wanted her whimpers, I wanted her moans, and I wanted her cries of pleasure as my own.

*They were the kindling to the raging fire that constantly burned for her.*

Nothing had ever felt this intense—this intimate. Everything with Sawyer felt as if I wouldn't breathe my next breath if I couldn't be with her. It was a frenzy I didn't want to leave. My cock, being the intelligent prick he was, found a way to nudge around the silk obscuring its home. Slowly sinking into her, Sawyer flexed around me, coating me in her liquid heat. The panties acted like a sleeve, making our connection tighter.

Looking down, I watched as I pulled out. My cock glistened with her wetness, highlighting the ink I had, and I watched entranced as I slid in and out. Sawyer continued to tug my hair, attempting to connect our mouths again. Her ankles dug into my ass as she yearned to pull us closer, her muscular thighs beckoning me.

Descending down, I took her mouth in a passionate kiss as I worked my hips. Sawyer's height on the dresser provided a perfect tilt, causing her to hit my pelvic bone. As we began to move together, the dresser shook with our movements, adding to the sound of our moans. Kissing down her neck, I sucked a section before licking it with my tongue as I roamed down her front.

She tasted of sugar and sunshine, and I ate it up. Sawyer had become the one essence I couldn't live without. The mounds of her breasts tempted me as they sat prettily in her bra. The dress had a rounded front, giving me the perfect access to snack on the tasty morsels.

I wanted to savor my treat, but Sawyer sought none of that. Pulling me tighter, she pleaded with me through her eyes and moans to deliver more. Lifting her up by the globes of her ass, I tilted her back further, allowing an even better angle. As I started to thrust deeper into her, the door to the room slowly opened. Neither of us stopped nor cared right this second.

Internally, I knew it had to be Rhett. I'd whispered to him my plan to whisk her away before the others saw and for him to meet us here when he could get away. I'd watched as he swallowed, my words affecting him, and I knew he'd be here eventually. I didn't even feel bad for the erection he probably had for the remainder of the time. It was part of life here, honestly. Living in a house with your sexy-as-sin girlfriend, you were bound to have a hard-on at least 90% of the time.

Trailing my tongue up to her ear, I whispered, "Now who's wishing they were feeling you wrapped around them?" I hadn't intended to taunt Rhett as I said it, but I'd heard his words that night in the fitness room, and my confused feelings at the time had taken it as a challenge.

This time, I was the one in the driver's seat, and I planned to milk it for all I could. I turned both our heads to take in our bystander. This position was one of power, as being the director of our sexual encounter was new to me. The first experience I had with strangers a few months ago was a distant memory. Back then, I'd felt self-conscious and unsure of what the play was despite their reassurances. Tonight, with the two people I trusted the most, I had all the confidence in the world.

I knew where I stood with them, and it heightened the sexual desire I experienced. During our first encounter together, I'd been hesitant, not knowing where I stood with Sawyer. It had been the most aroused I'd ever felt, and I hadn't even touched Sawyer during it. Watching them together had been erotic and had made me question my sexuality. I'd liked watching them move together; seeing Rhett's massive cock slide in and out of Sawyer had set me on fire.

But even now, as I looked at Rhett, I knew where we both stood on the matter. We enjoyed watching, we enjoyed almost performing for the other, and we would probably enjoy sharing her between us, something I hoped to try tonight. My bond with Rhett was unlike any other in my life. He was my best mate, my brother, but it ended there. We felt genuine love for one another and cared deeply, but outside the sexual pleasure we gained from our shared experience, we had no sexual desire for one another.

Looking into his eyes now, I knew I was right. We had an unbreakable bond cemented in a friendship that allowed our trust and vulnerability to translate into this situation. Rhett and I clearly loved one another, but we weren't *in love*. It wasn't like the other guys who had found something in one another, but it wasn't any less unique or important, in my opinion. Anytime you connected with someone intimately was special.

"What do you think, mate? Think we can bring her pleasure *together*?"

Rhett had been watching where Sawyer and I connected as I slid in and out of her, never stopping my movements. Our girl had her head thrown back, eyes closed as I tortured her with the slow pace, teasing each ripple of pleasure from her. My words had her head snapping up and eyes popping open as she looked between the two of us.

Grasping her chin, I brought her face to mine. "Think you can handle us both at the same time, love? Is that something you'd want?"

Sawyer licked her lips and nodded her head so fast, if I hadn't been holding it, she would've knocked into the mirror. A wicked smile pulled at my lips, and I liked all the feelings I could have with her. It didn't matter if my wild and reckless nature came out to play or my poetic prose; Sawyer accepted me, tats and all.

Voldemort had been so opposed to my ink that I'd gone a little overboard after the broken engagement in retaliation. I'd gotten five more, covering most of my chest from a tattoo artist I'd stalked on Instagram. I spent some time over one break in Kentucky getting them completed at his shop. Slade's artistry was the best I'd seen and had been well worth the trip.

The cock tats, on the other hand, had been an impulsive decision one night after feeling incredibly morose. Thankfully, it had turned out well, and after seeing Sawyer's reaction each time she caught sight of them, I was glad I'd done it.

"I think our vixen is feeling extra hungry tonight," I purred, locking my eyes with hers. Pulling out, I stepped back as Sawyer groaned from the loss of me. Smirking, I shucked my pants the rest of the way down my legs. Stepping back to her, I lifted the dress over her head, leaving her only in her undergarments. Rhett was still standing by the door, a frozen look on his face.

"Rhett, if you don't want to, you can just watch. Whatever you're comfortable with."

His eyes flicked to mine at the sound, and I watched as he wrestled with whatever plagued him. Slowly, I saw the fear leave him as he became resolute in his decision. Rhett reached back and pulled his shirt over his head with one hand. His muscles bulged as he did, and Sawyer's eyes were hooked on them. I slowly stroked my cock, feeling her wetness spread over me as I waited for him to approach.

His eyes were hooded as he took her in. Sawyer wore a soft pink lace bra that cupped her breasts snuggly. Never one to disappoint on the underwear front, her panties were the type that cut her butt cheeks into a V as they lifted them. They were pink with tiny donuts over them, and I could make out a little of the script on the front, leading me to believe it said something in regard to *cream-filled*. In her dorky cuteness, she was sexy as fuck.

Rhett made it to her, his jeans hung low on his hips and the button open, the zipper still up. He didn't say anything as he traced his finger up one arm and lowered the strap. Sawyer's breath hitched as Rhett dropped the other in the same fashion. I watched as he traced the curve of her mounds with the barest of pressure, feathering over her skin. Goosebumps broke out as she started to breathe faster in anticipation.

When he unhooked the contraption, her breasts spilled out, ready for action. Rhett began to kiss down her body, hooking his thumbs in her panties before pulling them down. Once they were off, he stood up and put his hands on his zipper, stopping before pulling it down. I watched in fascination as the liquid heat built between them. I never knew it could be this erotic to watch someone else give the girl I loved immense pleasure.

"Pull your knees up, baby. I want you to touch yourself, to show us how much this turns you on," Rhett commanded.

Sawyer didn't hesitate and had her legs spread wide, her pussy on display for us. I was transfixed as she parted her lips and plunged her fingers inside. Her thumb circled her clit, and I watched as her eyes bounced back and forth from him to me.

When he began to lower his zipper, she kept her eyes fixed as she drank him in, slipping her finger inside herself at the same tempo. Rhett stopped when he got to the base of his penis, but didn't move to push them off his hips. The whimper that left her was enough to force him to move, picking her up and wrapping her legs around him as he kissed her.

Watching two people in love lose themselves to one another should've made me feel left out, especially when I also loved the girl. It didn't, though. Instead, I felt privileged to share this intimacy with them and bear witness to the depth of their love. In this darkened room behind closed doors, freedom could be found. And here in this room, we were bare in every way.

Rhett turned to me, and an idea struck. Walking closer, I smoothed my hands over Sawyer's ass, grasping her knees in the crooks of my elbows. Rhett was a few inches taller than me, but it should work for us both in this position.

"Lean back on me, love," I directed, as she transferred her head to my shoulder. Sawyer wrapped an arm around my neck as my cock bobbed against her ass. Nodding to Rhett, I motioned for him to take her knees, and he appeared to understand the position I wanted to try. With us both standing, we could hold our girl between us and be in her at the same time.

Before he took her, he yanked down his jeans, kicking them out of the way. Grabbing her legs, he hooked her knees over his elbows before lining himself up, the angle perfect as he slid in. Their combined moan had me yearning for my chance to share the pleasure. Realizing I'd forgotten one crucial detail, I moved Sawyer to put her arms around Rhett's neck as he continued to lift her up and down.

Jogging over to the bathroom, I opened the drawer in the middle, hoping there was some lube in here. It seemed I was in luck as I found a small bottle. Snapping it open, I squeezed some onto my cock and spread it around. Squirting another handful into my palm, I placed it on the counter and headed back.

Moans of pleasure and skin slapping greeted me as I returned. Quickly, I joined in, Rhett having slowed his actions. I spread the cold liquid over Sawyer's rosette and slowly began to pump my finger in to loosen her. Once she was coated enough, I had her lean back on me again, her arm secured around my neck as I placed kisses on her lips.

"I missed you," she cooed, an orgasmic high on her face. Smiling, I kissed all of her face as Rhett held her steady. Using my hands to spread her ass cheeks, I began to push my dick in slowly. Her channel was warm and tight, and I could feel myself on the brink of an orgasm. Once I was seated, I nodded to Rhett, who started to push in the front. Sawyer moaned loudly with each inch he took, the vibration running down her body into my dick with each moan.

"Oh fuck, oh fuck," she chanted, tossing her head back and forth.

"Ssh, love. You got this. We got you."

Kissing her, I took her moans as my own as Rhett and I started to move. We found a rhythm holding her this way. She was practically weightless between us as we took turns pistoning in and out. With each thrust of his cock, I could feel it rub against the thin wall that separated us. The act itself was intoxicating, the tightness a level I'd never experienced before.

Sawyer's body tensed up before I felt her spasming around us. Tweaking her nipples, I thrust up one last time before unloading myself. It had been too much for me to hold off any longer. Rhett waited until I came down from the high, slowly pulling out of her. I held her still as he began to increase his pace and pound into her. I could feel his balls as they slapped her ass now, but not once did I find myself craving them to touch me more than they were.

We both seemed to have accepted the likelihood of sword

crossing in the act of sharing, but I didn't think either of us desired it without Sawyer between us. But I was making assumptions and would need to talk it out with him. Knowing one another as we did, though, I had confidence I was accurate in my assumption. A few minutes later, I felt his arms tense as he held her knees, and his movements stopped as he poured himself into her.

We were all panting as our orgasmic bliss started to subside. Moving Sawyer back to Rhett's chest, I walked back into the bathroom and started the shower so we could all rinse quickly. Thankfully, he'd followed me and walked into the water as it turned warm. Together, we rinsed off Sawyer as she stayed in his arms in a cocoon of bliss. Once she was clean, we took turns rinsing our bodies off, handing off our jellified girlfriend, and I laughed as I thought of her underwear.

It startled her, and she turned to me, a massive smile on her face. "I like that sound, your laugh. What were you laughing at, though?"

"I thought about your donut underwear and how it should've said 'all the jelly' instead of 'here's the cream' because we'd made your body jellified," I teased.

Stepping out of the shower, I sat her on the counter and helped dry her off with the towel Rhett handed me. Sawyer smiled, a twinkle in her eye. "Who says those are the only ones I have?"

"Touché' love. I can't wait to discover all the nerdy knickers you have and then promptly take them off you."

"Our first time, she had on Olaf ones, and I thought, 'who

is this crazy beautiful girl who can make snowmen look sexy?' I haven't been able to look away since, so I guess the real joke is on me." Rhett laughed loudly.

The sound was infectious, and Sawyer and I joined in, filling the space with our laughs. With minimum clothing on, we all climbed into Rhett's cavernous bed and slept peacefully. Life was coming together, and turning into what I had been fighting for—moments where everything made sense. Right here, in this bed, it worked, and it was all that mattered.

# forty-one

. . .

## oliver

SNEAKING OUT OF BED, I wanted to make a special breakfast for the house. Now that we were all back home, the place felt full of life and like we were cemented firmly as BOSH. I saw it every day in how we cared for Sawyer and one another. It wasn't always the big overtures or gestures, but in the small details. In the meals we made for someone, folding their clothes while they were out, or even remembering to grab their favorite snack at the store. Our house had become our home, and the heart of it was Sawyer.

Today would reveal the results of the prank war and see who'd be crowned the champions of 2020. It had been close, but I was confident the few we pulled yesterday would send us over the top. Nevertheless, it had been fun and an excellent way to distract from the impending doom we all felt breathing down our necks.

We knew it was coming, a time when we wouldn't feel safe, a time when we'd have to make hard choices, and a time when loyalties would be tested. That fact hadn't changed, and worrying about it nonstop wouldn't do anything but drive us crazy. One of the benefits of being an elite athlete was having the mindset to focus only on what was in front of you. Of course, the goal was always there, but focusing incessantly on it only made you careless in the now.

And in the now, it was prank wars and sexy time. I much preferred those, *especially* the sexy times.

Cracking an egg, I scooped out the yolk with the eggshell as I concentrated on keeping it out of the mixture. Arms wrapped around my bare torso from behind, breaking my concentration as the rough calluses teased my skin, sending shivers through me.

"Did you think you could sneak out that easily?" Ty's raspy voice whispered in my ear before planting a kiss on my neck.

"Well, yeah, I kind of did."

"I'll remind you, just as I did Sawyer. I might not be an official Agency man, Ols, but I've had *way more training* than you."

Dropping the shell into the bowl, I turned around into Ty's arms. Our relationship had progressed at a good pace since our talk. It felt freeing to touch and kiss him if I wanted. I didn't feel I had to keep this shield up anymore, and I could be 100% authentic. The freedom I had now amazed me with how great it felt to be unburdened by those things.

Staring into Ty's eyes, I anchored my hands on his hips, feeling the elastic of his boxers under my palms. That was when the thought penetrated my brain. Ty was in the kitchen in his *boxers*. In the kitchen! In just his boxers! My brain misfired, and I had to forcibly keep myself from looking down. Ty smirked, an unusual look compared to his usual calm demeanor, and hell, if I didn't find it sexy as fuck.

When he shuffled forward a little, I felt his cock brush against my own, and I bit my lip to stifle the moan I so desperately wanted to release.

"I like seeing the effect I have on you, Ols. Sometimes, I still have to pinch myself when I'm around you because I don't believe it's real."

Oh sweet mercy, why did he have to be so adorable on top of his sexiness? I had a sudden urge to turn him around and make him scream my name. The thought stunned me, and I tensed for a minute, which, unfortunately, made Ty think it was about what he said. He started to pull away, his face falling with each step he took, and my heart began to race in fear. No! I couldn't lose him; I'd just found him.

"I understand—" he started, but was caught off guard when I slammed my lips to his in an effort to keep him close. It was the first time we'd kissed without Sawyer around. It was different kissing a man, but it wasn't any less enjoyable. His morning stubble brushed against my chin as we both fought for dominance.

I'd easily gained the advantage when I initiated the kiss,

but now it seemed to be equal as our tongues swirled around one another's. Our hands were everywhere, and I couldn't think of anything other than what it felt like to be manhandled by him. Ty's hands were solid and wide, and he could grab parts of me in different ways. When he shoved my boxers down to cup my ass, my eyes rolled to the back of my head; it felt so *good*.

He was rough and aggressive in a way I'd never been with a woman, and I understood then what I'd been missing from my sexual explorations—besides the obvious fact of them not being Sawyer or Tyler. I'd thought I'd be the dominant one, the one to push him around and take control of things, but as Ty thoroughly tongue fucked my mouth, I knew I'd been incredibly wrong.

*And Ty was definitely tongue fucking me.*

There wasn't any other way to describe the intensity of the kiss than to be owned by his tongue as he swished and rolled it. When he finally pulled back for air, it took me time to regain my senses. Had the air always smelled this sweet? Did music always sound that melodious? Were those songbirds I heard in the background?

Blinking, I focused on the man in front of me who'd just decimated my heart with his lips. Forget fucking butterflies; Ty Mathews made me feel like a herd of wild horses had stampeded across my heart. Before I could say anything back to the man in my arms, I registered the voice of my little bite-size love.

"Ah, *man*. Did I miss the good stuff already? Like, hell, guys, that was *fucking hawt.*"

Grinning, Ty and I turned to take in Sawyer as she fanned herself. She was still in her pajamas, and if I hadn't already had an erection from Ty's kiss, the sight of her in my high school hockey shirt would have caused one.

Groaning, I kissed Ty's cheek and pulled away, straightening my boxers as I did to adjust my goods. Sawyer, licking her lips combined with the lust-filled haze coming from Ty, did nothing to douse my desire. Pointing at them both, I backed away as I tried to scoop out the pieces of eggshell I'd dropped.

"I wanted to do something nice for the house and make breakfast for the reveal of the results. You two throwing sexy catnip at me isn't helping. So please, for the love of French toast and egg white omelets, can we table this sex-a-thon for after? I'll be so down for that. We can even use the whipped cream!"

When they both started laughing, I wanted to be offended, but it had curbed their desire enough that they were no longer herding me into a corner where I couldn't escape their sex round-up. The two of them together were dangerous. And here I thought it would be me who'd corrupt one of them to throw off all adult responsibilities in lieu of sex! Take that, all those teachers and guidance counselors who said I didn't take things seriously!

Turned out, it just needed to be something I cared about. And our family, BOSH, was the most important thing in my life—even above hockey.

"It shouldn't be this sexy for you to tell us to act responsibly, you know." Sawyer grinned. "But alas, I shall keep my distance and offer you my services to get this breakfast of delicious food quicker! And then the sex, of course!"

Laughing, I grabbed her by the hips and placed her on the counter, and proceeded to direct them both as we got the breakfast underway. Thirty minutes later, and with a few layers of clothing added, we had a table full of food.

"Okay, Sawyer, you get Rhett and Elias. I'm not waking up that grump this early. Ty, you get Mateo, and I'll tackle Rey and Sor. The first one back to the table gets the first orgasm."

I took off before I'd finished, hoping to get an advantage as I raced up the stairs. I could hear Sawyer cursing about short legs and distance as she headed downstairs, but I didn't care at the moment. It was too funny to listen to her. Ty was hot on my heels as I took the stairs a few at a time. He had the advantage of his door being closer to the stairwell, but I was banking on both of them being together.

Springing down the hall, I knocked incessantly on the dynamic duo's door and was two seconds away from entering, their privacy be damned, when a sleepy Soren opened it.

"Where's the fire, Ollie?"

"No time to explain. Breakfast!"

I was halfway down the hall as I shouted the statement. Ty had finished his message to Mateo, who looked as equally asleep as Soren had, and it was neck and neck as we raced for the landing. Tickling his sides, I twisted him out of the way and nudged forward.

What I'd thought was my advantage ended up being my downfall. The tickling maneuver sparked Ty to remember my own crux with it. When his hands grabbed my ribs and started to move, I tensed up and curled into a fetal position to stop the painful action. My stupid move was biting me in the butt, or well, ribs.

"Fuck, stop." I laughed, gasping for air. His fingers released me, and he vaulted over me to head the rest of the way downstairs. I laid gasping on the landing as I watched him slide into the kitchen. Tears were streaming down my face at the fun of the race, despite having lost. Picking myself up, I leisurely jogged downstairs to congratulate Ty.

Except when I turned the corner, it was to find him sulking and a beaming Sawyer instead.

"I'm guessing you somehow won, pretty girl?"

"You better believe it, and I will collect on that orgasm!"

"But how?" Ty whined, but it only caused me to laugh more at his wounded puppy look.

"That's a secret I'll never tell."

"If you didn't tell them, though, that basically negates you winning," Ty tried to defend. However, Rhett and Elias turned the corner, Lucky trotting behind them a second later, stopped his rant. I assumed she hadn't needed to wake them up by their attire, but merely announced it was breakfast and skipped the rest of the way back up the stairs.

Sawyer's smug smile was too cute to hate, and Ty eventually kissed her, accepting his loss. I'd need to remember this for another time. It seemed to be a great motivator for them both. *And for me.* I couldn't deny that either.

The rest of the guys strolled into the kitchen a few minutes later, all bed rumpled and sleepy-eyed. Sawyer wasted no time and began to dig into the plates of food around the island. Everyone followed suit, and we soon found ourselves eating quietly together at the table. Once we all seemed to have filled our tummies, chatter returned, and I realized how normal this felt. This was my life, and I loved it. Every crazy-filled second of it.

"Since I wasn't an official member of the prank war, I've taken over the points and rules position from Rhett and will now share the final scores," Elias began, effectively stopping everyone as they listened.

"Before yesterday, team Ready to Rumble had a total of 80 points, and team Hot to Trot had a total of 82 points. Are there any discrepancies before we start?"

We were all on the edge of our seats as we waited to hear the final scores. When no one responded, Elias looked down at his phone to continue.

"Okay, Team Rumble, please share the pranks you pulled yesterday."

"We got Sawyer with the head in the jar." Soren chuckled, making Sawyer stick her tongue out at him in fun.

"And there were the caramel dipped onions," Henry added, making us all cringe at the disgusting level they'd been.

"Oh, and the last one was the balloon-filled conference room that had three sound makers that were playing "It's a Small World" on repeat." Rhett grinned.

Elias chuckled at that one as the rest of us tensed. It had taken forever to find those damn things, and by that time, the song had driven us all bonkers. If we ever made it to Disney

World one day, we'd need to steer clear of that ride, for I feared we all had PTSD from the song. It wouldn't be pretty, and the casualties alone would be messy.

"Ah yes, of course. The needle in the balloon stack. Okay, well, that brings your total to an even hundred points. Well done, Team Rumble."

Some hoots from them sounded out, and we smiled back. It was fun to win, but the important part was the fun we'd had throughout. At least, that was what I kept telling myself. As the only returning member on my team, I felt a lot of pressure to deliver for us. When I heard Sawyer mumble, *"should be Team Grumble"* I about lost it and realized it didn't matter, it had been successful.

"Now, Team Trot. What were the pranks you successfully pulled off?"

Sawyer grinned wide before she started on the list. We had pulled out all the stops yesterday and had gone a *tad* overboard.

"Well, there was the underwear exchange that Henry found himself in," she giggled, "and of course, the bubble wrap under the rug."

"My favorite," started Mateo, "was the Chewbacca Roar contest."

"Ah, so it was your idea," grunted Rhett, whose phone hadn't stopped ringing from people calling and roaring like the Wookie. The fact it brought him so much displeasure only made it even more hilarious. Which, by the laughter around the table and the few roars, everyone agreed.

"Don't forget about the harmonica on Soren's bumper!" Ty offered.

"Oh God, that's what it is! I couldn't figure it out! That was brilliant, actually. I kept hearing a whistle, but no clue where."

"Yes, and not to be left out, but my absolute favorite, sorry Soren, was the pink hair conditioner!" I boomed.

At my words, the whole table busted out into laughter as we recalled the look of horror Rey had sent to us after practice when he found Soren in the locker room. I should've felt bad, but he'd gotten me earlier in the week with toothpaste Oreos. I feared he'd forever ruined the cookie for me, it was only fair in my book.

"I kind of like it." Soren shrugged as he smoothed back his pink locks. It was kind of disappointing it didn't faze him and how he actually looked hot with pink bubblegum waves, but it had been funny, nonetheless.

"You were a good sport about it," Sawyer offered, kissing his cheek.

"With the calculations of the last events, it brings Team Trot to a total of 120 points! Our new winners are team Hot to Trot! Congrats!"

At Elias' words, our team jumped up and started dancing around the table, doing our victory lap. Soren placed crowns made out of toilet paper rolls on each of our heads. We all smiled as we leaned together for a picture and gave the other team a few loser jabs.

Despite losing, they were gracious and allowed us to boast and brag about our accomplishments. It was a great start to the morning, and later, when Sawyer collected her orgasm prize, it was an even greater start to my afternoon.

Things were going well, which meant the great equalizer was bound to strike soon. And when we woke the following day with a text from Samson stating they'd found the body of a girl, I knew our fun was officially over.

The Council had made their move, and we'd finally entered the endgame. Some of Elias' chess strategy rubbed off on me as I realized it was time to advance our pawn into a position of attack. The Council would learn that while we might be young, and few in numbers, we were strong because we had each other. The most dangerous opponent was always the one you didn't see coming.

# forty-two

. . .

## sawyer

WAKING up to a message about a dead body was not the wake-up I wanted. Ty and I headed out to meet Samson at the Agency building. I'd spoken to Madelyn about moving practice, and she'd been accommodating and told us to take the day off due to how well we'd been doing. She wanted us back early on Sunday morning, though. It was nice since I couldn't block out hours a day to deal with Council shit. At least with the new director on our side, things seemed to be equal.

"Do you think it's Jill?" I asked Ty. We'd been skirting around it all morning; no one was brave enough to ask it out loud.

"I don't know," Ty mumbled, tightening his hold on my

hand. "He didn't specify, which gives me hope that it's not, but also, why tell us then?"

"Yeah." I nodded absently as I watched the elevator climb. Samson had us meet him at the facility despite our grumblings about the security. When the elevator finally arrived on the correct floor, I gathered my courage to see what he had to show us. Dead bodies were not on my bucket list of things to see.

We found him waiting for us down the hall outside a door. When he heard our footsteps, Samson looked up, and I could see the stress on his face. I had a feeling the news wasn't going to be great. Hugging him, I realized when I pulled back how natural that had felt. I didn't even question it. I just saw someone I loved and hugged them—mind-blowing epiphanies before dead bodies were a lot for a morning.

"Hey, tiny dancer," he breathed into my hair. I felt his body relax at my hold, and I was glad I'd hugged him. I had a feeling Samson didn't let many people touch him, much less give him comfort, for that matter, making me want to do it even more.

"Hey, Brave Heart," I uttered, feeling he needed the reminder. Smiling, I pulled back and waited for him to tell us the reason for being here.

"Sorry to make you guys come here, but I felt it was important. It's not pretty, so prepare yourself."

He watched us as we nodded. I swallowed and grabbed Ty's hand, a feeling of apprehension filling me to the brim. Samson led us into a room that resembled what I expected a morgue would look like based on TV shows I'd seen. How odd was it that I related to things on TV as real experiences? The thought was jarring, and I realized how much I'd jumped down the rabbit hole in order to avoid what I was about to witness.

The room was cold and smelled of bleach, and I instantly plugged my nose. I guess it was preferable to dead bodies. A man in a lab coat at the table wrote down some things, presumably about the body on the table covered by a sheet. I was thankful it was covered. I didn't know if I could handle seeing one lie there all willy-nilly like. Fuck, my mind was spiraling into nonsense in an attempt to deal with the anxiety I was experiencing.

"She didn't report in the other day, so we sent someone to check up on her. When they got to her apartment, they found her like this. The reason why you're here is because of what the killer put on the body. It's graphic, and I hate to make you do this, but I think you need to see it."

Samson looked sincere, and I knew it was going to be bad, but if I needed to see this, then I would. I could do this. At least it was clear it wasn't Jill, and relief flowed through me at that realization. There was still time to find her. Trepidation in my steps, I shuffled forward with Tyler at my side as I kept my nose plugged. It would be handy in case I gagged too, I figured.

The first thing I noticed when the sheet was lifted was how pale her skin looked. Against the cold silver table, her skin contrasted greatly with it. Bracing myself, I shifted my eyes to her face, but was confused when I didn't know her.

She appeared petite, like me, with blonde hair and pale skin, but her face wasn't recognizable at all. Peeking up at Samson, the question was straightforward in my eyes.

"You don't know her. I wouldn't have brought you to see the body of someone you knew, Sawyer. I want to shield you from this part of my life as much as possible. She was an agent working undercover in town. Your paths might've crossed, but I doubt you would've ever spoken to her."

"Am I the only one who thinks—" I started, but was cut off by Ty.

"She looks like you? Yeah, I'd say she bears a slight resemblance."

"That's part of the reason why you're here and what we found on her stomach and arms," Samson admitted, swallowing as he nodded to the guy who'd been standing there silently.

He pulled the sheet the rest of the way back, and I stared as I took in her stomach. Carved into her skin were the words, "Time's up, Sariah." What was worst, up one arm was "I'm coming to collect," down the other was, "what's owed to me with interest."

"The amount of time it took someone to cut those letters is kinda astounding," I mumbled. My brain was doing that thing again where it focused on something ridiculous because if I let it dive into the fact a crazy lunatic sent me messages on dead bodies, I'd probably hide in a hole and never leave. On second thought, the guys could bring me food and water. I'd be fine.

Squeezing my eyes tight, I tried to push the images out of

my head. On the plus side, it wasn't anything grotesque that triggered my gag reflex, but it also seemed like it would be awhile before those words would be burned out of my retinas. Ty pulled me into his arms, and I went willingly. My brain was stuck on the fact someone had done this, had sent me a message via a dead girl.

A year ago, *hell, three months ago even,* the weirdest thing that happened in my life was whether Mrs. Smith's ambrosia salad was edible—man, I kind of missed those potluck dinners now that I thought about it. Rambling thoughts aside, it seemed like I needed to create a scale from naked cake pictures, to imaginary friends being your biological uncle, to sending messages via corpses. I hoped this was as weird as it got.

I didn't realize Ty had moved us out of the cold room until he pulled me onto his lap. That was when I knew we had to be in a different area, because if he thought about sitting down in there, he was truly missing the plot. Lifting my head, I recognized that we were back in Samson's office. Turning around, I faced my uncle.

"So that's creepy and all, but why did we have to come here? You could've sent me a pic of that, and I would've been happy about it."

"Because that wasn't the only thing I wanted you to see or need to give you and I didn't have time to do both. It was the only solution that made sense this morning on two hours of sleep," he answered, handing me a baggie with a note in it.

I noticed his eyes were heavy, and I felt bad for questioning him. It was in my nature to question everything now, and I had to learn when I could drop the defensive act. Samson had never purposefully put me in danger, so if I needed to be here, if it made it easier on the man working countless hours to save us, I could deal with having to see a dead body. Carefully, I grabbed the plastic sleeve, noticing a message written on paper and a picture. Spreading the plastic down on the desk, I leaned over it to try to make out the note.

*"See how good you could've had it."*

Looking at the photo, I realized it was a picture of Jill. She looked glassy-eyed and was loaded down with make-up. She looked well beyond her age as she sat provocatively in the picture. Her legs were posed together at least, but based on her stockings, negligee, and robe, she wasn't knitting. A man's arm wrapped around the back of her head, his hand in a possessive grip on her throat from the front. When I peered closer, her lipstick had smeared, and I could make out faint bruises on her skin. I'd even wager the glassiness in her eyes was a combination of tears and drugs to keep her malleable.

I felt a tear roll down my cheek, partly in sadness for the pain and horror Jill was suffering and partly because this was meant to be my fate. For whatever reason, I'd been given to people who loved me, and I didn't understand what made me different, and outside being the right "family" for the Council, I didn't honestly understand their obsession with me either. I was a ball of disgust, relief, and confusion as I stared at the photo.

It seemed Latimer was out of patience. It was laughable to think he could have easily snatched me a week ago at the hockey game. For someone so important to him, I didn't even register when I was right in front of him. It didn't think it was an act either. *He really didn't know me.* Which made me wonder if all this was really about Latimer, or perhaps, someone posing as him to use his influence?

It was starting to feel like it was the latter option, which only led me to *R*.

"What now, then? Were they able to trace anything to help us find Jill?" I asked. I'd moved back to Ty's arms, but I couldn't quit staring at the photo. It was mocking me, and I wanted to punch the man in the picture. I grabbed onto the anger and used it to light a fire in me. It would be far more useful than fear.

"It gives us a little more information than we had before, but I say this with the understanding that it doesn't go outside our trust circle. I've concluded that there's a lot of compromised agents here. I have a list of a few, but I don't believe for a second it's all there is. Until I know who we can trust, you don't talk to anyone in the Agency unless I've cleared them. Ty's father is clean, and Rey's father is working on something for me, but keep your info from him. He's not dirty, but better not to ply him with things they may use against him. Fin and Cohen, along with Ace, are clear, but other than that. No one. *Understand*?"

"Yeah." I gulped. Shit, this was getting worse by the minute. Samson passed me something across his desk, and if it was some other creepy gift, I'd need to talk to him about appropriate things to buy for nieces. Fortunately, it was just a charm. Picking it up, I saw it was a snowflake, and I smiled at it.

"Thanks. What's it for?"

"It's the newest technology to scan for bugs and send encrypted information, as well as a GPS tracker. I had it made for you, for um, your birthday," he stuttered. "Just tap the side here, and it will scan the area. If it vibrates, you're good; if it beeps two times, the area is compromised and not secure. Do it in your house multiple times a day in various places just to make sure no one is getting into your home. He's going to make a play soon, so keep this on you at all times." He paused, sucking in a breath. "I can't lose you again, tiny dancer."

Wrapping my hand around the charm, I nodded thoughtfully and took my chain off to add it with my dancer one. Ty assisted me in putting it back on, and I did feel oddly better. If something were to happen, they'd have a way to find me as long as my necklace stayed on. It wasn't foolproof, but it was better than nothing.

"Thanks, Samson."

"I wish I could take credit for it, but it was Mr. Reyes who developed it. I had Cohen make the charm for you, though." He shrugged. "Ty told me to be thoughtful when getting you a gift, so, yeah." He shuffled again, and I realized it made him uncomfortable to admit he had a sensitive side.

"Well, I still appreciate it."

Ty watched over my shoulder as I played with the two charms. I didn't want to make him more uncomfortable by talking about it too much, but I did love it.

"So, what now?" Ty asked.

He'd placed his chin on my shoulder as we faced Samson.

It should feel weird to be held like this in my uncle's office, but it didn't, and that made me happy on two fronts—that things were natural with all of us by now, and because my relationships were accepted by Samson.

"We stay the course. You guys keep focusing on training and let us worry about the rest. If I get something, I'll clue you in, but until we think they're going to make a move, there's not much for you all. But, if I had to guess, it would be at the competition like our intel says. It's the best chance they have at getting to you and where the Council will be gathered next."

His words left a hollow feeling in me with how true they felt. The Council was no longer hiding in the shadows, and because of that, they weren't going to be as careful, which could be good *and* bad. It seemed they were resorting to sending me twisted gifts, and the dead body was just the first sick grand gesture to be made. I was scared to think about what would be next.

# forty-three

. . .

## sawyer

DESPITE THE DEAD body's warning, there hadn't been any other messages or attempts. Everything had gone cold, and it had been a quiet four weeks. It was now mid-November, and the competition was upon us. Which meant Samson had been right *again*. This morning, I woke up focusing on all the good things in my life and tried to push the fear out of my mind.

Training had gone better than Henry or I had ever antici-pated. We were skating cleaner than ever, and with the help of Madelyn, we had a chance to make the Olympic team. Excitement bubbled up at the realization my childhood dream might begin today. It was bittersweet, like everything in my life that occurred nowadays. My parents wouldn't be present, but so many others would be in the stands cheering us on. Samson and Isla were attending, as well as Aggie and Charlie. It made my heart happy to see the people I cared about finding love in one another.

Samson and Isla's rekindled relationship was the stuff of romance books. After our dinner, Isla had practically been a permanent fixture in Oak Crest. Thankfully, she could run her non-profit virtually and wasn't missing too much not being in Seattle. She flew back and forth every couple of weeks for the things she couldn't manage via the internet. It was the happiest I'd seen Samson. He was a completely different person now he wasn't hiding in the shadows.

In a moment of vulnerability, he'd revealed I'd been the light pulling him out. The nervous twitch of his lip told me how hard it was for him to admit it, so for once, I didn't make a big deal out of it. Laughing it off, I told him he was dumb. I might've been a light in his world, but he was the one who'd taken the step forward into it. I wanted him to own his bravery. Samson had spent long enough hiding from everything that made him who he was, and I didn't want him to sacrifice anything else for me. My Brave Heart had become courageous.

Tucking my necklace under my leotard, I scanned the locker room. There were a few other girls here, but none of them appeared to be paying attention to me. It was nice, if not odd, after being at TAS where it felt like everyone watched me. I sat down on the bench and laced up my skates. My skirt fell over my legs, and I smiled as I took in the fabric. Fin had outdone herself on our ice dance outfits. She was

Houdini with time, but I wondered if it was more about staying busy to avoid something.

She'd been busy working with the Agency, and yet, it felt like something more was going on. Something she wasn't talking about or willing to confront. Asa continued to support her; his worry evident things weren't right between them. Sometimes I wanted to lock her in a room with Asa to make her talk, but it wasn't my relationship, and I had enough of that on my plate.

Having seven boyfriends was a full-time job. The only saving grace was everyone was so busy right now with training schedules, it somehow worked out where I spent relatively equal time with each of them. It'd been nice to have couple-time with my guys. I was utterly in love with all of them at this point and couldn't imagine my life without them. BOSH was my family.

Elias had gone back to his family's home a few times. He'd been hush-hush on the matter, stating the less we knew, the better. Elias found ways to be at the house when he could, and when he couldn't, the FaceTime calls were extra spicy. He was meeting us here today, and I was excited to see him. It had been over a week now, and I missed my reluctant knight. A throat clearing brought me out of my reverie, and I looked up to find a girl I didn't know.

"Hi."

"Hi, can I help you?"

"Oh, um, sorry." She blushed. "I'm just a fan, but um, there's a guy out there who asked for you. Said to head out when you were ready. He's really cute, too."

Smiling, I nodded my thanks and locked up my gear before exiting.

Rhett peeked his head around the door as I pushed it open. Laughing, I ran as fast as possible on my skates to him. The black and silver fabric swished with each step. It was longer than a standard figure skating dress, but the slits added great visual lines to my movements when we danced. The shimmery stones on the bodice sparkled, and I liked how Rhett responded to me in it.

"Wow, baby. You look, wow!"

"Thanks. Fin outdid herself."

Wrapping my arms around his waist, I hugged my gentle giant and soaked in his calming essence.

"You ready to kick some butt?"

"So ready," I beamed. Taking my hand, he pulled me down the hall, where I came face to face with all of my boyfriends. Lined up, they were all waiting for me.

"Ah, you guys!"

Hugging and kissing them one by one, I cherished the warmth they added to my life. When I reached Elias, I ran into his arms, kissing him the longest. When it started to get heated, a throat-clearing had us pulling apart. A slight blush appeared on my cheeks, but I didn't care. They were all here, and I'd missed this fucker.

Turning in his arms, I tried to hold the tears at bay. I didn't know why I was so emotional about this. It wasn't over the top or outlandish. I think competing for the first time in five years was getting to me more than I realized, and having their support meant the world to me.

"You guys are going to do great. Now, wipe those tears and go out there and wow us all," Soren commanded.

"Come on, Smalls, we got this."

Taking Henry's outstretched hand, I began in the direction of the arena. Glancing back over my shoulder, I waved at them as we disappeared around the corner.

"Okay, game face, Sawyer, game face," I coached myself to Henry's amusement.

"She's talking to herself. Better watch out. Sawyer's gone mental."

The last person I wanted to see before walking out on the ice, was now standing ahead of us in the concourse. Rolling my eyes, I pulled Henry's hand and moved further away from her. She'd purposefully waited for us since this wasn't even the time for her event. The bitch wanted to throw me off. Adelaide hadn't learned yet that I didn't care about her. Nothing she did or said affected me anymore. Didn't mean I wasn't going to take her down still, because I was. I just wasn't letting her control me any longer.

Madelyn came over and gave us a commiserating smile. While she hadn't come out and said anything, her opinion on QB appeared to be about the same as ours. I didn't blame her, especially when Bitchalide had been out in full force, making every decision Madelyn made difficult. Her pettiness at not getting picked by her parents to take over the position was ridiculous. It was funny in a sad way to watch the spoiled princess not get her way on something. How difficult she made it for everyone else was uncalled for. At this point, I felt only pity for the spoiled princess.

"Okay, we got the game plan, right? Focus on each other and tune out everything else. You guys are going to be great."

"Thanks, Coach."

Grinning warmly at the woman, I did feel confident in our performance. Her watch buzzed with the timer, alerting us to head to the rink. We made it a point not to watch the others before us because, either way, it would only make us paranoid. Instead, we stayed in our own bubble and listened to our music in our headphones over and over to the point it was ingrained. Handing off our things to her, we waited for the current pair to skate off the ice.

"Now entering the ice is a new dancing pair from Oak Crest, Utah—Sawyer Sullivan and Henry Reyes."

The announcer droned on, but I ignored him. The ice swished under my skates, and while it wasn't the freshest ice after a few hours, it wasn't the worst either. Our program wouldn't be affected by it, and that was all that mattered. The fabric caressed against my tights as I glided, and I felt as lightless as the material. My hands were poised, and I felt graceful as we took our positions apart from one another.

We weren't starting in a hold position. Instead, we were bucking tradition and following Scott and Tessa's footsteps from Canada and were about ten feet apart, facing one another. The music started, and the beat immediately had me moving. "Astronaut in the Ocean" by Masked Wolf wasn't traditional music either. The Olympic committee had approved music with lyrics at the 2018 Olympics, and it had opened the door for performers to branch out.

We collided into a joint spin before Henry twisted me up

to his shoulder. The movements were fluid, and we fell into the song and choreography. The music switched to "Heather" by Conan Grey in parts. It was a mashup that highlighted the two tempo changes we needed and had an edge of soft and dark that worked for our number. Henry had amazed me with the transitions and moves he wanted to try. With Madelyn's coaching and training schedule, we had perfected it.

Twirling around, we twizzled in perfect synchronicity, the feel of the ice echoing our slices. Every time we moved on the ice, I could forget about the Council and all the crap that went along with it. Here I could push my body to express my soul and not worry about the next thing coming for us. Skating had always been my passion, and when I skated, I unfailingly felt like the best version of myself.

As we joined hands for a combination spin, I watched everything blur around us. My focus was Henry as we shifted feet and kept spinning. I loved this spin, and doing it as a pair always made me feel empowered. It was like shedding the old skin and embracing what remained.

We moved into position for our sneak move. Reverse rotational lifts were illegal unless it was the woman lifting the man. For twelve seconds, I held Henry up with purely my core muscles. He was facing outward, upside, and holding onto me around the waist. My skates were open, knees slightly bent as I braced all his weight around my middle. Throwing my hands out, I counted the beats until I could flip him back. It took forever to achieve this move, but it was our best hope to score higher than our competition.

Flipping his feet down, Henry skated out, grabbed my

hand, and pulled me in for our last lift. Balancing my skate on his leg, I stood as I reached out with my hand and transitioned into a curve lift—the music and emotion connected with me as I hit each pose and motion. Ice dancing was all about the beauty of the movement, infusing the dance elements more than figure skating.

At the crescendo, I could feel my heart beating with each push-off of my skates and the adrenaline pumping through me. The emotions were heavy as I skated with my best friend and lover. I trusted him with my life, and that's what I believed made our skating partnership work flawlessly. When you trusted and knew someone intuitively, it was broadcasted in every piece of choreography. Hand over head, I skated under his arm and back again as we twisted together in a combo step spin move.

Henry and I skated in our own world, telling the story of our hearts and fears as we performed them on the ice. We went into our last moves of simultaneous choreographic spins, and I felt it. The moment when you knew you'd nailed something spectacular. As the song started to wind down, our movements matched, and we skated with our hands outstretched until they barely touched, fingertips grasping one another. As the last note played, Henry's touch on my hand lifted. I crumpled inward into a sit spin before ending in a pose.

It was quiet for a moment as the music stopped, making it more evident. No one moved; no one made a noise as they watched, captivated. It was the first time I'd looked at the crowd, and I looked to the spot I knew my family was. As I joined hands with Henry, the arena erupted. I didn't know who started it, but once the first clap sounded throughout the rink, there was a cacophony of them. The guys and our family were on their feet, whooping and hollering more than anyone else. It was a bit over the top for ice skating, but I didn't care and soaked in every minute of it.

As the attendants skated out, I realized how many roses and stuffed animals had been thrown down. Grasping Henry's hand tighter, we bowed a few more times before skating off. Madelyn was all smiles when we stepped onto the soft landing, handing us our skate guards as she did. She ushered us to the kiss and cry area as we hastily got ourselves in order. The skating attendant handed off an armful of flowers to me and another with letters and stuffies to Henry.

We'd had a good following before, so this wasn't a new thing for us, but this level was unknown. Henry and I stared at one another, disbelief and giddiness coursing through us. Kissing him, I wanted to remember this moment, no matter what happened. I realized skating again with him and competing was the dream. I didn't need gold medals or ribbons. I just needed my guys and friends—my BOSH.

Sitting down, Henry wiped the tears I hadn't realized were falling, and Madelyn had someone come and take the items from us, freeing our hands at least.

"Thank you," I mumbled, still in shock as we waited for scores.

In my mind, I knew we were competing. But it was like I hadn't believed it. This had all been out of reach for so long; I hadn't let myself hope for it. Now, I was in shock as everything sank in. When the scores started to come across the board, my mouth dropped open even further.

*Sullivan & Reyes-92.66*

Henry turned to me, and nothing would've stopped me from kissing him. Thankfully, nothing did, and we hugged and kissed in our enthusiasm.

"I knew it! You guys were going to be great, and you went out there and just blew everyone away!" Madelyn cheered.

Pulling back, I turned to our coach and friend, grabbing her hand to pull into our hug. When we'd hugged enough, we made our way out of the kiss and cry and back into the concourse. There we found the rest of our family and friends. More hugs and tears were passed as we all celebrated our scores. We'd made it to the finals and were currently in first place. There was still the free skate and four more pairs to go, but it was good. In fact, it was terrific.

Which meant, of course, Adelaide had to ruin it. We walked into a more crowded area where I happened to be holding Elias' hand when she appeared. Seeing me with him, the ugliest look crossed her face. She looked ridiculous anyway, with her sparkly red leotard and skates standing in the middle of a common area. Most people had on jackets or leggings, but not her; she wanted everyone to notice her every minute of the day.

"Eli! I can't believe you continue to consort with this floozy! I'm not waiting around any longer. It's over!"

"Bitchelaide, he was never with you. Move on. It's just sad at this point."

My mouth was hanging open, and I took in Mateo as he

took a stand against bullies. QB didn't know how to react as she turned, her mouth agape, only able to stare. The icing on the cake was when he patted her on the shoulder when we walked by. It was the funniest thing I'd ever seen and better than any witty comeback I would've had. Mateo had never looked sexier. Licking my lips, I watched him saunter off as dirty thoughts filled my head. Elias pulled me into his chest, whispering in my ear.

"Oh love, you liked that, didn't you? I think I know what I need to do for our next *workout*."

Elias had started calling our sexy shenanigans workouts since our first one had been in the fitness room, and we always felt like we'd been through a workout afterward. It was cute how he couldn't say fuck out loud, but of course, that made me only want to say it more for him.

Backing away, I winked. "If you're asking if I want to ask Mateo to join our fuckfest, you would be right."

Shaking his head at me, Elias grinned and followed. Just because we didn't actively hate one another anymore didn't mean I wasn't going to push his buttons. What was the fun in that? *Nothing*. It was more fun to get him riled up and then devour one another. Ollie caught me as I moved further away, and I snuggled under his arm, inhaling his spicy scent.

"Hey, bite-size. You were amazing out there. I think that was the second most amazing thing I've ever seen."

Knowing he was setting me up for a joke, I smiled, tilted my head up, and asked it anyway. "Oh yeah, hot stuff? What's the first?"

"You sucking Ty's cock while I drill you from behind."

Almost choking, my face heated as I recalled the time we'd done just that. "Yeah, I guess that can be first." I grinned when I finally had my coughing under control.

We made it to the box Aggie had gotten for all of us, and I went through another round of hugs from Charlie, Aggie, Samson, and Isla. Fin called, and we FaceTimed for a few minutes, along with Rowan and Rhonda. They hadn't been able to make it due to the distance but were watching online. Once I'd spoken to everyone, even Ace and Chloe, I was tired and sat back to watch the last of the skaters.

They were all talented, and with only one more couple to go, we had a marginal lead. It looked good for us to stay in first, or at least in second, ensuring we'd make it to the finals tomorrow. We'd all traveled to Colorado together from Utah and were staying in a hotel close by. BOSH had a huge suite, and the parental units had separate rooms on different floors. Samson had extra agents he trusted stationed around the arena and hotel.

He was working with Constance Berkshire, Ashlee's mom, to weed out the bad apples. Samson had confronted Constance after Ty had witnessed a secret conversation, and she'd spilled everything she knew. They had Ashlee, and it was another girl on our list to save. Along with Brandon Mathews and David Reyes, the four were working to over-haul the Agency. The benefit of the stress over the past month meant Samson had a better idea of who was on the side of good.

We expected the Council to make a move and were as prepared as we could be. Jill was still missing, and all the

544

leads we had on her had gone cold. After the story broke about him, Donnelly was in the wind and officially black-listed from the national ice skating committee. The FBI was hunting him for fraud and child pornography. They'd been able to retrieve enough of the files on his phone from what Fin had recovered, along with our clone one, to put together a case.

It was disappointing he was still free out there, but knowing the authorities were taking care of it and he would have severe consequences when found made it feel somewhat better. I was still waiting for that satisfying moment when he was captured, and I knew he wouldn't be able to harm anyone else.

When the last couple skated off to get their scores, I decided to take advantage of the distraction and use the restroom before the lines became ridiculous. Individual figure skating started after this, and we were going to stay and watch a few of our students who'd entered the competition. Hopefully, we'd be out of here before QB's time. Having to watch her skate was akin to dry shaving with a rusted razor —uncomfortable, painful, and left you needing a shot.

"I'll be right back. I just need to pee," I whispered to Ty. Kissing my cheek, he let me out of his lap, and I shuffled out the door. The bathroom was still empty when I got there, and I sighed in relief once I could go. I was one of those people who waited until the very last minute to relieve myself and then had to go so bad I was doing the pee-pee dance. Trying to go in a leotard was a bitch, and I cursed myself for waiting so long. Ah, sweet relief.

Redressing, I washed my hands and was happy to find my hair still in place. Fin had put it in a French braid crown at the butt-crack of dawn this morning before we left. That was a true friend to get up so early, considering the drive here was eight hours. I needed to ask what type of hair witchery she used to keep it intact. Wiping away the mascara under my eyes from the few tears I shed, I felt presentable again as I dried my hands and headed back to the suite.

I really should've been more aware. It wasn't like I didn't remember what was going on in our lives. Maybe it was the amount of time in between things that had made me forget. Or perhaps it was just the happiness clouding the fear I needed to have. Whatever the reason, I could only blame myself for the hand that went over my mouth as I stepped out the door and the prick I felt in my neck.

Blackness met me quickly, and I berated myself for being so foolish. I hoped our backup plan would be good enough.

My life depended on it.

# forty-four

. . .

## sawyer

WAKING to find Donald Donnelly standing over me, I had to stop from upchucking my lunch all over myself. My revulsion had to be evident on my face, and his sneer confirmed it. I tried to pinch myself to wake up, hoping this was merely a nightmare—it wasn't.

"Well, if it isn't *little Miss Slutville*," he breathed on me, spit falling onto my face. Disgust rushed through me, and I cringed away from him as best I could. Donald looked worse for wear. Being on the run hadn't been good to him. His hair was stringier, his skin had lost its color, and a layer of oil coated his skin. His clothes were worn and ripped in a few places, and he smelled like he hadn't showered in weeks.

Swallowing, I tried to clear my throat, but it was dry, and I felt incredibly parched. Logically, I deduced it was more than

Kris Butler

likely because of whatever drug they stuck me with. Logic was all I could allow myself to think.

"Where am I? Donald, are you here to rescue me?" I whispered. I hoped to play dumb and pretend I didn't know Donald was on the wrong side of things. It was all I could think to do. He'd been leaning down to sneer something at me but paused when he heard my request. It was enough to garner I'd piqued his interest. It was quickly squashed when a second voice spoke.

"Move away from the whore, Donnie. She's only trying to trip you up."

Ice filled my veins, and I knew then how much I'd underestimated her. Adelaide moved into focus and smiled evilly down at me.

"Looks like you ended up on your back, after all, Slutyer. Guess you won't be making the second program tomorrow. Too bad, really." She faked a tear with her finger, her smile wide as she did it. Adelaide looked manic, causing genuine fear to fill me. Apparently, she was desperate enough to do whatever it took to get back what she believed was owed to her.

"I see you understand now. You're going to be my ticket to the future I want. Donnie and I worked it out with someone who wants you. For some reason, he was willing to offer me a trade. They couldn't get to you with all your lovers around every corner or with the security your traitorous uncle set up. Fortunately, I had access *everywhere*. It was so easy once you were alone. You didn't even see me there, and all I had to do was plunge that needle into your neck, and

548

*boom*, down you went. I shoved some men's clothes on you, put a hat over your head, and sat your ass in a wheelchair." She cackled, and it was terrifying to watch her transform into this unhinged person.

"I watched as all your lovers scurried about in a panic when they realized you were missing. For guys who say they love you, they waited an awfully long time before noticing you were missing. Seems you're already losing their interest." She shrugged, inspecting her fingernails as if they held all the secrets of the world.

"You started to rouse at one point, but I still needed to perform, so I dosed you again. I had some random student watch you by saying you were my sick granddad. I went out on the ice and skated, and by the time I rolled your sorry ass out of the arena, they weren't checking who was coming and going. It'd been *hours*, and they still hadn't found you. It was pretty brilliant," she beamed.

"And I was waiting at the curb with a van, *voila*. Here we are," Donnelly interjected, wanting some credit.

"Why am I not surprised you two teamed up? You're both vile," I wheezed.

My mouth was going to be my biggest downfall. I knew this. And as the words floated out of my mouth, I was prepared for the blowback. Adelaide hated me and now had the opportunity to do whatever she wanted without anyone stepping in. She smacked me across the face, her eyes widening at the pleasure she received from making me hurt. Tears stung my eyes as I tried to focus on the room, my ears ringing with how hard she'd slapped me.

"Ow," I groaned.

"Keep running that mouth, Sawyer, and I'll remind you who the real queen is."

"You?" I laughed, despite knowing better. "You're *nothing*, Adelaide. It's why nothing you say affects me anymore. I already won. I have people who care about me and love me. What do you have? A crappy motel room and Donnelly?" I scoffed. "*Nothing*. Just. Like. You."

This time she punched me, and I blacked out from the force.

Rousing, I found myself gaining consciousness to the sounds of Director Douchebag and Bitchalide fucking right next to me. Seriously, I was rethinking my vow not to vomit as I registered the sounds. Closing my eyes tight, I willed myself to block it out. Unfortunately, my movement caught her attention, and I heard her make a comment despite my attempt to avoid sound.

"Oh fuck, Donnie, that feels so good when you fuck me with your fat cock. You have the best dick I've ever had. I bet you're making our guest jealous. Oh yeah, right there, daddy."

Gagging, I tried to go to my happy place to save my mind from being raped. Seriously, this was some fucked up torture technique. Bound at my hands and feet, I could barely move on the bed other than turning my head. Trying to focus on anything other than the two assholes rutting next to me, I took in the room I was stuck in. It was a typical shitty motel room, giving nothing away on my location. I literally could be anywhere with the basic wallpaper and art prints.

Taking in my person, I could make out what I was wearing: a sweatshirt and some pants. Based on the restrictiveness and bunching of the pants, it seemed I was still clothed in my skating outfit—double win. I prayed to all that was good in the world that my necklace was still on. Wiggling my legs, I tested my restraints, but they were secure. Queen Bitch had done her due diligence. Focusing on my guys and the routine Henry and I had performed today, I skated the program over in my head and tuned out the noise next to me.

It worked so well; I hadn't realized they'd finished. The slap on my other cheek had me gasping as I came back into my awareness.

"Bloody hell, skank. Do you have to keep slapping me so hard?" It'd been a reactive statement, and the moment it left my lips, I regretted it.

"How dare you use *his* words in front of me!" she roared, and this time, she punched me in the stomach.

Coughing, I tried to catch my breath as best I could while my hands and feet were bound. It wasn't easy, and it took a while to convince the bile to stay down. My stance on the whole non-violence approach was wavering. Elias had asked me what revenge I wanted on Adelaide a couple of weeks back, feeling I was owed that.

*"I have some plans for her from the things she played on me, love. But what do you need to set things right?" Elias brushed my hair behind my ear as I laid in his arms. He was so gentle with me, making each movement seem unique and careful.*

*"I feel bad for her, honestly. I have everything she wanted, and I'm happy. If she goes away, that's good enough for me."*

*"Where's the brutal throat punch Sawyer I heard all about?" he grinned.*

*"Shit, you heard about that?" I cringed. "Not one of my finer moments. Five bucks, it was Ollie who spilled the beans. But now, I don't think I could hit her. Her life is already sad enough. What would be the point?"*

Yeah, I was starting to find the point.

She yanked me up by my bound wrists, the plastic cutting into my skin with the force. I was disoriented for a moment; my equilibrium re-oriented itself to the new position. When I could focus, it was on a naked Adelaide pulling her hand back to strike again, and I braced myself for the blow. Eyes screwed shut; I was confused when I didn't feel it.

A new person held Adelaide's wrist in their grasp. "You mess her face up anymore, and they won't want her. Get yourself in check, Ade," the woman growled.

QB didn't like being addressed by this woman, but she listened nonetheless, moving and letting go of me. I fell back onto the bed, landing on the pillow. The woman towering over me looked familiar, but I couldn't place her. I heard her say, "sorry about this," right before feeling another pinch and everything went black again. *Seriously, this fucking sucked.*

This time when I woke, I was in a different room. The light filtering through the window was dim, but I could make out a few things around me. It was a bit nicer with burgundy furnishings, and the bed seemed comfier. Bonus, there wasn't anyone fucking next to me. When I reflexively went to touch my head, I realized I was no longer bound.

Wincing at the pain in my eye and cheek, I tried to sit up. Slowly, I braced my hands on the bed as I did, taking in the room. I was in a four-poster bed filled with pillows and a thick duvet. A small lamp sat near me on the right night-stand. Switching it on brought the room more into focus.

Studying my surroundings, my gaze tracked around the room, taking in the furniture. It was a basic setup of a bedroom: desk, bed, nightstands, dressers, and two doors that I assumed were a closet and bathroom. Gingerly, I climbed off the bed and made my way to the window. I pulled the curtains back but had no idea where I was based on the view.

Woods surrounded me, meaning we were somewhere far from civilization. Taking in my body, my stomach and face were tender from the abuse, but everything else seemed fine. I did have my dress on under the baggy man clothes QB had put on me. I hoped it meant I hadn't been violated yet.

It was sad I had to classify it with a yet, but I understood my reality. My brain drew possible outcomes of my situation to help me prepare. I would do what I needed to survive. I always had, and I wouldn't stop now. It was the 'living with yourself' afterward that gave me pause. Would the guys forgive me? Still love me? I couldn't doubt them. Their love wasn't empty or conditional. It would be my strength through this.

A slight sound had me turning, and I realized someone was in the room with me. When they called out my name in a whisper, I hurried over to them.

"Jill! Oh my God, are you okay?"

"Sorry," she rasped, blinking to focus.

She was in rough shape, causing tears to come to my eyes. Moving the hair out of her face, I took in her injuries. Her face looked worse than I assumed mine did, and that was saying something. Glancing back to the doors, I ran over to see where they led. The first one was locked, meaning it was the door leading to our escape. Moving on, I found the bathroom next. Opening doors and drawers, I found a stack of wash rags. Spotting a tub basin, I wondered if it would be better than just wet rags.

Starting the water, I added some oils and Epsom salt I found under the sink and hoped they'd help her. Once it was going, I rushed back to the bedroom and helped her up.

"Jill, I know you're hurt, and I want to help. I think a bath will feel better. Would that be okay?"

She mumbled something I couldn't decipher before nodding her head, so I helped her sit up. I felt terrible when she winced in pain, a cry caught in her throat. My own injuries were ignored as I helped her walk to the bathroom. By the time we made it, I was panting as well. Leaning against the counter for a few beats, I caught my breath before assisting her to sit on the edge of the tub. Helping her undress, I slowly lifted her clothes above her head. Her entire body resembled a giant bruise, and I hurt for this girl.

Silently crying for her, I helped her into the water and turned it off as she sank down. Jill was despondent and barely made any noise. I found a plastic container used to hold feminine products under the sink and dumped it. Gathering water in it, I poured it over her head. Gradually I was able to get her hair washed and clean her cuts.

She had several abrasions and scrapes and a few places where it looked like she'd been burned. I tried not to think about the redness or the swollen parts of her private areas or the bite marks around her breasts. But it was difficult not to imagine the horrors she'd been through.

These men were sick and evil, and vengeance like none other filled me to my gills. Helping her out of the tub, I dried her off and started to brush her hair. Once I was done, I started to search for some clothes when a presence stopped in the doorway. I scolded myself for not hearing them enter.

Their shadow darkened the floor, and I tensed, waiting to see what they were going to do. When they didn't say anything, I turned and found the woman who'd knocked me out. I stared at her, assessing as she stood there unmoving. She was thin, with stringy blonde hair, and I could make out track marks up her arms.

"You're not much of anything. I don't know what my son sees in you, to be honest, or these men here. You have a golden cunt, girl?"

"Whoa, I don't know who you are, but I don't care. That was rude."

She laughed this deep smoker's laugh that sent chills through me. This wasn't a woman to mess with. When her hand shook as she brushed her hair back, I realized she wasn't as fierce as she let on. I wasn't sure how she managed to stop QB from striking me, when a slight wind would blow her over. When I looked under the layer of makeup coating her face, I could see some similar traces of a certain golden-haired boy I loved.

"You're Pamela."

Lingering as I held Jill against me, we waited for her to respond or move out of our way. She snorted, but turned and walked back into the bedroom. The woman pounced on the bed like a teen girl and watched me as I sat Jill down on the couch.

"How is my son? Is he as good in bed as I got for him as a teen, or is he damaged goods now?"

Bitter bile coated my throat at her choice of words. "You're disgusting and not worthy to be his mother."

She laughed again; this one was a little colder. "You can judge me all you want, princess, but you'll be just as disgusting when these men are through with you. Word of advice, if you don't want to end up like her." She nodded, keeping her eyes on the piece of hair she was examining. "It's better not to fight back. She's a strong one, that girl. I'll give her that. She lasted longer than most. It took him six weeks to break her."

She hopped back off the bed and went to leave, turning to

impart one final message before she did. "You're to be dressed and ready for dinner in an hour. The outfits are labeled in the closet."

I realized my mistake of not overpowering her as the door slammed shut, jolting me out of my shock. I couldn't think further than hugging the girl next to me. Tears rolled down Jill's cheek, the bath and horrendous vulture having penetrated the fog she'd been in.

"I tried to be strong, Sawyer. I really did."

"Oh, sweetie, you're so strong. I'm so proud of you. Don't for one second think you're weak. You're still here, and that's all that matters. Don't listen to her. I'm going to get us out of here, and then we can get you help, okay?"

Jill nodded, tears streaming down her face, and I tried not to let the disbelief in her gaze affect me. She'd been here so long at this point, I felt guilty, but I couldn't have done anything. But this I could do. I could make sure we survived, and I could help her after. That was something I was capable of.

Moving to the closet, I found two dresses, two sets of shoes, and two undergarments. The rest of the space was empty. I guess they didn't want us to get any ideas of escape. I didn't want to think of the sinister reason—you didn't need clothes when you were dead or just a body to fuck.

Carrying the stuff out, I helped Jill dress into the red cocktail dress and brushed her hair back as I dried it. There was a little bit of makeup in the bathroom, so I covered up the bruises on her face as best I could. Once she was ready, I dressed quickly. My dress was an emerald green mid-length dress. If I wasn't so sickened by the reason for it, I might've liked it.

The door was unlocked with a few seconds left to spare as I slipped on the last heel. The man I'd hoped never to see again stood grinning down at me. *R.*

"Ah, my little pet. So good to have you back where you finally belong. We've had to be creative in the time we've missed you."

I didn't miss the way Jill flinched at his words, and I knew this man was part of the reason she looked the way she did. Helping her stand, I took her hand in mine and tried to offer the strength she needed to get through this dinner. When I'd changed, I'd finally been able to take a full count of myself, and I realized my necklace was gone. Besides the fact it was the GPS meant to save me, the sentimental value in those charms was invaluable. If Adelaide did anything with it, I would rain down trouble on her until she returned it.

"It's interesting, *R*," I snarled, "all the things you've done over the years to get me for Mr. Latimer led me to believe I was important to *him*. And yet, when I literally ran into the man, he didn't even know who I was. I found it odd as he looked at me with absolutely no recognition."

He stopped to stare at me, a look of uncertainty on his face at my remark. It seemed I was onto something.

"So, it got me thinking," I boasted, "it's not Mr. Latimer that wants me at all. It's *you*. He's a businessman who washed his hands of me years ago. But for some sick reason, you're obsessed with me, and I don't think Mr. Latimer even cares who the fuck I am."

I thought I'd finally put the pieces together and had the upper hand for once, as I noticed a lick of fear flash in his eyes. For one minute, I felt triumphant, arrogant in my boast to use this to my advantage.

"I always knew you were smart, Sawyer, or should I say, *Sariah*. I do prefer that name of yours, the one my Victoria gave you."

A man stepped into the room from the hallway, having stayed hidden there as I'd dressed down R. Jill turned inward at his voice, clinging to me, and I had no doubt he was responsible for her condition. This man was scary and gave off a feeling of something not being right. He was an apex predator, and I wanted to steer clear of him as everything in me screamed to "run." Swallowing, I asked the question I could tell he was dying for me to ask.

"Who?" I stumbled, swallowing; I tried again. "Who are you?"

"Ah, I'm hurt, Sariah, truly hurt. All this time with Victoria's journal, and you didn't put the pieces together. Tut, tut. Maybe I need to reconsider my statement about you being smart," he jeered.

Not once did he lose his perfect smile, and it only made his statement even more sinister. His eyes were dead, and cold settled into my bones at having to be in the same room with him.

"No? Nothing?" he pretended to ask when I didn't answer. Shaking his head in disappointment, he leveled me with his piercing blue gaze. "I'm Alek Hawthorne, princess."

What. The. Fuck.

# forty-five

. . .

*Four hours earlier*

## rhett

LOOKING BACK AT THE DOOR, I wanted to know how Sawyer felt about the last set of scores. The pair had come close, but Sawyer and Rey still held the lead. I was so proud of them and couldn't wait to celebrate back at the suite. When she still wasn't back a few minutes later, I went in search of her.

It was stupid, really. Someone should've gone with her to the bathroom. But with it only being a few feet from our box and guards on both ends, it felt relatively safe. I didn't see her out in the hallway, and when I looked down at the spots the guards were meant to be, only one was there. Fear gripped me at what that alluded to. Knocking on the door, I held back a moment in case I heard anything. The door opened from the inside, and for a second, relief flooded me. Except when I caught sight of the girl, it was a random person and not Sawyer, my hope fleeing.

"Excuse me, miss. Sorry, but was there anyone else inside? My girlfriend hasn't come out yet." I managed to ask in a somewhat polite voice. I wanted to yell and demand answers, but odds were this woman was an innocent bystander. Bringing her into this wouldn't do anything but make me look like a crazy person. Crazy people didn't get to help hunt for missing people, so I pushed down the urge to yell, focusing on what was important.

"No, sorry." She shrugged, moving away quickly.

Exhaling, I knocked again, and when no one answered, I pushed the door open a tad to see if anyone was near.

"Baby, are you in here?" I was about to go in when Ty's voice stopped me.

"Is Sawyer still in there?"

Shaking my head, he cursed under his breath and moved closer. Pushing the door open, I hesitantly stepped inside. I peeked below all the stalls but found them all devoid of legs. Ty followed me in and looked around the sink area. The whole restroom was empty. No one was in here. So, where was Sawyer?

"Rhett, look!"

Ty's voice was panicked, and when I followed his line of sight, I saw what had made it so. Lying against the wall behind the door was Sawyer's necklace. Scooping it up, the clasp was broken, and I didn't know if it had fallen off or been torn. Either way, it was no longer around her neck, meaning we'd lost her.

Shutting down my fear, I channeled my rage as I stormed out of the restroom. Adelaide was lingering nearby, a covert smile on her face, and I wanted to go and shake her down. I wouldn't put it past her to have something to do with this. Ty pulled me back to the box, and when I turned around to glance at Adelaide, she was gone.

When we returned to the group, everyone noticed the necklace clutched in my hand and the absence of the girl whose neck it was meant to be around.

"She's gone, isn't she?" Isla, her mother asked, her bottom lip trembling.

Glancing at her, I nodded, unable to answer. The rage bubbled up my throat, making it difficult to speak as I struggled to control it. I watched Samson shut down all his emotions, and I channeled him. Now wasn't the time to fly off the handle. If we were to find our heart, we needed to focus. The other guys seemed to agree because, as one, we all looked to Samson for our orders. Finally, I was able to utter something.

"Tell us what to do."

He nodded, pulling out his phone, typing in something before addressing us. "Can you bring me her necklace?"

Walking over to him, I watched as he pushed something, and when it vibrated, he let out a breath. "Okay, this room is secure. What do we know?"

"She went to use the restroom right before the last pair got their scores," Ty offered.

"So, we can estimate it's been around 20 to 30 mins. No one has seen her leave the building yet, so she has to be here somewhere. Let's break into teams and meet back in an hour with an update. Pair off into your buddy system," he directed, stopping as he strode across the room. "Elias, it's time."

Elias nodded, clearly understanding the command, and pulled out his phone. Everyone moved out as they teamed up. Waiting for my best friend, I wanted to know what the last message had been about. When he was done, he walked toward me, and we left the suite.

"I messaged my benefactor. He's on the alert if he hears anything. He'll have Samuel on the inside too and report back as soon as he gets word."

A small trace of tension left my chest, knowing we had people this time. The other guys branched off in one direction, so we went the other. We checked training rooms, janitor closets, concession stands, and every nook and cranny we came upon in the complex for over an hour. She hadn't been in any of them. When we got back to the box, it looked like everyone had the same luck we'd had.

"Well, she's either gone or somewhere we won't find her at the moment. It's time to activate the last phase of our plan."

"Samuel's in position," Mateo offered, reading from his phone.

"Mr. Hawthorne reported back and said he got word. There's been an emergency injunction to have the vote early. They're going to do it tonight after the opening dinner.

They've accelerated their plans for some reason, and I bet it has to do with Sawyer. When he becomes abreast of the location, he will let us know."

"It's better than nothing. *Fuck*. How did they get wind of this?" Samson cussed, and it made me admire him more to see him coming undone. I was a mess inside and was struggling, but at least I wasn't alone. It made it easier for some reason.

"So we, what, wait?" Henry's voice cracked, utter devastation in it.

"Until we have a location, all we can do is prepare. Let's head back to the hotel. We can change and get ready and set up a home base. We'll get her back even if I have to search every possible location on this planet. I can't—" Samson stopped, emotion clogging his voice.

Isla grabbed his hand, tears streaming continuously down her face. Samson gathered himself before he spoke again. Looking us all in the eyes, he made a promise, a vow.

"We won't lose her."

For some reason, I believed him, and I held onto that hope with everything in me.

Three hours later, we were sitting in our suite as we waited. A knock on the door brought Asa and Fin into the room. Milo had a helicopter and offered it up to them when he'd heard, allowing them to get here in half the time. It had been a nice gesture and one that made me like the guy marginally. Asa comforted his mother when he came in, nodding to the rest of us. Fin hugged me and then the others as she tried to keep, what I'd come to realize was her darkness hidden.

We hadn't hung out as much since Sawyer returned, and part of that was on me getting wrapped up in a girl. Before then, we'd spent almost every weekend hanging out. Over the course of a year, you got to know a person well. Fin was hiding something and wrestling with it on her own. Pulling her aside, I led her to the bedroom and shut the door. I leaned back against the door, crossing my arms, and stared.

It didn't take long. It never did. She was a sucker for the intense eyebrow to get her talking.

"What? Why are you looking at me like that?"

"Fin."

"Rhett," she mocked.

"Are you going to make me ask?"

"I don't know what you're talking about there, big guy."

"Hmm. Is that how we're going to play this?"

"Apparently, since I'm clueless," she huffed, fidgeting on the spot.

Tired of playing this game, I came out and asked her on the spot. "What are you hiding from everyone else, Fin?

"It's nothing."

Giving her another glare, she finally caved.

"I promise, it has nothing to do with *this*. It's just something I'm sorting out with my past."

"That's not an answer."

Her lip started to tremble, and I dropped the tough guy

act and crossed the room in two easy steps to her. Pulling her into my arms, I held my friend as she broke down, tired of carrying her struggles on her own. When she pulled back, I handed her a Kleenex, she wiped her eyes and blew her nose. I watched carefully as she sat on the bed, leaving space for me to join her.

In that room, amidst Sawyer being taken, Fin confided in me and shared her deepest pain. When she'd finished, I handed her another Kleenex as I gathered what I wanted her to hear.

"I'm sorry that happened to you, Fin, but you're not responsible for what's going on now. I know a small part of you thinks it, and I know another part of you thinks what you're feeling doesn't matter because there's something bigger going on."

She ducked her head, my observation being valid. "I just wanted to fix it on my own, you know." She shrugged, sniffling.

"I do. I get it. But I also know you can't do something like this on your own. It's eating you up carrying it around, and you're pushing everyone away that cares. Part of being a team and a family is sharing the burden. We might not be able to fix it for you, but we can support you through it. I know your best friend feels the same way. She's been worried about you. We all have. Including your boyfriend out there."

"God, I'm a horrible cow."

"Stop. This isn't pile-on-Fin hour."

She sat quietly for a few minutes, thinking everything

over, twisting the tissue in her hand. This was the part I was good at, allowing quiet space.

"You know you've changed since Sawyer's come into your life."

"Yeah. I think so." I smiled briefly. "She makes me want to be better."

"Sawyer does have that effect on people." She paused, before peering up at me, the fear evident in her eyes. "Can I ask one favor?"

Nodding, I waited for her to ask, knowing what she wanted.

"Let me tell them all on my terms and not under duress."

"I can accept that, as long as you do. Come on, let's see if they've heard anything new."

Standing, I turned to help her, but she shook her head. "I need a minute. I promise I'll be out in a second."

Giving her space, I quietly left the room. Everyone appeared to be in the same spots when I returned. Asa had been watching the door, his face dropping when he saw me. I watched as he wrestled with whether or not to ask me what was going on; he decided and walked over in the end.

"I don't want you to break her confidence. Can you tell me if she's in trouble? Do I need to worry about my girlfriend *and* my sister?"

I thought for a moment about the best way to answer his question. "She's not in danger if that's what you're asking."

He nodded, accepting my carefully worded answer. Fin wasn't in the type of trouble where someone was after her, but she was in over her head to a point. If she didn't ask for help soon, she would drown in the sea of darkness she was flirting with.

It was a few hours later when we finally got the call it was time to move. Mr. Hawthorne had sent a location to Elias with instructions to wait for his signal before we did anything. We loaded into a van Samson had delivered. Isla, Aggie, and Fin stayed back in the room, along with Asa and Mateo.

They were handling the computers and would give us visual information once we were in place. We had trackers that Samson had given us if any of us were separated. However, if it were anything like the last Council facility, there would undoubtedly be a device to block signals.

Pulling up to an empty warehouse, I wondered if we'd been duped into a trap. We looked around at one another, similar thoughts on all of our faces. When we heard screaming and gunshots, we ran from the van, not caring we hadn't been given the signal to go. Sawyer could be in there, and if she was, she was in danger. Every single one of us would willingly die for her.

Tonight, we might get our chance.

Mateo shouted at us through the comms, asking what our status was. Heavy pants were returned to him, ignoring his pleas as we headed into the warehouse. Except when we made it in, breathless in the cold air, it was empty.

"But," I stuttered, unable to finish, spinning around in a circle. A crushing sense of anxiety filled me at not being in the right place, and everything I'd been holding back exploded out of me. Grabbing the closest object, I threw it against the wall and watched it splinter everywhere. I went to throw the next thing and scream out my rage when a hand gripped me from behind.

"That's not going to help, mate," Elias said in a firm voice.

I opened my mouth to respond when the last voice I expected to hear spoke from the shadows.

"I would listen to your friend, *Son*."

# forty-six

. . .

## sawyer

I BLINKED at the man before me and tried to process the words he said. He was tall with a head of dark, slicked-back hair. His clothes and hygiene were impeccable, and nothing on his person was out of place—not a hint of stubble or stray nose hair. He had a square jaw and angular face that I couldn't seem to pull my focus from. He was menacing in a way that made the air around you cold, and caused fear to race through you.

I tried to be strong. I really did. But when I locked eyes with him, it was like he sucked all the good out of you with one look. Goosebumps rose on my skin, and my legs began to tremble in genuine fear. There was no humanity in his eyes. If pure evil had a human form, it would be in the shape of this man. Nothing in this scenario made sense now. If this was

Alek Hawthorne, then who the hell was Elias' benefactor? Had we all been led astray this whole time? Did that mean our plan was shit, and they wouldn't be able to find me?

Swallowing, I tried to keep the contents of my stomach down. Between all the vile things I'd witnessed the past few hours and whatever the hell they'd been injecting me with, it made it incredibly difficult. I could feel the bitterness at the top of my throat, and it took everything in me to keep it down. I couldn't seem to create enough saliva to keep wetting my throat.

Counting in my head, I tried to focus on the good things and calm myself. I pulled everything Mrs. Mary had taught me in therapy to the forefront and channeled it all into being strong, remaining calm, and staying in the present. If there was ever a do-or-die situation, it was now, and I needed every tool I had at my disposal.

Fear wanted me to crawl into a hole and hide, leaving behind everyone and everything that threatened me. Hope was a blazing light, telling me to hold on. The guys flitted through my vision, and I used their love to stay standing. I recalled the strength my parents had in those last moments to save me and embolden myself. I reflected on the sacrifices Samson and Charlie made over the years to keep me safe and provide for me to push down the bile. I used it all to lift my chin and stare him straight in the eyes.

Alek Hawthorne might be evil personified, but I was *Sawyer fucking Sullivan*. I didn't care about my genetics or family legacy. Those things meant nothing to me. I'd made myself and formed my own family. People loved me enough to risk their lives for mine. *I was a fucking original, and that was my power.*

Finding my strength, I unleashed all my sass. "And I care because?"

He appeared stunned for a second. Alek Hawthorne wasn't used to people not shrinking in fear from him. His eyes glinted, and despite knowing I'd made myself more interesting, I held my stare. I could see the desire he was getting from thoughts of breaking me. But I stayed firm despite the thorn in my side he'd become.

"Oh, Sariah, you're as delicious as I always knew you'd be. You've got Victoria's fire and Isla's grace. I can't wait to watch you break."

His words had no effect. I'd gone into my battle zone, and I was fully armed and protected. When I didn't even blink, I saw the first sign of doubt enter his eyes, but it was quickly replaced with his delight at how hard I was going to be. Alek Hawthorne wasn't one to be underestimated, and I'd have to be mindful of that. Now that he'd set his sights on me, I hoped Jill would at least get some reprieve.

Alek smiled and nodded to R, who had been standing back watching the scene. His lecherous stare did nothing to me now. He was a mere rodent with Alek around.

"Ladies, our guests are ready for their entertainment. Shall we?"

He motioned for us to head out into the hallway ahead of him. Keeping hold of Jill, I assisted her as we walked out. I tried to catalog my surroundings, but it was basic and plain with little details. It offered nothing in the form of information to use against our captors or even identify where our room had been. The realization that everything in this place was picked for an intended purpose left a sour taste in my mouth. Imagining people twisted enough to think of all the minute details they could use to weaken their prey astounded me.

And there was no doubt in my mind he viewed us as anything other than prey.

We came to a set of stairs, and I attempted to hold Jill and the railing. It was rough going as she'd retreated more into herself, leaning on me fully and leaving me to carry her weight. The assholes behind me weren't patient about my struggle, either. When we finally made it to the bottom, I was panting from the exertion. There was no way we could escape with Jill in her current condition. I was strong, but not 'carry another person through the forest' strong. Keeping my belief the guys were on their way, I straightened myself and pushed on.

"Do you have an actual name, R, or are you too unworthy to merit one?" I asked tauntingly.

The push on my back was the first indication he didn't like my comment. The second was when he pulled my hair, causing my head to snap back. I found him standing over me with my braid around his fist.

"Watch how you speak to me, *girl*." His spit flew onto my face, and I scrunched up my nose at it.

"Ew. You might want to see a doctor for that condition."

I seriously should shut up, but it was like my fight sensor had been intensified. Once I'd accepted I wasn't running, my need for self-preservation had fled. I watched in slow motion as he reared back, ready to strike me. Alek grabbed his hand, halting him before he could strike. I didn't want to be grateful to the prick, so I chose not to be. He probably only stopped him so he could do it.

Steeling myself, I waited to see how this would play out. Jill clung to me, her nails digging into my sides, but I bared it all, knowing I could handle this.

"Enough, Leon. Don't get angry at Sariah for being cleverer than you."

Oh, *Leon* did not like that comment at all if the sneer on his face was any evidence. Smirking, I waited for him to release my hair. He did, but not before pulling some strands loose; the asshole had to really tug with it being braided. Fucking hell, that hurt. Guys with short hair didn't understand the pain of having their hair pulled in that manner. I could use that rusty razor right about now—or a spoon, that would work to gouge out his eyeballs.

Oh, Fight Sawyer was feisty and a bit homicidal, it seemed.

Leon's face screwed up, a sneer on his lip. I had to hold myself back from laughing at his name and being put in his place by Alek. No part of me wanted to align with that monster in any shape or form, so I forced it down, focusing on my resolution to fight. At any rate, I wasn't on the verge of vomiting anymore. I kept the urge to massage the back of my head contained as I walked forward.

We came upon two wooden doors where a man in a suit stood guard. I had a brief flash of him dressed in 18th century period clothing with the powder wig and little tights, and I couldn't help the little giggle that slipped through. I felt a bit manic with everything—my defense to curbing the despair. If I sat and thought about all the shit going on right now, I'd break before Hawthorne even started his torture.

The guard looked at me curiously but kept his blank facade as he opened the door for us. The room we entered sobered me instantly. It was a formal dining room with a large table, and a sitting area to the side filled with couches and oversized chairs. Already seated in various spots were the remaining members of the Council—including my father.

I spotted Latimer, who again gave me a cursory glance before returning to his *companion*, and I used that term lightly. Interspersed between the men were girls. And I mean *girls*. They were sitting on laps or draped over the men, their bodies being groped by the members as they chatted.

I was easily the oldest, and the bile I'd finally contained threatened to slip back up. They were all dressed similarly to us in short cocktail dresses, but I picked up a detail I'd failed to notice earlier. Each girl was in a solid color, and each pervert they were "entertaining" had a corresponding pocket square. *It was a fucking matching game.*

Out of the corner of my eye, I tried to spy what color Alek had, but he was too far back for me to decipher. However, he'd been waiting to pounce as he cozied up from behind and whispered into my hair.

"Don't worry, Sariah, I like my girls nice and broken in. Though, from what I hear, you might already be there. For tonight; however, you're free game for anyone."

Swallowing, I kept my gaze straight ahead and willed myself not to let his words affect me. The guys were coming. They would find me. I knew it. I kept repeating my mantra over and over.

Alek ushered Jill and me over to sit in two empty seats on the couch. I took the opportunity to study the members while Mr. Hawthorne situated himself on his self-made throne in the center of the space. Some of the men appeared to have the women as mere accessories, whereas others enjoyed their "entertainment" with their hands slipped under skirts.

"Greetings, gentlemen. We will be proceeding to our dinner shortly and then on to our emergency vote. We will have the chapters on hand that can be present to cast, and everyone else will broadcast into our secure network. It should go smoothly, and we can put this threat to our reign behind us and continue thriving in our positions of power." Alek grinned.

"Here, here," one of them cheered, a drink raised. I think it was the Rothchild representative by default. The pictures we had were outdated, making it hard for me to pinpoint exactly who everyone was. Orson was easy, and Latimer. Fitzroy as well, and even Draven due to his resemblance to Victoria. That left Rothchild and Bellamy as the ones I didn't know. Neither looked like the counterparts I knew of their family line, so it was a gamble, but the tall nature of the one led me to think Rothchild.

Jill shook next to me, and I tried to comfort her the best I could, but there wasn't much I could do in a room full of predators looking for any sign of weakness.

"Until that time, we have our *entertainment* courtesy of the latest auctions. And," he looked at me pointedly, "while the green item is older than our average lot, she's been owed to me for many years and has finally been returned." He steepled his hands, leaning back in his chair, and I knew this next bit was part of his master plan to break me.

"Jayce, don't you recognize the one you lost me?" Latimer finally looked fully at me, taking me in head to toe, and a lascivious smile appeared. Before he could respond, Alek continued with his plan of attack. "But Orson, you must be enjoying this family reunion. She is *your* daughter, after all."

Abernathy gave me a cursory glance; a sneer pulled at his lips before switching to a cruel smile. "I think you mean *niece*, Alek." He laughed.

"Oh, you are quite right." He chuckled, slapping his knee, directing the next part to me. "I always forget you *stole* your brother's girl and then his sperm for the ultimate 'fuck you' for joining our enemies," Alek proclaimed.

The rest of the men roared in laughter, finding the confession humorous. Alek watched me the whole time as he hit me with that bit of information. My heart raced, and as much as I didn't want to reveal how much he affected me, he was getting to me. The surprise and pain covered my face, my inability to hold them back evident for all to witness. Alek sucked it up like a sponge, and I could almost see him growing in size with each emotion he pulled from me.

He was an emotional parasite, feeding on the husks of my pain.

"Peculiarly, Sariah has managed to connect herself to

almost every family in this room. It's curious, don't you think, how she managed to do that, having no knowledge of us?" He paused for dramatic effect, commanding the room as he did. "She's fucking quite a few of your family lines. Let's see, Richard, she's with your bastard, Jayce, your black sheep nephew, and Ronald, your degenerate cousin's boy. She's related to Orson by blood, and Nicholas, your daughter raised her for fifteen years."

The last man turned to me then, regarding me for the first time. An emotion I was surprised to see entered his eyes— love and *regret*.

"So tell me, Bill, is your family losing its touch? Why hasn't your nephew gotten in on her pussy? Is your family that incompetent?" Alek said, cold hatred infusing every word, sending chills up my spine. He didn't show any emotion on his face, but his words were filled with them.

"I-I-" Bellamy started to defend, stuttering before gathering himself. I didn't know if it was reassuring or not that these influential businessmen were as unraveled by Alek as I was. "I think the better question Alek," he restarted, confidence filling his voice now, "is what my family might know that has kept us away. How is a wisp of a thing like her capable of thwarting your resources for twentyish years? And when she does resurface, it's in the middle of our progeny?"

"Curious indeed," Alek responded, steepling his fingers. I had the feeling he was leading Bellamy into a trap. "What do you think is the reason then? What is this *knowledge* you've failed to share with the rest of the members?"

Bellamy swallowed, the realization he hadn't exactly

saved himself yet from the hot water. "Clearly, we have a spy in our midst."

"Oh? And who, pray tell, do *you* think it is? Because from where I'm sitting, it's looking more and more like... you."

"Alek! How could you think such a thing? We've been partners for Exousia Corp for thirty years now. You think *I* could be a spy that long?"

Alek assessed him with his unwavering gaze. I knew he didn't suspect Bellamy, but it was interesting to watch how he wielded his power over these men who were considered influential in their own rights. They might all be praying mantises, but Alek was the most dominant and wouldn't hesitate to eat his own kind. I'd watched a documentary once on the matter, and despite the nightmare-inducing graphics, it felt very similar to the dynamics in this room.

Slowly, Alek smiled, and I understood how much he'd orchestrated. He flipped his emotions so casually it could only mean one thing—this was all a game to him. The rest of us didn't even have the same board.

"Well, Bill, I guess time will tell, won't it. Now, gentlemen, pocket squares into the pot. It's time to choose your dinner companion."

I watched in horror as they all pulled the colored fabric from their suit jacket pocket and tossed it into a deep bowl in the middle of the table. It was all black and therefore cut out all the color from the inside, obscuring the squares as they fell. I watched as he added the green one that matched my dress but kept the red one for himself. Jill had been looking as well and gasped at the gesture.

"I believe, Orson, you're up first."

When Abernathy shifted his gaze to me, it caused Alek to chuckle. "Of course, if you get your daughter, I mean *niece*, you can redraw. Unless," he paused, a creepy smirk on his face, "you're into that. No judgment zone here."

I'd hit a new level of disgust as I stared in horror at what he was implying. Thankfully, Orson didn't seem to have *that* preference, though I did catch the leer Bellamy threw at me, and with how Alek had embarrassed him, I knew it wouldn't be a good dinner for me if I were his companion.

Orson drew a blue one, and a redhead walked over to him, sitting in his lap. I turned my head, not wanting to watch it even if he wasn't my biological father. I couldn't focus on that bit of information yet, on what it meant. My brain wouldn't allow me, afraid I would crumble into a puddle of emotional goo if I did. My minute of distraction cost me missing the next two who drew colors when I peered up.

"Richard." Alek motioned, and I watched with bated breath as he drew his square. I didn't know who I wanted to pick me. None of my options looked promising. When he pulled out the green, my stomach dropped. I stared frozen at the piece of fabric, unable to move.

"Sariah, you're to go to him."

Alek's words beckoned me forward, but I was frozen to the spot. "Last chance, Sariah, or I'll have Leon assist you, and I don't think you'll like his direction."

Standing, I shuffled my way over, not wanting to have R touch me. Thankfully Richard was on a couch, allowing me to avoid the sitting on the lap dilemma. I didn't think my body would be able to handle it. From the time it took me to move and sit down, the rest of the pocket squares had been drawn. Clearly, I was the only one with an issue, or the other girls were so conditioned already they fell in line quicker.

When I sat down, I started nervously twisting the watch Isla gave me around my wrist. I'd taken it off to skate per regulations, and Ty had held onto it for me. When we'd gotten to the box, I'd put it back on, catching Isla's eye when I had. She smiled and nodded, and I was glad I could make her happy by wearing it. It had become as integral to me as the necklace, and if I'd lost both of them, I feared how I would've responded.

Even now, it brought me comfort to have the watch and to twist it around, reminding me of the promise I made to Isla. She thought she wasn't brave, that I was more than her. But I understood the strength she needed to live the life she did with the secrets she had. This gift reminded me of a woman who found a solution and was strong and brave, and I could be too.

"So, you're the one who's created a shit ton of trouble for me with my worthless son and the Aldridge's?"

Taken aback by his words, I looked up at him, ready to defend Elias. "Say what you want about me, but *Elias* is far from worthless. Adelaide Aldridge is the worst type of person, and if you cared at all for your son, you would know that."

"Oh? How so?"

He leaned back, taking me in, as I started to respond. His

eyes dropped to my hands and halted when he took in my watch.

"She's—"

"Where did you get that watch?"

Raising my eyebrows, I waited for him to notice he'd cut me off. I might be considered these men's concubine, but it didn't mean they could talk to me like I was beneath them. I would give this jackass the same speech I'd given his son and enjoy it a lot more.

Shutting my mouth, I waited, looking down at my watch, unsure what he meant. Curiosity took over, and I answered. "This watch? My mother. But that has nothing to do with this."

*"It has everything to do with this."* He swallowed, and instead of the cocky businessman he'd been a few minutes ago, he now seemed nervous. Venturing toward the 'bite his head off all black widow style' nervous.

Looking at the watch closely, I tried to remember its importance, why she'd told me to wear it. *When you need it, you'll know.* When the memory came to me, I looked into his eyes, and hope filled me again.

Uttering the words inscribed on the watch, *"Inter spem et metum,"* I almost felt the air shift with their power.

The words fell from my lips, Richard nodding as I watched him gulp down his dread, setting into motion whatever they meant.

# forty-seven

. . .

## tyler

PANIC CRASHED into me as we gazed around the barren room; something wasn't adding up. Rhett started to unravel as a chair crashed into a beam, the sound causing me to jump with the echo. I kept turning in circles, hoping something would make sense when I saw it. Taking a step toward a section, I was caught off guard when a man stepped out of the shadows and spoke.

"I would listen to your friend, Son."

Rhett froze in his tracks, and we watched him turn to take in the man. Based on the stranger's words and resemblance, I presumed it to be his father. Rhett charged him, anger furrowing his brows, his muscles tense as he targeted the older man. Elias attempted to stop him but was too slow by the time he'd taken off, his fingers brushing his shirt as Rhett passed.

Samson, however, stood in Rhett's path, his back to him as he cocked a gun and pointed it. The stranger raised his hands, a smirk gracing his lips the whole time, like he thought we were cute. How this man was Rhett's father blew my mind. Other than appearance, there was no resemblance.

"I'm not here to harm you. I have a message, actually. You've all been invited to a dinner, and I'm to show you the way."

Samson studied the man, gauging his sincerity, a look of familiarity there. "Who sent you, Ryan?"

"The Council, of course." He smirked again, Rhett tensing. "There's an important vote tonight, and you're all *required* guests."

"You should've let me punch him first," Rhett seethed through his teeth. I wouldn't put it past him to go around Samson at this point and do it anyway.

"Fine, we'll bite. Where are you taking us?"

"You're already here. This way."

Rhett's father turned around and walked off, not caring if we followed or not. The guys all looked at one another, questioning, but we knew we were going. If it led to Sawyer, then there was no question.

"Mateo, we're headed somewhere," Samson covertly said into his mic.

"You're still strong so far. No other signs of body heat that we can tell. Cohen thinks there's something underground, and we might lose you once you step into what looks to be a steel elevator based on the blueprints he pulled up."

We fell into our rough formation of me and Ollie at the front, Henry and Soren in the middle, with Rhett and Elias flanking them. Samson brought up the rear as we headed into the dark shadows of the warehouse. He led us toward the area I'd spotted, and it looked like Mateo was right; it was a service elevator of some sort. The metal parts that connected had caught my eye. Pulling the doors apart, Ryan stepped in and waited with a bored expression.

"How did you get nominated to retrieve us?" Rhett asked, some of his anger fading now that we were moving

"Well, I'm working my way up, boy. Play your cards right tonight, and you could be on the right side of this as well."

I was proud of Rhett for holding back the comment I could see brewing in his eyes, but it didn't surprise me when I thought about it. Ryan was a means to Sawyer right now. As soon as he stopped being that, then he was fair game. I just hoped I was around to see him punch his dad. It would be epic.

The elevator came to a stop a few minutes later, jolting us all with the landing. Ryan pulled apart the sections and stepped through. Ollie hesitated for a minute before walking ahead as well. I wanted to grab his hand, but I knew we needed to do this part independently. Walking into a room of unknown entities, we couldn't afford to give anything away, no matter how much I wanted his comfort for myself.

We were ushered into a room where we found others gathered. I was surprised when I saw several Agency people among the crowd. Based on the tick in Samson's jaw, he wasn't. Recalling my training, I took in all my exit points, identified the most significant threats, and found the best advantage point. Moving there, I leaned back against the wall to wait. Based on everyone's stance in the room as they chatted and drank, it was clear they'd gathered for a reason, but it hadn't occurred yet.

Ollie propped himself next to me, his eyes on the crowd. "I haven't seen any of the Council members yet. Something is off about all this. Where's Mr. Hawthorne? Where's Samuel? Why would they just invite us in?"

"I don't know. It definitely is odd. Mateo, can you still hear us?"

When he didn't respond, I shook my head at Ollie. So it was like we'd assumed, a blocker was in place. Switching on the camera part, I hoped it would pick up something. I watched as the Co-Director of Operations, Mrs. Brooks, approached Samson. It was then I recognized her as the one I'd seen in the stairwell that day. We were close enough that I could hear most of their conversation.

"Samson, I guess what they say is true. Once you're Council, you never really leave it. I'm glad to see I was wrong about you. I'm sure your brother will be glad to see you've come to your senses."

Samson grunted, looking around the room, and ignored her. Some days I admired his boorish personality. It was interesting how when he stopped being an asshole to Sawyer, and our nickname game had stopped as well. We were protective of our girl and the people in her life. Now that we knew he loved her, he was given the respect he deserved.

When new people entered the room, we tried to hide so they wouldn't see us. Adelaide walked around, laughing as she talked with a man and woman. Upon closer inspection, I couldn't believe who she was with. Though, Bitchalide didn't appear to like being spoken to by the other woman, but was hand in hand with the ex-director.

"Bloody hell, could this room get any more incestuous?" Elias muttered when he noticed them.

"I think I'm going to throw up," Ollie gagged as we all watched Donnelly kiss Adelaide and then kiss the other woman, grabbing their asses as he did. Adelaide didn't like being shared, though, with another woman.

"Oh fuck," Soren cursed, and that was when we realized who the other woman was—Pamela.

"I think it just did," Rey mumbled to Elias.

Thankfully, the trio settled in a different vicinity of the room, and the space was large enough that unless we made it known, they hopefully wouldn't notice us until after we'd made our play. Unfortunately, that didn't look like it was in the cards for us. Seconds later, the room darkened, and a screen lifted that had been separating the rooms.

Only one man was highlighted; the rest of what looked to be a table cast into darkness. I squinted my eyes, trying to make out the shapes. I hoped to determine if this was the Council and if Sawyer was with them, but it was no use. Everything was too dark at this point.

"Greetings, C.O.U.N.C.I.L. Thank you all for being here

with us for the occasion of our special vote tonight. Now, I know some of you are wondering why an emergency vote is needed, and I will get to that. But first, my favorite part, let's remember why we do what we do."

Like some pre-programmed mass, they all chanted, "Control the Olympics and Utilize the Networks. Command the Industries and demand Loyalty. *Council of many, the voice of one, the goal of all."*

"I guess that tells us what Council stands for," Ollie muttered under his breath. I tried to stifle the laugh that wanted to come up my throat, causing me to cough instead. It was so like Ollie to bring humor to a tense situation. I think it was what had drawn me to him because he reminded me of Sawyer in that way.

"Ah, I do love hearing those words. We've all been so successful using the Greeks' philosophy and utilizing the networks provided to us through our athletes. It's truly amazing what we've become today, which brings us to our vote. Our way of life is being threatened," he paused, dramatic effect in tow. The crowd gave him what he wanted with an audible gasp. "I know, but somehow, the Agency inches closer than it ever has before. I've gathered you here tonight to put a stop to them once and for all."

We really shouldn't have been surprised. And yet, at the close of his words, lights illuminated around us, highlighting us to the crowd. Ryan wasn't trustworthy, yet we followed him right into the mousetrap, clouded by our need to save Sawyer.

"It seems we have *traitors* in our midst. Bring them forth."

We stood firm, turning and watching the people around us. Yet, the crowd moved us in a herd-like fashion. We were directed toward the center of the room, shoving and pushing coming from all around us. Falling to my knees after a brutal push, I observed the other guys as I stood. We were all fairing about the same as slurs were directed at us. Panic gripped me, and I worried about how we planned to get out of this.

Elias caught my look and shook his head no, to stay the course. Fighting every instinct in me, I let the crowd do their worst and not make a scene. We made our way toward the man cast in light. His arrogant smile grated on me, and I hoped one of us got to knock it down a peg.

"Thank you so much for being our guests tonight and helping to prove to our chapters the urgency needed in this vote," he spoke to us, bowing his head.

He nodded, and armed men surrounded us, trapping us where we were. Elias still shook his head, and I hoped his trust had been placed in the right person because it was starting to feel like we'd been played. The man up front turned back to the crowd, gaining their excitement as he fed off their frenzy for power, greed, and possibly blood.

"These men want to stop our way of life. They think they're smarter than us! Than me! They want to take what we've earned for themselves. What do we say to foes like this?" He cajoled the crowd, gaining their fervor with each frenzied pitch.

"*Imperium sine fine! Imperium sine fine!*" they shouted over and over into a chant.

We looked at one another, unsure what it meant. Elias said

it back and then translated it for us. *"Imperium sine fine. An Empire without an end."*

Why did that terrify me more than what C.O.U.N.C.I.L. had stood for? Once he had them eating out of his hand, he spoke again.

"We are never ending. There's nothing or no one who can stop us, for we are the ultimate authority. Even my company name shouts this at them, but they do not listen! For what does *Exousia* mean, but power and authority itself!" He chuckled, clearly impressed with his ideas, if not deranged. The man was unhinged, and I didn't understand how someone like him had escaped all our notice. Who *was* he?

"It's time to put an end to the Agency and become an even greater Council. Our emergency vote tonight isn't just to elect the board we need as an organization, but a vote to take us into the future. Not only would a vote for me keep me as the president of this board, but a vote for *me* is a vote for *America.*"

I tried to process what he meant about being the board president because I thought we'd already met him—Elias' benefactor. At the end of his statement, the remaining lights flicked on, illuminating the table he stood in front of and all its guests. Seconds later, ginormous signs dropped from the ceiling. The lunatic had uncanny timing with his lights and electronics. A hush fell over the room in reverence as we looked on at the posters.

*Alek Hawthorne for president.*

Blinking, I barely had time to take in the table and a blonde head that could be Sawyer when all Hell broke loose.

## sawyer

Mr. Fitzroy grabbed my hand and pulled me. When I'd uttered the phrase earlier, something in him had shifted. I still didn't know what it meant, but it had changed him. I watched as he went from the bored CEO to an anxious man before landing on a man with a purpose.

"Tell my son I'm sorry and that I love him. I lost my way over time, but he's the one mistake I didn't make. Tell him that at the end," he swallowed, an edge of pleading in his voice, "when it counted. *I chose the right side.*"

Nodding, I was confused until we were all ushered down a dark stairwell, taking us underground. We were spat out into a ballroom and clothed in darkness as we sat at a large table. Jill was a few seats over, worry on her face as we listened to Alek's speech. When I saw my guys and Uncle, or perhaps Father, pushed forward, courage boosted me.

When Alek revealed his lunatic plan, murmurs went around the room. The presidential election had occurred weeks ago, and a new candidate was already elected. Confusion clouded me as I tried to make sense of the man.

Tugging Richard's hand, I hoped to absolve him from whatever he felt was about to damn him. "It's never too late to make amends with him. You can still try. I don't have to be the one."

"If only it were that simple. I understand why he's enraptured by you now. You make him feel like a man worthy of love. I'm glad he'll have you by his side for what's to come."

Before I could respond, he pushed me behind him again, and I watched as he drew a gun and pointed it at the back of Alek.

"I don't think that will be possible, *Alek.*"

His voice was steady as he cocked the gun, and almost as if in slow motion, I watched in horror as he went to fire the weapon, only to see blood bloom on his own chest. Richard clutched the wound, the gun clattering to the floor. I vaguely remember hearing Elias yell for his father as he fell, following the gun down to the ground.

Screams echoed around me, but I ignored them as I kneeled next to him and tried to put pressure on the wound.

"Why? Why would you do that?"

I didn't realize I was crying until I felt tears drop onto my arms as I attempted to stop the bleeding. My hands were slick with it as I watched it gurgle out of him.

"Because of the code."

"I don't understand. Please, you can't die. I can't have your death on my conscience. If you're good, you should live. *You should live,*" I pleaded, not noticing the chaos all around me.

He lifted his hand, smearing blood on my face as he wiped a tear. "Good isn't always good, and bad isn't always bad, sweet girl. My death was foretold many years ago when I took the vow. Give my watch to Elias. He's the rightful bearer of it now. Don't forget to tell him... *tell him....*"

He trailed off, his hand dropping to his side as the life

drained out of him, and I let out the scream I'd been carrying around with me for years. In a moment of pure rage, I slipped off the watch and grabbed the gun that was still on the ground. Standing, I shot it into the sky to get *his* attention. Then pointed it at the one to blame for everything —Alek.

I had been so wrong. I could see it now. It wasn't Abernathy. It wasn't Latimer. It wasn't even Draven running off Victoria. This was all about *him*. He was the true evil, the one orchestrating this, and we were just pieces on a board he moved around as he pleased. I didn't understand chess the way Elias did, but I knew this.

The queen was the most powerful piece on the board. It was time I checkmated this motherfucker.

Cocking the gun again, I willed my arms to quit shaking. The blood on my hands made it difficult to hold on to, but I gripped it as tight as I could. What pissed me off was that Alek wasn't even worried. In fact, he started clapping as he looked at me with pity.

"Well done, Sariah. If only your mother were here to see you now. I do miss Victoria. She was the true love of my life. Too bad she was in love with my *fucking cousin* instead of me," he roared, some of his mania returning. I was starting to remember; her journal making more sense. It was becoming apparent to me now.

"But in the end, she found her way back to me like I knew she would. Oh, the years I had with her. Of course, I had to keep her locked up. I didn't want her running off again like she did last time. You know, she talked about you all the time, how strong you were, how I wouldn't find you. Well, jokes on you, Victoria!" he screamed again.

His hair was unkempt now, hanging down in his face. Spittle clung to his lips with each yell he made, and even his clothes seemed a little more disheveled. He was the most dangerous-looking man at that moment, coming unraveled from the inside out. There was not an ounce of humanity left; he was pure recklessness. It would only take one push, and he might kill us all in a fit of rage because he felt like it.

My own rage didn't care, and with each statement he made about Victoria, it only grew. Logic had no place alongside my anger.

"Have you figured it out yet, Sariah?"

When I didn't answer, he let out another maniacal laugh. "Oh, this is going to be good. I wish you could see your face when I tell you how I raped and killed your adopted mom. Oops. I guess I just did. Surprise!" He faked covering his mouth, his eyes full of mirth.

I was struggling not to pull the trigger. I wanted to, but something kept stopping me. I knew if I pulled it, I would be a murderer, and I didn't know if I could come back from that. Would it be worth it to lose myself? To lose the guys? Just to get revenge? Tears streamed down my face. Shouts sounded all around me, people calling my name, but I stayed focused on the one man in front of me.

"Liar. She died in the fire. You're just baiting me."

"Oh, princess—" he started, but I'd had enough of him using my father's nickname for me.

"Stop! Stop calling me that! It's not yours to use!"

He smiled wide at my interruption. "I can see you won't believe me. It's a good thing I like to have visuals for my presentations. Allow me."

He clicked a button, and a screen dropped, almost like he'd been prepared for this reveal. A picture of Victoria, older than I last saw her, filled the screen. I wanted to burn it from my eyes. It didn't make sense how it could be possible. She was tied to a bed, naked, abuse done to her.

The anger grew in me. She'd been alive all this time but held prisoner by this monster. It was the last push I needed to pull the trigger. Alek stared at me in glee, getting pleasure from my pain, wanting me to cross the line. Before I could pull it, the catalyst that would inevitably alter my life, a hand dropped on my shoulder in a comforting squeeze. It traveled down my arm to take control of the gun. Looking up, I found Nicholas Draven above me, his hands covering mine. When he nodded at me, I knew what he wanted, to let him have it.

"Let it be my burden to carry. She wouldn't want that for you. Let me give that to you and get my own vengeance. He was right about one thing. She would be so proud of the woman you've become."

Nodding, I let go as Nicholas took the gun from me to make the man who'd killed his daughter pay. However, that was when 'imposter Alek' strolled into the room, effectively halting everything as they all switched their gaze to him.

"Hello, *cousin*. It seems we have an even bigger score to settle."

Alek whirled around to take in the man, not caring he was giving his back to us, the ultimate sign of not seeing us as a threat. Dropping his head back in a laugh, he clapped for the imposter before addressing the man I'd known as Mr. Hawthorne, Elias' benefactor.

"Well done, cousin," he sneered. "But I'm afraid, *Logan*, that you're too late."

"That's where you're wrong, Alek."

In a move almost similar to the one Mr. Hawthorne—a Mr. *Logan* Hawthorne—had performed the first time I made his acquaintance, screens flicked to life all around the room. Alek rolled his eyes, not impressed with the theatrics.

"My own followers? Really, Logan. You've lost your touch. I'm bored of you already. Good riddance." He motioned, clearly expecting guards or something to happen. When nothing did, he screamed it louder. "Guards! Take him!"

"It's time I tell you a story, Alek."

He snapped his fingers, and the pictures on the screen changed from boardrooms of other Council chapters to news stations, heads of states, and it even looked like the Olympic committee if the rings in the background were anything to go by.

"You see, this whole time, thanks to my trusted associate," he said, nodding, and I spotted Samuel, who I hadn't noticed until then, tip his hat from the corner. "He's had a dummy feed up for you. You thought you were broadcasting this disaster to all the chapters tonight to prove your power, your *authority*. In actuality," he nodded again, and this time it switched to the same rooms as before, but they were being invaded by SWAT and secret agents from across the globe as they broke down doors and arrested people.

For the first time, I saw some of Alek's bravado falter as he watched his followers be rounded up. The screens flicked back, and Logan continued. "Your people were being arrested while you boasted to all the people in this room. To top it off, you sealed your own fate. Your egotism and arrogance at being the head of an empire, the man in the *watchtower*, left you open for attack. I used your own words against you. Each major news station, every head of state, and law enforcement agency has witnessed your lunacy tonight. You've lost it, cousin. *It's over.*"

"No!" he screamed, and faster than any of us thought possible, he grabbed Samson, who'd been sneaking around him. Holding a gun to his head, I watched fear enter Samson's eyes.

"Sariah, you can fix this. Tell them, tell them, or *Daddy* here gets it!"

Shaking my head, I didn't know what he wanted. What could I say that would absolve him of all the things he'd done? Tears flooded down my cheeks, mixing with the blood from Richard. I couldn't even see in front of me as I pleaded for Samson's life.

"No! Please, not him. I don't know what you want. I can't do anything."

"Yes, you can! You stupid girl. You have all these men fighting over you, and you don't even know the power you have."

"Orson, tell her, tell her how you drugged Isla and had

some escort you paid to seduce Samson here and then drugged him," he begged his new target. Alek waved the gun back and forth with each word, trying to get us to say what he thought we knew to save him.

"Just let him go, please!" I tried again.

"It's okay, tiny dancer. *I love you.*"

With Samson's words, my world stopped as the sound of the gunshot rang out. Dropping to my knees, everything in me gave out as the pain sliced through me. The room spun around when I felt arms wrap around me and pick me up, carrying me from the chamber of death.

"Sawyer, *tiny dancer*, ssh. It's okay. I'm okay."

Samson's voice pierced through the fog, and I opened my eyes and blinked to make sure I saw him correctly. *"Dad?"* I whispered.

"Yeah, tiny dancer. I guess so." He chuckled, his smile watery. "You'll have to explain that to me later, but it's over, Sawyer. It's over."

I hugged him tightly, wrapping my arms around his neck. We both cried, feeling the relief of that statement. When I felt arms grabbing me, at first, I thought someone had come to take me away from Samson. Their voices filled the space around me, and I gave in to the pull of my guys hauling me into their arms.

Mumbled words of love and thanks were shared as we took comfort in making it out of there. A phone was shoved in front of my face, and I saw Mateo. His relief was palpable as he took me in. Fin and Asa were also there, and while I couldn't make out all the words, I got the gist of what they were saying. They'd seen it all on camera, Logan Hawthorn having had Samuel link them in when everything was in place.

There was some yelling from Fin and some shocked looks from Asa as he realized Samson was our father, but all in all, everyone was relieved we'd made it out alive.

After all, we were BOSH, and we were together and alive —everything else was gravy.

# forty-eight

. . .

## sawyer

WAKING UP THE FOLLOWING DAY, a whirlwind of activity surrounded me from the moment my eyelids cracked open. Unfortunately, Henry and I had to withdraw from the competition thanks to the beating Queen Bitch gave me. I was in no shape to skate, physically or emotionally. The drugs were still making me drowsy, and the aftermath of everything had weighed heavily on me—the secrets, the lies, and the heartbreaking reality of so many unnecessary deaths.

Since the committee had been privy to the takedown, they allowed us a special 'extenuating circumstances' waiver. We had the option of using those scores at our next competition for the first portion, or they would allow us to skate the second half for a panel of judges in a month. We wouldn't medal from the event, but we'd get to carry our full scores with us.

In the end, we decided on the second option, wanting our points at the competition to mean something for the events that had occurred. So on a snowy Saturday in December, Henry and I skated our free skate and received a record-breaking score of 112.66. We were in a good position now to be eligible for the Olympic team. Things were coming together, despite being chaotic on a whole new level the following months. As the world agencies worked to unravel the years of corruption and deceit the Council had weaved throughout the world, we focused on healing our family.

Jill withdrew from school, and her parents were getting her help with a trauma therapist back in her home state of Illinois. We texted weekly, and she kept me updated on her progress. I was rooting for her. She admitted to having an affair with Donnelly, and the guilt and shame she had would take time to process. He'd groomed her, and she was starting to understand that. She was strong, and I knew I'd see her back on that ice someday. I would be there cheering her on when she did.

TAS itself was under different leadership after the scandal broke and was being rebranded. It turned out that Sasha—Mrs. Aldridge—had been connected to the Council and led the mini-board within the school. Dimitry turned out to be a decent guy in the end and divorced her the next day. Apparently, he'd been suspicious of her and Adelaide for some time, especially after Elias had disclosed Queen Bitch's actions during their engagement, and he'd started his own investigation into things.

With his findings and the video from the meeting, Adelaide's medals and titles were stripped from her. Dimitry was attempting to redeem the school and bring it back to what it was always meant to be, and so had decided to name it The Lux Brumalis Institute, Lux for short. It was a Latin word that meant "the light of winter." Mr. Aldridge wanted to bring light back into the sports we all loved and hoped this was the start. He even honored Victoria by naming the ice rink after her. Now, every time I trained, I felt like she was watching down on me.

"Smalls?" Henry walked into my room, a soft smile for me. I was curled up with a sleeping Mateo as I journaled. After waking from nightmares multiple times, the guys had convinced me to go back to therapy. It had been a good idea, all the events stirring up old wounds of trauma. I felt like I had a chance at healing now.

"Yes, Henry?"

"I was wondering," he said, grinning, "if you'd want to go skating?"

Furrowing my brow, I looked at him oddly. "Um, Henry, we skated this morning."

"Yes, but this would be pond skating."

Glee filled me as I nodded enthusiastically. My shaking woke my koala, his arms wrapped around me. The one nice thing about being kidnapped, the constant cuddle huddles now. It was a regular koala love-fest in my room twenty-four-seven now. Dislodging his tight grip, I kissed his forehead as he smiled at me.

"Wanna go pond skating?"

Mateo nodded, and we ended up spending the afternoon skating out in the open with the mountains around us. It was one of the most peaceful and enjoyable skates I'd ever had. Mateo was like a baby deer as he tried to figure out how to keep his feet from flying out from under him.

"I don't understand why this is so hard. I can ski. Surely, the same principles would apply!"

Watching his frustration, I laughed, enjoying the light moments with my guys, appreciating them for what they were. Getting justice against Adelaide had taken time. Despite being charged with kidnapping, drugging me, and attempted murder, she managed a plea bargain where she didn't serve any time. Those nights were hard as I screamed at the injustice of it all.

I wanted to let it go, move on with my life, but every time I thought of her punching me, rage would fill me. Rhett had replaced my clasp on my necklace, at least making that wrong right. Elias had worked with the DA to provide evidence of her crimes. When he'd initially asked me, I thought her being brought down a peg and losing everything that mattered would be enough, but it wasn't. She'd almost killed me, and it was a pain I struggled with.

I'd heard she'd been unable to find work, having never worked a day in her life and being quite inept with basic life skills. She was penniless and homeless and resorted to selling her body to make ends meet. Her father had disowned her, unable to deal with the horrendous acts she committed. When Elias received the news she'd been beaten and left for dead by one of her Johns, I wanted to feel bad for her, but I couldn't muster the energy to care.

That might make me a horrible person, but I didn't feel anything for her, not even pity. She hadn't wanted to change and blamed everyone else for her behaviors. I think that was what frustrated me the most—her inability to own her actions. At least now, she was out of my life and it was better off without her. I'd slept without nightmares that night.

Standing back, I watched Henry teach Mateo how to stay standing on his skates. Samuel and Ace were skating as well, and it'd been fun getting to know Mateo through Sam's eyes.

"Whatcha doing, Wildcat?"

Leaning back into Ty's arms, I tilted my head up. "Just enjoying being out here. It's beautiful. I feel so free here."

"Mmm. I like the sound of that."

"Yeah." I smiled at him. "Me too."

Ty kissed my nose, a blush tinting my cheeks at the cuteness. He pulled me into his arms, doing a spin with me. This was a familiar skate dance we did years ago. Skating, I kept finding pieces of me I thought had been lost. Maybe it was reclaiming things, or as the months passed, we continued to gain more and more closure.

Donald Donnelly's capture and subsequent arrest were a big part of that. Thankfully, there was no way he could escape his charges, and he was currently serving multiple life sentences along with a few other Council members.

During the scuffle with Alek and me, Rhett had knocked

out his dad with one punch. Oliver had become famous for the retelling of it, and Rhett didn't seem to mind. Every time I heard Ollie start with, "and then Rhett walked up casually, pulled his fist back, and bam!" smacking his fist into his hand. "His father didn't even have a chance to blink. It was that fast! The sound he made hitting the floor was epic!" I would catch a hint of a smile from Rhett.

With his grandmother's letters and his testimony, his father was charged with the murder of Granny Rothchild. I think that was the best feeling for Rhett, that he had gotten justice for her. He was still going through her will and what that meant for his life. We all planned to take a trip to the house after school ended to see its condition. Personally, I was looking forward to going to warm California and the beach regardless of what the place looked like.

Soren's mother had managed to escape the round-up the first night, having slipped out of the meeting when things started to go south. Pamela always seemed to find a way to survive until it finally caught up with her. I never told Sor she had a part to play in my kidnapping, not wanting to put that guilt on him. A few months after the takedown, he'd gotten a phone call that she'd been found dead—overdose.

Henry and I went to the funeral with him, feeling it was important to say goodbye. Soren didn't cry once, saying he'd made peace with what she'd done years ago and was only attending out of goodwill. I didn't mention I heard him crying at night sometimes; instead, I would hug him tighter the following day and love him harder. We all had our burdens to carry, but it didn't have to be alone.

When Soren had to face his abuser, Morano, on the stand, he'd been strong. Having closure from his abuse healed something in him. I'd always thought he was my sunshine, never realizing the shadows he still carried. Once he shed the weight of his past and mother, he was luminescent. Soren sparkled so much now, I joked about him becoming a vampire. He laughed it off, but he never did deny it.

Oliver's family had tried to mend bridges with him after everything settled. He tried, he really did, but after one dinner with them, it was apparent they didn't care about him and only wanted to use him to improve their status and gain favor. Suddenly, it was okay to have a son who was a famous hockey star, despite never supporting him throughout his whole career. On top of their reaction, when they discovered he was bisexual, they sealed their fate, and Ollie washed his hands of them. Ollie was happy to have it off his conscience so he could move on with his life.

I watched him hit a puck into the net against Rhett, and I knew he'd finally accepted every part of himself. The freedom reflected in his eyes was sexy. Throwing his arms up in a cheer, I laughed at the joy he routinely expressed. Ollie was our loveable goofball, fuckboy no more.

Elias had the hardest battle. In the end, his father had saved me and done his best to make things right. Elias cried in my arms one night after I revealed what Richard's dying words had been. He struggled to align the different versions of his father together. The father who'd been fair but distant. The Council member who'd committed atrocious things. The hero who'd sacrificed himself.

Elias guilted himself, believing if he hadn't pulled away but maybe tried harder, they would've had a better relationship. It took him a while to let go of his guilt. He finally realized it wasn't all on him and not something he could carry around forever. I think it gave him comfort, at least, to know the man his father was when it had counted, just like his dad wanted. I was just sad they missed out on that when he was alive.

When things had settled, Isla had finally revealed to me what the watch and words represented. She explained how she'd sought the refuge of an organization that turned out to be known as the Order. *Imperium in Imperio*—the order within an order. The group within the Agency that Ashlee had spoken of the night Fin was taken.

The words I'd said, *inter spem et metum*, meant 'between hope and fear' in Latin. It was the calling card of the Order, and when uttered, you had to answer. Fear was the warning, and hope was the way out, for in the place between hope and fear, progress and change could be made if you were willing. I liked that idea because I often got lost in the fear, and now hope would be my compass.

Elias had inquired about his father's involvement in the Order, and it turned out he'd initially been sent as an agent of change. They'd heard rumblings of a chapter making claims and grandiose visions, and Richard was to help direct it in a different direction. Unfortunately, Alek had gotten his claws into him and brainwashed him into choosing power and greed.

Elias held on to the hope that his father's continuation to

wear the watch all those years awarded him some goodwill. It didn't absolve Richard from the awful things he'd done or allowed to be committed, but it showed there was still hope for him. Had he lived, I liked to think he would've been able to redeem himself.

The Council had started as a way of change in the world but had been corrupted over time. Their original acronym stood for 'Change ourselves until no change is left.' It saddened me that what had started as a network of progress had been corrupted into an ugly state of affairs. But I guess that was all of history. Until someone stood up against it, corruption got away with endless atrocities.

I hated that my family had been the ones to pay the price.

Rey's mother, Sofia, brokered a deal for a short prison stay and community service in exchange for testifying against the Council. Her statements were some of the leading points in putting away the remaining members, like Latimer, Bellamy, and Abernathy. Fitzroy died that day, and Draven had been the one to pull the trigger in the end, killing Hawthorne when the shot had gone off, getting his vengeance.

Nicholas Draven was an unexpected surprise. I struggled with my emotions surrounding him. When he reached out and asked to see me, I almost didn't go. It was Elias who convinced me to hear him out, saying he wished he'd tried more with his father. So, I did. It took a while, but we came to a level of understanding and worked on building a relationship. I learned he loved Victoria very much and only joined the Council as a way to protect her. He'd been the oldest member; his daughter having gone to school with most of the chapter leaders.

He wasn't a good man, though, and didn't try to hide his misdeeds, somewhat gaining my respect. Nicholas had spent several years in Brazil developing weapons and technology for the highest bidder, regardless of their intended use. It was easy for him to switch to manufacturing it for the Council. He'd known all along Alek was dangerous.

The disappearance of time in Victoria's journal was after Alek had attempted to kidnap her. She'd gone on the run, her father having helped her hide until they created a plan. When she returned, he'd reached out to Alek about joining. Draven was able to keep her away from him then and even sent her to work undercover at Latimer's, believing they were working on a scheme to overtake the others' business.

When she'd disappeared again, he'd feared Alek had finally been successful. Until one day, he received a photo with no return address. It had a picture of me as a baby being held by Victoria. He knew then she was safe and happy. Nicholas told me he worked as hard as possible to ensure we were hidden after that, including keeping the Reyes on the payroll for protecting Victoria.

He'd been working to keep us off Latimer and Alek's radar. When Leon blackmailed the Reyes' on Alek's authority, Nicholas had been away on business and missed it. The regret in his eyes was heavy, and I had the suspicion he blamed himself for Victoria's death. If he hadn't left town, maybe he would've seen the double cross in enough time to stop it. It was the turning point for Nicholas, though, and he'd worked to make amends ever since. Starting with assisting the FBI in gathering evidence against Alek. He'd been the one to reach out to Logan five years ago after her supposed death.

It had been the catalyst for his change. To learn she'd been alive almost this whole time as a slave to Alex had been too much for him to let go. He didn't regret killing Alek. It wasn't the first blood on his hands, and he was willing to pay the price for that action. He told me he felt safer knowing I lived in a world where Alek Hawthorne no longer was. I agreed with him, even if I kept it to myself. Jill's photo and state I'd found her in still haunted me.

Draven was charged with murder, and he hadn't taken the plea deal offered to him. He wanted to do what was right for me, to show me he was a worthy man. So through a jail visitation room once a month, I was getting to know my adoptive grandfather. It was a bit surreal, but for a woman who'd loved me enough to endure so much pain, I could get to know her father.

"Come on, love. We're dividing up into teams. I have a sneaky suspicion I'll want you on mine." Elias pulled my hand, directing me over to the center. It was five on five, and we broke apart to play pond hockey. Slapping the puck out from Rhett, I stuck out my tongue as I did a low spin and sped off toward the goal, laughing the whole way at his dumbstruck look. Henry cheered from the goal, not caring we were on opposite teams.

Henry and Fin were healing. They'd started family therapy with their parents, needing to work on all the lies and deceit over the years. Sofia acknowledged to me the part she'd played and how her actions had led to the death of my father and the kidnapping of my mother. I didn't blame her, and part of me had forgiven her, but it was hard to be around her. Henry understood and didn't pressure me, struggling himself.

Shockingly, Mateo's family was completely clear of any Council or Agency involvement. His only connection had been through Samuel. After the televised scandal, his mom had called and demanded he leave this 'sin hole' at once. Watching him stand up to his mom had been hot. Well, I assumed he had because it was in Spanish so I had no clue. But listening to the tone of his voice and his level of authoritativeness, well, let's just say I showed him exactly how he made me feel after it. Now, when he used that voice on me and called me *"Dulzura,"* it immediately got my motor running.

Samuel scored a goal, and we all cheered as he skated around, throwing his arms in the air. He continued working for Logan, despite the Council and Agency being dissolved. It was fun adding people to our group and watching Mateo reconnect with his friend. I was happy he'd been able to reclaim that part of his history.

The biggest scandal was undoubtedly the reveal of both organizations to the public. Samson's Hail Mary turned out to be the same as Elias'—Logan. When he reached out to his old friend, they used their contacts to set up the coinciding takedowns of the chapters and publicize it. It'd been hard for Samson to out the secret organization at first, having spent most of his life serving it. Logan convinced him by reminding Samson of the reason he'd joined in the first place—stop the Council and protect those he loved. Once he reconciled that, Samson brought charges against so many operatives it'd been shut down in a day as they sorted through the mess.

Samson had decided to create his own security firm—Alpha Security Solutions—once everything had settled with the investigations. He now worked with the people he trusted, like Tyler's father and even Logan through his foundation, H.M.E. Samuel and Ashlee Berkshire were also assisting in setting it up, as well as Cohen. Henry's dad was even working on new technology for them. All in all, it was a lower-risk job with a stable home base and fit his needs better.

Cheering sounded behind me, and I was scooped up into a set of arms as they skated around the pond. Chuckling, I hung onto Ollie as he did his victory lap.

"You're the best thing that ever happened to me, pretty girl." He sat me down, kissed me quickly, and then joined back into the play. Shaking my head, I decided to take a breather, the many layers I wore making me overheated.

Sitting down, I unwrapped my scarf and discarded my mittens and hat. "Mind if I join you, Sis?"

"Nope."

Asa sat, and I leaned into him, his smell familiar to me now. We'd continued our sibling nights, and I looked forward to them every week. We were as close as most siblings now, and it was a bond I never knew how much I'd missed out on.

The talk with Samson about what Alek had divulged had

been painful to share. Samson's realization of how his brother not only drugged and violated him but stole his semen had changed something in him. Especially when he thought of all the years, his brother had stolen from him with his family. Samson had advocated vehemently for Orson to receive the maximum penalty, and we were all right there with him. Orson didn't deserve ever to be free.

Through it all, he'd been happy to know the truth finally. He and Isla had rekindled their love and started to build a life together. Asa struggled differently with the news than me. He had to reconcile the father he'd known wasn't his father and that he could have a relationship with Samson. It was awkward for them both, and I grieved for the years we all missed out on at the hands of that madman.

Fin continued to say everything was fine, but I saw the cracks. She continued to pull away. Despite her promise to Rhett, she gave us excuses that she could handle it. She dismissed it and said in the grand scheme of things, her issue wasn't significant. Rhett hadn't broken her confidence, as much as I wished he would. It was frustrating, as her friend, to watch her suffer and not be able to do anything about it when I could see her pain. I had to keep reminding myself I couldn't do it for her. I could only be there when she was ready. It was only a matter of time before she splintered, and I would be there to help pick up the pieces.

"Mom sold the house in Seattle. She'll officially be a resident of Utah next week."

"That's great. I can't wait to see her more."

"Me too, Sis, me too."

Smiling up at him, I never got tired of him calling me that. A loud crash had us both looking at the ice. Ace had collided with Rhett and had fallen flat on his back. The guys gave him a hard time while Rhett held out his hand, not caring in the slightest. The guys had embraced Ace, forgiving him for any deceit, and acknowledged his role in our successful escape.

He and Chloe continued to be my coffee crew, and we now had weekly sessions with Rowan and Fin when she felt like it. It was good to have time outside of the guys, especially when I spent the time laughing.

The coffee guy had been questioned by Samson and found to be innocent in the end. He thought he was helping a father and daughter connect and hadn't intended anything harmful. It was still weird when we saw him at the coffee shop, so we all tried to go when we knew he wouldn't be there.

"Charlie getting nervous?"

"No." I smiled fondly. "He's as steady as always. Speaking of, we should head back. Tomorrow is going to be a busy day."

Standing, I let out a whistle, grabbing all the guys' attention. "Let's roll out! We've got a wedding in the morning, and I need my beauty sleep."

The guys laughed but gathered all their gear, piled back into the cars, and headed for the Monroe Mansion. Utah continued to amaze me with how it could be cold enough in the mountains for frozen ponds and warm enough in the center of town for flowers to bloom. Aggie's garden was in full spring bloom and the site of the nuptials the next day. It was going to be beautiful, and I couldn't be happier.

For Charlie and Aggie, of course.

Despite Charlie giving his blessing to Soren back in October, none of us were ready for that life change. We loved one another and were happy with how things were. That was enough for now.

Charlie had officially sold the rink and moved here before Christmas. Their romance was one for the storybooks. Tomorrow, they would become husband and wife, and I was standing up with Charlie. I'd never seen him smile so much and had a feeling I'd need to change his name from Grump soon.

They were to have a small ceremony in Aggie's backyard, and Alfred, the butler, was officiating. Once I got over my fear of him, I thanked him for his efforts in saving my life. He wasn't as scary anymore, and I'd catch a rare smile now and then. I guess I'd just add him to my collection of grumps and wear him down.

The school year ended in a few weeks, and we were on the precipice of deciding what our future would look like. None of us knew if we wanted to stay another year in Oak Crest and help Lux get back on track, or if it would be better to cut our losses and move on. We had plans we wanted to explore outside of this place, which was both exciting and daunting.

Ollie had given in to his desire to attend culinary school and had started some classes on the weekend, loving every minute of it. I wasn't complaining about the delicious food he brought home either.

Rhett had submitted his graphic novel he'd been working

on for years when I'd found it one afternoon. It was a big step for him out of his comfort zone. Granny Rothy had inspired him to push forward with his dreams, providing him with the money to do whatever he wanted.

Soren and Mateo were both still happy with training students, having loved their sports but not sure they wanted to compete again. Lux offered them both the opportunity to do something they loved without pressure.

Henry had shared more of his music, and with Soren and my encouragement, was submitting them to record labels. He was focused on our Olympic dreams first, but it never hurt to explore.

Tyler, in essence, had the toughest decision. His father had extended him a position in Samson's company working security. I think a part of him enjoyed it, but he was scared of what it would mean to step out of what he knew with hockey. Right now, he was happiest where he was, and that was what mattered.

Elias had started fighting in amateur matches and had one coming up in Chicago at a new fighting arena, Upswing. We were excited about attending with him and advancing his career. I was hoping to visit with Jill while I was there too.

Despite the horrors we'd faced down, this place had a lot of good memories and that was what we chose to focus on.

The evening had passed in a blur of food, stories, and laughter. Aggie had invited us all to stay for the weekend in the mansion, and it was an invitation I wouldn't refuse. This home was special to both of my moms and now me. Every time I was here, I felt connected to a part of Victoria I hadn't known. I liked discovering new things through Aggie, Isla, and even Nicholas. It kept her memory alive.

Samson had gone with me to the graves he had made for them. It had been hard, but it did give me closure. I thanked my dad for loving me and protecting me with his life and promised to make him proud. Samson held me for a long time, both of us tearful, as we watched the sunset behind their graves.

Zipping up the side, I turned and twisted as I watched the material swish around me. The dress was a light pink and resembled the one from *The Sound of Music*, in the infamous gazebo scene. Performing that scene later with one of the guys was so on my bucket list. Ollie would join me; of that, I was confident.

"Smalls, hurry up! You're going to miss it all!"

"I'm coming. I'm coming." I smiled as I opened the door and took in my seven dates. They were all dressed similarly in gray suits, and the devilish looks they leveled at me made it slick between my legs before I knew what was happening. Biting my lip, I debated what to do.

"None of that, Wildcat. We have a man to marry!"

Ty grabbed my hand and dragged me out to the garden, where everyone else waited. Lucky was even here with his little tie and pillow to carry the rings on. It was a perfect day, and as my family gathered around to celebrate, I had an odd realization.

Despite everything the Council had taken from us, we'd found a way to survive and thrive in a world set out to use us. Their attempts at world domination had led me to find happiness and love. When I thought about how different things this May were than the last, well, it wasn't even comparable.

I once was a girl with multiple names but no identity or family.

These days, I was a woman loved beyond measure with more family than I could've ever dreamed of having. My future was on the rise, and I knew now clearly who I was.

I was *Sawyer fucking Sullivan*, and this was my story to tell. Life wasn't perfect, but it was my perfect, and that was all that mattered.

# epilogue

. . .

## sawyer

THE SOUNDS of the ocean crashing against the shore had become the background noise of my life for the past week. The soothing surge of the waves as they swelled and receded made me feel like the earth was breathing. It was relaxing here, at Granny Rothy's house, and I daydreamed what it would be like to live here. To wake up every day to the sound of seagulls, the feel of sand between my toes, and some of the most beautiful sunsets over the water I'd ever seen.

We'd finished dinner earlier, and now I rested against the porch railing as I looked out at the sea, a light breeze tossing my hair and dress to and fro. The guys were laughing in the background as they played cards, their friendly camaraderie the soundtrack of my heart. Life seemed simpler here, and maybe it was a lie, but it was definitely the appeal. After the past year, I'd embrace simplicity any day. Arms wrapping around my waist were the first indication I'd been spotted, the nose trailing up my neck the second.

"Dulzura, I missed you."

*If happiness had a sound, it would be this moment as contentment filled me.*

Leaning back against Mateo's chest, an instant smile graced my face. His steadiness and confidence were a constant, his sweetness underlying it all. Tilting my head a little, I could see him in the waning light as he watched the ocean with me.

"So I've been thinking," he started.

"Mmhm."

"And I think there's something new I'd like to try."

"Mmhm," I murmured, smiling inwardly.

I loved his sexual confidence and all the things he'd wanted to explore with me. Each one felt like I got to experience it again for the first time because I was doing it with him. He pulled my hips closer, his hard cock now wedged between the crack of my ass.

"First, I want to kiss all over your body in the moonlight. Then I want to see if we can make all the others jealous by the sounds we produce, and um…"

He trailed off, and I knew his request would be fun if he'd gotten shy about it now. Seeming to not find the words, his hands drifted down my thigh and snuck under my dress. His hand caressed my inner leg, and I had to focus on the horizon to not shift my legs. With Mateo, sometimes I led and showed him, and other times I needed to give him the chance to find his way. I had a suspicion this was one of the times I needed to let him discover.

In a barely-there touch, his fingertip grazed me and stopped when he didn't feel any material. A mischievous smirk lifted my lips as I imagined the thoughts racing through his mind. I'd decided since it was our last night before other guests arrived, I wanted to see if I could entice my boyfriends into, well, basically, an orgy.

Yep, I said it. I wanted a fucking orgy. After all the books Soren and I read this past year, it was the one thing we hadn't done as BOSH.

Everyone was comfortable now in our relationship, no longer caring who was in the room or walked by mid orgasm. We barely even locked doors unless someone needed alone time. Mateo's request seemed to match perfectly with my goal, and I began to formulate a plan.

"Dulzura," he purred, his voice now husky with sexual need, "why aren't you wearing any panties?"

Turning in his arms, I brought my face closer to his to answer. "What's the fun in wearing them when you have seven boyfriends? I figured I'd be helping you all out."

"You think you're cute when you're cheeky, don't you?"

"Oh sweetie, I'm always cute."

"That you are," he bent down and nipped my neck, sucking on my favorite spot. I held in the moan, not wanting to alert the guys too soon. I wanted to give Mateo his fantasy first, and then I could get mine.

"I think I know the perfect spot for your request."

Taking his hand, I casually walked with him down the

little beach hill to the lounge bed below. Granny Rothy had lived in a freaking mansion on the coast. She even had her own private beach, and the next house was a mile away. It was still the beach, so we could be caught, but the lounge was tucked in a secluded area by the hot tub on the lower deck.

Yeah, this house was on steroids. It hosted twelve bedrooms, fifteen toilets, two kitchens, a pool, hot tub, fitness room, movie room, library, and even a conservatory where greenhouse plants grew. It had been kept in working order by a trust and household staff over the years. Rhett had given them the week off when we got here, which had been good for the sexcapades. No school, no work, and no training for the week outside of working out had given us a lot of time to christen the home. I doubt Granny Rothy had that in mind when she left it to him, or maybe she did. She sounded like a sassy broad who didn't take shit.

Dropping Mateo's hand, I pushed one strap off my shoulder and then the next one as I walked back to the bed. Pushing it over my breasts, I let the dress drop to the deck before I sat down, the stars starting to twinkle now the sun had set. Mateo watched me as I relaxed back, completely naked, a hunger brewing in his eyes.

"What are you waiting for? Come explore."

He instantly jumped, his clothes discarded as he made it to me. Placing one knee down next to me, he'd never looked more like a predator than he did now.

"Dulzura, you've been naughty. Are you ready to be a little more?"

I nodded, because who needed words when there was a

sexy nerd above them?. Without hesitation, he dived down to my mouth and captured my lips in a fierce kiss, leaving me breathless as he pulled away. I was about to complain and drag him back when his mouth found my nipple instead. Sucking it into his mouth, he expertly distracted me as he pushed me back onto the bed. Working my body over, I let him get his wish of kissing me in the moonlight as I writhed in pleasure. When he got to my core, he peeked up, his glasses a little askew from his ministrations.

"There was one thing I wanted to try. It's just hard for me to say."

"Sweetie, nothing you could say would make me embarrassed or think differently about you. I promise."

"Okay, I was wondering if we could try mutual oral sex stimulation simultaneously."

My brain faltered, his words confusing me for a minute as I tried to work out what he meant. "Are you asking if we can sixty-nine?"

His cheeks tinted, but he nodded his head, his gaze steady as he waited. Grinning wide, I bounced up and wrapped my arms around his neck. "Oh, yes! I'd love to."

Mateo's embarrassment faded, and the hunger took over as he kissed me again. Pushing him down, I moved, so I was now facing his cock as it strained upward. I watched as he took his glasses off, setting them to the side before I straddled his head. Gently, I lowered myself, afraid to suffocate him until he had his bearings.

"Dulzura, you're going to have to get lower than that.

You're not going to hurt me. In fact, I want nothing but your smell and taste around me."

He purred the last bit, and it took all my willpower not to slam my hussy vagina down onto his face. Dropping myself lower, I focused on the delicious dessert in front of me as I sank down. His tongue tentatively reached out, and I instinctively rolled my hips, seeking more. Giving in, I descended the rest of the way as I began to lick his cock.

My tongue devoured him as I swirled it around his thick shaft, his taste invading my mouth. Sucking him down, we both started to get into the rhythm as we 'mutually orally stimulated' one another. At one point, I found myself humming my moan more than I was sucking, so I focused back on making him cum first.

Grabbing his balls in my hand, I fondled them as I fisted the base with the other. My arms were braced on his thighs as I rolled my hips on his face. His hands had grasped my ass, using it to move me as he willed. Somehow, I managed to win the race, and I felt his hot cum hit the back of my throat a moment later. Licking my lips, I felt smug as I always did after a successful blow job.

Mateo wrapped his arms around my waist and lifted me, so I was now actively sitting on his face. The direct contact gave him more room to work with, and my moans could now be heard as I rode him. Grabbing my breasts, I fell into the sensations as he ate me out like a champ. Within seconds, I was coming around him, my thighs unintentionally squeezing his face as I did.

When I came back to reality, I opened my eyes and found

six pairs staring back with hunger, and a victorious smile spread across my face. Group orgy, here I come.

Moving off Mateo, he sat up and took in the sight too. Giving my best come hither stare, I leaned back as I quirked a finger. For a second, no one moved, and I started to think I'd been wrong, but in a flash, they all moved at once and started undressing. Mateo stayed where he was, a languid smile on his face. Peeking at him, he gave me a look, and I couldn't help but laugh.

"I think I was bamboozled into making a fantasy of yours come to life, Dulzura," he flirted, "and I'm honored to have been chosen as tribute."

Chuckling more, I tackled him back to the bed and kissed his face all over between my laughs. My mistake was taking my eyes off the advancing hungry mob as they finished undressing and descended on the bed. My hips were grabbed, and I was pulled flush against a hard chest as tattooed arms wrapped around me.

"Love, you've been naughty, and I think it's time you—"

Something wet hit me as the sounds of snores woke me. The realization that I'd fallen asleep came crashing into me. Mateo was next to me, his arm wrapped around me tightly as I tried to orientate myself. We were still naked and on the lounge bed, my memory and dream overlapping, so I couldn't determine what was real.

Based on my position and nakedness, I could assume the sexy times with Mateo had been real, but the group part had been a dream. *Damn.* I was really looking forward to having an all-you-can-dick buffet. Something wet hit my arm this time, and I remembered what had woken me in the first place and stopped my dream orgy too.

Glancing down, I found a white patch on my arm. Scrunching my nose, I looked up to see what it was when it happened again. Only this time, it landed right on my forehead. Screeching, I jumped up as I tried to run from the devil bird that was shitting all over me. As I ran frantically about, my arms waving over my head, I'd forgotten two critical things.

1) I was buck naked

2) My family was due to arrive today.

So as I ran around in the sand like a lunatic, I rounded the bend and ran smack dab into the middle of Aggie, Charlie, Fin, Asa, Samson, Isla, Rhonda, and Rowan. I stopped, frozen in my tracks as I tried to process what was going on. The men all cursed and covered their eyes as the women laughed at my plight. And that was the moment I remembered my nudity.

Fucking hell.

Well, what can you do when you're naked and covered in bird poo poo, having committed the most grievous code orange of your life?

You remember who you are, and you own that shit. Literally.


The End.
Turn the page for a sneak peak at Finley's book, along with a bonus scene

# bonus scene

. . .

## soren

"LOVE, you've been naughty, and I think it's time you pay up."

"Oh? What do I need to pay?"

Sawyer panted, her body trembling with need as Elias dominated her. It was a side of him I hadn't witnessed before. The rest of us stood back, almost like we were waiting to be directed, or perhaps just transfixed by the erotic nature of Elias clasping Sawyer's neck. It was hot on a whole new level. I wouldn't admit it out loud, but even I was turned on by Elias at that moment.

Rey brushed against my arm, the movement had goose-bumps erupting all over my body, my nerves already on standby for what was to come. When we'd heard her moans, it was like a siren's call drawing us near, and as the group we were, the six of us stood and followed. There hadn't been hesitation on anyone's part, and it reminded me how far we'd come since the discussion around the table ten months ago. The amount of time didn't match the life we'd lived or the emotions we felt, but at the same time, almost a year with these people had me excited for what else was to come.

And right now, I hoped it would be me.

Grabbing Rey's hand, I pulled us to the bed, unable to stand by and watch any longer. I was a doer, and I wanted to *do*. My movement had Ollie and Ty surging forward as well, but Rhett stayed back, happy to only watch for now. Mateo smirked at me, the expression fitting him more and more as he'd grown into his confidence. I winked, throwing him off and he blushed, and I couldn't help the smile covering my face.

When he realized I was messing with him, he smiled back. Mateo, Rey, and I had grown closer as friends, and I appreciated the quiet solitude he brought to my life. I never would've thought he and I would be so similar in ways, but we were, and the bond we shared had become special to me. Sawyer's eyes opened at our movement, her desire thick as Elias trailed kisses down her throat. His hands grasped her breasts, and I lounged back as I took in the show.

It was difficult to know which direction to look as Rey started to stroke himself. Giving in to what my body wanted, I pulled his face to mine and sealed our lips in a fiery kiss. He met me with exuberant passion, and I found myself falling back onto the bed. I lost sight of everyone else as we kissed one another.

# ollie

Pinching myself, I blinked when it hurt, not expecting this to be real. Ty's deep chuckle next to me had me looking up into his hooded eyes.

"Oh, *this is very real*, Ols."

He licked his lips, my whole body shuddered in desire at the motion. Sawyer's moans drew my attention, and I turned back to our girl splayed out as Elias consumed her pussy. Ty nibbled on my neck, his dick pressed against me, urging me forward, directing me to join the fun. Crawling onto the bed, I kissed Sawyer, needing to feel her. Some days I was still amazed that this beautiful girl loved me as much as I loved her.

Her eyes opened, a smile gracing her lips when she saw it was me. It was the greatest confidence booster. Sawyer reached her hands up and clasped my face, pushing my hair back.

"I thought only guys did that?" I grinned.

Laughing, she kissed me, not responding other than to tell me how she felt with her mouth. Ty closed in behind me as he started to pepper kisses down my spine. Moans could be heard all around us, the ocean a backdrop to our fun. It was so peaceful here, a perfect hideaway from the world.

When Ty's hand smoothed over my ass, I found myself shuddering again. His hand traveled around the front, finding my cock dripping and ready for him. Squeezing, he started to pump me, and I couldn't hold my moan back any longer.

*"Fuck, Ty."*

Moving my hands down Sawyer's body, I tweaked her nipples and rolled them over on my thumb. The peaks stood up at attention, and I leaned forward to lick them. Mateo had made his way to the other side, and I relinquished a nip for him to partake in. Her breast in hand, Mateo kissed her as he fondled her mound. He dropped down to lick her chest, and I watched as Rhett moved into position. I stopped, frozen for a second, when I caught sight of his monster cock. Blinking, my face must've looked comical because I heard Sawyer giggle at my reaction. Ty moved up closer, grasping my dick firmly, and whispered in my ear.

"I know. *Fucking huge.*"

For some reason, I found Ty talking about Rhett's third leg hot. As he whispered the words, he bit into my shoulder, and I found myself erupting. I wanted to feel embarrassed about it, but when Ty leaned over me and started to lick up my cum, I found myself growing hard again. Once he was done, he peeked up, a look of pure satisfaction on his face, and I tackled him to the bed.

When Ty had topped me the first time in the kitchen, it had stunned me how hot I'd found it, but it didn't mean I couldn't dominate him as well from time to time. Pushing him back, I grazed my hands down his abs and sucked his cock deep into my throat in one movement. His dick jumped in my mouth, shocked at the sudden feeling, and I vowed to make him cum as quick as I had.

I never thought giving pleasure could be as fulfilling as

receiving, but as I watched Ty throw his head back in ecstasy, I found myself hard as steel again.

## mateo

After almost a year together, I'd found myself comfortable being intimate within a group. At first, I'd worried I'd be left out, not being part of a pair or even having the dynamic Elias and Rhett had, but it hadn't been the case. Typically, I found myself with Rey and Soren, but there were times when it was me and Ty, or me and Rhett. Kissing Sawyer's body, I traveled down her, wanting to cover her with my kisses.

Elias pulled back and urged me to take over. He laid back now, watching the rest of us as we all fell into a sexual frenzy. Lifting Sawyer's legs, I brushed my cock against her wet folds, coating myself in her juices. Pushing in, I paused for a second like I always did, remembering the first time I'd felt her around me. Tight heat wrapped around me, and I dropped my head back at the sensation.

I started to move, her moans becoming louder around Rhett as I pistoned into her. Earlier, a fantasy had come to life, and now it was the perfect encore showing me life was better than any dream. With Sawyer and the guys, the possibilities were endless. I watched as Rey and Soren moved closer and took hold of her legs as I continued to hold on to her hips. With them spreading her open more, I moved faster as I slid in and out. Locking eyes with my Dulzura, I fell head over heels into bliss as I came. No matter how many times I felt her around me, it was never enough.

"I love you," I whispered, her eyes telling me everything my heart knew. Lounging back, I was officially done after two orgasms, and I watched the rest of BOSH fall deeper into the sexual frenzy.

## sawyer

My dream had become a reality, and as my third orgasm rolled through my body, I started to wonder if I'd bitten off more than I could chew. Sex filled the air, our moans combining with the waves to create the perfect backdrop for our lovemaking. Rhett pulled out of my mouth, and I felt Elias move up behind me. His desire was thick as he palmed my ass, pulling me back into him. Elias always surprised me in the bedroom, showing me a dominant side I craved so much.

"Love, I think it's time you saw how many cocks you could have at once. Are you up for the challenge?"

"If it's up, I want to ride it!" I laughed. Elias looked at me before laughing, shaking his head at my nonsense.

"We shall see about that, love."

Like a switch, I saw the change in him as he began directing everyone. Mateo gave me a coy smile from the side, spent after two orgasms, and nodded he was okay watching. Our ability to communicate had improved so much, we could read each other with a look most of the time. I trusted he was good and focused back on all the cocks as they started to surround me. I suddenly felt overwhelmed, and a hysterical laugh escaped.

"Love, trust us, okay?"

Looking into Elias' eyes, I found love and safety and knew I'd be taken care of. Nodding, I waited for him to direct us, our captain emerging for our dickventure.

Without words, he directed Rhett to his back and helped me straddle the monster. Every time I felt him in me, I always felt victorious at conquering the beast. From this angle, I felt even fuller, filling me up all the way. Bracing my hands on his abs, I petted the beautiful things, distracting myself.

Soren wiped my lip, and I looked up, wondering what he was doing.

"You had some drool there, sweet pea."

I stared at him, aghast at the accusation, but when I felt it roll down my chin, I shrugged, not caring in the slightest. Rhett had the most amazing abs. They were ab-azing and always made me abnotized. We all had our weaknesses, and mine was Rhett's abs.

"Baby, you keep looking at me like that, and I have half a mind to steal you away and fuck you until you can't walk."

Sadly, I did think about it for half a second, but then I remembered my cock-a-palooza going on right now, and I shut it down. Hands grabbed my hips, pulling me into the hard body behind me, their warm breath sending shivers down my spine.

"It's time to have some fun, bite-size."

Grinning, I dropped my head back and peered up at Ollie. He looked down at me, love and devotion on his face, and I melted. When Ty peeked over his shoulder, I smiled wider, loving having them all here like this. It was epic.

Elias handed Ollie and Ty something, but I was soon distracted when Elias moved me forward. He was like the puppet master, moving us all together into the positions he wanted. I found a pierced cock in front of my face, and I couldn't help but stick my tongue out and lick it. As soon as I did, I found my hands grasping two more cocks, and everyone began to move. Peeking up, I found Henry and Soren on one side of Rhett and me. As I stroked Henry and sucked Soren, Rhett moved me up and down on him in small bursts.

With Ollie and Ty behind me, it left Elias as my other dick in hand. Squeezing, I heard him hiss as I pulled my hand down slowly. His hands rubbed my back as he smoothed them over me until he found my front and pinched my nipple. I couldn't turn my head to shout at him, and it became a game to see who could spur the other one on first. Every squeeze I gave him, he would pinch my nipples back, and I found myself panting around Soren's thick cock in my mouth.

Another hand snaked down between Rhett and me and found my clit, and it helped distract me from the cold liquid on my back entrance. Ollie began to work me over, and I was overwhelmed with so many sensations I didn't know where to focus. Hands, tongues, and cocks were touching almost every part of me, and it was the most stimulating experience I'd ever had.

Ollie started to push in more once he had me ready, and I paused my other movements as I adjusted. I heard his moan and I was kind of sad I couldn't watch him and Ty. I loved watching my men together, and being with them all had me on the edge quickly. Once Ollie was seated, everything ramped up, my body on full tilt of cock. It was all the peen, all the time as I became stuffed full.

Sensation exploded, and I felt the tightness between Rhett and Ollie's dicks as they see-sawed in and out of me. Soren had taken over my mouth and was thrusting into me. My hands still managed to work as I squeezed and pumped the two dicks in my hands. My nipples and clit were pinched, and I found myself losing consciousness when everything exploded in me.

## elias

Sawyer looked beautiful between us all. Spread wide over Rhett's dick with Ollie, she appeared to be in cock heaven. Her hand continued to squeeze and stroke me, and I found myself heading in the direction I hadn't expected to so soon. This was the first time we'd been one big group, and while it was a little cramped space-wise, it hadn't been awkward. By this point, we'd all been together enough and were comfortable in our relationships with Sawyer, helping to make us feel stable.

Sawyer's body began to spasm and set off a ricochet of orgasms. One by one, we all fell victim to our sex Goddess. I somehow managed to move her into my arms, and we all laid on the lounge bed, naked under the stars. None of us were self-conscious, and no one even cared that our bodies touched or overlapped. We'd survived the Council and bitchy drama queens; we could manage complete vulnerability with one another.

A sigh escaped Sawyer, and I looked down at her and found her smiling. "Everything alright, love?"

"Everything is perfect. I thought this was a dream. I'm glad it wasn't."

"Love you, baby," Rhett mumbled before drifting off to sleep. The rest of the guys of BOSH echoed out their own sentiments, and we fell fast asleep in our cuddle huddle.

# stiletto sins

. . .

*This is a precursor of what is to come and will be slightly different in Stiletto Sins.

## finley

EVERYONE LAUGHED and celebrated as Rhett blew out his candles. The big grump had a smile on his face and I knew I'd never seen him happier. The house we were staying in was magnificent and the ocean was literally right outside the back door. I should be happy. I should be able to enjoy this time with my friends, but all I could think about was how miserable I was.

Asa placed his arm around me, drawing me close, and I forced a smile. He'd been the absolute best over the past year —caring, patient and understanding. I knew this was hard on him and yet he let me figure it out at my pace. The worst part of it, I wished he hadn't been so nice about it because then I wouldn't feel as guilty. But I'd fallen in love with him for a reason, and now I was punishing him for it. It wasn't fair, and I knew it.

This wasn't how it was supposed to be. My life was moving forward, but I still felt stuck in the same perpetual loop. On paper, my life was perfect. I had a boyfriend I loved. My best friend was back in my life, and my brother was pursuing his dreams. Things with my parents were improving, and I felt I had an honest relationship with them for the first time ever. And ultimately, we were safe now. The Council and the Agency had been disbanded.

So why did I continue to feel on edge? Why did I flinch every time someone knocked on the door or came in with a "you'll never believe this?" Why did I find myself constantly thinking about boys I shouldn't? The whys had built up to an oppressive weight and I was suffocating. I walked along a perpetual ledge, constantly balancing as I waited for the other shoe to drop.

*Funny since shoes were what got me into this mess in the first place.*

Sleep evaded me, the nightmares a constant presence, adding to my constant state of hyperarousal. To top it off, I'd been keeping secrets for months now. How Asa was still with me, I didn't know. How anyone had put up with my sour moods and distance only proved how much better they all were than me.

*I didn't belong.*

Not with the things I'd done. Not with my past.

I couldn't stay. This trip had been the last push I needed to convince myself things had to change. In order to live the life

I wanted, to feel happy… I had to finish what I'd started when I was seventeen. I had to face *him*. The only thing standing in my way was me, and it was time I faced the sins of my past instead of running.

*Except I had to run now.*

I had to put distance between me and the people I loved—especially Asa. He was too good, too pure, and I couldn't taint him with the sins of a misguided youth. No, this couldn't come back on him. I didn't think we'd survive it, and losing him that way would crush me.

It was better for me to go now. This way, I could control the fallout, and perhaps once I was done, once I'd completed my mission, we could start again. It was the only sliver of hope I'd allow myself to hang on to.

"Want to go with everyone to the beach? I think there were some sea turtles laying their eggs?"

Turning into him, I kissed his cheek as I tried to hide the tear that was falling. "I've got a headache. I'm going to call it a night, but you should go."

He assessed me, trying to gauge my feelings. "I can go with you."

Shaking my head, I cupped his cheek. "No, it's okay. I promise I'm fine. Go, have fun and make sure none of them get into trouble. I don't think anyone can deal with seeing Sawyer naked again." I chuckled, trying to distract him.

Asa grimaced, recalling how we'd been greeted this morning before responding. "Are you sure?"

"Positive."

"Okay. I'll check on you in a bit then."

He kissed my cheek before walking off with the group. I waved, trying to hold in my emotions, not wanting them to see what I was feeling. I needed this time to make my escape.

Quietly, I slipped off to the room we were staying in for the weekend. Pulling the letter out of my bag, I placed it on his pillow. Tears dropped onto it as I tried to wipe them away. It was cowardly to leave this way, but I wouldn't have the courage to do it if I didn't. Changing quickly, I grabbed my bag and tiptoed down the stairs to the front door. Tears trailed down my face as I left everything I knew behind.

With determination, I opened the door and walked through. Dressed in all black, I blended into the night as I crept down the driveway. It might be an escape, but I could still look fashionable. At the end of the road, I spotted the car idling for me. A warm sensation filled my body at him coming through, but I shoved it away.

I knew this would hurt; leaving this way was a punch to the gut, but I'd run out of options. If I didn't do this, if I didn't go now, I'd always be watching over my shoulder, waiting for *him*.

I would never be happy—not until he'd been dealt with.

Shoving my bag into the tiny trunk, I opened the door to the expensive sports car.

"You get out okay?"

"Yeah. No one saw me. Thanks," I paused, swallowing, "for doing this for me."

"You know I'm here for you, Finley, whatever you need. Besides, it's kind of my thing to be the one to save you."

Smiling, I tried to ignore the confused butterflies erupting at his words. It didn't matter, though. They were there, swirling around with everything else I felt guilty about. *I was tired of feeling guilty.* Buckling up, I settled in for the drive and pulled out the list I'd made.

1. Find him
2. Take him down
3. Make him pay

At one time, he'd been my salvation, until he became my damnation. My sins were dark, and my spirit broken, but I was no longer weak. It was time I remembered who I'd been. It was time I returned to Oblivion.

And this time, my stilettos weren't just sinful. No, this time, they would be *deadly*.

# afterword

I find myself shedding a few tears as I write this letter to you, my faithful readers. How is that a story I thought of one night when I felt emotionally wrought has resonated with so many of you? Some days it feels surreal that this is my life now. I get to write stories and share them with people! There have been good moments, stressful times, and even some days I cried throughout this process. But, the good things have outweighed the bad, and it's the passion of you all that spurs me to keep trekking away.

Writing the last scenes of this story were harder than I expected. I laughed, cried, and got goosebumps as I wrote this book, cheering them on as their story unfolded. The part where Sawyer stands up and is like, *"I'm Sawyer Sullivan, and I'm an original,"* chills, even now. It was the accumulation of everything I felt bringing my girl to accepting her worth and power. I hope you all have found that as well.

I've learned so much about myself from writing, and I feel I've grown in my ability. I know there are issues with Damaged Dreams, and I plan to address those at some point and release a box set with all kinds of juicy scenes. So, make sure to stay tuned for that, more than likely at the beginning of next year before Fin's Duet. I hope you are excited about her story and what else is to come from this world.

Well, that is all folks, The Council Series is complete. Sawyer and the BOSH boys got their justice and happy ending. If you felt I was a "big ole meanie," as one of my alpha readers said for the ending, well, I have a surprise for you! **Sign up for my newsletter, and you'll get the group orgy Sawyer hoped for!**

Hopefully, you will also check out the dark contemporary stories I have releasing in the next few months. Pride is my Rapunzel retelling mixed with the deadly sin of Pride. She's a stripper, and there's a lot of dancing! It deals with sexual abuse, so if that's a trigger, then beware, but if you read this book, then you're probably good to read Pride.

The series I'm extremely excited about is Dark Confessions. The first book is Dangerous Truths and will be out in August! I can't wait for you to sink your teeth into it. It's very different from these books, but I hope you will like it all the same.

Stay tuned and follow me on social media, where you can stay up to date on all my new releases. I often will do polls as well, so if you're hurting for a Charlie novella, a Jill spin-off, or even Ace, then let me know! I can be persuaded with hot guy pics and nice words, or just yell at me like Erica does, that works too!

Thank you from the bottom of my heart for taking the time to read this series and sharing it with others. There is a lot of fun Council merch added to my Redbubble store, so make sure to check it out! Everyone needs a cuddle huddle!

Until next time, stay sassy!

# acknowledgments

This book was a labor of love, and I tried to give it the time and love it needed. There are several people I need to thank because I know I wouldn't have kept going otherwise. Drumroll, please.

First up are the two ladies who get the brunt of my crazy.

Emma, go ahead and grab that tissue because I know you will cry, or sorry, your allergens are about to act up. There, better. Thank you for being the best cheerleader, my ride or die girl, and some days my literal sunshine. I never knew I needed a friend like you until I found ya. You're more than just my alpha reader and PA, but my bestie and sister for life. You're the whole damn package, girl!

Cat, none of this would've even happened if you hadn't told me last August I could. You pushed me to step out of my comfort zone and find my voice. It's a gift I will always cherish. Becoming your friend and doing this with you has been the cat's pajamas, as I like to call you. Thank you for showing me the ropes and being the support I needed when I felt like it was crap. You're the strength and critique I need to keep me balanced. You're stuck with me for life! Your friendship is irreplaceable.

Second are my ladies, who aren't afraid to tell me how it is while also demanding more thirsty scenes. 😌 You guys should thank them too for squeezing out a new epilogue for you all.

Becki, you crack me up and never back away from telling me how you truly feel. I respect that so much and value you as a reader and friend. I will try to get you more throat punches in the future.

Shawna, thank you for understanding the story and knowing when I need to add something. Your thirsty comments make me laugh, and I always look forward to them. You are a great cheerleader.

Jillian, thank you for jumping in on this one, but being a huge fan and supporter from the very beginning. You loved sweet Mateo from the start, and I hope he showed you his confidence in this book. Thank you for being the sweetest and spotting all my missing letters!

Marla, thank you for your constant feedback and love for these guys. You always have the time for me and let me share my ramblings. Thank you for being that listening ear and encouragement.

To all my ARC readers, thank you for taking the time to read this and pumping it up. I love seeing your edits on Instagram and can't wait to see what you got for me. A couple of you have reached out over the months, and your kind words (or shouts) genuinely do make my day. Thanks for making this little indie author feel a blimp of recognition through your support. You all rock my socks!

Thank you to Jillian, Kylie, and Sandy for helping me start

a list of names for our group some of their ideas that you might've seen are: Winter Operatives, Code Orange Pack, Council Breakers, Winter Warriors, Winter Wonders, and Ice Breakers.

To Megan who won the birthday giveaway to be named in the book, I hope you enjoyed your little shoutout in helping with Lucky's gift!

To all the readers where ever you are, thank you for loving Sawyer and the gang!

Before I get to my husband, who hates being last, which obviously means I have to do it on purpose now, I have one last shoutout.

To Kristin, the first person to buy all three paperbacks, thank you! You're officially in a book! Hope you loved this one and aren't too scandalized!

To my husband, thank you for understanding my incessant need to write and edit and write and edit nonstop and on repeat. And while I hope you never read these, I know your little work friend will share some details. May you know how much I love you. From stressful deadlines to internal pressures I place on myself to feelings of doubt, you never once told me to quit or give it up. That means the world to me, so thank you. To the moon and back, babe.

# bosh bells & epic fails

A Christmas Council Novella

# Bosh Bells

## AND
## EPIC FAILS

## KRIS BUTLER

*To all the magical Christmases we've had, and all the ones to come. May you never stop wishing for Christmas Miracles.*

# blurb

I've heard that surviving the first major holiday was the true test of a relationship.

What about when you had seven of them? No one told me that I'd need to cram for the holidays! If I made it through them without a code orange moment, it would be a true Christmas miracle! I was doubtful even Santa could grant that one.

Between gifts, sledding, and some hot apple cider, my usually quiet Christmas transformed into one of epic proportions; which wouldn't be complete without giant Santas, a house full of trees, and a Christmas party that turned into a competition. (If you guessed Ollie and Fin were behind this, you'd be right!)

Add in some Christmas ghosts, and well, it wouldn't be BOSH if there weren't some fails and bells along the way.

Join Sawyer and the gang in this twist on *The Christmas Carol* that will have you laughing, crying, and fanning yourself before the end. While it is a continuation of a completed series, it is not needed to have read it in order to enjoy this Christmas rom-com. This book is intended for readers 18+

due to content and language. It also includes a why-choose relationship with LTGBQ+ characters within. If that's not your thing, then no worries, there are several other amazing stories in this anthology for you to enjoy. From BOSH, Lucky, and me, Merry Christmas.

# prologue

. . .

SNOW BEGAN FALLING SOFTLY outside the window as I watched, and I couldn't help but become excited. The first snowfall of the season was always something to celebrate. I'd been excited all day, the smell in the air, and I knew it would be soon. Everyone thought I was crazy when I announced it, but I could; I could smell the snow. Maybe it was the one weird gift I had, but it was mine, no matter how much other people tried to convince me otherwise.

Arms wrapped around me from behind, snuggling into my neck, and I rested back in his arms. "You were right. It's snowing." He chuckled, giving in to my amazing gift.

"Mmhmm."

"You can be smug about it. I clearly haven't learned to respect this weird gift of yours over the years. Though, I think I just like to give you a hard time. It's my favorite pastime."

"That you do!" I acknowledged, laughing. "I like it, though. It keeps me humble."

"How hard was it for you to say that?"

"So, hard!" I admitted, laughing even more. "I like to flaunt my wins so much. At least you're a good sport about it. I can't say that for everyone else."

"Well, that's because I'm obviously the more mature of the bunch."

Turning in his arms, I smiled up at him. "Oh, is that what it is? And here, I just thought it was because you liked having sex with me." A burst of air left him in a guffaw at my words, causing me to smile even wider.

"Well, there is that, but I thought that went without saying." He bent down to kiss me, and like every time our lips touched, I fell even more in love with him.

"Hey guys, sorry to interrupt, but this one is starving, and the others are clambering to open gifts." The interrupter held up a baby, tears streaming down her sweet face as she reached out to me, her little lip quivering. "Mama."

Heart-melting, I left the embrace of my husband and took my child. "Thanks, go ahead and start, and I'll be out after I finish feeding her."

The guys both turned, but my husband stopped, giving me a knowing look. "Don't fall asleep or get caught up in that journal of yours."

"Me? Never! I'll be down in a bit."

They both nodded, knowing smiles on their faces as I sat back in the rocking chair, the blonde beauty already sucking away at my breast. Smoothing her hair away, I thought of all the dreams I had for her, all the hopes and wishes for her future. Despite what my husband had warned against, I grabbed the notebook off the side table, the pen already on the last page I'd gotten to, reading over what I'd written earlier.

Once she had her fill, her little baby coos the soundtrack to my thoughts, I laid her down in the temporary crib we had set up at my parents. Laying across the bed, I started to write, telling her the story of how I fell in love. When I'd written for a while, I knew I had one more thing to say before I closed it, bargaining with time to close my eyes for just a few quick minutes.

*My Dearest,*

*By now, I hope you can see how much we all love you, and I hope that whatever happens in your life, you too have love. I think there is magic at Christmas that doesn't exist at any other time, so I hope you embrace and love it as much as I do. And if for whatever reason I don't get to spend a million Christmas' with you, may you always have these. For what is Christmas without magic bells and epic fails?*

*Boring.*

*Merry Christmas, dearest one.*

*Love,*

*Your mother*

# one

Sawyer

DECEMBER 2020

Christmas music rang out through the store as I ran around the corner, hiding behind a large blow-up penguin. It hadn't been my brightest idea to start a game of hide-and-seek tag in the largest Christmas store known to man, but after two hours here, I'd gotten bored. Ollie and Soren had easily fallen into my trap and were playing with me. We'd all come with Rhett to the megastore a few towns over, thinking it would be fun to pick out Christmas decorations for the house. It was BOSH's first Christmas, after all.

None of us had understood the implications of that request.

Out of all the people who'd be a Christmas snob, I never expected it to be Rhett, our resident grumpy bear. Elias had given me an eyebrow raise when I suggested we'd all go, but he'd kept his mouth shut. I'd be paying that favor forward later when I teased him and then left him with some Christmas blue balls to match the decor.

Challenge accepted, Elias.

Rhett had a mile-long list, and everything had to be a specific brand, color, and aesthetic. It was cute for the first hour, but by hour two, I wanted to poke my eyes out with the candy-cane-shaped lights. Peeking around the massive Chilly Willy, I didn't hear the person who snuck up behind me, the motor of the blower covering their footsteps.

"Gotcha!" Ollie chuckled, grabbing me on the sides and hauling me up into his arms. Squealing, I didn't fight it and went easily as he spun us around. Throwing my arms around his neck, I smiled up at my ginger-bearded boyfriend. Ollie had the rugged hockey player look down, and right now, with his hair longer and his beard growing out, he was a delectable sight to behold. I'd added flannel shirts to my Christmas shopping list and had some plans to live out some lumberjack fantasies.

"Hey, boyfriend."

"Hey, pretty girl."

His smile was brilliant as he leaned down and kissed me. We might've gotten lost in our kiss as the sound of a throat clearing brought us back to the land of snowflakes and mistletoe.

"You guys are so busted."

Leaning against the shelving of every shaped wreath imaginable, stood Tyler. His golden-brown hair flopped against his forehead, his green eyes pierced me as he stared. I motioned with my finger, and he walked over, a sly smile on his face.

"Well, what do we have to do in order to avoid being in trouble?" I asked, batting my eyelashes.

"Oh, wildcat. I can think of so many things… but Rhett is up at the checkout, and he's waiting for you to bring the items you three hooligans said you were getting half an hour ago." He gave me a pointed look, clearly knowing we'd been up to no good and not gathering any items like we'd said.

"Oops."

"Yeah, oops. Luckily, I'm a good boyfriend, and I got it for you. So, let's go before Papa Elf gives us all workshop duty or something," he muttered, turning in the opposite direction. Ollie set me down, and we followed Ty together. When he started to shake his rear extravagantly in front of us, we both chuckled, appreciating the view.

"Now, that's some hot crossed buns!" Ollie whistled.

"Not again with the Christmas puns," I groaned, rolling my eyes. Ollie had been non-stop with his Christmas jeers.

"It's not even a Christmas one, babe," Tyler yelled over his shoulder, winking.

Ollie peered down to me with a raised brow, and I shrugged. "I don't know what they are," I whispered, and Ollie chuckled, not admitting if he knew or not. Doubtful.

Thankfully, he didn't make any further punny statements. As soon as it hit midnight on November 30, my world had become a tidal wave of red and green. I hadn't celebrated a real Christmas in years, and *never* to this extreme. Victoria had been festive, but even this was a level all of its own.

Rhett had lists upon lists, and within twenty-four hours our house had started to become a Winter Wonderland. He'd even gone and helped his mom with the B&B. It was a whole new side to him I never would've expected. It was cute, if not slightly annoying, when I didn't put the correct amount of ornaments in one section of the tree.

With the new additions in our lives, the Brotherhood of Sawyer's heart, or BOSH as we'd shortened it, Rhett had decided some new decor and trees were due to represent all of us. There were already four trees in the house, and now we were adding two more. As much as I griped about it though, it was beautiful inside and out, and it did feel like a magical Christmas world inside.

I told Rhett he should hire himself out to decorate for people, but he hadn't been interested. I guess he only liked doing it for places he had a connection to, his annoyance for people outside of our circle shining through.

We came around the corner and found Mateo and Rhett waiting for us. My sweet nerd smiled before heading down the checkout lane to grab a cart. His glasses concealed his eyes, his dark floppy hair falling across his forehead, but I could tell he was amused with me, chuckling softly as he went. The two with me handed off the items we'd gathered and escaped down the aisle with Mateo as well.

"Traitors!" I hissed.

They only laughed, not caring as they escaped to the safe zone. Rhett stood waiting, his famous eyebrow raised, as I crept closer. I couldn't read his emotions from here, so I kept scooting along, dragging my feet a minuscule amount closer.

"Baby, why am I not surprised you were the one creating a ruckus?"

"Who, *me*? I'd never! You've got me mistaken."

He shook his head, a grin spreading on his face as I neared. The damn boy knew it was my weakness, and I sighed, finishing my trek to him. Rhett took the ribbon I held and dropped it and the other items on the conveyor belt. He kept staring at me, his eyes boring into me, ignoring everyone else.

The cashier scanned the items, slowly bagging them as she looked me over. I couldn't tell if she was annoyed I'd held up her lane or if it was because I was with all the guys. Either way, I didn't care. I'd had enough of girls giving me the stink eye to last a lifetime. Wrapping my arms around Rhett's waist, I clung to him like a barnacle. My arms barely reached around him, my fingers locked for maximum effect.

Rhett looked down at me while he paid and just patted me on the head. He scowled at the cashier as she tried to get his attention, and it only made me love him even more. He was a grumpy old man at times, but he was mine. They all were.

Once she handed him back his card and receipt, he went to shove it in his pocket but was stopped by my presence on his body. "Baby, I need to put this in my pocket."

"Use mine. I'm not moving."

Chuckling, he reached down, but instead of putting the items in my pocket like I asked, he lifted me by the ass, pulling me up in one motion. This man and his arm muscles, Lord have mercy!

Yipping, I gripped around his neck, wrapping my legs around his waist. "You know, grump, I probably look like your disobedient child like this." I twisted myself, so I was on his back instead of like a toddler on his hip. He grunted as I koala'd my way around but didn't stop me.

As we exited the store, a cider stand was near the door, and I eagerly pointed at the hot beverages. Rhett didn't say anything but walked over and handed her some money. He went to grab a cup, but she slapped his hand, and he pulled back in alarm. I was about to go off on the lady when she picked up a decorated cup with a lid and presented it to me.

"For the lady, may it bring all of your Christmas wishes." She bowed her head as I took it, and I looked at Rhett as I hung over his shoulder. He smirked at me, finally letting me down.

"Thanks."

She didn't say anything else but turned to wait on the next customer. The weird thing was she let them pick their cup. Rhett and I exchanged a look, but the cold had me shaking off the weirdness and jumping in the truck that pulled up. We'd borrowed one to get the trees because Rhett insisted these two be real ones. Oliver was in the driver's seat, looking sexy as fuck behind the wheel. Henry sat in the passenger seat, but climbed out and got in the back with me when he noticed Rhett. There was no way Rhett would fit back here with his 6'7" frame.

The rest of BOSH was in an SUV up ahead, idling at the front of the entrance waiting for us. Ollie took off as soon as we were all situated, and I laid my head against Henry as I sipped my drink. It tasted different than any cider I'd had before, but it was tasty, and I found it gone within a few minutes. Since we had a bit of a drive, I snuggled closer to Henry and closed my eyes, the guys' conversation lulling me to sleep.

"How long has she been sleeping?" I heard a voice ask in the distance.

"For about six hours. She slept through lunch and dinner. When I checked on her again to see if I could get her to eat something, I noticed her fever. Is she going to be okay?"

A wet cloth was placed on my forehead, and the coolness felt nice against my skin. I blinked my eyes open to find the guys, along with Rhonda, Rhett's mom, crowded around the bed. I tried to focus on them all, but it was hard, everything was fuzzy around the edges. Suddenly, a sharp pain in my abdomen had me sitting up with a gasp. The person who'd been leaning over me barely had time to move out the way before I nailed them with my forehead.

"Ow," I cried out, clutching my stomach.

"Where does it hurt, Sawyer?"

"It's like a sharp pain," I gasped. "Fucking hell," I winced. "Sorry, Rhonda."

"It's fine, sweetie. Does anything else hurt?"

"No, but I really need to pee."

"Okay, I'll help you," she offered, reaching for my hand.

"Okay."

She had the guys clear out while she helped me to the bathroom, and the most excruciating pain imaginable pierced through me as I peed.

"Fuck, oh my God, that burns something fierce."

Breathing through the pain, I gingerly wiped and waddled to the sink. Bracing my hands on the counter, I took some deep breaths until I could fully stand and wash my hands. Wobbling to the door, I opened it and found Rhonda waiting for me.

"Any symptoms?"

"Um, yeah, it burns when I pee," I cringed.

She chuckled. "Rowan wanted to name our WiFi network that," she joked and then realized I wasn't in the mood to appreciate the hilariousness of that. "Well, sweetie, I think you have a UTI. Honestly, I try not to think about what you get up to with all of those boys, but yeah…"

It was at that moment I realized what she was implying, which meant, of course, I had to make it worse, code orange style and word vomit all over her, awkward Sawyer style. "I haven't even had a proper orgy! This is so unfair."

Realizing the words I'd just shouted at my boyfriend's mom, I groaned, covering my face. Thankfully, Rhonda was the coolest and only laughed. "Honey, more power to you if you can wrangle them all. Come on, we're gonna need to call in a prescription. Rest and relaxation are in order for the next few days until the worst of it passes."

Nodding, I shuffled to the bed. I was glad someone had called her. Isla and Sampson, my newfound biological parents, would've been way more embarrassing to have to discuss this with. Samson might've even tried to shoot one of the guys. It would be better to keep this on the down-low to save me ultimate humiliation from my parents.

Getting comfortable in the blanket and pillow masterpiece Soren had made while I'd been in the bathroom, I was surprised when there was a knock at the door. Looking up, I found the last person I expected to be there—Mr. Hawthorne. I glanced at him curiously, but he only nodded in greeting.

Mr. Hawthorne was in his forties, with blonde white hair, crystal blue eyes, and clean-shaven, he always took me by surprise. He was dressed in one of his typical expensive suits, looking out of place in my bedroom. As always though, his smile was kind and welcoming.

"Mr. Hawthorne, what can I do for you?"

"Please, Sawyer, call me Logan. I was wondering if I could have a moment of your time?"

"Um, now's not the best. I'm not feeling the greatest."

"Oh, of course. I'm sorry you're under the weather. Perhaps, I could just drop this off then, and we could talk more when you're feeling better?"

He raised a brown leather journal wrapped in twine and holly. "Um, sure." I didn't fear him anymore, but he was still a stranger to me for the most part. I knew he was important to my adoptive mom, so I wanted to give him the benefit of the doubt. He'd also inevitably saved us all, so there was that to consider. It was just awkward, when my vagina felt like it was on fire, trying to have a heart-to-heart with the man.

"This was your mother's, or Victoria's. I thought you

675

might like it. It's about some of her better moments here before everything became about taking down the Council. Isla and Samson are in it as well. I thought you'd be able to get to know a different side of her, and them. And well, perhaps, me too. I'd like to be in your life if you'd let me."

He seemed so sincere, I could hardly say no, even if the thought made me a little uncomfortable. "That's kind of you. Thank you. When I'm feeling better, maybe we could get some hot chocolate or something?"

"That'd be nice. You know, your mother always said cider and hot chocolate had magical qualities about them at Christmas. It would be nice to share some of that magic with you."

He handed me the journal before squeezing my shoulder, making his way out the door. I didn't have much time to open it before the guys returned, arms full of food and their own pillows and blankets. Rhonda returned and told me there would be some medication delivered soon and to rest up.

"You okay, bite-size?" Ollie asked as he snuggled up behind me. I grimaced slightly as I was moved, my abdomen still feeling painful.

"I'll survive. Though, I'm mad at all of you."

The seven of them turned, shocked expressions on their faces. "Why? What did we do, sweet pea?" Soren, my golden snowboarding Adonis asked, his handsome face creased in confusion.

"You all hypnotized me with your dicks, and now it burns when I pee," I cried.

Of course, they all found that hilarious, the fuckers. Huffing, I curled onto my side and ignored them as I opened the journal and began to read about the first woman I called mom, Victoria, while the sounds of "A Christmas Carol" played in the background on the TV. At some point, my head drooped, my eyes closed, and I fell asleep on top of the journal.

# two

. . .

### Sawyer

I WAS DREAMING. I knew I was dreaming, but it didn't stop the dream from happening. No matter what I tried, I couldn't wake myself. Pinching my arm for the millionth time, I gave up when nothing happened. At least I wouldn't bruise in my dream, right?

Accepting I was in a dream state, I looked around the room I'd found myself in, wondering what in the hell was going on and how I found myself here. This seriously had to be a dream.

Why did I believe I was dreaming?

Well, I didn't usually wake up with a penis between my legs!

Okay, scratch that. I sometimes woke up with a penis between my legs, but it wasn't like *this*. Nope, not like this at all.

Looking down, I checked again, and sure enough, the

foreign appendage was still there. Was this what happened when you had a UTI? I'd never read about this online before. Perhaps no one spoke about it because it was too weird to comprehend. There could be hundreds of girls out there walking around with a dick now, too afraid to say anything.

Or maybe it had been that cider? Now that I thought more about it, the whole exchange with the women had been weird. The way she'd slapped Rhett's hand and made sure I had a specific cup, it could only mean she'd doped me!

Unless this was all part of my high fever delusion? When I thought about it, I did feel flushed.

Feeling relieved at the notion it was all some weird delusional fever dream, I decided to accept the opportunity to be a guy for a time. Looking closer at the room I was in, I could guess it was a dorm, and my roommate was still fast asleep. I peeked over to see if I could recognize him, but it was too dark to tell.

The realization I was in a dorm room stood out to me. Why would I dream about being in a dorm room? I hadn't even been in the dorms on campus that I could recall. My feverish delusion had apparently been smoking crack. Perhaps I needed to venture out more than just around campus or read more books. Now, that was an idea! Mine and Soren's book club was my favorite type of book club, after all.

The alarm next to the bed of the boy I was peering at started to go off, and I jumped back just in time to avoid being smacked with his arm as he reached out and turned it off. I was impressed he only needed it to go off once, and then was *bam!* awake. He rolled over, catching me staring at him as I stood frozen to the spot. His white-blonde hair was tousled over his forehead, and his crystal-blue eyes regarded me with suspicion as he swung his legs over the edge of the bed.

"Chase, why are you standing over me?"

Stuttering, I managed to get some words out, "You can see me?"

The boy gave me a weird look, turning up his lips in a rye smile. "Of course I can see you. You're standing two feet in front of me. Did you hit your head or something? Coach will be pissed if you're off your game. Move. I'm grabbing the shower since you seem to be taking your time this morning."

"Coach?"

The boy stood, pushing around me, and walked to a dresser on the far side of the room to grab clothes. My question had him turning around, doubt in his gaze now as he assessed me. "Yeah, Coach. For the hockey team? Seriously, did you eat strawberries or something?"

I blinked. Man, I had weird dreams. I must be channeling Ollie and Ty with the hockey team. "Strawberries?" I mumbled, but the boy shook his head, his brow creased as he headed to the other door in the room.

Sitting down, I tried to pinch myself again, but still, nothing happened, and actually, it was beginning to hurt. Looking up, I jumped back in fright when a ghostly version of Aggie, my mothers' mentor and tea-loving friend, appeared.

"Aggie! What are you doing here? What's going on?"

"Oh, sorry, dear, running a bit late. I never do seem to

make it on time to these things. Nevertheless, you're here, and I'm here, might as well get on with it."

"And where exactly is here?"

"The past, of course!" She exclaimed as if that cleared it up.

"The past… who's past exactly?"

"Ah, well, *that* I'm afraid I can't tell you. Rules and all." She shrugged her ghostly shoulders, and I wanted to shake them. "But," she hedged, and I gritted my teeth in annoyance. I didn't find this side of Aggie fun, at all. Bring me back the grandmotherly version any day. "I am allowed to tell you that you have a day to figure out what you're supposed to learn from this."

"Wonderful, and here I thought waking up with a penis was the weirdest thing that would happen to me today."

"I did think that was rather genius of me." She giggled, and I wondered if she'd been spending too much time with me. "Enjoy!" Aggie gave a finger wave and poofed out of the room.

Yep! I've clearly lost it. Sighing, I braced my head in my hands as I contemplated the craziness of my delusion. Penis growing, Aggie poofing—Holy facial hair, batman!

Feeling my face, I stood to take in the man beard I had in the small mirror on the wardrobe door. Considering I was a teenager, it was pretty impressive. The door opened causing steam to roll out and my mysterious roommate returned. Of course, he found me fondling myself in the mirror and rolled his eyes at me.

"You're so obsessed with that beard, man."

"What's not to like?" I chuffed, wanting to stand up for whoever I was.

"It's scratchy and makes you look old."

"Well, maybe I like it."

"Whatever, man. You better get a move on it."

He'd been dressing as we spoke, and I realized when he finished, he was fully dressed now. Jumping, I opened the wardrobe fully and pulled out a uniform. At least it made it easy. Except as I hopped down the hall chasing him, putting on my shoe to try and catch up, I found myself cursing the invention of ties. Who thought teenagers knew how to tie a tie! What was wrong with these people?

Righting myself once I had my shoe on, I dug around in the bag to see if I could find a phone, anything to give me a clue to who I was and what past I was stuck in. I should've looked in the room more, but my roommate extraordinaire hadn't waited, and I didn't want to be clueless about who I was and lost. I could only deal with so many unknowns before I gave up and I didn't want to be stuck here, or as a boy, in case this wasn't a dream.

"Dude, wait up!" My roommate scoffed at me but stopped, waiting as I turned the corner, chasing him half-dressed.

"Chase, fix your clothes before you get a demerit! Honestly! It's like you woke up a different person or some-thing!" He huffed at me but grabbed my clothes and began to fix them as he straightened my shirt collar. It was then I saw his bag with the name tag on the side.

*Logan Hawthorne.*

Holy shit! I had gone back in time. What year did that make it then? I blinked, the time not coming to me as I tried to recall. Maybe I wasn't supposed to know, a time travel precaution so you didn't screw up timelines or something. Though, I wasn't me, so how much could I screw up? Actually scratch that. I was me, just not in my body. I could screw up a whole lot.

Logan straightened my tie and turned to walk the other way, and I had to jog to catch up again. More kids filtered in around us as we neared a building, and I looked to see if I recognized anyone. Not that I would, but it was one of those habitual things you seemed to do when faced with a crowd— look for a familiar face, so you didn't feel alone. Or at least it was something I did.

I was surprised when I actually found one.

Victoria—my adoptive mother.

I stopped in my tracks when she approached, but her eyes were only for Logan. Swallowing, I tried to think of something extraordinary to say to my mother. I hadn't seen her in over five years, and there had been countless times I'd wanted to tell her something. But standing in front of her teenage self, they all seemed to evaporate.

"You okay there, Chase?"

I realized she was talking to me a moment later, and I nodded, not trusting my voice not to come out sounding like I would cry. She glanced at Logan, and he rolled his eyes, clearly fed up with my weirdness.

"I think he had some bad cheese or something." He placed his arm around her shoulders, drawing her into him.

It was weird seeing my mom with someone who wasn't my adoptive dad, Scott. But she looked so happy, I couldn't fault her happiness, especially knowing how their story ended.

They began to walk toward the double doors I assumed led to a cafeteria, and for some reason, it struck me that we were at what now was The Aldridge School. Everything looked familiar but not exactly the same. Updates and renovations had occurred from whenever this was to current.

Shit, I wondered if there was an underground site here already?

Someone bumped into me, pushing me along, and I dropped the thought as I caught up to Logan and Victoria. I smiled at her, trying to keep it cool. I didn't want to weird her out since I was currently in the body of a teenage boy. I followed through the food line, grabbing some cereal and milk, not sure I could eat with this much occurring at once. My mind swirled all around as I tried to gather all the information I could.

It had to be the reason I hadn't considered until we got to the table that I'd be smacked in the face with my biological parents as well. Samson and Isla were already seated at the table and were... kissing. I stopped midway to my chair, my jaw opening as I took in the scene in front of me.

"You okay there, dude?" Logan nudged me, and I closed my mouth, nodding. I couldn't quit staring at them though. So, when they pulled apart, Samson found me watching and raised an eyebrow in such a similar move to Rhett that I almost choked.

It also brought the realization the guys weren't with me,

and I sobered, focusing on my breakfast. I tried to eavesdrop as I crunched my cereal, intent on learning what I needed to so I could return back to my time and the men I loved. It seemed there was a Christmas party tonight and a gift exchange. I hoped whoever I traded bodies with had been a planner and already bought a gift. No way could I manage to do that for someone I didn't even know.

Everyone started to gather up their stuff and get up, so I rushed to swallow the last of my food, downing my juice. I didn't know if I'd get another chance, and maybe if I drank something different, it would reverse whatever voodoo spell that lady had placed on me in case that was the cause. An elbow nudged me and I found myself staring at Victoria.

"Oh, um, hi." Why were my cheeks reddening? I wanted to push my hair back, the nervous energy needing an outlet, but the short tresses I had as a boy didn't really lend to the fidgeting action. The realization my mother might think I was flirting with her, had me sobering, and I cleared my throat, standing tall.

That was when the fact I was tall, like really, really tall, sunk in. At this height, I had to look down at her, her head coming to only my upper chest, and I found her smiling kindly at me.

"I know you have practice now," she started, and I inwardly began to freak out at the thought. "But I was hoping afterward, we could go into town and you could help me pick out the hockey thing I'm getting Logan."

"Oh, yeah, sure. Um, I'll text you?"

Victoria tilted her head, her nose scrunched up in confusion. "Text?"

Shit! This was the 90's or something. "Oh, ha! Just kidding, who has minutes, am I right?" I spluttered as I tried to remember what form of communication they used back then. Every movie I'd ever seen that took place in the late '90s began to scan across my brain. They definitely had cell phones in Clueless, maybe no one used them here. Wait, what was that messaging thing they used? AWOL? No, that was something else.

"You're so funny, Chase. Just call my dorm phone or send me a message on AIM if I'm online. Just don't tell Logan, it's a surprise."

Nodding, I waved as she left, stunned and feeling like the biggest idiot. If I didn't figure out how to get back to my time, I would never survive in the '90s. Nope, it wouldn't work at all. I was a product of my generation and I needed my technology. The thought of not having Netflix had my whole body trembling.

Glimpsing around, I noticed everyone was gone, and I cursed. I needed to find my way to the hockey rink if I did have practice. In no way did I want to screw this guy's life up just because he'd been unfortunate enough to have me steal his life. Shitballs, I hope he wasn't in my body!

Cringing at that though, I headed out of the cafeteria. Two seconds later, I shrieked, jumping back when Aggie appeared directly in front of me in all of her ghostly fashion. "Oh my God, woman! You're going to actually kill me if you don't start announcing yourself!"

"Oops, sorry, dear. I'm still getting the hang of it. Have you figured out what you need to do yet?"

"Seriously? It's been like an hour since I last saw you!"

"And?"

"Ugh, no. I haven't. I'm late for practice and I don't know where that is, and then I have to go shopping with my future adoptive mom, who probably thinks I have a crush on her because I can't stop blushing or losing my words. Why was I sent back here? Can't you just help me out?"

"Sorry, dear. It doesn't work that way. You've gotta figure it out for you."

"Ugh, fine. Is there anything you can do?"

"Oh, I know!" She snapped her fingers and I was immediately transported to the hockey locker room. For the first time in my life, I didn't want to be. Naked dudes, upon naked dudes, surrounded me, and I stumbled my way to a spot near the wall that was free so I could shut my eyes and avoid all the juvenile peen.

"Chase! Come on. What is with you today?" Logan yelled out, slapping me on the back as he stalked off.

"I'm coming," I grumbled, throwing my bag onto the bench. Thankfully, I knew how to put on all the hockey gear, having played with Ty several times in high school. As long as I wasn't the goalie, I'd be fine. Pucks flying at my head wasn't a situation I wanted to be in regardless if I was 6 ft something. Once the room cleared out, I looked around and found a locker with the name Chase O'Daniel on it. Lacing up the black skates, I finished up and wobbled out the door, one of the last people left inside.

A whistle blew as I stepped onto the ice, and it immediately made me miss Ty and Ollie. The memory of Oliver taking me to the rink to show off flashed through my mind, and how it ended with me kissing Tyler made me smile. That had been a good day.

"Boy, what's got you smiling?" An older man bellowed, and I sobered, realizing he was talking to me.

He gave me a perplexed look when I didn't move, so I scurried, getting in line with the others, and began to run through the drills with everyone else. Amazingly, my natural balance from figure skating over the years lent to me not falling on my ass. Not to mention, hockey was so much easier at this height! Moves I usually struggled with, I found I could do easily now, my long arms and leg strength adding to the effortlessness of each movement.

Somehow, I managed to survive the practice, resulting in a dripping, sweaty mess a few hours later. I followed the horde back to the locker room and remembered to shut my eyes this time to avoid the free dong smorgasbord I was about to walk into.

Gathering my stuff, Logan gave me another weird look, his hands on his hips as he stared at me, his blue eyes observing me closely. However, there was no way I would be showering with that many teen boys. Nope! Gonna have to pass on that experience. Logan kept looking at me, waiting for a response.

"I, uh, got a thing. I'll, um, see you later."

He nodded slowly, his face scrunched up in thought as I practically ran out of the locker room, my head in my bundle of clothes as I made my way out. Once I hit the outside air, I slowed, relieved to be out of the stinky boy fest. Unfortunately, a few seconds later, Logan caught up to me, a question on his lips.

"What's going on with you? You're acting weird."

"What? Me? Nah, I'm cool."

"Uh-huh. What's up?"

"Nothing! I swear. I just didn't feel like being around that many dicks! Okay?"

"Are you homophobic or something, Chase?" He stepped back, his face changing to disgust at the thought, and I filed that away. It seemed Logan was all for love, even as a teen.

"What? No! Ugh, this is going in the wrong direction. I had some bad cheese last night or something, remember? And now I have tummy problems. So, you know, I gotta take a shit and I'm a nervous pooper. Happy?"

He stopped in his tracks and I took the advantage to stalk off, hiding my face as best I could without long hair. Seemed even when I was in a different body, I still had code orange moments, even if this was a size 12 foot in the mouth one.

Thirty minutes later, I'd showered alone, changed, and was now trying to figure out this archaic system of sending a message on AIM. Clicking on the AOL icon, I groaned when the icon wheel spun as it loaded, taking over ten minutes to open. Seriously, the patience of this generation. No wonder none of them had it now when it came to driving. They'd spent it all as teenagers waiting for dial-up internet and pages to load.

When it finally came online, I searched through the

contacts, but of course, no one had an easily identifiable user-name. After flicking through *bootysmak*, *hockeylover009*, and *iceskatersarebetter*, I gave up, deciding to take my chances at the girl's dorm instead. Thankfully, the dorms were in the same place as they were now, and I found it easily. However, I kept forgetting I was no longer a girl, but a boy now. The dorm mom at the front desk kindly reminded me.

"Excuse me, young man! Boys are not permitted on the upper floors!"

I stopped, face flaming at my blunder. "Sorry ma'am, um, I'm here to see Victoria." I left it at that because I couldn't remember if she went under her real last name here or if she had a different one, her name changing over the years almost as impressive as mine had been.

"Hmph," she snorted, but nodded, pointing to a waiting area.

I waved thanks, and took a seat, wiping my sweaty hands down the legs of my jeans. Geez, boys sweated a *lot*. I could already feel it building under my armpits, and I'd reeked after that two-hour practice. Why did I think it smelled so good on my guys? Must be a pheromone thing, because I did not find myself smelling seductive and masculine at the moment.

"Chase!"

I stood as Victoria descended the stairs, shuffling my feet as I waited, again not knowing how to interact with her. I'd spent fifteen years of my life with the woman, but at the moment, she felt like a stranger. We walked in silence for a few minutes and I thought about all the things I'd wanted to ask my mom, but hadn't gotten the chance to after the night my world had changed. But now that I stood here with her in my presence, none of it seemed important anymore.

"So, um, Logan, you seem to like him, huh?"

Victoria looked up at me, probably curious as to why I asked but nodded. "Yeah, I do. He's much better than his cousin."

Her whole body did a shiver and it hit me that Alek was here as well. I whipped around, afraid he would be directly behind me, wanting to kidnap me. Of course, he wasn't there, but the dreadful feeling his name dredged up stayed, and an even bigger sense of urgency to return to my timeline hit me. I didn't want to be in a place where he existed.

"You don't like him either?"

"No!" I shouted, then immediately cleared my throat, toning it down. "No."

"That's smart of you. Most of the other boys hang on to all of his words acting like he's a fucking king, especially, Robert." She rolled her eyes, and I so badly wanted to tell her everything that would transpire. But I didn't. I couldn't risk screwing anything up and not being where I was twenty-odd years later, lying in a bed surrounded by men who loved me.

As much as I wished Victoria could escape what life had in store for her, I knew I couldn't sacrifice everything else for it. The mother I'd known wouldn't want me to do that either. She'd sacrificed her life for mine, after all.

We arrived at the store in town a few minutes later, and she led me over to the wall of sticks she was considering. The problem now I realized was I had no knowledge of hockey sticks. Looking at them all against the wall, I started to panic when I couldn't tell the difference between the red one or the black one outside of color.

"Um, you know what. Hockey sticks are lame and impersonal. You should get him…" I nervously scanned the store, hoping something would stick out to me. Out of the corner of my eye, I saw something shiny at the front. Walking over to it, I found myself drawn there like a magpie, that or the ghost of Aggie jumping up and down pointing to it led me there. You take your pick.

"How about one of these with his jersey number on it?' I picked up the dual crossing hockey sticks keychain and held it out to her. She looked at it, and smiled, nodding.

"Yeah, you're right. This would be much better. Thanks, Chase." She hugged me briefly, then headed to the engraving station to personalize it. I'd wanted to hold on for longer when she'd wrapped her arms around me, but figured it would've been weird. Instead, I tried to remember how she smelled and felt to lock away in my vault of memories for my mom.

She returned a few minutes later, a huge grin on her face as she carried the small gift bag. "Come on, coffee's on me."

We walked out of the store together, and around the corner to the coffee shop, and I almost tripped when I saw which place it was—the coffee shop I'd met my friend Ace at.

The door jingled when we entered, the sound eerily familiar. It looked similar to how it did now, not much had changed in the years. The espresso machine looked dated, or I guess, it wasn't for the current time period.

693

"What are you thinking?" she asked, peering out the corner of her eye.

"I know you said coffee, but I'm kind of feeling tea. It's something I used to do with my mom." My voice dropped, becoming soft at the end, and I tilted my head away so she wouldn't see the tears that were wanting to spring to life. I couldn't cry here.

"Oh, that sounds perfect. I love a good pot of tea."

Relieved, I smiled and nodded. She ordered one she liked, and we took it over to a table, sitting down and arranging our dishes. It felt nice, even if I was a boy, to do this.

"You said you do this with your mother?"

"Yeah, we would have heart to hearts and tea. It was nice. She died a few years ago, though. So, it's been a while." I shrugged, concentrating on fixing my tea, knowing if I looked at her then, I would sob my eyes out.

"Oh, I'm so sorry Chase, that's awful. But wait, I thought your mom visited last month for the alumni thing?"

She asked, and my head snapped up in panic. "I mean my grandmother. She was like a mom to me."

"Oh, that's cool. I'm not that close to my grandmother, and my mother died when I was eight. My family hasn't always been the best of people, though. My dad, he's very strict and hard to please. I came to this school to be my own person, but he's wanting to pull me back again. Just when I think I can make different choices for myself, I find myself falling back into old habits."

I nodded, understanding what she meant. "I've felt that way before. Once, I was in a new place, and I felt like I couldn't trust anyone. Life was really lonely during that time, but I survived. Then I came here, and there were all these amazing new people and I had to decide if I wanted to trust them or keep living a life where I was only half living."

"How do you get past the fear?"

"I don't think you do. Life is always scary. I think the more important thing is who you have in it to help you through it. I know my life is fuller now because of them."

"You're very insightful, Chase. I'm glad I got this chance to get to know you better."

"Yeah, you too. And listen, if I act differently after this, it's just because it's hard to be vulnerable."

"Oh, sure."

I relaxed at her acceptance, not wanting to set Chase up for failure. We drank the rest of our tea in silence for a while. I wasn't sure why Victoria had fallen silent, and I was kicking myself for being so different from the real Chase and potentially making it awkward for him. When nothing but leaves remained in our teacups, we grabbed our coats and started to walk back toward campus.

"I think I'm going to do it," she said eventually. "You've given me the courage to pave my own way, and I'm going to take it."

"Wow, that's awesome. I'm glad I could be helpful."

"You really were. I'm glad we did this. I feel like we're better friends now. I'm happy I got to before we all left school."

"Me too, me too."

Something in my chest tingled at the feeling, the sound of

bells ringing in the air, and I wondered what the sensation meant. I didn't get the chance to explore since the next second I spotted Aggie, and she winked before snapping her fingers. I prayed I'd learned what I needed to send me back to my body and timeline. But most importantly, to my BOSH boys.

# three

. . .

Sawyer

THIS TIME when she transported me, it was thankfully back
to my own body and bed. Gasping, I sat up with a start, relief
washing through me at the familiar bedding and surroundings. A shadow moved in the corner, and I swiveled, the
momentum causing me to almost fall out of bed. Thankfully,
an arm wrapped around me, pulling me back down to safety.

"Babe? You feeling better?" A sleepy Soren mumbled,
cracking his eyes open at me. I was so excited to see him, I
bent down, kissing him passionately for a minute. He took
my kiss as my answer and rolled me under him.

"I'm gonna take that as a yes," he confirmed when he
pulled away. His eyes lit up, his blonde hair falling down
around his face as he stared down at me in delight. I tucked
the hair back behind his ears, the tresses touching his shoulders now.

"I like your hair this length. Gives me something to grab onto."

He raised his eyebrow, his pupils dilating at the thought, and he thrust his lower half into me. "Is that so?"

Soren bent down to nibble my neck when the pain returned, and I grimaced. "Ow, ow, ow."

He moved off me at lightning speed, and I rolled into a ball, clutching my stomach. "Shit, this pain makes me almost not want to have sex ever again. Ugh, I have to pee, and if it hurts again, I'm cursing you all!"

Soren only chuckled, not taking my threat seriously before he scooped me up and carried me to the bathroom. "Thanks, but there's no way you're staying in here."

"No worries, sweet pea. Golden showers aren't my thing. Yell if you need anything, though. I'm sorry you're going through this. I'll get you some water and meds for when you're out."

Nodding, I gave him a brief grimace before the door closed. Bracing for the pain, I gritted my teeth as I emptied my bladder. It wasn't as painful as the first time, but it wasn't a walk in the park either. Washing my hands, I was relieved when I found my green eyes, blonde hair, and no facial hair staring back at me. I'd assumed I'd returned to myself when Soren hadn't freaked out when he was making out with a 6ft bearded guy, but then again, he was pansexual, so he loved me for who I was as a person and not my gender. That was comforting, actually.

Still, it was nice to have my body back, short stature and

all. "It'd been nice being 6ft tall, Chase. Hope I didn't screw anything up for you."

With that, I exited and found a lot more people in my room than when I'd left it. "You're all courageous to show your faces after I just had to breathe through peeing," I pouted.

"Love, we feel awful, so we're here to cheer you up. A whole day where you can decide what you want to do. If you're feeling up to it." Elias looked at me, the challenge thinly threaded through his words, the familiar fire burning inside, and not in my vagina this time.

"Hmm, I might be up for it. My fever appears to be gone, though it made me have the craziest dream. You guys won't believe it."

"I once dreamt I had tiny hands like a T-rex," Ollie stated, demonstrating as he tried to grope his boyfriend, Ty, making us all chuckle.

"Well, I don't know what it means," I admitted, walking over and sitting on the bed, "but mine was weirder."

"How so? I'm impressed you remember it too," Henry asked.

I turned to him, and he pulled me closer. "I woke up in a boy's body and back in time. I got to meet my biological parents and Victoria as teenagers. I'm guessing the combination of reading her journal and watching old Christmas movies." I shrugged, not wanting to admit I didn't think it was only just a dream. It had felt so real. But, even if it was all a fever-induced delusion, it was nice to see my mom again.

"Wow, that's pretty out there," one of them said, but I

snuggled into Henry, not caring. I fell asleep again with the hope I wouldn't wake up in a different person's body.

Thankfully, when I woke up later, I was still me. After another dose of antibiotics, I felt back to my usual self and took the guys up on doing something. I really wanted to go to the ice castles, but they wouldn't be open until January, so we added it to our excursion list for next year.

Instead, I found myself staring at a 1,200 ft wide lane of snow, on top of a mountain, as people careened down it in colorful tubes. "This was a bad idea."

"You're not scared, are you, *Dulzura*?" Mateo pulled me closer to him, my sweet, nerdy boyfriend having stayed by my side.

"Um, maybe, a little."

"You'll do great. You've skied. This will be even easier."

"Yeah, you're right. It just seems so much faster."

"Yeah, but I think you'll love it. Come on, it's our turn."

He tugged on my hand, pulling me toward the front, our tubes dragging behind us. I watched as a few of the guys took off, heading down the slope. Swallowing my fear, I nodded, and we dropped our hands and grabbed the handles of our tubes.

"Belly?"

"Belly," I agreed. Smiling, I faced the front, and we counted together. "One, two, three." We took off, jogging a few feet before we launched ourselves into the air. A scream ripped from my lungs, the rush of the exhilaration filtering through me as we flew. With a thump, we landed close together, skidding a few feet as our momentum took us sliding through the snow.

Laughing, I turned my head to see Mateo. "Okay, this is awesome." He smiled, and I returned to paying attention to where I was headed, not wanting to run into anyone. That would so be my luck.

Rhett and Elias were waiting at the bottom, and I heard the other four behind me. Rhett bent down when I stopped, scooping me up. I would never get over him doing that. "You have fun, baby?"

"I did! Let's go again."

"Smalls, we gotta do the two-person one, or all go in tandem!" Henry shouted as he and Soren came to a stop. Ollie and Ty were behind them a few seconds later, and we all headed to the lifts together. We spent the next few hours taking turns, trading off who went down the slope. By the time we left, we were all smiles and worn out.

Ty held my hand as we waited for Rhett to pull the car up. It was dark now, the sun having set off in the distance. The mountain was lit up with lights allowing tubers to continue to sled.

"Today was a lot of fun, wildcat."

Tilting my head up, I smiled wide as I agreed. He bent down, kissing my nose, and I couldn't help the blush that rose to my cheeks. Ty was so sweet at times, and he made me feel all the butterflies. Arms wrapped around from behind me, encasing us both, and I looked up to see Ollie.

"Hey boyfriend," I cooed, loving how much Ollie had changed since he'd told us about his family.

"Hey girlfriend, hey boyfriend," he sang back. He reached over my head, kissing Ty before looking back at me. For a second, I'd been completely enclosed in their arms, like a Ty & Ollie igloo and it was nice.

"So, I was thinking," Ollie started, and Ty and I groaned. "Hey! Not all my ideas are bad." Ollie attempted to pout, but he couldn't pull it off. Mainly because he couldn't stop his own laugh from bubbling up. "Anyway," he continued, ignoring us, "we should have a party at the house. But make it like a Christmas extravaganza. We'll have a bunch of contests. Cookie baking, gingerbread house making, snowman creating, Christmas charades, ornament decorating, and oh, we'll end it with a Secret Santa party!"

I looked at Ty, and he had the same look of disbelief as I did on my face. "What's the catch, because all that sounds fun?"

Ollie looked down at me, a twinkle in his eyes, and I knew this was where the twist would be. I didn't think Ollie could do anything without making it into something extreme. "Ye of little faith, Sawyer." His grin did not go away, though, and instead, it spread wider, and I wondered what the hell he was up to. If I knew Oliver Windsor as well as I thought I did, he'd wait until we were all gathered and agreeing to it before he dropped the bomb on us. I guess he'd learned that trick from his family and the training through the Council.

Hopefully, he would use it for good and not to embarrass me, one of his favorite pastimes. I did that well enough on my own.

It had been a whole week since the body switch and UTI fiasco. I was officially through all my antibiotics, and it no longer burned when I peed, thankfully. As much as I said I wasn't ever going anywhere near their dicks again, the week of no sex was getting to me. At first, the guys were respectful and kept their distance. But once I'd been back to basic working order, their touch hazing began.

And it was hazing, no matter how they tried to spin it.

They were all slowly driving me mad with the torture. It had been almost a full week of nothing but edging! In the beginning, I hadn't noticed. Their casual grazes seemed innocent and nothing out of the ordinary. But by mid-week, they'd dropped all pretense and were straight out revving me up and then backing away. Each and every single one of them, even my sweet Mateo.

"You've been corrupted, Mateo," I panted as he casually passed his hand over my center as he nonchalantly took some popcorn from the bowl. Which was nowhere near my vagina, mind you.

"*Oh*? Whatever do you mean, *Dulzura*?"

"Don't you dare '*Dulzura*' me! What's going on? Either you've all gone crazy from no sex for a week, or there's something to be won by edging me this hard. Though, I wouldn't put it past Ollie or Soren whispering in your ear either."

His hand stopped midway to his mouth, and he glanced at me, gulping. "Uh, Wh-aa-tt?"

"Ha! I knew it!" I jumped up and straddled him, knocking the popcorn to the floor, not caring if it scattered everywhere. "Two can play this game, babe. So, what's it going to be? Are you going to tell me, or will I have to torture it out of you?"

"I don't know what you're talking about," he hedged, but I saw the way his Adam's apple bobbed as he swallowed, along with his cock hardening beneath me. Leaning down, I nipped his ear before whispering into it.

"You really want to play this game, *Teo*?" I rocked into him, and his breath caught on a gasp in his throat. His hands planted firmly on my hips, and he didn't stop me as I rocked again before pulling back. I'd started to call him Teo in moments when we were alone, and I found he liked it, his dick thickening even more as I pressed into it.

Heat seared me from his eyes, his glasses a little skewed from the movement. Slowly, I began to lift my shirt over my head, my breasts on display right in front of him, and he groaned. Taking his hands from my hips, I placed them on the mounds, encouraging him to explore. Mateo had come a long way in the time we'd been together, but sometimes he was still shy until we were in the heat of the moment.

"Sawyer, you're the most beautiful woman I've ever seen. Some days, I pinch myself to make sure I'm not dreaming, but there's no way my imagination is this creative."

He leaned forward, his breath skirting my skin, and my

nipple pebbled at the sensation. I ran my fingers through his hair, loving how curly it was becoming. All of my guys had the best hair, and I wouldn't admit I was half jealous of it. The silky strands fell through my fingers, and I pressed the tips of them into his scalp, alternating pressure. Mateo groaned, the vibration echoing around my breast in the process, and I rocked forward, needing some friction.

"You ready to tell me?" I knew I wasn't being fair as my hand skirted down his chest, but they'd been touching me all week and then leaving me hanging. I'd use my womanly wiles if it got me both the D and information. When my hand grazed his jeans, I rubbed the length of him, and his breath hitched more. In his excitement, he bit my nipple, and I was the one moaning this time.

"Oh, God."

The need in me rose to a new level, and I no longer cared about information. I just needed him in me. Slipping my hand down his pants, I found his cock ready, and began to stroke. He was hard as steel, his head falling back as I stroked him. Unzipping his pants, I freed him, giving his dick a few good strokes.

"*Dulzura*," he moaned, his fingers tightening on my hips where they'd returned to.

Lifting up on my knees, I pushed my sleep shorts over and lowered myself on him. When he felt me start to slide down, his head snapped up, hunger in his eyes. Mateo's fingers tightened on my hips, and he pulled me the rest of the way down. Together, we moaned at the connection, both needing it. Kissing him, I mussed his hair as my arms tangled around his head, pulling us closer, knocking his glasses off in the process.

Mateo took over, thrusting up as we worked together to climax, our breaths panting out between kisses. When he bent down to kiss my neck, I opened my eyes and found a grinning Soren to the side of the couch. Feeling extra needy, I beckoned him to me as Mateo used my ass to direct me. He'd at least gotten comfortable around a few of the guys by this point, Soren and Henry being the ones he felt the closest to, so I didn't think he'd care if he joined in. Leaning forward, I whispered in his ear, making sure it was okay.

"Soren's here. Care if he joins?"

He lifted his head slightly, looking over my shoulder, shaking his head no. Soren took it as the all-clear and began to strip as he moved closer. An idea sprung to my mind, and I wondered if Mateo would be game.

"Teo, feel like checking off another thing on your sex bucket list?"

He smiled, trusting me to guide him. "If it's with you, I'm always willing."

This sweet boy, he killed me sometimes with how pure he could be. Cupping his face, I spread my thumb over his cheek, just enjoying the moment between us for a second. His eyes closed at the touch, his lashes fluttering against his cheeks. He had the most beautiful long lashes. Kissing his nose, I slowly slipped off him and discarded my clothes entirely.

Soren's hand fell to my hips, his cock jutting between my ass, the piercing rubbing me there. Instinctively, I arched my back at the feel of him. Pulling his head down, I wrapped my arm around the back of his neck so I could whisper into his ear. "Let's help Mateo pop his anal cherry... with *me*."

Soren lifted his head, a smile on his face at the idea. He kissed my shoulder and pulled away to hopefully grab some lube. Mateo had chucked his jeans and shirt, his lean body on display as he watched me walk toward him. He had a way of making you feel like every time was the first time and that he would never get enough. It was addictive and something I hoped he never lost.

Reaching out a hand, I pulled him to his feet, our naked bodies touching as he came closer. "I think it's time you claim the last hole." His eyes grew big, but he nodded, a smile forming.

Soren returned and picked me up, throwing me over his shoulder, surprising me at the swiftness. "Ah! Soren!"

"I got you, sweet pea." He tossed the bottle of lube to Mateo and laid down on the couch, pulling me with him. Snuggling in close, I kissed his neck, his golden skin a tempting sight. I knew Mateo had to be nervous, so I focused on Soren but lifted my ass up, so Mateo could reach me.

His hand shook at first, but when I didn't back away, he kept exploring, letting his fingers dip into my wetness, plunging his fingers deep while I made out with my golden sunshine boyfriend. Tentatively, he began to spread my hole, using my own juices to lubricate and prepare. I lost myself in kissing Soren, his cock piercing rubbing against my clit with each rocking forward. I heard Mateo's breath as he started to push forward, and I tried to stay still, giving him what he needed. I moaned out, the pressure finally beginning to satiate the need I've felt all week.

When he was seated, he groaned, his hands stilling on my hips. Lifting my head, I peeked over my shoulder, and I found him breathing heavily, his eyes closed. "You okay, Teo?"

"So good."

Giggling, I wasn't prepared for when Soren decided to slide into me from the front, his piercing rubbing me in all the best ways as he did. My giggle morphed into a moan, and I fell back to Soren's chest, letting them hold me up at this point. They began to move together, finding a rhythm, and it was everything I'd been needing. It didn't take me long, the orgasm having built to a precipice for a while, and I fell over the edge, bursting into a cacophony of tingles. When I opened my eyes, I was surprised to find Henry had joined us.

He winked at me, then bent down to kiss me, all the while thrusting his dick in Soren's mouth. Every time I saw those two together, I simultaneously melted and became aroused. I loved the love they held for one another, their connection genuine.

"I love you, Smalls," he whispered, pulling back from the kiss.

As the three of them worked, I found myself beginning to rise up again. The air smelled of sex, our bodies slapping together in the most delicious ways, our moment full of love and heat. I knew without a doubt I loved all three of them. Each time we were together, it wasn't just a carnal thing, but a declaration of our love for one another too.

I could tell they were close now, and when Mateo banded his arm around my midsection and pulled me closer to him, I knew he was about to cum. He kissed me quick, staring into my eyes as he thrust deep once and stalled. The hand on my hip tightened as he spilled inside of me, and I watched as he came undone.

Soren thrust up, hitting me in the best way, and I tipped over quickly, the feeling so exhilarating, it felt like I was falling. A minute later, Henry's groan followed, and our bodies stilled, nothing but the sound of our breaths in the room. When I opened my eyes, I realized I was on the floor. I looked around, the guys a mess of tangled limbs with me. They all laughed at my confused expression.

"I thought we were on the couch?"

"We were, Smalls. Somehow when you and Soren came, your body trembled so much from the orgasm that it tilted us over the edge.

"Huh, so I guess when it felt like I fell, I was really falling."

They burst out laughing with me, the moment too light-hearted not to. As our laughter died down, I heard someone coming closer to where we all were. None of us had the energy to move though and we'd all seen each other naked, so we weren't concerned at the moment.

However, when a screech rang out, I knew the day had finally come. Finley had walked in on her brother post-sex.

"No, no, no! Shit balls! I did not need to see my brother's balls! I'm scarred for life. I need some brain bleach!"

"It could be worse, Fin," I started, sitting up. "He could've been balls deep in me." She lifted her hand a smidge to glare at me. Her eyes were squinted so hard, I didn't know how she even saw me.

"That is not funny, Sawyer Sullivan! Don't forget I can get you back. I'm dating your brother too, after all."

Cringing, I held up my hands, not wanting to picture that. We might have only known we were siblings for a few months, but no one wanted to see their twin's balls.

"How about we all get dressed and quit talking about balls," Henry grumbled, not keen on his sister talking about sex. She stuck her tongue out at him, even with her hands still covering her eyes. I hoped to get to their level one day with Asa.

"Speaking of balls," Soren started, and we all groaned. "What? I was going to suggest making some coconut ones." He cheesed, and I rolled my eyes, not buying it.

We all dressed and joined Finley in the kitchen, where she told us why she'd come over as we made coconut balls. Apparently, there was a rival party on the same night as ours, and she wanted to rally, making ours the best. Throughout the night, I never remembered to get Mateo to tell me what they were planning.

# four

. . .

Sawyer

THE NEXT TIME the crazy Freaky Friday thing occurred, I was walking through town with Elias. One minute I was enjoying my hot chocolate and holding his hand; the next, I was slipping on ice. My foot went up, my momentum sending me backward, but I never hit the ground. Instead, I landed on a bed. A very soft bed, in fact.

Feeling the sheets, they were silky, and the texture felt nice under my hands as my fingernails dragged across them. The realization I had nails, something I never had in real life, had me bringing my hand in front of my face. Except, I couldn't see. Or well, I could see, but it was blurry. Sitting up, I couldn't make out anything else in the room; it was all blobs and muted colors.

Glancing around, I found a nightstand close by, and I reached out, hoping to find some glasses, assuming I'd woken up in the body of someone who was practically blind.

I really should've paid more attention to Mateo when he woke up because as I reached out to find the object, I knocked it off, sending it to the floor.

Fucking great.

Throwing my legs to the side of the bed, I tentatively placed my feet down on the ground, making sure I didn't step on them. When it was free of objects, I put the rest of my weight down and stood. Squatting, I started to feel around for the glasses, excited when my hand connected with them. Pulling them up, I placed them on my face, and the room finally came into focus.

It looked like a hotel room, and I wondered where I was this time. Standing, I looked for any signs of my where-abouts. There was a notepad on the floor next to the night-stand I'd knocked the glasses off. I picked it up and sighed in relief. I was still in Oak Crest Peak. In fact, I was at Rhett's mom's B&B. An awkward thought entered my head, and I rushed to the door in my room, hoping it was a bathroom. When I saw my reflection in the mirror, I relaxed. Phew! I hadn't woken up as my future mother-in-law or sister-in-law. That would've been hella awkward.

Instead, I was a woman with dark hair, average height and body, and wearing a pink silk pajama camisole and short set. The glasses I'd found sat crooked on my nose, and I straightened them, remembering the nails. Looking down at my hand, I took in the beautiful french manicure with a little diamond on the ring fingers.

The door opening from the other side had me turning in shock as a man, a very familiar and bare-chested man, entered. He was rubbing his eyes, so he hadn't seen me yet. He was only partially dressed with a pair of lounge pants on, but I was thankful he was at least wearing them. Thankfully, they weren't the grey sweatpants my guys wore that I drooled over. I'd be upset if *those* had been ruined for me.

"Mr. Hawthorne!" I screeched, covering my eyes. I heard him stop, and I peeked through my fingers, finding him gaping at me.

"Gwen, apologies, the door wasn't locked. Let me know when you're finished."

He spun, shutting the door behind him, and I found myself breathing a sigh of relief again. Well, at least some things had been cleared up for me. I was someone named Gwen and staying in a joint suite with Mr. Logan Hawthorne. Logan appeared to be the common denominator from my previous body-switching experience so far.

Using the bathroom quickly, I knocked on his door and then scurried out of mine, closing it behind me. I heard the other side open a few seconds later, and I stepped away, not wanting to eavesdrop while my pseudo-uncle relieved himself. In fact, I should get dressed and figure out what year I was in and see if I could manage to get Aggie to show.

Pulling open the wardrobe on the far wall, I found it full of fashionable dresses. Whoever Gwen was, she had style. Selecting a deep red sheath dress, I found a drawer of under-garments and hosiery. Screwing up my nose at the hose, I decided to brave it without. Seriously, those things were evil. Sorry, Gwen.

I ignored the idea I was wearing someone else's underoos

713

because, actually, Gwen's body was the one wearing them, not mine, so it was only a mental thing. When I heard the shower turn off in the bathroom, I waited a few minutes until I heard his door open and close.

"No courtesy knock, huh, Logan?"

Popping my head in, I checked it was clear and made sure to lock the other door this time. Quickly, I got ready, styling my hair as best as I could and applying the makeup as professionally as I was able. Finley always helped me with this stuff, so without her here, I was lost. "Sorry, Gwen," I muttered again, cringing.

Unlocking the door on Logan's side, I hurried out of the bathroom again and exited the other door. I was brought out into a sitting room area and found Mr. Hawthorne sitting at a table, drinking a cup of coffee. I didn't know how to act; I wasn't sure who I was to him. As far as I knew, he was single, but again, I didn't know what year it was. I should've looked for a phone while I'd been in the room. I turned to go back and look when he called out, stopping me.

"Gwen, everything okay? You seem a little off this morning?"

Spinning, I gawked at him, not sure what to say. "I, um, just didn't sleep well. That's all. I'm gonna grab my phone." I pointed back toward my room, hoping what I'd said wasn't too out there like last time.

He raised his eyebrow at me, and I froze, scared I'd stepped in it again. "I mean," I started, backpedaling.

"It's over here, where I told you to leave it last night so you wouldn't work."

"Right, you did say that."

Walking toward it, I tried to hide my face, the heat rising to the surface at making a fool of myself in front of him, even if he didn't know it was really me. Every moment in this man's presence had been weird. I'd verbally assaulted him the first time I ever met him, the second he'd watched me almost shoot his cousin, and the third had been when I had a UTI. Between waking up as his roommate in the past, and his pseudo roommate whenever this was, I was beginning to suspect my assumption it was connected to him was true.

I spotted the familiar device on the console table, and I sighed in relief at recognizing the model. It had to be around the same time as my own. Unplugging it, I clicked on the calendar and relaxed when I found I was still in the year 2020. Okay, so same year, different body. Not as horrible to deal with.

Scrolling through the phone, I tried to figure out just who I was to the man. I started with pictures, but Gwen didn't have much in her albums besides photos of a fluffy white cat, shoes, and dresses. Next, I clicked on her messages, but they were mostly from Logan about work and people who appeared to be her family. Okay, so she must work with, or for Mr. Hawthorne.

The problem was, I had no clue what he did other than take down corrupt agencies. A knock on the door had me jumping, but I recovered and walked over to it. When I opened it, I had to restrain myself from hugging the woman standing there.

"Good morning, Ms. Norton. I wanted to check that you

and Mr. Hawthorne had a good evening and if you needed anything else from me today?"

"Oh, it was wonderful, thank you."

"Excellent. Will there be any special meal requests or requirements this evening?"

"Um," I stuttered, turning my head, peering at Logan, who gazed at me, an odd expression on his face. "Any special requests?"

"You know all my preferences, Gwen. That's why you're my assistant."

"Right, yes, that." I nodded, pointing a finger in acknowledgment.

Glancing back at Rhonda, I tried to hide the grimace, and stepped out into the hall, pulling the door behind me. "I'll have to get back with you. I'm having a little bit of a memory issue this morning, and nothing is ringing a bell."

"Okay, dear. Just let me know."

She patted my hand, the familiar gesture making me calm even if she didn't know it was me. Tapping the phone in my hand, I wondered if Gwen took notes on things. I opened it up to search when a ghost of Charlie appeared directly in front of me.

"Oh, God!" I gasped, clutching my chest as I stepped back, hitting the wall. Rhonda stopped, looking back at me in concern, her face worried as her eyes creased.

"You okay, dear?"

"Yes, sorry, thought I saw a spider, but it was just a shadow," I said, awkwardly chuckling. "I'm good."

"Okay." She accepted my response, but walked off, giving me furtive glances as she did.

Once she was gone, I gave my former guardian the stink eye. "What do you think you're doing, old man?"

"Waiting until you were dressed and away from spectators, Sawdust. I didn't particularly want to walk in on you, you know." He waved his hand up and down, and I cringed at the thought, even if it wasn't really me.

"Yeah, okay. Good call. But what are you doing here? What's going on? I thought I was hallucinating when Aggie visited, but now you too? Am I secretly in a coma somewhere?"

"No, Sawdust, you're just experiencing reality from a different perspective."

"Thanks, that clears it up so much," I deadpanned, leveling him with a look that clearly stated I wasn't buying it. I started to ask a question when the door opened, and Logan looked at me strangely.

"Who are you talking to?" he asked, looking up and down the hallway.

"Oh, just taking some dictation notes." I waved the phone in front of his face, my smile a bit manic, but I was struggling to keep it together.

"Are you sure you're okay, Gwen? You're acting strangely."

"Totes, fine." I cringed as soon as the words left my mouth, but I owned it, walking back into the room. Wonderful. Charlie had given me no info on what I needed to do to get out of here, and I was stuck with a man that gave me hives. And this time, I wouldn't have either of my mothers here to distract me.

Sitting down at the table, I buttered a croissant and stuffed it in my mouth. Chewing, I turned to Logan, who had a piece of bread held halfway to his mouth, gaping at me.

"What?" I mumbled, then remembered I had food in it. Grabbing some coffee, I filled a cup and swallowed, turning to look at him again. "Something on my face?"

He cleared his throat, shutting his mouth as he shook his head. "No, sorry. It's just, I don't think I've ever seen you eat carbs before."

Looking at the croissant in my hand, I almost pouted at the thought of not getting to enjoy it. I didn't want to disrespect Gwen's body, but maybe she deserved a day where she got to eat a carb. Shrugging, I finished the croissant, enjoying every last bite. Logan cleared his throat, and I turned to him, hoping he'd give me some information on what in the world I was supposed to do here.

"Are you ready for our meeting?"

Swallowing, I nodded, wiping my hands on the napkin. "Yes, um, let me grab my things real quick."

He tilted his head slightly, the stoic man watching me closely, and I tried to get up from the table gracefully and walk back to the room without falling on my face. When I shut the door, I sighed back against it. Charlie needed to get his ghost butt in here and tell me what the fuck was going on.

"Charlie," I whispered. When he didn't appear, I hissed it, "*Charlie.*" Still nothing. Stomping my foot, I let the expletives rip. "Old man! Get your ass in here, pronto. I'm not naked, and I need your help. Aggie was such a better ghost friend than you! Is there a Ghost HR I can complain to?"

He finally popped up, right in front of my face, the turd! Jumping back, I knocked my head on the door. "Ow."

Charlie crossed his ghost arms smugly and dared me to say anything. "You *rang*?"

"Don't give me any of that crap, sir! Now, do your mojo thing and tell me what the heck I'm supposed to do! I can't ruin this woman's life."

He rolled his eyes but snapped his fingers, and I was transported to a conference room. Seriously! I was going to have to talk with him about his attitude. Thankfully, I didn't make any noise when I came to my awareness and peered around the room. I checked the phone in my hand and realized a few hours had passed. Logan was sitting at the long conference table, scribbling some notes down in a leather portfolio. He looked up and found me watching him.

"Gwen, did you hear me? My next appointment is here."

"Yes, sir, sorry."

Standing, I smoothed the dress material down and started for the door, hoping it would be obvious where I needed to go and grab this visitor. Thankfully, there were only a few other doors and an open area for a lobby when I exited. A man stood in a suit looking at the wall, so I hoped he was the one I was meant to get.

"Sir?"

He turned, and I almost tripped over myself when it was Elias. He looked so handsome in his attire. He smiled at me when I said his name and walked toward me.

"Gwen, so good to see you." He reached out to grab my hand, and I mistook it and hugged him. Awkwardly. He patted my back, but I found it hard to let him go. He cleared his throat, and I pulled back, my face flaming.

"Um, sorry. Christmas cheer and all that. This way," I blurted, spinning toward the door.

He tilted his head oddly at me but thankfully didn't comment. I berated myself to get it together as we made our way into the conference room. I'd been hopeful when I saw him, thinking it would give me some clues why I was Gwen, but as they started talking about business, I found myself zoning out. Shit. I was going to get this woman fired! Focusing back in, I tried to listen to what they were saying. When I heard my name, I perked up.

"How's Sawyer doing?" Logan asked.

"She's good. Still adjusting, but she's on the mend."

"That's good, that's good."

"Are you going to attend the Christmas party?" Elias asked, watching his mentor.

"Oh, no. I don't think I'll have time." Logan cleared his throat and began to pick up papers, avoiding Elias. Okay, this was interesting.

"You sure you're not just avoiding getting to know her?"

"What would ever make you think that, Elias?" Logan smirked.

"Oh, I don't know, Mr. Hawthorne, the fact you seem to be avoiding getting to know her."

"She doesn't want to get to know me. I'm no one to her. I was in love with her adoptive mother, but I failed them both in the end. I can't believe Alec had her, I—" he stopped, taking a breath. He looked up at Elias, searing him with a sharp look. "I gave her the journal. There's not much more I can do. I'm not going to force myself on her. She's already had that done by too many others."

"Hmm, that sounds admirable, sir, in theory. But I know for a fact, Sawyer doesn't realize how much you've looked out for her and how you kept her off the Council's radar for those five years she was in Iowa. Or how you faked her death to provide her with that reprieve."

I sucked in a breath. Elias was right. I had no idea Logan had been so instrumental in my life. I knew Samson had interfered; his role had been easy to identify, but this. I didn't know what to think. He was a stranger to me, but it seemed I meant a great deal to him, or at least my mother had.

"It doesn't matter, Elias."

"If you say so, sir." He gathered his stuff, and I wanted to follow him out and ask him about us; if everything else in this reality was the same. But I stayed put, the temptation was too great and I didn't want to mess up anything.

"Gwen?"

Looking up, I found Logan staring at me expectantly. "Yes, sir?"

"I asked if you were ready to head out?"

"Oh, yes." I stood, gathering the few things around me I hoped were Gwen's and followed him out of the room. I spotted Charlie leaning his ghost body on the counter, and when he saw me, he snapped his fingers, winking, and I was teleported again. He was getting coal this year, for sure!

When I opened my eyes, I found us at what appeared to be a children's home. Logan was standing next to me in the corner, his arms crossed as he watched the children talk to Santa. An older woman with grey hair walked over, a big smile on her face, grasping his arm when she was close.

"Mr. Hawthorne, we can't thank you enough for all you've done for us. The kids are having a wonderful Christmas. Are you sure I can't announce you so they can all tell you thanks?"

He shook his head no. "That's not necessary. I'm glad they're having a good Christmas, though, and I enjoy seeing them happy. That's the only thanks I need. Please let my assistant know if you need anything else in the upcoming year."

"Of course, Mr. Hawthorne. Have a Merry Christmas."

He titled his head once and headed for the door. I followed, smiling at the woman who patted me on the arm as I passed. "He's a good man. Take care of him."

I nodded, not sure how to take what she was saying. When I went out the door, the cold air whipped around me, and I cursed myself for not wearing the hosiery now and scurried to the car that was waiting. Logan was standing next to the door, holding it open for me. I scooted in, and he followed me, the car taking off as soon as his door closed.

"We have two more places to go, and then you can have the rest of the night off, Gwen."

I nodded, not sure what to say. He peered out the window, lost in his own world. We ended up going to a children's ward and a soup kitchen. Each visit, he refused to be acknowledged but enjoyed watching the people getting to celebrate the holiday. At the last place, a woman walked up to him, taking his hand.

"Mr. Hawthorne. I just wanted to thank you for your assistance in getting the city to back down on the closure of this place. You really were the Hail Mary we needed."

"Of course, Sherry. It's what I do, after all."

"Well, you went above and beyond. We wouldn't be able to help all these families without you."

"I'm just glad you're enjoying the holiday. Please let me know if you need anything else, but you shouldn't be hearing from them anymore."

"Thank you. Merry Christmas, Mr. Hawthorne."

He tilted his head again, not saying anything as he set off toward the door. I followed him closely, information rolling through my head. "You paid off the city, didn't you?"

"I don't know what you mean, Gwen. I met with them and renegotiated the terms. That's all."

"Mmhmm."

He kept walking, dropping the subject. I still didn't know what I was meant to do here, but I was learning a lot about the enigma that was Mr. Hawthorne. Logan did a lot for people but never wanted the credit for it. And yet, he seemed lonely. I wondered how much he'd closed himself off after my mother's disappearance from his life, the knowledge of her death another burden he carried.

The car pulled up to the B&B, and he made no move to get out but turned to me when I didn't either.

"You're free to go for the evening, Gwen. It's Christmas

Eve, go and spend it with your friends. I know you have plans."

I nodded but stopped. "What about you, Mr. Hawthorne?"

"I'll be fine."

I opened the door and stepped out of the car, turning before I closed the door. "Merry Christmas, Logan."

He looked up but didn't say anything, and I shut the door. It took off as soon as I was clear from it, and I wasn't surprised when I found Charlie standing next to me. He had a sad look on his face as he watched the car disappear. He held out his arm this time for me, looking at it for me to take.

"You'll want to hold on for this one."

The moment my hand touched his ghostly arm, we were transported to a cemetery. At least, I no longer felt the cold, and I wondered if I was now a ghost version of myself. When we stopped next to where the black car I'd just exited was rolling to a stop, I figured I'd guessed right.

Logan stepped out, a bundle of white roses in his arms as he made his way toward a grave. Charlie nodded for me to follow. Cautiously, I did, despite not needing to be quiet since he couldn't see me. Something about being in the cemetery made me want to be, though, in order to respect the sanctity of this place.

When he came to a stop in front of a new headstone, I had a pretty good guess who it was for. I wondered when he had this done and why he hadn't told me. He placed one rose on top of the stone and the rest at the foot. He crouched down, brushing the snow off so he could read it.

"Hey Tori, I hope you like your new resting place. I finally got the call today that the stone was here. I'll tell Sawyer tomorrow, but selfishly, I wanted to be the first to see you. You'd be so proud of the daughter you've raised. She reminds me so much of you. It almost makes me feel twenty years younger. Some days I wish we were, and all the different choices I could've made were still out in front of me. But I know that's unfair. Our paths were the ones we were meant to take, even if I don't like how they ended. I miss you, and I'm sorry that in the end, I wasn't able to save you too. I hope I can at least make it up to you by keeping her safe."

Tears rolled down my face, and ghost Charlie patted my back, handing me an invisible handkerchief. When I gave it back, he placed his arm out, and we were transported again. This time it was back in the B&B. Logan sat in front of a fire, a tumbler of whiskey in his hand, the lights off. I could hear the TV, a newscaster giving the weather report.

"It's going to be a cold Christmas, but the snow will be perfect for everyone's Christmas sledding or skiing activities."

"He's alone on Christmas?" I asked, looking up to Charlie. He nodded, placing his hand over mine.

"He's always alone."

With that, he winked, and I was whisked away again. This time, when I landed, my back hit the snow as I was transported back into my body.

# five

## Sawyer

"AND SHE'S DOWN!" I blinked, trying to orient myself to the world around me. Snow fell around me as I laid in it, the cold, wet feeling beginning to absorb through my layers. A face appeared above me, his sparkling chocolate eyes shining down on me.

"You okay, baby?"

"Mmhmm. I think so."

"You got hit with that snowball pretty hard."

Rhett reached down, lifting me, and setting me on my feet, brushing the snow off. I blinked again, trying to align myself back to my time frame. A tear escaped, the remnants of the last thing I'd seen with Logan hitting me. Rhett wiped it away, squatting down to my height to look at me.

"Sawyer, are you okay? Did you get hurt?"

"I'm fine. Just emotional, sorry."

"You don't have to apologize, baby. Is this too much too soon?" he asked, but before I could answer he continued to mutter under his breath. "I knew this would be a bad idea. I should've told them all no." Rhett carried on for a few minutes this way, including several methods of how he wanted to maim Ollie, concluding in me giggling at his creativity.

"No, I promise," I assured, cupping his face."I've just been thinking a lot about Victoria. I've been reading her journal, and it's made me feel closer to her, but it's also made me miss her more, you know?"

Rhett nodded, rubbing his face against my gloved hand. "Yeah, baby, I get that."

"And, well, it's made me wonder about Logan. He was important to her, and he helped save us all. Maybe I should get to know him more. I feel like he might be alone." I bit my lip, not wanting to admit I knew the truth, that he was alone.

I was still having a hard time reconciling the time jumps to reality. I could easily explain away the first one, the weird cider and medication making it plausible as a dream. But now, I had no idea how I could walk, drink hot chocolate, slip on ice, and then wake up in the snow? This time it felt like I'd missed a whole day.

The rest of the guys came over when they realized we weren't joining back in the massive snowball fight I'd apparently woken myself in.

"Sawyer? You okay?" Soren asked, a little out of breath as he looked me over in concern.

"Yeah, fine."

"Let's head inside, guys. I think that's enough practice for today."

"Practice?" I asked but then immediately regretted it when everyone looked at me in concern.

"Alright, Smalls, let's go. Coach Maggie will kill me if we miss any more practices since we have an invitational coming up next month."

I nodded absently, following them all inside. Finley was there baking with my brother, Asa, when we entered the kitchen.

"Sawyer, save me! Your best friend is a cookie nightmare!" He cringed, as Fin laughed, swatting him in jest.

"Ah, you've been introduced to Finley 'bossy pants' Reyes?"

"Hey! I'm not bossy! I just happen to want things a certain way. There's nothing wrong with that," she huffed, planting her hands on her hips. I watched as she joked, all smiles, but I saw the strain behind it and wondered if I'd pushed my best friend too far.

"You're right, Fin. You're amazing."

She smiled, but I could still see a little anxiety around the edges, and I wanted to kick myself. I needed to check in with my friend to make sure I hadn't screwed anything up between us. Since she'd been taken and drugged, Fin had been maintaining that she was fine and hadn't skipped a beat, and we all let her. She was so good at showcasing what we wanted to see, I forgot how she dealt with difficult things.

She didn't. Fin was an avoider, and tended to bury things, thinking it would go away if she ignored it. I knew from experience how that strategy never worked. I'd have to steal her away and go to the ice cream place Asa had taken me. Nobody could be sad when eating sprinkles. Plus, the woman's magic at guessing the perfect combination was too awesome to miss out on.

"How did your practice go?" she asked, changing the subject.

"Good until Sawyer got hit in the face with a snowball."

"Who do I need to beat up?" she huffed, narrowing her eyes at the guys. Laughing, I walked over and hugged my bestie, glad to have her back in my life after five years. Her arms wrapped around me, and we held each other for a few seconds, both just needing the comfort, apparently. I held her tight, wanting to infuse my own comfort into her.

"Thanks, Fin, but I'm fine, promise." Pulling back, I watched her nod as I observed her, giving her a look only best friends had. The one that said we had a gab session in our future. "So, what are you baking?"

Asa launched into the different kinds of cookies they'd been working on, and Ollie huffed and walked over, taking control. "This is the wrong kind of flour, and you're doing the icing incorrectly. Here, hand over the spatula."

When Ollie went all bossy in the kitchen on his knowledge of baked goods, it always made me hot and bothered. He was so funny and jokey any other time, but was all business when it came to hockey and baking. I loved watching him geek out over different recipes and was always willing to be his test subject.

As Ollie took over, Finley outlined the schedule for "training" for the rest of the week for us. Apparently, part of her plan to make our party the best was to make it into a weekend competition between the houses. Only Fin would consider a competition a way to solve someone else having a party the same night. I didn't know how she had the time or the energy to do everything to the level she did, but she was Fin, and she always made it awesome.

We broke off into two units and began to tackle the rest of her list. I was paired up with Elias as we attempted to build a gingerbread house.

"Love, I don't think that's how it's supposed to work." I stood back, looking at the piece of gingerbread I'd just added, using the frosting to seal them together.

"What do you mean?" I kept staring at it, but I couldn't see anything wrong with it outside of being wobbly. He walked over, a sexy smile on his face, and I fell into his gaze, still getting used to seeing Elias enamored with me instead of our fighting.

He wrapped his arms around my waist and pulled me to him, placing his head on my shoulder. Elias held me for a few minutes before he said anything.

"This is better."

"So, you had me thinking I'd put a piece of the house up wrong when really, you just wanted an excuse to hold me?" I scoffed but laughed, not at all mad about it.

"Hmm, that doesn't sound like me."

"I do like this position better too, but it might be hard to win the contest if both of our arms are occupied."

"I've already won in life, love. I don't need to win anything else."

He kissed my cheek, and my heart took off at his words, the butterflies filling me every time I thought about Elias Turner. A realization occurred as we stood there looking at our crooked gingerbread house.

"Speaking of, what can you tell me about Mr. Hawthorne, or I mean, Logan?"

"That was not what I'd expected you to ask." He chuckled. "He's been a mentor to me for a long time. Our relationship has changed over the years, but he's pretty private, keeping most of his personal life to himself. Logan is generous and smart, and I've yet to beat him in chess. I know he loved your mom and hasn't ever recovered from her leaving. He's been single for as long as I've known him, only pictured with his assistant, Gwen, or occasionally some other upper-class women at events. Nothing ever permanent."

"Gwen, yes, of course."

"You know Gwen?"

"Um, I'm sure I met her once."

"Hmm, well, she's the only one I know to be consistent in his life. She travels with him everywhere. Logan keeps busy, always working on a bunch of different projects through his foundation. He has a knack for helping people out of tough situations. Outside of work, he plays hockey on occasion, enjoys bourbon, brandy, and whiskey, and has a penchant for fast cars. Other than that, he's a closed book."

Nodding, I filed the info away, determined to learn more about the man I was beginning to care for. Finishing our gingerbread house, I didn't know if it was fortunate or unfortunate we didn't meet Fin's expectations. She left us with a disapproving eyebrow, as she went in search of her next gingerbread builders. I excused myself from the Christmas festivities and took some solace in my room, Lucky joining me on the bed.

Laying on my stomach, I petted him as I prepared myself to dive further into my mother's past. Pulling out the journal, I hoped to uncover more about the man my mom had loved first.

*Today, Logan and I went to get hot chocolate together. I know I'm falling in love with him. I just don't know how to tell him. At least he liked the keychain I'd picked out with Chase. I'd been nervous, thinking the better bet was the hockey stick, but as Chase had said, he had a lot of those, and the keyring was more sentimental. When I hugged Chase later at the party, telling him thanks, he looked at me weirdly and said, "sure." I swear, boys do not make sense.*

Shut the front door! I stopped reading as the realization of the incident I'd body swapped with had been real. Or had I only read about it before and osmosis was at work, the words seeping into my brain as I slept? Looking back at the journal, I kept reading for more clues.

*The pressure my father is placing on me continues to increase, and I know I'll have to make a decision soon. I want to tell Logan, but I'm worried that doing so will put him in danger or invite him into a fight that isn't his. He wants to be an environmentalist and have a family he comes home to. I know his life has been displaced most of his life, and he wants to settle down in one place and go to sleep in the same bed each night. If I tell him what I'm going through, it will change the future he wants for himself.*

*I don't know if I'm ready to destroy his dream yet.*

The reality of the situation, how Logan's life was irrevocably changed anyway and set on a completely different course, hit me, making me feel even more for the man. I could no longer deny the facts. Even if my out-of-body experiences weren't real and only my imagination, the realities of Logan's life told the truth.

He was alone, and I had an idea on how to change it.

I'd fallen asleep with Lucky on my bed, and when I woke, the light in the room had faded, indicating it was evening. Checking my phone, I found a few messages from the guys and Fin. Some of them were going out to grab more supplies, and others were finishing their last-minute shopping. I hope some part of me had managed to get shopping done because I couldn't remember at this point with all my possible time jumping what I had and hadn't done. Let's pray it was when

I was in Gwen's. Stretching, I got up and decided to go see who I could find. Lucky lifted his head but decided to stay where he was all curled up in my blankets. I swear, that dog was a comfort hog, always finding the squishiest places to curl up in.

Walking down the hall, I found the first few rooms I checked empty. When I walked into Ollie and Ty's room, I stopped, immediately turned on by the scene I came across. The first thing I noticed was a naked ass. The second was the hands palming said ass as they rocked into one another. Ty's boxers fell just below his cheeks, his upper body bare as he and Ollie kissed one another, and grinded their lower halves. Their moans and movements were erotic, and I found myself panting from the view alone.

I debated on what to do. Did I jump in and join them? Did I stand here and just watch? Or perhaps, I would have some solo play while I viewed?

Ollie and Ty continued to rock into one another, and I knew I wouldn't be able to leave. Decision made, I took my shirt off as I tiptoed closer and pushed my shorts and underwear down as well. I was headed to the chair when an arm snaked out and pulled me close. Gasping, I looked down at my captor and found both of them taking me in with hungry eyes.

"You weren't thinking of only watching, were you, wildcat?"

"Well, yeah, I mean, I was going to have some solo play because you're both too hot not to."

"You hear that, babe? Sawyer thinks we're hot."

"Hmm, what I heard was, she was going to touch herself to us."

As they were discussing what I'd planned to do, Ollie's hand slipped lower, cupping the globes of my butt. Ty's hand smoothed up my back, sending tingles over my spine. They both worked my body over with their touches while rocking into one another and having a mundane conversation at the same time.

"I don't know, I think what she was saying was… " I tuned them out, Ollie's hands dipping lower now, and I spread my feet a little, lifting up to give him the angle I wanted. When his finger brushed my wetness, I moaned, and they both stopped their nonsensical arguing and turned to me.

"Oh, someone is ready to play. What do you say, Ty? How should we play with our girlfriend?"

"Hm, I have some ideas."

They hauled me up on the bed, and I landed in the middle with both of them on the side of me. I pouted, though, the beautiful man sandwich now gone.

"What's wrong, bite-size?" Ollie asked, teasing me with his nickname for me.

"I liked watching you two together. It's why I didn't interrupt. You guys were sexy, and I wanted to watch the show."

"Mm, is that so?" He leaned forward, taking my breast into his mouth, and I surrendered to his touch for a second before I refocused.

"Yes," I panted.

"Okay, wildcat. We'll put on an appetizer for you, and then you can be our main course."

Nodding, I licked my lips in anticipation as Ty rolled across me, shucking his boxers completely off this time. I focused on his cock, and watched it as it bounced with his movements, completely entranced by it as it moved. Ollie laughed at me, but I wasn't embarrassed, shrugging as I wiped away the drool. I didn't call it dicknotized for nothing. All these beautiful peens to enjoy, it was bound to happen.

Ollie shoved off his boxer briefs, his cock jumping up and ready to join the party as well. I moaned at the sight, my hands already starting to travel my body. Leaning on my side, I placed my head in my hand and bent one leg up so I could watch and have access.

It didn't take them long to fall back into their passionate kiss, and I marveled at how beautiful it was to watch them both embrace this relationship between them. Ty rocked into Ollie again, their dicks rubbing up against one another with each thrust. Slowly, I drifted my hand down, finding my center soaking wet and using some of my own lubrication to swirl around on my finger before I started rubbing my clit.

I loved how they kissed, their tongues and hands more aggressive with one another as they sought what they wanted. Dipping lower, I found my pussy hot and throbbing as I plunged two fingers inside. Licking my lips, I moved my fingers in and out, and I found my eyes closing as I began to approach my orgasm. Pushing faster, I laid my head on the pillow so I could pinch my nipple, squeezing my breast to my chest as I built up speed. Opening my eyes to watch them before I tumbled, I was surprised to find they'd stopped, both panting as they watched.

The look in their eyes held wanton passion for me, and it sent me careening over the edge. As soon as I tumbled, they both snapped and pulled me into them, no longer willing to leave me out. Ollie kissed me, his playful tongue skipping all around as he devoured my mouth. His hands were in my hair, possessively gripping my head as he reminded me I was his too. Ty moved down and began to alternate between sucking Ollie and licking me.

I could hear us both moaning as he changed back and forth, and I was a gasping mess. But this time, I needed more.

"Fuckety fuck, I need someone to fuck me hard, *now*."

"Well, when you ask so nicely," Ollie teased, chuckling. He stopped, his face turning serious for a minute, and pulled me close to whisper. "I'm ready to take a step with Ty, but I'm a little nervous. Would you help me, babe?"

Smoothing his auburn hair back, I nodded, kissing his nose. "Of course, Ollie bear. What do you need me to do?"

Ty had other plans, though, and a side I didn't often see from him emerged, knowing what Ollie really needed. "Are you doubting me, Ols? You know what position to take. On your back, legs braced."

Ty's voice came out darker than usual, a little domineering in his tone, and I found myself wanting to obey as well. Ollie whimpered, doing as he said, and I saw how his cock jutted up at the thought. Reaching over, I stroked him, and his head rolled back, eyes fluttering closed. Ty winked at me as he got the lube out, and began to prep Ollie. They were each other's firsts, and I knew this had to be a momentous occasion for them. I was honored to be part of it.

Tilting my head in the other direction, I stroked Ollie and cupped his cheek. His eyes opened, looking straight at me as he smiled softly, at such odds to his usual cocksure one. Leaning forward, I captured his lips with mine, the gentleness of our kiss being a healing balm to my soul. When I felt him tense a second later, I kissed him deeper, wanting to distract him from the uncomfortable part. Squeezing his cock at the base, I slowly drew my hand up as I swirled my tongue with his.

Ollie pulled away when it became too much, panting as he tried to center himself. "You're doing great, Ols. Fuck, it feels amazing. I'm almost there. Just, hold on." Ty's words reassured him, and I watched as he took a deep breath and let it out. Once Ty was seated, they both stilled. I looked to Ty to see what he wanted me to do next.

"Your choice, wildcat. You can lay back on his chest and ride him or sit on his face?" He smirked, and I couldn't help but laugh at the mischievous nature he was displaying. The feeling of still needing one of them in me rose, and I found myself straddling his chest and laying back as I braced my legs outside his. It was a bit of a jungle gym, but it worked and when I slid onto his waiting cock, Ollie and I groaned, my pussy still wet from my orgasm. Wrapping my arm around his neck, he banded one under my breasts, and we locked our lips together.

They somehow managed to communicate when to move, and they both started to rock. I could feel each of Ty's thrusts into Ollie as they pushed me in the opposite direction. It felt like a reverse see-saw in a sense, but it was the most incredible orgasmic see-saw that had ever been invented.

"Fuck, I'm not going to last much longer. Watching you two and feeling you so tight around me, I'm about to explode," Ty moaned.

"Same," was the only word Ollie managed to get out before he pushed me down on his cock, holding me in place as his whole body tensed. Thankfully, Ty was still aware of enough to flick my clit, helping to send me over the edge again. When Ty came a moment later, I worried he might pass out as his eyes rolled back. He fell to the side a second later, and we all three laid there a sweaty, naked, and cummy mess.

"I gotta catch you guys in action more often if that's the result."

"Is it you catching us if we knew you were there the whole time?" Ty asked, lifting his head slightly with a smile.

"Semantics," I mumbled, causing Ollie to laugh, the rumbles lifting me as the vibrations traveled through my body as well.

"I think I'm dick drunk," he finally slurred, causing Ty and me to laugh with him.

"I just thought of your next t-shirt slogan," I mumbled, my eyes getting heavy.

"Oh?"

"Dick the halls and messy balls."

"Babe, that doesn't even make sense."

"Sure it does."

"No, it would be better as Dick the balls with howls of jolly."

"How is that better?"

"It actually rhymes!"

"You're both hopeless."

"Love you too."

The three of us managed to play silly Christmas sex games the rest of the night, and I never had so much fun thinking of words to rhyme with balls.

# six

. . .

Sawyer

WHEN IT HAPPENED THIS TIME, I was more prepared, expecting the switch. What I hadn't been ready for, though, was finding myself on an airplane. At least I wasn't flying the plane. That would've been a disaster. I wasn't sure what the rules were for these alternative timelines either. If I'd mess up something in my future, would it still happen? Or even if I could die here and not in my timeline?

It was too complicated to fathom. Stay alive, Sawyer. That was my motto. One that had served me well so far in life considering the amount of people who'd wanted me dead at one time or another.

Taking in my form, I had to guess I was a nurse or someone in the medical field based on my attire. I wore blue scrubs and comfortable shoes. Whoever I was this time, they were about my same height, and I'd guess older, the wrinkles on my hands pointing in that direction. Glancing around, I didn't see anyone else near me, and I had a brief second where I wondered if this was how I died—alone on a plane in the future. Fuck, I sure hope that wasn't how I went down.

It was a private plane, the open and elegant space different from any commercial flight I'd taken. Twisting in my seat, I pushed up the window screen and was met with the night sky, lights of a city below. We'd either just recently taken off or were landing soon. A door opened from behind me, and I turned, finding my father walking toward me.

Samson looked older as well, probably in his late sixties. He'd greyed a lot but still had a full head of hair. His face was scruffy, the unshaven look patched with grey as well. When he saw me watching, he nodded and took a seat across the way from me.

"He's resting but will probably need more medication when we land."

I nodded, not wanting to sound like an idiot since I didn't know who he was referring to. The plane started to descend, the overhead speaker coming on and announcing our arrival in Salt Lake City, Utah. Well, at least we were still close to Oak Crest Peak.

When we landed, I unbuckled and followed Samson, hoping he'd know what was going on since I hadn't had a visit from my always helpful ghost friend yet. He started down the steps but stopped when he noticed me following him. Giving me a curious look, he stopped on the step.

"Don't you need to check on the patient and help him off the plane?"

I froze, oops. "Yes, I just wanted to see if it was raining. Holy shit, I'm British."

Samson squinted at me, more concerned now. "You feeling okay, Ethel?"

Nodding quickly, I realized my immediate mistake when my head didn't snap back like usual, and I found myself dizzy, needing to grab onto the railing, so I didn't fall. Once it cleared, Samson appeared like he was about to offer me to sit down, and I didn't want that, so I turned and huffed down the aisle to the back room I assumed my "patient" was in.

Opening the door, I quickly entered, shutting it behind me, and I found myself in a dark room. There was a bed and a body laid in it, hooked up to an IV and a bunch of other wires that hooked into a machine. It beeped, causing me to jump, and I startled myself, clutching my chest. I decided to ignore the wetness I felt below. Fuck, was this what happened to women? I was not looking forward to that. Hopefully, I wouldn't be in this body long, determined to figure out my purpose before I had to deal with it.

"Hello."

"Shit balls!" I jumped, squealing a little as the curse flew from my mouth. I spun around and found my ghost friend. She was a little girl, sitting on the edge of the bed and swinging her feet. Thankfully, they didn't seem to actually make contact with the bed, keeping it from moving with her movements. She was cute, about five, her blonde hair in braids on the side of her head. She could be me for all I knew. The resemblance was uncanny.

"Um, sorry, don't repeat that."

She giggled, watching me. "You're funny."

"Ha, sure, little girl. Are you here to help me? Can you get us from the plane to wherever we're going? I don't know how to do any of this medical stuff, and I'm bound to kill him if it's left to me."

She shrugged her shoulders, and I tried to rein in the urge to shake her tiny frame for answers. Whatever ghost training they did, needed to be revamped! Or were the people in my life just insufferable? Yeah, probably fair.

"I don't remember being this stubborn," I muttered, only making her giggle again.

Sighing, I turned to the man, not sure I wanted to find out who it was, but I needed to so I could get back to my time-line. Besides, I was 98% sure I knew.

Stepping closer, I peeked around the machine and found Logan Hawthorne. He looked awful. Rail thin, with a sickly pallor, it wasn't surprising to see him needing all these machines. A pit formed in my stomach, and I swallowed as I tried to figure out what to do. Maybe I just needed to be there for him?

Picking up his hand, I patted it, unsure what to say. He blinked his eyes open at my touch, a strained smile crossing his lips.

"Ethel, are we here?"

Nodding, I didn't trust myself to say anything else until I could swallow the tears, my sinuses burning as I tried to hold them back.

"Yes, sir. We've landed. Samson is getting the car, I believe. I'm to help you get off the plane."

Somehow, I'd known what to say, or at least how to fake it. Logan nodded, so I'd been close enough, at least.

"Very well. Help me sit up, and then I'll get myself into the chair." He nodded to the corner, and I saw what he was referring to. Relief rushed through me. I wasn't going to need to carry him out of here. I'd been wondering if I needed to find that slide thing they used when planes crashed. Knowing my luck, I'd break this old gal's hip in the process. That couldn't be good karma.

Focusing back on Logan, I could tell it pained him to ask for help, and I bet his insistence to get into the chair by himself was for his own pride. I panicked for a second when I went to unhook him but realized there was only one thing other than the IV hooked up to him, and he pulled it off with ease. Grabbing under his armpits, I helped him sit up, and when he felt stable, I turned to grab the chair. The little girl was now sitting in it, watching me. I shooed her, and she shook her head.

"Ugh, you're annoying. I really hope you're not me." She giggled at my statement but still didn't move.

"You say something, Ethel?" Logan asked.

"Nope, sir."

I pulled the chair and pushed it closer to the bed, and ignored her sitting in it. She could get a face full of bum for all I cared. I noticed the IV hook on the back of it as I pushed, so I transferred the bag over when I stopped, feeling proud of myself for figuring it out. I looked down at Logan watching me.

"You seem different today, Ethel."

"Oh? Same, ol' me." Curses! These damn observant men.

"Hmm, well, for one, you're way more chipper than usual, and two, you never call me sir. It's usually ol' chap or dear."

I paused with my fiddling, panic surging through me. "Ha, ha. You got me, sir, I mean, dear. I was testing your togetherness, and well, yay, you passed. You have it together!" I might've done a little jazz hands, but I'd deny it if anyone asked.

"Hmm, I think my illness has taken a toll on you, Ethel. At least it will be over soon, and you can have some time off."

I stopped, looking up at him, shock registering over my face. "Wh-at?"

"Don't give me that, Ethel. You know what this trip is, my last hoorah." He started coughing, the activity taking a lot out of him, and he pointed to a bag as I stood gaping. Shutting my mouth, I grabbed it and opened it, looking inside. A million bottles littered the inside, and I had no clue which to give him. I pulled one out, the name Eloxatin not meaning anything to me.

"The Tramadol, please."

With relief, I looked for the one he said and found it, handing it to him. He looked at the bottle and then at me. "Um, Ethel. I can't open these, you know that. My grip isn't what it used to be since the chemo. Plus, I need water."

"Right, sorry."

I grabbed it back from him, twisting it forcibly when it went flying, pills scattering everywhere. I looked up, worried I'd just ruined everything when a smile broke out over his face, and he laughed. It was a simple guffaw, but it sounded hearty, and I found myself relaxing and smiling.

"So, sorry, Logan. I don't know what's gotten into me. Maybe a little jet-lagged. Here let me clean this up."

I started picking up the pills, putting them back into the bottle. The little girl jumped out of the chair and picked one up. I watched as her little hand went to put it in her ghost mouth.

"No!" I shouted, causing Logan to jump and topple over. "Fucking hell! This would be the perfect time to use your ghost fingers and get me out of this mess!"

The ghost child giggled, putting the pill in her mouth, and then snapped her finger, the little shit.

I was transported to a room, thankfully, not the one on the airplane. I was glad my thoughts were still American. How odd would it be if I suddenly started thinking, "bangers and mash! My rocket is skint!" Or, "the baine is bawling! I'm chuffed to bits!" I'd have no idea what I was doing *or* thinking then. Though, it would be the perfect time to use some of Elias' cuss words.

Peering around the dark room, I'd guess it was still night-time. Shoving off the covers, I wobbled to the side of the bed, the muscle definition I was used to missing from my legs. Balls, this sucked. I was not looking forward to getting older now. Rocking myself up, I hobbled over to a door, the standard check myself out in the mirror routine becoming common at this point.

I looked about how I felt—rough. My hair was shorter, a classic bob cut. It was a dark color, no grey insight. I'd guess I was maybe in my 60's, but I sucked at guessing ages, so who knew. I still had a little youthfulness to me, but the bags under my eyes, the bird's nest in the back of my hair, and the paleness of my skin made me want to rub moisturizer all over myself. I was so going to up my game with a good skin-care routine when I got back to being me. Sorry, Ethel.

Since I was dressed, I decided to explore and hoped to gather information while everyone was asleep. It was the only reason I could find the child ghost would send me here. I couldn't exactly do anything else. I found some house shoes and a robe back in my room, and thankfully, a brush. Once I was moderately respectable-looking, I peeked out the door, finding it clear.

The first room I came to was a standard living room and the next a kitchen. My stomach growled, and I wondered when the last time Ethel had eaten. Taking a detour, I started to rummage through the fridge when I heard someone come up behind me.

"Couldn't sleep either, Ethel?"

Thankfully, I'd heard Samson. Otherwise, I might've dropped everything I'd just gathered. Turning, I took the items I held to the counter. "Nope. Jet lag is a real bitch." I cringed when I realized I said bitch. Samson merely chuckled but grabbed a glass from one of the cabinets and filled it with water from the tap. I kept making a sandwich, and when I finished, I found him watching me.

"My daughter makes the same type of sandwich," he mused.

I paused with it at my mouth, stopping before I took a

bite, the realization slamming into me. Crunching down on the bite of Nutella, pecans, and ham, I tried to think of a plausible reason. "She must watch the same cooking show," I finally uttered through my bite, smiling with the food in my mouth, making my cheeks puff out.

"Logan's right. You're different, Ethel."

"Jet lag." I shrugged, like that explained everything.

"Hmm."

"So, how's Logan? Is he feeling better?"

"He's dying, Ethel. You know this."

I coughed, almost choking on the bite I'd just taken. The Nutella stuck to the roof of my mouth as the bread turned to sawdust. I didn't know Logan all that well yet, and this was the future, but something about the news made me sad, and well, apparently, Ethel was a crier. Once they started, she was sobbing, big loud mouthfuls of wheezing, mournful sounds. Samson panicked and patted my back, hoping it would calm me. I waved him off, taking the glass of water he'd sat down instead.

"Sorry, I thought you knew Ethel. You were there when he got the news."

"I, sorry, it just still hits me, you know? I can't imagine a life without him."

"You seem awfully close to Logan for only working for him for 2 months now."

"Well, that's my gift. I care too much."

He nodded, not buying it.

"So, yeah, he's dying. I guess I blocked it out."

"He should've died weeks ago, according to the doctors,

but I think he's been hanging on to make it here. His life hasn't been an easy or happy one. I think he's been alone more than he's been with people. I thought once we took care of the Council, he'd slow down, put some roots down. But it was like he worked harder, pushed himself more, and everyone else went on living life without him. I was so caught up in rediscovering my own family that I didn't even notice. He risked his life, and then we all forgot about him."

Samson had tears in his eyes, and when he noticed me watching, he turned and filled the water glass back up. Grief for a life that hadn't even been lived yet hit me. "What about his assistant, Gwen? Wasn't she in his life? And all the organizations he helped?"

"Gwen? Oh, yeah, she left after a few years. I think she was in love with him and kept waiting for him to notice, but he never did. She met someone else and moved, no longer free to keep following him around. He never found anyone to fill her spot and began traveling alone after that."

*Always alone.* The words ghost Charlie had said echoed in my head.

I started blubbering again. "That's just really sad." Samson looked like he was going to panic again and handed me a tissue. "Thanks." Blowing my nose, I reined in the emotions. Fuck, what if Ethel was like menopausal, and that was what the waterworks were for? Or was it the opposite?

"So, why are we in Utah?"

"I think you hit your head, Ethel."

"Maybe." I shrugged, taking another bite to shut myself up.

752

"This is where Logan wanted to die. You called me three days ago, telling me his plan, and asked me to join you. Apparently, I was the only number in his phone book that answered."

The thought of that was even more sorrowful.

"So, I rescheduled some things, and you guys picked me up yesterday. He wants to go sledding down some mountain he never got around to and then be buried next to Victoria."

Nodding, I swiped a tear off my cheek. I'd read something about sledding in the journal the other day. So, at least that tracked. Samson stood for a few more minutes, collecting his thoughts, before tossing the rest of the water back and gesturing goodnight as he headed back to his room.

I sat down on the stool, wondering what I needed to do here. I'd come out here to find information and stumbled upon things I hadn't really wanted to know. But I guess that was the point.

The child ghost appeared next to me on the other stool. I didn't jump this time, expecting it.

"Why am I seeing this? Why didn't I ever get to know him?"

She shrugged, spinning back and forth on the chair.

"Why are you my ghost companion? You're no help at all."

Huffing, I turned back to stare out the big window on the back of the house. The sun was starting to rise, the surrounding area becoming visible in the dawn light. We were near a mountain, the backdrop showing a few in the distance as the snow fell around us. It was peaceful.

"Mama sad. She cried when papa called."

I turned on the stool, looking at the little girl. "Mama?" I asked, but she only nodded.

"What was she sad about?"

"Never trying."

"Never trying what?"

She shrugged. "That's all I heard her tell daddy."

"What's your daddy's name?"

She smiled, her little kid smile, and I knew she wouldn't tell me. I watched her grab a cookie before looking at me, waving. Her last words made my heart skip a beat before she snapped me back to my timeframe.

*"Bye, mommy."*

# seven

. . .

Sawyer

A GASP ESCAPED me as I came back to myself this time, the tears falling down my face at the scene I'd just left. Except apparently, I'd managed to cry from my whole body in the time I'd been gone, the tears streaming down my entire body. Opening my eyes, I sighed in relief when it was only the water from the shower pouring down over me and not tears escaping my body. That would've been a weird thing to develop.

"Baby? Are you okay?"

Rhett's voice rang out through the bathroom, and when a sob escaped, he immediately stepped into the shower, clothes and all. Wrapping his arms under me, Rhett scooped me up into him, holding me close to his chest. I couldn't stop crying, and I didn't know why it was hitting me so hard. My words came out in a mumbling mess of nonsense, making it impossible for Rhett to understand anything I said. So, he simply rocked me in his big arms in the world's best teddy bear hug.

When I finally calmed down, he wiped my cheeks. It was then I realized we were sitting on the edge of the tub and no longer in the shower.

"How about I draw you a bath and wash your hair?" he asked.

Memories of the last time soothed me, and I knew it would bring me the soft reassurance I was okay that I needed. Nodding, Rhett stood up and sat me on the counter so he could turn on the bath and put some bubbles in. He peeled off the wet shirt he wore, and I watched as his back muscles bunched, moving together as he twisted.

Fucking hell. I think my mind conveniently forgot how sexy this man was at times so I could get work done. Because each time he showed me his body, it was like getting slapped upside the head with a sexy stick. At 6'7", the man was all muscled perfection. His Greek heritage provided him with thick dark hair, some intense eyes, and his golden bronze skin, making up one delicious man. His grumpy nature had to be the only thing that kept women away, because Rhett was as delicious as man candy got.

"Like what you're seeing, baby?"

Peering up, I realized he'd turned his head to look back at me while I'd been staring at his butt. Shrugging, I smiled and licked my lips. His famous eyebrows that had their own language lifted as heat flared in his eyes. It was like he remembered I was sitting on the counter, naked, all of a sudden. Rhett turned off the water, the massive tub half full, and I wondered how long I'd been out of it staring at his butt. Eh, worth it.

Apparently, I'd dozed off again because Rhett lifted my chin with his finger, the heat no longer there as he stared down at me in concern. "Come on, let's take a bath, and you can tell me what's troubling you."

He picked me up again, placing me in the warm water, before stepping back. I started to whine, thinking he was leaving when he smirked, unzipping his pants instead. He peeled the wet fabric from his legs and then scooped them up with his shirt and walked into the shower to hang them to dry. It was the simple things like this that always surprised me about Rhett. He was meticulous and thoughtful, never rushing anything as he took time and care to pay attention to the details. I knew it was from years of taking care of his mom and sister, especially after Rowan had been diagnosed with Lupus, but I still found it sweet as fuck.

Moving forward, I made space for him to slip into the water behind me, the level rising to almost the top now, and I understood why he hadn't filled it all the way, again making me smile and go all gooey for the man. Leaning back on his chest, I sighed in contentment.

"Sometimes I wonder if you're even real, you know."

"Why is that?" he asked while scooping up water to pour over my hair.

"Because of this. You're romantic and sweet, caring and protective, and sexy as all get out. You were the first to suggest I could date you all and didn't get mad when I kissed

Mateo. You care for all the guys and always make sure everyone is safe. You're the mother hen of the group."

"I'm just being me, nothing special I'm doing."

"And yet, the fact you don't realize that what you do without thinking it's special, makes you even more special. You don't do it for applause or accolades, but because you care. I'm just glad I met you and get to be part of it."

"Baby, you're my whole world. I didn't think girls like you existed, but I hoped, and then you swaggered out of an airport, hitting me with all your confidence, and I couldn't help but fall in love with you right then. Of course, I would do whatever I needed to make sure I got to be with you. The fact we've all made our own little family, has just made life better."

He kissed my temple, my eyelids fluttering closed at the sweet gesture. Rhett Taylor was one of a kind, and I was glad he was mine. Rhett proceeded to wash my hair, taking care to rinse and lather each strand. I never felt as cared for as I did when I was in the arms of my guys. They truly made me feel adored, all the years of self-doubt and feeling replaceable, washed away a little more each day.

When he'd rinsed out all the suds, he pulled me back to his chest, and I laid there, listening to his heartbeat for a while. Finding my words, I said the things I'd feared out loud.

"I don't know if it's real or if I've been having weird hallucinations since the day at the Christmas store, but I've been experiencing moments where I'm not myself. And each time, I'm someone in Logan's life."

"Mr. Hawthorne's?"

"Mmhm."

"Are you saying…?" he asked, not finishing his sentence, the words croaking on his tongue.

Laughing, I shook my head understanding his fear. My cheek rubbed up against his pec with the motion, and I smiled at the sensation, the smoothness was a soft balm to my face.

"No, it's not like that. I told you, no more dicks for me. Besides, he's like an almost father to me, I guess. No, what I'm saying is that each little experience gave me some insight to who he is. I might've been dreaming it all, but it felt real. And…" I stopped, not sure how to formulate the last bit.

"And?"

"I think, no, *I know*, that I'm meant to be a part of his life. He needs me, all of us probably. Logan's all alone. He never got over Victoria and then made his life a mission to help others and take down the Council. When we all needed him, he was there, saving us. And now, he's just what? Pushed to the side because he's done his part?"

"I don't think anyone meant to. It's been a bit of a whirlwind since that day, baby."

"You're right, I know you are, but I also feel guilty. When he stopped by the other night, I didn't really want him here. I felt weird that he was trying to form some relationship with me because he dated my adoptive mom back in high school."

"I think you're being too hard on yourself. It's a natural reaction to someone you don't know that well. Most of your life has been about hiding who you are and not trusting people. Until you arrived here, that is."

"True. I guess I forget it's my natural reaction because all of you bulldozed into my life, and I never looked back."

"It's not too late to reach out to him."

"Yeah, I'm going to. I fear if I don't, then he'll live a short and lonely life, dying with only Samson and a nurse as witnesses. I don't want that for anyone."

"Yeah, Samson isn't the best conversationalist."

The laugh escaped me, and I looked up at my mountain of a man. "Those words did not just escape you?"

"Why? Because I'm not allowed to make jokes or make fun of the fact I'm also not a conversationalist unless it's with you?" He raised his eyebrow, and I laughed again.

"I love you, Rhett Taylor."

"I love you, Sawyer Sullivan, to the moon and back."

"To the moon and back."

Sitting at the counter, I waited for Elias to get back. He'd gone into town apparently to do something for my dad. Just thinking that thought had me realizing how much my life had changed in a few short months. Coming to Utah, to The Aldridge School, to train the junior level figure skaters had been the best decision of my life. Not only had it given me the answers I'd sought for the past six years now, but it also brought all these incredible people into my life. I had a twin brother, a mother and a father, and seven boyfriends. Not to mention reconnecting with my best friend and making other ones with Rowan, Ace, and Chloe. With Charlie moving here and dating Aggie, everyone important to me was here. It was odd how such an unassuming place had become my home.

My life was full and overflowing with people I cared about.

But I still had room for Logan.

I'd pushed him away earlier, thinking he was trying to connect out of his guilt for my mother. I didn't think I needed anyone else in my life. And maybe I didn't. But he did. Logan needed someone to pull him into their sphere and not let him escape with a polite, "thank you, but I'm fine."

I wouldn't forget him.

Elias walked in, and I jumped up, scaring Lucky, who'd been asleep at my feet, in the process. He scattered to a standing position and we both ran to Elias. Wrapping my arms around him, I peered up at his face. My distinguished boyfriend looked down at me, a wry smile on his face.

"Love, what can I do for you?"

"Help me save Logan."

"Save Logan? From what?"

"Loneliness. It's awful, Elias. We all forget him, and then he dies alone, only Samson and his nurse there to witness it."

"I don't know what you're talking about, Sawyer, but I believe you. What do you need help with?"

I smiled wide. "I love you. Thank you for not fighting me."

"I happen to only enjoy fighting with you in the bedroom nowadays," he said, bending down to kiss me.

The urge to give in to the desire in his eyes at that moment and throw caution to the wind was strong. But the look of Logan on his last day, the grief and regret I saw in my dad's eyes, and the words of the little girl about not trying haunted me, and I knew I couldn't rest until I knew he wouldn't die alone. If not for those reasons, for Victoria. She'd been my first mom, after all, loving me as her own, and now it was time for me to love someone she'd once thought she'd have forever with.

"First, I need Gwen's information."

"Easy. Next?"

"How do you feel about sledding?"

Elias quirked his eyebrow in question, and I grinned, the plan coming to me after reading more of Victoria's journal.

"Why do I get the feeling this isn't your typical sledding like we did the other day?"

"No, that was tubing for fun. This is extreme."

"Well, loving you is a bit of an extreme sport, so you know I'm in."

"Seriously, who knew this sweet guy was under all the bullshit in the beginning? I'll never forget how you thought I was a 'rando hook-up,' though." I laughed, the sound traveling through my whole body.

"I was a tosser, love. Obviously, I needed the love of a sassy pixie to set me straight."

"Well, save all the sweet words for now. We've got a trip to plan." Kissing him on the nose, I pulled him over to the conference room. We didn't have to use it anymore for Operation Toe Pick, so it had reverted back to a regular meeting space.

I already had the information for the mountain and the plan to get everyone to the Christmas Party. Elias looked over it, a smile coming to his face.

"Alright, love. This is brilliant." He handed me his phone as he went back to looking at the details.

Pulling up the details for Gwen, I took a deep breath as it rang. When she answered, it took me a moment to respond as the sound of her voice sent a familiar chill down my spine.

"Um, hello, Gwen. This is Sawyer, Sawyer Sullivan."

"Oh, yes, Elias' girlfriend. How can I help you, Sawyer?"

"Well, you see, my adoptive mother Victoria, she and Logan were very close, and I'd like to get to know Logan better. He brought me her journal last week, and well, one of the things mentioned in there is how Logan and Victoria had plans to go to some crazy mountain and drink hot chocolate by the fire. And well, I want to make that happen."

"I don't think I understand. Why are you calling me then? Do you need Mr. Hawthorne?"

"No, you're who I needed. First, I wanted to make sure you keep him in Oak Crest Peak and put our Christmas party on his schedule. And second, to cancel anything he had for the weekend."

"But... "

"I know, he'll probably be mad, but I'll take the blame. This is important. I feel if I don't take this chance, then I'll never get it."

She was quiet for a few seconds, and I bit my lip as I waited.

"You care about him?"

"I do. I don't want him to be alone or forgotten."

"Okay, I'll do it then."

"Thank you, Gwen."

"You're welcome, Sawyer. Is there anything else I could do for you today?"

"Yes."

"Okay, what is it?"

"Make sure you schedule yourself as well. I'd like you to come with Logan to the party."

"B-u-u-t-t, me?" she sputtered.

"Yes." I smiled, nodding to myself, not caring she couldn't see me. "It's important I get to know you too, and I'd like you to be here."

"Oh, well, that's very kind of you. I just don't know if Mr. Hawthorne will like that."

"Well, too bad. It's for me. Please, Gwen? It's Christmas, and you can't be alone on Christmas."

"Well, I guess you make a valid point."

"So, you'll come too?"

"Yes, I'll come. Just send me the details."

"I will. Thanks again. Bye."

"Bye. And Sawyer," she hesitated, before finishing, "thank you."

She hung up, but I heard the thanks for what it was, and it filled me with warmth, the Christmas cheer and sense of magic wrapping around me. This was what life was meant to be like all the time. Christmas just reminded us it was possible.

I turned back, Elias watching me. "Do you have some free time?" He nodded, and I took his hand, pulling him out to the garage, only stopping briefly to get my boots and coat.

"Where are we going, love?"

"Shopping!"

"I feel like this is a setup."

"Nah. I hate shopping most of the time, but this will be fun. First, we gotta stop at the pet store for Lucky. And then I have a perfect idea for my secret Santa and a gift for Logan."

"Hmm, I guess I could grab a thing or two."

"See, I'm a life saver."

"You're something alright."

Sticking out my tongue, I laughed, knowing Elias was only pretending to hate shopping, and in fact, loved it. He just had to grumble about it first.

We made it to the pet store a few hours later, and I smiled when Megan greeted me. I'd like to deny she knew me on a first-name basis, but since October, when I'd picked up the gift for Elias, I'd been back at least once a week. It was a bad habit, but I kept finding new things for him to love. Lucky was the most stylish and well-pampered dog in Oak Crest.

"Hey, Megan. Just picking up some last-minute gifts for the pooch."

"You got perfect timing, Sawyer. I was just about to call you to say your customized gift was done."

"Yay! That's perfect."

"Do I want to know?" Elias asked, a smile on his lips, though.

"Nope."

I picked up a few things I'd been eyeing, avoiding Elias, knowing I'd cave if he tried. When she brought it out a few minutes later, I shoved it in the bag, not wanting Elias to see it until it was time. I placed the other few things I wanted on the counter and paid quickly, ready to get home.

Walking out of the store, for a brief second, I flashed to the first time I'd been here and how R had shown up, threatening to kidnap me. Gah, I was so glad he'd been taken care of. Getting into the car, a message from Gwen came through, the final piece in place.

> **Gwen**: It's on his schedule and I booked him off. He'll just think it's something he's forgotten. Everything is set.
> **Me:** Perfect. Thanks again, Gwen. See you on Friday.
> **Gwen:** You're welcome. See you then.

Smiling, I sang along to the Christmas songs on the drive home, hopeful Christmas magic existed and would grant me this one wish this Christmas.

# eight

. . .

Sawyer

IT WAS the perfect Winter Wonderland as we walked through the house one last time before the final day of competitions started. Rhett had been working overtime this week to get the house even more "Christmasey," if that was even possible. Though, somehow, he managed to squeeze in one more tree and a 6ft Santa that scared the shit out of me every time I walked around the corner.

"Ho, ho, ho." He chuckled, and my body shivered at the sound of his voice, making me want to kick him in his anima-tronic junk. If I could, I'd roast his chestnuts on an open fire any day.

"It's cute how much you hate that thing," Henry whispered in my ear.

"Yeah, well, it's a larger version of Chucky just waiting to come alive and bash my brains out."

"Smalls, I don't understand half the crazy things your mind makes up, but it always entertains me."

"That's what I'm here for, the entertainment," I snarked, then cringed, not meaning for it to come out so sharp.

Henry, of course, heard it and pulled me to him. "Hey, what's really going on?"

"I'm just worried he won't show."

"He'll show. Gwen confirmed and everything. Now, tell me, what's really wrong?"

I peered up at Henry, his eyes softly showing me his patience and love, and I sighed, knowing he was right. Wrapping my arms around his waist, I snuggled close to him, just needing the boy who loved me first, to hold me.

"I'm scared he won't like me. I'm a bit much. I say the wrong things and tend to go either all in or nothing at all in things. What if he thinks I'm not worth it and regrets saving me? He could've spent all that time looking for Victoria instead. I'm also just sad she's not here. The past Christmases were hard, but they also felt like any other day. Until I met Charlie, I didn't even get a present. This will be my first Christmas with family and friends, making me miss both of them so much more. You remember what they used to be like at Christmas?" I asked, blinking the tears off my eyelashes.

Henry nodded, wiping them before they could fall. "Yeah, I do. I wondered if this would be hard for you. Your mom, Victoria, she had a way at Christmas. She didn't go hog crazy on the decorations, but she always made sure to make it special with the events and things. Where do you think Fin stole all of her ideas?"

Thinking about that, I smiled, liking that she'd made an impact on my two best friends and neighbors, even back then.

"And your dad, actually, are we calling him Scott or Brent?"

"Um, I dunno. I guess Scott, that's who he was to me. Victoria became a whole other person, and reading her journals and learning about her life, it just felt right to call her that, I suppose. My dad didn't really change much other than his name. I don't know him as Brent."

"Fair. Well, Mr. Brennon," he teased, winking, "he was the best at lights. Scott went all out each year, and no matter how much my dad tried to beat him, yours won the neighborhood award each year."

"Yeah, Christmas was always fun even if we spent a lot of it practicing for our competitions. I always loved the little traditions we did."

"Then let's incorporate some of them now. You can keep the spirit of Victoria and Scott with you, even now that you have a room full of family. I know Samson and Isla would understand. Besides, you're doing a big one tonight for Logan. I think that will help once he's here to see it."

"You're right. Thank you."

"Anytime, Smalls. I just have one question."

"Okay?"

"Who did you get for secret Santa?"

"I'm not telling!"

"Fine!" Henry rolled his eyes, a playful smile on his lips. "Come on. I think the gingerbread and cookie-making contests are wrapping up. All that's left after that is the present wrapping and ornament decorating. Fin's got everyone on a schedule, so all the parents should be arriving in thirty minutes or so."

"Yeah, okay. Just one thing." I smiled, stealing his words.

"Yes, Smalls?"

"You going to kiss me under this mistletoe, Henry Alexander Reyes?"

"I'll kiss you everywhere."

"Good answer."

Leaning down, he kissed me softly, his lips pressing into mine, and I tasted the mint from the candy cane he'd had earlier. Henry was the epitome of first kisses and loves. "Love you."

"Love you too, Smalls."

We walked into the dining room and heard the judges scoring the gingerbread houses, and amazingly, Soren and Mateo had come in first place, with one of the Ashleys and her roommate coming in second. I still needed to figure out which Ashley was which and not just refer to them as one of the Ashleys. With Adelaide gone, they'd become friendly toward us, no longer part of her 'Alphabets' girl group.

Henry pulled me into the kitchen, and we found the cookie baking/decorating contest going strong. Ollie had insisted Ty help him, but as I watched Ty lick more frosting off his finger than what made it onto the cookie, I wondered if Ollie had made that decision dick-drunk. The fact he kept looking at Ty and blushing made me realize he didn't care. It was a softer side of the fuck boy persona, and I found myself loving all the ways Ollie kept growing and surprising me.

The blonde judge was being a little handsy as she walked between the two guys, and a part of me wanted to march up to her and show her who they were with, but Henry tugged me, locking me to his side. Of course, Ollie handled it better than I ever could have in the end.

"Ma'am, I did not give you consent to touch my chest. It may be on display, but it's not for you to have your way with me. Not to mention, my boyfriend is standing right there."

The girl blushed, embarrassed, and began to apologize profusely. Ollie turned and winked, and I knew I had nothing to worry about. Not to mention how hot it was to see him stand up for consent. My whole soapbox spiel I'd given him my first week here when he'd undressed me with his eyes seemed to really stick.

Fake wiping a tear, I joked as I looked up at Henry. "Our Ollie is growing up."

Shaking his head at me, we kept walking through the house, meeting Rhett, Elias, Finley, and Asa as they came in from outdoors. The other events were held at the other houses to spread out the congestion and make it fair for home-field advantage or something.

"Hey, how did we fare?"

"Elias and Rhett got first place in the snowman building contest, and Asa and I got second in Christmas Carol charades," Fin answered as she removed her coat. All three guys gave me big eyes at her news, and I knew my bestie was not taking that news well. Fin did not like to lose.

"Asa, maybe you can help Henry with the ornament decorating in my place?"

"Sure, sis."

He kissed my cheek as he walked past, squeezing my shoulder as I approached Fin. She was messing with all the coats, straightening them every which way. I still hadn't had an opportunity to talk to her. It looked like now was my time.

"Hey, I'm sorry you didn't win."

"It's fine."

"Fin, cut the crap. I know how much you hate to lose. I have a scar on my shin that says so."

She laughed, but then tears started to flow, and I pulled her into my arms. "Hey, what's going on, really? I don't think this is all really about charades."

"I'm just, I don't know what I'm doing anymore, Saw. I can't seem to get my groove, and I'm messing up everything. I don't even know why your brother puts up with me. I'm a mess."

"None of that. Asa loves you. It's clear as day. And you're not messing up everything. You do so much. I imagine it's just all catching up with you. I think you need to stop spinning so many plates in the air and focus on a few things and see if that's easier."

"It's more than that, though," she whispered, looking at me with fear in her eyes. Fin opened her mouth to profess whatever had been weighing on her for the past two months when the door opened, cold air blowing in and bringing with it both our parents. She quickly wiped her eyes and turned to greet everyone, the perfect and poised Finley back on display.

"Mom, Dad, I'm so glad you made it. Samson and Isla, it's so good to see you too," she greeted, hugging them all.

"Mr. and Mrs. Reyes." Hugging Fin and Henry's parents, I helped take their coats and directed them where to go. Samson and Isla had hung back, waiting to give me a hug in private.

"Hey Mom, Dad, it's good to see you too." I embraced them both, always amazed each time I got to. Learning I was adopted two weeks before my sixteenth birthday, I never thought I'd get to say that to my biological parents after the story my parents had told me. To be here now was one of the best things about the past three months.

"When does the competition end and the party begin?" Isla asked.

"It should be in about twenty minutes. The ornament decoration and wrapping contest were the last events, and they just started."

"Excellent, point me in the direction of some cookies. Ollie promised me some good ones!" Samson exclaimed, rubbing his hands together. The change in him was remarkable since the whole takedown. Remembering kicking him in the junk like I had when he'd made me mad had me laughing now.

"Come on, I'll show you."

I grabbed Isla's arm and pulled her with me into the living room. "Thanks for your help in getting everything together."

"Oh, sweetie, it was my pleasure. Victoria and Logan were my friends too. This means just as much to me."

Nodding, I laid my head on her shoulder as we watched

the last of the competitions. Finley stood off by herself, watching Asa and Henry, her fidgeting making me anxious from observing her. Charlie and Aggie were competing in the gift wrapping, and watching Charlie try to get a ribbon to curl had me chuckling. Finley exhaled in relief and relaxed even more when the time was called, and Henry and Asa came in second. I assumed it meant we had enough points, but I hadn't been keeping up, like Fin apparently was.

A few minutes later, one of the new board members announced the winners. In third place was Ashley's house, second place was one of the hockey guys' houses, and we all held our breath as we waited to hear who'd won.

"And in first place, Rhett Taylor's group." We all cheered, the first official Christmas BOSH extravaganza a success. Hoots and hollers rang out around us, as we all congratulated the teams.

"Well, that's all folks, now the Christmas parties will begin, but our hosts of this house have asked everyone who isn't family to clear out as they have something else planned. However, everyone is welcome back tomorrow for a surprise. Merry Christmas."

"Merry Christmas," rang out, as everyone began to pick up their belongings, hugging friends goodbye. Once they were all gone, we all jumped into action, running around the room to pick up things that had been knocked over or moved. Five minutes later, we all ran back into the living room, panting but in place for when he was to arrive. I spotted Rhonda and Rowan to the side, and was glad everyone had made it.

**Gwen:** We just pulled in.
**ME:** Perfect. Just walk in and go straight.

"That was Gwen. They're here. Places everyone! Places!"

We were probably a sight to behold as we all ran around attempting to get into a hiding spot. I didn't know why I thought a surprise Christmas carol party would be the entrance he needed, but something in Victoria's journal had made me think it was the right move, and Rhett had helped me decorate the front room to fit it.

*Tonight, Logan took me to a Christmas village. He held my hand the whole time, and it was one of the most magical nights. It was simple, but that was what I liked about it. We talked, and for that one night, I could pretend I wasn't a girl from a family that sold weapons to the highest bidder, among other criminal activities. We walked around, taking in the sights, talking about our favorite things about Christmas. I confessed that one of the things I missed about Christmas at home was my mother's snow globe collection. My father had bought her one each year, and even after she died, he still did. My father wasn't always the best, but he loved my mom, and Christmas was when he showed it the most. Logan listened intently, not interrupting once, and after my story, he dragged me to a store.*

*It was a little antique shop, but there was a wall of snow globes in the back. He told me to pick out the first one for my collection, and he'd buy me a new one each year until I had my own room full of them because that was my dream.*

*It was the happiest and saddest moment because I knew it*

*would never come to be, but this snow globe, the one he bought me tonight, will go with me everywhere. The tiny figure skater on ice with snowflakes on it is a perfect representation of my time here, and I'll cherish it forever. If only I could take the boy with me too. At least, I'll have my memories. It would have to be enough.*

I remembered the snow globe she spoke of, and she would pull it out every Christmas. I wish I still had it, but running away in the middle of the night didn't leave much time to dig through the Christmas decorations. So instead, we all went out and bought a snow globe, making a room full of them to represent all of us and the Christmas we'd spend with each other from here on out, making Victoria's room come alive. It was probably dorky, but I hoped he liked it. It was my way of saying I wanted him to be part of our tradition too. Henry was right, I could feel Victoria in this room, and I hoped it meant Logan could as well.

"Gwen, are you sure the party was to take place here? It's too quiet."

"Sawyer said her house. Just go, Logan. I'm sure it's fine."

I smiled at the fact Gwen was giving him grief and hoped he'd see the woman in his life for what she could be. I didn't want him to miss out on things, living life alone. I couldn't fix his love life, but I hoped my willingness to be in his life showed him he could also open his heart for others.

When he stepped into the room, the music started playing softly, and I suddenly felt weird, like I was waiting to propose to him or something. Motioning for the others to join me, I smiled when his eyes landed on me. They started to sing behind me, staying in their spots as their caroling of "Have Yourself a Merry Little Christmas" became a soft backdrop to the scene.

"Sawyer, what's going on?"

"Merry Christmas, Logan."

"Merry Christmas. I still don't understand what's going on."

"Well, since no one will join me," I groaned, narrowing my eyes at the people hiding, "I guess I will have to share myself. Sorry, it sounded like a good idea in my head, but now I feel like I'm waiting for you to take me to a dance or something." Blowing out a breath, I relaxed when he smiled at my word vomit. "I read the journal you gave me, and I wanted to thank you for giving me that piece of her. I read about the time you took her to the Christmas village and how you bought her—"

"A snow globe," he answered, a realization falling over his face.

"She did keep her promise to pull it out each year. And we had fun picking a new one each year. She ended up with over twenty before we had to leave them all behind." My voice croaked on the last part, and I stopped to gather myself so I wouldn't break into tears. Before I could, though, Sofia, Henry and Fin's mom, stepped out, a box in her hand.

"Actually, I think I might have something for you. After you guys left, I was tasked to box up all of your belongings for the Agency, and well, look for clues for the Council." She stopped, clearing her throat. Talking about her dubious past was still difficult for her. "I didn't find anything worth turning over to the Council, your father had done a good job not leaving any clues, but I did take a few personal items when packing that I thought you might want someday, if we were ever to cross paths. I didn't remember until I got Fin's message, and well, I think you might want this."

She handed me the silver box, and I knew immediately what it was. Nodding, I turned to Logan with it. "Well, it looks like we do have one more to add. Would you do the honors and mark your spot in our snow globe family? And well, our family as well?"

Logan stared for a long moment, and I worried he'd say no, and my anxious need to fill the quiet exploded out of me, code orange style, and I awkwardly emotion-filled word vomited all over him.

"I'm not like propositioning you or anything. I mean, you're a lovely looking man, but you're kind of old and dated my mom, and I don't know if you two like you *know*, and yeah, I can't do that. Besides, I already have my own cock express, and it's pretty full. I just didn't want you to be alone and thought it would be cool to do something, but if it's too much, just tell me, and I'll shut up. Shit. I'm doing that thing where I make it worse, aren't I?"

Face flaming, I didn't resist the arms of Elias or Ty, who were the closest to me, as they cuddled me in my embarrassment. Everyone else laughed, and I heard Charlie, Samson, and Asa make comments about not wanting to know anything about me and dicks ever again. Once the laughter died down and I pulled my head out of Ty's armpit, I found Logan smiling at me.

"This is the best Christmas gift you could ever give me. Would it be weird to ask for a hug?"

"Not at all. Iif you can accept me saying awkward as fuck things, then you deserve a hug."

Elias and Ty let me go, and I handed the box to Gwen when I walked forward, smiling at her. It was weird seeing this side after being her, but I'd keep that to myself. Logan opened his arms, and I hugged him, and it felt right. He smelled of hot chocolate and peppermint, and I immediately felt comforted. When I stepped back, I didn't miss the mistiness in his eyes.

"I think you're up, old chap," Samson said, handing Logan the snow globe. He took it, looking around the room to find the perfect spot. When he walked up to the mantel and placed it, I smiled.

"Perfect."

"Okay, now that the mushy stuff is out of the way, it's time for some secret Santa shenanigans!" Fin directed,

"And food!" Ollie shouted.

Everyone cleared out, leaving Samson, Isla, and me with Logan. "There's one more thing. Tomorrow, we're all going to Mt. Crest Peak, and we're all going to do the plunge together."

Logan's eyebrows raised, his mouth open as he looked between the three of us in shock. "But, I don't understand. I thought it was closed?"

"It is closed because we reserved it."

"That was something…" he started, before trailing off.

"Victoria mentioned you wanted to do it together, so

we're all going to do it in her honor. What do you say, Uncle Logan?"

He froze, and I wondered if I'd stepped in it again until he rushed forward, pulling me into another hug, the tears no longer content to stay in his eyes. "Thank you, I never realized how much I missed her until you showed me it was okay to."

It was the perfect thing for him to say, and I knew without a doubt that from here on out, Logan would be part of our group, our family. It was the best Christmas gift I could've gotten.

# nine

. . .

Sawyer

IT COULDN'T HAVE BEEN MORE than a few hours when someone was waking me up. We'd stayed up late, exchanging gifts, and just being together under the Christmas lights. Rhett had strung them up in the movie theater, and once all the grown-ups had left, we'd congregated there to celebrate together. We stayed up until the early hours, and I barely made it to Rhett's bed before I fell asleep.

I was about to roll over and give someone my best grinch impersonation for waking me up when I came eye level with a red bow. A red bow that was attached to a very erect cock, pointing right at me. Blinking, I covered my eyes and then moved my hand to ensure I wasn't imagining things. I even touched my body to make sure I was in the right one this time.

"Baby, is there a reason you're playing peek-a-boo with my cock?"

Rhett's voice had me looking up into his eyes, an unusual carefree smile on his face. Sitting up, I licked my lips when I realized I was still me.

"Not particularly, just, you know, making sure I wasn't imagining it, and honestly, I didn't expect it from you. Not that I'm complaining, I'm just shocked."

"I can affirm you're not hallucinating. I won the stupid game Ollie made up, and the prize part of it meant having to wear this stupid thing. But," he stopped, his eyes heating even more. "It also meant I got you for Christmas morning. So, are you going to unwrap your present? Or do I have to keep standing here with this stupid bow on my dick?"

"She hasn't even noticed me." The slight British accent had me turning around where I found Elias sitting on the other side of the bed, reindeer antlers on his head, and a red circle nose covering the tip of his tattooed cock.

"What in the Christmas Hell is going on?"

"Well, apparently, you can't get your stocking stuffed by Santa without riding his reindeer too."

"That is the corniest Christmas joke, but sign me up for whichever list gets me this!"

"Then come and unwrap your gift."

Turning, I crawled on my knees toward Rhett, who stood at the end of the bed. He was stark naked, only the red bow on his cock and a Santa hat on his head. He was hands down the sexiest Santa I'd ever seen. The shirt I'd fallen asleep in rode up over my hips with my movements, and I heard Elias groan behind me, my ass now in his face, bare.

"Bloody hell, love."

I smiled, finally reaching my target, and I plucked the bow off of Rhett's tip, placing it on my head instead. Leaning forward, I licked up his length, and he groaned, his monster cock bobbing right in front of me. When I felt Elias' hands on me, I joined in the moaning, my lips wrapping around Rhett, taking him as far as I could. Rhett's fingers threaded in my hair, and he helped guide my mouth down over him.

Elias surprised me a second later, and I jerked forward a little when I felt his finger tracing a line up my slit, the wetness already gathering there. "You're always so wet, love."

I couldn't respond, my mouth full of Rhett's dick, but as Elias began to play with me below, I felt my eyes roll to the back of my head as I attempted to take Rhett further. I was probably only half to three-fourths of the way down, his palm holding the base.

We stayed in this position for a few minutes as I sucked Rhett's monster cock, and Elias plunged his fingers into my pussy from behind. I was beginning to feel the start of an orgasm when in some weird coordinated movement, I was beginning to expect from the duo, Elias pulled out of me, and Rhett stepped back, and I wondered what they were up to now. The two of them had discovered their enjoyment of watching and performing in front of others, as well as sharing me between them. They didn't cross swords, but it was still always an epic fuckfest.

"It's time to tell Santa what you want, baby." Rhett grinned as he sat back on the bed, patting his leg for me to climb on.

"I just can't take you seriously with the puns." I laughed but moved over to him anyway. When I got there, he turned me, so I was facing Elias, my back to his chest. Holding me tight to him, I spread my legs over his thick thighs as I lowered myself down. Each time I took Rhett in me, I was always amazed at the capacity the vagina could stretch to. Moaning, I stopped once I was fully seated, needing a second to pant through the sensation of being fully stuffed.

"Shit, fuck."

"With that mouth, you're being awfully naughty. I think it's time I show you what happens to naughty girls," Elias whispered, inching closer to me. I was locked into Rhett's arms, my legs positioned on the outside of him, stretching me wide. Rhett started to plunge in me, and I was helpless to do anything but moan out my pleasure. I went a little dick-dazed as usual, the room fading into nothingness as Rhett fucked me with short thrusts. When I felt a finger on my clit, I opened my eyes to find Elias smirking at me.

He cupped my cheek, bringing our lips together, and kissed me passionately while I fucked his best friend. The exoticness of that thought, the feel of his finger on my magic button, and the huge cock pistoning into me ignited the orgasm that had started to build, sending me careening over the edge. Neither of them let up, and I soon found myself bent over on my elbows as Rhett grabbed my hips and pulled me down on his dick with greater force.

It was the perfect eye-level position for Elias to tease me with his tattooed cock, and rub the tip over my lips as he stroked himself. Sticking my tongue out, I tried to capture it, but he kept mocking me, only bringing it forward when my mouth was closed and pulling back each time I tried to take more. Rhett's movements had me moaning out as he thrust forward, and I peeked over my shoulder to see him intently watching where he slid in and out of me.

When I turned back, I found Elias waiting, and this time when I stuck my tongue out, he didn't budge, and I was able to take him into my mouth. Each of Rhett's thrusts pushed me onto Elias, and I found the perfect rhythm to suck him. When Rhett was close, he pulled me up, locking his arm around me again, but this time he tilted my head back so he could look in my eyes and kiss me.

His hand traveled down to my clit, and as his tongue tangled with mine and he rubbed my nub, I felt him stutter in me, thrusting up once more before he locked me down on him as he came. Rhett moaned into the kiss, only pausing briefly before he kept on kissing me, riding out the orgasm as his tongue devoured my mouth. I began to spasm around him, my second orgasm leaving me a boneless mess. When he stopped, he carefully pulled me off him and laid me on the bed.

Elias was waiting for me and pulled me to him. Gently, he brushed the hair back off my face, cupping my cheek as he leaned forward to kiss me too. "I'll never grow tired of kissing you, love."

My heart swooned as his lips met mine in a passionate kiss, and I soon found my body craving to be closer to him. Hitching my hip over his, I wrapped my arms around his neck, needing to feel every inch of my body next to his. Elias slid into me easily at the angle, and in a move unlike him, he slowly thrust in and out of me in short movements. This was what I was beginning to discover about Elias.

Most of the time, our lovemaking was the passionate, rough, dominating, make you scream in a few seconds type of fucking, and every now and then, he would also do the sweet, make you so wet, heart-melting ones. It was the perfect representation of him, and I loved every minute of our time together.

Rolling me onto my back, he put my ankles on his shoulders before he moved back, leaning on his haunches, lifting my ass up off the bed. "It's a good thing I'm flexible," I moaned as Elias began to fuck me at a fast pace.

"It's a great thing, love," Elias barely panted out before he pounded into me harder, his grunts echoing around the room. The reindeer antlers on his head bounced with each thrust, and I found myself watching them, wondering how long they'd stay on. Soon, my eyes were closing as I drew close to the edge, and when he pushed into me one more time, I lost consciousness as I orgasmed again, so close together.

I was wrapped up between Elias and Rhett when I came to, one in the front and one in the back. Rhett faced me, and I smoothed my hand over his cheek as he watched me.

"Well, Santa, what's your decision? Am I on the naughty list? Am I your favorite ho, ho, ho?"

"Baby, you're on all the lists and always my favorite everything."

"I don't think that makes sense, but I'll take it."

"Love, go to sleep for a little longer before we have to go and try not to die falling down a mountain."

"Okay, Grinch."

"I don't even care what you call me if it gets me some more sleep. I think you stole all my energy with that fucking."

"Oh, so I'm a succubus now?"

"Ssh, sleep."

"Fine."

Somehow we did manage to sleep for another hour and then were woken up by the other guys. Ollie was like a kid, excited for Christmas morning, and he'd even made us all special Christmas cinnamon rolls that were amazing. It was one of the best Christmas mornings, as we all sat around drinking coffee and eating buns in our onesie Christmas pajamas Soren had gotten all of us. As Lucky lounged in his bed, his own Christmas shirt on, I knew I wanted this a million more times.

A few hours later, I found myself staring down at the 100 vertical foot drop, and I was beginning to question my sanity. Logan was pumped, though, the biggest smile I'd ever seen on the man as he looked out all around him. It was only this fact that got me to sit on the sled, wrapping my arms tight around Soren, who was in front. I figured the snowboarder had the best odds at keeping me safe, but it could just be wishful thinking.

"You ready, sweet pea?" Soren asked, patting my thick gloves with his.

"No, but let's do this." His chuckle didn't comfort me, but I looked over at Logan on his, and he winked before he pushed off, and I knew I'd do this a hundred times if it meant he wouldn't take his last breath on this mountain alone. Taking my own deep breath, I squeezed Soren's middle, and we took off.

I'd like to say I enjoyed it once we were going, but that would be a lie. It was as terrifying as I'd thought, and that was coming from someone who was used to flying through the air, spinning, and then landing on thin blades of metal, on ice.

If I never had to sled down that mountain again, it would still be too soon. Ty apparently felt the same, so when everyone else opted to go again, he stayed down at the lodge with me.

"Thanks for sticking back, though I would've been fine to sit here by myself."

"Are you kidding? I didn't want to go again, but now I get the bonus of cuddling you all to myself. Come on, let's get some hot chocolate and make this fantasy a reality."

Chuckling, I followed him to the stand, the woman operating it looking familiar. When I went to grab a cup, she stopped me, handing me one instead. I looked at her, realizing she'd been the lady back at the Christmas store. Opening my mouth to ask her if she'd been the cause of my body-swapping issue, the question got stuck on my tongue. Instead, I heard the tinkling of bells as my hand wrapped around the cup, and somehow, I knew, my task was done, and I wouldn't be swapping places anymore.

She winked and then moved on to the next customer. I stood frozen for a second, Ty tugging the hand he held, and I followed in a daze. He picked a comfortable couch in front of the fireplace, with the Christmas tree next to it by a big bay window. As the soft Christmas music played, I curled into his arms, sipping my drink, and I knew that this was only the beginning of all the wonderful Christmases I would have, and I couldn't wait to see what epic tales and fails they brought. Because what was Christmas without a bit of magic, a dash of laughter, and a heap of love.

"I think BOSH Christmases are my favorite."

"Mine too, wildcat. Mine too."

As I stared out the window, the familiar feeling came over me, and I turned to Ty, a smile on my face. "It's going to snow."

"Oh? How do you know?"

"I just do. It's something my mom taught me."

"Hmm, I don't know if I believe you."

"Well, you'll see."

"I think that's my favorite part."

"Why?"

"Because seeing means I get to be there, and anywhere with you is where I want to be."

"Well, I'm glad. Merry Christmas, Ty."

"Merry Christmas, wildcat. One of many more to come."

As I snuggled close and waited for the rest of my boyfriends and family to return, I knew that no matter what, we would always have this, and it was the perfect wish I could ever have for myself. Only it was better than a wish because it was already true.

# epilogue

. . .

CLOSING THE JOURNAL, I smiled at the last passage, knowing that the tradition would continue. If my life had taught me anything, it was that traditions and family were the things you could hold onto. Life would be messy, love might get complicated, and sometimes evil would triumph, but if you held steadfast to the ones you loved, nothing could take that away.

"You ready, babe?"

"Yeah, I just need to check on the twins real quick."

"I'll go with you." Nodding at my husband, I took his hand, and we walked into their room together. The twins were sleeping soundly. I brushed back the blonde hair, a soft smile on my face as I stared down at my daughter. My son snoozed next to her, his little cheeks rosy from being out in the snow all day. My husband pulled me close to him, and we both stood, watching them breathe for a few seconds, content to relish in the joy of our children.

Picking up the silver snow globe, I turned the dial. The sweet melody played out quietly as snow fell down around an ice skater. Setting it back on the shelf, I grabbed my husband's hand, walking out to join the rest of our family. Before I shut the door, I whispered, "Merry Christmas, Victoria. Merry Christmas, Logan."

*Today, we played in the snow, and the two of you had so much fun. You both laughed so much when you got to go sledding with Grandpa, and when your favorite Uncle showed up, you were bouncing so much, I thought you would take off like a rocket into the sky. Grandma and Nanna visited, and you all made so many cookies. I think we have enough for a week! The best part, though, was picking out your snow globe and adding it to the Christmas village we'd created. I love doing that with you each year, and I hope it's something you continue to do as well. Sleep well, my loves. I love you both so much.*

*Love*

*Your mother*

# bonus epilogue

· · ·

Henry/Rey

SMALLS GIGGLED as Ollie tackled her to the ground, the pillow bed around us providing a soft landing. The adults had just left, and we'd all congregated here to do our Secret Santa exchange. We'd drawn names in an attempt to decrease our holiday shopping, but I know most of the guys hadn't stuck with the rule. Soren had ordered Christmas onesies for everyone, and even though I hadn't drawn Sawyer, I'd still gotten her a gift too.

It was still fun to do the Secret Santa though, especially because Fin and Asa had joined in. I liked seeing my sister happy, and I wanted to get to know Asa more. Both because he was Small's brother, but also because he was dating my sister. I knew it was important to both of them.

"You okay?" Soren asked as he wrapped his arms around me. I never thought I'd be the one snuggled, but when your boyfriend was taller and broader than you, I seemed to keep finding myself in his arms. Not that I was complaining about it.

"Yeah, I'm just reminiscing and all that."

"Hmm," he mumbled into my neck and I had to remind my dick my sister was in the room. Soren didn't appear to have the same reservations and brushed his hard cock against me. Groaning, I pulled away, needing the distance to stop me from turning around and ravishing him.

"Okay, let's circle up and start unwrapping!" Fin clapped, and everyone followed her lead. Sitting down on the pillow, I smiled when Smalls sat next to me.

"Can I sit here? I feel like I haven't seen you as much lately."

"Smalls, you never have to ask. Sit your cute butt down." She stuck her tongue out at me, but happily sat. I linked our fingers together, happy to be spending this Christmas with her. Soren sat on my other side, stretching his long legs out in front of him, and leaning back on his arms. He'd turned himself at an angle so he was behind me, his shoulder touching mine. Soren was determined to kill me with the small things, no doubt about it.

"Alright, so, I think it'd be fun if we open the gift and then try to guess who it's from first before we're told."

"Yes, Fin, we understand. We all got the 10 emails you sent about not putting who it was from on the tag. Now, can we start?" Sawyer teased, smiling at her.

"Ugh, alright. Here," she said, picking up a gift and handing it to Ollie. "Looks like you're first." Fin sat down then, and it was the first time I noticed her anxiety peeking through. Hmm.

"Yippee! I get to go first. It better be good," Ollie shouted, pulling me from my observation of Fin. He tore into the beautifully wrapped gift, paper pieces flying everywhere. He was such a kid at heart and was the perfect person to start. Everyone watched with huge smiles on their faces, his exuberance filling the air with Christmas cheer as we waited to see what he got.

"It's a… " he unfolded the material and read it, a joyful laugh leaving him. "*'I'm a weird dough.'* Oh shit, this is good. It's an apron, and it's punny." He beamed wide as he turned it and showed the rest of us, chuckles ensuing as well at the gift. Cupping his chin, he peered around at everyone. "Hmm, who would've picked this out for me. Sawyer?" he asked.

"Nope, afraid not." She grinned, shaking her head.

"Well, fuck, I have no clue then. Who was it? I need to hug the genius behind this!"

"Now I don't want to say," Elias muttered, but Ollie heard and grinned wide. He launched his 6ft frame up and at the broody asshole before he could refuse, wrapping the man in a big bear hug.

"Oof." Elias patted him on the back, giving everyone a wide-eyed stare. "I'm glad you like it," he said, clearing his throat. "There's a gift card in the pocket for some baking utensils I didn't understand but felt you should pick out."

"Ahh, I knew you got me, Eli-Cat!"

"Do I even want to know?"

"You're like an alley cat, all skittish, but leave out some food, and you become all soft and purring."

"Uh, sure, mate. Can you get off me now?"

"Oh, sorry!" Ollie moved back, a slight blush on his face, and I found it endearing knowing the once brute could find something sentimental.

"Okay, great, well, Ollie, pick a gift for someone to unwrap," Fin suggested, wanting to move the game along.

We watched as he critically moved back and forth, looking at all the packages. Finally, he bent down and selected a red gift bag with black tissue paper sticking up. Inwardly, I smiled smugly, attempting to hold my laughter in. He read the nametag and grinned toward Ty. "You're up, stud."

Ty shook his head but took the bag. Tossing out the paper, he lifted the item up for everyone to see.

"Well, I think I know who my Secret Santa was," he commented, looking toward me. I couldn't hold back the laughter anymore and fell over, as it tumbled out of me. Ty held up a pair of boxers and socks that had my face on them, and I'd scrunched up my nose, indicating something smelled terrible. Cackles went out around the room, and I found myself laughing so hard, I couldn't breathe for a second.

When I finally managed to calm down, I wiped tears from my eyes. "Sorry, I couldn't help myself."

Ty had pulled the socks on and pulled the boxers over his pants, posing with his hip out. "What? I think your face looks great on my feet."

When the laughter died down again, he walked into the center of our circle and grabbed a flat gift in basic brown wrapping. "Mateo," he read, grinning before he walked it over to him. Sitting up, he blushed a little before accepting it. He'd come a long way since his first day here, but there were moments he still became shy around everyone, especially if he was put on the spot.

Unwrapping it carefully in a very Mateo way, he took his time and made sure not to bend the corners. When he unfolded the paper, he stared at the gift in his lap quietly for a moment, taking it in. I leaned around Soren so I could see what it was.

"Wow, it's beautiful. Thank you, Rhett."

The man in question simply nodded. "I thought you could use it for the tattoo you'd talked about getting."

"I will, thank you. It's simply perfect." Mateo held it up now for everyone to see. It was a combination of different elements from Disney movies all mashed together. It really was cool to see Simba on a magic carpet with Jiminy Cricket on his shoulder. Rhett was talented.

"Outside of Ollie, you guys are no fun," Fin huffed, crossing her arms that the last two people had immediately guessed.

"You said no name on the outside. You didn't say anything about the gift itself," I teased. Fin stuck her tongue out at me but settled back against Asa.

"Well, I guess I'll pick then," Mateo cut in, quickly selecting a box wrapped in Christmas trees and handing it to Asa.

Unwrapping it, Fin peered over as he did, waiting to see what his gift was. The music continued to play in the background, the lights Rhett had hung adding the perfect Christmas ambiance. Asa laughed, the sound jolly as he turned the box of hot sauces around. We'd all recently discovered his penchant for spicy things.

"I love this. Especially because of what they're named. Too Hot to Handle, Ass Blaster, Nukey No-No, and Choke Your Chicken hot sauce. This is great. I can't wait to try them out."

"Just maybe stay away from me when you try the Ass Blaster one. I don't need any of that," Fin teased. Asa beamed at her, and I could tell how much he loved her, his eyes displaying all of his feelings. He leaned forward and kissed her cheek before turning to guess who had his name. I relaxed when I realized I hadn't wanted to punch him when he kissed her. I guess I approved.

"Hmm, I'm going to go with Soren?"

"Nope."

"It was me!" Ty barked, and Asa turned to his teammate, bumping fists with him.

"Well, thanks, man. I love it. Okay, I guess I get to pick the gift next." He sat the sauces down and leaned forward, picking up a purple gift bag with snowflakes on it. "This one is for you, Finster."

"Ah, thanks." She smiled big before pulling out the paper and holding up a coffee mug. She read it and then turned it around for us to see. "I code like a girl. Try to keep up."

"Oh, that's cool," Sawyer said, smiling at her friend.

"And there's a bunch of pens and post-it notes inside with

the same phrase. Hmm," she muttered, tapping her finger on her chin as she looked around the room. "Soren?"

"Why does everyone think you got them?" I mumbled, a little sour despite my gift being obvious.

"Obviously, because I'm thoughtful and kind," Soren responded, kissing my cheek, brightening my mood.

"It was me," Mateo admitted in a soft voice. Fin grinned wide and got up and hugged him. "Thank you." He nodded, his cheeks reddening some.

"Now, let's see, I'm going to pick this one," Fin sang, plucking up a small box wrapped in silver wrapping paper.

"It's for you, bestie." Sawyer sat up straighter, stretching her hand out to grab it. I knew what this one was, and I turned to watch her open it. Smalls unwrapped it quickly but was mindful not to tear anything in the process. She opened the small box, lifting the lid to uncover a rope bracelet with an oval shape in the middle. I felt Soren casually move his arm behind me, and in the next second, the oval lit up, causing Smalls to gasp.

She peered up, looking around the room to find who was the gift giver. "I mean, I want to say Soren too, but everyone else has been wrong, so maybe, Ollie?" she guessed.

Oliver chuckled, shaking his head. Soren lifted his wrist, showing an almost identical bracelet on his wrist, only in black rope instead of the rose gold Smalls was in. He pushed the center again, and the light on hers lit again, and a smile came to her face.

"They're 'thinking of you' bracelets. Whenever you think of me, or I of you, we just hit the center, and it will light the other person's bracelet, letting them know the other is thinking of them."

"Oh my God, I love it!" Smalls launched herself over me, wrapping her arms around Soren's neck. I smacked her butt since it was on my lap, and she squealed at the sensation. Smalls turned her head, her eyes narrowing at me, but was cut off by Fin.

"As sweet as that is, I don't want to see any of what else is about to occur. I've already been scarred enough for a thousand lifetimes."

"Haha, Fin."

"No fair, I want one of those," Ollie pouted.

Soren rolled his eyes. "I'll send you the link."

Smalls crawled to the center and grabbed a present. There were only four left, the pile diminishing with each gift. I started to go through who had been revealed in my head to see if I could figure out who might have my name.

"Here, Elias, this one has your name on it." Smalls tried to hide her smile, but it was evident to me at least she'd been his Secret Santa. The corner of his lip lifted, and he took the gift from her, waiting for her to sit back down before he opened it.

Unwrapping the present, which had been wrapped with Christmas dogs in funny Santa hats, he took his time, much to Sawyer's dismay. She was practically bouncing on her knees as she waited for him to pull out the gift. The first item he brought out was a small disc held by a string, and if I had to guess, it was an ornament. He read it, smiling before looking at her.

"It's perfect, love."

He turned it around for us to see, and we all leaned in close to read it. "Most paw-some dog dad" was engraved with a sketched drawing of Lucky below it. Smalls beamed, happiness almost protruding from her pores. The second item he brought out was a travel mug. Elias read it, a guffaw leaving him as he did. "Thanks for picking up my poop. I ruff you."

Everyone joined in with the laughing as Sawyer bounced in joy. "That one's technically from Lucky." Elias nodded, looking over to the dog, who was conked out under a bed of pillows.

"Well, I appreciate it. Clever girl picking it up right under my nose too."

"Yep! I told Megan to wrap it up so you wouldn't see."

"I love it. They're both perfect. Thanks, love." She nodded. Elias got up to grab the next gift but walked over and kissed her briefly first. I watched as she blushed, and I pulled her into me, loving seeing her finding her happiness.

"I love you, Smalls." She tilted her head up, peering at me.

"Love you too, Henry." I kissed her nose, and we both turned to look at what gift he had grabbed. He picked up another gift bag, this one with an ugly sweater pattern on it, and handed it to Rhett.

We all watched as the giant grump opened his gift. He pulled out a black t-shirt and grunted when he read it, a smile breaking out over his face. "This is clearly Ollie, but I actually like it, so thanks."

Ollie laughed, nodding as we all waited for Rhett to share. He turned it around, and it said, "This is my normal face." It had an outline of a frowny face on it under the words, and we all laughed along with him when we saw that. Rhett placed the shirt back in the bag before he leaned over and grabbed one of the remaining two gifts. His long arms allowed him to reach the pile without even having to move.

"Damn," Smalls whispered, and I swear she licked her lips too.

"Henry," he read, handing the gift to Elias to pass over toward me. Once it made it past a few people, it made it to me, and I smiled as I unwrapped the box. It was heavy, and as I lifted the lid off, I was stunned by what I found.

Beautiful blank sheets of music paper laid in the box. There was a note on top of it. "So you can keep making beautiful music for all of us to hear."

"Wow, I'm so amazed. If I didn't know better, I'd say it was from Soren too," I joked, trying to dispel some of the tears that wanted to fall at the thoughtful gift. Looking around, I tried to remember who was left. Only Fin and Asa remained if I'd done it correctly. Swallowing, I looked to my sister. "You?" She smiled but shook her head. Shock registered in me before I looked at Asa.

"Asa, wow, thank you. It's a perfect gift."

"You're welcome. I know you don't want to sing, but I thought your song at the birthday party was great, and I wanted to help you follow your dream. Plus, you owe me a song for next year, so I figured I'll make sure that happens."

Laughing, I nodded, grinning from ear to ear. "You got it, man."

"Well, that leaves one person, Soren," Fin stated, biting her lip as she held out the gift. I couldn't place what would make my sister nervous until I realized she wasn't just getting a gift in the game, but it meant something to her to buy it for my boyfriend.

"Thanks, Fin. I'm sure I'll love it."

She sat back down, and we all watched eagerly as the last present was opened. Soren pulled four boxes, laughing as he did, and sat them down. He turned them around, and I realized what they were, Funko Pops from Schitt's Creek.

"These are amazing, Fin. They'll go perfect with my others."

She grinned happily, sagging in relief that he'd loved it. I picked them up, looking them over and recalling how I'd been so confused about my feelings for him when we started the show. Leaning over, I kissed his cheek, happy to be where we were now. "Merry Christmas, Sor."

"Well, that's our cue to head out," Fin said, interrupting our moment. She pulled Asa up, and they gathered their gifts, saying their goodbyes to everyone. Kissing her cheek, I held her close, hoping she knew how much I loved her.

"I love you, little sister."

"I love you, big brother."

Pulling back, I observed her eyes, trying to answer the questions I didn't know to ask.

"I'm okay. Promise."

Nodding, I let her go and watched as she left with Asa.

Before exiting the room, he stopped, looking back and giving me a look. For a second, brother to brother, we shared a look, and I knew he'd look after her, just as he knew I'd look after Sawyer. Nodding, I accepted his concern for what it was, the knowledge giving me a solace of hope Fin would rebound from this and let us in. If not, I didn't know if she'd be able to survive the fallout this time.

Shaking the morose thoughts, I leaned back into Soren's arms, the rest of the BOSH crew around me, and I snuggled in for a long winter's nap. Or at least, a Christmas Eve one. Rhett had set up movies, the lights dimming as they began to play. Over the next few hours, one by one, everyone began to fall asleep, either choosing to head up to bed or hunkering down in the Christmas dreamland.

As my eyes fluttered closed, I couldn't help but think, "Merry Christmas to all, and to all a good night."

**Want to know how the BOSH gang developed? Read their story in the Council Series, and Fin's next year in Stiletto Sins.**

# from the author

To all my readers, new and old, I hope you enjoyed this Christmas Novella, and it filled you with all the squishy feels. If you're a new reader, check out their story, and for all the BOSH fans, there's more to come in this world in 2022, so make sure to stay tuned to see what's next.

Thank you to Emma, Amber, Kayla, and Tory for helping me get in the Christmas spirit and make sure the story was true to the characters, and adding that bonus epilogue.

# box set bonus

## A Council Series Bonus

Possible spoilers for the Dark Confessions series lie ahead.

# bonus

KRIS BUTLER

# one

. . .

**sawyer**

AN ARM BRUSHED against my bare back, pulling me toward the naked body behind me. Smiling, I didn't fight it as I went, knowing I'd enjoy whatever they were up to.

"Good morning, love," Elias purred, melting my heart.

"Hey there, winner." I could feel him smiling on my back as he kissed my shoulder.

"It's nice to hear you say that," he admitted, and I rolled over, wanting to see into his eyes.

"You earned it, babe, and now you're on your way to getting a sponsor and team. I'm so proud of you. Nicco appeared excited about working with you. I don't understand how all of that works, but it seemed like a big deal."

He smoothed the hair off my face, tucking it behind my

ear. "It is. This would move me into becoming a professional fighter once I get enough fights and wins under my belt."

"You guys, it's too early for conversation," Henry whined from behind me. I loved how he still wasn't a morning person.

"Too bad, you need to get up," Rhett said from the doorway, a towel wrapped around his waist. I sat up, licking my lips as I took him in.

"No time, baby. You guys have warmups soon. You need to shower and eat before you meet Madelyn at the rink." Pouting, I knew he was right, but I really wanted to eat the delicious man in front of me instead.

Thankfully, Rhett was in full mother hen mode and just gave me a disapproving look before shaking his head and turning on the light. He walked over to the suitcases and pulled out his clothes, tossing the towel onto my face. He was already pulling his jeans up by the time I got it off.

"No fair," I huffed, climbing out of the middle of the bed. Now that I was awake, I desperately wanted that shower. Last night had been fun celebrating Elias' win, and I didn't want to start off a competition with cum on various body parts. The two guys behind me in bed groaned as I crawled, and I couldn't help but shake my bum in their faces, making them groan.

I found Henry tossing off the covers and pulling on his pants before standing when I climbed off. Elias was laid back, his tattoos on display, as he stared at me with lust in his eyes. I debated crawling back into bed when Rhett took me by the shoulders and moved me toward the bathroom, shutting the door behind me.

"You got fifteen minutes, baby."

Sighing, I jumped into the shower he had ready for me and quickly went through my routine as I started to get myself focused for the day. We needed this last competition to have enough points to be considered for the Olympic team. If today went well, then we could be training for Vansojieng. It felt so surreal, a dream I never thought I'd get back coming to fruition.

I only wish my parents were here to see it as well.

Drying off, I brushed my hair, wishing Fin was here. She always did my hair and makeup so nicely. I was still mad at her for leaving the way she did, but if I focused on it now, I'd lose my concentration for today, and I couldn't let myself slip now. We'd come too far, worked too hard, to lose sight of what was in front of us. Fin would come back when she was ready, and I'd kick her butt when she did. Until then, I had to trust she was safe.

Dressed in loose workout clothes and my hair pulled back in a low bun, I exited the bathroom to find food and a smoothie waiting for me. "You're the best, Rhett." I pulled him down, leaning up on my toes so I could kiss his cheek. The man was too tall for me to reach him otherwise.

"Anything for you, baby. You got ten minutes." He slapped my butt, winking at me as I scarfed the high protein plate of food down and then chugged the shake. They had been a constant thing he'd done for me since the first day I moved in, and I'd be the first to admit I was addicted to them.

Whether it was the taste, the ingredients, or the drool-worthy man who made them for me, I'd never know.

Slipping on my shoes, I picked up my bag and looked for Henry. I found him at the breakfast bar, scarfing down his own plate of food, his hair damp on his forehead. I hated how quickly guys could get dressed versus me, and I wasn't even someone who fixed my hair without assistance! The whole act of having to blow-dry and straighten it really sucked the time away.

He looked up, smiling at me as I made my way over. "What are you grumbling about?" he asked, putting the last bite into his mouth.

"The unfairness of being a girl sometimes," I replied, not realizing I'd been grumbling the whole way over. Henry snorted, jumping off the stool, and came over to pull me into his arms.

"I miss her too," he said, realizing what my grumpy mood was really about. Relaxing into his arms, I let him hold me for a moment, knowing I needed to center myself for this day more, or we'd be toast before we even stepped foot onto the ice.

Kissing the top of my head, he drew back, taking my hand and tugging me toward the door. I peeked into the open bedroom door and found Elias had fallen back asleep. Rhett was taking us to the rink, and then I guess he would either come back and grab Elias, or he'd find his own way there later.

Stepping out of the main doors, we found Rhett waiting for us in the rental car. Quickly, we got in and buckled so he could take off. I knew we had plenty of time to get where we needed, but Rhett was always early to things. He pulled out into the Chicago traffic, and I went to my pre-competition meditation place, where I began to zone out all the noises around me, pushing away the inherent thoughts and running through the routine repeatedly in my head.

Popping in music as well, I laid back, focusing on what I needed to do, letting everything else fade away. Today, I was confident that Henry and I would make a dream occur.

# two

. . .

## rey

WE'D BEEN DOING our warm-ups and running through the complex lifts and twists we needed to go through the past few hours before our routine. We'd already run through the program twice now and just needed to keep our muscles warm before we headed out to compete.

Lifting Smalls one last time, I dropped her down, feeling confident about the lift. "We got this, Smalls." She nodded, smiling wide, throwing her arms around my neck in exuberance.

"I think so too."

A few of the other skaters nodded hellos as we made our way off the ice, needing to rest now that we'd warmed up. Madelyn was waiting for us, a broad smile on her face as we approached. She'd become more than a coach to us over the past seven months, landing herself in our odd family.

It was crazy to think of everything that had happened last winter and where we were now. I was glad to be done with the Council and free to live our lives the way we wanted.

"That was great, you guys. I have high hopes you will blow the competition out of the water here. This could be it!" she jumped up a little in excitement, making us smile too. Sawyer gave her a quick hug before taking the water bottle she had for us.

"Thanks, Coach. I feel good too."

"Okay, well, you have a few minutes to rest, and then we need to head over to the tunnels."

Nodding, we both drank the rest of the water and began to do some stretches. Once we were limber, we placed our skate guards on and grabbed our bags. Rhett and Elias were both waiting outside the practice rink when we emerged. Madelyn nodded to them, waving them over to walk with us.

"Your fan group is much smaller today," she teased.

"Yeah, unfortunately, some of the others had to stay back at Lux to help with camps and obligations for the next school year."

"Have you decided yet what you're doing?" she asked curiously. She'd taken over the interim director position for the skating program for the past school year but was now back to coaching full-time. She had three potential chances to land at the Winter Olympics.

"It kind of depends on how today goes. Mr. Aldridge said

we could wait and see. He'd love to have us back but understands that the Olympics aren't something you pass up."

"That's nice of Dmitry," Madelyn said, nodding with a soft smile, and I wondered if she had a crush on the quiet man. Dmitry had been working overtime since the scandal broke to redeem the school. "Well," she cleared her throat, "let's head over to the tunnel."

As we walked, I filled my lungs up with oxygen and then slowly let it out. I heard Smalls doing the same as we fell into our competition meditative zone.

Swinging my arms, I pumped the blood back into them, moving them back and forth to keep them loose. Once we were done with our final stretches, I pulled Smalls to me, resting my forehead on hers. Together, we breathed in sync, centering ourselves to be one.

Madelyn tapped me on the shoulder, cueing that it was time to go. Squeezing Swayer's hands, we broke apart and moved toward the opening, where we could see the light and hear people as we moved closer.

The announcer must've said our names as we entered the ice, with applause and cheers rising as we stepped out. As always with Sawyer, a sense of rightness flooded me as we held onto one another and skated into position. The way she moved, the gentle caress of her blades against the ice, was a sound I'd never tire of hearing. It was filled with memories of a long-forgotten youth and unrealized dreams, of yearning and strength, of love.

It was the soundtrack to all my best moments with Sawyer on the ice.

The music began to play through the speakers, and we fell into our program like a well-known lover. It truly was an extension of us at this point, having skated this short program so many times, that it was as natural as breathing.

Lifting Smalls, she extended her leg, gripping my arm, and I placed my feet perpendicular so I could twirl us counterclockwise. The air around us moved, the color of our costumes bleeding into the space around us as purple seemed to envelop us in a cocoon.

When I'd done three spins, I moved to lower her into the next drop, her legs wrapping around my waist as she fell back, her arms spread. After a sixteen count, I spun her out, taking her hand as we went into side-by-side spins together. We had a few more difficult moves, but the program, as always, was flying by as we skated together.

The crowd around us was a distant blur as we continued to skate, hand in hand, over the whole of the rink. Moving into our final moves, I looked at her, knowing that no matter what, we'd already succeeded in our dreams because we were here together, and that was my favorite place to be.

As we spun, dancing together as the song began to end, I pulled her close, holding her to me. "I love you more than anything, Sawyer, I just want you to know that."

Her hand cupped my cheek, her eyes alive with the thrill of finishing a program well, a massive grin on her face. "And I'm the luckiest girl because of that. You're one in a million, Henry. Love you too."

The applause reminded us we were on the ice still, so we

bowed, waving and smiling toward the crowd. Skating off, I waited until we were back in the tunnel before pulling her to me, kissing her with enough passion to heat a thousand suns.

I didn't need to hear our scores because I'd already won.

# three

. . .

## sawyer

THE HIGH OF the short program going well had me feeling giddy. I almost wished we hadn't made plans with Jill afterward.

"Don't give me that look," Henry moaned, grabbing me by the waist and dragging me to him. His cock began to grow against my belly, making my pussy clench with need. His eyes bore into me like they wanted to see inside my skull and find the best ways to turn me on. Licking my lips, I was about to yank him closer when a phone vibrated loudly on the bench, making us jump.

Sheepishly, I picked up the phone, swiping the notification. "They're outside. She has some friends she wants to introduce us to. Come on, maybe we'll have time for some more sexy times after lunch."

Henry laughed, grabbing both of our gear bags, and I skipped ahead, opening the door and grinning wide at Jill. While we'd been talking weekly on the phone, keeping up to date on how she was doing, it was different seeing her in person, and I could tell this place had been good for her.

She turned when she heard the door, a squeal leaving her as she rushed toward me, and I braced myself for the impact. Her tiny arms wrapped around me, and I returned the hug, smiling into the embrace. While I wasn't this close with all of my students, going through the ordeal we did together had bonded Jill and me, and she'd become like a little sister.

"Jill! Oh my God, you look so good!"

"You guys were amazing! Like, I couldn't take my eyes off you for one second. You're going to make it. I just know it." She finally pulled back, tears developing in her eyes as she stared at me. "I'm just so happy to see you."

I embraced her one more time, squeezing hard for good measure. Henry walked up, patting her on the head in his awkward with teen girls way.

"Hey, Jill."

"Coach Rey, it's good to see you. I was telling Sawyer how amazing you guys were."

"Thanks, we enjoy skating with one another." He turned to me, love shining in his eyes.

"I hope to find that someday," she sighed. "Come on, I want you to meet two friends I've made. This was their first ice skating competition."

She tugged at my hand, drawing us closer to the other

two teens at the end of the hall. They looked vaguely familiar, but I couldn't place them.

"Imogen, Jude, these were my skating coaches, Rey and Sawyer. Sawyer saved my life once." She blushed, and I couldn't help but put an arm around her again. The girl needed more hugs. I loved that she wasn't shying away from the trauma, though. I could tell how much her therapy was helping her bit by bit, and it made me proud of her for fighting through the dark stuff. I knew from experience that therapy wasn't always rainbows and deep breathing. Most of the time, it sucked because you had to face the things you wanted to avoid to make progress. Therapy was not for the faint of heart.

"Wow, you guys were amazing. I've never skated before, but I'm pretty sure I'd look like one of those baby deers when they first stand up," Imogen said, smiling kindly at us. I liked her and knew that Jill had picked some good friends.

The boy snorted, pulling her close. "I've just started to learn hockey from one of my dads."

"That sounds like a story," I teased, and he laughed, shrugging his shoulders.

"I have five, some people think that's weird, but I love our family. We're misfit penguins."

"Aw, that's so cute. Your mom must be the woman I met last night, Loren?" I asked, snapping my fingers at why they looked familiar now.

His eyes widened, and he looked at Imogen with a little bit of fear. I understood that look, so I rushed to decrease his anxiety. "We were there last night. One of my boyfriends was fighting. Steel?"

At that, they both deflated, smiling. "Oh yeah, now that you mention it, I remember seeing you in the VIP lounge. Steel was good."

"Did you say *one* of your boyfriends?" the girl asked, a teasing glint in her voice. Jill rolled her eyes, dragging her friends toward the exit.

"Come on. I'm starving. Sawyer can tell you about her seven boyfriends when we get some food in us."

"Seven!" Imogen shouted, her eyes going wide, but she smiled, a look coming over her as a plan developed in her mind.

Nudging Henry, I whispered, "Oh, I know that look." He nodded, laughing with me. We followed them out, happy to let them lead, since we had no idea where we were. A burly guy in a suit broke off from the wall as we exited, following behind us.

"You have a babysitter?" I asked, catching up next to them.

Imogen rolled her eyes, but nodded. "Yeah, there's been a few incidents, and my brothers are a bit overprotective. You get used to it. Topher's good about staying back and letting us do our thing as long as we don't try to run off."

She was so matter-of-fact about it, I knew there was a story there, but it wasn't mine to uncover. We ended up at a little bistro that wasn't far from the arena. The smells of fresh bread, coffee, and baked goods greeted us as we entered.

"I love that you can walk to just about anywhere in this city."

"Yeah, it makes it nice," Jude said, a heavy look entering his eyes for a second that I recognized. It didn't surprise me that Jill had connected with people who knew darkness. She saw the pain they carried matching her own. It made me happy for the three of them that they had found one another.

The rest of the meal was fun as we shared stories about skating and learned how Jill's life was going without having to train all the time.

"I'm learning so many new things about myself. It was hard at first, I missed skating, but I wasn't ready to go back to the ice yet. My therapist suggested I try out different things to see if they sparked something in me. It was how I found myself at the youth center. When they had to find a new building, it felt even more vital to be part of something rein-venting itself. That was when I met these two. They were there every day, painting, cleaning, and doing just about anything they could to make the place a home for kids. I don't know. I guess it made me want to be part of something that people felt so passionate about. It gave me a sense of belonging that I'd been missing."

Imogen squeezed Jill's hand, and I had to admit, it had hit me in the feels as well. "That's beautiful, Jill. I'm so proud of you. You've really worked hard to not let the past and the horrors of last year define you." I hugged her again, the tears leaking from my eyes. Henry handed me a napkin when I pulled back, and I chuckled, wiping my eyes.

"Gah, okay, no more weepy stuff." The table laughed,

helping to break the heavy stuff. "We need to head back so we can prepare for tomorrow. You able to make that one too?" I asked, not wanting to put pressure on her but hoping to see her one more time.

"Absolutely. I'm your fan club's president here. It's my duty."

Picking up our trash, we headed to the door, saying our goodbyes. "It was nice to meet you both. I'm glad that Jill's made some good friends. That's something you can never take for granted."

After a few more hugs and promises to touch base tomorrow, the three of them and their shadow walked off in the other direction. I leaned against Henry, watching them go, a little sad.

"I'm glad we got to see her. She's doing great," Henry said, kissing my hair.

"Yeah. She really is." Shaking off the sad feelings, I wrapped my arm around his waist. "Come on, let's head back, and maybe we can try out that tub in the master bedroom."

"You have the best ideas, Smalls."

Laughing, we jogged the rest of the way to the hotel, our gear lightly bouncing us with each step.

# four

· · ·

## rhett

I WAS thankful Sawyer had something to do after her short program yesterday, because it allowed me to finalize all the plans for the surprise party. We probably should've learned after the disaster of the last two times we'd tried to surprise Sawyer that it always ended up in a mess. But there was something about planning and trying to do something for your woman that made me keep trying.

"Mate, relax. She has no idea," Elias said, chuckling. He patted me on the back as he walked into the sitting area of our hotel room. He'd pretended to be asleep again this morning when I'd taken them, but had gotten up the moment we left to pick up the first batch of arrivals. Asa, Samson, and Isla were chatting around a table as they ate some food.

Charlie and Aggie were meant to be here in an hour, along

with the last of BOSH. I was worried their plane would be delayed, and then we'd miss them skating. It was a battle between wanting to surprise her and not wanting to miss her performance. I wasn't sure which I was willing to sacrifice if it came down to it.

"Alright, well, I guess I'll head to the airport. Elias will make sure you all get to the arena." I waved, making my way toward the door.

The drive to the airport was quick, at least. I'd rented a van since we had such a large party, and it would make it easier to get back and forth from places without having to take multiple cars. Trying to park the eighteen-passenger monstrosity was a whole other thing. Giving up on the space I'd been trying to back into, I sped off around a curve, waiting until I found a floor of the parking garage that was basically empty, and I could park long ways across three spots. It was a dick move, but hopefully, it wouldn't affect anyone before leaving.

Jumping out, I jogged toward the stairs and hurried down them as I counted the floors. By the time I reached the platform for travelers, I was slightly out of breath. I'd chalk it up to the Chicago air. It was different than in Utah.

Much to my relief, as I stepped into the airport, I spotted Ollie's ginger head standing high above the rest of the crowd. He nodded, waving when he saw me, nudging the others to turn in my direction. When they neared, I hugged my brothers, happy to see them after being away for a few days. It was so odd how familiar and used to one another's presence we'd gotten after almost a year.

"Rhett!" Ollie cheered, the first to embrace me.

Soren, Tyler, and Mateo followed suit, smiling as they shifted their luggage. I looked around, realizing Charlie and Aggie weren't here yet.

"Did you guys happen to spot Charlie? Were you not on the same plane?" Anxiety began to crawl up my throat that something had happened to them.

"Calm yourself, Rhett," Aggie jeered, walking around the tall athletes of BOSH and hugging me. I sighed in relief, happy everyone was here.

"Hey, Aggie." I smiled as I patted the petite woman, happy she finally let me call her shortened name.

"Alright, hands off my wife," Charlie said, chuckling. "I'm ready to see my girl."

The other guys nodded, and I smiled, knowing this would work out. Leading them through the crowd, I cringed a little when we got to the stairs, realizing I was on the ninth floor. Thankfully, the elevator dinged, saving me from having to haul Aggie and Charlie up them over my shoulders.

We squeezed into the space, managing to make it since no one had a lot of luggage. The ride was quiet, and I knew we were all anxious to make it to the arena so we wouldn't miss their performance. When we stepped off the elevator, my face heated a little when one of the airport security carts was parked next to my half-hazard job.

"Um, sorry, sir. I was in a bit of a hurry, and I'm not used to parking this."

The man laughed, waving me off, looking pleased that we hadn't been gone forever. He waited until we were in and pulling away, though, before he left, and I wondered if he expected us to camp out there. Once we started down the ramps, the van broke out into laughter, easing some of the tension in my chest.

"That had to be the worst parking job in the history of horrible parking," Ollie said, slapping the seat.

"You can try to park this beast then," I grumbled, not really caring. I was just happy we were all back together.

"Does Sawyer or Henry suspect anything?" Soren asked.

"No. Not that I can tell. They were both focused on today."

"That's good. I'm looking forward to their surprised faces. I feel like every other time we've tried this, it's ended in an epic failure," Mateo said, reiterating my earlier thoughts.

"Yeah, same."

I filled the van in on the past day and how they'd done. Of course, they'd watched it, but it felt nice to talk about it and give them my thoughts.

"You really think this will be it?" Charlie asked, fidgeting a little with his hands next to me.

"Yeah. Madelyn agrees too. This is going to make them eligible for the Olympic team. After that, she pretty much thinks they're a shoo-in."

Excited chatter rose up as everyone talked about how amazing that would be. I pulled up to the arena, showing the badge I'd gotten the day before to grant us access. When I managed to park the van in a single space this time, I couldn't help but smile smugly at Oliver. He, of course, just laughed, loving giving me a hard time.

When we entered the VIP box, we had a few moments later, all of us were slightly out of breath. We were rewarded with the emcee coming on and announcing Sawyer and Henry.

"Perfect timing," Samson said, standing to greet us. We all moved closer to the glass to see them better as their music started.

Even though I'd seen them perform this a hundred times now, I never got bored. Henry and Sawyer were magnetic on the ice, pulling you into the story they were weaving. You felt like you got to witness something special by watching them and were an honored guest.

Each dip and spin, twirl, and flick had me captivated. I didn't think I'd ever grow tired of watching them skate with one another. It was more than just a long program. It was an experience of love that they weaved into every aspect.

We all watched enamored, quietly holding our breath as they went into the last section. The box exhaled together as applause broke out when they finished, along with whoops and cheers. As they skated off the ice together, the box emptied, all of us wanting to get to them as fast as possible to celebrate. Madelyn had set up a room for us to use once they were clear of the kiss and cry section.

Stepping into the room I'd spent yesterday decorating with Elias, I cringed at how bland it looked. In moments like these, I missed Fin and couldn't wait to wring her neck for thinking it was okay to leave without saying anything. But that was another story for another day.

Samson turned on the TV when we entered, and we all

huddled around it, waiting to hear the scores. We all began clapping again when they flashed up, knowing they'd done it. They'd secured themselves an invite.

Waiting the next several minutes was excruciating as we all tried to stay still and quiet. I could hear Sawyer before she opened the door, bringing a smile to my face.

"I don't understand. Do they want us to take pictures? Can we do this later, Madelyn? I really just want to see my guys."

"Just trust me, okay. It will be quick."

I could hear her sighing as she pushed the door open, Henry behind her. When they spotted all of us, they both stopped, frozen.

"Surprise!" everyone shouted, rushing to them.

Our movement was the key to freeing them from their frozen stance as they charged toward us, too, and we tried to make a thirteen-person hug. Which, of course, did not work at all.

"Okay, let's back up, give them some room, and then we can all hug them without smothering them," I suggested.

Thankfully, everyone seemed to agree, backing up and giving Henry and Sawyer space. When it was finally my turn, I lifted Sawyer up, clinging to her. "Congrats, baby. I'm so proud of you."

"Stop, Rhett. I'm already crying."

"Never. I'll never stop telling you how amazing you are or how proud I am of your achievements. I love you, Sawyer."

She pulled back, her face a red splotchy mess, but she'd never looked more beautiful. "I love you too, you big sap."

She kissed me, and I wished I could've deepened it, but between her biological parents and surrogate grandparents in the room, I decided not to push it.

"Thank you," she said as I placed her down. "This is the best gift anyone could have given me. I'm so happy everyone was here for this. I just…"

"I know," I said, knowing she meant Fin.

She shook her head, wiped her eyes, kissed me quickly on the cheek before moving on to the next person.

Standing back, I let myself relax, knowing that my plan had been successful and I had made the woman I loved happy. Charlie nudged me, pulling me from my musings.

"You did good, Son." He clapped my shoulder, and I realized how much I'd needed to hear that from a male figure. Nodding. I thanked him, feeling a piece of bitterness I hadn't known still existed dissolve at his words.

Looking around the room at all the people in my life this year, I knew without a doubt it would be amazing, and I was ready for it.

# five

. . .

## sawyer

WE SOMEHOW MADE it back to the hotel in the crazy big van Rhett had gotten. It had been fun, even if I worried we might drive him insane halfway home with our singing. Some people just didn't appreciate van karaoke.

Hugging my parents, brother, and pseudo grandparents bye, I walked the rest of the way to the room with my guys.

"I'm so glad you were all there for that. I hadn't known how much I wanted to see you all after until we stepped off the ice, and I thought I'd have to wait another day. Thank you for coming and changing whatever you had to."

Soren pulled me close, kissing me on the head as Rhett unlocked the door. "We hated missing it, so we all made sure to make the long program. Us being together as a family was important. Especially to celebrate." He wiggled his eyebrows at me, and I giggled, feeling so full of life at the moment. From the skating high to being surprised by my loved ones, I wasn't sure anything could top this night.

When we stepped back into our hotel room, I fully expected clothes to start falling and my body to be ravished. I wasn't expecting to find a table, torture equipment, and a man I barely knew standing there smiling at me.

"Um, what is this?" I asked, looking at the guys. It was Elias who stepped toward me, taking my hand.

"Love, this past year has taught us all how precious life is, and while we're all still young and you can't legally get married to all of us, we thought a different approach might be more BOSH's style anyway. Nicco had wanted to talk with me about a tattoo idea, and it sparked something in me, and I knew what we all should do. Since most of you are athletes and jewelry can be a hindrance to training, how does a tattooed ring sound as a symbol of our love instead?"

I shrieked, jumping up and wrapping my arms and legs around him. He caught me, letting out a huff as he stepped back. His body was firm beneath, and I had to focus on it so my eyes wouldn't start leaking again. The damn things were malfunctioning all over the place today.

Kissing his face, I nodded, looking around at the other guys. "You guys want to do this?"

"Of course, bite-size," Ollie said, coming up and kissing my cheek.

"You're up first," Elias said, dropping me back to my feet.

"Oh, okay, wow, um, do I need to prepare for this?" I

started to rub my hands on my pants, sweating as I thought about the needle.

"Come on, love, I'll hold your hand," Elias teased, but I gripped him, taking it for what it was—a lifeline.

I looked up at the man, the name finally making sense. "Oh, hey. You tattoo and promote fighters?" I asked, nervously sitting in the chair. He smiled kindly, but I could tell he was mischievous, the look in his eyes belying the fact he was trying to calm me.

"Among other things. I like to stay busy." I nodded like that made complete sense, my hand shaking as he took it, cleaning the area and tilting my hand to get a good feel of the area he had to work with.

"Her hands are pretty tiny. I'd suggest maybe just a heart over the top part here for better clarity."

"A heart, yeah, I could do that," I said, my voice far away even to my own ears. I realized then he hadn't been talking to me, but the guys, as they began to converge, mumbling. When Rhett showed him an idea, Nicco nodded, beginning to pull out his equipment, screwing the ink onto the gun.

"It's just going to feel like a pinch. It will be over before you know it. You just have to hold still, okay?"

"Hey, Wildcat," Ty's calm voice said, turning my face to his. "I think I finally decided about the next school year."

"Oh?" I asked, jumping a little when I heard the gun turn on. Licking my lips, I tried to focus on Tyler's beautiful green eyes. "What did you decide?"

"I talked with Dmitry, and he's agreed to let me do more of a part-time coaching this year. He'd like for me and Ollie to stay for this school year so we can train and acclimate the new coaches he's bringing in. It looks like there will be three new coaches, so he didn't want to lose everyone. With Asa still up in the air, I could tell he was struggling, so I was happy we could find a compromise. I won't have to do any of the overnight games, meaning I'll be home more and can help out my dad, giving me a chance to see if it's what I want to do. At the end of the school year, I can choose to stay or go with no pressure either way."

"That's great, Ty. I'm so happy for you. I think it will be a great thing for you. Oh shit!" My eyes went huge as I realized something. "If Henry and I don't teach, then we can't all live together anymore." Tears came to my eyes, and I started to panic. I didn't think I could do training for the Olympics and teaching, even if only part-time.

"Actually," Henry said, walking over. "I have a solution, but first, check out your first tat, Smalls." He beamed at me, and I realized the noise of the gun had stopped. I must've really been focusing on Tyler to not even notice.

Carefully, like I was afraid to spook a tiger or something, I turned my head slowly toward Nicco. I found him grinning at me, his arms crossed over his chest.

"Go ahead, look." He tilted his head at my finger, and I braved it, peeking down.

Gasping, I pulled my hand closer to have a better look. It was simple and a little red at the moment, but I could tell how beautiful it would be. It was the heart with wings symbol that Ollie had used for our BOSH shirts. Tears fell down my cheeks, and at that point, I just let them, no longer trying to ignore the fact I was a happy crier.

"I love it," I said, looking up to meet Nicco's eyes. "Thank you."

He smiled, nodding. "Okay, short stuff, move it, or I'll tattoo you somewhere else."

I had never jumped out of a chair so quick in my life, scooting away from him, knowing he'd do what he said. He seemed like the type not to make idle threats.

The guys chuckled at me as I moved toward Henry, wanting his news. Ollie jumped into the chair, his torture time up now.

Turning away from the sight, I knew I couldn't deal with watching them get tattooed. I never thought I'd be so averse to the process, but needles were not my thing.

"You were saying?" I asked once we were further enough away. I didn't think they could grab me and hold me down for more.

"Dmitry said if we do a few pop-up clinics, he would convince the board to let us stay in our housing and treat our house as 'married couple' rules so we wouldn't have to worry about finding a new place. He wants to keep the other guys as much as he can for the next year in whatever capacity. He knows our time will be limited now, but he's hoping that keeping us close will keep the others."

"He's not wrong," a voice said, wrapping their arms around me and pulling me into their chests. I peeked up, finding Soren standing there. "We go where you go, sweet pea. I think outside of Mateo and I, everyone else will be on part-time status this school year." He kissed my forehead, and I sighed into the sensation.

"I'm just glad we're all going to be together. That's what counts. And yeah, tell him that works for me. Madelyn okay to stick around Utah?"

Henry laughed, nodding. "Um, yeah. She was excited. I think there might be something between her and Dmitry."

"Shut up! No way." I thought about it and could see it then. Dmitry was an attractive guy, and now that his harpy of an ex-wife was out of the picture, it would be good for him to find someone nice.

"So, Elias will finish his doctorate between fights, Rhett's working on his graphic novel, and Ollie is taking his cooking classes. We really have all found our own path." I sighed into Soren's arms, the love for my guys flowing through me and what our future held.

"So, how long does it take to tattoo eight people?" I mused, biting my lip and squirming a little.

Henry looked at me, his eyes heating with lust as he stepped closer. "Who says we can't start now, and they join in?"

"Rey, you're up," Ollie shouted, jogging over. "I like what you're thinking, though; I'll be sure to warm Sawyer up as she sits on my face."

He grabbed me out of Soren's arms and lifted me up bridal style, jogging the rest of the way as he carried me to the bedroom. "Sometimes it pays to be first, babe." He winked before tossing me onto the bed, and I knew this night would be epic.

# six

. . .

## oliver

SAWYER'S FACE broke out into a smile as she landed on the bed, her tiny body bouncing as she giggled. Crawling over her, I stopped to stare down at her, taking in her beauty.

"You take my breath away every day, Sawyer. Even after all this time, I still pinch myself some mornings to make sure it's real."

"Oh, Ollie." She leaned up, kissing my nose. My eyes closed voluntarily as she brushed a piece of my hair back. I nuzzled into her neck, breathing in her pear scent.

"You always smell good enough to eat," I said, licking her neck. "Which I think I will do right now."

I didn't waste time moving lower, yanking her leggings and panties down in one go. She yelped, and it made me smile wider as I pulled them off the rest of the way, finding her wet and glistening for me.

"Fuck, bite-size." Falling back onto the bed, I scooted up and pulled her onto my chest. She giggled at the move, peering down at me now.

"Well, hello there, good sir."

"Get into position, and I'll show who's a good girl," I growled, needing her to move up so I could taste my cream.

Sawyer gasped, obliging to my request as her thighs landed on the sides of my head. She only hovered for a second before she lowered, a happy purr rumbling out of me as she landed where I wanted her.

Moaning into her pussy, I clasped her thighs, drawing her closer to me. Licking her plump lips, I spread them with my tongue as I began to lap up her wetness. She enveloped me as I closed my eyes, drowning in the sensation of having her this close.

Moving one hand, I spread her lips more, pressing my thumb over her bud, using some of her own juices to swirl it around her clit. Sawyer's moans above me had my cock hardening at a rapid pace, and I was soon regretting not freeing myself before I laid down. As she rocked into me, though, I soon forgot about the tightening of my jeans and focused on the beautiful woman sitting on my face.

Losing myself in the pleasure I was giving Sawyer, I lost track of time as she began to spasm around me, coating my face with her cum. Moving to plunge my fingers into her more, I jumped when hands ran up my legs, gripping my thighs.

"Have you been pleasuring our girl well, Ollie?" Ty purred, some of the slight dominance he exhibited coming out to play.

"Mmhmm," I mumbled, the vibrations making Sawyer gasp.

"What do you say, Wildcat? Should I lick Ollie like he's licking you?"

"Yes, please do, but I want to watch," she breathed, spinning herself around before I could grasp what was happening.

She peeked down at me, winking before sitting back down over my mouth, facing Ty this time. I tried to focus on plunging my fingers and swirling my tongue, but the anticipation of what was happening was killing me. My zipper began to lower slowly, and I felt the immediate relief of my cock being freed from its restraints.

"Fuck, yes, that," I moaned, causing Sawyer to laugh.

Ty began to lick and suck me as I did the same to Sawyer and the room became filled with moans. I was on the verge of tipping over when the door opened, and Soren made an announcement.

"Time to share, guys." Sawyer laughed but moved off my face, eager to have her lovers fill her up, I suspected. Soren already stood naked, his pierced cock on display. I wondered how much it hurt and if Nicco did piercings as I looked at it. Though I suppose I'd have to lay off any bedroom activities while it healed, and that didn't sound like fun, so I shoved that curiosity aside and focused back on what he wanted us to do.

"I'll take the bottom. You guys get top," Soren stated, moving to lay on the bed. Sawyer happily sank onto his ready cock, a long moan leaving her as he filled her. Ty draped his arms around me, and we watched them together for a few moments, enjoying seeing our girl pleasured.

When he nipped my ear, I turned, looking into his green eyes. They sparkled back at me, and I knew what he wanted. Smiling, I pecked his lips. "Okay."

He handed me the bottle of lube, and I moved over to Sawyer, squirting some on my dick and her backside. Slowly, I pressed my finger in, stretching her as she adjusted to my size. Moving it back and forth, I added another, her moans of ecstasy, the music to my wet dreams.

"Ready, bite-size?" I asked, nudging her with the tip of my cock.

"Mmhmm," she mumbled, her head thrown back as she rocked on Soren.

Steadily, I pushed in, feeling her warmth surround me, stopping as I became overwhelmed. Tyler took the opportunity to begin to prep me, and the first drop of the liquid had me moving an inch closer, making her and Soren gasp at the pressure.

It didn't take Tyler long to work me up, and soon he joined our fuckfest, pushing his cock into me. His arm braced around my chest, pulling my face back to him.

"Fuck her good, Ols. I want to hear her scream our names." He kissed me, biting my tongue before pulling back, tightening his grip on my hips. I followed suit, taking his order to heart as I began to plunge into Swayer, rocking back when Soren would rock forward. When Rey appeared next to Soren on the bed, I didn't even blink, not surprised.

We were so focused on the desire coursing through our bodies that a mariachi band could be playing next to me, and I'd probably miss it, too concentrated on Sawyer's ass and Ty's cock to care about anything else.

"Shit, I'm coming," Ty groaned, drawing back one last time before he slammed into me, holding himself to me tight. He bit into my shoulder with a roar, sending me toppling over the hill into my own orgasm as I pumped into Swayer, my balls drawing tight. Panting, I felt her tighten around me, and I knew it meant she'd orgasmed as well.

Falling to the bed, Ty and I lay there for a second as the three of them found their own releases. We scooted over when Mateo and Elias walked in next, letting them have their time with Sawyer. Ty got up, pulling me to my feet, and we padded over to the bathroom.

He turned on the shower, pulling me with him. We just stood under the spray for a few minutes, letting the waterfall over our heads, basking in the afterglow.

Grabbing some soap, I cleaned myself up and then moved to Ty, wanting to take care of him too. He cupped my cheek, looking at me with reverence, and I wondered what I ever did to deserve him.

"I love you, Ollie." He kissed me softly once, pulling me back to step under the water to wash off the suds.

"I love you, Ty." Smiling, we stepped out of the shower and dried off. Rhett had Sawyer on her knees when we entered the room as she sucked Elias' cock. Mateo, Soren, and Rey were all passed out on the other side of the bed, spent.

The paranoid part of me that still worried the Council would return any moment to steal away our happiness had me stepping out into the sitting area to ensure the doors were locked and everything was secure. When I was satisfied, I pulled Tyler into my arms and laid down next to him, knowing that we were BOSH for life no matter where this life took us. We had the tattoos to prove it.

# seven

. . .

## sawyer

STRETCHING, I yawned as I grabbed my bags, eager to get off the plane. My body ached in all the best ways after being well-fucked last night. It was a feeling I'd grown addicted to and one I wouldn't give up any time soon.

Mateo knocked my shoulder, and I looked up, finding him smiling at me. "I was just thinking about the first time I met you at this airport."

"Oh, God!" I giggled, the memory coming to me.

A few of the other guys turned at the sound, curious looks on their faces. As we stepped outside into the Utah air, I realized how right it felt to be here. Taking a deep breath, I pulled that mountain air deep into my lungs, filling them up before I slowly let it out. It was still summer, not a hint of snow in sight, but it had that feeling of crispness about it that I loved.

"Whatcha doing, baby?" Rhett asked, stopping.

"Breathing in home."

He smiled at that, glancing around. "Rowan should be around here somewhere. She insisted on meeting us."

At the news, I looked around, searching for her. When I saw a tiny white fluff ball zooming toward me, I bent down, knowing I'd been right. She'd brought Lucky to us.

He collided with me, giving me kisses as he eagerly jumped around, sniffing me for any new smells. When Elias bent down, too, he gave him the same treatment, licking his face with doggy wet kisses, making Elias laugh at his exuberance.

"It's good to see you too, bud."

Gathering the squirming fluff ball into my arms, I took a second to look around at the place that had become my home this past year. When I'd stepped off the plane from Iowa, I was hopeful for a fresh start, a place to find answers and start living my life again. I had no idea the incredible men and women who would become my family awaited me a few feet right from where I stood.

As I looked over to where I first laid eyes on Rhett, I found my giant lover standing in the same spot, lifting that eyebrow that had started it all. This time, I didn't have to wonder what they were saying; this time, I knew.

I was loved and happy with my whole future ahead of me. It was everything I had hoped for and so much more.

**The End**

Though, you might catch some of your favorite characters this summer and fall in Stiletto Sins, and the new Council spinoff, Lux Brumalis.

# also by kris butler

## the council series

(completed series)

Damaged Dreams

Shattered Secrets

Fractured Futures

Bosh Bells & Epic Fails

## the order duet (council spinoff)

Stiletto Sins

## dark confessions

Dangerous Truths

Dangerous Lies

Dangerous Vows

Reckless (Cami's Novella)

Relentless (Nat's Novella)

Dangerous Love

# tattooed hearts duet

Tattooed Hearts Completed Duet

Riddled Deceit (Part 1)

Smudged Lines (Part 2)

# music city diaries

Beautiful Agony

# vacation romcom

Vibing

# sinners fairytales

(standalone)

Pride

# about the author

Kris Butler

Kris Butler writes under a pen name to have some separation from her everyday life. Never expecting to write a book, she was surprised when an author friend encouraged her to give it a try and how much she enjoyed it. Having an extensive background in mental health, Kris hopes to normalize mental health issues and the importance of talking about them with her characters and books. Kris is a southern girl at heart but lives with her husband and adorable furbaby somewhere in the Midwest. Kris is an avid fan of Reverse Harem and hopes to add a quirky and new perspective to the emerging genre. If you enjoyed her book, please consider leaving a review. You can contact her the following ways and follow Kris's journey as a new author on social media.

CPSIA information can be obtained
at www.ICGtesting.com
Printed in the USA
JSHW062314140722
27990JS00001B/2

9 781958 746035